THE MAHABHARATA

PRAISE FOR THE SERIES

'The modernization of language is visible, it's easier on the mind, through expressions that are somewhat familiar. The detailing of the story is intact, the varying tempo maintained, with no deviations from the original. The short introduction reflects a brilliant mind. For those who passionately love the Mahabharata and want to explore it to its depths, Debroy's translation offers great promise . . .'

—*Hindustan Times*

'[Debroy] has really carved out a niche for himself in crafting and presenting a translation of the Mahabharata . . . The book takes us on a great journey with admirable ease.'

—*Indian Express*

'The first thing that appeals to one is the simplicity with which Debroy has been able to express himself and infuse the right kind of meanings . . . Considering that Sanskrit is not the simplest of languages to translate a text from, Debroy exhibits his deep understanding and appreciation of the medium.'

—*The Hindu*

'Overwhelmingly impressive . . . Bibek is a truly eclectic scholar.'

—*Business Line*

'Debroy's lucid and nuanced retelling of the original makes the masterpiece even more enjoyably accessible.'

—*Open*

'The quality of translation is excellent. The lucid language makes it a pleasure to read the various stories, digressions and parables.'

—*Tribune*

'Extremely well-organized, and has a substantial and helpful Introduction, plot summaries and notes . . . beautiful example of a well thought-out layout which makes for much easier reading.'

—*Book Review*

'The dispassionate vision [Debroy] brings to this endeavour will surely earn him merit in the three worlds.'

—*Mail Today*

'Thoroughly enjoyable and impressively scholarly . . .'

—*DNA*

'Debroy's is not the only English translation available in the market, but where he scores and others fail is that his is the closest rendering of the original text in modern English without unduly complicating the readers' understanding of the epic.'

—*Business Standard*

'The brilliance of Ved Vysya comes through.'

—*Hindustan Times*

THE MAHABHARATA

Volume 8
(Sections 78 to 86)

Translated by
BIBEK DEBROY

PENGUIN BOOKS
An imprint of Penguin Random House

PENGUIN BOOKS

USA | Canada | UK | Ireland | Australia
New Zealand | India | South Africa | China

Penguin Books is part of the Penguin Random House group of companies
whose addresses can be found at global.penguinrandomhouse.com

Published by Penguin Random House India Pvt. Ltd
7th Floor, Infinity Tower C, DLF Cyber City,
Gurgaon 122 002, Haryana, India

First published by Penguin Books India 2013
This edition published 2015

10 9 8 7 6 5 4 3 2

ISBN 9780143425212

Typeset in Sabon by Eleven Arts, New Delhi
Printed at Repro India Limited

www.penguin.co.in

For Suparna

Ardha bhāryā manuṣyasya bhāryā śreṣṭhatamaḥ sakhā
Bhāryā mulam trivargasya bhāryā mitram mariṣyataḥ
Mahabharata (1/68/40)

Nāsti bhāryāsamo bandhurnāsti bhāryasamā gatiḥ
Nāsti bhāryasamo loke sahāyo dharmasādhanaḥ
Mahabharata (12/142/10)

Contents

FAMILY TREE

Bharata/Puru Lineage

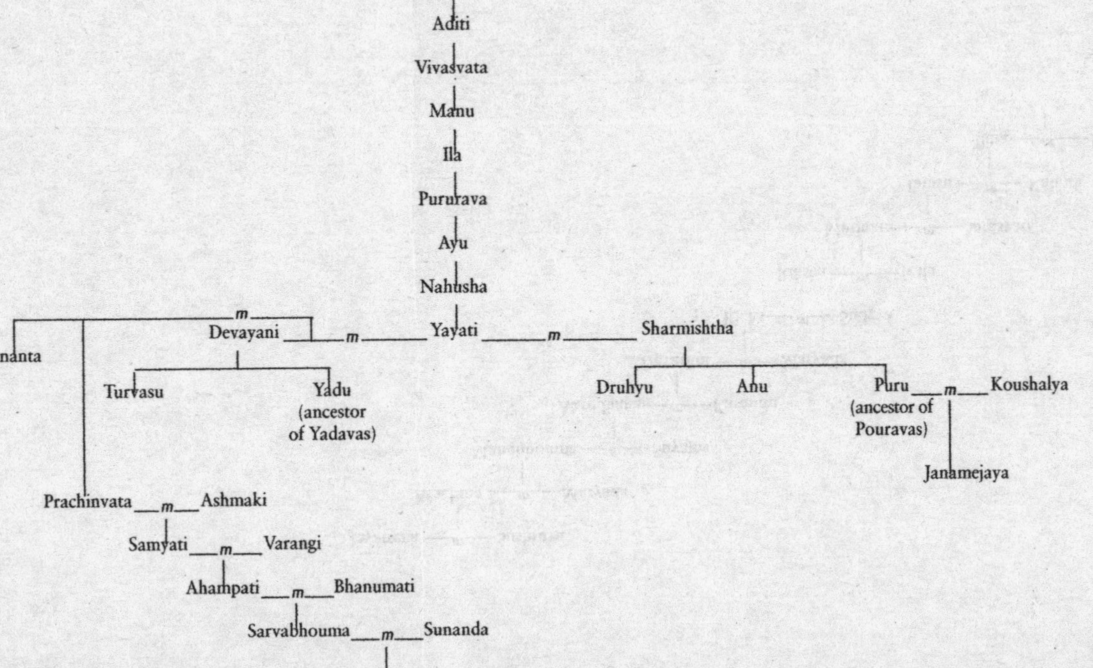

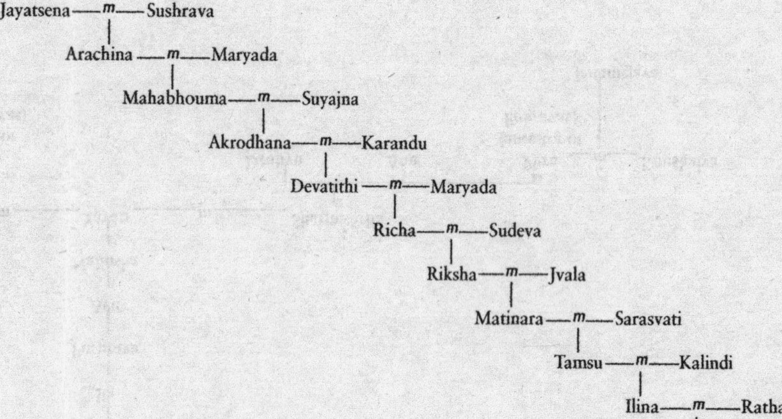
Jayatsena —m— Sushrava
Arachina —m— Maryada
Mahabhouma —m— Suyajna
Akrodhana —m— Karandu
Devatithi —m— Maryada
Richa —m— Sudeva
Riksha —m— Jvala
Matinara —m— Sarasvati
Tamsu —m— Kalindi
Ilina —m— Rathantari

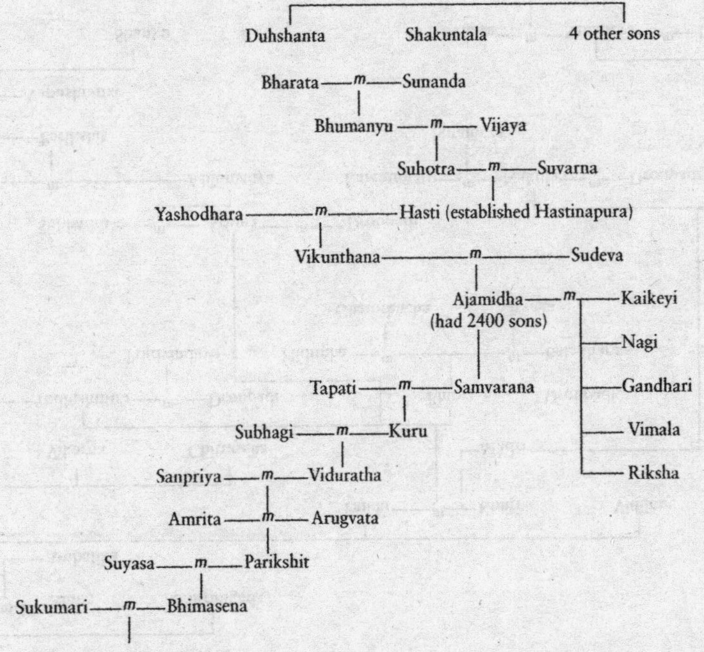
Duhshanta
Shakuntala
4 other sons
Bharata
m
Sunanda
Bhumanyu
m
Vijaya
Suhotra
m
Suvarna
Yashodhara
m
Hasti (established Hastinapura)
Vikunthana
m
Sudeva
Ajamidha
(had 2400 sons)
m
Kaikeyi
Nagi
Gandhari
Vimala
Riksha
Tapati
m
Samvarana
Subhagi
m
Kuru
Sanpriya
m
Viduratha
Amrita
m
Arugvata
Suyasa
m
Parikshit
Sukumari
m
Bhimasena

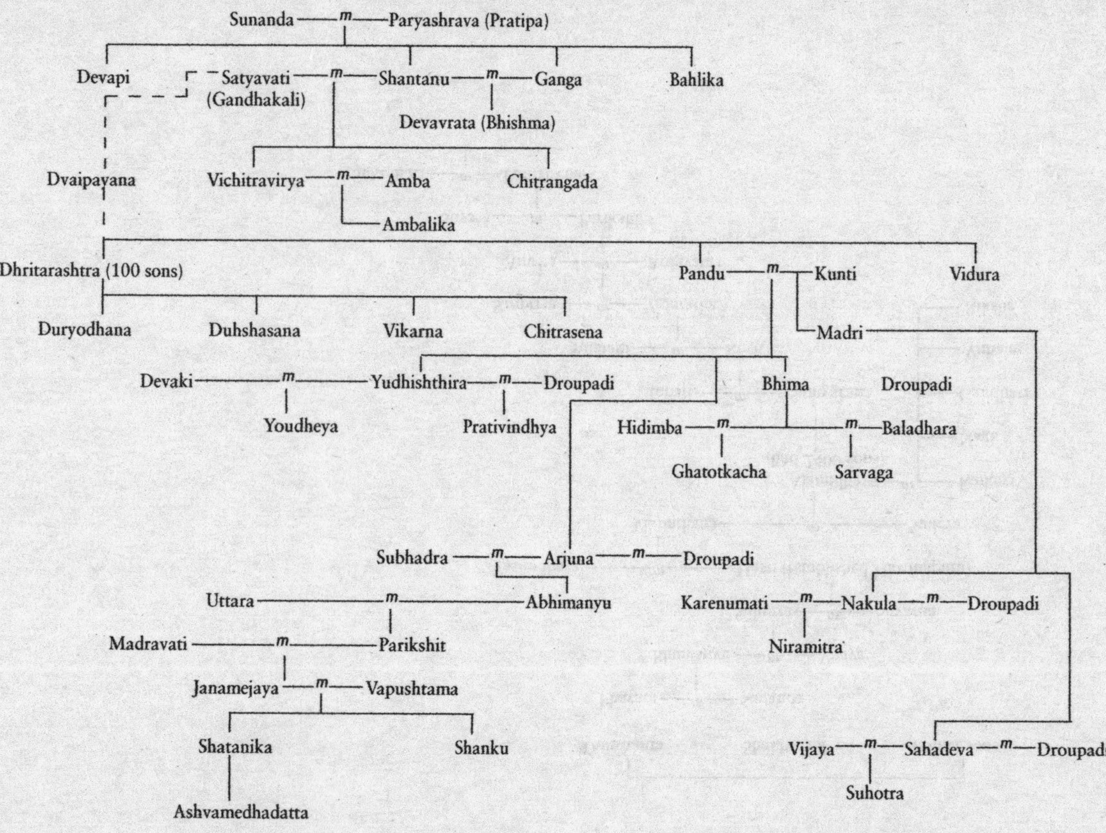
Sunanda
m
Paryashrava (Pratipa)
Devapi
Satyavati
(Gandhakali)
m
Shantanu
m
Ganga
Bahlika
Devavrata (Bhishma)
Dvaipayana
Vichitravirya
m
Amba
Chitrangada
Ambalika
Dhritarashtra (100 sons)
Pandu
m
Kunti
Vidura
Duryodhana
Duhshasana
Vikarna
Chitrasena
Madri
Devaki
m
Yudhishthira
m
Droupadi
Bhima
Droupadi
Youdheya
Prativindhya
Hidimba
m
m
Baladhara
Ghatotkacha
Sarvaga
Subhadra
m
Arjuna
m
Droupadi
Uttara
m
Abhimanyu
Karenumati
m
Nakula
m
Droupadi
Madravati
m
Parikshit
Niramitra
Janamejaya
m
Vapushtama
Shatanika
Shanku
Vijaya
m
Sahadeva
m
Droupadi
Ashvamedhadatta
Suhotra

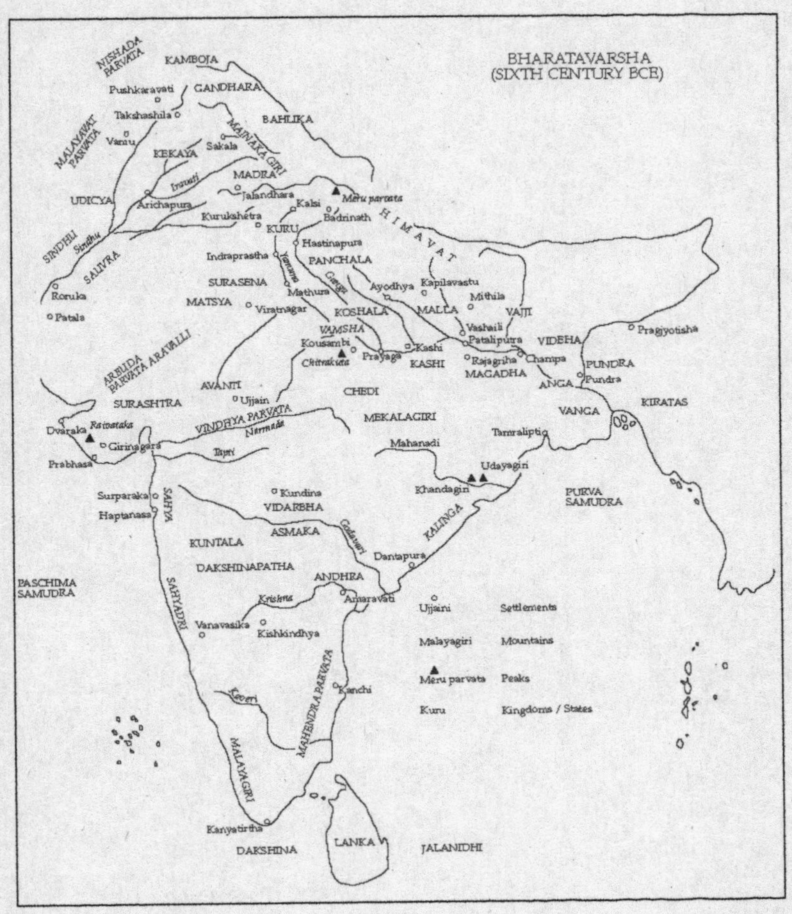

BHARATAVARSHA
(SIXTH CENTURY BCE)
NISHADA PARVATA
KAMBOJA
Pushkaravati
GANDHARA
Takshashila
BAHLIKA
MALAYAVAT PARVATA
Vanu
MAINAKA GIRI
Sakala
KEKAYA
MADRA
Iravati
Meru parvata
UDICYA
Arichapura
Jalandhara
Kalsi
Badrinath
HIMAVAT
Kurukshetra
KURU
SINDHU
Sindhu
Hastinapura
SALIVRA
Indraprastha
Yamuna
PANCHALA
Ganga
SURASENA
Mathura
Ayodhya
Kapilavastu
Roruka
Mithila
MATSYA
Viratnagar
MALLA
VAJJI
Patala
KOSHALA
Vashali
Pragjyotisha
VAMSHA
Pataliputra
VIDEHA
Kousambi
Kashi
ARBUDA PARVATA ARAVALLI
Prayaga
Champa
Chitrakuta
KASHI
Rajagriha
PUNDRA
MAGADHA
Pundra
AVANTI
ANGA
Ujjain
CHEDI
SURASHTRA
KIRATAS
VANGA
VINDHYA PARVATA
MEKALAGIRI
Dvaraka
Raivataka
Narmada
Tamraliptia
Girinagara
Mahanadi
Tapti
Prabhasa
Udayagiri
Khandagiri
Surparaka
Kundina
PURVA SAMUDRA
SAHYA
VIDARBHA
Haptanasa
KALINGA
Godavari
ASMAKA
KUNTALA
Dantapura
DAKSHINAPATHA
ANDHRA
PASCHIMA SAMUDRA
SAHYADRI
Krishna
Amaravati
Ujjaini
Settlements
Vanavasika
Kishkindhya
Malayagiri
Mountains
MAHENDRA PARVATA
Meru parvata
Peaks
Kanchi
Kaveri
Kuru
Kingdoms / States
MALAYAGIRI
Kanyatirtha
LANKA
JALANIDHI
DAKSHINA

Acknowledgements

Carving time out from one's regular schedule and work engagements to embark on such a mammoth work of translation has been difficult. It has been a journey of six years, ten volumes and something like 2.25 million words. Sometimes, I wish I had been born in nineteenth-century Bengal, with a benefactor funding me for doing nothing but this. But alas, the days of gentlemen of leisure are long over. The time could not be carved out from professional engagements, barring of course assorted television channels, who must have wondered why I have been so reluctant to head for their studios in the evenings. It was ascribed to health, interpreted as adverse health. It was certainly health, but not in an adverse sense. Reading the Mahabharata is good for one's mental health and is an activity to be recommended, without any statutory warnings. When I embarked on the hazardous journey, a friend, an author interested in Sanskrit and the Mahabharata, sent me an email. She asked me to be careful, since the track record of those who embarked on unabridged translations of the Mahabharata hasn't always been desirable. Thankfully, I survived, to finish telling the tale.

The time was stolen in the evenings and over weekends. The cost was therefore borne by one's immediate family, and to a lesser extent by friends. Socializing was reduced, since every dinner meant one less chapter done. The family has first claim on the debt, though I am sure it also has claim on whatever merits are due. At least my wife, Suparna Banerjee (Debroy) does, and these volumes are therefore dedicated to her. For six long years, she has walked this path of dharma along with me, providing the conducive home cum family environment that made undistracted work possible. I suspect Sirius has no claim on the merits, though he has been remarkably patient at the times when he has been curled up near my feet and I have been translating away. There is some allegory there about a dog keeping company when the Mahabharata is being read and translated.

Most people have thought I was mad, even if they never quite said that. Among those who believed and thought it was worthwhile, beyond immediate family, are M. Veerappa Moily, Pratap Bhanu Mehta and Laveesh Bhandari. And my sons, Nihshanka and Vidroha. The various reviewers of different volumes have also been extremely kind and many readers have communicated kind words through email and Twitter, enquiring about progress.

Penguin also believed. My initial hesitation about being able to deliver was brushed aside by R. Sivapriya, who pushed me after the series had been commissioned by V. Karthika. And then Sumitra Srinivasan became the editor, followed by Paloma Dutta. The enthusiasm of these ladies was so infectious that everything just snowballed and Paloma ensured that the final product of the volumes was much more readable than what I had initially produced.

When I first embarked on what was also a personal voyage of sorts, the end was never in sight and seemed to stretch to infinity. There were moments of self-doubt and frustration. Now that it is all done, it leaves a vacuum, a hole. That's not simply because you haven't figured out what the new project is. It is also because characters who have been part of your life for several years are dead and gone. I don't mean the ones who died in the course of the actual war, but the others. Most of them faced rather tragic and unenviable ends. Along that personal voyage, the Mahabharata changes you, or so my wife tells me. I am no longer the person I was when I started it, as an individual. That sounds cryptic, deliberately so. Anyone who reads the Mahabharata carefully is bound to change, discount the temporary and place a premium on the permanent.

To all those who have been part of that journey, including the readers, thank you.

The original ten volumes were published sequentially, as they were completed, between 2010 and 2014.

Introduction

The Hindu tradition has an amazingly large corpus of religious texts, spanning Vedas, Vedanta (*brahmanas*,[1] *aranyakas*,[2] Upanishads,), Vedangas,[3] *smritis*, Puranas, dharmashastras and *itihasa*. For most of these texts, especially if one excludes classical Sanskrit literature, we don't quite know when they were composed and by whom, not that one is looking for single authors. Some of the minor Puranas (Upa Purana) are of later vintage. For instance, the Bhavishya Purana (which is often listed as a major Purana or Maha Purana) mentions Queen Victoria.

In the listing of the corpus above figures itihasa, translated into English as history. History doesn't entirely capture the nuance of itihasa, which is better translated as 'this is indeed what happened'. Itihasa isn't myth or fiction. It is a chronicle of what happened; it is fact. Or so runs the belief. And itihasa consists of India's two major epics, the Ramayana and the Mahabharata. The former is believed to have been composed as poetry and the latter as prose. This isn't quite correct. The Ramayana has segments in prose and the Mahabharata has segments in poetry. Itihasa doesn't quite belong to the category of religious texts in a way that the Vedas and Vedanta are religious. However, the dividing line between what is religious and what is not is fuzzy. After all, itihasa is also about attaining the objectives of *dharma*,[4]

[1] Brahmana is a text and also the word used for the highest caste.

[2] A class of religious and philosophical texts that are composed in the forest, or are meant to be studied when one retires to the forest.

[3] The six Vedangas are *shiksha* (articulation and pronunciation), *chhanda* (prosody), *vyakarana* (grammar), *nirukta* (etymology), *jyotisha* (astronomy) and *kalpa* (rituals).

[4] Religion, duty.

artha,[5] *kama*[6] and *moksha*[7] and the Mahabharata includes Hinduism's most important spiritual text—the Bhagavad Gita.

The epics are not part of the *shruti* tradition. That tradition is like revelation, without any composer. The epics are part of the *smriti* tradition. At the time they were composed, there was no question of texts being written down. They were recited, heard, memorized and passed down through the generations. But the smriti tradition had composers. The Ramayana was composed by Valmiki, regarded as the first poet or *kavi*. The word kavi has a secondary meaning as poet or rhymer. The primary meaning of kavi is someone who is wise.

And in that sense, the composer of the Mahabharata was no less wise. This was Vedavyasa or Vyasadeva. He was so named because he classified (*vyasa*) the Vedas. Vedavyasa or Vyasadeva isn't a proper name. It is a title. Once in a while, in accordance with the needs of the era, the Vedas need to be classified. Each such person obtains the title and there have been twenty-eight Vyasadevas so far.

At one level, the question about who composed the Mahabharata is pointless. According to popular belief and according to what the Mahabharata itself states, it was composed by Krishna Dvaipayana Vedavyasa (Vyasadeva). But the text was not composed and cast in stone at a single point in time. Multiple authors kept adding layers and embellishing it. Sections just kept getting added and it is no one's suggestion that Krishna Dvaipayana Vedavyasa composed the text of the Mahabharata as it stands today.

Consequently, the Mahabharata is far more unstructured than the Ramayana. The major sections of the Ramayana are known as *kanda*s and one meaning of the word kanda is the stem or trunk of a tree, suggesting solidity. The major sections of the Mahabharata are known as *parva*s and while one meaning of the word parva is limb or member or joint, in its nuance there is greater fluidity in the word parva than in kanda.

The Vyasadeva we are concerned with had a proper name of Krishna

[5] Wealth. But in general, any object of the senses.
[6] Desire.
[7] Release from the cycle of rebirth.

Dvaipayana. He was born on an island (*dvipa*). That explains the Dvaipayana part of the name. He was dark. That explains the Krishna part of the name. (It wasn't only the incarnation of Vishnu who had the name of Krishna.) Krishna Dvaipayana Vedavyasa was also related to the protagonists of the Mahabharata story. To go back to the origins, the Ramayana is about the solar dynasty, while the Mahabharata is about the lunar dynasty. As is to be expected, the lunar dynasty begins with Soma (the moon) and goes down through Pururava (who married the famous apsara Urvashi), Nahusha and Yayati. Yayati became old, but wasn't ready to give up the pleasures of life. He asked his sons to temporarily loan him their youth. All but one refused. The ones who refused were cursed that they would never be kings, and this includes the Yadavas (descended from Yadu). The one who agreed was Puru and the lunar dynasty continued through him. Puru's son Duhshanta was made famous by Kalidasa in the Duhshanta–Shakuntala story and their son was Bharata, contributing to the name of Bharatavarsha. Bharata's grandson was Kuru. We often tend to think of the Kouravas as the evil protagonists in the Mahabharata story and the Pandavas as the good protagonists. Since Kuru was a common ancestor, the appellation Kourava applies equally to Yudhishthira and his brothers and Duryodhana and his brothers. Kuru's grandson was Shantanu. Through Satyavati, Shantanu fathered Chitrangada and Vichitravirya. However, the sage Parashara had already fathered Krishna Dvaipayana through Satyavati. And Shantanu had already fathered Bhishma through Ganga. Dhritarasthra and Pandu were fathered on Vichitravirya's wives by Krishna Dvaipayana.

The story of the epic is also about these antecedents and consequents. The core Mahabharata story is known to every Indian and is normally understood as a dispute between the Kouravas (descended from Dhritarashtra) and the Pandavas (descended from Pandu). However, this is a distilled version, which really begins with Shantanu. The non-distilled version takes us to the roots of the genealogical tree and at several points along this tree we confront a problem with impotence/sterility/death, resulting in offspring through a surrogate father. Such sons were accepted in that day and age. Nor was this a lunar dynasty problem alone. In the Ramayana, Dasharatha of the solar dynasty also had an infertility problem, corrected through a sacrifice. To return to the genealogical tree, the Pandavas won the Kurukshetra war. However, their five sons through Droupadi were killed. So was Bhima's son Ghatotkacha, fathered on Hidimba. As was Arjuna's son Abhimanyu, fathered on Subhadra. Abhimanyu's son Parikshit inherited the throne in Hastinapura, but was killed by a serpent. Parikshit's son was Janamejaya.

Krishna Dvaipayana Vedavyasa's powers of composition were remarkable. Having classified the Vedas, he composed the Mahabharata in 100,000 shlokas or couplets. Today's Mahabharata text doesn't have that many shlokas, even if the Hari Vamsha (regarded as the epilogue to the Mahabharata) is included. One reaches around 90,000 shlokas. That too, is a gigantic number. (The Mahabharata is almost four times the size of the Ramayana and is longer than any other epic anywhere in the world.) For a count of 90,000 Sanskrit shlokas, we are talking about something in the neighbourhood of two million words. The text of the Mahabharata tells us that Krishna Dvaipayana finished this composition in three years. This doesn't necessarily mean that he composed 90,000 shlokas. The text also tells us that there are three versions to the Mahabharata. The original version was called Jaya and had 8,800 shlokas. This was expanded to 24,000 shlokas and called Bharata. Finally, it was expanded to 90,000 (or 100,000) shlokas and called Mahabharata.

Krishna Dvaipayana didn't rest even after that. He composed the eighteen Maha Puranas, adding another 400,000 shlokas. Having composed the Mahabharata, he taught it to his disciple Vaishampayana. When Parikshit was killed by a serpent, Janamejaya organized a snake-sacrifice to destroy the serpents. With all the sages assembled there, Vaishampayana turned up and the assembled sages wanted to know the story of the Mahabharata, as composed by Krishna Dvaipayana. Janamejaya also wanted to know why Parikshit had been killed by the serpent. That's the background against which the epic is recited. However, there is another round of recounting too. Much later, the sages assembled for a sacrifice in Naimisharanya and asked Lomaharshana (alternatively, Romaharshana) to recite what he had heard at Janamejaya's snake-sacrifice. Lomaharshana was a *suta*, the sutas being charioteers and bards or raconteurs. As the son of a suta, Lomaharshana is also referred to as Souti. But Souti or Lomaharshana aren't quite his proper names. His proper name is Ugrashrava. Souti refers to his birth. He owes the name Lomaharshana to the fact that the body-hair (*loma* or *roma*) stood up (*harshana*) on hearing his tales. Within the text therefore, two people are telling the tale. Sometimes it is Vaishampayana and sometimes it is Lomaharshana. Incidentally, the stories of the Puranas are recounted by Lomaharshana, without Vaishampayana intruding. Having composed the Puranas, Krishna Dvaipayana taught them to his disciple Lomaharshana. For what it is worth, there are scholars who have used statistical tests to try and identify the multiple authors of the Mahabharata.

As we are certain there were multiple authors rather than a single one, the question of when the Mahabharata was composed is somewhat pointless. It wasn't composed on a single date. It was composed over a span of more than 1000 years, perhaps between 800 BCE and 400 ACE. It is impossible to be more accurate than that. There is a difference between dating the composition and dating the incidents, such as the date of the Kurukshetra war. Dating the incidents is both subjective and controversial and irrelevant for the purposes of this translation. A timeline of 1000 years isn't short. But even then, the size of the corpus is nothing short of amazing.

* * *

Familiarity with Sanskrit is dying out. The first decades of the twenty-first century are quite unlike the first decades of the twentieth. Lamentation over what is inevitable serves no purpose. English is increasingly becoming the global language, courtesy colonies (North America, South Asia, East Asia, Australia, New Zealand, Africa) rather than the former colonizer. If familiarity with the corpus is not to die out, it needs to be accessible in English.

There are many different versions or recensions of the Mahabharata. However, between 1919 and 1966, the Bhandarkar Oriental Research Institute (BORI) in Pune produced what has come to be known as the critical edition. This is an authenticated text produced by a board of scholars and seeks to eliminate later interpolations, unifying the text across the various regional versions. This is the text followed in this translation. One should also mention that the critical edition's text is not invariably smooth. Sometimes, the transition from one shloka to another is abrupt, because the intervening shloka has been weeded out. With the intervening shloka included, a non-critical version of the text sometimes makes better sense. On a few occasions, I have had the temerity to point this out in the notes which I have included in my translation. On a slightly different note, the quality of the text in something like Dana Dharma Parva is clearly inferior. It couldn't have been 'composed' by the same person.

It took a long time for this critical edition to be put together. The exercise began in 1919. Without the Hari Vamsha, the complete critical edition became available in 1966. And with the Hari Vamsha, the complete critical edition became available in 1970. Before this, there were regional variations in the text and the main versions were available from Bengal, Bombay and the south. However, now, one should stick to the critical edition, though there are occasional instances where there are reasons for dissatisfaction with what the scholars of the Bhandarkar Oriental Research Institute have accomplished. But in all fairness, there are two published versions of the critical edition. The first one has the bare bones of the critical edition's text. The second has all the regional versions collated, with copious notes. The former is for the ordinary reader, assuming he/she knows Sanskrit. And the latter is for the scholar. Consequently, some popular beliefs no longer find a place in the critical edition's text. For example, it is believed that Vedavyasa dictated the text to Ganesha, who wrote it down. But Ganesha had a condition before accepting. Vedavyasa would have to dictate continuously, without stopping. Vedavyasa threw in a counter-condition. Ganesha would have to understand each couplet before he wrote it down. To flummox Ganesha and give himself time to think, Vedavyasa threw in some cryptic verses. This attractive anecdote has been excised from the critical edition's text. Barring material that is completely religious (specific hymns or the Bhagavad Gita), the Sanskrit text is reasonably easy to understand. Oddly, I have had the most difficulty with things that Vidura has sometimes said, other than parts of Anushasana Parva. Arya has today come to connote ethnicity. Originally, it meant language. That is, those who spoke Sanskrit were Aryas. Those who did not speak Sanskrit were mlecchas. Vidura is supposed to have been skilled in the mlechha language. Is that the reason why some of Vidura's statements seem obscure? In similar vein, in popular renderings, when Droupadi is being disrobed, she prays to Krishna. Krishna provides the never-ending stream of garments that stump Duhshasana. The critical edition has excised the prayer to Krishna. The never-ending stream of garments is given as an extraordinary event. However, there is no intervention from Krishna.

How is the Mahabharata classified? The core component is the couplet or shloka. Several such shlokas form a chapter or *adhyaya*. Several adhyayas form a parva. Most people probably think that the Mahabharata has eighteen parvas. This is true, but there is another 100-parva classification that is indicated in the text itself. That is, the adhyayas can be classified either according to eighteen parvas or according to 100 parvas. The table (given on pp. xxiii–xxvi), based on the critical edition, should make this clear. As the table shows, the present critical edition only has ninety-eight parvas of the 100-parva classification, though the 100 parvas are named in the text.

Eighteen-parva classification	*100-parva classification*	*Number of adhyayas*	*Number of shlokas*
(1) Adi	1) Anukramanika[8]	1	210
	2) Parvasamgraha	1	243
	3) Poushya	1	195
	4) Pouloma	9	153
	5) Astika	41	1025
	6) Adi-vamshavatarana	5	257
	7) Sambhava	65	2394
	8) Jatugriha-daha	15	373
	9) Hidimba-vadha	6	169
	10) Baka-vadha	8	206
	11) Chaitraratha	21	557
	12) Droupadi-svayamvara	12	263
	13) Vaivahika	6	155

[8] Anukramanika is sometimes called anukramani.

Eighteen-parva classification	*100-parva classification*	*Number of adhyayas*	*Number of shlokas*
	14) Viduragamana	7	174
	15) Rajya-labha	1	50
	16) Arjuna-vanavasa	11	298
	17) Subhadra-harana	2	57
	18) Harana harika	1	82
	19) Khandava-daha	12	344
		Total = 225	Total = 7205
(2) Sabha	20) Sabha	11	429
	21) Mantra	6	222
	22) Jarasandha-vadha	5	195
	23) Digvijaya	7	191
	24) Rajasuya	3	97
	25) Arghabhiharana	4	99
	26) Shishupala-vadha	6	191
	27) Dyuta	23	734
	28) Anudyuta	7	232
		Total = 72	Total = 2387
(3) Aranyaka	29) Aranyaka	11	327
	30) Kirmira-vadha	1	75
	31) Kairata	30	1158
	32) Indralokabhigamana	37	1175
	33) Tirtha-yatra	74	2293
	34) Jatasura-vadha	1	61
	35) Yaksha-yuddha	18	727
	36) Ajagara	6	201
	37) Markandeya-samasya	43	1694
	38) Droupadi-Satyabhama-sambada	3	88
	39) Ghosha-yatra	19	519
	40) Mriga-svapna-bhaya	1	16
	41) Vrihi-drounika	3	117
	42) Droupadi-harana	36	1247
	43) Kundala-harana	11	294
	44) Araneya	5	191
		Total = 299	Total = 10239
(4) Virata	45) Vairata	12	282
	46) Kichaka-vadha	11	353
	47) Go-grahana	39	1009
	48) Vaivahika	5	179
		Total = 67	Total = 1736

Eighteen-parva classification	*100-parva classification*	*Number of adhyayas*	*Number of shlokas*
(5) Udyoga	49) Udyoga	21	575
	50) Sanjaya-yana	11	311
	51) Prajagara	9	541
	52) Sanatsujata	4	121
	53) Yana-sandhi	24	726
	54) Bhagavat-yana	65	2055
	55) Karna-upanivada	14	351
	56) Abhiniryana	4	169
	57) Bhishma-abhishechana	4	122
	58) Uluka-yana	4	101
	59) Ratha-atiratha-samkhya	9	231
	60) Amba-upakhyana	28	755
		Total = 197	Total = 6001
(6) Bhishma	61) Jambukhanda-vinirmana	11	378
	62) Bhumi	2	87
	63) Bhagavad Gita	27	994
	64) Bhishma vadha	77	3947
		Total = 117	Total = 5381
(7) Drona	65) Dronabhisheka	15	634
	66) Samshaptaka-vadha	16	717
	67) Abhimanyu-vadha	20	643
	68) Pratijna	9	365
	69) Jayadratha-vadha	61	2914
	70) Ghatotkacha-vadha	33	1642
	71) Drona-vadha	11	692
	72) Narayanastra-moksha	8	538
		Total = 173	Total = 8069
(8) Karna	73) Karna-vadha	69	3870
(9) Shalya	74) Shalya-vadha	16	844
	75) Hrada pravesha	12	664
	76) Tirtha yatra	25	1261
	77) Gada yuddha	11	546
		Total = 64	Total = 3315
(10) Souptika	78) Souptika	9	515
	79) Aishika	9	257
		Total = 18	Total = 771

Eighteen-parva classification	*100-parva classification*	*Number of adhyayas*	*Number of shlokas*
(11) Stri	80) Vishoka	8	194
	81) Stri	17	468
	82) Shraddha	1	44
	83) Jala-pradanika	1	24
		Total = 27	Total = 713
(12) Shanti	84) Raja-dharma	128	4509
	85) Apad-dharma	39	1560
	86) Moksha Dharma	186	6935
		Total = 353	Total = 13006
(13) Anushasana	87) Dana Dharma	152	6450
	88) Bhishma-svargarohana	2	84
		Total = 154	T otal = 6493
(14) Ashva-medhika	89) Ashvamedhika	96	2743
(15) Ashra-mavasika	90) Ashrama-vasa	35	737
	91) Putra Darshana	9	234
	92) Naradagamana	3	91
		Total = 47	Total = 1061
(16) Mousala	93) Mousala	9	273
(17) Mahapra-sthanika	94) Maha-Prasthanika	3	106
(18) Svargarohana	95) Svargarohana	5	194
Hari Vamsha	96) Hari-vamsha	45	2442
	97) Vishnu	68	3426
	98) Bhavishya	5	205
		Total = 118	Total = 6073
Grand total = 19	Grand total = 98 (95 + 3)	Grand total = 2113 (1995 + 118)	Grand total = 79,860 (73787 + 6073)

Thus, interpreted in terms of BORI's critical edition, the Mahabharata no longer possesses the 100,000 shlokas it is supposed to have. The figure is a little short of 75,000 (73,787 to be precise). Should the Hari Vamsha be included in a translation of the Mahabharata? It doesn't quite belong. Yet, it is described as a *khila* or supplement to the Mahabharata and BORI includes it as part of the critical edition, though in a separate volume. In this case also, the translation of the Hari Vamsha will be published in a separate and independent volume. With the Hari Vamsha, the number of shlokas increases to a shade less than 80,000 (79,860 to be precise). However, in some of the regional versions the text of the Mahabharata proper is closer to 85,000 shlokas and with the Hari Vamsha included, one approaches 95,000, though one doesn't quite touch 100,000.

Why should there be another translation of the Mahabharata? Surely, it must have been translated innumerable times. Contrary to popular impression, unabridged translations of the Mahabharata in English are extremely rare. One should not confuse abridged translations with unabridged versions. There are only five unabridged translations—by Kisori Mohan Ganguly (1883–96), by Manmatha Nath Dutt (1895–1905), by the University of Chicago and J.A.B. van Buitenen (1973 onwards), by P. Lal and Writers Workshop (2005 onwards) and the Clay Sanskrit Library edition (2005 onwards). Of these, P. Lal is more a poetic trans-creation than a translation. The Clay Sanskrit Library edition is not based on the critical edition, deliberately so. In the days of Ganguly and Dutt, the critical edition didn't exist. The language in these two versions is now archaic and there are some shlokas that these two translators decided not to include, believing them to be untranslatable in that day and age. Almost three decades later, the Chicago version is still not complete, and the Clay edition, not being translated in sequence, is still in progress. However, the primary reason for venturing into yet another translation is not just the vacuum that exists, but also reason for dissatisfaction with other attempts. Stated more explicitly, this translation, I believe, is better and more authentic—but I leave it to the reader to be the final judge. (While translating 80,000 shlokas is a hazardous venture, since Ganguly and Dutt were Bengalis, and P. Lal was one for many purposes, though not by birth, surely a fourth Bengali must also be pre-eminently qualified to embark on this venture!)

A few comments on the translation are now in order. First, there is the vexed question of diacritical marks—should they be used or not? Diacritical marks make the translation and pronunciation more accurate, but often put readers off. Sacrificing academic purity, there is thus a conscious decision to avoid diacritical marks. Second, since diacritical marks are not being used, Sanskrit words and proper names are written in what seems to be phonetically natural and the closest—such as, Droupadi rather than Draupadi. There are rare instances where avoidance of diacritical marks can cause minor confusion, for example, between Krishna (Krishnaa) as in Droupadi[8] and Krishna as in Vaasudeva. However, such instances are extremely rare and the context should make these differences, which are mostly of the gender kind, clear. Third, there are some words that simply cannot be translated. One such word is dharma. More accurately, such words are translated the first time they occur. But on subsequent occasions, they are romanized in the text. Fourth, the translation sticks to the Sanskrit text as closely as possible. If the text uses the word Kounteya, this translation will leave it as Kounteya or Kunti's son and not attempt to replace it with Arjuna. Instead, there will be a note explaining that in that specific context Kounteya refers to Arjuna or, somewhat more rarely, Yudhishthira or Bhima. This is also the case in the structure of the English sentences. To cite an instance, if a metaphor occurs towards the beginning of the Sanskrit shloka, the English sentence attempts to retain it at the beginning too. Had this not been done, the English might have read smoother. But to the extent there is a trade-off, one has stuck to what is most accurate, rather than attempting to make the English smooth and less stilted.

As the table shows, the parvas (in the eighteen-parva classification) vary widely in length. The gigantic Aranyaka or Shanti Parva can be contrasted with the slim Mousala Parva. Breaking up the translation into separate volumes based on this eighteen-parva classification therefore doesn't work. The volumes will not be remotely similar in size. Most translators seem to keep a target of ten to twelve volumes when translating all the parvas. Assuming ten volumes, 10 per cent means roughly 200 chapters and 7000 shlokas. This works rather well for Adi Parva, but collapses thereafter. Most translators therefore have Adi Parva as the first volume and then handle the heterogeneity

[9] Krishna or Krishnaa is another name for Droupadi.

across the eighteen parvas in subsequent volumes. This translation approaches the break-up of volumes somewhat differently, in the sense that roughly 10 per cent of the text is covered in each volume. The complete text, as explained earlier, is roughly 200 chapters and 7,000 shlokas per volume. For example, then, this first volume has been cut off at 199 chapters and a little less than 6,500 shlokas. It includes 90 per cent of Adi Parva, but not all of it and covers the first fifteen parvas of the 100- (or 98-) parva classification.

* * *

The Mahabharata is one of the greatest stories ever told. It has plots and subplots and meanderings and digressions. It is much more than the core story of a war between the Kouravas and the Pandavas, which everyone is familiar with, the culmination of which was the battle in Kurukshetra. In the Adi Parva, there is a lot more which happens before the Kouravas and the Pandavas actually arrive on the scene. In the 100-parva classification, the Kouravas and the Pandavas don't arrive on the scene until Section 6.

From the Vedas and Vedanta literature, we know that Janamejaya and Parikshit were historical persons. From Patanjali's grammar and other contemporary texts, we know that the Mahabharata text existed by around 400 BCE. This need not of course be the final text of Mahabharata, but could have been the original text of Jaya. The Hindu eras or *yuga*s are four in number—Satya (or Krita) Yuga, Treta Yuga, Dvapara Yuga and Kali Yuga. This cycle then repeats itself, with another Satya Yuga following Kali Yuga. The events of the Ramayana occurred in Treta Yuga. The events of the Mahabharata occurred in Dvapara Yuga. This is in line with Rama being Vishnu's seventh incarnation and Krishna being the eighth. (The ninth is Buddha and the tenth is Kalki.) We are now in Kali Yuga. Kali Yuga didn't begin with the Kurukshetra war. It began with Krishna's death, an event that occurred thirty-six years after the Kurukshetra war. Astronomical data do exist in the epic. These can be used to date the Kurukshetra war, or the advent of Kali Yuga. However, if the text was composed at different points in time, with additions and interpolations, internal consistency in astronomical data is unlikely. In popular belief, following two alternative astronomers, the Kurukshetra war has been dated to 3102 BCE (following Aryabhatta) and 2449 BCE (following Varahamihira). This doesn't mesh with the timelines of Indian history. Mahapadma Nanda ascended the throne in 382 BCE, a historical fact on which there is no dispute. The Puranas have genealogical lists. Some of these state that 1050 years elapsed between Parikshit's birth and Mahapadma Nanda's ascension. Others state that 1015 years elapsed. (When numerals are written in words, it is easy to confuse 15 with 50.) This takes Parikshit's birth and the Kurukshetra war to around 1400 BCE. This is probably the best we can do, since we also know that the Kuru kingdom flourished between 1200 BCE and 800 BCE. To keep the record straight, archaeological material has been used to bring forward the date of the Kurukshetra war to around 900 BCE, the period of the Iron Age.

As was mentioned, in popular belief, the incidents of the Ramayana took place before the incidents of the Mahabharata. The Ramayana story also figures in the Mahabharata. However, there is no reference to any significant Mahabharata detail in the Ramayana. Nevertheless, from reading the text, one gets the sense that the Mahabharata represents a more primitive society than the Ramayana. The fighting in the Ramayana is more genteel and civilized. You don't have people hurling rocks and stones at each other, or fighting with trees and bare arms. Nor do people rip apart the enemy's chest and drink blood. The geographical knowledge in the Mahabharata is also more limited than in the Ramayana, both towards the east and towards the south. In popular belief, the Kurukshetra war occurred as a result of a dispute over land and the kingdom. That is true, in so far as the present text is concerned. However, another fight over cattle took place in the Virata Parva and the Pandavas were victorious in that too. This is not the place to expand on the argument. But it is possible to construct a plausible hypothesis that this was the core dispute. Everything else was added as later embellishments. The property dispute was over cattle and not land. In human evolution, cattle represents a more primitive form of property than land. In that stage, humankind is still partly nomadic and not completely settled. If this hypothesis is true, the Mahabharata again represents an earlier period compared to the Ramayana. This leads to the following kind of proposition. In its final form, the Mahabharata was indeed composed after the Ramayana. But the earliest version of the Mahabharata was composed before the earliest version of the Ramayana. And the events of the Mahabharata occurred before the events of the Ramayana, despite popular belief. The proposition about the feud ending with Virata Parva illustrates the endless speculation that is possible with the Mahabharata material. Did Arjuna, Nakula and Sahadeva ever exist? Nakula and Sahadeva have limited roles to play in the story. Arjuna's induction could have been an attempt to assert Indra's supremacy. Arjuna represents such an integral strand in the story (and of the Bhagavad Gita), that such a suggestion is likely to be dismissed out of hand. But consider the following. Droupadi loved Arjuna a little bit more than the others. That's the reason she was denied admission to heaven. Throughout the text, there are innumerable instances where Droupadi faces difficulties. Does she ever summon Arjuna for help on such occasions? No, she does not. She summons Bhima. Therefore, did Arjuna exist at all? Or were there simply two original Pandava brothers—one powerful and strong, and the other weak and useless in physical terms. Incidentally, the eighteen-parva classification is clearly something that was done much later. The 100-parva classification seems to be older.

The Mahabharata is much more real than the Ramayana. And, therefore, much more fascinating. Every conceivable human emotion figures in it, which is the reason why it is possible to identify with it even today. The text itself states that what is not found in the Mahabharata, will not be found anywhere else. Unlike the Ramayana, India is littered with real places that have identifications with the Mahabharata. (Ayodhya or Lanka or Chitrakuta are identifications that are less certain.) Kurukshetra, Hastinapura, Indraprastha, Karnal, Mathura, Dvaraka, Gurgaon, Girivraja are real places: the list is endless. In all kinds of unlikely places, one comes across temples erected by the Pandavas when they were exiled to the forest. In some of these places, archaeological excavations have substantiated the stories. The war for regional supremacy in the Ganga–Yamuna belt is also a plausible one. The Vrishnis and the

Shurasenas (the Yadavas) are isolated, they have no clear alliance (before the Pandavas) with the powerful Kurus. There is the powerful Magadha kingdom under Jarasandha and Jarasandha had made life difficult for the Yadavas. He chased them away from Mathura to Dvaraka. Shishupala of the Chedi kingdom doesn't like Krishna and the Yadavas either. Through Kunti, Krishna has a matrimonial alliance with the Pandavas. Through Subhadra, the Yadavas have another matrimonial alliance with the Pandavas. Through another matrimonial alliance, the Pandavas obtain Drupada of Panchala as an ally. In the course of the royal sacrifice, Shishupala and Jarasandha are eliminated. Finally, there is yet another matrimonial alliance with Virata of the Matsya kingdom, through Abhimanyu. When the two sides face each other on the field of battle, they are more than evenly matched. Other than the Yadavas, the Pandavas have Panchala, Kashi, Magadha, Matsya and Chedi on their side. The Kouravas have Pragjyotisha, Anga, Kekaya, Sindhu, Avanti, Gandhara, Shalva, Bahlika and Kamboja as allies. At the end of the war, all these kings are slain and the entire geographical expanse comes under the control of the Pandavas and the Yadavas. Only Kripacharya, Ashvatthama and Kritavarma survive on the Kourava side.

Reading the Mahabharata, one forms the impression that it is based on some real incidents. That does not mean that a war on the scale that is described took place. Or that miraculous weapons and chariots were the norm. But there is such a lot of trivia, unconnected with the main story, that their inclusion seems to serve no purpose unless they were true depictions. For instance, what does the physical description of Kripa's sister and Drona's wife, Kripi, have to do with the main story? It is also more real than the Ramayana because nothing, especially the treatment of human emotions and behaviour, exists in black and white. Everything is in shades of grey. The Uttara Kanda of the Ramayana is believed to have been a later interpolation. If one excludes the Uttara Kanda, we generally know what is good. We know who is good. We know what is bad. We know who is bad. This is never the case with the Mahabharata. However, a qualification is necessary. Most of us are aware of the Mahabharata story because we have read some version or the other, typically an abridged one. Every abridged version simplifies and condenses, distills out the core story. And in doing that, it tends to paint things in black and white, fitting everything into the mould of good and bad. The Kouravas are bad. The Pandavas are good. And good eventually triumphs. The unabridged Mahabharata is anything but that. It is much more nuanced. Duryodhana isn't invariably bad. He is referred to as Suyodhana as well, and not just by his father. History is always written from the point of view of the victors. While the Mahabharata is generally laudatory towards the Pandavas, there are several places where the text has a pro-Kourava stance. There are several places where the text has an anti-Krishna stance. That's yet another reason why one should read an unabridged version, so as not to miss out on these nuances. Take the simple point about inheritance of the kingdom. Dhritarashtra was blind. Consequently, the king was Pandu. On Pandu's death, who should inherit the kingdom? Yudhishthira was the eldest among the brothers. (Actually, Karna was, though it didn't become known until later.) We thus tend to assume that the kingdom was Yudhishthira's by right, because he was the eldest. (The division of the kingdom into two, Hastinapura and Indraprastha, is a separate matter.) But such primogeniture was not universally clear. A case can also be established for Duryodhana, because he was Dhritarashtra's son. If primogeniture was the rule, the eldest son of the Pandavas was Ghatotkacha, not Abhimanyu. Before both were killed, Ghatotkacha should have had a claim to the throne. However, there is no such suggestion anywhere. The argument that Ghatotkacha was the son of a rakshasa or demon will not wash. He never exhibited any demonic qualities and was a dutiful and loving son. Karna saved up a weapon for Arjuna and this was eventually used to kill Ghatotkacha. At that time, we have the unseemly sight of Krishna dancing around in glee at Ghatotkacha being killed.

In the Mahabharata, because it is nuanced, we never quite know what is good and what is bad, who is good and who is bad. Yes, there are degrees along a continuum. But there are no watertight and neat compartments. The four objectives of human existence are dharma, artha, kama and moksha. Etymologically, dharma is that which upholds. If one goes by the Bhagavad Gita, pursuit of these four are also transient diversions. Because the fundamental objective is to transcend these four, even moksha. Within these four, the Mahabharata is about a conflict of dharma. Dharma has been reduced to *varnashrama* dharma, according to the four classes (*varna*s) and four stages of life (*ashrama*s). However, these are collective interpretations of dharma, in the sense that a Kshatriya in the *garhasthya* (householder) stage has certain duties. Dharma in the Mahabharata is individual too. Given an identical situation, a Kshatriya in the garhasthya stage might adopt a course of action that is different from that adopted by another Kshatriya in the garhasthya stage, and who is to judge what is wrong and what is right? Bhishma adopted a life of celibacy. So did Arjuna, for a limited period. In that stage of celibacy, both were approached by women who had fallen in love with them. And if those desires were not satisfied, the respective women would face difficulties, even death. Bhishma spurned the advance, but Arjuna accepted it. The conflict over dharma is not only the law versus morality conflict made famous by Krishna and Arjuna in the Bhagavad Gita. It pervades the Mahabharata, in terms of a conflict over two different notions of dharma. Having collectively married Droupadi, the Pandavas have agreed that when one of them is closeted with Droupadi, the other four will not intrude. And if there is such an instance of intrusion, they will go into self-exile. Along comes a Brahmana whose cattle have been stolen by thieves. Arjuna's weapons are in the room where Droupadi and Yudhishthira are. Which is the higher dharma? Providing succour to the Brahmana or adhering to the oath? Throughout the Mahabharata, we have such conflicts, with no clear normative indications of what is wrong and what is right, because there are indeed no absolute answers. Depending on one's decisions, one faces the consequences and this brings in the unsolvable riddle of the tension between free will and determinism, the so-called karma concept. The boundaries of philosophy and religion blur.

These conflicts over dharma are easy to identify with. It is easy to empathize with the protagonists, because we face such conflicts every day. That is precisely the reason why the Mahabharata is read even today. And the reason one says every conceivable human emotion figures in the story. Everyone familiar with the Mahabharata has thought about the decisions taken and about the characters. Why was life so unfair to Karna? Why was Krishna partial to the Pandavas? Why didn't he prevent the war? Why was Abhimanyu killed so unfairly? Why did the spirited and dark Droupadi, so unlike the Sita of the Ramayana, have to be humiliated publicly?

***

It is impossible to pinpoint when and how my interest in the Mahabharata started. As a mere toddler, my maternal grandmother used to tell me stories from *Chandi*, part of the Markandeya Purana. I still vividly recollect pictures from her copy of *Chandi*: Kali licking the demon Raktavija's blood. Much later, in my early teens, at school in Ramakrishna Mission, Narendrapur, I first read the Bhagavad Gita, without understanding much of what I read. The alliteration and poetry in the first chapter was attractive enough for me to learn it by heart. Perhaps the seeds were sown there. In my late teens, I stumbled upon Bankimchandra Chattopadhyay's *Krishna Charitra*, written in 1886. Bankimchandra was not only a famous novelist, he was a brilliant essayist. For a long time, *Krishna Charitra* was not available other than in Bengali. It has now been translated into English, but deserves better dissemination. A little later, when in college, I encountered Buddhadeb Bose's *Mahabharater Katha*. That was another brilliant collection of essays, first serialized in a magazine and then published as a book in 1974. This too was originally in Bengali, but is now available in English. Unlike my sons, my first exposure to the Mahabharata story came not through television serials but comic books. Upendrakishore Raychowdhury's Mahabharata (and Ramayana) for children was staple diet, later supplanted by Rajshekhar Basu's abridged versions of both epics, written for adults. Both were in Bengali. In English, there was Chakravarti Rajagopalachari's abridged translation, still a perennial favourite. Later, Chakravarthi Narasimhan's selective unabridged translation gave a flavour of what the Mahabharata actually contained. In Bengal, the Kashiram Das version of the Mahabharata, written in the seventeenth century, was quite popular. I never found this appealing. But in the late 1970s, I stumbled upon a treasure. Kolkata's famous College Street was a storehouse of old and second-hand books in those days. You never knew what you would discover when browsing. In the nineteenth century, an unabridged translation of the Mahabharata had been done in Bengali under the editorship of Kaliprasanna Singha (1840–70). I picked this up for the princely sum of Rs 5. The year may have been 1979, but Rs 5 was still amazing. This was my first complete reading of the unabridged version of the Mahabharata. This particular copy probably had antiquarian value. The pages would crumble in my hands and I soon replaced my treasured possession with a republished reprint. Not longer after, I acquired the Aryashastra version of the Mahabharata, with both the Sanskrit and the Bengali together. In the early 1980s, I was also exposed to three Marathi writers writing on the Mahabharata. There was Iravati Karve's *Yuganta*. This was available in both English and in Marathi. I read the English one first, followed by the Marathi. The English version isn't an exact translation of the Marathi and the Marathi version is far superior. Then there was Durga Bhagwat's *Vyas Parva*. This was in Marathi and I am not aware of an English translation. Finally, there was Shivaji Sawant's *Mritunjaya*, a kind of autobiography for Karna. This was available both in English and in Marathi. Incidentally, one should mention John Smith's excellent abridged translation, based on the Critical Edition, and published while this unabridged translation was going on.

In the early 1980s, quite by chance, I encountered two shlokas, one from Valmiki's Ramayana, the other from Kalidasa's *Meghadutam*. These were two poets separated by anything between 500 to 1,000 years, the exact period being an uncertain one. The shloka in *Meghadutam* is right towards the beginning, the second shloka to be precise. It is the first day in the month of Ashada. The yaksha has been cursed and has been separated from his beloved. The mountains are covered with clouds. These clouds are like elephants, bent down as if in play. The shloka in the Valmiki Ramayana occurs in Sundara Kanda. Rama now knows that Sita is in Lanka. But the monsoon stands in the way of the invasion. The clouds are streaked with flags of lightning and garlanded with geese. They are like mountain peaks and are thundering, like elephants fighting. At that time, I did not know that elephants were a standard metaphor for clouds in Sanskrit literature. I found it amazing that two different poets separated by time had thought of elephants. And because the yaksha was pining for his beloved, the elephants were playing. But because Rama was impatient to fight, the elephants were fighting. I resolved that I must read all this in the original. It was a resolution I have never regretted. I think that anyone who has not read *Meghadutam* in Sanskrit has missed out on a thing of beauty that will continue to be a joy for generations to come.

In the early 1980s, Professor Ashok Rudra was a professor of economics in Visva-Bharati, Santiniketan. I used to teach in Presidency College, Kolkata, and we sometimes met. Professor Rudra was a left-wing economist and didn't think much of my economics. I dare say the feeling was reciprocated. By tacit agreement, we never discussed economics. Instead, we discussed Indological subjects. At that point, Professor Rudra used to write essays on such subjects in Bengali. I casually remarked, 'I want to do a statistical test on the frequency with which the five Pandavas used various weapons in the Kurukshetra war.' Most sensible men would have dismissed the thought as crazy. But Professor Rudra wasn't sensible by usual norms of behaviour and he was also a trained statistician. He encouraged me to do the paper, written and published in Bengali, using the Aryashastra edition. Several similar papers followed, written in Bengali. In 1983, I moved to Pune, to the Gokhale Institute of Politics and Economics, a stone's throw away from BORI. *Annals of the Bhandarkar Oriental Research Institute (ABORI)* is one of the most respected journals in Indology. Professor G.B. Palsule was then the editor of ABORI and later went on to become Director of BORI. I translated one of the Bengali essays into English and went and met Professor Palsule, hoping to get it published in ABORI. To Professor Palsule's eternal credit, he didn't throw the dilettante out. Instead, he said he would get the paper refereed. The referee's substantive criticism was that the paper should have been based on the critical edition, which is how I came to know about it. Eventually, this paper (and a few more) were published in ABORI. In 1989, these became a book titled *Essays on the Ramayana and the Mahabharata*, published when the Mahabharata frenzy had reached a peak on television. The book got excellent reviews, but hardly sold. It is now out of print. As an aside, the book was jointly dedicated to Professor Rudra and Professor Palsule, a famous economist and a famous Indologist respectively. Both were flattered. However, when I gave him a copy, Professor Rudra said, 'Thank you very much. But who is Professor Palsule?' And Professor Palsule remarked, 'Thank you very much. But who is Professor Rudra?'

While the research interest in the Mahabharata remained, I got sidetracked into translating. Through the 1990s, there were abridged translations of the Maha Puranas, the Vedas and the eleven major Upanishads. I found that I enjoyed translating from the Sanskrit to English and since these volumes were well received, perhaps I did do a good job. With Penguin as publisher, I did a translation of the Bhagavad Gita, something I had always wanted to do. *Sarama and Her Children*, a book on attitudes towards dogs in India, also with Penguin, followed. I kept thinking about doing an unabridged translation of the Mahabharata and waited to muster up the courage. That courage now exists, though the task is daunting. With something like two million words and ten volumes expected, the exercise seems open-ended. But why translate the Mahabharata? In 1924, George Mallory, with his fellow climber Andrew Irvine, may or may not have climbed Mount Everest. They were last seen a few hundred metres from the summit, before they died. Mallory was once asked why he wanted to climb Everest and he answered, 'Because it's there.' Taken out of context, there is no better reason for wanting to translate the Mahabharata. There is a steep mountain to climb. And I would not have dared had I not been able to stand on the shoulders of the three intellectual giants who have preceded me—Kisori Mohan Ganguli, Manmatha Nath Dutt and J.A.B. van Buitenen.

Bibek Debroy

Souptika Parva

Souptika Parva refers to incidents that take place during the night. The word *supta* is used both as a noun and an adjective and, in this context, means events that take place when people are asleep. The parva is named accordingly. In the 18-parva classification, Souptika Parva is the tenth. In the 100-parva classification, Souptika Parva constitutes Sections 78 to 79. Souptika Parva is a short parva and only has eighteen chapters. In the numbering of the chapters in Souptika Parva, the first number is a consecutive one, starting with the beginning of the Mahabharata. And the second number, within brackets, is the numbering of the chapter within Souptika Parva.

SECTION SEVENTY-EIGHT

Souptika Parva

This parva has 515 shlokas and nine chapters.

Chapter 1284(1): 66 shlokas
Chapter 1285(2): 33 shlokas
Chapter 1286(3): 35 shlokas
Chapter 1287(4): 33 shlokas
Chapter 1288(5): 38 shlokas
Chapter 1289(6): 34 shlokas
Chapter 1290(7): 66 shlokas
Chapter 1291(8): 151 shlokas
Chapter 1292(9): 59 shlokas

In the night, Ashvatthama sees an owl kill sleeping crows and decides that the Pandavas and Panchalas should be killed in the night, while they are asleep. Kripa and Kritavarma try to dissuade Ashvatthama, but fail. Ashvatthama worships Shiva and Shiva enters his body. Ashvatthama kills Dhrishtadyumna, Shikhandi, Uttamouja, Yudhamanyu, other Panchalas and Droupadi's sons. This information is conveyed to Duryodhana and Duryodhana dies.

Chapter 1284(1)

'Sanjaya said, "Together, those brave ones[1] then headed in a southern direction. At a time when the sun was about to set,

[1]Ashvatthama, Kripa and Kritavarma.

they reached the camp.[2] They unyoked their mounts and were terrified. They went to a deserted region and entered it. They were not very far away from where the soldiers were encamped. They were mangled, all over their bodies, with sharp weapons. They let out long and warm sighs and thought of the Pandavas. They heard the fierce roars emitted by the Pandavas, who were desirous of victory. Fearing that they would be pursued, they again fled in an eastern direction. However, after travelling for some time, they were thirsty and their mounts were exhausted. Those great archers could not tolerate what had happened and were overcome by anger and vindictiveness. They were tormented that the king[3] had been killed and rested for some time."

'Dhritarashtra said, "O Sanjaya! The task that Bhima performed is deserving of honour. He brought down my son, who possessed the strength of ten thousand elephants. He was young and could withstand the *vajra*. All beings were incapable of slaying him. O son of Gavalgana![4] Men cannot overcome destiny. In the battle, the Parthas clashed against my son and brought him down. O Sanjaya! It is certain that my heart is made out of stone. Despite having heard about the death of one hundred of my sons, it has not shattered into one thousand fragments. When their sons have been slain, what will become of this aged couple?[5] I am not interested in dwelling in the dominion of the Pandaveyas. O Sanjaya! How can I? I have myself been a king. I have been the father of a king. How can I be a servant who follows Pandaveya's commands? O Sanjaya! I have commanded the entire earth and have placed my feet on its head. How can I be reduced to this difficult state of being a servant? O Sanjaya! How can I bear to hear Bhima's words? He has single-handedly killed one hundred of my sons. The words that the great-souled Vidura spoke have come to be true. O Sanjaya! My son did not act in accordance with those words.

[2]The camp of the Kouravas.

[3]Duryodhana.

[4]Sanjaya was the son of Gavalgana.

[5]Dhritarashtra and Gandhari.

O son![6] My son, Duryodhana, has been slain through *adharma*.[7] O Sanjaya! What did Kritavarma, Kripa and Drona's son do?"

'Sanjaya replied, "O king! After those on your side had travelled a short distance, they saw a fierce forest. It was full of many trees and creepers. They rested there for some time and those supreme horses obtained water. At the time when the sun was setting, they entered that great forest. It was full of large numbers of many kinds of animals and many birds. There were diverse trees and creepers and it was full of many kinds of predatory beasts. There were many beautiful ponds, full of water. These were covered with hundreds of lotuses and blue lotuses. Having entered that terrible forest, they glanced around in different directions. They saw a banyan tree[8] there, with many thousands of branches. O king! Approaching that banyan tree, those *maharatha*s, best among men, saw that it was the best among trees. They descended from their chariots there and unyoked the horses. O lord! As is decreed, they washed themselves and performed the evening rites. At that time, the sun had reached Mount Asta,[9] the best of mountains. Night, the creator of the entire universe,[10] manifested itself. In every direction, the sky was beautiful to behold. It was ornamented with planets, *nakshatra*s and stars.[11] Beings which are powerful and roam during the night began to howl. Beings that roam during the day were overcome by sleep. Because of the shrieks of beings that roam in the night, it became extremely fearful. Predatory beasts were delighted and the night became terrible. Kritavarma, Kripa and Drona's son sat down together. It was the

[6]The word used is *tata*. This means son, but is affectionately used towards anyone who is younger or junior.

[7]In the duel with the clubs, Bhima struck Duryodhana below the waist and on the thighs, something not sanctioned by the code of fair fighting. This has been described in Section 77 (Volume 7).

[8]*Nyagrodha*, the banyan tree, the Indian fig tree.

[9]Mountain behind which the sun sets.

[10]Because there was darkness before the universe was created.

[11]Nakshatras are specific, while stars are general. There are twenty-seven specific nakshatras and some of these are collections of stars, rather than individual stars. Therefore, stars are mentioned in addition to nakshatras.

beginning of that terrible night and they were overcome by grief and sorrow. They sat down under the banyan tree and sorrowed about the destruction that had encompassed the Kurus and the Pandaveyas. Their limbs were overtaken by sleep and they lay down on the surface of the ground. They were greatly exhausted and wounded by many arrows. Maharatha Kripa and Bhoja[12] succumbed to sleep. They deserved happiness and did not deserve this misery. However, they slept on the surface of the ground. O great king! They slept, overcome by exhaustion and sorrow.

'"O descendant of the Bharata lineage! But Drona's son was flooded with wrath and intolerance. He could not sleep and sighed like a snake. He could not obtain any sleep and was tormented by anger. The mighty-armed one glanced at the forest, which was terrible to behold. He glanced towards the forest, inhabited by many beings. The mighty-armed one saw the banyan tree, inhabited by tens of thousands of crows.[13] Thousands of crows spent the night there. O Kouravya! Resorting to separate perches, they slept happily. In every direction, those crows were at ease and slept. He[14] saw that an owl, terrible in appearance, suddenly arrived. Its shriek was horrible and it was gigantic in form. Its eyes were tawny and its plumage was reddish brown. Its nose and talons were extremely long. It possessed the speed of Suparna.[15] O descendant of the Bharata lineage! Making only the slightest bit of noise, that bird approached the branches of the banyan tree. The bird descended on the branch of the banyan tree and having descended, killed an extremely large number of crows. It tore away the wings of some and severed the heads of others. With the talons on its feet, it broke the legs of others. It was powerful and in a short while, destroyed the ones it could see. O lord of the earth! Every side of that banyan tree was strewn with limbs and bodies.

[12]Kritavarma.

[13]The word used is *vayasa*. This means crow, but can be applied to a bird in general. However, subsequently, the word *kaka* is used. This specifically means a crow.

[14]Ashvatthama.

[15]Garuda's name.

Having slain the crows, the owl was delighted. It was the destroyer of its enemies and had acted against its enemies as it willed.

'"On witnessing the deceitful act perpetrated by the owl in the night, Drona's son began to think and arrived at a conclusion. 'For the battle, this bird has given me an instruction. I wish to destroy the enemy and it is my view that the time has come. The victorious Pandavas are incapable of being slain by me. They are powerful and full of enterprise. They are strikers who accomplish their objectives. But, in the king's[16] presence, I pledged to kill them. I will destroy myself, like an insect engaged in entering a fire. If I fight through fair means, there is no doubt that I will lose my life. However, there will be success through deceit and great destruction of the enemy. People who are skilled about sacred texts also abundantly praise certain methods over those that are uncertain. There will be words of censure and reprimand from the worlds. But a man who has embarked on the dharma of kshatriyas must bear them. The Pandavas, firm in their enmity, have committed acts of deceit at every step, even though they have been censured and reprimanded by everyone. On this, those who have thought about dharma have sung a song earlier and it has been heard. They knew about what was right and proper and recounted these shlokas. "The forces of the enemy must be struck, whether they are exhausted, shattered, eating, retreating or entering.[17] Whether they are sleeping in the middle of the night, whether their paths of progress have been destroyed, whether their warriors have been slain and whether the forces are hesitant or not, one must act in the same way."' Thinking in this way, Drona's powerful son resolved to slay the Pandu and Panchala warriors while they slept.

'"Having arrived at this cruel decision and thinking about it repeatedly, he awoke Bhoja and his maternal uncle,[18] who were asleep and told them. They were overcome with shame and did not reply. Having thought for some time, in a voice that was distracted and

[16]Duryodhana, described in Section 77 (Volume 7).

[17]Their camps.

[18]Kripa. Kripa's sister, Kripi, was Drona's wife and Ashvatthama's mother.

choking with tears, he[19] said, 'King Duryodhana was immensely strong and the only brave one. He has been killed. It is for his sake that we were engaged in this enmity with the Pandavas. He was the lord of eleven armies.[20] He fought single-handedly with many wicked ones and was brought down by Bhimasena, who acted with the valour of a shudra. Vrikodara also performed an inferior and extremely cruel deed. He kicked the head of one who had been consecrated with his feet. The Panchalas are roaring, singing and laughing at this. In their joy, they are blowing on hundreds of conch shells and beating on their drums. That tumultuous sound of musical instruments is mixing with the blare of conch shells. Those fierce sounds are borne by the wind and are filling the directions. The horses are neighing and the elephants are trumpeting. The brave ones are roaring like lions and that great sound can be heard. From the eastern direction,[21] those fierce sounds of rejoicing can be heard. The clatter of chariot wheels can be heard and it makes the body hair stand up. The Pandavas created great carnage among the sons of Dhritarashtra and the three of us are the only ones who have survived. Some of them possessed the life force of one hundred elephants. Some of them were skilled in the use of all kinds of weapons. But they have been killed by the Pandaveyas. I think that this is destiny. There is no doubt that deeds lead to such an end. Even if one performs extremely difficult deeds, this is the outcome of that. If your wisdom has not been clouded by your confusion, given this great calamity, decide and tell us about the best course of action.'"'

Chapter 1285(2)

'"Kripa said, 'O lord! Your words are full of reason and we have heard everything that you have said. O mighty-

[19] Ashvatthama.

[20] *Akshouhinis*.

[21] Ashvatthama, Kripa and Kritavarma had also eventually headed towards the east.

armed one! But listen to some words I am about to tell you. All men are tied down by two things, restrictions[22] and deeds. There is nothing superior to destiny and human action. O supreme one! Success does not come from destiny, to the exclusion of deeds. Nor do deeds alone succeed. Success comes from the union of the two. Everything, whether it is superior or inferior, is tied down by these two. Whether it is engagement, or whether it is withdrawal, everything is seen to depend on these.[23] What fruits are obtained when rain showers down on a mountain? What fruits are obtained when rain showers down on a ploughed field? Both exertion with an unfavourable destiny and a favourable destiny without exertion are always unsuccessful. What I have said earlier is correct. If the destiny of rain showers down on a field that has been properly tilled, seedlings of great qualities result. Human success is like that. Sometimes, having made up its mind, destiny follows its own course. However, according to their capacity, the wise resort to manliness. O bull among men! All human objectives are accomplished by those two.[24] Engagement and withdrawal are seen to be the result of this. One can resort to manliness, but success depends on destiny. One undertakes tasks based on that and consequent fruits follow. In this world, it is seen that the enterprise of skilled humans, if unaccompanied by destiny, are completely unsuccessful. That is the reason why lazy and ignorant men disapprove of enterprise. But this does not appeal to those who are wise. On earth, deeds are often seen to be unsuccessful. However, the lack of action is also seen to lead to the great fruit of misery. No one can be seen to obtain what he desires without action, nor is there one who obtains nothing after exertion. An industrious person is capable of sustaining life. A lazy person never obtains happiness. In this mortal world, it is often seen that industrious people want to ensure their own welfare. If an industrious person undertakes action and fails to obtain the fruits, he is not reprimanded in the slightest possible way. However,

[22]In the sense of destiny.

[23]This probably implies engaging in action and withdrawing from action.

[24]Human action and destiny.

if one does not undertake action and yet obtains fruits, he is usually censured and hated. A person who disregards this and acts in a contrary way, injures himself. That is what intelligent people say. Enterprise does not give rise to fruits because of two reasons, either because manliness is lacking, or because destiny is deficient. If there is a lack of enterprise, no task ever becomes successful. If an industrious and skilled person acts, after bowing down to destiny, the accomplishment of objectives is never baffled. This is also true of those who serve the elders and after asking them, act in accordance with their beneficial words. If, after asking those who are revered by the aged, one resorts to enterprise, one always obtains supreme success. It is said that this is the root of success. If one listens to the words of elders and then engages in tasks, one soon obtains all the fruits. However, a man who seeks to obtain his objective because of passion, anger, fear and avarice has no control and is soon dislodged from his prosperity. This Duryodhana sought to obtain his objective because of his greed. He was not far-sighted. He began a task that was not approved of. He was foolish and did not think. He disregarded the beneficial words of the intelligent and sought the counsel of those who were wicked. Though he was dissuaded, he engaged in an enmity with the Pandavas, who were superior to him in qualities. Right from the beginning, he was evil in conduct and could not control his meanness. He did not follow the advice of his friends and has been tormented through this catastrophe. We also followed that wicked man. That is the reason we have confronted this great and terrible calamity. This great calamity has overtaken me now. Even if I use my intelligence, I cannot fathom what is good for us. A man who is confused should ask his learned well-wishers. Having asked them, he should act in accordance with their words. Therefore, let us unite and go to Dhritarashtra, Gandhari and the immensely intelligent Vidura. Let us ask them. Asked by us, they will tell us what is beneficial for us next. We should then act according to what they say. That is my firm view. One should never embark on a task that will lead to disaster. If one resorts to enterprise and that task is unsuccessful, one should certainly deduce that the task is not favoured by destiny.'"'

Chapter 1286(3)

'Sanjaya said, "O great king! On hearing Kripa's auspicious words, which were full of dharma and artha, Ashvatthama was overcome with sorrow and grief. He burnt with misery, like a blazing fire. He formed a cruel resolution in his mind and replied to both of them. 'The quality of intelligence varies from man to man. But depending on his own wisdom, each one is satisfied with what he has. In this world, everyone thinks his own intelligence to be supreme. Each person reveres his own understanding and praises it a lot. Each person bases himself on praising his own wisdom. Everyone criticizes the intelligence of others and always honours and praises his own. To accomplish an objective, if they hold similar views, they are then satisfied with each other and show each other great honour. But when, because of destiny, those same men face a hardship, they oppose each other's understanding. This is especially the case because human intelligence is affected by lack of thought. Since the wisdom is clouded, their understanding differs. A skilled physician diagnoses the disease properly and then applies a medicine to correctly cure it. In the same way, men use their intelligence to accomplish their objective. Even if they use their own wisdom, they may be censured by other men. On this earth, when one is young, one's intelligence is often clouded. It is different in middle age. And in old age, a different kind of intelligence is agreeable. O Bhoja![25] When one confronts great calamity or when prosperity is equally great, it is seen that a man's intelligence is confounded. In the same person, depending on the state of intelligence then, what is once regarded as wisdom at one time is regarded as the reverse at another. Having used one's wisdom and intelligence to determine what is virtuous, one should then try to accomplish the objective. O Bhoja! All men determine what is virtuous and then cheerfully act accordingly, even if that action leads to death. Having determined their own reasoning and wisdom, all men act in different kinds of ways, thinking these to be beneficial. As a result of the calamity, I

[25]Kritavarma.

have arrived at a resolution today and I will tell both of you about this. It will dispel my sorrow. Having created beings, Prajapati[26] ordained tasks for them. He assigned different qualities for each of the varnas—supreme self-control to brahmanas, great energy to kshatriyas, skill to vaishyas and servitude of all varnas to shudras. A brahmana without self-control is not virtuous. A kshatriya without energy is the worst. An unskilled vaishya is censured, as is a shudra who is not devoted. I have been born in a brahmana lineage that is greatly revered. However, because of misfortune, I am engaged in the dharma of kshatriyas. Knowing the dharma of kshatriyas, if I now resort to the conduct of brahmanas and perform an extremely great deed, that will not be virtuous for me. I have wielded a divine bow and celestial weapons in the battle. Having seen my father slain, how will I speak in any assembly? Today, I will follow my desires. I will resort to the dharma of kshatriyas and follow in the footsteps of the king[27] and my immensely radiant father. The Panchalas desired victory and will sleep comfortably tonight. They will cast aside their armour and will be full of delight. They will think that they have defeated us and will be tired and exhausted. While they are comfortably sleeping in their respective positions in their camps, I will perform the extremely difficult task of attacking their camp. I will attack their camp when they are senseless, as if dead. I will slaughter them with my valour, like Maghavan[28] against the *danava*s. Today, I will use my valour and slaughter all of them together, with Dhrishtadyumna at the forefront, like a blazing fire amidst kindling. O supreme ones! Having slain the Panchalas, I will obtain peace. While roaming around amidst the Panchalas and slaughtering the Panchalas, I will be like the enraged Rudra, the wielder of the Pinaka,[29] acting against beings. Having severed and slain all the Panchalas today, I will then wrathfully take the battle to the sons of Pandu and afflict them. Today, I will strew the earth with the bodies of all the Panchalas. I will strike

[26]Brahma.

[27]Duryodhana.

[28]Indra.

[29]Pinaka is the name of Shiva's bow or trident.

them down, one by one, and free myself of my debt to my father. The footsteps of Duryodhana, Karna, Bhishma and Saindhava are difficult to follow, but the Panchalas will tread along those. Tonight, before the night is over, I will use my strength to grind down the head of Dhrishtadyumna, king of the Panchalas, treating him like an animal. O Goutama![30] While the sons of the Panchalas and the Pandus are sleeping tonight, I will use my sharp sword to crush them. O immensely intelligent one![31] When the Panchala soldiers are sleeping tonight, I will slaughter them. Having succeeded in my task, I will be happy.'"'

Chapter 1287(4)

'"Kripa said, 'O one without decay! It is through good fortune that you have decided to take revenge. Even the wielder of the vajra himself is incapable of restraining you. When it is morning, both of us will follow and accompany you. However, cast aside your armour and standard and rest tonight. When you advance against the enemy, I and Satvata Kritavarma will armour ourselves and follow you on our chariots. O best among *rathas*! United with us, you will use your valour to slaughter the enemy, the Panchalas and their followers, in the encounter. You are capable of doing this through your prowess. But rest during the night. O son![32] You have not slept for a long time. Sleep during this night. O one who grants honours! You are exhausted and without sleep. Rest, and then clash against the enemy in the battle. There is no doubt that you will slay them. You are the best among rathas! When you grasp your supreme weapons, no one is capable of defeating you, not even the gods, with

[30]Kripa.

[31]This is in the singular and is specifically addressed to Kripa.

[32]The word used is tata. This means son, but is affectionately used towards anyone who is younger or junior.

Agni's son.[33] When you advance angrily in the battle, with Kripa and Kritavarma, which warrior is capable of fighting against Drona's son. Not even the king of the gods. Let us overcome our exhaustion and lack of sleep. Let us get over our anxiety. When the night is over and it is morning, we will kill the enemy. There is no doubt that you possess divine weapons. So do I. Satvata is a great archer and is always skilled in fighting. O son! We will unite and advance against the enemy. We will strike and kill them in the battle and obtain complete happiness. However, you should rest first. Sleep happily during the night. O supreme among men! When you advance, Kritavarma and I will unite and follow you. We are archers and can scorch the enemy. When you advance swiftly on your chariot, we will armour ourselves and station ourselves on our chariots. You will go to the camp[34] and proclaim your name in the battle. You will fight against the enemy and cause great carnage. When it is morning and the day is clear, you will create that carnage. You will roam around, like Shakra destroying the great asuras. You are capable of destroying the Panchala formations in the battle. You will be like the enraged slayer of all the danavas,[35] against the army of the *daitya*s. When you are united with me in the battle and are protected by Kritavarma, the lord who is the wielder of the vajra is himself incapable of withstanding you. O son! Neither I, nor Kritavarma, will ever retreat from an encounter without having defeated the Pandus in the battle. We will kill all the inferior and united Panchalas and Pandus in the battle and return. Or we will be killed by them and go to heaven. When it is morning, we will aid you through every possible means. O mighty-armed one! O unblemished one! I am telling you this truthfully.'

'"The maternal uncle of Drona's son thus spoke these beneficial words to him.[36] O king! But having been thus addressed by his maternal uncle, his eyes became red with rage. He replied, 'If a man

[33]The text uses the word Pavaki, Pavaka's (Agni, the fire god) son. This means Kartikeya.

[34]The camp of the Panchalas and the Pandavas.

[35]Probably meaning Indra.

[36]Though not explicitly stated, this is Sanjaya speaking again. Ashvatthama's mother was Kripi, Kripa's sister. Kripa was hence his maternal uncle.

is afflicted and intolerant, how can he sleep? This is also true of someone who is thinking about artha and kama. Behold. I confront all these four reasons today. Even one of these four can destroy my sleep in the night, not to speak of the grief of someone like me who remembers the slaughter of his father. My heart is tormented now and I can find no peace during the day or at night. In particular, all of you have witnessed the wicked way in which my father was killed and this is tearing at my vitals. On this earth, how can someone like me remain alive even for an instant, after hearing the words the Panchalas spoke to me when Drona was killed? Without killing Dhrishtadyumna, I am not interested in remaining alive. Since he and the united Panchalas killed my father, they deserve to be slain by me. On hearing the lamentations of the king with shattered thighs,[37] is there anyone who is so cruel that his heart will not be tormented? On hearing the piteous words of the king with the shattered thighs, whose eyes will not overflow with tears? While I am alive, the side of my allies has been defeated. This increases my sorrow, like a torrent of water flowing into an ocean. I am single-mindedly focused on this now. How can I sleep happily? They are protected by Vasudeva and Arjuna. O maternal uncle! I think that even the great Indra cannot withstand them. I am incapable of restraining myself from this course of action. Nor do I see anyone in this world who can restrain me from this course of action. The messengers have told me about the defeat of my friends and the victory of the Pandavas. My heart is tormented. While the enemies are sleeping, I will cause carnage among them today. Then, bereft of fever, I will rest and sleep.'"'

Chapter 1288(5)

'"Kripa replied, 'Men who are not in control of their senses indeed find it difficult to understand everything about dharma and artha, even if they serve these. That is my view. In that

[37]Duryodhana.

way, it is certain that an intelligent person who has not studied humility understands nothing about dharma and artha. A person, who exercises self-control and serves,[38] without countering what is accepted by everyone, learns all the sacred texts and is intelligent. But there may also be an insolent, evil-souled and wicked man. He disregards destiny and what is beneficial and performs many wicked deeds. A well-wisher is a protector and seeks to dissuade from committing sin. One who is dissuaded obtains prosperity. However, one who is not dissuaded faces ill fortune. Just as a person whose intelligence is confused can be restrained through good and bad words, a well-wisher is capable of restraining a person and preventing him from facing a hardship. If an intelligent well-wisher[39] is about to perform a wicked deed, wise ones must use all their capacity to repeatedly restrain him. Therefore, set your mind on what is beneficial and control yourself. O son![40] Act in accordance with my words, so that you do not have to repent later. Following dharma, in this world, the slaughter of those who are sleeping is not applauded. This is also true of those who have cast aside their weapons and have abandoned their chariots and horses, those who say, "I am yours,"[41] those who seek refuge, those who have loosened their hair[42] and those whose mounts have been killed. O lord! The Panchalas have cast aside their armour. All of them will sleep peacefully in the night, unconscious, like those who are dead. If a wicked person acts hostilely against them in that state, it is evident that he will be immersed in a large and fathomless hell, without a boat to aid him. In this world, you are famous as the best among those who know all about weapons. Since you have been born on earth, you have not committed the slightest transgression. When the sun rises tomorrow and illuminates all beings, you will again be like a sun and defeat the enemies in the battle. This reprehensible

[38]In the sense of serving superiors, elders and preceptors.

[39]In the sense of friend.

[40]The word used is tata.

[41]As a token of surrender.

[42]Again as a sign of surrender.

deed is impossible in someone like you. It will be like a red spot on a white sheet. That is my view.'

'"Ashvatthama said, 'O maternal uncle! It is exactly as you have instructed me now. However, they have earlier shattered that bridge[43] into a hundred fragments. In your presence, the lords of the earth have witnessed it. When he had cast aside his weapons, my father was brought down by Dhrishtadyumna. Karna was supreme among rathas. When the wheel of his chariot was submerged and he faced a great difficulty, he was slain by the wielder of Gandiva. In that way, Bhishma, Shantanu's son, had cast aside his weapons and was without arms. Placing Shikhandi in front of him, the wielder of Gandiva slew him. In that way, Bhurishrava, the great archer, had decided to cast aside his life in the battle. Disregarding the cries of the lords of the earth, Yuyudhana[44] brought him down. In the encounter, Duryodhana clashed against Bhima with the club. While all the lords of the earth looked on, he was brought down through adharma. He was alone there, and was surrounded by many maharathas. That tiger among men was brought down by Bhimasena through adharma. The messengers have recounted the lamentations of the king with shattered thighs. I have heard them and it tore at my vitals. In similar fashion, the wicked Panchalas have also resorted to adharma and have broken the bridge.[45] Why don't you reprimand those who have broken all the rules? They slew my father. I wish to kill the Panchalas, while they sleep in the night. I do not care whether I am born as a worm or an insect. I will now swiftly do what appeals to me. I will quickly hasten towards that. Otherwise, how can there be sleep? How can there be happiness? I have made up my mind to kill them. The man who can dissuade me has not been born, nor will he be born.'"

'Sanjaya said, "O great king! Having spoken these words, Drona's powerful son yoked his horses alone and set out in the direction of the enemy. The lords, the great-minded Bhoja and Sharadvata, spoke

[43]Of dharma.

[44]Satyaki.

[45]Of dharma.

to him. 'Why are you yoking them to your chariot? What do you wish to do? O bull among men! We will accompany you tomorrow. We are with you, in joy and in sorrow. You should not doubt us.' However, Ashvatthama remembered the slaughter of his father and was enraged. He told them everything about what he desired to do. 'My father slew hundreds of thousands of warriors with his sharp arrows. When he had cast aside his weapons, he was brought down by Dhrishtadyumna. I will kill him in that situation today, when he has cast aside his armour. A wicked deed will be committed against the wicked son of Panchala. Like an animal, the wicked Panchala will be slain by me today. He will not attain the worlds obtained by those who are killed with weapons. That is my view. Swiftly fasten your armour and seize your swords and bows. O best among rathas! O scorcher of enemies! Wait here for me.' Having spoken these words, he ascended his chariot and left in the direction of the enemy. O king! Kripa and Satvata Kritavarma followed him. Those three advanced in the direction of the enemy. They blazed like fire with kindling in a sacrifice. O lord! They went to the camp, where all the people were sleeping. On his supreme chariot, Drona's son reached the vicinity of the gate."'

Chapter 1289(6)

'Dhritarashtra asked, "O Sanjaya! On seeing Drona's son in the vicinity of the gate, what did Bhoja and Kripa do? Tell me that."

'Sanjaya replied, "Summoning Kritavarma and maharatha Kripa, Drona's son approached the gate of the camp, overcome with rage. He saw a gigantic being there, as resplendent as the sun and the moon. He saw him stationed there, guarding the gate, and the sight made the body hair stand up. He was clad in attire made out of tiger skin and copious quantities of blood flowed from it. The upper garment was made out of black antelope skin and a serpent was the sacred thread. The arms were thick and large and wielded many kinds of weapons. A giant snake was like an armlet. His face was like a blazing garland. His gaping and fearsome mouth possessed terrible fangs. He possessed thousands of eyes and was wonderfully ornamented. It is impossible to describe his form or his attire. In every way, the mountains would be shattered if they looked at him. Large flames issued everywhere, from his mouth, his nose, his ears and his thousands of eyes. From those energetic flames, hundreds and thousands of Hrishikeshas[46] emerged, holding conch shells, *chakra*s and clubs. For all the worlds, that extraordinary being was terrifying. On seeing him, Drona's son was not distressed, but showered him with divine weapons. But the gigantic being devoured all the arrows that were shot by Drona's son, like the mare-headed fire[47] devouring the agitated waters. On seeing that his torrents of arrows had been rendered unsuccessful, Ashvatthama hurled a blazing javelin that was like the flames of a fire. The javelin blazed at the tip. But striking him, it was shattered. It was like a giant meteor, striking against the sun at the time of the destruction of a *yuga* and falling down from the firmament. Ashvatthama swiftly unsheathed a shining sword. It possessed a golden handle and was as radiant as the sky. It was like a flaming serpent emerging from a hole. The intelligent one then hurled that supreme sword at the being. On striking against the being, it disappeared like a puff of air. Drona's son became angry. He hurled a flaming club that was like Indra's standard. However, the being devoured this too. When all the weapons were destroyed in this way, Ashvatthama looked around and saw that the sky was covered with many Janardanas. Devoid of all weapons, Drona's son beheld this extraordinary sight. He remembered Kripa's words and repenting, said, 'He who does not listen to the pleasant and beneficial words of well-wishers, has to sorrow later, when he is overtaken by a calamity. I did not listen to their words. A person who is driven by violence and seeks to kill, violating the injunctions of the sacred texts, is dislodged

[46]Krishnas.

[47]*Vadava* is a mare and the subterranean fire, in the waters, is *vadavamukha*, shaped like a mare's head.

from the path of dharma and treads along crooked paths. One should not release weapons at cattle, brahmanas, the wives of kings, friends, a mother, a preceptor, an aged one, a child, one suffering from disease, one who is blind, one who is sleeping, one who is frightened, one who has just awoken, one who is intoxicated, one who is a lunatic and one who is distracted. In earlier times, the preceptors have always instructed men in this way. But I have transgressed the eternal path indicated in the sacred texts. I have begun to tread along a path that should not be followed and have faced this terrible calamity. The learned ones have said that there is no calamity greater than retreating from a great task out of fear, once one has embarked upon it. Using my strength and prowess, I am unable to accomplish the task I wished to. It is said that human tasks are not superior to destiny. A man may perform a task. However, if destiny does not render it successful, it is said that he is dislodged from the path of dharma and confronts a calamity. When one begins a task, but withdraws from it because of fear, learned ones say that this is known as defeat. Because my attempt was evil, this great fear has come upon me. Otherwise, Drona's son would never have retreated from an encounter. This extremely great being has arisen like the staff of destiny. Even though I think about it in every way, I do not understand who he is. It is certain that my wicked intelligence has made me embark on a course of adharma. As a consequence, he is seen to counter me in this way. Therefore, it has been ordained by destiny that I should retreat from this encounter. There is nothing that can be undertaken unless destiny is favourable. Hence, I will now seek refuge with the lord Mahadeva. I will seek refuge with Kapardin,[48] the lord of the gods and Uma's consort. He will save me from this terrible staff of destiny that is destroying me. He is adorned in a garland of skulls. He is Rudra Hara, who plucked out Bhaga's eyes.[49] That god surpasses all the gods in austerities and in valour. I will therefore seek refuge with Girisha, the wielder of the trident.'"'

[48]Shiva's name.

[49]Rudra and Hara are Shiva's names. At the time of Daksha's sacrifice, Shiva plucked out Bhaga's eyes. Girisha is also Shiva's name.

Chapter 1290(7)

'Sanjaya said, "O lord of the earth! Having thought in this way, Drona's son descended from the seat of his chariot and bowed down in obeisance.

'"Drona's son said, 'I seek refuge with Ugra,[50] Sthanu,[51] Rudra, Sharva, Ishana, Ishvara, Girisha,[52] the god Varada,[53] Bhava,[54] the undecaying Bhavana,[55] Shitikantha,[56] Aja,[57] Shakra, Kratha, Kratuhara,[58] Hara, Vishvarupa,[59] Virupaksha,[60] Bahurupa,[61] Umapati,[62] Shmashanavasina,[63] Dripta, the lord who is Mahaganapati,[64] Khattangadharina,[65] Munda,[66] Jatila[67] and Brahmachari. He is the one who has to be carefully thought of in the mind. He is the one who those of limited intelligence find extremely difficult to attain. In the sacrifice, I offer myself as a gift to the destroyer of Tripura.[68] He is the one who has been praised. He is the one who deserves to be praised. I am praising the irresistible

50The fierce one.

51The immobile one.

52The lord of the mountains.

53Varada means one who is the granter of boons.

54The excellent one, the one who brings into existence.

55Meaning, the creator of the universe.

56The one with a dark neck.

57The one without birth.

58The destroyer of a sacrifice, referring to Daksha's sacrifice.

59One whose form is the universe.

60The one with deformed eyes.

61One with many forms.

62Uma's consort.

63One who dwells in cremation grounds.

64*Gana*s are demonic beings who are Shiva's followers. Ganapati is the lord or leader of ganas, while Mahaganapati is a great Ganapati.

65The wielder of *khattanga*, a staff with a skull at the top.

66The one with a shaved head.

67The one with matted hair.

68City of the demons, destroyed by Shiva.

one, who has hides as his garment. O Vilohita![69] O Nilakantha![70] O Aprikta![71] O Durnivara![72] O Shukra![73] O Vishvasrija![74] O brahman! O brahmachari! You are the one who follows vows. You are always engaged in austerities. You are infinite. You are the objective of austerities. You have many forms. You are the lord of ganas. You are three-eyed. You are the one who loves your attendants. You are the one towards whom the lord of the ganas always looks.[75] You are the lord of Gouri's heart.[76] You are the father of Kumara. You are tawny. You have a bull as your mount. Your body is like your garment. You are extremely fierce. You are eager to adorn Uma. You are greater than everything. You are supreme. There is nothing that is greater than you. You are the lord of all arrows and weapons. You are the southern horizon. You are clad in golden armour. You are the god who is adorned with the moon on his head. O god! I meditate supremely on you. I am facing this great calamity now, one that is extremely difficult to counter. You are the purest of the pure. I am offering all the elements in my body as a gift to you in this sacrifice.' On realizing that this was the great-souled one's intention and that he had made up his mind to give himself up, a golden altar appeared before him.[77]

'"O king! A wonderful fire manifested itself on the altar. The flames enveloped the directions, the sub-directions and the firmament. Many beings also manifested themselves there. They possessed flaming mouths and eyes. They had many feet, heads and arms. They were like elephants and mountains, with giant faces. There were forms like dogs, boars and camels. There were mouths like horses,

[69]The deep-red one.

[70]The blue-necked one.

[71]The one who is not mixed.

[72]The irresistible one.

[73]The seed.

[74]The creator of the universe.

[75]Here the lord of the ganas means Kubera. That is, Kubera looks towards Shiva.

[76]Gouri is another name for Uma/Parvati.

[77]Before Ashvatthama.

jackals and cows. There were faces like bears and cats and mouths like tigers and leopards. There were faces like crows, mouths like apes and faces like parrots. Some possessed mouths like giant snakes. Others had mouths that were white in complexion and like those of swans. O descendant of the Bharata lineage! Some possessed mouths like woodpeckers and faces like blue jays. There were mouths like tortoises and alligators, mouths like porpoises. Some had mouths like giant sharks.[78] Others had mouths like whales. Some had mouths like lions, or faces like curlews. Others possessed mouths like doves or pigeons. Others had mouths like snakes. Some had ears on their hands. Others had thousands of eyes and hundreds of stomachs. O descendant of the Bharata lineage! There were those without flesh, with mouths like wolves[79] and mouths like hawks. Some had no heads. O king! Some had terrible mouths like bears. Eyes and tongues blazed. There were others with flaming mouths. O king! There were others with faces like sheep and mouths like goats. There were those with the complexion of conch shells, with mouths like conch shells and ears like conch shells. Some wore garlands of conch shells. Others had voices like conch shells. Some had matted hair, five tufts, or were shaven. Others had lean stomachs. There were four teeth and four tongues. Some had conical ears, or were diademed. O Indra among kings! Some wore grass on their bodies. Others had curly hair. Some wore headdresses and crowns. Others had beautiful mouths and were ornamented. Some wore lotuses and white lotuses, others were decorated with lilies. They were full of greatness and there were hundreds and thousands of them. Some had *shataghnis*[80] and chakras in their hands. Others had clubs in their hands. O descendant of the Bharata lineage! There were those with catapults and nooses in their hands, others with bludgeons in their hands. Some girded quivers on their backs, full of colourful arrows. They were indomitable in battle. They were with standards, pennants, bells and battleaxes. Some raised giant nooses in their hands. Others

[78]The word used is *makara*.

[79]The word used is *koka*. This can mean wolf, frog, or house-lizard.

[80]Unidentified weapon that could kill one hundred people at one go.

had maces in their hands. Some had pillars in their hands. Others had swords in their hands. There were those with snakes around their crowns. Others had giant snakes as their armlets and were adorned in colourful ornaments. Some were covered with dust. Others were covered with mud. All of them were attired in white garments and garlands. Some had blue limbs. Others possessed orange limbs. Some had faces that were shaven. With complexions like gold, those cheerful companions played on musical instruments like drums, conch shells, smaller drums, *jharjharas*,[81] other drums and trumpets. Some sang. Others danced. Those immensely strong ones jumped, leapt and whirled around. They ran swiftly and fiercely, the hair raised up by the wind. They were like crazy and giant elephants and roared repeatedly. They were extremely terrible, fearsome in form. They had spears and swords in their hands. Their garments were of many different colours. They were adorned with colourful garlands and unguents. They wore beautiful armlets decorated with jewels and their arms were raised up. They were brave and the slayers of enemies. They could withstand. But it was impossible to withstand them. They drank blood and ate fat and marrow. They sustained themselves on flesh and entrails. Some had hair that was tied up in tufts. Some had earrings. Some were thin. Others had thick stomachs. Some were extremely short. Others were extremely tall. Some were strong and extremely terrible. Some were terrible to look at. Others had drooping lips. Some possessed long penises. Others had knotted bones. Some wore extremely expensive crowns. Others were matted or shaven. They were capable of bringing down the sun, the moon, the planets and the nakshatras on the ground. If they so desired, they were capable of slaughtering the four types of beings.[82] They were always without fear and were capable of tolerating Hara's frowns. They were successful in doing whatever they wanted. They were the lords of the lords of the three worlds. They were always engaged in

[81]Kind of musical instrument, a variety of drum.

[82]Those born from wombs, those born from eggs, those born from sweat (insects and worms) and plants and trees.

sporting. They were the lords of speech. They were always devoid of malice. Having obtained the eight kinds of prosperity,[83] they were no longer overcome by wonder. However, the illustrious Hara was always amazed at their deeds. He was always devotedly worshipped by them in thought, words and deeds. In thought, words and deeds, he devotedly protected them like sons. There are other angry ones who always drank the blood and fat of haters of the brahman. They always drank *soma*, which has four kinds of taste.[84] They worshipped the wielder of the trident through learning, brahmacharya, austerities and control and obtained Bhava's presence. The illustrious Maheshvara, with Parvati, oversees the past, the present and the future. With the large number of demons, the illustrious lord enjoys the past, the present and the future.

'"They laughed in many kinds of ways. They slapped their arms and roared loudly. They played musical instruments. All this made the universe resound. Those extremely radiant ones praised Mahadeva and approached Drona's great-souled son, increasing his glory. They wished to test his energy and witness the carnage in the night. They had terrible and fierce clubs, tridents and swords in their hands. Those large numbers of demons were terrible in form and approached from every direction. On seeing them, fear was generated in the three worlds. However, on seeing them, the immensely strong one wasn't distressed. Drona's son had a bow in his hand. There were guards made from the skins of lizards on his fingers. He offered himself as a sacrifice to the one to whom sacrifices were offered.[85] Bows and arrows were the sacred kindling there. O descendant of the Bharata lineage! In that act of sacrifice, his own self was the oblation. Drona's powerful son used mantras of pacification. In great anger, he offered himself as a sacrifice to

[83]Compassion, forgiveness, cleanliness, lack of jealousy, altruism, lack of greed, purity and self-control.

[84]There are actually six kinds of taste—sweet, sour, salty, pungent, bitter and astringent. Here, bitter and astringent are probably being left out.

[85]Meaning, Shiva.

the one to whom sacrifices are offered. The undecaying Rudra is the performer of terrible deeds. Having performed this terrible deed, he joined his hands in salutation. Worshipping the great-souled one, he said, 'I have been born in the lineage of Angirasa. I am offering myself as a sacrifice. O illustrious one! I am offering myself as an oblation into the fire. Please accept me as a sacrifice. O Mahadeva! Devotedly, I am offering myself to you, as supreme kindling. With you in front of me, I am doing this in this time of difficulty. You are the soul of the universe. All beings are in you and you are in all beings. All the chief qualities are combined and vested in you. O lord! You are the refuge of all beings. I am offering myself as an oblation to you. O god! Accept me, since I am unable to defeat the enemy.' Having spoken these words, Drona's son ascended the altar, into the blazing fire. Overcome by anger, he controlled his soul and entered the one with the black trails.[86] He presented himself as an oblation, with his arms raised up.

'"On seeing him immobile, the illustrious Mahadeva himself smiled and said, 'Krishna, who is unblemished in his deeds, has worshipped me through truth, purity, sincerity, yoga, austerities, rituals, endurance, devotion, fortitude, intelligence and speech. Because of this, there is no one who is dearer to me than Krishna. I have tested you so as to show him honour. I have protected the Panchalas and exhibited many different kinds of maya. I have protected the Panchalas and have shown him honour. However, they have been overtaken by destiny and can no longer remain alive now.' Having spoken these words to the great archer, the illustrious one entered his body.[87] Before entering, he gave him a supreme and sparkling sword. Penetrated by that illustrious one, he again blazed in energy. Because of the energy created by the divinity, his body became powerful. As he attacked and advanced towards the camp of the enemy, many invisible beings protected him. He was like the lord of the gods[88] himself."'

[86]The fire.

[87]Shiva entered Ashvatthama's body.

[88]Mahadeva.

Chapter 1291(8)

'Dhritarashtra asked, "When Drona's maharatha son headed towards the camp, were Kripa and Bhoja frightened? Did they retreat? Were they restrained by the inferior guards and did they run away? Did those maharathas think that they[89] were irresistible and refrain? Or did they crush the camp and kill the Somakas and the Pandavas? Did they follow Duryodhana's supreme footsteps in the encounter? Were they slain by the Panchalas and did they lie down on the ground? What tasks did those two accomplish? O Sanjaya! Tell me that."

'Sanjaya replied, "Drona's great-souled son headed towards the camp and Kripa and Kritavarma stationed themselves at the gate of the camp. O king! On seeing that those two maharathas were ready to make efforts, Ashvatthama was delighted and softly spoke these words. 'If the two of you try, you are sufficient to destroy all the kshatriyas, not to speak of the remaining warriors, especially when they are asleep. I will penetrate the camp and roam around like Death, so that not a single man escapes from me with his life.' Having said this, Drona's son penetrated the large camp of the Parthas. Casting aside all fear, he entered through a spot where there was no gate. The mighty-armed one knew the spot and entered. He quietly approached Dhrishtadyumna's abode. Having performed great deeds in the battle, they[90] were extremely exhausted and slept at ease, surrounded by their own soldiers. O descendant of the Bharata lineage! He entered Dhrishtadyumna's abode. Drona's son saw that Panchala[91] was lying down, as if he was dead. He was on a large and excellent bed, covered by an expensive and silken sheet. This was covered with excellent garlands and was fragrant with the aroma of incense. The great-souled one was calmly sleeping, devoid of any fear. O lord of the earth! He awoke the sleeping one with a kick of his foot. With the touch of the foot, the one who was indomitable in battle awoke. The

[89]The opponents.
[90]The Panchalas.
[91]Dhrishtadyumna.

one with an immeasurable soul recognized Drona's maharatha son. As he was rising from his bed, the immensely strong Ashvatthama seized him by his hair and pressed him down on the ground with his hands. O descendant of the Bharata lineage! He was crushed down with great force. Because of consternation and sleep, Panchala was unable to resist then. O king! He pressed him down on his throat and his chest with both his feet. Though he roared and writhed, he[92] was about to kill him like an animal. He tore at Drona's son with his nails and gently said, 'O son of the preceptor! Slay me with your weapon. Do not delay. O best among men! By doing this, let me go the worlds of the virtuous.' Having heard the words that he had spoken, Drona's son replied, 'O worst of your lineage! There is no world for those who slay their preceptor. O evil-minded one! You do not deserve to be killed by any weapon.' Having spoken thus, like a lion against an elephant, he angrily struck the brave one in his inner organs with extremely fierce kicks of his feet. O great king! As he was being killed in that abode, the brave one's cries woke up the women and the guards. They saw that his body was being crushed by someone with superhuman valour and took that being to be a demon. Therefore, out of fear, they did not raise an alarm. Having dispatched him to Yama's eternal abode, the energetic one approached his extremely handsome chariot and ascended it. O king! He emerged from that abode and made the directions resound. The powerful one left for other parts of the camp on the chariot, wishing to kill the enemy.

'"When Drona's maharatha son had left, all the women and the guards let out cries of lamentation. On seeing that the king, Dhrishtadyumna, had been killed, they were overcome with great sorrow. On hearing their shrieks, all the kshatriyas awoke. The bulls among kshatriyas swiftly approached and asked, 'What has happened? Tell us.' O king! The women had been terrified at the sight of Bharadvaja's descendant.[93] In distressed voices that choked with tears, they said, 'Swiftly follow him. We do not know whether it

[92]Ashvatthama.

[93]Ashvatthama.

was a *rakshasa* or a human. He has killed the king of Panchala and is now stationed on his chariot.' At this, the foremost among warriors violently surrounded him. On seeing that they were descending on him, he uprooted all of them with *rudrastra*.[94] Having slain Dhrishtadyumna and all his followers, he saw that Uttamouja was sleeping nearby, on his bed. He attacked him and forcefully pressed down on his throat and his chest with his feet. He thus killed that scorcher of enemies, while he was shrieking. Thinking that he had been killed by a rakshasa, Yudhamanyu approached. He raised a club and powerfully struck Drona's son in the chest. However, he[95] rushed towards him, and seizing him, flung him down on the ground. As he writhed, he slew him like an animal. Having slain that brave one, he attacked the others. O Indra among kings! Wherever those maharathas slept, quivered, trembled and strove, he killed them like animals at a sacrifice. He grasped his sword and separately killed many others. Skilled in fighting with the sword, he roamed along different paths in various parts of the camp. He saw army divisions and killed those who were sleeping in the midst of those divisions. They were exhausted and had cast aside their weapons. He uprooted all of them in a short instant. With that supreme sword, he brought down warriors, horses and elephants. All his limbs were covered with blood and he was like Death, created by Destiny. Drona's son raised his sword and made them tremble. He struck them with three different motions of the sword[96] and was covered in blood. He was covered in red and fought with that blazing sword. His form was superhuman and he was resplendent and extremely terrible. O Kouravya! Those who were awakened were confused by the noise. On seeing Drona's son, they were distressed and glanced towards each other. On beholding his form, the kshatriyas, the destroyers of enemies, thought that he was a rakshasa and closed their eyes. Assuming a terrible form like Yama, he roamed around in that camp.

[94]Divine weapon named after Rudra, Shiva.

[95]Ashvatthama.

[96]In *Dhanurveda*, there were many techniques (motions) of fighting with the sword and it is not immediately obvious which three are meant.

'"He saw Droupadi's sons and the remaining Somakas. O lord of the earth! Frightened by the noise and hearing that Dhrishtadyumna had been killed, Droupadi's maharatha sons grasped bows in their hands. Without any fear, they countered Bharadvaja's son with storms of arrows. The Prabhadrakas awoke. With loud roars, they and Shikhandi struck Drona's son with arrows that possessed stone heads. On seeing that they were raining down showers of arrows, Bharadvaja's descendant roared powerfully and wished to kill the ones who were extremely difficult to defeat. Remembering the death of his father, he became extremely angry. He swiftly descended from his chariot and rushed against them. In that encounter, he picked up a giant shield that had the marks of one thousand moons and also a large and shining sword that was decorated with gold. With that sword, the powerful one roamed around and attacked Droupadi's sons. O king! In that encounter, the tiger among men struck Prativindhya[97] in the abdomen and killed him. Slain, he fell down on the ground. The powerful Sutasoma[98] struck Drona's son with a javelin and again attacked Drona's son with a sword. However, the bull among men severed Sutasoma's arm, with the sword in it. He struck him again in the side and with his heart shattered, he fell down. Nakula's valiant son, Shatanika, picked up a chariot wheel. Using both his hands, he flung it with great force and struck him[99] in the chest. However, after the wheel had been flung, the brahmana attacked Shatanika. He lost his senses and fell down on the ground and he severed his head.[100] Shrutakarma[101] picked up a club and attacked him. He attacked Drona's son and severely struck him on the left side of his head. However, with that supreme sword, he struck Shrutakarma on his face. Slain and bereft of his senses, he fell down on the ground, with his face disfigured. At this sound, the brave Shrutakirti[102] seized a giant

[97]Droupadi's son through Yudhishthira.

[98]Droupadi's son through Bhima.

[99]Ashvatthama.

[100]Ashvatthama severed Shatanika's head.

[101]Droupadi's son through Sahadeva.

[102]Droupadi's son through Arjuna.

bow. He attacked Ashvatthama and countered him with a shower of arrows. However, he countered that shower of arrows with his shield. O king! He then severed his head, with the earrings, from his body. The slayer of Bhishma,[103] together with all the Prabhadrakas, armed themselves with many weapons and attacked the brave and powerful one from all sides. He[104] used his bow to strike him between the eyebrows with an arrow with a stone head. At this, Drona's extremely powerful son was filled with great rage. He attacked Shikhandi and cut him down into two pieces with his sword. Having killed Shikhandi, the scorcher of enemies was enraged and powerfully attacked all the large numbers of Prabhadrakas. He also attacked the remaining troops in Virata's army. Wherever the immensely strong one saw the sons, grandsons and well-wishers of Drupada, he created a terrible carnage. He attacked many other men and killed them, one after the other. Drona's son was skilled in executing motions with the sword and struck them down with his sword.

'"They saw Kali,[105] with red eyes and a red mouth, adorned in red garlands and smeared with crimson paste. She was attired in a single red garment and had a noose in her hand. She had a tuft on her head. They saw that dark night stationed before them, as if she was smiling. She seemed to have tied up men, horses and elephants in a terrible bond. She seemed to tie up many dead bodies with nooses in their hair and bear them away. O venerable one! The foremost among warriors were sleeping and in their dreams saw them borne away by the night, as they were constantly struck by Drona's son. Since the battle between the Kuru and the Pandava soldiers had commenced, they had always seen that female deity and Drona's son in their dreams. They had already been slain by destiny and later, they were brought down by Drona's son. He roared frightfully and terrified all the beings. Those brave ones remembered the Kali that

[103]Shikhandi.

[104]Shikhandi.

[105]The text uses the word Kaali, a natural translation being the goddess. However, since the goddess Kali is unusual in the Mahabharata, a dark personification of the night is also possible.

they had seen earlier. As they were oppressed by destiny, that is what they thought. Because of those roars, hundreds and thousands of archers in the camp of the Pandaveyas woke up. Like Death created by Destiny, he severed the feet of some and the thighs of others. He shattered the flanks of others. As they were crushed severely, they emitted piteous sounds of lamentation. O lord! The earth was covered by them and there were others who were crushed by elephants and horses. Some exclaimed, 'What is this? Who is this? What is this noise? Who has done this?' As they wailed thus, Drona's son became their destroyer. He angrily destroyed the Pandus and the Srinjayas, who were without weapons and armour. Drona's son, supreme among strikers, dispatched them to the world of the dead. They were without weapons and awoke, overcome by fear. Some were blind with sleep and bereft of their senses. They seemed to vanish there.[106] Some were paralysed in their thighs. Others were full of lassitude and lost their energy. They lamented in great fright and began to kill each other. Drona's son once again ascended his chariot, the one that made a thunderous noise. With the bow in his hand, he used arrows to dispatch many others to Yama's eternal abode. Other best among men sought to approach him again. But while they were still at a distance, those brave ones were offered up to that terrible night. He crushed many with that fierce chariot. He showered the enemy with many diverse kinds of arrows. Yet again, he grasped that extremely wonderful shield marked with the signs of one hundred moons[107] and the sword that possessed the complexion of the sky, and roamed around. In that encounter in the camp, Drona's son was indomitable. O Indra among kings! He agitated them, like an elephant in a large lake. O king! Many warriors were awoken by the noise, still somewhat unconscious. They were afflicted by sleep. They were afflicted by fear. They ran around, here and there. There were those who couldn't find a voice and others who shrieked. There were those who screamed a lot and those who screamed little. Some could not find their weapons and their garments. Others had dishevelled

[106]Killed by Ashvatthama.

[107]The earlier reference was to one thousand moons.

hair and could not recognize each other. There were others who awoke and were terrified. Some wandered around aimlessly. Some released excrement. Others released urine. O Indra among kings! The horses and the elephants tore off their bonds. Others clung to each other and crated a great melee. Some men were frightened and lay down on the ground. As they fell down there, the elephants and the horses crushed them.

'"O bull among men! While this was going on, the rakshasas were satisfied and screamed in delight. O best among the Bharata lineage! O king! The large number of delighted demons emitted roars and filled all the directions and the sky with that loud noise. On hearing the woes of lamentation, the elephants and horses were frightened. O king! They freed themselves and as they fled, they crushed the men in the camp. As they ran here and there, a dust arose from their feet and this doubled the darkness of the night in the camp. Because of the darkness that was created, all the people were confounded. They could no longer recognize their fathers and their sons. Nor did brothers recognize their brothers. Elephants attacked elephants that were without riders and horses attacked horses. O descendant of the Bharata lineage! They attacked, broke and crushed each other there. As they were mangled and fell down, they killed each other. As they fell down, they brought down others and crushed them. The men were unconscious, sleepy and covered in darkness. Driven by destiny there, they killed those on their own side. Those in charge of gates abandoned the gates. Those in charge of divisions abandoned the divisions. To the best of their capacity, they fled. They were unconscious and no longer knew the directions. O lord! Without knowing, they destroyed each other. Their senses robbed by destiny, they cried out for their fathers and their sons. As they fled in various directions, they abandoned those on their own side and their relatives. Other men screamed and called out to each other by the names of their lineages. There were others who lamented as they fell down on the ground. Drona's son was crazy in that encounter. Recognizing them, he brought them down.

'"There were others who were repeatedly struck and lost their senses. Those kshatriyas were afflicted by fear and tried to run away from the camp. Terrified and seeking to preserve their lives, they emerged from the camp. In the vicinity of the gate, they were killed by Kritavarma and Kripa. They were devoid of weapons, implements and armour. Their hair was dishevelled and they joined their hands in salutation. They trembled on the ground and were terrified. They begged to be set free. O great king! But those who emerged outside the camp were not set free by the evil-minded Kripa and Hardikya. They also wanted to do that which would please Drona's son. Therefore, in three places, they set fire to the camp. O great king! When the camp was thus lit, Ashvatthama, the one who delighted his father, roamed around with the sword, exhibiting the dexterity of his hands. Some brave ones attacked, others ran away. The best of brahmanas used his sword to rob all those men of their lives. The valiant one severed some warriors in the middle with his sword. Drona's son angrily brought them down, as if they were stalks of sesamum. Men, horses and the best of elephants shrieked in grievous tones. O bull among the Bharata lineage! They fell down and were strewn all over the ground. Thousands of men were slain and fell down. There were many headless torsos which were seen to rise and then fall down again. Arms with weapons and armlets, and heads, were severed. O descendant of the Bharata lineage! There were thighs that were like the trunks of elephants, and arms and feet. The backs of some were mangled, and the heads of others. The flanks of others were mangled. Drona's son attacked them all, while some retreated. He severed the bodies of some men at the middle and sliced off the ears of others. He struck others on the shoulders and pressed down the heads of some into their bodies. While he roamed around, slaughtering many men, the terrible night was covered in darkness and seemed to become even more fearful. Some still had some life left. Other men were slain in thousands. There were innumerable elephants and horses on the ground and it looked terrible. It was full of *yaksha*s[108] and rakshasas. It was terrible because of the chariots, the horses and the elephants. As Drona's son angrily severed them, they fell down on the ground.

[108]Yakshas are semi-divine species and companions of Kubera, the god of treasure.

Some screamed for their mothers, others for their fathers, and still others for their brothers.

'"Some exclaimed, 'The angry sons of Dhritarashtra could not accomplish this in the battle. While we were sleeping, the evil-acting rakshasas have done this.[109] As long as he is protected by Janardana, Kounteya is incapable of being vanquished by gods, asuras, *gandharva*s,[110] yakshas and rakshasas. He is devoted to brahmanas. He is truthful in speech. He is controlled. He is compassionate towards all beings. Partha Dhananjaya does not kill one who is sleeping, one who is distracted, one who has cast aside his weapons, one who has joined his hands in salutation, one who is running away, or one whose hair is dishevelled. These rakshasas, evil in their deeds, are perpetrating these terrible acts on us.' Lamenting in this way, many men lay down. The lamentations of men and the shrieks of others died down in a short while. That great and tumultuous sound was pacified. O lord of the earth! The earth was sprinkled with blood and because of that, the large and fierce dust swiftly disappeared. Thousands of men were bereft of enterprise and writhed around in agony. As they fell down, those men were angrily killed, like Pashupati[111] amidst animals. There were some who clung to each other as they lay down. There were others who ran away. Some tried to hide, while others tried to fight. However, Drona's son brought all of them down. They were burnt by the flames and slaughtered by him. O Indra among kings! Before half of the night was over, that large army of the Pandavas was conveyed by Drona's son to Yama's abode. That night increased the delight of creatures that roam around in the night, though it caused a terrible carnage among men, elephants and horses. Many different kinds of rakshasas and *pishacha*s were seen there. They fed on the flesh of men and drank the blood. They were fierce, tawny and terrible. They had teeth like stone and were covered with blood. Their hair was matted and their thighs were long. They had five feet and large

[109]They had not realized that it was Ashvatthama.

[110]Gandharvas are celestial musicians and semi-divine.

[111]Shiva.

stomachs. There were those with five fingers, harsh and malformed, with terrible roars. Some had knees that were like jars. Others were short in stature, blue in the throat and fierce. They were extremely cruel and hideous. They were abominable and came with their sons and wives. Rakshasas of many different kinds of forms were seen there. They cheerfully drank the blood. Others danced around in large numbers. They exclaimed, 'This is great. This is pure. This is tasty.' There were also carnivorous creatures that subsisted on flesh. They fed on the fat, marrow, bones, blood, oily substances and other parts of the body that they regarded as excellent meat. Other demons[112] drank the fat that flowed and danced around. There were terrible and fierce carnivorous creatures that fed on flesh, with many kinds of mouths. They came there, in tens of thousands, millions and tens of millions. There were gigantic rakshasas terrible in form, the performers of cruel deeds. They were delighted and satisfied at this destruction. O lord of men! Many such demons assembled.

'"When it was morning, Drona's son desired to leave the camp. His body was covered in human blood and the sword was still in his grasp. O lord! It was as if the sword had become one with his hand. Having destroyed the men, he was resplendent in that carnage of men. He was like a fire that consumes all beings, when the destruction of a yuga is near. O lord! Drona's son accomplished the task that he swore to undertake, but walked along an undesirable path. He followed an extremely difficult path and forgot the fever on account of his father. The camp was asleep, when he had entered in the night and killed. In a similar silence, the bull among men emerged. With the other two,[113] the valiant one emerged from the camp. O lord! He joyfully told them what he had accomplished and delighted them. They also told him about the pleasant deeds that they had undertaken and about how they had destroyed thousands of Panchalas and Srinjayas. They roared in delight and slapped their palms. In this way, that night caused a great destruction of men among the Somakas. While they were asleep and unconscious, this

[112]*Kukshila*, a specific kind of evil spirit.

[113]Kripa and Kritavarma.

terrible and fearful destruction took place. There is no doubt that the course of destiny cannot be crossed. Those who caused a great carnage of men amongst us were thus slain."

'Dhritarashtra asked, "Why did Drona's maharatha son not accomplish such a great deed earlier? He did not achieve such a feat, though he was firm in ensuring the victory of my son. Why did he perform this task after my son had been killed? After all, Drona's son is a great archer. You should tell me this."

'Sanjaya replied, "O descendant of the Kuru lineage! This was certainly because of terror and fright. Drona's son could accomplish this deed because the Parthas, the intelligent Keshava and Satyaki were not present.[114] In their presence, even the lord of the Maruts[115] would have been unable to kill them. O king! O lord! And this kind of conduct was possible because the men were asleep. Having caused that extremely great carnage of men among the Pandavas, those maharathas[116] met each other and exclaimed, 'This was fortunate. It was good fortune.' Those two congratulated Drona's son and embraced him. In great delight, he[117] spoke these supreme words. 'All the Panchalas have been slain and all of Droupadi's sons. The Somakas and all the remaining Matsyas have been slain by me. Having accomplished this deed, let us immediately go to the spot where the king[118] is. If he is still alive, we will give him this pleasant news.'"'

Chapter 1292(9)

'Sanjaya said, "Having killed all the Panchalas and all the sons of Droupadi, they together went to the spot where Duryodhana

[114]In Section 77 (Volume 7), we have been told that the Pandavas, Krishna and Satyaki had gone to the Kourava camp.

[115]Indra is the lord of the Maruts.

[116]Ashvatthama, Kripa and Kritavarma.

[117]Ashvatthama.

[118]Duryodhana.

had been struck down. Having gone there, they saw that there was still some life left in the king. Having descended from their chariots, they surrounded your son. O Indra among kings! His thighs had been shattered. He was unconscious and was alive with great difficulty. They saw him lying down on the ground, vomiting blood through his mouth. He was surrounded by a large number of carnivorous beasts and their forms were terrible. There were a large number of jackals nearby, wishing to devour him.[119] He was restraining those carnivorous beasts, which wished to feed on him, with a great deal of difficulty. He was writhing on the ground and was suffering from severe pain. The great-souled one was lying down on the ground, covered in his own blood. In great grief, the three remaining heroes, Ashvatthama, Kripa and Satvata Kritavarma, surrounded him. Those three maharathas were also covered in blood and sighed. Surrounded by them, the king looked like a sacrificial altar surrounded by three fires. They saw the king lying down there, in a state that he did not deserve. Those three were overcome by great sorrow and wept. They wiped the blood from his face with their hands. On seeing the king lying down in the encounter, they wept in compassion.

'"Kripa said, 'Since he is covered in blood, there is nothing that is too difficult for destiny. Duryodhana was the lord of eleven armies.[120] He has been struck and is lying down. Behold. He loved the club and that club has fallen down on the ground, near him. Its complexion is like that of gold and it is adorned with gold. From one battle to another, this club never abandoned the brave one. Even now, when the illustrious one is about to go to heaven, it has not abandoned him. Behold. Decorated with molten gold, it is lying down near the brave one, like a wife lying down near her beloved, in accordance with dharma. This scorcher of enemies used to be ahead of all those whose heads had been consecrated.[121] Behold the progress of time.

[119]After he was dead. The word used is *shalavrika*, which we have interpreted as jackal. It is also possible to break this up into *shala* and *vrika* and interpret it as jackals and wolves separately.

[120]Akshouhinis.

[121]That is, kings.

He has been brought down and is now devoured by dust. Earlier, he slew many enemies and made them lie down on the ground. That king of the Kurus has now been brought down by the enemy and is lying down on the ground. Hundreds of kings used to bow down before him in fear. He is now lying down on a bed meant for brave ones, surrounded by predatory beasts. For the sake of wealth, this lord used to be worshipped by the kings earlier. Shame. He has been struck and is lying down. Behold the progress of time.'"

'Sanjaya said, "O supreme among the Bharata lineage! On seeing the best of kings lying down, Ashvatthama wept piteously. 'O tiger among kings! You were spoken of as the foremost among all archers. You were Samkarshana's[122] disciple and in a battle, you were the equal of the lord of riches.[123] O unblemished one! How did Bhimasena find a weakness in you? O king! You were always powerful and skilled and he was evil in his soul. O great king! There is no doubt that time is the most powerful on this earth. We see that you have been brought down by Bhimasena in the encounter. How did that happen? You have known about all forms of dharma. Vrikodara is inferior and wicked. There is no doubt that the wicked one slew you through deceit. Time is impossible to cross. He summoned you to a duel in accordance with dharma. However, Bhimasena used adharma to shatter your thighs with a club. Having brought you down through adharma, he kicked your head with his foot. Shame on Yudhishthira, since he ignored the act of that wicked one. There is no doubt that all warriors will censure Vrikodara's act in the encounter, as long as living beings continue to exist. He brought you down through deceit. O king! The valiant Rama, descendant of the Yadu lineage, always used to say that there was no one who was equal to Duryodhana in fighting with the club. O king! O descendant of the Bharata lineage! Varshneya[124] used to take pride in you. The lord used to say, "In fighting with the club, Kouravya is my worthy

[122]Samkarshana is Balarama's name.

[123]Kubera.

[124]Balarama.

disciple." You have obtained the end that supreme rishis applaud as the objective of a kshatriya. You have been slain and are headed towards that objective. O Duryodhana! O bull among men! I do not grieve on your account. I grieve because Gandhari and your father have lost their son. They will sorrow and roam around the entire earth as beggars. Shame on Varshneya Krishna and the evil-minded Arjuna. They pride themselves on their knowledge of dharma and ignored it when you were brought down. What will all the Pandavas tell the kings? How was Duryodhana slain in this shameless way? O Gandhari's son! You are blessed that you have been brought down in an encounter. O bull among men! In accordance with dharma, you were advancing towards the enemy. Gandhari's sons have been slain. Her kin and relatives have been killed. What will be her plight and that of the invincible one who possesses the sight of wisdom?[125] Shame on Kritavarma, maharatha Kripa and me. Placing the king ahead of us, we should have also gone to heaven. You have been generous in granting all the objects of desire. You have been a protector engaged in the welfare of the subjects. Shame on us, worst among men, since we have not followed you. O tiger among men! It is because of your valour that Kripa's house, and mine and that of my father, have always been full of jewels and servants. It is through your favours that we, with our friends and our relatives, have performed the best of sacrifices and given away copious quantities of gifts. With you at their head, all the kings have departed now. These riches are like stones now. Where will those like us go? O king! The three of us are not headed towards the supreme objective. We are not following you. We are deprived of heaven. We are deprived of riches and we are remembering your good deeds. Since we are not going with you, what will we do now? O best among the Kurus! There is no doubt that we will roam the earth in our sorrow. O king! Without you, how can there be peace? How can there be happiness? O great king! You will leave this place and meet the maharathas.[126] You will honour them, according to excellence and according to seniority. You will honour

[125]Dhritarashtra.

[126]Those who have died earlier.

the preceptor,[127] the one with the best standard among all archers. O lord of men! In the course of the conversation, tell him these words of mine, that I have killed Dhrishtadyumna today. Embrace King Bahlika, the great maharatha, and Saindhava, Somadatta and Bhurishrava, and also the best of kings, who have gone to heaven before you. Tell them these words. Embrace them and ask about their welfare.' These were the words that he spoke to the king, who was unconscious and whose thighs were shattered. Ashvatthama then glanced at him and again spoke these words. 'O Duryodhana! If you are still alive, listen to this welcome news. There are seven Pandavas left and three on the side of the sons of Dhritarashtra. There are the five brothers and Vasudeva and Satyaki. Other than me, there are Kritavarma and Sharadvata Kripa. All the sons of Droupadi have been killed and also Dhrishtadyumna's sons. O descendant of the Bharata lineage! All the Panchalas have been killed and the remaining Matsyas. Behold the revenge that has followed their deed. The sons of the Pandavas have been killed. While they were sleeping in their camp, the men and the mounts have been killed. O lord of the earth! I penetrated the camp in the night and killed Dhrishtadyumna, the one with the wicked deeds, as one would slay an animal.' Hearing those pleasant words, Duryodhana found composure in his mind.

'"Having regained his senses, he spoke these words in reply. 'I have not been able to achieve this, or Gangeya, or Karna, or your father. Engaged in my welfare, you have done this today, together with Kripa and Bhoja. You have slain the inferior commander,[128] together with Shikhandi. Because of this, I honour you, as an equal of Maghavan.[129]O fortunate one! May you be prosperous. We will meet again in heaven.' Having spoken these words, the great-minded king of the Kurus became silent. The brave one abandoned sorrow on account of his well-wishers and gave up his life. They embraced the king and were embraced by him. They repeatedly glanced towards him and then ascended their own chariots. Having heard the piteous

[127]Drona.
[128]Dhrishtadyumna.
[129]Indra.

lamentations of your son, when it was morning, overcome by grief, I left for the city.[130] O unblemished one! When your son went to heaven, I was overcome with sorrow. The divine sight that the rishi had given me was instantly destroyed."'[131]

Vaishampayana said, 'Having heard about the death of his son and his kin, the king[132] let out long and warm sighs and became immersed in deep thoughts.'

[130]Hastinapura.

[131]Vedavyasa had given Sanjaya divine sight, so that he could witness events without physically being present and also divine the thoughts of others.

[132]Dhritarashtra.

SECTION SEVENTY-NINE

Aishika Parva

This parva has 257 shlokas and nine chapters.

Chapter 1293(10): 30 shlokas
Chapter 1294(11): 30 shlokas
Chapter 1295(12): 40 shlokas
Chapter 1296(13): 20 shlokas
Chapter 1297(14): 16 shlokas
Chapter 1298(15): 33 shlokas
Chapter 1299(16): 36 shlokas
Chapter 1300(17): 26 shlokas
Chapter 1301(18): 26 shlokas

Aishika is a reed, or blade of grass and this parva is named after Ashvatthama invoking a divine weapon on a reed. Bhima pursues Ashvatthama, to exact vengeance. Ashvatthama and Arjuna invoke their brahmashira *weapons, which threaten to destroy the worlds. Arjuna withdraws his and Ashvatthama's is diverted towards the wombs of the Pandava women. Ashvatthama's weapon destroys Uttara's foetus (Parikshit), but Parikshit will be revived by Krishna. Ashvatthama gives up his gem.*

Chapter 1293(10)

Vaishampayana said, 'When night had passed, Dhrishtadyumna's charioteer went to Dharmaraja and told him about the carnage that had taken place when everyone was asleep. "O great king! They were sleeping in their own camps in the night, assured and unattentive. Droupadi's sons, and those of Drupada, have been killed in the camp by the wicked Ashvatthama in the night, together with the cruel Kritavarma and Goutama Kripa. In that way, thousands of men, elephants and horses have been destroyed, with lances, javelins and battleaxes. Nothing is left of your army. It was like a giant forest severed with a battleaxe. O descendant of the Bharata lineage! I heard the great uproar raised by your troops. O lord of the earth! From among those soldiers, I am the only one who is left. O one with dharma in his soul! I somehow managed to escape from Kritavarma, when he did not notice." On hearing those inauspicious words, the invincible Yudhishthira, Kunti's son, was overcome with sorrow on account of his sons and fell down, senseless. As he was falling down, Satyaki advanced and grasped him, as did Bhimasena, Arjuna and the Pandavas who were Madri's sons.

'Having regained his senses, Kounteya was overcome with great sorrow. "Having defeated the enemy, a conqueror is thereafter brought to distress by destiny.[1] Even those with divine sight, find it difficult to fathom the course of prosperity. Those who were defeated have triumphed. And we, who were victorious, have been conquered. Having slain our brothers, friends, fathers, sons, well-wishers, relatives, advisers and grandsons, we were triumphant. But we have now been defeated. Adversity is like prosperity. And prosperity is seen to be like adversity. Our victory may have the form of a triumph, but our victory is actually a defeat. Having won, I later have to lament, like an evil-minded person. How can I think of this as a victory? I have been defeated by the enemy. Shame on a victory that has resulted from the death of well-wishers. We were unmindful and have been conquered. There were those for whom we committed wicked deeds and they have been conquered by those who were in search of victory.[2] In the encounter, they escaped from the fangs of barbed and hollow arrows and the tongues of swords,

[1]Yudhishthira is speaking these words.

[2]Referring to the enemy.

from terrible bows and the slapping of bowstrings against palms. Karna was an angry lion among men, one who never retreated from battle. They escaped from him and have been slain while they were distracted. The chariots were like lakes. The showers of arrows were like waves. The ornaments[3] were like gems. The mounts were like furrows.[4] The javelins and swords were like fish. The standards and elephants were like crocodiles. The bows were the whirlpools. The giant arrows were the foam. The encounter was like the strong swell of the tide when the moon rises. Drona was like an ocean. The twang of his bowstring against his palm was like the clatter of an axle. They overcame all that, using their weapons as boats. While distracted, those princes have now been killed. In this world of the living, there is nothing that causes the death of men as much as mindlessness. When a man is distracted, prosperity abandons him from every direction and he is immersed in adversity. Bhishma was like a giant conflagration. His white standard was like a fire at the tip. The arrows were like flames, fanned by the great wind of his anger. The twang of his giant bowstring against his palm was like the clatter of an axle. The many kinds of armour and weapons were like oblations being offered. In the great battle, the large army was like dead wood before him. Having withstood the force of those weapons, the princes have now been slain through mindlessness. If a man is distracted, he cannot obtain learning, austerities, prosperity and great fame. Behold. The great Indra enjoyed all the happiness and sacrifices after slaying the enemy attentively. The kings, sons and grandsons were like Indra. Behold. They have been slain, especially because they were distracted. They were like prosperous merchants who had crossed an ocean, but were destroyed because they were careless over an inferior stream. While sleeping, they were killed by those intolerant ones. There is no doubt that they are in heaven now. I sorrow for Krishna.[5] How will that virtuous one handle the ocean of grief that she will be submerged in now? On hearing that

[3]Worn by the warriors, the comparison is with gems in the ocean.

[4]In the waves.

[5]Krishnaa, Droupadi.

her brothers, sons and her aged father, the king of Panchala,[6] have been killed, it is certain that she will be distressed and fall down on the ground, unconscious. Her body emaciated with grief, she will lie down. How will she be able to tolerate that grief and sorrow? She is one who deserved happiness. On hearing about the destruction of her sons and the slaughter of her brothers, she will be scorched, as if by a fire." The king of the Kurus lamented in this way.

'He then spoke these words to Nakula. "Go and bring the unfortunate princess here, with all her maternal relations." The king was like Dharma and Nakula accepted the words that had been spoken to him, in accordance with dharma. He swiftly went on a chariot to the queen's residence, where the wives of the king of Panchala also were. Having sent Madri's son, Ajamidha,[7] together with his well-wishers, was overcome by distress and grief. Weeping, he left for the spot where his sons had fought, a place that was still frequented by a large number of demons. Having entered that inauspicious and terrible place, he saw his sons, well-wishers and friends. They were lying down on the ground, their bodies wet with blood. Their bodies were mangled and their heads had been severed. On witnessing that extremely hideous sight, Yudhishthira, foremost among those who uphold dharma, wept loudly. Along with a large number of his followers, the foremost among the Kouravas lost his senses and fell down.'

Chapter 1294(11)

Vaishampayana said, 'O Janamejaya! On seeing that his sons, brothers and friends had been slain in the encounter, his[8] soul was immersed in great grief. The great-souled one was overcome

[6]Drupada was killed much earlier, by Drona in Section 71 (Volume 6), though Droupadi might not have known this.

[7]Yudhishthira's name.

[8]Yudhishthira's.

by deep sorrow. He remembered his sons, grandsons, brothers and relatives. His eyes were full of tears. He trembled and was senseless. The well-wishers became extremely anxious and comforted him.

'At that time, when it was morning, Nakula brought Krishna[9] there, on a chariot that was as radiant as the sun. She was extremely distressed and he brought her with him. She had gone to Upaplavya and had heard the extremely unpleasant news there, that all her sons had been destroyed. She was miserable. She trembled like a plantain tree stirred by the wind. Having approached the king, Krishna was afflicted by grief and fell down on the ground. Her face, with eyes like full-blown lotuses, was afflicted by misery, as if the sun had been covered by darkness. On seeing that she was falling down, the angry Vrikodara, for whom truth was his valour, approached her and grasped her in his arms. The beautiful one was comforted by Bhimasena. Krishna wept and addressed Pandava, together with his brothers. "O king! It is through good fortune that you will now enjoy the entire earth. Following the dharma of kshatriyas, you have offered your sons to Yama. O Partha! It is through good fortune that you have obtained the entire earth and do not remember Subhadra's son,[10] who was skilled and whose gait was like that of a maddened elephant. While residing in Upaplavya, I heard that my brave sons had been brought down, in accordance with dharma. It is good fortune that you do not remember this with me. I have heard that they were slain while they were sleeping, by Drona's son, who acted wickedly. O Partha! That sorrow is tormenting me, as if I am in the midst of a fire. Drona's son acted in a wicked way. O Pandavas! Listen to me. If, in an encounter today, you do not exhibit your valour and destroy him and his followers, and he remains alive in the encounter, I will resort to *praya*[11] here. Drona's son must be made to reap the fruits of his wicked deed." Having spoken these words to Pandava Dharmaraja Yudhishthira, the illustrious Krishna sat down there.

[9]Droupadi.

[10]Abhimanyu.

[11]Act of giving up one's life by fasting to death.

'On seeing that his beloved queen had sat down there, *rajarshi* Pandava, with dharma in his soul, replied to the beautiful Droupadi. "O beautiful one! O one who knows about dharma! Your sons and your brothers have followed dharma and have attained their ends in accordance with dharma. You should not grieve. O fortunate one! Drona's son has gone to a forest that is far away. O beautiful one! How do you think that he can then be brought down in a battle?" Droupadi replied, "I have heard that Drona's son possesses a natural jewel on his head. I wish to see that jewel brought to me, after the wicked one has been slain in an encounter. O king! I have formed a resolution that I will live only if that is placed on your head." Having spoken these words to the Pandava king, the beautiful Krishna angrily approached Bhimasena and spoke these words. "O Bhima! You should remember the dharma of kshatriyas and save me. Slay the one whose deeds are wicked, like Maghavan against Shambara.[12] There is no other man who is equal in valour to you. All the worlds have heard that when the Parthas confronted a great calamity in the city of Varanavata, you were the refuge.[13] When we saw Hidimba, you were the refuge again.[14] In the city of Virata, I was severely oppressed by Kichaka. You saved me from that calamity, like Maghavan saved Poulami.[15] O Partha! You have performed many other great deeds earlier. O destroyer of enemies! Slay Drona's son now and be happy." In this way, she lamented a lot, in misery and grief. The immensely strong Kounteya Bhimasena could not tolerate this. He climbed onto his great chariot, which was wonderfully decorated with gold. He grasped his colourful and wonderful bow, bowstring and arrows. Having appointed Nakula the charioteer, he embarked on the task of killing Drona's son. He brandished his bow and arrows and swiftly

[12]Shambara was a demon killed by Indra.

[13]A reference to the incidents in Section 8 (Volume 1).

[14]The incidents of Section 9 (Volume 1). However, Droupadi wasn't around then.

[15]Kichaka was slain by Bhima in Section 46 (Volume 4). Maghavan is Indra and Indra's wife is Shachi or Poulami, the daughter of Puloma, a demon. Indra killed Puloma.

goaded the horses. O tiger among kings! Those horses were as swift as the wind. Thus urged, they proceeded swiftly. The one without decay spiritedly left the camp on his chariot. The valiant one quickly followed the footsteps that Drona's son had taken and the route that his chariot had taken.'

Chapter 1295(12)

Vaishampayana said, 'When the invincible one had departed, Pundarikaksha, bull among the Yadu lineage, spoke these words to Yudhishthira, Kunti's son. "O Pandava! Your brother is overcome with sorrow on account of his sons. O descendant of the Bharata lineage! The descendant of the Bharata lineage has left alone, wishing to kill Drona's son. O bull among the Bharata lineage! Among all your brothers, Bhima is the one you love most. He is headed towards a calamity. Why are you not doing something about it? Drona, the destroyer of enemy cities, instructed his son about a weapon named brahmashira. It is capable of burning down the earth. That great-souled and immensely fortunate one possessed a standard that was foremost among that of all archers. The preceptor gave it[16] to his beloved Dhananjaya. His son was unable to tolerate this.[17] The great-souled one knew that his son was reckless. The preceptor knew about all forms of dharma and gave it to his son with reluctance. He spoke to his son and imposed this restriction on his son. 'O son! Even if you confront the greatest of catastrophes in a battle, this weapon should never be used, especially against humans.' The preceptor, Drona, spoke these words to his son. Later, he again added, 'O bull among men! You will not stay along the path of the righteous.' On hearing the unpleasant words of his father, the evil-souled one gave up hope of obtaining all kinds of fortune. Tormented by sorrow, he

[16]The weapon.

[17]That it had been given to Arjuna.

began to roam around the earth. O best among Kurus! O descendant of the Bharata lineage! At that time, you were in the forest. He came to Dvaraka and was supremely honoured by the Vrishnis. While he dwelt in Dvaravati,[18] he once came to me, while I was alone along the shores of the ocean. He smiled and told me, 'O Krishna! My father, the preceptor of the Bharatas, has given the weapon named brahmashira to me. It was obtained by Agastya, for whom truth was his valour, after performing the fiercest of austerities. It is worshipped by the gods and the gandharvas. O Dasharha! It is with me now, as it used to be with my father. O supreme among the Yadu lineage! I will give that divine weapon to you, if you give me the chakra weapon in return, one that is capable of destroying enemies in battle.' O king! He affectionately joined his hands in salutation and addressed these words to me. O bull among the Bharata lineage! He carefully sought that weapon from me. 'Gods, danavas, gandharvas, men, birds and serpents together are not equal to one-hundredth part of my valour.[19] I possess this bow, this spear, this chakra and this club. I will give you whichever of these weapons you cherish. Whichever one you wish, whichever you can raise and use in battle, take that from me, without giving me any weapon in return.' The mighty-armed one wished to rival me and told me that he wanted the chakra. It possessed an excellent nave and one thousand spokes. It possessed the essence of the vajra and was made out of iron. At this, I asked him to take the chakra. He violently seized the chakra with his left hand. O one without decay! However, he was incapable of moving it from its spot. He then attempted to seize it with his right hand. He made every kind of effort and tried every means to grasp it. But though he used all his strength, he was incapable of raising it or moving it. Drona's evil-minded son made the supreme of efforts. O descendant of the Bharata lineage! Exhausted, he then desisted. When he gave up all such intentions, I spoke these gentle words to the insensible Ashvatthama. 'He is regarded as the supreme one among gods and humans. He is the wielder of Gandiva, the one

[18]Dvaravati is another name for Dvaraka.

[19]Krishna spoke these words to Ashvatthama.

with the white horses. The supreme of apes sits astride his standard. He is Jishnu. He defeated and satisfied Shankara, the one with the blue throat and Uma's consort, the god who is the lord of the gods, himself in a duel.[20] There is no other man on earth whom I love as much. There is nothing that I cannot give him, even my wives and sons. O brahmana! He is unblemished in his deeds. Even such a well-wisher like Partha has never spoken such words to me earlier, the likes of which you have spoken.[21] I observed extremely terrible brahmacharya for twelve years, on the slopes of the Himalayas. I worshipped through austerities. Rukmini[22] observed similar vows and gave birth to my son named Pradyumna, who is as energetic as Sanatkumara.[23] He is like me. But even he has never asked for this great and divine chakra. You have sought it like a foolish person. The extremely strong Rama[24] has never spoken such words to me. Nor have Gada and Samba asked for what you have asked.[25] Nor have the other Vrishni and Andhaka maharathas who dwell in Dvaraka earlier asked for what you have asked. The son of the preceptor of the Bharatas is revered by all the Yadavas. O best among rathas! O son![26] Who, will you fight with this chakra?' Having been thus addressed by me, Drona's son spoke these words in reply. 'O Krishna! O great one! After worshipping you, it was my intention to fight with you. That is the reason I desired the chakra, worshipped by gods and danavas. O lord! Had I obtained it, I would have become invincible. I tell you this truthfully. O Keshava! That is the truth. I have not obtained that extremely rare object of desire. O Govinda! I am about to depart. Speak auspicious words to me now. You are a bull among the Vrishnis and you wield this chakra, with the

[20]Described in Section 31 (Volume 2).

[21]That is, Arjuna never asked for those weapons.

[22]One of Krishna's wives.

[23]One of the four mental sons born to Brahma. Sanatkumara is believed to have been born as Pradyumna.

[24]Balarama.

[25]Gada was Krishna's brother. Samba was Krishna's son, through Jambavati.

[26]The word used is tata. It means son, but is affectionately used for anyone who is younger or junior.

excellent nave. There is no one on earth who can receive this chakra.' Having spoken these words, Drona's son received a couple of horses and riches from me. The child also took many kinds of jewels. He is angry and evil in his soul. He is fickle and cruel too. He knows about the weapon brahmashira. Therefore, Vrikodara needs to be protected from him."'

Chapter 1296(13)

Vaishampayana said, 'Having spoken these words, the foremost of warriors, the one who delighted all the Yadavas, mounted his giant chariot, which was stocked with every kind of weapon. It was yoked to two excellent horses from Kamboja and they had golden harnesses. The shaft of that excellent chariot had the complexion of the rising sun. Sainya was yoked on the right and Sugriva was yoked on the left. Meghapushpa and Balahaka were yoked on the flanks.[27] This divine chariot had been constructed by Vishvakarma[28] and was decorated with many jewels. A flagpole with powers of maya was raised up and Vinata's son[29] was resplendently stationed there, like rays radiating from the solar disc. The enemy of the snakes was seen on that flag, like truth personified. Hrishikesha, with a standard that was the best among those of all archers, ascended the chariot and so did Arjuna, the performer of truthful deeds, and the Kuru king, Yudhishthira.[30] On either side of Dasharha, those great-souled ones dazzled. The wielder of the Sharnga[31] bow was like Vasava on that chariot, with the two Ashvins on either side. Having ascended the

[27]These are the names of Krishna's horses. Sainya and Sugriva, the two main horses, were on the inside. Meghapushpa and Balahaka were on the extreme left and extreme right.

[28]The architect of the gods.

[29]Garuda. Garuda sits astride Vishnu's standard.

[30]Arjuna and Yudhishthira ascended the same chariot.

[31]The name of Vishnu/Krishna's bow, literally meaning a bow made out of horn.

chariot that was honoured by the worlds, Dasharha goaded those excellent horses to pick up speed. Urged by the bull among the Yadus, and with the two Pandaveyas on it, those horses swiftly bore that excellent chariot along. The horses of the one who wielded the Sharnga bow were extremely fast. As they sped, there was a great sound, like that of birds descending in the sky.

'Bhimasena, the great archer, was travelling fast. O bull among the Bharata lineage! However, in a short while, those tigers among men caught up with him. Kounteya[32] blazed in anger and he rushed towards the enemy. Though those maharathas caught up with him, they could not restrain him. While those handsome and firm archers looked on, using his extremely fast and tawny steeds, he headed towards the banks of the Bhagirathi.[33] He had heard that Drona's great-souled son, the slayer of his sons, would be there. He saw the cheerful, illustrious and great-souled Krishna Dvaipayana Vyasa there, seated with rishis. He also saw Drona's son seated near them, with dust covering the tips of his hair. The perpetrator of evil deeds was covered in clarified butter and was dressed in a garment made of *kusha* grass. Kounteya grasped his bow and an arrow and rushed towards him. The mighty-armed Bhimasena exclaimed, "Wait. Wait." Drona's son saw the one with the terrible bow dashing towards him, with a bow and an arrow. He saw his two brothers and Janardana stationed behind him. He was distressed and thought that he had met his end. However, since his soul was never distressed, he thought of the divine and supreme weapon. Drona's son grasped a reed in his left hand and invoked that celestial weapon on it.[34] In the presence of those brave ones, who also possessed divine weapons, the intolerant one released it, uttering the terrible words, "To bring an end to the Pandavas". O tiger among kings! For the sake of confounding all the worlds, Drona's powerful son spoke these words and released that weapon. A fire was generated in that reed and it seemed to consume the three worlds, like Yama at the end of time.'

[32]Bhima.

[33]Ganga.

[34]Divine weapons could be invoked on any object with the use of mantras.

Chapter 1297(14)

Vaishampayana said, 'From the signs, Dasharha had understood what Drona's son intended. The mighty-armed one spoke to Arjuna. "O Arjuna! O Pandava! O Arjuna! In your mind, you have the knowledge of the divine weapon that was instructed to you by Drona. The time to use it has arrived. O descendant of the Bharata lineage! It is needed to save yourself and your brothers. You should release it, since it is capable of countering all weapons." Having been thus addressed by Keshava, Pandava, the destroyer of enemy heroes, swiftly descended from the chariot and grasped his bow and an arrow. The scorcher of enemies spoke words of welfare, addressed to his preceptor's son, then to himself and all his brothers. He bowed to the gods and all his preceptors. Meditating and pronouncing auspicious words, he released that weapon, so as to pacify the other weapon. That weapon was violently released by the wielder of Gandiva. It blazed with great flames, like the fire that arises at the end of a yuga. In a similar way, the weapon released by Drona's son was fierce in its energy. It blazed in great flames, surrounded by a disc of energy. There were many peals of thunder and thousands of meteors fell down. A great fear was generated in all the beings. The firmament was enveloped in that great noise and seemed to be covered in a terrible garland of fire. The entire earth, with its mountains, forests and trees, trembled. That weapon was stationed there, scorching the worlds with its energy. The two *maharshis*, Narada, with dharma in his soul, and the grandfather of the Bharatas,[35] showed themselves then. They sought to pacify the two brave ones, Bharadvaja's descendant and Dhananjaya. Those two sages were learned in all forms of dharma and had the welfare of all beings in mind. Those two supremely energetic ones stationed themselves between those two flaming weapons. Those two illustrious and supreme rishis were incapable of being assailed by anything and were like two blazing fires themselves. They could not be touched by any living being and they were revered by the

[35]Vedavyasa.

gods and the danavas. For the sake of the welfare of the worlds, they pacified the energies of the weapons.

'The two rishis said, "The maharathas who have fallen down earlier were knowledgeable about many weapons. These weapons should never be used against humans. Why have you invoked them?"'

Chapter 1298(15)

Vaishampayana said, 'O tiger among men! On seeing those two energetic ones,[36] who were like fires, Dhananjaya quickly withdrew his divine arrow. He joined his hands in salutation and spoke to the best of rishis. "This weapon was used by me to pacify the other weapon. Once I withdraw this supreme weapon, all of us will be destroyed. It is certain that Drona's son, the perpetrator of wicked deeds, will consume us with the energy of his weapon. The two of you are like gods. You should think of a means so that we, and all the worlds, are saved." Having spoken these words, Dhananjaya again withdrew his weapon. In an encounter, it is difficult for even the gods to do this.[37] With the exception of Shatakratu himself, no one other than Pandava was capable of withdrawing a supreme weapon, once it had been released in a battle. Once invoked, it was full of Brahma's energy. With the exception of someone with a cleansed soul and someone who was a brahmachari, no one else was capable of withdrawing it. If a person is not a brahmachari, and having released the weapon, wishes to withdraw it, the weapon will sever his head, with that of his descendants. Arjuna had followed the vows of a brahmachari. He had obtained a weapon that was difficult to get. However, he had never invoked it, not even in a time of great calamity. Pandava followed the vows of truth. He was brave and a brahmachari. He was obedient to his superiors. It

[36]Narada and Vedavyasa.

[37]To withdraw a weapon, once released. Knowledge of a divine weapon meant not just knowledge about its release, but also knowledge about its withdrawal.

was because of this that Arjuna was capable of withdrawing that weapon again.

'Drona's son saw that the two rishis were stationed in front of him. However, in the encounter, he was incapable of again withdrawing that terrible weapon. In the encounter, he was incapable of restraining that supreme weapon. O king! Distressed in his mind, Drona's son addressed Dvaipayana. "I was distressed because I confronted a great calamity. I was scared of saving my life. I released the weapon out of fear. I was scared of Bhimasena. In attempting to kill Dhritarashtra's son, he acted in accordance with adharma. O illustrious one! Bhimasena resorted to falsehood in the battle. O brahmana! Though I have not cleansed my soul, this is the reason I invoked this weapon. I do not have any interest in withdrawing it, even now. Once this celestial weapon has been released by me, it is invincible. O sage! I have invoked it with the energy of the fire and with mantras, 'To bring an end to the Pandavas'. Therefore, it has been created for the destruction of the Pandaveyas. It will now destroy all the sons of Pandu who are alive. O brahmana! With my senses destroyed by anger, I have committed a wicked deed. Created by me in this encounter, this weapon will slaughter the Parthas."

'Vyasa replied, "O son![38] Partha Dhananjaya knew about the weapon brahmashira. However, he did not release it out of rage, or to slay you in this encounter. In the encounter, he wished to pacify the weapon that had been released by you. Arjuna released it, and withdrew it again. He obtained instruction in the use of *brahmastra* from your father.[39] However, the mighty-armed Dhananjaya was compassionate and did not deviate from the dharma of kshatriyas. He possesses fortitude and is virtuous. He has knowledge of all the weapons and is righteous. Why do you wish to kill such a person and his brothers? In a spot where the weapon named brahmashira is countered through the use of another supreme weapon, in such a

[38]The word used is tata.

[39]Here, brahmastra seems to be equated with brahmashira. However, brahmastras were used in the Kurukshetra war. This is the only instance of brahmashira being used. The two weapons were presumably different.

kingdom, it does not rain for twelve years. The mighty-armed Pandava is capable. However, because he had the welfare of all subjects in his mind, he did not counter your weapon with his. You, the Pandavas, you, and the kingdom must always be protected. O mighty-armed one! That is the reason you should withdraw that divine weapon. Get rid of this rage and let the Pandavas always be without disease. Rajarshi Pandava[40] does not wish to win through the use of adharma. You possess a gem on your forehead. Give that to me. Once you have given that, the Pandavas will grant you your life in return."

'Drona's son said, "The Pandaveyas possess jewels and there are riches obtained by the Kouravas. However, this gem that belongs to me is superior to both of those. When this is worn, there is never any fear from weapons, disease, hunger, lack of protection, gods, danavas and serpents. Nor is there fear from large numbers of rakshasas, or fear from thieves. This is the kind of energy that is vested in this gem and I should never give it up. O illustrious one! Take it. However, what should be done next? Here is the gem. But the reed invoked by me is invincible and it will descend on the wombs of the Pandaveyas."[41]

'Vyasa replied, "Do this and do not turn your mind to any other task. Release this towards the wombs of the Pandaveyas and desist."'[42]

Vaishampayana said, 'Ashvatthama was severely afflicted. At this, on hearing Dvaipayana's words, he released that supreme weapon in the direction of the wombs.'

Chapter 1299(16)

Vaishampayana said, 'The perpetrator of wicked deeds acted accordingly and released it. On discerning this, Hrishikesha cheerfully spoke these words to Drona's son. "In earlier times,

[40]Yudhishthira.

[41]That is, the Pandava women.

[42]The brahmashira weapon was thus diverted towards the wombs.

Virata's daughter, the daughter-in-law of the wielder of Gandiva,[43] had gone to Upaplavya. A brahmana who followed vows had seen her there and had said, 'When the Kurus are destroyed, a son will be born to you. That is the reason the one in your womb will be known by the name of Parikshit.'[44] The words of that virtuous one will be true. When everyone is destroyed, there will again be a victorious son." On hearing the words of Govinda, supreme among the Satvata lineage, Drona's son became greatly angry and replied in these words. "O Keshava! You are saying this because of your partiality and this shall not be true. O Pundarikaksha! My words will never be false. O Krishna! The weapon that has been invoked by me will descend on the womb of Virata's daughter, the one that you wish to protect."

'Vasudeva replied, "This supreme weapon is invincible and will indeed descend. The foetus will be born dead. However, it will revive and live till a long age. All the learned ones know that you are wicked and a coward. You have always been engaged in evil and wicked deeds. You survive by killing those who are children. That is the reason you will reap the fruits of your wicked deeds. You will roam around the earth for three thousand years. You will never have a companion and will never be able to converse with anyone. You will be alone and have no aides. You will roam through diverse countries. O wicked one! You will never find a station amidst men. You will have the stench of pus and blood. You will dwell in desolate regions and in wildernesses. O evil one! You will roam around, ridden with every kind of disease. Parikshit will come of age and obtain the Vedas and the vows. The brave one will obtain knowledge of all the weapons from Kripa Sharadvata. He will know about all the supreme weapons and base himself on the dharma of kshatriyas. He will have dharma in his soul and protect the earth for sixty years. On top of this, the mighty-armed one will be the king of the Kurus. O extremely evil-minded one! That king will be known by the name

[43]The daughter is Uttara, married to Abhimanyu.

[44]This is derived from the word *parikshina*, which means something that has been destroyed or lost.

of Parikshit. O worst of men! You will look on. Behold the power of my austerities, energy and truth."

'Vyasa said, "You disregarded us and perpetrated this terrible deed. This has been your conduct, though you were a virtuous brahmana.[45] That is the reason there is no doubt that the excellent words spoken by Devaki's son will come true. You have resorted to the path of inferior deeds."

'Ashvatthama replied, "O brahmana! Together with you, I will dwell among men.[46] O illustrious one! Let Purushottama's[47] words come true."'

Vaishampayana said, 'Drona's son gave the gem to the great-souled Pandavas. While all of them looked on, with an unhappy state of mind, he left for the forest. Having destroyed their enemies, the Pandavas placed Govinda, Krishna Dvaipayana and the great sage, Narada, ahead of them. Obtaining the natural gem that Drona's son possessed, they swiftly rushed towards Droupadi, the spirited one having made up her mind on praya. Those tigers among men used well-trained horses that were as fleet as the wind. With Dasharha, they again returned to their camp. The maharathas quickly descended from their chariots. They saw Krishna[48] Droupadi, afflicted by great misery. She was overcome by sorrow and grief and was cheerless. With Keshava, the Pandavas approached her and stood around her. Having been instructed by the king, the immensely strong Bhimasena gave her the celestial gem and spoke these words. "O fortunate one! This is your gem. The slayer of your sons has been vanquished. Arise. Give up this sorrow and remember the dharma of kshatriyas. O dark-eyed one! O timid one! When Vasudeva left on his mission of peace and had yoked his mounts,[49] you had spoken these words to Madhu's slayer.[50] 'I do not have husbands. I do not have sons. I do not have

[45]That is, born as one.

[46]Vedavyasa was immortal and so was Ashvatthama.

[47]Purushottama is Krishna's name.

[48]Krishnaa.

[49]Described in Section 54 (Volume 4).

[50]Vishnu killed a demon named Madhu.

brothers. O Govinda! You are also not there. The king wishes for peace.' Those were the firm words you spoke to Purushottama. You should now remember those words, which were in accordance with the dharma of kshatriyas. The wicked Duryodhana, who stood in the way of the kingdom, has been slain. I have drunk the blood of the trembling Duhshasana. We have repaid our debts to the enemy. There is no one to wound us with words. We have defeated and released Drona's son, so as to honour brahmanas. O queen! His fame has been destroyed. Only his body remains. He has been separated from his gem. He no longer possesses any weapons on earth."

'Droupadi replied, "I only wished to repay my debts. The son of the preceptor is my senior too. O descendant of the Bharata lineage! Let the king fasten the gem on his head."'

Vaishampayana said, 'The king acted accordingly and followed Droupadi's words. He received it and fastened it on his head, regarding it as something that had been left for him by his preceptor. The lord bore that divine and supreme gem on his head. The great king was radiant, like a mountain, with the moon on top. The spirited Krishna,[51] afflicted by sorrow on account of her sons, arose. Dharmaraja asked the mighty-armed Krishna.'

Chapter 1300(17)

Vaishampayana said, 'When all the soldiers were asleep and were destroyed by the three rathas, King Yudhishthira grieved and spoke these words to Dasharha. "O Krishna! All my sons were maharathas. Drona's son was wicked, inferior and blemished in his deeds. How could they be slain by him? In a similar way, Drupada's sons were accomplished in the use of weapons. They were brave. They could fight with hundreds and thousands. How could they have been brought down by Drona's son? Dhrishtadyumna was the best

[51]Krishnaa.

among rathas. In the forefront of the battle, Drona, the great archer, could not stand before him. How could he have been slain? O bull among men! What act had the preceptor's son accomplished, that he could single-handedly slay all of them in the camp?"

'Vasudeva replied, "There is no doubt that Drona's son had sought refuge with the god of the gods, the lord without decay, the lord of everything. That is the reason he could slay many, though he was single-handed. If Mahadeva is pleased, he can even grant immortality. O bull among the Bharata lineage! I know about Mahadeva's true nature and about the many deeds that he performed in ancient times. O descendant of the Bharata lineage! He is the beginning, the middle and the end of beings. Everything in this entire universe moves because of his deeds. The lord, the grandfather, wished to create beings and saw him first. He told him, 'Without any delay, create beings.' Having been thus addressed, the one with the tawny locks[52] saw that beings would have defects. For a very long time, the immensely ascetic one submerged himself in water and tormented himself through austerities. The grandfather waited for a very long period of time. So as to generate beings, he then created another being through his mental powers. On seeing that Girisha was submerged in the water, this being told his father,[53] 'I will generate beings only if no other being has been born before me.' His father told him, 'There is no other being who has been born before you. Sthanu is submerged in the water. You can confidently do what you have to do.' That being then created seven Prajapatis, Daksha and the others.[54] All of them created the four kinds of beings.[55] Having been created, all the beings were hungry. O king! They violently rushed towards the Prajapatis, wishing to devour them. As they were about to be devoured, in search of succour, they fled to the grandfather. 'O illustrious one! Please save us from these. Decree some means

[52]Shiva.

[53]Brahma.

[54]Prajapati means lord of beings and the Prajapatis were also creators of beings. The number of Prajapatis varies, from one text to another.

[55]Those born from wombs, eggs, sweat (worms/insects) and plants/trees/herbs.

for their sustenance.' He then assigned them the forests, the herbs and all immobile objects. Among mobile beings, the strong could feed on the weak. Having been assigned a means of sustenance, all the beings were satisfied and went away to wherever they had come from. O king! They cheerfully multiplied themselves, within their own species. When the beings prospered, the preceptor of the worlds[56] was pleased. However, the eldest one arose from the waters and saw all these beings. He saw many different kinds of beings, who were extending through their own energies. The illustrious Rudra angrily planted his *linga*, so that it penetrated the earth and remained stationed there. Brahma wished to pacify him and spoke these words to him. 'O Sharva! Why did you remain inside the water for such a long period of time? Why have you made your linga penetrate inside the earth?' Thus addressed, he angrily replied to the preceptor of the worlds, 'Someone else has created these beings. What will I do with this?[57] O grandfather! Through my austerities, I have created food for the beings. The herbs will always multiply and so will the beings.' Having angrily spoken in this way, Bhava was cheerless and went away. The immensely ascetic one tormented himself through austerities on the foothills of Mount Munjavat."'[58]

Chapter 1301(18)

'Vasudeva said, "When the yuga of the gods was over,[59] the gods resolved to perform a sacrifice in accordance with the dictates of the Vedas. They made all the due preparations. The foremost among the gods thought of an appropriate place where the sacrifice could be performed. Amongst themselves, the gods apportioned out the shares of the objects offered at the sacrifice.

[56]Brahma.

[57]The linga.

[58]Mount Munjavat probably had a lot of *munja* grass.

[59]This probably means, when *satya yuga* or *krita yuga* was over.

O lord of men! Despite knowing about Rudra and about his true nature, the gods did not determine a share for Sthanu. On knowing that the immortals had not thought of a share for him at the sacrifice, Krittivasa[60] quickly determined to obtain a share and created a bow. There are sacrifices for the worlds, sacrifices with rituals, sacrifices performed in households and eternal sacrifices that involve the five elements.[61] Sacrifices performed by men are the fifth kind. Kapardi[62] constructed a bow for the sake of a sacrifice that was a sacrifice for the worlds. He created a bow from the elements and it was five cubits long. O descendant of the Bharata lineage! *Vashatkara*[63]constituted the bowstring. He wished to destroy the four limbs of the sacrifice.[64] Therefore, Mahadeva angrily grasped his bow. He went to the spot where the gods had assembled. On seeing the undecaying brahmachari arrive there with the bow, the goddess earth was distressed. The mountains began to tremble. Winds did not blow. Though offered kindling, fires would not blaze. The nakshatras, in their circle in the sky, were anxious and roamed aimlessly. The resplendent sun and the moon lost the radiance in their discs. The entire sky was enveloped in great darkness. The gods were distressed and confused. The top of the sacrificial altar could no longer be seen. Rudra used his arrow to pierce the sacrifice in the heart. Thus attacked, the sacrifice assumed the form of a deer and fled, together with the fire. O Yudhishthira! In that form, it roamed around in the sky. However, Rudra pursued it in the firmament. When the sacrifice was attacked in this fashion, the gods lost their senses. Having lost their senses, the gods could not distinguish anything. Using the curved end of the bow, Tryambaka[65] then angrily tore out Savita's arms, plucked out Bhaga's eyes and gouged out Pushana's teeth. The gods, and all the parts of the sacrifice, fled. Some whirled

[60]Literally, the one attired in skins. Shiva's name.

[61]The five great elements are ether/sky, air, fire, water and earth.

[62]The one with matted hair, Shiva's name.

[63]The sacred exclamation of *vashat*.

[64]This is probably a reference to the four kinds of chants and priests involved in any sacrifice, associated with each of the four Vedas.

[65] The three-eyed one, Shiva's name.

around, as if they had lost their lives. Having driven all of them away, Shitikantha[66] laughed. He used the extremities of his bow to paralyse and obstruct the gods. When the immortals shrieked, the bowstring broke. O king! When the bowstring was severed, he violently brandished his bow. The best of the gods was without a bow and the gods, together with the sacrifice, approached him and sought refuge with him. They sought the lord's favours. The illustrious one was pleased and cast his anger aside into a body of water. O lord! That is the fire in the water, which always dries it up. O Pandava! He returned Bhaga's eyes, Savita's arms and Pushana's teeth and the sacrifice was also restored. Everything was well, exactly as it had been earlier. The gods thought of all the oblations as his share. O lord! When Bhava[67] was enraged, the entire universe was in disarray. When he was satisfied, everything was hale again. He[68] was gratified with the valiant one.[69] That is the reason all your maharatha sons have been killed, and so have many other brave Panchalas and their followers. In your mind, you should not think that this has been done by Drona's son. This was because of Mahadeva's favours. Now do whatever task must be done next."'

This ends Souptika Parva.

[66]The one with the blue throat, Shiva's name.
[67]Shiva's name.
[68]Shiva.
[69]Ashvatthama.

Stri Parva

Stri Parva is a parva concerning women. This parva is so named because it is about the grief of the women and the funeral ceremonies performed by the women and the survivors. In the 18-parva classification, Stri Parva is the eleventh. In the 100-parva classification, Stri Parva constitutes Sections 80 to 83. Stri Parva has twenty-seven chapters. In the numbering of the chapters in Stri Parva, the first number is a consecutive one, starting with the beginning of the Mahabharata. And the second number, within brackets, is the numbering of the chapter within the parva.

SECTION EIGHTY

Vishoka Parva

This parva has 194 shlokas and eight chapters.

Chapter 1302(1): 37 shlokas
Chapter 1303(2): 23 shlokas
Chapter 1304(3): 17 shlokas
Chapter 1305(4): 15 shlokas
Chapter 1306(5): 22 shlokas
Chapter 1307(6): 12 shlokas
Chapter 1308(7): 20 shlokas
Chapter 1309(8): 48 shlokas

Vishoka means the end of sorrow, or to be freed from sorrow. This parva is named after Vidura's attempt to dispel Dhritarashtra's sorrow.

Chapter 1302(1)

Janamejaya asked, 'O sage! When the great king Dhritarashtra heard that Duryodhana and all the soldiers had been killed, what did he do? What did the great-minded Kourava king, Dharma's son,[1] and the other three, Kripa and the others,[2] do? I have heard about Ashvatthama's deed and the curses that were

[1]Yudhishthira.

[2]Kripa, Kritavarma and Ashvatthama.

imposed on each other.[3] Tell me what happened next and what Sanjaya said.'

Vaishampayana replied, 'When his one hundred sons had been killed, Dhritarashtra, the lord of the earth, was miserable and tormented by sorrow on account of his sons. He was like a tree deprived of its branches. He was deep in reflection and overcome by his thoughts. The immensely wise Sanjaya went to him and spoke these words. "O great king! Why are you grieving? Sorrowing does not help. O lord of the earth! Eighteen akshouhinis have been destroyed. The earth has been rendered bare and is almost empty. The lords of men had assembled from many directions and many countries. With your sons, all of them have confronted their death. It is necessary to perform the funeral rites of the fathers, the sons, the grandsons, kin, well-wishers and preceptors, in the due order." On hearing those piteous words, the invincible one[4] was afflicted because of the death of his sons and grandsons and fell down on the ground, like a tree struck by a storm.

'Dhritarashtra said, "My sons have been killed. My advisers have been killed. All my well-wishers have been killed. It is certain that I will roam around the earth in grief. Bereft of my relatives, how will I now live this life? I am like a decayed and aged bird whose wings have been clipped. I have lost my kingdom. My well-wishers have been slain. I am blind too. O immensely wise one! I am like the one with rays,[5] when it is dim and does not shine. I did not listen to the words of the well-wishers, or the advice of Jamadagni's son,[6] devarshi Narada, or Krishna Dvaipayana. In the midst of the assembly hall, Krishna spoke beneficial words to me. 'O king! There has been enough of enmity. Restrain your

[3]Ashvatthama was cursed. His imposing a curse refers to his act of destroying the foetus in Uttara's womb.

[4]Dhritarashtra.

[5]The sun.

[6]Parashurama.

sons.' Because I was evil-minded, I disregarded those words and it torments me severely. I did not listen to the words, full of dharma, that Bhishma spoke. On hearing about Duryodhana's death, when he was roaring like a bull, and of Duhshasana's slaughter, Karna's catastrophe and the setting of the sun that was Drona, my heart has been shattered. O Sanjaya! I am suffering like a fool. I do not recall any evil deeds that I have performed, which could lead to these fruits now. It is certain that I have committed sins in my earlier lives. Because of that, the creator has acted so as to give me this share of grief. This consequence of the destruction of my friends and all my relatives, the destruction of my well-wishers and allies, has been brought about by destiny. Where is another man on this earth who is as miserable as I am? Therefore, the Pandavas will now see me, rigid in my vows, following the long road that extends towards Brahma's world."'

Vaishampayana said, 'Thus did he lament, thinking about his many sorrows. To dispel the king's sorrows, Sanjaya spoke these words. "O king! O best among kings! Abandon your grief. You have heard about the certainty of the Vedas and the sacred texts from many seniors and about what the sages told Srinjaya in ancient times, when he was tormented by grief on account of his son.[7] O king! When your son was young and insolent, you disregarded the words that were spoken to you by your well-wishers. You were avaricious and desired the fruits and did not act in accordance with what was good for you. Your advisers were Duhshasana, the evil-souled Radheya,[8] the evil-souled Shakuni and the evil-minded Chitrasena.[9] They were thorns and they made the entire world full of thorns for

[7]The Critical edition does not tell us who Srinjaya was, what the sages told him, and when Dhritarashtra heard it. The story has been excised from this part of the Critical edition and is about a king named Srinjaya, whose son was killed by thieves. Narada consoled him by telling him the histories of sixteen kings who had to die. But Narada's account appears later.

[8]Karna.

[9]Duryodhana's brother.

themselves.[10] O descendant of the Bharata lineage! Your son did not act in accordance with the words of Bhishma, eldest among the Kurus, or Gandhari, or Vidura. He did not act virtuously, in accordance with dharma. Instead, he always spoke of war. He took all the kshatriyas to their destruction and increased the fame of the enemies. You were in the midst as a neutral and did not say anything that should have been said. You were the main beast of burden, but you did not bear your proportionate load. Right from the beginning, a man should adopt the appropriate course of action. One should not strive for something earlier, which one has to repent later. O king! Because of your affection towards your son, you were only interested in pleasing him. You have subsequently arrived at a state of repentance and you should not sorrow. There are those who only see the honey and not the fall. Like you, they sorrow when their greed for honey dislodges them.[11] One who searches for gain obtains sorrow. One who sorrows does not obtain happiness. One who sorrows does not obtain prosperity. One who sorrows does not obtain the supreme objective. A man who starts a fire and then covers it up in a garment, sorrows when he is scorched. Such a person is not regarded as learned. The Parthas were a fire. You and your sons fanned it with the wind of your words. You sprinkled the flames with the clarified butter of your greed. When it was kindled, your sons fell into it like insects. They were scorched by Keshava's flames. You should not sorrow. O king! Tears are flowing down from your face. This is not in accordance with the sacred texts and the learned ones do not praise it. It is said that they are like sparks and scorch men. Therefore, use your intelligence to conquer your anger. Get a grip on yourself." O scorcher of enemies! When the

[10]The text uses the word *shalya*, which means thorn or stake. Shalya was also the king of Madra and it is also possible to interpret the shloka in the sense of Shalya, as a proper noun. However, there is no suggestion that Shalya ever offered advice to Dhritarashtra and that it was rejected, though Shalya eventually fought on the side of the Kouravas. We have therefore taken the word shalya to be a common noun.

[11]The image is that of a man who climbs a tree for honey and falls down.

great-souled Sanjaya had consoled him in this way, Vidura showed his earlier intelligence and again spoke to him.'

Chapter 1303(2)

Vaishampayana said, 'With words that were like *amrita*, Vidura dispelled the sorrow of Vichitravirya's son, the bull among men. Listen to what he said.

'Vidura said, "O king! Arise. Why are you lying there? Get a grip on yourself. This is the final outcome[12] of everything that is mortal—mobile and immobile. Everything that is stored is dissipated. Everything that rises falls down again. Everything that is united is separated again. Death is the end of life. O descendant of the Bharata lineage! O bull among kshatriyas! Since Yama attracts both those who are brave and those who are cowards, why should these kshatriyas not fight? A man who does not fight—dies. A man who fights—lives. O great king! When one's time has come, no one can transgress it. O king! You should not grieve over those who have been killed in the battle. If the sacred texts are proof, they have attained the supreme objective. All of them studied. All of them observed the vows. All of them were destroyed when they were headed forwards.[13] What is there to sorrow over? They were generated from beyond your sight.[14] They have again gone beyond your sight. They were not yours. You are not theirs. What is there to sorrow over? A person who is killed obtains heaven. A person who kills obtains fame. Both of these possess many qualities. There is no failure in battle. Indra will create worlds that will satisfy their desires. O bull among men! They will become Indra's guests. Mortals do not go to heaven through sacrifices that are

[12]Death.

[13]That is, they were not retreating.

[14]Before they were born.

rich in donations, austerities or learning. Brave ones go there by being slain in battle. Beings go through thousands of mothers and fathers and hundreds of wives and sons.[15] Whom do they belong to? Whom do we belong to? From one day to another, those who are stupid face thousands of reasons for sorrow and hundreds of reasons for fear, but not those who are learned. O supreme among the Kuru lineage! There is no one who is loved by time, nor anyone time hates. Time looks upon everyone neutrally and everyone is dragged away by time. Life, beauty, youth and stores of riches are temporary and this is also true of good health and consorting with those one loves. A learned person is not interested in these. One should not sorrow over something that affects the entire country and not a single person alone.[16] If something no longer exists, it will have no return. If one sees some powerful antidote to sorrow, one can act. But if there is no medicine against sorrow, one should not think about it. It does not abandon someone who is thinking. Instead, it only becomes stronger. Because they confront something they do not like and because they are separated from something they like, men of limited intelligence are united with mental grief. There is no artha, dharma or happiness that will result from your sorrowing. As long as one has tasks to accomplish, one should not deviate from those objectives.[17] In particular, men who achieve one kind of prosperity and then another, and continue to be dissatisfied, are confused. The learned are satisfied. Mental sorrow is dispelled through wisdom and physical suffering through medicines. That is the capacity of knowledge. One should not become the equal of a child. When a man lies down, his earlier deeds lie down next to him. When he stands, they stand next to him. When he runs, they run with him. In whichever state one performs a deed, good or bad, in exactly that state the fruits of that deed are obtained."'[18]

[15]In successive births.

[16]That is, death.

[17]In this context, dharma, artha and happiness, not dharma, artha and kama.

[18]The meaning of this shloka is not very clear.

Chapter 1304(3)

'Dhritarashtra asked, "O immensely wise one! Because of what you have spoken well, my sorrow has been dispelled. But I again wish to hear the true purport of your words. How do learned ones free themselves from their mental grief, when they come in contact with something that is injurious, or when they are separated from something that is good?"

'Vidura replied, "Whenever the mind is free from unhappiness and happiness—that is when a learned one obtains peace and attains a good objective. O bull among men! Whatever we think of is not permanent. The world is like a plantain tree. It has no essence.[19] Learned ones say that the bodies of mortal beings are like houses. They are destroyed by time. But the single being that is inside[20] is beautiful. Men cast aside clothes, whether they are old or new, and wear other clothes that they like. Bodies occupied by souls are like that. O Vichitravirya's son! Beings obtain a life of unhappiness or one of happiness, depending on the deeds they have themselves undertaken. O descendant of the Bharata lineage! Depending on their deeds, they obtain heaven, happiness and unhappiness. Whether he can control it or not, he bears his own load. An earthen pot may be shattered once it has mounted on the wheel,[21] once some work has been done on it, once work on it has been completed, once it has been taken down but is still wet, once it is dry, once it has been fired, or once it has been taken down and is being used. O descendant of the Bharata lineage! The bodies of souls are used like that. Some are destroyed in the womb, some after being born, some when they are a day old, some when they are half a month old, some when they are a month old, some when they are a year old, some when they are two years old, some in youth, some in middle age and some in old age. Depending on their earlier deeds, beings come into being

[19]Because there is no wood in a plantain tree.

[20]The atman.

[21]The potter's wheel.

and cease to be. This is the way of the world. What is the reason to sorrow? O king! O lord of men! It is like beings sporting in the water. Some leap up and others are submerged. In that way, in this unfathomable earth, some leap up and others are submerged. One is tied down and has to enjoy the fruits of one's deeds. Only those of limited intelligence suffer on this account. Those who are wise remain established in the truth and search for what comes at the end of this life. They understand why beings come together and attain the supreme objective."'

Chapter 1305(4)

'Dhritarashtra asked, "O supreme among eloquent ones! Life is unfathomable. But how does one understand it? I wish to hear about it. Tell me truthfully. I am asking you."

'Vidura replied, "O lord! Listen to everything about beings, about their birth and other deeds. On earth, for some time, a being dwells as an embryo.[22] When the fifth month is over, flesh is formed. Within the womb, all the limbs are then formed within a month. The being dwells in the midst of all this, smeared with flesh and blood. Because of the force of the wind, the feet are upwards and the head is downwards. It faces great difficulties as it approaches the gate of the vagina. Accompanied by earlier deeds, it is afflicted by the contraction of the vagina. Having been freed from this,[23] he sees the other calamities in this world. Evil demons grab him, like dogs after a piece of meat.[24] If he is still alive, in a subsequent phase, he is grasped by diseases. He is tied down by his own deeds. He is bound down in the noose of senses and afflicted by the succulent addiction

[22]The text uses the word *kalala*. An embryo goes through stages of development, progressively, kalala, *arbuda*, *peshi* and so on. So kalala is the first stage in am embryo's development.

[23]Having been born.

[24]These are demons that afflict infants, newly born children.

to them. O lord among men! He confronts various temptations. He is repeatedly tied down by these and is never satisfied. He does not realize when he arrives in Yama's world. In the course of time, he dies and Yama's messengers drag him around. Those who are inarticulate in speech utter good and bad words through their mouths. Like that, the atman ties down the atman and fails to comprehend this.[25] Thus, people are destroyed and are overcome by avarice. They become crazy because of greed, anger and pride. They do not understand their own atman. He finds pleasure in having been born in a good lineage and censures those who have been born in an inferior lineage. He is vain in the pride of prosperity and censures those who are poor. He reprimands others as stupid, but does not look at his own self. He inflicts teaching on others, but does not teach himself. This world of mortals is not permanent. Since the time of birth, whoever follows dharma in all his activities, attains the supreme objective. O lord of men! He who understands all this and acts accordingly, follows the path of liberation and obtains it."'

Chapter 1306(5)

'Dhritarashtra said, "If the unfathomable path of dharma is difficult to understand, tell me everything in detail about the path of intelligence."

'Vidura replied, "After bowing to the one who created himself,[26] I will tell you this. This is what the supreme rishis said about the unfathomable mysteries of life. There was a brahmana in this great world. He reached an impenetrable forest that was full of large and carnivorous beasts. Terrible, large and hungry beasts were scattered in every direction, in the form of lions, tigers and elephants. They led

[25]This is a difficult shloka to translate. The meaning is not evident and some liberties have been taken in the translation.

[26]Brahma.

to a fear that was like that of death. On seeing them, his heart began to beat faster. O scorcher of enemies! His body hair stood up and he didn't know what to do. He swiftly ran around that forest, here and there. He glanced in all the directions, wondering where he could find refuge. Afflicted by fear, he searched for an opening through which he might run away. The brahmana could not go very far and could not disassociate himself.[27] He saw that the terrible forest was surrounded by a net on every side and that an extremely terrible-looking woman was embracing it with her arms. Five-headed serpents rose up, like mountains. The giant forest was covered by large trees that touched the sky. In the midst of that forest, there was a well that was covered. It was strewn with creepers and the mouth was hidden under a covering of grass. The brahmana fell into that hidden store of water. He was entwined in that net of creepers and hung there. He was like a giant jackfruit, hanging from its stalk. He hung there, with his feet facing upwards and his head facing downwards. At that time, he faced another difficulty there. He saw a giant elephant at the edge of the well. It possessed six faces and moved on twelve feet. It was dark and speckled. It was gradually advancing, through those creepers and trees. As he hung from the branches of the tree, the branches were also covered by many kinds of bees. They were terrible in form and fearful. They had collected honey earlier and were returning to their hive. O bull among the Bharata lineage! They repeatedly went out to collect honey. Beings find it tasty. However, a fool is not satisfied with it. Many streams of honey always flowed there. The man who was hanging there, continuously drank from these flows. But though he was in this difficulty and though he drank, his thirst was not satisfied. He kept desiring it and repeatedly satisfied himself by drinking it. O king! His hopes of remaining alive were ignited. Black and white rats gnawed through the tree, on which, the hopes of the man remaining alive were based. That desolate forest was full of carnivorous beasts and an extremely terrible woman. There were serpents at the bottom of the well and an elephant at the edge. Because of the rats, there was the fifth fear of falling from

[27]From those beasts.

the tree.[28] Because of his greed for the honey, the bees represented the sixth great fear. Thus did he dwell, having been flung into this ocean of life. Without approaching knowledge, he did not abandon his hope of remaining alive."'

Chapter 1307(6)

'Dhritarashtra said, "Indeed, that was a great sorrow, to dwell in such difficult circumstances. How could he have found pleasure there? O supreme among eloquent ones! How could he have been satisfied there? How can one dwell in a place where one faces a contravention of dharma?[29] How can that man escape from this great fear? Tell me everything about this and I will try to do what is right. Great compassion is generated in me and I wish to save him from that state."

'Vidura replied, "O king! That was only a metaphor, cited by those who know about salvation. Using it, a man can enjoy a good end in the world of the hereafter. That desolate forest is the unfathomable cycle of life. The carnivorous beasts that were mentioned are diseases. A woman, giant in form, was established there. The wise speak of her as old age, destructive of complexion and beauty. O king! The well is the body that souls occupy. The giant serpent which dwells there is time. He is the destroyer of all beings and takes away everything from the body. In the midst of that well there was a creeper there and the man hung onto it. That is the hope for remaining alive, which all those with bodies possess. O king! The elephant with six faces is said to be the year. Its faces are said to be the seasons and its feet are the months. Those who think about beings say that the rats which are

[28]Carnivorous beasts, serpents, the elephant and the terrible woman being the other four.

[29]There is a contravention because in that difficult situation, the brahmana cannot pursue the usual dictates of dharma.

[30]Hence black and white.

always gnawing at the tree are days and nights.[30] The bees there are said to be desire. From it, there are many flows that stream down as honey. Humans submerge themselves in those juices of desire. Those who are learned say that the wheel of life circles in this way. That is the reason wise ones sever the noose that ties them to the wheel of life."'

Chapter 1308(7)

'Dhritarashtra said, "O one who can see about the true nature of things! You have told me about an appropriate account. I wish to be again delighted by listening to your words, which are like amrita."

'Vidura replied, "Listen. I will again tell you about that path in detail. On listening to this, accomplished ones are freed from the cycle of life. O king! A man who is on a long journey is exhausted and dwells somewhere for some time. O descendant of the Bharata lineage! In that way, those who are limited in their intelligence pass through this cycle of life and dwell in many wombs.[31] However, those who are learned are freed. That is the reason those who are learned in the sacred texts speak of this[32] as the journey. The learned describe this unfathomable life as a forest. O bull among the Bharata lineage! Those who are mortal have to return to this world, whether they are mobile or immobile. But one who is learned is not enamoured of this. The learned speak of the physical and mental diseases of mortals, whether they are direct or indirect, as carnivorous beasts. O descendant of the Bharata lineage! Those with limited intelligence are not disturbed by the large carnivorous beasts of their own deeds, even though they are always afflicted and attacked by them. O king! Even if a man escapes from these diseases, he is subsequently enveloped by old age, destructive of beauty. Without any support in any direction, he is submerged in the great mire of many kinds of sound, forms,

[31]In successive births.

[32]The cycle of rebirth.

tastes, touch and scent. Years, seasons, months, fortnights, days, nights and *sandhyas*[33] progressively take away beauty and vitality. These are the different manifestations of time, but those with limited intelligence do not know about them. It is said that all beings here have their deeds written on them.[34] The body of a being is like a chariot. The soul is said to be the charioteer. The senses are said to be the horses. Deeds and intelligence are the harnesses. He who dashes behind those swift horses is whirled around on a wheel on this cycle of life. However, a charioteer who controls them with his intelligence does not return.[35] It is said that the chariot which confounds those with limited intelligence belongs to Yama. O king! O lord of men! It gives what you yourself have obtained—destruction of the kingdom, destruction of well-wishers and the destruction of sons. O descendant of the Bharata lineage! This subsequent craving[36] only leads to sorrow. In the course of a supreme sorrow, a righteous person should look upon the grief as medicine. One who is firm in controlling his soul can escape from that sorrow in a way that valour, prosperity, friends and well-wishers cannot. O descendant of the Bharata lineage! A brahmana who resorts to friendship and good conduct has three horses to depend on—self-control, renunciation and lack of distraction. A man who is stationed on that mental chariot and controls the reins of good conduct, discards all fear of death. O king! He goes to Brahma's world."'

Chapter 1309(8)

Vaishampayana said, 'When the supreme among the Kuru lineage heard the words that Vidura had spoken, he was tormented by

[33]The time that joins day and night, the morning and the evening twilight.
[34]Past deeds.
[35]That is, is not reborn.
[36]In the sense of repentance after an event.

grief on account of his sons. He lost his senses and fell down on the ground. His relatives, Krishna Dvaipayana and Kshatta Vidura, saw that he had fallen down on the ground, unconscious. O descendant of the Bharata lineage! Sanjaya, other well-wishers and trusted gate keepers sprinkled him with cold and pleasant water and fanned him with palm leaves. They carefully rubbed his body with their hands. Dhritarashtra remained in this state for a very long period of time. After a long period of time, the lord of the earth regained his senses. Overcome by thoughts of his sons, he lamented for a very long period of time. "Indeed, shame on being a man and on everything that man receives. The roots of perennial unhappiness result from this. O lord! This great misery that one obtains from the destruction of one's sons and from the destruction of prosperity, kin and relatives is like poison, or the fire. It is scorching my limbs and destroying my wisdom. O supreme among brahmanas! Overcome by this, a man thinks that death is superior. Confronted by this calamity and faced with this misfortune, this is what I will do now."[37] Having spoken these words to his great-souled father, supreme among those who know about the brahman, Dhritarashtra was overcome by great grief and was stupefied. O lord of the earth! The king was silent and was immersed in thought.

'On hearing his words, the lord Krishna Dvaipayana, spoke these words to his son, who was tormented by misery on account of his sons. "O Dhritarashtra! O mighty-armed one! Listen to what I am telling you. You are learned. You are intelligent. You are skilled about dharma and artha. O scorcher of enemies! There is nothing that should be known that is not known to you. There is no doubt that you know that everything mortal is temporary. Everything in the world of the living is temporary and there is no state that is eternal. O descendant of the Bharata lineage! Since life ends in death, why are you grieving? O Indra among kings! You were a witness to the creation of this enmity. Your son was the cause, but the working of destiny made him act in that way. O king! It is certain that the

[37]End his life. Dhritarashtra is addressing Krishna Dvaipayana Vedavyasa. Dhritarashtra was Vedavyasa's son.

destruction of the Kurus was destined. Why are you sorrowing over brave ones who have headed towards the ultimate objective? O mighty-armed one! The great-souled Vidura knew about this. O lord of men! That is the reason he made every effort towards peace. But it is my view that even if one tries for a long period of time, no being is capable of deviating from a path that destiny has laid down. I have myself heard what the gods wanted done. I will tell you about this. How will you regain your composure?[38] In the past, I had swiftly gone to Indra's assembly hall. Having recovered from exhaustion, I saw the assembled residents of heaven there. The foremost of devarshis, with Narada at their head, were there. O lord of the earth! I saw the Earth there too. She had gone before the gods because she wanted a task to be accomplished. Having approached the assembled gods, the Earth said, 'In Brahma's abode, you had promised to accomplish a task for me.[39] O immensely fortunate ones! You should quickly act accordingly.' On hearing her words, Vishnu, revered by the worlds, laughed and in that assembly of the gods, spoke these words to the Earth. 'The eldest of Dhritarashtra's one hundred sons is known by the name of Duryodhana. He will accomplish your task. Once he becomes the king, your task will be done. Because of him, all the lords of the earth will assemble in Kurukshetra. Wielding firm weapons, those strikers will kill each other. O goddess! Your burden will be destroyed in that clash. O beautiful one! Swiftly go to your own place and bear up the world.' O king! This was your son, born in Gandhari's womb as a part of *kali*,[40] to become the cause of the destruction of the worlds. He was intolerant, fickle, wrathful and difficult to control. Because of the work of destiny, his brothers were created and they were similar. His maternal uncle, Shakuni, his beloved friend, Karna, and all the

[38]This is a literal translation, the sense being that Vedavyasa will tell Dhritarashtra once he has regained his composure.

[39]In Section 6 (Volume 1), Earth went to Brahma, requesting that she should be saved from the depredations of the asuras on earth.

[40]The word kali has different meanings, including connotations of *kali yuga*. Here, it is best understood as the personification of strife, dissension, discord.

kings who allied with him were also generated on earth to ensure destruction. O mighty-armed one! Narada knew the true reason behind all this. O lord of the earth! Your sons were destroyed because of their own crimes. O Indra among kings! You should not sorrow. There is no reason to grieve. O descendant of the Bharata lineage! The Pandavas have not committed the smallest of crimes. Your evil-minded sons brought injury to earth. O fortunate one! There is no doubt that Narada recounted all this earlier, in Yudhishthira's assembly at the time of the rajasuya sacrifice.[41] 'The Pandavas and the Kouravas will clash against each other. O Kounteya! Since that will happen, do what you must.'[42] On hearing Narada's words then, the Pandavas sorrowed. This is the entire truth and eternal mystery about the gods. O lord! How can your sorrow be dispelled? How can you be compassionate towards your own life?[43] Knowing what has been ordained by fate, you should be affectionate towards the sons of Pandu. O mighty-armed one! This is what I had heard earlier. It was recounted at Dharmaraja's rajasuya, supreme among sacrifices. When I told Dharma's son this secret, he tried to avoid the battle with the Kouravas. However, destiny was stronger. O king! Destiny can never be crossed and no being, mobile or stationary, can cross Yama. O descendant of the Bharata lineage! You are devoted to tasks and possess the best of intelligence. You know that beings come and go. Nevertheless, you are confounded. You are tormented by grief and are repeatedly losing your senses. If King Yudhishthira knows about this, he will cast aside his life. The brave one is always compassionate, even towards inferior species. O Indra among kings! How will he not feel compassionate towards you? O descendant of the Bharata lineage! Retain your life out of compassion towards the Pandavas. I am instructing you to refrain from your proposed course of action. If you act in this way, you will attain fame in this world.

[41]The rajasuya sacrifice has been described in Section 24 (Volume 2). In Section 25 (Volume 2), Narada remembers these events, but does not actually recount them.

[42]This is Vedavyasa quoting Narada.

[43]And not give it up.

O son! The dharma that you will gain will be like what can be got by tormenting with austerities for a long time. Because of sorrow on account of your sons, the flames are blazing. O great king! Every time they do so, use the water of your wisdom to quench them." Hearing these words of the infinitely energetic Vyasa, Dhritarashtra thought for some time.

'He then replied, "O supreme among brahmanas! I am overcome by a great net of grief. I no longer know myself and am repeatedly losing my senses. Having heard your words about this being ordained by destiny, I will retain my life and no longer sorrow." O Indra among kings! On hearing Dhritarashtra's words, Vyasa, Satyavati's son, instantly disappeared.'

SECTION EIGHTY-ONE

Stri Parva

This parva has 468 shlokas and seventeen chapters.

Chapter 1310(9): 21 shlokas
Chapter 1311(10): 23 shlokas
Chapter 1312(11): 30 shlokas
Chapter 1313(12): 15 shlokas
Chapter 1314(13): 19 shlokas
Chapter 1315(14): 22 shlokas
Chapter 1316(15): 20 shlokas
Chapter 1317(16): 59 shlokas
Chapter 1318(17): 30 shlokas
Chapter 1319(18): 28 shlokas
Chapter 1320(19): 21 shlokas
Chapter 1321(20): 32 shlokas
Chapter 1322(21): 14 shlokas
Chapter 1323(22): 18 shlokas
Chapter 1324(23): 42 shlokas
Chapter 1325(24): 28 shlokas
Chapter 1326(25): 46 shlokas

This section is named after the women. When the Pandavas meet Dhritarashtra and Gandhari, Dhritarashtra wants to crush Bhima to death, but is offered an iron image instead by Krishna. Vedavyasa dissuades Gandhari from cursing the Pandavas. Gandhari's glance distorts Yudhishthira's nails. Slain warriors and funeral rites are described. Gandhari curses Krishna.

Chapter 1310(9)

Janamejaya asked, 'After the illustrious Vyasa had departed, what did King Dhritarashtra do? O brahmana rishi ! You should tell me that in detail.'

Vaishampayana replied, 'O best among men! After he[1] heard this, for a long time, he was conscious and thought. He then asked Sanjaya to yoke[2] and told Vidura, "Quickly bring Gandhari and all the women of the Bharata lineage here. Bring my sister-in-law, Kunti, and all the other women here." Thus did the one with dharma in his soul speak to Vidura, who was knowledgeable about dharma. With his intelligence clouded by sorrow, he[3] climbed onto the chariot.

'Gandhari was stricken by grief, but was goaded by the words of her husband.[4] With Kunti and the other women, she rushed to where the king was. Approaching the king, they were overcome with great sorrow. They greeted each other and cried grievously. Kshatta,[5] who was himself suffering even more, comforted them. The voices of the women were choking with tears. He made them ascend their vehicles and left the city. In all the houses of the Kurus, loud lamentations were heard. The entire city, including the children, was afflicted by grief. Those women had earlier not been seen, not even by the large numbers of the gods. With their lords slain, they were now seen by ordinary men. Their beautiful hair was dishevelled and they cast aside their ornaments. Clad in single garments, those women ran around hither and thither, without protectors. The houses were as beautiful as white mountains and they emerged from these. They were like those leaving homes in mountains, when leaders of the herds had been slain. Large numbers of women emerged. O king! They ran around in sorrow, like young girls in an arena. They held onto each other's arms and wept, lamenting their sons, brothers and fathers. They were seen there, as if the world was being destroyed at the end of a yuga. They lamented and wept and ran around here and there. They were senseless because of sorrow and did not know what they should do. Earlier, the women used to be bashful, even before their friends. They were shameless now and appeared in single garments

[1]Dhritarashtra.
[2]The chariot.
[3]Dhritarashtra.
[4]There is some abruptness and break in continuity in the text here.
[5]Vidura.

before their mothers-in-law. Earlier, they used to console each other in times of grief, even if it was of a mild kind. O king! Distracted by sorrow now, they ignored each other.

'The king was surrounded by thousands of such lamenting ones. He left the city in distress and quickly headed towards the field of battle. With the king at their head, artisans, traders, vaishyas and those who earned a living from all kinds of work emerged outside the city. At the destruction of the Kurus, the women cried and lamented in piteous tones. A loud noise arose and oppressed the world. It was as if beings were being scorched when the time for the end of a yuga has arrived. The beings thought that they were being destroyed. At the destruction of the Kurus, all the citizens became extremely anxious. O great king! They were devoted to them and cried in severe grief.'

Chapter 1311(10)

Vaishampayana said, 'When they had only gone a distance of one *krosha*,[6] they saw the maharathas—Sharadvata Kripa, Drona's son and Kritavarma. They saw the king, the lord who possessed the sight of wisdom. With voices choking with tears, sighing and weeping, they said, "O great king! Your son has performed an extremely difficult deed. O king! With his followers, the lord of the earth has gone to Shakra's world. Out of Duryodhana's army, the three of us are the only rathas who have escaped. O bull among the Bharata lineage! All the other soldiers have perished." Having addressed the king in this way, Kripa Sharadvata spoke these words to Gandhari, who was afflicted by sorrow on account of her son. "He fought without any fear. He slew large numbers of the enemy. Your son has been killed after performing heroic deeds. It is certain that they have obtained the worlds that can be conquered through

[6]Measure of distance between 3 and 4 kilometres, 4 kroshas are equal to 1 *yojana*.

sparkling weapons. They are roaming around with radiant bodies there, like immortals. Not a single one of them retreated from fighting with the brave ones. They never joined their hands in salutation. They were slain through weapons. This is said to be the ancient and supreme objective of kshatriyas. Since they have been slain through weapons in a battle, you should not sorrow. O queen! Their enemies, the Pandavas, have nothing to be delighted about. With Ashvatthama at the forefront, listen to what we have done. We heard that Bhimasena had killed your son through the use of adharma. We entered the camp of the sleeping Pandus and created a great carnage. With Dhrishtadyumna at their head, all the Panchalas have been killed. Drupada's sons and Droupadi's sons have been brought down. We massacred large numbers of your son's enemies. Then the three of us fled from the battle, because we were incapable of remaining there. The Pandavas are great archers and will come here quickly.[7] They will be full of intolerance and enmity and will seek to exact vengeance. On hearing that their sons were killed while they were distracted, those illustrious and brave bulls among men will swiftly search out our footsteps. Since we have acted injuriously against them, we are not interested in remaining here. O queen! We seek your permission. Do not sorrow unnecessarily. O king! We seek your permission. Resort to supreme fortitude. You must ensure that the dharma of kshatriyas alone remains established." O descendant of the Bharata lineage! Having said this, Kripa, Kritavarma and Drona's son circumambulated the king. They glanced towards the intelligent king Dhritarashtra. Those great-souled ones swiftly urged their horses towards the Ganga.

'O king! All those maharathas took each other's leave and anxiously left in three different directions. Kripa Sharadvata went to Hastinapura. Hardikya went to his own kingdom and Drona's son went to Vyasa's hermitage. Those brave ones departed, glancing towards each other. Those great-souled ones were frightened at having injured the sons of Pandu. O great king! Having met the king

[7]These sentences suggest that the events of Section 79 (Volume 7)never happened and there is some inconsistency.

before the sun had risen, those brave ones, the scorchers of enemies, departed in different directions, as they willed.'

Chapter 1312(11)

Vaishampayana said, 'When all the soldiers had been slain, Dharmaraja Yudhishthira heard that his aged father had left from Gajasahvya.[8] O great king! With his brothers, he sorrowed and was afflicted by grief on account of his sons. He went to the one who was overwhelmed with grief on account of his sons. He was followed by the brave and great-souled Dasharha,[9] Yuyudhana[10] and Yuyutsu.[11] They were followed by the extremely grief-stricken Droupadi, who was oppressed by sorrow, and also the frightened Panchala women who had assembled there. O supreme among the Bharata lineage! Along the banks of the Ganga, he[12] saw large numbers of women shrieking and lamenting, like female ospreys. Thousands of them wept and surrounded the king. They raised their arms in lamentation and uttered pleasant and unpleasant words. "How can a king who knows about dharma commit such an act of violence now? He has slain his fathers, brothers, preceptors, sons and friends. O mighty-armed one! What was in your mind when you killed Drona and your grandfather, Bhishma, and when you slew Jayadratha? O descendant of the Bharata lineage! What is the use of the kingdom when you cannot see your fathers and brothers, the invincible Abhimanyu and Droupadi's sons?" The mighty-armed one went past the ones who were shrieking like female ospreys.

[8]Another name for Hastinapura.

[9]Krishna.

[10]Satyaki.

[11]Dhritarashtra's son through a vaishya woman. Yuyutsu had sided with the Pandavas.

[12]Yudhishthira.

'Dharmaraja Yudhishthira showed homage to his eldest father.[13] In that way, those destroyers of enemies[14] also honoured their father, in accordance with dharma. All the Pandavas announced their names to him. However, the father was afflicted because his sons had been killed. Oppressed by grief, he embraced Pandava[15] reluctantly. O descendant of the Bharata lineage! He embraced Dharmaraja and comforted him. Like a fire that wished to burn, he then looked for the evil-souled Bhimasena. The fire of his anger was fanned by the wind of his sorrow. He wished to burn down the forest that was Bhimasena with his sight. However, Hari[16] realized that he[17] harboured ill intentions towards Bhima. He pushed Bhima aside with his arms and presented an iron Bhima. Through signs, the immensely intelligent Hari had understood his intentions in advance. The immensely wise Janardana had therefore thought of a contrivance. The strong king grasped the iron Bhimasena with his arms, thinking it to be Vrikodara. The king possessed the strength and force of ten thousand elephants. When he grasped the iron Bhima and shattered it, his own chest was mangled and blood began to flow from his mouth. Covered with blood, he fell down on the ground, like a *parijata* tree,[18] with blossoms at the ends of its branches. The learned *suta*, Gavalgana's son,[19] seized him and asked him not to act in this way. He spoke words to pacify and comfort him. The great-minded one abandoned his anger and overcame his rage. Full of sorrow, he repeatedly exclaimed, "Alas, Bhima! Alas!" On knowing that he had overcome his rage and was full of sorrow because Bhimasena had been killed, Vasudeva, supreme among men, spoke these words to him. "O Dhritarashtra! Do not grieve. Bhima has not been killed by you. O king! It was an iron image that has been brought down by you. O bull among the Bharata lineage! I knew that you were

[13]In the sense of Pandu being the younger father.

[14]The other Pandavas.

[15]Yudhishthira.

[16]Krishna.

[17]Dhritarashtra. Dhritarashtra wished to crush Bhima with his embrace.

[18]The coral tree.

[19]Sanjaya.

overcome by rage. So I dragged Kounteya away, when he was in the jaws of death. O tiger among kings! There is no one who is as strong as you. O mighty-armed one! Where is the man who can withstand being crushed by your arms? When someone has been crushed by your arms, he cannot escape alive, just as one cannot escape alive when one has confronted Death. O Kouravya! Therefore, I got your son to construct this iron image of Bhima and offered it to you.[20] Because you were tormented by sorrow over your sons, your mind had deviated from dharma. O Indra among kings! That is the reason you wished to kill Bhimasena. O king! However, it would not have been proper for you to kill Vrikodara. O great king! Your sons will never become alive again. Therefore, you should condone everything that we have done and approve of it. Do not unnecessarily have this sorrow in your mind."'

Chapter 1313(12)

Vaishampayana said, 'The attendants then arrived, so as to clean him.[21] Once he had been cleaned, Madhusudana again spoke to him. "O king! You have studied the Vedas and many sacred texts. You are learned in the Puranas and the dharma of kings. O immensely wise one! Though learned, you did not follow their injunctions. O Kourava! You knew that the Pandavas were superior in strength and valour. A king is firm in his wisdom only if he detects crimes himself and obtains what is most beneficial, depending on the time and the place. A person who is told about what is beneficial, but does not accept the good and reject the bad, confronts a calamity and has to repent later. O descendant of the Bharata lineage! Consider the course of action that you followed. O king! You did not control yourself and were under Duryodhana's control. This is because of your own

[20]No further details are given about the 'son'. If son is to be interpreted strictly, Krishna must have asked Yuyutsu to construct the image.

[21]Dhritarashtra.

crimes. Why did you wish to kill Bhima? Therefore, control your anger and remember your own evil deeds. In his insolence, the inferior one[22] had Panchali[23] brought to the assembly hall. Bhimasena killed him to avenge that enmity. Look towards your own transgressions and those of your evil-souled son. O scorcher of enemies! The blameless Pandus were abandoned by you." O lord of men! Thus did Krishna recount the entire truth.

'Dhritarashtra, lord of the earth, replied to Devaki's son. "O mighty-armed one! O Madhava! It is as you have described it. O one who has dharma in his soul! The affection towards my son made me deviate from my patience. That tiger among men[24] is powerful and has truth as his valour. O Krishna! It is fortunate that Bhima was protected by you and did not come between my arms. I am no longer distracted. My anger has gone. My fever has been dispelled. O Keshava! I wish to embrace the brave middle Pandava.[25] Those Indras among kings have been slain. My sons have been killed. My refuge and my pleasure are now vested with the sons of Pandu." He wept and embraced Bhima, Dhananjaya and Madri's two sons, the brave men. He touched their limbs, comforted them and gave them his blessings.'

Chapter 1314(13)

Vaishampayana said, 'Dhritarashtra granted them leave. All the brothers, bulls among the Kurus, together with Keshava, went to Gandhari. The unblemished Gandhari was oppressed by grief on account of her sons. When she recognized Dharmaraja Yudhishthira,[26] who had slain his enemies, she wished to curse him.

[22]Duryodhana.
[23]Droupadi.
[24]Bhima.
[25]Bhima.
[26]Gandhari was blindfolded.

However, the rishi who was Satyavati's son[27] got to know in advance about her wicked intentions towards the Pandavas. He touched the fragrant and pure waters of the Ganga. With the speed of thought, the supreme rishi then arrived at the spot. With his divine sight, he could see and understand what was in the minds of all living beings. The immensely ascetic one blessed his daughter-in-law and told her that this was not the time for cursing. It was the time for peace. "O Gandhari! You should not have anger towards the Pandavas. Obtain peace and control your passion. Listen to my words. Desiring victory, your son spoke to you eighteen days ago. 'O mother! I am going to fight with the enemy. Pronounce auspicious blessings on me.' Desiring victory, he repeatedly beseeched you. O Gandhari! You said, 'Where there is dharma, there is victory.' O Gandhari! Earlier, I cannot remember your words ever having come false. You are prudent. O spirited one! Remember those words of dharma that you uttered earlier. O one who always speaks the truth! Control your anger and do not behave in this way."

'Gandhari replied, "O illustrious one! I do not hate them. Nor do I desire that they should be destroyed. But the sorrow on account of my sons is powerful and I am distracted. I must protect the Kounteyas now, just as Kunti does, and just as Dhritarashtra will protect them. This destruction of the Kurus has come about because of the crimes of Duryodhana, Shakuni Soubala, Karna and Duhshasana. Bibhatsu[28] has committed no crime, nor have Partha Vrikodara, Nakula and Sahadeva, and certainly not Yudhishthira. Wishing to fight, the Kouravyas destroyed each other. They fought with each other and killed each other. However, what I find unpleasant is the deed Bhima undertook while Vasudeva looked on. The great-minded one challenged Duryodhana to a duel with the clubs. As they roamed around in many ways in the encounter, he realized that he was superior in skills.[29] He struck him below the navel and my anger increases because of that. The great-souled

[27]Vedavyasa.

[28]Arjuna.

[29]Bhima realized that Duryodhana was superior in skills.

ones were knowledgeable about dharma and have been instructed about dharma. To save their lives, how could those brave ones have abandoned it in the encounter?"'

Chapter 1315(14)

Vaishampayana said, 'On hearing her words, Bhimasena was frightened. Entreating Gandhari, he spoke these words to her. "Whether I acted in accordance with dharma or in accordance with adharma there, it was because of fear and with a desire to save myself. Therefore, you should forgive me. If I fought in accordance with dharma, there was no way I could have stood up to your immensely strong son. Hence, I acted in an unfair way. The valiant one was the only one left from among the soldiers and having killed me in the encounter with the clubs, would have obtained the kingdom. That is the reason I did what should not have been done. The princess Panchali was in her season and was in a single garment. You know everything about what your son told her then. Without taking care of Suyodhana, we would not have been able to enjoy the earth, with its oceans, unfettered. That is the reason I did what should not have been done. Your son caused us injury, when he exposed his left thigh to Droupadi in the assembly hall.[30] O mother! Your son acted in a wicked way and that is the reason he had to be killed by us. At that time, we abided by the instructions of Dharmaraja. O queen! It was your son who generated that great enmity. We are the ones who always suffered in the forest. That is the reason I did what I did. Having seen the end of that enmity and having killed Duryodhana in the battle, Yudhishthira has obtained the kingdom and we have overcome our rage."

'Gandhari said, "O son! You have praised my son and this is not about your killing him. He did everything that you have recounted. O

[30]At the time of the gambling match, described in Section 27 (Volume 2).

descendant of the Bharata lineage! When Vrishasena killed Nakula's horses in the battle, you drank the blood from Duhshasana's body.[31] This was a terrible deed, befitting those who are not *arya*s, and condemned by those who are virtuous. You performed a cruel deed. O Vrikodara! How could you have done it?"

'Bhimasena replied, "One should not drink the blood of someone else, not to speak of one's own. There is no difference between one's own self and one's brother. O mother! Do not sorrow. His blood did not pass beyond my teeth and my lips. Vaivasvata[32] knows this. My hands were smeared with his blood. I cheered my brothers, who were terrified on seeing that Nakula's horses had been slain by Vrishasena in the battle. At the time of gambling with the dice, he had seized Droupadi by the hair. I had spoken words in anger then and those were in my mind.[33] O queen! Had I not accomplished my pledge, I would have been dislodged from the dharma of kshatriyas till eternity. That is the reason I did what I should not have done. O Gandhari! You should not believe that this was a crime and censure me. In earlier times, when your sons injured us, you did not restrain them."

'Gandhari said, "You were not defeated and you killed one hundred of this aged one's sons. Why did you not spare one, one who had committed the least crimes? O son! We are aged and have lost our kingdom. He would have been our successor.[34] For these blind and aged ones, why could you not have saved a single one? O son! Had you left one, I would not have felt this sorrow at your having slain our sons, as long as you acted in accordance with dharma."'

[31]Vrishasena was Karna's son. This wasn't quite the way it happened. These incidents are from Section 73 (Volume 7), Karna Parva. Vrishasena killed Nakula's horses after Bhima had drunk Duhshasana's blood. The incidents occur in different chapters; Vrishasena killed Nakula's horses in the subsequent chapter.

[32]Yama.

[33]Bhima swore to drink Duhshasana's blood, described in Section 27 (Volume 2).

[34]There is a nuance that a translation cannot capture, the word in question being *santana*. This means son or daughter. But it also means continuous flow, which is the reason an offspring is called santana, ensuring the continuous line of succession.

Chapter 1316(15)

Vaishampayana said, 'Gandhari was angry. She was afflicted at the slaughter of her sons and grandsons. Having said this, she asked, "Where is King Yudhishthira?" Trembling and with his hands joined in salutation, Yudhishthira, Indra among kings, approached and spoke these gentle words to her. "O queen! I am Yudhishthira, the violent slayer of your sons. I deserve to be cursed. I am the reason behind this destruction on earth. Curse me. After slaughtering my well-wishers in this way, there is no purpose to my life, or in this kingdom and these riches. I am foolish and a slayer of my well-wishers." Having spoken these words, he was frightened and approached close. Gandhari said nothing, but sighed, long and deep. Yudhishthira lowered his body down and fell at her feet. She was knowledgeable about dharma and could see dharma. Through the band of cloth, the queen could see the tips of the king's fingers.[35] The king's nails had been handsome, but now became malformed. On seeing this, Arjuna hid behind Vasudeva. O descendant of the Bharata lineage! They[36] were restless and moved around. However, Gandhari's rage was gone and she comforted them, like a mother.

'Those broad-chested ones took her leave and together, went to see their mother Pritha,[37] the mother of brave ones. Having not seen her sons for a long time, she had been anxious about her sons. The queen covered her face with a piece of cloth and wept. Thus, with her sons, Pritha shed tears. She saw that they had been wounded from the blows of many weapons. In many ways, she repeatedly touched her sons. She sorrowed for the grief-stricken Droupadi, who had lost her sons. She saw that Droupadi had fallen down on the ground and was weeping. Droupadi said, "O noble lady! Where have all your grandsons, together with Subhadara's son,[38] gone? You are an

[35]Because Dhritarashtra was blind, Gandhari always wore a blindfold.

[36]All the Pandavas.

[37]Kunti.

[38]Abhimanyu.

ascetic and they have not seen you for a long time. They have not come to you now. Without my sons, what good will the kingdom be to me now?" The large-eyed Pritha comforted her. She raised Yajnaseni,[39] who was weeping and was afflicted by grief. With her, and with her sons following her, Pritha, who was suffering herself, went to Gandhari, who was suffering even more. With her sister-in-law, Gandhari spoke to the illustrious one.[40] "O daughter! Do not grieve. Behold. I am also miserable. I think that this destruction of the worlds has been goaded by destiny. It came about inevitably and naturally, and made the body hair stand up. When Krishna was unsuccessful in his entreaties,[41] the immensely intelligent Vidura had spoken some great words and those have come to pass. One should not sorrow over something that is inevitable, especially something that has already occurred. One should not sorrow over those who have been killed in a battle. I am in the same state as you are. Who will comfort me? It is because of my crimes that the best of our lineage have been destroyed."'

Chapter 1317(16)

Vaishampayana said, 'Having said this about the destruction of the Kurus, with her divine eyesight Gandhari saw everything there. She was immensely fortunate and was devoted to her husband. She was his equal in observing vows. She was always engaged in fierce austerities and was truthful. Maharshi Krishna,[42] the performer of auspicious deeds, had granted her many different kinds of boons, including the strength of divine knowledge. The intelligent one[43] could see things that were far away and not near, such as the bravest

[39]Droupadi.

[40]Droupadi.

[41]A reference to Krishna's mission of peace, described in Section 54 (Volume 4).

[42]Vedavyasa.

[43]Gandhari.

of men lying down in the field of battle. This made the body hair stand up. It was strewn with bones and hair and there were torrents of blood. Many thousands of bodies were scattered around in every direction. There were elephants, horses, chariots and warriors, completely covered in blood. There were bodies without heads and a large number of heads without bodies. It was strewn with elephants, horses and the bravest of men, deprived of their lives. The place was populated by jackals, wild crows, ravens, herons and crows. It was full of rakshasas, maneaters and delighted ospreys. Inauspicious jackals howled and it was populated by vultures.

'Dhritarashtra, lord of the earth, obtained Vyasa's permission. With all the sons of Pandu, with Yudhishthira at their head, with Vasudeva and the king who had lost his relatives[44] leading the way, and assembling all the Kuru women, he[45] went to the field of battle. The women, who had lost their lords, approached Kurukshetra. They saw their slain sons, brothers, fathers and husbands there. They were being devoured by predatory beasts there, by jackals, wild crows, crows, demons, pishachas, rakshasas and many kinds of beings that roam around in the night. The women saw that place, which was like Rudra's sporting ground. As they descended from their extremely expensive vehicles, they screamed. The women of the Bharata lineage were miserable and saw a sight that they had not seen earlier. Some roamed around amidst the bodies. Others fell down on the ground. They were exhausted and without their protectors. Some lost their senses. The women of the Panchala and Kuru lineages were extremely miserable. Their minds were numb because of the sorrow, and in every direction, they screamed.

'Subala's daughter[46] was knowledgeable about dharma. She looked at that terrible field of battle. Having seen the destruction of the Kurus, she approached Pundarikaksha Purushottama and spoke these sorrowful words. "O Pundarikaksha! Look at these

[44]It is not clear who this king is. It can only be Satyaki, though Satyaki is rarely described as a king.

[45]Dhritarashtra.

[46]Gandhari.

daughters-in-law, whose lords have been slain. O Madhava! Their hair is dishevelled and they are shrieking like female ospreys. They arrived together, remembering the bulls among the Bharata lineage. They are running around separately now, after their sons, brothers, fathers and husbands. O mighty-armed one! These are the mothers of heroes and their sons have been killed. Some are the wives of heroes and the brave ones have been killed. The place is beautiful with those tigers among men, Bhishma, Karna, Abhimanyu, Drona, Drupada and Shalya. They were like blazing fires. The great-souled ones wore golden armour, decorated with molten gold and gems. They wore armlets and bracelets on their arms. They were ornamented with garlands. Spears, clubs, sparkling and sharp swords, arrows and bows were released from the arms of the brave ones. Large numbers of delighted carnivorous beasts have assembled in some places. In some places, they are sporting. In others, they are lying down. O lord! O brave one! Behold. That is how the field of battle looks. O Janardana! As I look at it, I am tormented by grief. O Madhusudana! The Panchalas and the Kurus were like the five elements.[47] I never thought that they would be destroyed, or that they would be killed. Thousands of eagles and vultures are tearing apart the best of armour, and dragging and devouring the mangled bodies. Who could have thought of the destruction of Jayadratha, Karna, Drona, Bhishma and Abhimanyu? O Madhusudana! They were regarded as those who could not be killed. I see them slain now. They are being devoured by vultures, herons, wild crows, hawks, dogs and jackals. Those wrathful ones were stationed under Duryodhana's command. Behold those tigers among men now. They are like fires that have been pacified. All of them deserved to lie down on soft and clean beds. They have been destroyed now and are lying down on the bare ground. At the appropriate time, they were always praised by bards. They are now hearing the many horrible and inauspicious howls of jackals. Those illustrious and brave ones used to lie down on beds earlier. Their limbs used to be smeared with the paste of sandalwood

[47]The sense is that the five elements (earth, air, fire, water, sky) are not destroyed. So the Kurus and the Panchalas would not be destroyed either.

and aloe. They are now lying down in dust. Vultures, jackals and crows are tearing away their ornaments. They are repeatedly emitting inauspicious and hideous howls. There are bows, arrows, yellow swords and sparkling clubs. They were cheerful and prided themselves on fighting. They are radiant, as if they are still alive. There were many who were extremely handsome, but have been torn apart by carnivorous beasts now. Some possessed eyes like bulls and are lying down, wearing golden garlands. Others, with arms like bludgeons, are still holding their clubs. The brave ones are lying down facing them, like women along their beloveds.[48] Others have dazzling armour and sparkling weapons. O Janardana! Thinking that they are still alive, the predatory beasts are not oppressing them. Other great-souled ones have been dragged away by the predatory beasts. Golden garlands have been scattered around in every direction. Those fierce jackals have attacked the illustrious ones who have been slain. Thousands of necklaces have been flung away from their necks. All of them would be praised by bards in the second half of the night.[49] In the other half, accomplished minstrels would praise them with many offerings. These excellent women are miserable with grief and are lamenting them now. O tiger among the Vrishni lineage! They are severely afflicted by sorrow and are despondent. O Keshava! The faces of these excellent women are like red lotuses. They are handsome and beautiful, but have dried up now. Some others are no longer crying. They are grief-stricken and reflecting. Miserable, the women of the Kuru lineage are rushing here and there. The women of the Kuru lineage possess golden complexions, like that of the sun. But because of the anger and the tears, the faces now have the hue of copper. Having lamented a lot, some have become quiet. The women no longer know what another one is lamenting. Some have lamented and shrieked for a long time. Those brave ones are now trembling with sorrow and are casting aside their lives. On seeing the many bodies, they are shrieking and lamenting. Others,

[48]The clubs are being compared to women lying down alongside their beloved husbands.

[49]The text uses the word *apararatri*, meaning the second half of the night.

with delicate hands, are beating on their heads with their hands. The earth is beautiful, strewn here and there with fallen heads and hands and heaps of other kinds of limbs that have been severed. There are horrible heads without bodies and bodies without heads, a sight that arya women should not see. On seeing this, they are delighted and confused at the same time. Affixing a body to a head, they are glancing at it senselessly. Miserably, they are saying, "This is not he. He is somewhere else." There are hands, thighs, feet and other parts that have been cut down by arrows. Joining them, they are overcome by misery and are repeatedly losing their senses. There are other bodies without heads, devoured by animals and birds. On seeing these, some of the Bharata women are not recognizing that these are their husbands. O Madhusudana! Others are seeing their brothers, fathers, sons and husbands, killed by the enemy, and are beating their heads with their hands. There are arms holding swords and heads wearing earrings. The earth is impassable because of the mire that the flesh and the blood have created. These unblemished women do not deserve unhappiness and have not been touched by misery earlier. The earth is scattered with their brothers, fathers and sons. O Janardana! Look at the large numbers of Dhritarashtra's daughters-in-law. Those young women, with excellent hair, are like a herd. O Keshava! What greater misery can manifest itself before me, than that all these women should appear in this form and act in this way? O Keshava! It is certain that I have performed wicked deeds in my earlier lives, since I see my sons, grandsons and brothers killed." Lamenting in this way, she saw her slain son.'

Chapter 1318(17)

Vaishampayana said, 'Oppressed by grief, Gandhari then saw Duryodhana. She suddenly fell down on the ground, like a severed plantain tree in a forest. Having regained her senses, she repeatedly lamented again. On seeing Duryodhana lying down, covered in blood, Gandhari embraced him and lamented piteously. "Alas! Alas, son!" She was afflicted by grief and lamented, her senses overwhelmed. His extremely broad collar bones were decorated with a golden necklace. Oppressed by grief, she sprinkled him with tears flowing from her eyes. Hrishikesha was near her and she spoke these words to him. "O lord! This war, which would lead to the destruction of relatives, presented itself. O Varshneya! At that time, this best of kings joined his hands in salutation and spoke to me. 'O mother! In this clash that has arisen between relatives, you must pronounce words of victory over me.' O tiger among men! Knowing everything about the catastrophe that he had brought on himself, I told him, 'Where there is dharma, victory exists there. O son! O lord! Since you are fighting without any confusion, you are certain to obtain the worlds that can be conquered through weapons.' O lord! Having spoken this earlier, I am not mourning him. I am sorrowing over the miserable Dhritarashtra, whose relatives have been killed. O Madhava! Look at my son. He was intolerant and the best among warriors. He was skilled in the use of weapons and was indomitable in battle. He is lying down on a bed meant for heroes. Those whose heads were consecrated[50] would advance ahead of this scorcher of enemies. He is lying down in the dust now. Behold the progress of time. It is certain that the brave Duryodhana has attained an end that is not very easy to obtain. He is lying down forwards,[51] on a bed loved by heroes. The lords of the earth used to honour and delight him earlier. Earlier, the best of women used to fan him with the best of whisks. He is now being fanned by the best of birds, with their wings. The strong and mighty-armed one is lying down here. Truth was his valour. He was brought down by Bhimasena in the encounter, like an elephant by a lion. O Krishna! Look at Duryodhana lying down, his body covered with blood. O descendant of the Bharata lineage![52] He has been slain by Bhimasena, with an upraised club. O Keshava! Earlier, the mighty-armed one brought eleven akshouhinis

[50]That is, kings.

[51]The sense being that he did not retreat.

[52]Since Krishna is being addressed, this is a clear typo.

into the battle. He has now been conveyed to his destruction. This Duryodhana was a maharatha and a great archer. He is lying down. He has been brought down by Bhimasena, like a tiger by a lion. He was foolish and disrespected Vidura and his father. He was stupid and wicked and disrespected the aged. That is the reason he has fallen prey to death. He was stationed on this earth for thirteen years, without any rivals. My son was the lord of the earth. He has been slain and is lying down on the ground. O Krishna! I will not see the earth ruled by Dhritarashtra's son. O Varshneya! It used to be full of elephants, cattle and horses. But this did not last for a long time. O mighty-armed one! I will now see it ruled by others. O Madhava! There will no longer be elephants, cattle and horses. How can I remain alive? Behold. There is a greater hardship for me than the slaying of my son. With the brave ones killed in the battle, these women are around me. O Krishna! Look at Lakshmana's mother.[53] She possesses beautiful hips, but her hair is dishevelled. She is lying down in Duryodhana's arms and is like a golden altar. When the mighty-armed one was alive earlier, it is certain that this spirited child would nestle herself in his excellent arms and pleasure herself in those arms. How is it that my heart is not shattering into a hundred fragments? I have seen my son, together with his son, slain in the battle. The unblemished one is inhaling the fragrance on the head of her blood-stained son.[54] The one with the beautiful thighs is caressing Duryodhana with her hand. How can that spirited one not sorrow over her husband and her son? She is sometimes looking at her son and sometimes at him.[55] The long-eyed one is beating her head with her hands. O Madhava! She is falling down on the breast of the brave king of the Kurus. Her complexion is like that of a white lotus. Since the ascetic one had earlier wiped the faces of her son and her husband, she seems to be between two white lotuses too.[56] If the sacred texts and what we have heard is true, then it is

[53]That is, Duryodhana's wife. Lakshmana was Duryodhana's son.

[54]Lakshmana.

[55]Duryodhana.

[56]Duryodhana and Lakshmana.

certain that the king has obtained the worlds that can be conquered through the strength of arms."'

Chapter 1319(18)

'Gandhari said, "O Madhava! Look at my one hundred sons. They were never exhausted in a battle. In the battle, most of them were killed by Bhimasena's club. But there is something that is causing a greater grief to me now. With their sons slain, my young daughters-in-law are running around with dishevelled hair. Their ornamented feet used to roam around on the terraces of palaces earlier and must touch the ground, wet with blood, now. As they are whirling and roaming around, crazy and tormented by grief, they are scattering vultures, jackals and crows. There is another one there, unblemished in her limbs. Her waist can be encircled by the hands. On seeing this terrible sight, she is miserable and has fallen down. O mighty-armed one! My mind can no longer find peace after I have seen the princess, Lakshmana's mother, the daughter of a king. Some see their brothers, others see their husbands and sons slain, lying down on the ground. On seeing that they have fallen down, they are grasping their arms with their own beautiful arms. O unvanquished one! There are middle-aged women and aged ones. With their relatives killed in the terrible clash, they are weeping. Listen. O immensely strong one! Exhausted and confused, they are clinging onto the seats of chariots and the slain bodies of elephants and horses. O Krishna! Behold. There is another one who has picked up the head of her relative, severed from his body. It is beautiful, has an excellent nose and is decorated with earrings. O unblemished one! I think that their crimes in their earlier lives must have been severe. And I, possessing limited intelligence, must have done the same as well. O Janardana! That is the reason we are being repaid by Dharmaraja.[57]

[57]This Dharmaraja does not mean Yudhishthira. It means Yama.

O Varshneya! Good and evil deeds can never be destroyed. O Krishna! Look at them. They are in the best of ages. They possess beautiful breasts and stomachs. They have been born in noble lineages. They are modest. Their eyelashes, eyes and hair are dark. Confused by sorrow and grief, they are gaggling like a gaggle of geese. O Madhava! They are shrieking like cranes and are falling down. O Pundarikaksha! The faces of these women are like blooming lotuses. Their faces are perfect and the sun's sharp rays are hurting them. O Vasudeva! My sons were as proud as crazy elephants, and jealous. Ordinary men are now looking at the women from the inner quarters.[58] The shields are marked with the signs of one hundred moons. The standards have the complexion of the sun. The armour is golden. The breast-plates are made out of gold. O Govinda! Behold the blazing helmets of my sons as they lie down on the ground. They are like fires into which oblations have been offered. Duhshasana is lying down here, brought down by the brave Bhimasena, the slayer of enemies, with a club that killed heroes. His limbs are drenched with the blood that has been drunk. O Madhava! At the time when Droupadi was afflicted by the gambling, she had urged him on and he[59] remembered that.[60] O Janardana! To please his brother and Karna, when Panchali was won over by the dice in the assembly hall, he[61] had spoken harsh words to her and to Sahadeva, Nakula and Arjuna. 'O Panchali! You are our servant and our wife. Quickly enter our house.' O Krishna! At that time, I had spoken to King Duryodhana. 'O son! Shakuni has been grasped by the noose of death. Abandon him. O extremely stupid one! Understand that your maternal uncle loves a conflict. O son! Swiftly abandon him and make peace with the Pandavas. O extremely stupid one! You do not comprehend. Bhimasena is intolerant. The sharp words that

[58]*Avarodhana*, the inner or women's quarters of a palace, where the royal ladies resided.

[59]Bhima.

[60]The incidents described in Section 27 (Volume 2).

[61]Duhshasana.

you have spoken are like inflicting iron arrows and flaming torches on an elephant.' However, he[62] was cruel and proud and struck with words that were like stakes. He released his poison, like a snake towards bulls. Duhshasana is lying down here, stretching out his arms. He has been killed by Bhimasena, like a giant bull by a lion. Bhimasena was extremely intolerant and did something that was extremely gruesome. In the battle, he angrily drank Duhshasana's blood."'

Chapter 1320(19)

'Gandhari said, "O Madhava! This son of mine, Vikarna, was revered as being wise. He was slain and is lying down on the ground. Bhima did this one hundred times. O Madhusudana! Vikarna is lying down in the midst of some elephants. He looks like the sun in the autumn sky, surrounded by dark-blue clouds. His hands bore the marks from wielding a giant bow and are encased in finger-guards. Why are they being mangled by vultures now? O Madhava! His ascetic wife is trying to ward off the vultures that are after meat. But though she is continually trying, the child is incapable of warding them off. O bull among men! Vikarna was brave and young and a leader of troops. He was used to happiness. He deserved happiness. O Madhava! He is lying down in the dust. In the encounter, his inner organs have been mangled by barbed arrows, hollow arrows and iron arrows. However, Lakshmi has still not abandoned this best of the Bharata lineage. Durmukha did not retreat and is lying down slain, after killing large numbers of the enemy in the battle. He has been killed by the brave one[63] in the encounter, by one who accomplished his pledge. O Krishna! Half of his face has been eaten up by carnivorous beasts. O son!

[62]This probably means Duryodhana, but could also mean Duhshasana.

[63]Bhima.

But you are shining more brightly, like the moon on the seventh lunar day. O Krishna! With a face like this, how could this brave one be brought down in the battle? How could my son be slain by the enemy and made to bite the dust? O amiable one! No one was capable of standing before Durmukha. He had conquered the world of the gods. How could he have been slain by the enemy? O Madhusudana! Chitrasena has been slain and is lying down on the ground. Look at this son of Dhritarashtra's. He was the best of archers. He is still adorned in colourful garlands and ornaments. Grief-stricken young women are weeping and are seated around him, together with large numbers of predatory beasts. The sound of the weeping of women mixes with the roars of carnivorous beasts. O Krishna! This seems to be an extraordinary and wonderful sight to me. The young Vivimshati was a leader of troops and was always served by the best of women. O Madhava! He is lying down in the mud and the dust now. The brave one was slaughtered in the encounter and his armour was shattered by arrows. More than twenty vultures have surrounded Vivimshati now. In the encounter, the brave one penetrated the Pandava formation. Having penetrated, he is now lying down, like a virtuous man. O Krishna! Look at Vivimshati. His face has a smile. He possesses an excellent nose and excellent eyebrows. He is like the lord of the stars.[64] Vasava's women have surrounded that prosperous one.[65] He seems to be sporting with gandharvas and thousands of celestial maidens. Duhsaha was brave and the ornament of assemblies. He was the one who slew brave soldiers. He was the one who destroyed the enemy. What about him? Duhsaha's body is completely covered by arrows. He looks like the slope of a mountain, covered by blossoming *karnikara* trees. His radiant garlands are golden. His armour is blazing. Though he is dead, Duhsaha looks like Mount Shveta, when it is ablaze."'

[64]The moon.

[65]In heaven.

Chapter 1321(20)

'Gandhari said, "O Madhava! O Dasharha! He was as proud and haughty as a lion.[66] He was said to possess one-and-a-half times the qualities, strength and valour of his father and you. He single-handedly penetrated the extremely impenetrable battle formation of my son. He was the one who caused death to others, but has himself come under the subjugation of death. O Krishna! He was Krishna's[67] son and was infinitely energetic. I see that though Abhimanyu has been slain, his radiance has not diminished. This daughter of Virata's[68] is the daughter-in-law of the wielder of Gandiva. This distressed child is sorrowing over her brave husband. The unblemished one is grieving. O Krishna! With her husband dead, the wife, Virata's daughter, has approached him and is wiping his face with her hands. The neck of Subhadra's son has three lines[69] and the face above it is like a blooming lotus. The illustrious one[70] is inhaling its fragrance. The beautiful one is desirable in her beauty and is embracing him. She used to be bashful earlier. But she has now lost her senses, as if she has drunk *madhvika* liquor. O Krishna! She has removed the golden armour and is glancing at his body, covered with wounds. O Krishna! The child is glancing at him and speaking to you. 'O Pundarikaksha! This one had eyes like yours and has been brought down. O unblemished one! He was your equal in strength, valour and energy. He was your equal in beauty. But he has been brought down and is lying down on the ground. He was extremely delicate and was used to lying down on the skins of *ranku* deer. His body is on the ground now. Does it not cause torment? With armlets, his hands are like the trunks of elephants, hardened from bowstrings. As he is lying down, with golden bracelets, those large arms are outstretched. He is

[66]This is a reference to Abhimanyu.

[67]Meaning Arjuna's.

[68]Uttara.

[69]The text uses the word *kambu*, which can be translated as a neck with three lines, or as a neck that is like a conch shell.

[70]Uttara.

certainly sleeping happily, tired out through many kinds of exertion. As I am lamenting in grief, he is not speaking to me at all. Where has the noble one gone, abandoning the noble Subhadra, his fathers, who are like the gods, and the grief-stricken me?' She has placed his head on her lap, as if he is still alive, and is removing the blood-smeared hair with her hands. She is asking, 'You are Vasudeva's sister's son. You are the son of the wielder of Gandiva. In the midst of the battle, how could those maharathas slay you? Shame on the perpetrators of that cruel deed—Kripa, Karna, Jayadratha, Drona and Dronayani.[71] They have caused this hardship. Did all those bulls among rathas not possess hearts? They surrounded a child and killed him and brought me this sorrow. The Pandavas and the Panchalas were looking. Though he possessed protectors, how was that brave one killed, as if he had no protectors? On seeing that he was killed by many, as if he had no protector, how is the brave Pandava,[72] tiger among men, still alive? Without the lotus-eyed one, how will the Parthas obtain any delight from getting this large kingdom or from the defeat of their enemies? You have earned worlds through your weapons, your dharma and your self-control. Let me swiftly follow you there and protect me there. It is always extremely difficult to die before one's time has come. I am extremely unfortunate. Despite seeing you slain in the battle, I am still alive. O tiger among men! You have gone to the world of the ancestors. In a gentle and smiling voice, which beautiful one will you greet there, as if she were I? In heaven, there is no doubt that you will crush the hearts of the apsaras, with your great beauty and your smiling words. O Subhadra's son! When you attain those auspicious worlds and meet the apsaras and spend time in pleasure with them, remember the good deeds that I did. O brave one! You were destined to spend only six months of your life with me.[73] In the seventh month, you have confronted your death.' As she is speaking these miserable and pointless words, the women of the Matsya king's[74]

[71]Ashvatthama.

[72]Referring to Arjuna.

[73]Abhimanyu and Uttara were married six months before the war.

[74]Meaning Virata.

lineage are pulling Uttara away. Having pulled the grief-stricken Uttara away, they are themselves overcome with sorrow, on seeing that Virata has been killed. They are weeping and lamenting. He is lying down, covered with blood, mangled by Drona's arrows. Virata is being torn apart by vultures, jackals and crows. Those dark-eyed ones are helpless and distressed and are incapable of restraining those birds from tearing Virata apart. Those women have been scorched by the sun and are exhausted from their endeavours. They are pale and their bodies have lost their beauty. Look at the children who have been killed—Uttara,[75] Abhimanyu, Sudakshina from Kamboja[76] and the handsome Lakshmana. O Madhava! Behold. They are lying down in the forefront of the warriors."'

Chapter 1322(21)

'Gandhari said, "This Vaikartana was a maharatha and great archer. He is lying down in the battle, as if a blazing fire has been pacified through Partha's energy. Behold Vaikartana Karna. He was one who slew many *atiratha*s. However, he has been brought down and is lying down on the ground, his limbs covered with blood. The great archer and maharatha harboured an enmity for a long time and was intolerant. The brave one has been slain in the battle by the wielder of Gandiva and is lying down. When my maharatha sons fought with the Pandavas and terrified them, they placed him at their head, like elephants with a leader of the herd. He was like a tiger in the battle, against the lion Savyasachi. He has been brought down, like an elephant by a crazy elephant. O tiger among men! When that brave one has been killed in the battle, his wives have assembled and have surrounded him, with their hair dishevelled. They

[75]Virata's son, Uttara, not the daughter, Uttaraa.

[76]This does not fit. Sudakshina from Kamboja was killed by Arjuna in Section 69 (Volume 6). However, he was not a child.

are weeping. Dharmaraja Yudhishthira was always anxious about him. Because of his worry, he could not sleep for thirteen years. The enemy could not assail him in a battle, like foes against Maghavan. His heat was like that of the fire at the time of the destruction of a yuga. He was as steady as the Himalayas. O Madhava! The brave one was the refuge for Dhritarashtra's son. He has been slain and is lying down on the ground, like a tree shattered by a storm. Behold Karna's wife, Vrishasena's mother. She has fallen down on the ground and is lamenting and weeping in piteous tones. 'It is certain that the preceptor's curse followed you.[77] That is the reason the earth swallowed up the wheel of your chariot. Then, in the midst of the enemy in the battle, Dhananjaya's arrow severed your head.' Alas! Shame! When Sushena's mother[78] has seen the mighty-armed Karna, with gold-decorated armour plates and who was never dispirited, she has fallen down, senseless. She is extremely miserable and is weeping. There is little left of the great-souled one. The predatory beasts have devoured his body. It is not a pleasant sight and is inauspicious, like the moon on the fourteenth day of *krishnapaksha*. She is writhing on the ground, where she has fallen. She is distressed and has arisen again. She is inhaling the fragrance of Karna's face. Tormented because her sons have been killed, she is weeping."'

Chapter 1323(22)

'Gandhari said, "The one from Avanti was brought down by Bhimasena.[79] Though he had many relatives, he is like one without relatives, and is being devoured by vultures and jackals. O

[77]Karna's preceptor, Parashurama, cursed him.

[78]Sushena was Karna's son.

[79]This doesn't quite fit. The famous ones from Avanti were Vinda and Anuvinda. However, they were killed by Arjuna, not Bhima. There was no famous warrior from Avanti who was killed by Bhima.

Madhusudana! Look at him. He created great carnage among the enemy. Covered with blood, he is lying down on a bed meant for heroes. Behold the progress of time. Jackals, herons and carnivorous beasts are separately tugging at him. The brave one advanced in the battle and is lying down on a bed meant for heroes. The women from Avanti have surrounded him and are weeping.

'"Pratipa's son, the great archer, Bahlika, has been slain by a broad-headed arrow. O Krishna! Look at the spirited one. He is like a sleeping tiger. Though he has been slain, the complexion of his face is extremely radiant. It is like the full moon that has arisen on the night of the full moon.

'"Vriddhakshatra's son was brought down in the battle by the son of the chastiser of Paka.[80] He was tormented by sorrow on account of his son and was accomplishing the pledge that he had made,[81] ensuring that it came true. Look at Jayadratha, who has been slain. Though he was protected, the great-souled one defeated eleven armies.[82] The spirited one was full of insolence and was the lord of Sindhu and Souvira. O Janardana! Jackals and vultures are devouring Jayadratha. They are howling and are dragging him into deep hollows. The women from Sindhu, Souvira, Gandhara, Kamboja and *yavanas*[83] have surrounded the mighty-armed one and are trying to save him. O Janardana! Jayadratha should have been killed by the Pandus when he seized Krishna[84] and ran away, together with the Kekayas. Out of respect for Duhshala,[85] they released Jayadratha then. O Krishna! In that case, why did they not show her respect again? She is my young daughter and is lamenting in great grief. She is trying to kill herself and is censuring

[80]The chastiser of Paka is Indra and Indra's son is Arjuna. Vriddhakshatra's son is Jayadratha.

[81]This is a reference to Arjuna's vow, made when Abhimanyu was killed.

[82]Arjuna defeated the eleven Kourava akshouhinis.

[83]Identified with Greeks, Ionians.

[84]Krishnaa, Droupadi. Jayadratha's abduction of Droupadi has been described in Section 42 (Volume 3).

[85]Jayadratha's wife, Duryodhana's sister.

the Pandavas. O Krishna! What can be a great misery for me than this? My young daughter has become a widow and the husbands of my daughters-in-law have been killed. Alas! Shame! Look at Duhshala. She seems to be without sorrow and fear. Searching for her husband's head, she is running hither and thither. He restrained all the Pandavas, when they looked for their son.[86] He slew a large number of soldiers and has himself come under the subjugation of death. The brave one was extremely difficult to defeat and was like a crazy elephant. The women, with faces like the moon, have surrounded him and are weeping."'

Chapter 1324(23)

'Gandhari said, "O son![87] This Shalya has been slain and he is lying down. He was Nakula's maternal uncle. In the battle, he was killed by Dharmaraja, who is knowledgeable about dharma. O bull among men! He always tried to rival you, everywhere. That maharatha king of Madra has been slain and is lying down. O son! He controlled the chariot of Adhiratha's son in the battle. For the sake of the victory of the sons of Pandu, he deprived him of his energy.[88] Alas! Shame! Shalya's face is as beautiful as the full moon, but wild crows have pecked at it and wounded it. His eyes are like the petals of lotuses. O Krishna! His complexion is like that of molten gold and the tongue that is sticking out of his mouth is golden. But it is being devoured by the birds. Shalya, the adornment of an assembly, has been slain by Yudhishthira. The women from the lineage of the king of Madra have surrounded him and are weeping. These kshatriya

[86]When Abhimanyu penetrated the formation, Jayadratha guarded the entry and prevented the Pandavas (Arjuna was away) from entering. This has been described in Section 67 (Volume 6).

[87]The word used is tata.

[88]Shalya had promised to sap Karna's energy in the battle.

women are clad in extremely fine[89] garments and approaching that bull among kshatriyas and bull among men, the king of Madra, are shrieking. With Shalya having been brought down, those women are stationed around him. They are like cows that desire a bull that has got mired in the mud. Look at Shalya, supreme among rathas. He was one who provided refuge to others. Mangled by arrows, he is lying down on a bed meant for heroes.

'"This powerful King Bhagadatta resided in a mountainous region. He was foremost among those who wielded goads on elephants. Having been brought down, he is lying down on the ground. A golden garland decorated his head and though he is being devoured by carnivorous beasts, it is still radiant on his hair. The battle between him and Partha was certainly terrible. It was fierce and made the body hair stand up, like that between Shakra and Bali. The mighty-armed one challenged Partha Dhananjaya and fought with him. Having advanced towards that calamity, he was brought down by Kunti's son.

'"There was no one on earth who was equal to Bhishma in valour and prowess. Bhishma has been struck and is lying down. O Krishna! Look at Shantanu's son lying down, like the sun in his radiance. He has been brought down by destiny, like the sun from the sky at the end of a yuga. In the battle, this valiant one scorched the enemy with the energy of his weapons. O Keshava! This sun among men has set, like the sun sets. The brave one is lying down on a bed of arrows. He was Devapi's equal in dharma.[90] Look at him. He is lying down on a bed meant for heroes, one that is liked by brave ones. This supreme bed is strewn with barbed arrows, hollow arrows and iron arrows. He is lying down, like the illustrious Skanda entering and lying down on a clump of reeds.[91] Gangeya's excellent pillow is not stuffed with cotton. It was given to him by the wielder of Gandiva and is made out of three arrows. The immensely illustrious one protected his

[89]The word used is *sukshma*, which is difficult to translate in a single word, because it has multiple meanings. While 'fine' is acceptable, there is also a sense of subtle, sheer, short and insignificant.

[90]Devapi was Shantanu's elder brother.

[91]Skanda was born in a clump of reeds.

father's injunction and held up his seed.[92] O Madhava! Shantanu's son, the unmatched warrior, is lying down. O son! He had dharma in his soul. He knew about dharma, as it has been laid down in continuous tradition.[93] He was mortal, yet immortal.[94] He still has life in him. In battle, there was no one else as accomplished, learned and valorous as him. Bhishma, Shantanu's son, has been brought down by the enemy and is lying down now. The brave one always spoke the truth. He was learned about dharma. When he was asked by the Pandavas, he himself told them about his means of death in the battle. When the lineage of the Kurus was destroyed, he again resurrected it.[95] Together with the Kurus, the immensely intelligent one has been defeated and has departed. O Madhava! Now that Devavrata,[96] bull among men and an equal of the gods, has gone to heaven, whom will the Kurus ask about dharma?

'"He was Arjuna's teacher and preceptor, and Satyaki's too. Look at the one who has been brought down—Drona, the supreme preceptor of the Kurus. His knowledge of the four types of weapons[97] was like that of the lord of the gods. O Madhava! Drona was as immensely valorous as Bhargava.[98] It is because of his favours that Bibhatsu Pandava could perform an extremely difficult deed.[99] All

[92]Bhishma remained celibate, so that Shantanu could marry Satyavati.

[93]Passed down from one generation to another.

[94]Bhishma could choose the time of his death.

[95]This could be a reference to Bhishma's remaining celibate, so that Shantanu could marry. However, it is probably a reference to Bhishma's marrying Vichitravirya to Ambika and Ambalika.

[96]Bhishma's original name.

[97]Leaving aside divine weapons, these four categories are *mukta* (those that are released from the hand, like a chakra), *amukta* (those that are never released, like a sword), *muktamukta* (those that can be released or not released, like a spear) and *yantramukta* (those that are released from an implement, like an arrow).

[98]Parashurama.

[99]It is not clear what this is a reference to. Given the context, it probably means the defeat of Drupada by the Pandavas (in the enmity between Drona and Drupada), or Arjuna's saving Drona from a crocodile. Both incidents have been described in Section 7 (Volume 1).

his weapons could not protect him and he has been slain and is lying down. With him at the forefront, the Kurus challenged the Pandavas. He was foremost among the wielders of weapons. However, Drona himself has been severed by weapons. He scorched the soldiers, like a moving fire. But he has been slain and is lying down on the ground, like a fire whose flames have been pacified. O Madhava! The bow in his hands is still intact and so are his arm-guards. Though he has been slain, Drona seems to be alive. O Keshava! As with Prajapati at the beginning of everything, the four Vedas and all the weapons never abandoned the brave one. His auspicious feet deserved to be honoured and were honoured by bards and worshipped by hundreds of disciples. But they are now being dragged by jackals. O Madhusudana! Drona was slain by Drupada's son.[100] Kripi[101] is full of misery and the sorrow has made her lose her senses. Look at her. She is weeping in distress. Her hair is loose and her face is cast downwards. She is tending to her dead husband, Drona, supreme among the wielders of weapons. O Keshava! Dhrishtadyumna shattered his body armour with his arrows in the battle. Her hair is matted and she is a brahmachari. She is tending to Drona. Overcome with grief, Kripi is performing the funeral rites. The delicate and illustrious one's husband has been slain in the battle. Fires have been lit, in the proper way, on every side of the funeral pyre. Drona was placed on this and those who were learned about *sama*s chanted the three samas.[102] O Madhava! Brahmacharis with matted hair[103] are hurling bows, javelins and the seats of chariots into the funeral pyre. Many other weapons will also burn with these. Having placed the infinitely energetic Drona on it, they are praising him and weeping. There are others who are quietly mouthing the three kinds of samas. Like a fire being offered into a fire, Drona is being

[100]Dhrishtadyumna.

[101]Drona's wife.

[102]Sama (*saman*) is a metrical hymn, not necessarily belonging to the Sama Veda. The number three probably means that hymns from the Rig Veda, the Sama Veda and the Yajur Veda were chanted.

[103]Drona's disciples.

offered as an oblation into the fire. Drona's brahmana disciples have circumambulated the pyre, keeping it to the left. With Kripi in front, they are now headed towards the Ganga."'

Chapter 1325(24)

'Gandhari said, "Look at Somadatta's son, brought down by Yuyudhana.[104] O Madhava! From a close distance, many birds are tugging away at him. O Janardana! On account of his son, Somadatta is tormented by sorrow and is seen to be censuring Yuyudhana, the great archer. Bhurishrava's mother is overcome by grief. The unblemished one is comforting her husband, Somadatta.[105] 'O great king! It is through good fortune that you have not seen this terrible destruction of the Bharatas. This fearful carnage of the Kurus was like that at the end of a yuga. Your brave son had a sacrificial altar on his standard and donated a lot. He performed many rites and sacrifices. It is through good fortune that you have not seen him slain now. Your daughters-in-law are fearfully lamenting a lot, like female cranes near an ocean. O great king! It is through good fortune that you do not hear them. They are clad in single garments and the dark hair on their heads is dishevelled. With their sons slain, with their lord slain, the daughters-in-law are running around. That tiger among men is being devoured by carnivorous beasts. His arm was severed and brought down by Arjuna. It is good fortune that you are not seeing this. Together with Bhurishrava, Shala was brought down in the battle.[106]

[104]Yuyudhana is Satyaki and Somadatta's son is Bhurishrava.

[105]There is a problem of consistency. Somadatta, Bhurishrava's father, seems to be alive. But in the shlokas that immediately follow, he seems to be dead. Satyaki's killing of Bhurishrava has been described in Section 69 (Volume 6). In some non-Critical versions, following this, Satyaki also killed Somadatta.

[106]Shala, Bhurishrava's younger brother, was killed by Shatanika in Section 69 (Volume 6).

It is through good fortune that you do not see all your widowed daughters-in-law now. Somadatta's great-souled son possessed a golden umbrella and a sacrificial altar on his standard. They were shattered on the terrace of his chariot. It is good fortune that you have not seen this.' With Bhurishrava slain by Satyaki, his dark-eyed wives have surrounded their husband. They are grieving. They are lamenting a lot, afflicted by grief on account of their husband. O Keshava! They are falling downwards towards the ground. Alas! This is terrible. How could Bibhatsu have performed such a fearful deed? The brave one performed sacrifices and while he was distracted, he severed his arm.[107] Satyaki perpetrated a deed that was more wicked. He[108] was attacked when he had controlled his soul and was ready to give up his life. O Madhava! 'You followed dharma. You are alone. But you were finally slain by two who followed adharma.' This is what the wives of the one with the sacrificial altar on his standard are screaming. The wife of the one who had a sacrificial altar on his standard has a waist that can be circled by two hands.[109] She has placed her husband's arm on her lap and is lamenting piteously. This arm used to untie her girdle. It used to crush her thick breasts. That arm used to caress her navel, her thighs and her loins and remove her lower garment. Partha is the performer of unblemished deeds. In Vasudeva's presence, while he[110] was fighting with another one in the battle and was distracted, he was brought down. That beautiful one may be silent, but is censuring you. 'O Janardana! When you are in an assembly, what will you say and tell them? Will you yourself say that Arjuna performed a great deed, or will the one with the diadem say so?' The co-wives are sorrowing over their husband and her in the same way, as if they are her daughters-in-law.[111]

[107]Arjuna severed Bhurishrava's arm while he was distracted in the sense of fighting with another, that is, Satyaki. This has been described in Section 69 (Volume 6).

[108]Bhurishrava.

[109]Earlier, the wives were in the plural. Here, it is in the singular.

[110]Bhurishrava.

[111]The co-wives are sorrowing both about Bhurishrava and about the principal wife.

'"Shakuni, the king of Gandhara, was powerful. Truth was his valour. He was slain by Sahadeva, a maternal uncle by a sister's son.[112] He was earlier fanned with two whisks that had golden handles. He is now lying down and is being fanned by the wings of birds. He used to perform many hundreds and thousands of different kinds of maya. However, his maya has been consumed by the energy of the Pandavas. He was wise about deceit and vanquished Yudhishthira through the use of maya in the assembly hall.[113] He won the extensive kingdom and has won the right to be reborn. O Krishna! Birds have surrounded Shakuni on every side. The deceitful one became accomplished for the sake of bringing about the destruction of my sons. He is the one who was addicted to this great enmity with the Pandavas. He has brought about the death of my sons, his own self and that of his followers. O lord! My sons have conquered worlds through their weapons. In that way, this evil-minded one has also won worlds through weapons. O Madhusudana! Even there, because of his evil intelligence, he will create dissension between my sons and the brothers."'

Chapter 1326(25)

'Gandhari said, "Look at the invincible Kamboja, who was like a covering for Kamboja.[114] O Madhava! He possessed shoulders like a bull. He has been slain and is lying down in the dust. His arms used to be smeared with sandalwood paste and are covered with blood now. When his miserable wife saw them, she lamented in grief. 'These arms were as thick as clubs. They possessed auspicious palms and fingers. When I was in their embrace, I used to be full of desire. O lord of men! Without you, what will be my end now?' Her relatives are far away and she is without a protector. Her voice

[112]Shakuni was Gandhari's brother and this is maternal uncle by extension.

[113]A reference to the gambling match.

[114]Sudakshina.

is exceedingly melodious. Even when they are scorched by heat, the beauty of many kinds of garlands does not vanish. In that way, though these women are exhausted, beauty has not abandoned their bodies.

'"O Madhusudana! The brave king of Kalinga is lying down. Look at his immensely large arms, encased in blazing armlets.

'"O Janardana! Jayatsena was the lord of Magadha. Look at him. He is surrounded by the weeping women from Magadha. O Janardana! They possess long eyes and excellent voices. Their lamentations are pleasant to hear and are confounding my mind. They have thrown away all their ornaments. They are weeping, oppressed by grief. Each of the women from Magadha possessed her own bed. But they are lying down on the ground.

'"Brihadbala was the prince and lord of Kosala. He has been separately surrounded by these women, who are weeping over their husband. The arrows of Krishna's son were struck with the strength of his arms and they are plucking them out from his body.[115] As they are doing this, they are miserable and are repeatedly losing their senses. O Madhava! All of them are overcome by the heat and the exhaustion. Their faces are as beautiful as wilting lotuses.

'"All the five brave brothers from Kekaya were slain by Drona. They are lying down, wearing beautiful armlets. They were headed towards Drona. Their armour was made out of molten gold. Their standards, chariots and garlands were coppery in hue. They are illuminating the ground, like blazing and radiant fires.

'"O Madhava! Look. Drupada was brought down by Drona in the battle. He was like a giant elephant, slain in the forest by a giant lion. O Pundarikaksha! The king of Panchala's umbrella is large and pale. It is shining, like the sun in the autumn sky. The wives and daughters-in-law of the aged Drupada are miserable. Having burnt the king of Panchala, they are circumambulating him, keeping him to the right.

'"The great archer, Dhrishtaketu, was a bull among the Chedis. The brave one was killed by Drona. Bereft of their senses, the women

[115]Krishna means Arjuna here. Arjuna's son is Abhimanyu, Brihadbala having been killed by Abhimanyu in Section 67 (Volume 6).

have moved him. O Madhusudana! Having countered Drona's weapons, the great archer was crushed. He has been slain and is lying down, like a tree brought down by a river. The brave maharatha, Dhrishtaketu, was the lord of Chedi. Having slain thousands of enemy in the battle, he has been slain and is lying down. The birds are tugging at him and his wives are tending to him. O Hrishikesha! The king of Chedi has been slain, with his forces and his relatives. Truth was his valour and the brave son of the daughter of Dasharha is lying down.[116] The beautiful women have placed the king of Chedi on their laps and are weeping. O Hrishikesha! His son has an excellent face and beautiful earrings. Look at him. He has been mangled by Drona with many arrows in the battle. As long as his father was fighting with the enemy, it is certain that he did not abandon him. O Madhusudana! He has never moved from that brave one's rear. O mighty-armed one! In that way, my son's son, Lakshmana, the destroyer of enemy heroes, followed his father.

'"O Madhava! Look at Vinda and Anuvinda from Avanti. They have fallen down. They are like flowering shala trees, destroyed by a storm at the end of winter. Their armlets and armour are golden. They wield arrows, swords and bows. Their eyes are like those of bulls. They are lying down, with unblemished garlands.

'"All the Pandavas, together with you, cannot be killed. They were freed from Drona, Bhishma, Vaikartana Kripa, Duryodhana, Drona's son, maharatha Saindhava, Somadatta, Vikarna and the brave Kritavarma. Those bulls among men could have slain even the gods with the force of their weapons. However, they have been killed in the battle. Behold the progress of time. O Madhava! It is certain that there is no burden that is too heavy for destiny, since these brave ones, bulls among kshatriyas, have been slain by kshatriyas. O Krishna! When you came to Upaplavya and returned unsuccessfully again, my spirited sons were already

[116]Dhrishtaketu was the son of Shishupala. Thus, he was the king of Chedi. However, Shishupala's mother was Shrutadeva. She was from a Yadava (Dasharha) lineage and Dhrishtaketu was descended from the Dasharhas on this side.

killed.[117] That is what Shantanu's son and the wise Vidura told me then. 'Do not show any affection towards your sons.' O son! What they saw, was certain to have come true. O Janardana! In a short while, my sons were consumed and became ashes."'

Vaishampayana said, 'Having said this, Gandhari was oppressed by grief and fell down on the ground. O descendant of the Bharata lineage! Her senses were distracted by her grief and she abandoned her fortitude. Because she was overcome by sorrow on account of her sons, her body was overcome by rage. With her senses distressed, Gandhari ascribed the blame to Shouri.[118]

'Gandhari said, "O Krishna! The Pandavas and the sons of Dhritarashtra were malicious towards each other. O Janardana! Why was their destruction ignored by you? You were capable. You had many servants and were stationed with a large army. Both sides were capable of listening to your words. O Madhusudana! You wilfully ignored the destruction of the Kurus. O mighty-armed one! Therefore, you will have to reap the fruits of what you have done. O wielder of the chakra and the club! I have earned something through my austerities and through serving my husband. You may be difficult to fathom. But through that, I am cursing you. The relatives, the Kurus and the Pandavas, slaughtered each other. O Govinda! Since you ignored this, you will slay your own relatives. O Madhusudana! When thirty-six years have elapsed, your relatives will be killed, your advisers will be killed and your sons will be killed. You will wander around in the forest. You will confront a horrible death. With the sons slain, with the kin and relatives killed, your wives will be tormented, as the women of the Bharata lineage are now."'

Vaishampayana said, 'Having heard these terrible words, the great-minded Vasudeva smiled a little and replied to Queen Gandhari. "O beautiful one! No one other than me can destroy the circle of the Vrishnis. O kshatriya lady! I know what has already been decided. You have acted in accordance with what has been

[117]A reference to Krishna's mission of peace, described in Section 54 (Volume 4).

[118]Krishna.

ordained. The Yadavas cannot be killed by any other men, or by gods and danavas. They will confront their destruction at each other's hands." When Dasharha said this, the Pandavas lost their senses. They became extremely anxious and no longer wished to remain alive.'

SECTION EIGHTY-TWO

Shraddha Parva

This parva has forty-four shlokas and only one chapter.

Chapter 1327(26): 44 shlokas

Shraddha is a funeral ceremony for dead relatives and this parva is named after that. The dead warriors are cremated and their funeral rites performed.

Chapter 1327(26)

'Vasudeva said, "Get up! O Gandhari! Arise! Do not sorrow unnecessarily. The Kurus have confronted destruction because of your crimes. Your evil-souled son was jealous and extremely insolent. You honoured Duryodhana and thought that his evil deeds were virtuous. But they were cruel, full of enmity and harsh. They transgressed the commands of seniors. You committed the sin yourself. Why are you trying to blame it on me? If one sorrows over someone who is dead, something that has been destroyed, or something that has already happened, one imposes sorrow on a sorrow and thereby, causes a double calamity. A brahmana lady gives birth for austerities, a cow for a draught animal, a mare for running, a shudra for a servant and a vaishya for animal husbandry. However, a princess like you gives birth for slaughter."'

Vaishampayana said, 'On again hearing Vasudeva's unpleasant words, Gandhari became silent. Her eyes were anxious and full of tears. Rajarshi Dhritarashtra had dharma in his soul and dispelled the darkness caused by limited intelligence. He asked Dharmaraja Yudhishthira, "O Pandava! You know the number of soldiers who are alive. If you know the number of those who have been slain, tell me." Yudhishthira replied, "One billion,[1] twenty thousand and sixty-six crore—that is the number slain in this battle of kings.[2] O Indra among kings! In addition, twenty-four thousand, one hundred and sixty-five brave ones are missing." Dhritarashtra asked, "O Yudhishthira! Where have those best of men gone? Tell me. O mighty-armed one! It is my view that you know everything." Yudhishthira replied, "They cheerfully offered their bodies as oblations in the supreme battle. Truth was their valour and they have gone to worlds that are like that of the king of the gods. O descendant of the Bharata lineage! Those who were cheerful in their minds, thinking that everyone is mortal, were slain in the battle and have encountered the gandharvas. Those who were unwillingly stationed in the battle and wished to be spared have been slain with weapons and have gone towards the *guhyakas*.[3] However, there were great-souled ones who were weakened and deprived of weapons. They were abandoned by others and severely afflicted. Even then, they attacked the enemy. Though they were severed by sharp weapons, they were devoted to the dharma of kshatriyas. Those extremely radiant and brave ones were slain and went to Brahma's abode. O king! There were some who were slain in the field of battle without doing anything remarkable. They have

[1]*Ayuta* is ten thousand. The text says ten ayuta ayuta, that is one billion.

[2]The total is thus 1,660,020,000. This cannot readily be converted into eighteen akshouhinis. One akshouhini had 21,870 chariots, 21,870 elephants, 65,610 horses and 109,350 foot soldiers. But the number of soldiers per chariot, per elephant or per horse is not known.

[3]Guhyakas are semi-divine species, companions of Kubera. This is a less desirable end.

obtained the region of Uttarakuru."[4] Dhritarashtra asked, "O son! What is this strength of knowledge, through which you can perceive like a *siddha*?[5] O mighty-armed one! If it can be heard by me, tell me about it." Yudhishthira replied, "Because of your instructions, I roamed around in the forest earlier. In that connection, I visited the *tirtha*s and obtained this blessing.[6] At that time, I saw devarshi Lomasha and acquired this knowledge. Earlier, through the yoga of knowledge, I had obtained divine sight."

'Dhritarashtra said, "O descendant of the Bharata lineage! There are people who have relatives and those who do not have relatives. Let the bodies of all those be burnt in accordance with the proper rites. Some have no one to perform the rites and fires have not been lit for some. O son! For whom can we perform the rites? There are many rites to be performed. O Yudhishthira! There are those who have obtained the worlds through their deeds, but are being dragged here and there by birds and vultures."'

Vaishampayana said, 'Having been thus addressed, the immensely wise Yudhishthira, Kunti's son, instructed Sudharma,[7] Dhoumya,[8] the suta Sanjaya, the immensely intelligent Vidura, Kouravya Yuyutsu and all the servants and charioteers, with Indrasena[9] at their head. "Perform the funeral rites for everyone. Let the bodies of those who have no one to look after them not be destroyed." Having heard Dharmaraja's command, Kshatta,[10] suta Sanjaya, Sudharma, Dhoumya, Indrasena and the others brought sandalwood, aloe, yellow fragrant wood, clarified butter, oil, fragrances and cotton garments. They made piles of woods and these expensive objects. They added

[4]Uttarakuru, as a real *dvipa* (continent) is to the north of Jambudvipa and to the north of Mount Meru. However, Uttarakuru is also described as a region that is not on earth, but as a region attained after death.

[5]A siddha is someone who has obtained success, in the sense of having obtained higher knowledge.

[6]The visit to the tirthas has been described in Section 33 (Volume 3).

[7]The family priest of the Kouravas.

[8]The family priest of the Pandavas.

[9]Yudhishthira's charioteer.

[10]Vidura.

the shattered chariots and other implements. O descendant of the Bharata lineage! Having carefully prepared the pyres and observed the prescribed rites, they burnt the foremost among the kings, following the due order—King Duryodhana and his one hundred brothers, Shalya, King Shala, Bhurishrava, King Jayadratha, Abhimanyu, Duhshasana's son, Lakshmana,[11] King Dhrishtaketu, Brihanta, Somadatta, more than one hundred Srinjayas, King Kshemadhanva,[12] Virata, Drupada, Panchala Shikhandi, Parshata Dhrishtadyumna, valiant Yudhamanyu, Uttamouja, the king of Kosala, Droupadi's sons, Shakuni Soubala, Achala, Vrishaka,[13] King Bhagadatta, the intolerant Karna Vaikartana and his sons, the great archers from Kekaya, the maharathas from Trigarta, Ghatotkacha, Indra among rakshasas, Baka's brother,[14] King Alambusa, King Jalasandha and hundreds and thousands of other kings. O king! Flows of clarified butter were poured and the blazing fires burnt them. For some of those great-souled ones, sacrifices meant for the ancestors were performed. Some chanted sama hymns. Others sorrowed over the ones who were dead. The sounds of women weeping mixed with the sama chants. During that night, a lassitude overcame all beings. The blazing fires flamed, without any smoke. They were seen to be like planets surrounded by clouds in the firmament. There were those who had come from many countries and had no one to tend to them. On Dharmaraja's instructions, Vidura brought all of them together and piled them in thousands of heaps. Pyres were lit with wood, sprinkled with oil and they were attentively burnt. Yudhishthira, king of the Kurus, performed the rites for them. After this, with Dhritarashtra at the forefront, he went towards the Ganga.'

[11]Duryodhana's son.

[12]This is a strange mention, because Kshemadhanva has only been mentioned in passing in Section 63 (Volume 5) and has no role to play in the actual war.

[13]Achala and Vrishaka were Shakuni's brothers.

[14]The rakshasa Alayudha.

SECTION EIGHTY-THREE

Jala-Pradanika Parva

This parva has twenty-four shlokas and only one chapter.

Chapter 1328(27): 24 shlokas

Jala is water and pradana is to give. After the cremation, this parva is named after the observation of water-rites and the offering of water to the dead warriors. Kunti also tells the Pandavas that Karna was their elder brother.

Chapter 1328(27)

Vaishampayana said, 'They reached the auspicious Ganga, desired by pious people. It had large lakes and beautiful banks, with large wetlands and large forests. They took off their ornaments and upper garments and offered oblations to fathers, grandsons, brothers and relatives. The noble women of the Kuru lineage offered water to their sons and all the others. They wept in great sorrow. Those who knew about dharma performed the rite of offering water for their well-wishers. The wives of heroes offered water for heroes. The Ganga had excellent passages to the water and seemed to extend out even more. The banks of the Ganga were beautiful, full of these wives of heroes. It was like a giant expanse of water. But it was not at all pleasant.

'O great king! Kunti was suddenly overcome by grief. She wept. In a soft voice, she spoke these words to her sons. "There was a brave and great archer. He was a leader of leaders of rathas. He was marked with the auspicious signs of a hero and was killed by Arjuna in the battle. O Pandavas! You thought of him as the son of a suta and as Radheya.[1] In the midst of the formations, the lord was as radiant as the sun. Staying at the front, he fought against all of you and your followers. He roamed around, gathering all of Duryodhana's troops behind him. There was no one on earth who was his equal in valour. He was devoted to the truth. He was brave. He did not retreat from a battle. The one with unblemished deeds was your brother. Perform the water-rites for him. He was your eldest brother, born from the sun god. He possessed earrings and armour.[2] He was brave. He was like the sun in his radiance." All the Pandavas heard these unpleasant words spoken by their mother. They sorrowed over Karna and became even more distressed.

'Sighing like a serpent, the brave Yudhishthira, Kunti's son, spoke to his mother. "No one but Dhananjaya could withstand his shower of arrows. How did he earlier become your son, born from a god? All of us were tormented by the strength of his arms. He was like a fire inside a garment. How did you hide him? The strength of his arms was fierce and the sons of Dhritarashtra worshipped him. No one but Kunti's son, ratha among rathas,[3] could have taken that away from Karna. He was supreme among all the wielders of weapons. He was our eldest brother! How did you, earlier, give birth to someone with such extraordinary valour? Alas! By keeping this a secret, you have killed us now. We had been afflicted on account of our relatives and Karna's death has added to that. Abhimanyu was destroyed. Droupadi's sons were killed. The Panchalas were destroyed and the

[1]The son of Radha.

[2]The natural earrings and armour Karna was born with.

[3]Meaning Arjuna.

Kurus were brought down. But this sorrow, that touches us now, is a hundred times greater than that. Sorrowing over Karna, it is as if I am being consumed by a fire. There is nothing that we could not have obtained, not even something that is in heaven. This fierce destruction that has enveloped the Kurus would not have occurred." In this way, Dharmaraja Yudhishthira lamented a lot. O king! Having lamented, loudly and softly, the lord performed the water-rites. All the men and women there, on both his sides, cried violently as he performed the water-rites. Out of affection for his brother, Yudhishthira, the wise lord of the Kurus, had Karna's wives, attired in their garments, brought there. Then, with them, the one with dharma in his soul performed the funeral rites. Having done this, with his senses in a whirl, he emerged from the waters of the Ganga.'

This ends Stri Parva.

Shanti Parva

Shanti Parva is the twelfth in the 18-parva classification and is the longest parva of the Mahabharata. In the 100-parva classification, Shanti Parva constitutes Sections 84 to 86. This parva has 353 chapters. In the numbering of the chapters in Shanti Parva, the first number is a consecutive one, starting with the beginning of the Mahabharata. And the second number, within brackets, is the numbering of the chapter within Shanti Parva.

SECTION EIGHTY-FOUR

Raja Dharma Parva

This parva has 4,509 shlokas and 128 chapters.

Chapter 1329(1): 44 shlokas
Chapter 1330(2): 29 shlokas
Chapter 1331(3): 33 shlokas
Chapter 1332(4): 21 shlokas
Chapter 1333(5): 15 shlokas
Chapter 1334(6): 12 shlokas
Chapter 1335(7): 41 shlokas
Chapter 1336(8): 37 shlokas
Chapter 1337(9): 37 shlokas
Chapter 1338(10): 28 shlokas
Chapter 1339(11): 28 shlokas
Chapter 1340(12): 36 shlokas
Chapter 1341(13): 13 shlokas
Chapter 1342(14): 39 shlokas
Chapter 1343(15): 58 shlokas
Chapter 1344(16): 26 shlokas
Chapter 1345(17): 23 shlokas
Chapter 1346(18): 38 shlokas
Chapter 1347(19): 23 shlokas
Chapter 1348(20): 14 shlokas
Chapter 1349(21): 19 shlokas
Chapter 1350(22): 15 shlokas
Chapter 1351(23): 16 shlokas
Chapter 1352(24): 30 shlokas
Chapter 1353(25): 33 shlokas
Chapter 1354(26): 36 shlokas
Chapter 1355(27): 32 shlokas
Chapter 1356(28): 58 shlokas
Chapter 1357(29): 141 shlokas
Chapter 1358(30): 42 shlokas
Chapter 1359(31): 47 shlokas
Chapter 1360(32): 24 shlokas
Chapter 1361(33): 12 shlokas
Chapter 1362(34): 36 shlokas
Chapter 1363(35): 32 shlokas
Chapter 1364(36): 46 shlokas
Chapter 1365(37): 43 shlokas
Chapter 1366(38): 49 shlokas
Chapter 1367(39): 49 shlokas
Chapter 1368(40): 22 shlokas
Chapter 1369(41): 18 shlokas
Chapter 1370(42): 12 shlokas
Chapter 1371(43): 17 shlokas
Chapter 1372(44): 16 shlokas

Chapter 1373(45): 20 shlokas
Chapter 1374(46): 35 shlokas
Chapter 1375(47): 72 shlokas
Chapter 1376(48): 15 shlokas
Chapter 1377(49): 80 shlokas
Chapter 1378(50): 36 shlokas
Chapter 1379(51): 18 shlokas
Chapter 1380(52): 34 shlokas
Chapter 1381(53): 27 shlokas
Chapter 1382(54): 39 shlokas
Chapter 1383(55): 20 shlokas
Chapter 1384(56): 60 shlokas
Chapter 1385(57): 45 shlokas
Chapter 1386(58): 30 shlokas
Chapter 1387(59): 141 shlokas
Chapter 1388(60): 52 shlokas
Chapter 1389(61): 21 shlokas
Chapter 1390(62): 11 shlokas
Chapter 1391(63): 30 shlokas
Chapter 1392(64): 29 shlokas
Chapter 1393(65): 35 shlokas
Chapter 1394(66): 37 shlokas
Chapter 1395(67): 38 shlokas
Chapter 1396(68): 61 shlokas
Chapter 1397(69): 71 shlokas
Chapter 1398(70): 32 shlokas
Chapter 1399(71): 14 shlokas
Chapter 1400(72): 33 shlokas
Chapter 1401(73): 26 shlokas
Chapter 1402(74): 32 shlokas
Chapter 1403(75): 22 shlokas
Chapter 1404(76): 37 shlokas
Chapter 1405(77): 14 shlokas
Chapter 1406(78): 34 shlokas
Chapter 1407(79): 43 shlokas
Chapter 1408(80): 20 shlokas
Chapter 1409(81): 41 shlokas
Chapter 1410(82): 30 shlokas
Chapter 1411(83): 67 shlokas
Chapter 1412(84): 54 shlokas
Chapter 1413(85): 11 shlokas
Chapter 1414(86): 33 shlokas
Chapter 1415(87): 33 shlokas
Chapter 1416(88): 38 shlokas
Chapter 1417(89): 29 shlokas
Chapter 1418(90): 25 shlokas
Chapter 1419(91): 38 shlokas
Chapter 1420(92): 56 shlokas
Chapter 1421(93): 19 shlokas
Chapter 1422(94): 38 shlokas
Chapter 1423(95): 13 shlokas
Chapter 1424(96): 21 shlokas
Chapter 1425(97): 23 shlokas
Chapter 1426(98): 31 shlokas
Chapter 1427(99): 50 shlokas
Chapter 1428(100): 18 shlokas
Chapter 1429(101): 47 shlokas
Chapter 1430(102): 20 shlokas
Chapter 1431(103): 41 shlokas
Chapter 1432(104): 52 shlokas
Chapter 1433(105): 53 shlokas
Chapter 1434(106): 24 shlokas
Chapter 1435(107): 27 shlokas
Chapter 1436(108): 31 shlokas
Chapter 1437(109): 28 shlokas
Chapter 1438(110): 26 shlokas
Chapter 1439(111): 29 shlokas
Chapter 1440(112): 86 shlokas
Chapter 1441(113): 21 shlokas
Chapter 1442(114): 14 shlokas
Chapter 1443(115): 20 shlokas
Chapter 1444(116): 22 shlokas

Chapter 1445(117): 44 shlokas
Chapter 1446(118): 28 shlokas
Chapter 1447(119): 20 shlokas
Chapter 1448(120): 54 shlokas
Chapter 1449(121): 57 shlokas
Chapter 1450(122): 55 shlokas
Chapter 1451(123): 24 shlokas
Chapter 1452(124): 69 shlokas
Chapter 1453(125): 34 shlokas
Chapter 1454(126): 52 shlokas
Chapter 1455(127): 10 shlokas
Chapter 1456(128): 49 shlokas

Raja is king and raja dharma is the dharma of kings. Knowing that Karna was Kunti's son, Yudhishthira sorrows over him and Narada recounts the story of Karna being cursed and his exploits. Yudhishthira wishes to leave for the forest, but is dissuaded. He is asked to learn about dharma from Bhishma and enters Hastinapura. Yudhishthira is crowned. Bhishma teaches Yudhishthira about raja dharma, the dharma of the four varnas and the four ashramas.

Chapter 1329(1)

Vaishampayana said, 'Having offered water to all the well-wishers, the descendants of the Pandu lineage, Vidura, Dhritarashtra and all the women of the Bharata lineage, dwelt there. The great-souled sons of the Kuru lineage wished to spend a month of mourning outside the city.[1] When King Dhritarashtra, with dharma in his soul, had performed the water-rites, the great-souled siddhas, supreme brahmarshis, Dvaipayana, Narada, the great rishi Devala, Devsthana and Kanva, with their supreme disciples, and many other brahmanas who were accomplished in wisdom and learned in the Vedas and all the *snatakas*[2] in the householder stage, came to see the supreme among the Kuru lineage. When they came, the great-souled one[3]

[1]This was a period of purification.

[2]Snatakas are those who have completed their studies (the brahmacharya stage) and are about to enter the householder stage (*garhasthya*).

[3]Yudhishthira.

worshipped them, in accordance with the prescribed rites. The maharshis seated themselves on extremely expensive seats. They accepted the honours that were appropriate for the occasion.[4] In due order, they seated themselves around Yudhishthira. The king was on the sacred banks of the Bhagirathi and his senses were overcome with grief. Hundreds and thousands of brahmanas consoled him.

'At that time, Narada consulted the sages and spoke words that were appropriate for the occasion to Yudhishthira, with dharma in his soul. "O Yudhishthira! Through the valour of your arms and the favours of Madhava, you have resorted to dharma and have conquered the entire earth. It is through good fortune that you have escaped from this battle, which was fearful for the worlds. O Pandava! It is perhaps because you are devoted to the dharma of kshatriyas that you have not rejoiced. O king! Once you have slain your enemies, will you not please your well-wishers? Having obtained this prosperity, I hope that grief is not standing in the way."

'Yudhishthira replied, "Resorting to the strength of Krishna's arms, the favours of the brahmanas and the strength of Bhima and Arjuna, I have conquered the entire earth. But this great grief is always circulating in my heart. Because of my avarice, I have caused a great carnage of my relatives. I have caused the death of Subhadra's son and Droupadi's beloved sons. O illustrious one! To me, this victory seems to be a defeat. What will my sister-in-law, Varshneyi,[5] tell me? When Hari Madhusudana returns, what will the residents of Dvaraka tell Krishna? With her sons slain and her relatives killed, Droupadi is distressed. She has always been engaged in our welfare. This is grieving me exceedingly. O illustrious one! O Narada! Let me tell you about something else. Kunti kept this as a secret and this is also a reason for my sorrow. He possessed the strength of ten thousand elephants and on this earth, was an atiratha in battle. His gait was like that of a sporting lion. He was wise and compassionate. He was generous and endeavoured

[4]This was a time of mourning.

[5]Subhadra, Abhimanyu's mother, descended from the Varshneya lineage.

about his vows. He was the refuge of the sons of Dhritarashtra. He was proud and fierce in his valour. He was intolerant and always arrogant. From one encounter to another, he flung us away. He was swift in the use of weapons and colourful in fighting. He was accomplished and extraordinary in his prowess. He was secretly born from Kunti's womb. He was our brother, from the same womb. When the water-rites were performed, Kunti said that he was the son of the sun god. He possessed all the qualities, and in earlier times, was cast into the water. The world thought of him as Radheya, the son of a suta. But he was Kunti's eldest son and our brother from the same mother. Greedy for the kingdom, I have ignorantly caused him to be killed in the battle. This is consuming my limbs, like a mass of cotton in a fire. Partha, the one with the white horses, did not know that he was a brother. Nor did Bhima and the twins know this. However, the one who was excellent in his vows knew this. We have heard that Pritha went to him earlier.[6] She wished to ensure our welfare and told him, 'You are my son.' But that great-souled one did not listen to Pritha's wishes. Much later, we have heard that he spoke these words to his mother. 'I am incapable of abandoning King Duryodhana in the battle. If I do that, I will be ignoble, cruel and an ingrate. If I act according to your wishes and conclude an alliance with Yudhishthira, people will say that I am frightened of the one with the white steeds in a battle. Having defeated Vijaya[7] and Keshava in the battle, I will then conclude an agreement of peace with Dharma's son.' This is what we heard. Pritha again spoke to the one with the broad chest. 'Then fight with Phalguna, but grant me safety for my other four sons.' The intelligent one joined his hands in salutation and told his trembling mother, 'Even if the other four sons come under my control, I will not kill them. O mother! Whether Partha is slain by Karna, or whether I am slain by Arjuna, it is certain that you will continue to have five sons.' Out of great affection for her sons, the mother told the son, 'As you desire their safety, ensure the safety of

[6]This has been described in Section 55 (Volume 4).

[7]Arjuna.

your brothers.' Having said this, Pritha took his leave and returned home. Our brave brother has been slain by Arjuna, a brother by a brother. O sage. Neither Pritha, nor he, ever divulged the secret. The brave and great archer was brought down by Partha. O supreme among brahmanas! I only got to know later that he was our brother. O lord! Pritha told us that Karna was our eldest brother. I have caused my brother to be slain and this is greatly paining my heart. Had Karna and Arjuna both been my aides, I would have been able to defeat even Vasudeva. When I was oppressed by the evil-souled sons of Dhritarashtra in the assembly hall, my anger was suddenly pacified on seeing Karna. This is despite the harsh and bitter words we heard from him in the assembly hall at the time of the gambling match, spoken for the sake of bringing Duryodhana pleasure. When I glanced at his feet, my wrath was destroyed. It seemed to me that Karna's feet were like those of Kunti's. I wished to determine the reason for this similarity between Pritha and him. But in spite of thinking about this, I did not understand. During the battle, why did the earth swallow up the wheel of his chariot? Why was my brother cursed? You should tell me this. O illustrious one! I wish to hear everything, exactly as it happened. You know everything that is to be known in this world, that which has happened, and that which will occur."'

Chapter 1330(2)

Vaishampayana said, 'Having been thus addressed, the sage Narada, supreme among eloquent ones, recounted everything about how the son of a suta had been cursed.

'"O mighty-armed one![8] O descendant of the Bharata lineage! It is exactly as you have said. There is nothing that could have stood against Karna and Arjuna in a battle. O king! What I am

[8]Though not explicitly stated, this is Narada speaking.

about to tell you is unknown to even the gods. O great king! O lord! Therefore, listen to what happened in earlier times, about how the kshatriyas would be cleansed by weapons and would go to heaven. To engender that dissension, he was created in a virgin womb. He was energetic as a child and came to be known as the son of a suta. He went to the best of the Angirasa lineage, your preceptor,[9] to learn about the science of war.[10] O Indra among kings! He thought of Bhima's strength, Phalguna's dexterity, your intelligence, the humility of the twins, the friendship that the wielder of Gandiva has had with Vasudeva since childhood and the devotion of the subjects and was tormented. From childhood, he formed a friendship with King Duryodhana. This is because of the enmity he always bore towards you and natural destiny. He saw that Dhananjaya was superior to everyone in learning about dhanurveda. Karna secretly went to Drona and spoke these words. 'I wish to know about brahmastra and the secrets of releasing and withdrawing it. It is my view that I should become Arjuna's equal in battle. It is certain that the affection you bear towards your disciples is equal to what you bear towards your son. Because of your favours, make me accomplished and skilled in the use of weapons.' Drona was partial towards Phalguna. He also knew about Karna's wickedness. Having been thus addressed by Karna, he replied, 'The brahmastra can only be known by a brahmana who is observant of the vows, or by a kshatriya who has performed austerities, and by no one else.' Having been thus addressed by the best of the Angirasa lineage, he honoured him and took his leave. He then quickly went to Rama[11] on Mount Mahendra. Having approached Rama, he lowered his head in obeisance before him and said, 'O Bhargava! I am a brahmana.' This earned him respect. Rama welcomed him and asked him everything about his *gotra*.[12] He was extremely delighted at this warm welcome. Karna resided

[9]Drona.

[10]Dhanurveda.

[11]Parashurama.

[12]Gotra can loosely be translated as family lineage.

on Mahendra, supreme among mountains, and met gandharvas, rakshasas, yakshas and gods there. There, in the proper way, he obtained all the weapons from the best of the Bhrigu lineage. Because of this, he was loved by the gods, the gandharvas and the rakshasas.

'"Once, near that hermitage, he was roaming around on the shores of the ocean. The son of the suta was wandering around alone, with a sword and a bow in his hand. O Partha! There was a person who was knowledgeable about the *brahman* and who performed the *aghnihotra* sacrifice every day. Unwittingly, he killed his *homadhenu*.[13] Having unwittingly performed this deed, Karna went and repeatedly told the brahmana, so that he might be pacified, 'O illustrious one! I have unwittingly killed your cow. Please show me your favours.' However, the brahmana censured him and angrily spoke these words, 'O wicked one! O evil-minded one! You should be killed. Therefore, reap this fruit. You have always sought to rival someone[14] and you have been striving against him every day. Because of this crime, when you are fighting with him, the earth will swallow up the wheel of your chariot. O worst of men! When you clash against your foe and are distracted because the wheel of your chariot has been devoured by the earth, he will exhibit his valour and sever your head. O stupid one! Leave this place. Just as you were distracted when you acted against me, another person will sever and bring down your head while you are distracted.' He again tried to secure the favours of that supreme among brahmanas. He gave him cattle, riches and jewels. However, he[15] again said, 'Nothing in all the worlds will be able to falsify the words spoken by me. You can go, or stay, or do whatever else you wish to.' Having been thus addressed by the brahmana, Karna was distressed and hung his head down. Terrified, he returned to Rama and thought about this in his mind."'

[13]Agnihotra is a sacrifice where oblations are offered to the fire. A homadhenu is a cow that yields milk for the oblations.

[14]Arjuna.

[15]The brahmana.

Chapter 1331(3)

'Narada said, "The tiger among the Bhrigu lineage[16] was pleased with the strength of Karna's arms, affection, self-control and the service he showed towards his preceptor. He was also excellent in austerities. Therefore, in the proper way, that supreme of ascetics[17] taught him everything about brahmastra, about its release and means of withdrawal. Having obtained this knowledge, Karna was delighted and dwelt in the hermitage of the one descended from the Bhrigu lineage. His valour was extraordinary and he strove to learn dhanurveda.'

'"One day, the intelligent Rama was wandering around near the hermitage, with Karna. He was afflicted because of the fasting and was also confident of Karna's affection. Therefore, Jamadagani's descendant went to sleep with his head on his lap. While the tired preceptor was sleeping, a terrible worm approached Karna. It fed on phlegm, fat, flesh and blood and was terrible to the touch. With blood-stained teeth, it penetrated his thigh. Because of fear on account of his preceptor,[18] he was unable to kill it, or fling it away. O descendant of the Bharata lineage! His thigh was pierced by that worm. But scared that his preceptor would wake up, the son of a suta ignored it. Karna bore that pain with fortitude and ignored it. He did not tremble and continued to bear Bhargava. Eventually, the blood from the limbs touched the extender of the Bhrigu lineage. The energetic one awoke and in torment, spoke these words. 'Alas! I have become impure. What have you done? Cast aside your fear and tell me the truth about what has happened.' Karna then told him how the worm had bitten him. Rama also saw that the worm looked like a pig. It had eight feet and sharp teeth and was covered with bristles that were like needles. It was known as Alarka and it shrivelled.[19]

[16]Parashurama.

[17]Parashurama.

[18]Fear of waking up Parashurama.

[19]Alarka is a mythical animal that looks like a boar and has eight legs.

As soon as Rama looked at it, the worm gave up its breath of life. It shrunk in the blood that it had drunk and it was extraordinary.

'"At that time, a rakshasa was seen in the sky. It was gigantic in form and was terrible in visage. Its neck was red, its limbs were dark and it was riding on the clouds. Its wishes having been satisfied, it joined its hands in salutation and addressed Rama. 'O tiger among the Bhrigu lineage! May you be well. I will go where I had come from. O supreme among sages! You have saved me from this hell.' Jamadagni's mighty-armed and powerful son replied, 'Who are you? How did you descend into hell? Tell me about it.' He said, 'Earlier, in the yuga of the gods,[20] I was a great asura named Praggritsa. O father![21] I was of the same age as Bhrigu. I forcefully abducted Bhrigu's beloved wife. Because of the maharshi's curse, I became a worm and fell down on earth. Your great grandfather[22] angrily spoke these words to me. "You will subsist on urine and phlegm. O wicked one! You will live a life that is like hell." I asked him, "O brahmana! When will this curse come to an end?" At this, Bhrigu told me, "There will be Rama, born of the Bhrigu lineage, and he will free you." It is because of this that I attained such a wicked end. O virtuous one! But having met you, I have been freed from that evil birth.' Having said this, the giant asura bowed before Rama and departed.

'"Rama angrily spoke these words to Karna. 'O foolish one! No one who has been born as a brahmana can endure such great suffering. Your patience is like that of a kshatriya. I wish to hear the truth.' Karna was frightened of being cursed. He sought his favours and said, 'O Bhargava! Know me to be between a brahmana and a kshatriya, born as a suta.[23] People on earth speak of me as Radheya Karna. O brahmana! O Bhargava! Pardon me. I was greedy for the weapons. A father isn't just the biological one. The lord, who is a

[20]Meaning satya yuga.

[21]The word used is tata.

[22]Meaning, Bhrigu. Bhrigu's son was Chyavana, Chyavana's son was Ourva, Ourva's son was Richika, Richika's son was Jamadagni and Jamadagni's son was Parashurama.

[23]A suta was born from a kshatriya father and a brahmana mother.

preceptor and gives one the Vedas and learning, is also one such. That is the reason why, in your presence, I described myself as a Bhargava.' The foremost among the Bhrigu lineage was incensed at this and he[24] had fallen down on the ground, trembling, distressed and hands joined in salutation. However, he[25] smiled and said, 'You acted in this false way because of your greed for weapons. O stupid one! In a different place, when the time for your death has come, you will be engaged in a fight with someone who is your equal and the brahmastra will not manifest itself before you. The qualities of a brahmana will never remain with someone who is not a brahmana. Leave this place, since this is not meant for an untruthful one like you. There will be no kshatriya on earth who will be your equal in battle.' Having been thus addressed by Rama, he took his leave and departed. He went to Duryodhana and said, 'I have become accomplished in the use of weapons.'"'

Chapter 1332(4)

'Narada said, "O bull among the Bharata lineage! Having thus obtained weapons from the descendant of the Bhargava lineage, together with Duryodhana, Karna amused himself. On one occasion, many kings assembled at a *svayamvara* ceremony organized by Chitrangada, the king of Kalinga. O descendant of the Bharata lineage! There was a prosperous city named Rajapura there. For the sake of the maiden, hundreds of kings assembled there. On hearing that all the kings had gathered there, Duryodhana also went there on his golden chariot, accompanied by Karna. At that svayamvara, a great festival was organized. O supreme among kings! Many kings came there for the sake of the maiden. O great king! Shishupala, Jarasandha, Bhishmaka, Vakra, Kapotaroma, Nila, Rukmi, firm in

[24]Karna.

[25]Parashurama.

his valour, Srigala, who ruled over a kingdom of women, Ashoka, Shatadhanva and the valiant Bhoja were among them. O descendant of the Bharata lineage! There were many others who resided in the southern directions, preceptors from among the *mlecchas*[26] and kings from the east and the north. All of them were adorned in golden armlets and were decorated in garlands made out of molten gold. All of them possessed radiant bodies and were crazy in their pride, like tigers. O descendant of the Bharata lineage! When all those kings had seated themselves, the maiden entered the arena with her nurse, guarded by eunuchs. O descendant of the Bharata lineage! While the names of the kings were being recounted, the beautiful maiden passed by the son of Dhritarashtra.[27] Kouravya Duryodhana could not tolerate that he had been passed by. Ignoring all the kings, he asked the maiden to stop. Protected by Bhishma and Drona, he was intoxicated by his valour. He lifted the maiden up onto his chariot and challenged the kings. O bull among men! Karna wielded a sword and had donned arm-guards and finger-guards. Riding on a chariot, the best among all wielders of weapons guarded him[28] from the rear. O Yudhishthira. There was a tumult and a loud sound arose among the kings, as body armour was donned, chariots were yoked and they angrily attacked Karna and Duryodhana. They released showers of arrows, like clouds on a mountain. With razor-sharp arrows, Karna brought each of their bows, with arrows affixed to them, down on the ground. Deprived of their bows, some advanced, raising other bows. Some attacked with arrows. Others grasped javelins and clubs. Karna was supreme among strikers and oppressed them with his dexterity. He slew many charioteers and defeated the kings. At this, they themselves picked up the reins of their mounts and said, 'Go away.' Devastated in their hearts, the kings abandoned the battle. Protected by Karna, Duryodhana was assured. Bringing the maiden with them, they cheerfully returned to the city of Nagasahvya."'

[26]Barbarians, those who do not speak Sanskrit.

[27]In a svayamvara, the princess passed by all the kings, choosing the one she wanted. By going past Duryodhana, she rejected him.

[28]Duryodhana.

Chapter 1333(5)

'Narada said, "Having learnt about Karna's strength, King Jarasandha, the lord of Magadha, challenged him to a duel. Both of them knew about the use of divine weapons and a battle commenced between them. In the encounter, they showered down many kinds of weapons on each other. Their arrows were exhausted. They were without bows. Their swords were shattered. The powerful ones descended on the ground and started to wrestle with each other with bare arms. While fighting with him in that terrible duel with bare arms, Karna was about to sever the two parts of the body that had been brought together by Jara.[29] O descendant of the Bharata lineage! On seeing that his body was about to face this hardship, the king cast aside all enmity and spoke these affectionate words to Karna. 'I am pleased.' He gave Karna the city of Malini. O tiger among men! Before this, the one who had defeated his enemies had ruled over Anga. But now, Karna, the afflicter of enemy forces, also began to rule Champa, after having obtained Duryodhana's permission. You know about all this. Thus, through the power of his weapons, he became famous on earth. For the sake of your welfare, the king of the gods begged his divine and natural armour and earrings from him.[30] The extremely revered one was confounded by the maya of the god and gave away his natural earrings and armour. Deprived of his earrings and natural armour, while Vasudeva looked on, he was slain by Vijaya. There was the brahmana's curse and that of the great-souled Rama. There was the boon that he had granted Kunti and Shatakratu's maya. Bhishma disrespected him and described him as only half a ratha.[31] Shalya sapped his energy. There was Vasudeva's policy. In a battle, the wielder of Gandiva obtained the divine

[29]Jarasandha was born in two parts and was united and brought together by a *rakshasi* named Jara, thus obtaining his name. The story has been recounted in Section 22 (Volume 2).

[30]Indra persuaded Karna to part with the natural armour and earrings. This has been described in Section 43 (Volume 3).

[31]Recounted in Section 59 (Volume 4).

weapons of Rudra, the king of the gods, Yama, Varuna, Kubera, Drona and the great-souled Kripa. That is the reason Vaikartana Karna was slain, though he was as radiant as the sun. This is the way your brother was cursed and deprived by many. However, since he has met his end in a battle, you should not sorrow over that tiger among men."'

Chapter 1334(6)

Vaishampayana said, 'Having spoken these words, devarshi Narada stopped. However, rajarshi Yudhisthira was overcome by sorrow and continued to think. The brave one was distressed in his mind and his head hung down in sorrow. He sighed like a serpent and his eyes were full of tears. Kunti's limbs were also overcome with sorrow and grief had robbed her of her senses. However, she spoke these sweet and important words that were suitable to the occasion. "O Yudhishthira! O mighty-armed one! You should not grieve. O immensely wise one! Conquer your sorrow and listen to my words. O supreme among those who uphold dharma! Earlier, I tried so that he might let you know that he was your brother and so did the sun god, his father. In front of me, the sun revealed himself in a dream to him and told him words that a well-wisher who desired his benefit and prosperity would say.[32] But despite our entreaties and our affection, I or the sun god did not succeed. We could not persuade him. Nor could we persuade him to unite with you. He was under the subjugation of destiny and was engaged in fanning the enmity with you. He was engaged in causing you injury. So he was ignored by me." When his mother said this, Dharmaraja's eyes filled with tears. With his senses clouded by tears, the one with dharma in his soul spoke these words. "I am extremely distressed because you kept this a secret." Tormented by extreme grief, the immensely energetic

[32]This has also been described in Section 55 (Volume 4).

one cursed all the women of the world, "Henceforth, they will not be able to keep a secret." The king remembered his sons, grandsons, relatives and well-wishers and his heart became extremely anxious. He lost control over his senses. Because he was overcome by sorrow, he was like a fire with smoke. Tormented and oppressed, the king yielded to despair.'

Chapter 1335(7)

Vaishampayana said, 'Yudhishthira, with dharma in his soul, was anxious and unconscious because of his sorrow. He remembered maharatha Karna and tormented by grief, sorrowed over him. Overcome by grief and sorrow, he sighed repeatedly.

'He was oppressed by grief and on seeing Arjuna, spoke these words. "Had we survived by begging in the city of the Vrishnis and the Andhakas, we would not have confronted this catastrophe and would not have deprived our relatives of all their menfolk. Our enemies have been successful in their objectives and the Kurus have obtained what they tried for. We have ourselves slain those who are our own. What fruits of dharma will we obtain? Shame on the conduct of kshatriyas and shame on the strength that chests hold. Shame on the intolerance that has taken us to this calamity. Forgiveness, self-control, purity, lack of enmity, lack of selfishness, non-violence and truthfulness in words are to be praised. Those who dwell in the forest practise these. But because of our greed and our delusion, we have resorted to arrogance and insolence. We have been brought to this state because of our hunger for a trifling kingdom. Even sovereignty over the three worlds will not delight us now, since we can see that those of our relatives who desired the flesh of the earth[33] have been slain. They did not deserve to be killed and were like the earth. But they have been slain for the earth. Having given

[33]The word flesh is being used in a figurative sense.

them up, deprived of prosperity and with our relatives killed, we remain alive. We are not dogs. But like dogs, we fought over meat. That flesh has now been destroyed and so have those who would have eaten the meat. We shouldn't have abandoned those who have been killed for the sake of the entire earth, heaps of gold or for all the cattle and horses. They were full of desire and passion. They were overcome by wrath and intolerance. They climbed onto the road to death and have gone to Vaivasvata's[34] eternal abode. For the sake of their sons, fathers seek a lot of welfare on earth. They observe austerities and brahmacharya, chant and practise renunciation. In a similar way, mothers conceive after fasts, sacrifices, vows and auspicious ceremonies and bear them for ten months. 'If they are born safely and remain alive after they are born, if they are full of strength, they may give us happiness in this world and the next.' In pursuit of fruits, this is what those pitiable ones hope for. Those young sons, decorated with earrings, have been killed. At a wrong time, those hopes have become unsuccessful and have been abandoned. They have not enjoyed the pleasures of the earth. They have not repaid their debts to the ancestors and the gods. They have gone to Vaivasvata's eternal abode. When they were born, the parents had wishes for them. But those kings have been slain when they became full of strength and beauty. They were full of desire and intolerance and experienced anger and delight. None of them enjoyed any of the fruits of birth. Because of our deeds, the Panchalas and Kurus who have been killed, and those of us who have not been slain, will obtain the worst of worlds. We will be known as the ones who caused the destruction of the world, even though we were deceived by Dhritarashtra's son. He was skilled in deceit. He was full of enmity and subsisted through the use of maya. Though we had never caused him injury, he always used falsehood towards us. We have not succeeded in vanquishing them, nor have they defeated us. They have not enjoyed the earth, nor women, singing and music. They paid no attention to their advisers, nor did they listen to those who knew about the sacred texts. They could not enjoy the jewels, the earth

[34]Yama's.

or the wealth they had obtained. When he[35] saw our prosperity, he turned pale, ashen and lean. This was reported to King Dhritarashtra by Soubala.[36] Because of his affection, the father remained established in the ways of the son. He disregarded his father, Gangeya and Vidura. There is no doubt that Dhritrashtra is in the same state as I am. He did not control his inauspicious and greedy son who was overcome by desire. With his brothers, Suyodhana has fallen from his blazing fame. He has hurled these two aged ones[37] into the flames of grief. The evil-minded one was always full of enmity towards us. Which other relative, born into a noble lineage, would speak to well-wishers they way he did? In the presence of the one from the Vrishni lineage, the inferior one, wishing to fight, used such words.[38] We have also been destroyed for an eternal period because of our own sins. Like the sun, we have scorched all the directions with our energy. That man, full of enmity towards us, came under the clutches of an evil planet that gave bad advice.[39] Because of Duryodhana's deeds, our lineage has been brought down. Having slain those who should not be slain, we will earn censure in this world. King Dhritarashtra made that evil-minded one the lord of the kingdom. He was wicked in his deeds and the exterminator of the lineage. Therefore, he[40] is grieving now. The brave ones have been slain. The wicked deed has been done. The prosperity has been destroyed. Having slain them, our anger has been overcome. This sorrow is restraining me now. O Dhananjaya! A wicked deed can be countered through a beneficial one. The sacred texts say that someone who has renounced does not perform a wicked deed again. The sacred texts say that someone who has renounced does not have to go through birth and death. Having attained perfection, that person, firm in his resolution, unites with the brahman. O Dhananjaya! He attains the knowledge of the sages and

[35]Duryodhana.

[36]This has been described in Section 27 (Volume 2).

[37]Dhritarashtra and Gandhari.

[38]The one from the Vrishni lineage is Krishna. This is a reference to the incidents in Section 54 (Volume 4).

[39]This is probably a reference to Shakuni.

[40]Dhritarashtra.

is without any sense of opposites.[41] O scorcher of enemies! I will take my leave from all of you and go to the forest. O destroyer of enemies! The sacred texts say that someone with possessions is not capable of attaining the best forms of dharma. I can see that. Because I desired possessions, I committed wicked acts and the sacred texts say that this can cause birth and death.[42] I will give up my possessions and the entire kingdom. I will depart, completely free, bereft of sorrow and devoid of fever. With the thorns having been removed, you rule over this pacified earth. O best of the Kuru lineage! This kingdom and the pleasures are not for me." Having spoken these words, Dharmaraja Yudhishthira stopped and the youngest Partha[43] replied.'

Chapter 1336(8)

Vaishampayana said 'Arjuna spoke, like a reviled person who is not ready to forgive. He was firm in his speech and valour and spoke these proud words. Indra's son was terrible in his valour and revealed his fierce aspect. The immensely energetic one laughed and repeatedly licked the corners of his mouth. "Alas! What misery! What a great calamity! This is supreme frailty. Having performed a superhuman deed, you now wish to abandon this supreme prosperity. The enemies have been slain and the earth has been obtained by practising one's own dharma. Having killed one's foes, but for foolishness, why should one give everything up? When has a eunuch or one who procrastinates ever obtained a kingdom? Overcome with rage, why did you kill all the lords of the earth? A person desiring to live through begging can never use his deeds to enjoy anything. Even if he tries to be powerful, his fortune is destroyed and he is never renowned in the world as someone who possesses sons and animals.

[41]Sentiments like unhappiness and happiness, like and dislike, friend and foe.
[42]That is, cause the cycle of death and rebirth.
[43]Arjuna.

O king! If you resort to this wicked means of subsistence through mendicancy and abandon this prosperous kingdom, what will people say? O lord! Why do you wish to abandon all enterprise, giving up all your fortune? Like an ordinary person, why do you wish to roam around as a beggar? You have been born in this lineage of kings and have conquered the entire earth. Yet, because of your confusion, you wish to give up dharma and artha and want to go to the forest. When you have gone, if wicked people destroy the sacrificial offerings, the consequence of that sin will devolve on you. Nahusha[44] said, 'It is not desirable to possess nothing. Without riches, cruel deeds are perpetrated. Shame on poverty.' You know that the practice of rishis is not to keep anything for tomorrow. But that which is known as dharma is established on the basis of riches. When someone's riches are stolen, his dharma is also stolen. O king! Who amongst us will pardon an act of our riches being robbed? If a poor person stands next to one's own self, that poor person is abused. Poverty causes degradation in this world and you should not praise it. O king! One who is degraded sorrows. One who is poor sorrows. I cannot see any difference between one who is degraded and one who is poor. Here and there, all the rites are extended and accumulated through wealth, like streams flowing down mountains. O lord of men! Dharma, kama and heaven result from artha. Without artha, the world will not be able to sustain its life. Like an inferior river[45] during the summer, all the rites of a person with limited intelligence are destroyed in the absence of wealth. One who possesses riches possesses friends. One who possesses riches possesses relatives. One who possesses riches is a man in this world. One who possesses riches is learned. A person who doesn't possess riches is incapable of obtaining riches only by desiring it. Riches follow riches, like elephants follow mighty elephants.[46] O lord of men! Dharma, kama, heaven, delight, anger, learning, self-control—all of these result from artha. The lineage

[44]Yayati's father, an ancestor.

[45]One that dries up during the summer.

[46]There is probably an implicit image of tame elephants being used to ensnare wild ones.

is extended because of artha. Dharma is spread because of riches. O supreme among men! A person without riches does not possess either this world, or the next. One without riches cannot perform the acts of dharma. Dharma flows from riches, like mountainous streams from mountains. O king! A person is not called lean when his body is lean. He is lean when he is lean in horses, lean in cattle, lean in servants and lean in guests. Consider this according to the right principles. Look at the gods and the asuras. O king! The gods prosper after having slain their own relatives.[47] If one does not take away the riches of others, how can one observe dharma? The wise ones have determined this in the Vedas. The learned ones have said that one must study the three kinds of knowledge[48] and always make efforts to accumulate wealth and perform sacrifices. It is through violence and enmity that all the gods have obtained their stations in heaven. This is what the gods resorted to, and these are the eternal words of the Vedas. One must study, one must perform austerities, one must perform sacrifices and one must officiate at the sacrifices of others. But all these become better when one takes objects away from others. Nowhere do we see any wealth that has not been taken away from others. This is the way in which kings conquered the earth. Having conquered, they say that the wealth is theirs, just as sons say that the wealth of their fathers is their own. The rajarshis who have obtained heaven have proclaimed this to be dharma. In the overflowing ocean, water spreads out in the ten directions. In that way, wealth that emanates from a royal lineage spreads throughout the earth. Earlier, the earth belonged to Dilipa, Nriga, Nahusha, Ambarisha and Mandhata.[49] It belongs to you now. O king! A prosperous sacrifice, with all the donations given, now awaits you. If

[47]The gods and the demons are descended from the same father, the sage Kashyapa.

[48]The Rig Veda, the Sama Veda and the Yajur Veda.

[49]Dilipa was a famous king from the solar dynasty and was the father of Raghu. Nriga was the son of Ikshvaku and also belonged to the solar dynasty. Nahusha was the father of Yayati and belonged to the lunar dynasty. Ambarisha was from the solar dynasty and so was Mandhata.

you do not perform that sacrifice, you will cause offence to the gods. If a king performs a horse sacrifice and offers donations, everyone becomes purified because of that. Vishvarupa[50] Mahadeva performed a great sacrifice at which everything was offered. He offered all the beings as oblations and then offered himself. That is the eternal path of prosperity and we have heard that there is no other end that is possible. This is the great path known as *dasharatha*.[51] O king! Do not follow any other route."'

Chapter 1337(9)

'Yudhishthira said, "Listen attentively for an instant. Cast your mind and your hearing towards your own inner self. If you listen to my words in that way, you will find them to be acceptable. You will not be able to take me back to the path travelled by the prosperous again. I will leave. I will abandon the path of ordinary pleasures and depart. I will travel alone along that path of tranquility. If you ask me what that is, I will tell you. Even if you don't wish to ask me, I will tell you. Listen. I will discard the pursuit of ordinary pleasures and torment myself through great austerities. I will dwell in the forest, sustaining myself on fruits and roots, and roam around with animals. I will pour oblations into the fire at the right time and perform ablutions at the right time. I will emaciate myself by eating little. I will cover myself with skins and rags and wear matted hair. I will endure cold, wind, heat and bear hunger, thirst and exhaustion. I will grind down my body through the prescribed austerities. In the forest, I will cheerfully listen to the pleasant notes, high and low, of the animals and birds that live there. They are pleasant to the mind and the ear. I will inhale the delicate fragrance of blossoming

[50]Shiva's name.

[51]Dasaratha means ten chariots. It is possible that this originally read *dasharatra*, meaning a sacrifice that lasted for ten nights.

trees and creepers. I will observe the many beautiful forms of those who live in the forest. I will not offend the sight of those who have resorted to *vanaprastha*[52] and dwell there with their families. I will act so that I do not cause anything unpleasant to them, not to speak of those who live in villages. I will live alone and pass my time in contemplation, eating that which is ripe and that which is unripe.[53] I will satisfy the ancestors and the gods with wild fruits, water and eloquent words. I will follow the fiercest of rites prescribed for those who dwell in the forest. Serving in this way, I will await the end of my physical existence. Or, I will dwell alone and spend my night under different trees. I will shave my head and beg for a living, destroying my body. I will be covered with dust and seek shelter in empty houses. I will find an abode near the root of a tree and abandon everything that is pleasant and unpleasant. Sorrow and delight, praise and censure, will be equal for me. I will have no desire and be free of any sense of possessiveness. Opposites will mean the same and I will have nothing to receive. I will find pleasure in my own atman. I will find serenity in my own atman. I will be like one who is dumb, blind and deaf. There will be no occasion for me to have conversations with anyone else. I will not injure any of the four kinds of beings,[54] mobile and immobile, as they are engaged in their own dharma. I will behave equally towards all those who have life. I will not laugh at anything, nor will I frown at anything. My face will always be cheerful and all my senses will be well controlled. I will not ask anyone about the route. I will travel along any path and not wish to go to any special country or direction. I will advance impartially and not glance back. I will be upright and cautious, so that I avoid and do not frighten anyone along the path. Nature is most important and food and drink will take care of themselves. I will not think about all the opposite sentiments[55] that stand against

[52]The stage of life when one retires to the forest.

[53]A reference to fruits.

[54]Those born from wombs, those born from eggs, those that are trees and plants and those born from sweat (insects and worms).

[55]Like happiness and unhappiness, pleasure and pain.

this. If even a little bit of succulent food is not available at first, I will roam around and seek to find it in seven houses.[56] But I will go at the time when there is no smoke, when the pestles have been put away, when the coal in the fire has died down, when food has been eaten, when the handling of the pots is over and when all the mendicants have gone. At one time, I will roam around and beg from two to five houses.[57] I will roam around the earth, freeing myself from the noose of desire. I will be like one who does not wish to live. I will act like one who is about to die. I will not find delight or sorrow in either life or death. If someone severs one of my arms and another person smears the other with sandalwood paste, I will not think of doing good things to the latter and harming the former. There are acts that are done to improve the state of one's life. I will abandon all of them. Blinking my eyes, I will give up attachment to all of them and abandon all the acts that are connected to the senses. When I have abandoned all resolution, I will purify myself well. I will have freed myself from all attachment and will have passed beyond all bonds. I will not be under the subjugation of anything and will follow the dharma of the wind.[58] I will roam around without any attachment and will obtain eternal satisfaction. It was because of my greed and ignorance that I performed extremely wicked deeds. There are men who perform good and wicked deeds because they are tied down, through cause and effect, to their relatives.[59] When the lifespan is over, the body is almost completely decayed. They then receive the fruits of those wicked deeds, but no one except the doer obtains the consequence.[60] The wheel of life goes on in this way, like the turning

[56]The shloka is cryptic and needs explanation. If food is not available in the first house, he will go to a second house, then to a third house and so on, up to seven such houses. He will beg for food at these houses.

[57]The idea is not to beg from too many houses.

[58]That is, be as free as the wind.

[59]The cause and effect refers to deeds in earlier lives affecting this life and deeds in this life affecting future lives.

[60]The relatives do not bear the consequences of wicked deeds, even if those wicked deeds are done for the relatives.

wheel of a chariot. This collection of beings meet each other. This collection of beings acts. Birth, death, old age, disease and pain are without any substance and transient. On this earth, one who can discard them is happy. The gods fall down from heaven and so do the maharshis from their appointed spots. Which person, if he desires to know about the reason and truth behind existence, would then desire to exist?[61] A king may perform many kinds of deeds, in accordance with the rites and auspicious signs. But that king will be bound down by the slightest bit of action. For a long time, this amrita of wisdom has presented itself before me. Therefore, I desire it and want the eternal and certain state, from which one does not decay. I will conduct myself in this virtuous way and roam around, without any connection to the material world. I will fearlessly place my body on that path."'

Chapter 1338(10)

'Bhima said, "O king! Your understanding has become clouded, just like a scholar of the Vedas who has limited intelligence and recites passages from the Vedas, without realizing their true purport. O bull among the Bharata lineage! If you had made up your mind to be lazy and censure the dharma of kings, then what has been gained from this destruction of the sons of Dhritarashtra? Forgiveness, compassion, pity and non-violence—with the exception of you, there is no one who treads the path of kshatriyas who is tied down by these. Had we got to know that your intentions would be of this type, we would never have picked up our weapons and killed anyone. We would have roamed around and sustained ourselves through begging, until it was time to free ourselves from our bodies. This terrible battle between the kings would not have taken place. The wise ones have said that everything is meant to

[61]In this cycle of birth, death and rebirth.

sustain life. Everything, mobile and immobile, is food to sustain life. Therefore, anyone who stands in the way of obtaining the kingdom must be slain. Those who are wise and learned about the dharma of kshatriyas have said this. Those killed by us were wicked. They stood in the way of the kingdom. O Yudhishthira! Having slain them, we should follow dharma and enjoy the earth. We are like a man digging a well, who stops in his task before having reached the water, and is therefore only covered in mud. We are acting like someone who climbs a tall tree for honey, but falls down and dies before he has been able to obtain it. We are acting like a man who sets out on a great journey with high hopes, but who despairs and returns. O supreme among the Kuru lineage! We are acting like a man who slays his enemies and then kills himself. We are acting like someone who is hungry, but having obtained food, does not eat it because he does not feel like it. We are acting like someone who is driven by desire, but having obtained a beautiful woman, does not perform the act. However, we are the ones who should be censured. We are the ones who are limited in our intelligence. O king! O descendant of the Bharata lineage! We have followed you, merely because you are the eldest. We possess the strength of arms. We are accomplished in our learning. We are spirited. But because we follow the words of a eunuch, we are like ones who are incapacitated. We are the refuge of those who do not have a refuge. However, our prosperity will be destroyed and our objectives will be unsuccessful. When people see us in this way, what will they think of us? It has been instructed that renunciation should be resorted to in times of distress, by someone who has been overtaken by old age, or by someone who has been defeated by his enemies. Those who are accomplished in wisdom do not recommend renunciation in a situation like this. Those who are subtle in discernment think that this is a transgression of dharma. Therefore, how can you resort to a state that is not recommended for you? You should censure it too, and not faithfully accept it.[62] Men who are without prosperity and riches, those who are atheists, have propounded this view about the learning in the Vedas. This is

[62]The state of *sannyasa* or renunciation.

falsehood in the garb of truth. If a man who is capable resorts to this state of shaving his head, he is deluding himself. He is resorting to false dharma. Though he subsists, he does not live. Then again, though he is capable of sustaining sons, grandsons, gods, rishis, guests and ancestors, he decides to lead a solitary life of happiness in the forest. Even animals, boars and birds cannot obtain heaven in this way. People do not say that this is an auspicious way of life. O king! If one could obtain success only through sannyasa, then mountains and trees would have swiftly obtained success. They are always seen not to cause injury towards others and are based on sannyasa. They have no possessions and always live on their own. If success can be obtained through one's own fortune[63] and not that of others, one should undertake action. There can be no success without action. Aquatic creatures have no one but themselves to sustain. If that is the criterion, they would obtain success. Notice that everyone in this universe is preoccupied with his own tasks. Therefore, one should act. There can be no success without action."'

Chapter 1339(11)

'Arjuna said, "O bull among the Bharata lineage! On this, an ancient history is recounted, the conversation between the ascetics and Shakra. Some brahmanas abandoned their homes and went to the forest. They had still not developed beards.[64] Though they were born in good lineages, they were stupid and followed the wrong path. They thought that they were following dharma and decided to observe brahmacharya. They abandoned their homes and their fathers. Indra took pity on them. Adopting the form of a golden bird, the illustrious one came to them and said, 'Men who eat leftover food perform an extremely difficult task. The lives of those who

[63] A reflection of past deeds.

[64] That is, they were young.

perform such meritorious acts should be praised. They are foremost among those who follow dharma and obtain the best of success and objectives.'[65]

'"The rishis replied, 'Aha! This bird is praising those who eat leftover food. It must be praising us, since we subsist on leftover food.'

'"The bird said, 'I am not praising you. You are covered in mud and dust. You are wicked ones who eat impure food. You are not the ones who eat leftover food.'

'"The rishis replied, 'We think that the path that we are following is the best. O bird! Tell us what is beneficial. We have great faith in you.'

'"The bird said, 'If you do not doubt me and do not cause a division in your own selves,[66] then I will speak words that are truly beneficial.'

'"The rishis replied, 'O father![67] We will listen to your words. You know about different paths. O one with dharma in your soul! Instruct us. We wish to be taught by you.'

'"The bird said, 'The cow is the best among quadrupeds and gold the best among metals. Mantras are the best among words and brahmanas the best among bipeds. Mantras determine the sacraments for a brahmana as long as he lives, from the time of birth to the time when he dies and is at the cremation ground. The rites of the Vedas are the supreme path towards heaven. All deeds are said to become successful through mantras. In this world, the firm words of the Vedas signify success, depending on the months, half-months, seasons, the sun, the moon and the stars.[68] In this life, all beings are attached to action in accordance with this. This[69] is sacred and the greatest stage

[65]It is easy to miss the sense. Leftover food is food left over after gods, ancestors and guests have had their share. That can be done even if one is a householder. Indra is making the point that one can be a householder and still follow dharma.

[66]By suppressing the good inner inclinations with bad ones.

[67]The word used is tata.

[68]This is extremely cryptic and brief. What is probably meant is the following. Those who die during *shuklapaksha* attain the world of the sun. Those who die during krishnapaksha attain the world of the moon. Those who are completely free attain the world of the stars after death.

[69]The state of the householder.

of life and is the field for success. What path is followed by men who censure action? They are stupid, evil and are deprived of artha. Those foolish ones subsist, but have abandoned the eternal path followed by the lineage of the gods, the lineage of the ancestors and the lineage of Brahma.[70] They traverse a path not approved by the sacred texts. O ascetics! Therefore, this is the asceticism you should endeavour to follow. The offering of shares to the eternal lineages of the gods, the ancestors and Brahma and servitude to preceptors are said to be the most difficult of tasks. Having performed such difficult tasks, the gods obtained supreme prosperity. That is the reason I am telling you that the burden of a householder is an extremely difficult one to take up. There is no doubt that this is the best form of austerity for beings. It forms the base. Everything is established on the rules prescribed for a family. O brahmanas! Those who are not selfish and those who have gone beyond opposite sentiments say that this is the best form of asceticism. People say that going to the forest is a middling kind of asceticism. Those who live on leftovers and following the rites, morning and evening, divide up the food among relatives, attain an end that is extremely difficult to obtain. They first give to guests, gods, ancestors and relatives. They then eat the remnants and are said to be those who live on leftovers. They are established in their own dharma. They are excellent in their vows and are truthful. They become the preceptors of the worlds and are revered by everyone. They do not suffer from envy. They attain the world of heaven, Shakra's heaven. Those people perform extremely difficult deeds and dwell there for an eternal number of years.'

'"On hearing his words, which were full of dharma and artha, they abandoned the path of non-believers[71] and resorted to the dharma of householders.[72] O one who cannot be assailed! Therefore, you should also resort to eternal patience. O supreme among men! With all the enemies slain, rule over the entire earth."'

[70]Those who follow such a path do not attain the worlds of the gods, the ancestors or Brahma.

[71]The word used is *nastika*. Though this is often translated as atheist, it actually means non-believer.

[72]This is Arjuna speaking again.

Chapter 1340(12)

Vaishampayana said, 'On hearing Arjuna's words, Nakula glanced towards the king, who was supreme among those who upheld all forms of dharma. The immensely wise one was broad in the chest and mighty-armed.[73] His eyes were coppery red and he was temperate in speech. The scorcher of enemies spoke these words to his brother. "The gods established their fires in Vishakhayupa.[74] O great king! Know that the gods decided to base themselves on action. O king! The ancestors gave life to both believers and non-believers. However, consider that they performed deeds in accordance with the prescribed rites. Know that those who censure the Vedas[75] have been dislodged and are extreme non-believers. O descendant of the Bharata lineage! A brahmana who abandons what is stated in the Vedas, despite all his action, does not attain the path of the gods and the vault of heaven. O lord of men! There are brahmanas who are learned and have carefully determined everything stated in the Vedas. Listen. They say that this[76] is the best stage of life. Wealth must be acquired in accordance with dharma and must be given away in the best of sacrifices. O great king! A man who thus perfects his soul is said to be one who truly renounces. However, a person who ignores this source of happiness is established on a higher plane, in the sense that he abandons his own self.[77] O great king! O lord! That is a *tamasa* kind of renouncing.[78] There may be a sage who does not have an abode. He roams around and finds refuge at the root of

[73]This is a description of Nakula.

[74]*Yupa* is a sacrificial altar and Vishakhayupa is a place towards the north where the gods set up their sacrificial altar.

[75]The rites prescribed in the Vedas.

[76]The status of a householder.

[77]This higher plane is being spoken of disparagingly, rather than approvingly. That higher plane is a reference to life beyond death. In the process, the person abandons his own self because he abandons his own body and deprives it of sustenance.

[78]Of the three qualities (*guna*), *tamas* is the worst and represents darkness and ignorance.

a tree. He does not cook and is always engaged in yoga. O Partha! He is one who renounces, but is a mendicant.[79] O lord of the earth! There may be a brahmana who disregards anger and delight and does not indulge in passions. He studies the Vedas. But such a person who renounces only serves his preceptor.[80] O king! The learned ones have considered all the ashramas[81] on a scale and have said that three of them on one side are equal to the stage of being a householder on the other. O descendant of the Bharata lineage! Having considered, the maharshis, who know about the objectives of the worlds, determined that this was the path towards artha, kama and heaven. O bull among the Bharata lineage! Someone who acts in accordance with these sentiments is one who truly renounces. Like a foolish person, he does not abandon his house and head for the forest. There are also those false ones, who are like bird-catchers trying to catch dharma. But because they cannot get rid of desire, the king of death[82] binds them around the neck with the noose of death. It is said that action done through pride does not lead to fruits. Tranquility, self-control, austerities, generosity, truthfulness, cleanliness, honesty, sacrifices, fortitude and dharma are always spoken of as the rites followed by rishis. Acts undertaken for the sake of gods, ancestors and guests are praised. O great king! In this mode of life, the three fruits are obtained.[83] One who follows this, observed by the brahmanas, and does not deviate, is one who renounces and never confronts catastrophe in anything. O king! The unblemished Prajapati[84] created beings. The one who is tranquil in his soul thought that they would worship him with sacrifices and perform sacrifices, with many kinds of

[79]Although not very clearly stated, the sense is that this is also not approved of. In any event, this is not meant for a kshatriya.

[80]Again, not meant for kshatriyas.

[81]The four stage of life—brahmacharya (celibate stage of being a student), garhasthya (the stage of being a householder), vanaprastha (retiring to the forest) and sannyasa (renunciation).

[82]Yama.

[83]This mode of life is that of a householder. The three fruits are dharma, artha and kama.

[84]Brahma.

gifts. Creepers, trees, herbs, animals fit to be sacrificed and oblations and other objects required for sacrifices were also created for the sake of sacrifices. The task of performing a sacrifice constrains those who are in the householder stage.[85] That is the reason the status of being a householder is a difficult task to perform and is not easy to obtain. O great king! There are householders who possess animals and grain, but do not sacrifice. Eternal sin awaits them. Some rishis say that studying is a sacrifice, others that knowledge is a sacrifice. There are others who perform great sacrifices in their minds. O king! There are brahmanas who become one with the brahman by adhering to the path that involves the act of giving. The residents of heaven envy them. O lord of men! There are many kinds of jewels that have been collected. By not giving them away in a sacrifice, you are thinking like a non-believer. For someone who has a family, I do not see any renouncement except through *ashvamedha*, rajasuya or *sarvamedha*.[86] O father![87] There are also other sacrifices revered by brahmanas. O great king! Perform those, like Shakra, the lord of the gods. When a king commits the sin of being distracted, bandits plunder. When the subjects have no refuge, the king is said to be overcome by kali.[88] O lord of the earth! If we do not give away horses, cattle, servant maids, adorned she-elephants, villages, countries, fields and houses to brahmanas, our consciousness will be destroyed by selfishness and we will be like kings overcome by kali. Kings who do not give and do not offer refuge obtain their share of sin. They enjoy unhappiness, never happiness. If you do not perform a great sacrifice, if you do not sacrifice to the ancestors, if you do not bathe in the waters of tirthas and instead depart, to roam around, you will face destruction, like a cloud that is dispersed and blown away by the wind. You will be dislodged from both the worlds[89] and be stationed between them. One who casts aside all attachment in his mind, internal and external,

[85]Because wealth is required to perform sacrifices.

[86]Ashvamedha is a horse sacrifice, rajasuya is a royal sacrifice and sarvamedha is a universal sacrifice.

[87]The word used is tata.

[88]In the sense of kali yuga, or strife and discord.

[89]This world and the next.

is one who truly renounces, not one who simply goes away. O great king! A brahmana who follows these rites prescribed for brahmanas is never dislodged.[90] The prosperous enemies have been swiftly slain in the battle, like the army of the daityas against Shakra. O Partha! Devoted to your own dharma, why should you grieve? O king! This is what has earlier been recommended in the sacred texts and practised by the righteous. You have conquered the earth through the valour and dharma of kshatriyas. O Indra among men! You know about mantras! Give it away and you will ascend the vault of heaven. O Partha! You should not sorrow now."'

Chapter 1341(13)

'Sahadeva said, "O descendant of the Bharata lineage! One does not obtain success by casting aside external objects. Even if one casts aside physical parts of the body, success may or may not occur.[91] There are those who cast aside external objects, but still desire them from inside the body.[92] Let the happiness that results from that kind of dharma devolve on those who hate us, not on us. There are those who cast aside both objects and the physical body. Let the happiness that results from that kind of dharma devolve on our well-wishers, but not on us. There are two *akshara*s in death and three aksharas in the eternal brahman. '*Mama*' is death and '*na mama*' is eternal.[93] O king! The brahman and death both dwell inside one's own self.

[90]This does not quite fit, since there is not much point invoking recommended conduct for brahmanas.

[91]An interpretation that is not obvious should be mentioned. External objects are those outside the body and those are being juxtaposed not just with physical parts of the body, but those that are internal to the body, that is, the mind.

[92]That is, the mind.

[93]Akshara is syllable, though there are some differences between the English syllable and the Sanskrit syllable, because of the way Sanskrit syllables are constructed. Mama has two syllables and means 'it is mine'. Na mama has three syllables and means 'it is not mine'. The sense of ego and ownership leads to death and its reverse leads to the eternal truth.

They are invisible inside beings and there is no doubt that they cause them to struggle. O descendant of the Bharata lineage! If it is certain that the soul cannot be destroyed, then, by destroying the bodies of beings, one does not cause any violence. On the other hand, if the soul is generated with the body and is also destroyed with the body, then the path of all these rites is completely futile. Therefore, a virtuous man should renounce internally and intelligently follow the path that has been followed by his ancestors earlier.[94] If a king obtains the entire earth, with all its mobile and immobile objects, and yet does not enjoy it, his life is certainly fruitless. O king! There may be a man who lives in the forest and survives on wild fare. However, if he still has attachment towards objects, he lives within the jaws of death. O descendant of the Bharata lineage! Consider the brahman that is naturally within all beings. A person who can see that characteristic is freed from great fear. You are my father. You are my mother. You are my brother. You are my preceptor. Therefore, you should pardon me for this distressed lamentation that is the consequence of sorrow. O protector of the earth! O supreme among the Bharata lineage! What I have spoken may be true or false. But know that it results from devotion towards you."'

Chapter 1342(14)

Vaishampayana said, 'Kunti's son, Dharmaraja Yudhishthira, did not speak, while his brothers spoke many things about what the Vedas had said. Droupadi, supreme among women, was beautiful. She had large eyes and was descended from an extremely noble family. She addressed the Indra among kings. The king was seated like a bull, surrounded by his brothers. They were like lions and tigers and he was like the leader of a herd of elephants. She knew about dharma

[94]A meaning can be inferred. Since one does not know whether the soul is eternal or not, one ignores that debate and follows the path traversed by ancestors.

and could discern the nature of dharma. Though she was always cherished by the king, she was always somewhat haughty, especially towards Yudhishthira. Having been invited, the wide-hipped and extremely beautiful one glanced towards her husband[95] and spoke these gentle words. "O Partha! These brothers of yours are as parched as *stoka* birds.[96] They are stationed here and are warbling, but you do not pay them any attention. O great king! They are like crazy and large elephants. Gladden them with appropriate words. They have always suffered from sorrows. O king! Earlier, you were with your brothers in Dvaitavana and they were oppressed by the cold, the wind and the heat. Why did you speak such words to them? 'Desiring victory in the encounter, we will slay Duryodhana in the battle and enjoy the entire earth, which is capable of granting every object of desire. O scorchers of enemies! We will deprive the rathas of their chariots and kill the mighty elephants. We will strew the field of battle with chariots. We will perform many grand sacrifices, at which a lot of gifts will be given away. Our sorrow of dwelling in the forest will become happiness.' O supreme among those who uphold dharma! These were the words you yourself spoke then. O brave one! How can you then shatter their minds now? A eunuch cannot enjoy the earth. A eunuch cannot obtain wealth. There cannot be sons in a eunuch's house, just as fish cannot exist in mud.[97] A kshatriya without the staff of punishment does not shine. There is no prosperity without the staff of punishment. O descendant of the Bharata lineage! Without the staff of punishment, a king's subjects do not obtain happiness. O supreme among kings! Friendship towards all beings, donations, studying and austerities are dharma for a brahmana, not for a king. The wicked must be countered. The virtuous must be protected. Together with not running away from a battle, this is the supreme dharma for kings. A person who possesses both forgiveness and anger, who gives

[95]Yudhishthira.

[96]Stoka is another name for the *chataka* bird, which waits for the rains and is believed to survive on drops of water.

[97]Deprived of water.

and also takes, who frightens and also grants freedom from fear and who chastises and also rewards—such a person is said to know dharma. You have not obtained the earth through learning, donations, conciliation, sacrifices or bribery.[98] The forces of the enemy had brave ones who were ready to strike, with elephants, horses and chariots. It was larger in three parts.[99] It was protected by Drona, Karna, Ashvatthama and Kripa. O brave one! It has been destroyed by you. Therefore, enjoy the earth. O great king! O tiger among men! O lord! You used a rod to crush Jambudvipa, with its many countries.[100] O lord of men! You also used a rod to crush Krounchadvipa, equal to Jambudvipa and to the west of the great Meru. O lord of men! You used a rod to crush Shakadvipa, equal to Krounchadvipa and to the east of the great Meru. O tiger among men! To the north of the great Meru is Bhadrashva, equal to Shakadvipa. You crushed it with your rod. There were many countries between one dvipa and another dvipa. O brave one! You immersed yourself in the ocean and crushed them with your rod. O descendant of the Bharata lineage! These were the immeasurable deeds that were performed by you. O great king! The brahmanas honoured you. But despite that, you are not pleased. O descendant of the Bharata lineage! Look at your brothers and delight them.

[98]The Critical edition says *utkocha*, meaning bribery. Many non-Critical versions say *samkocha*, meaning fear or cowering down. Given the context, samkocha fits better.

[99]This is difficult to figure out. The traditional interpretation has been that the Kourava army was superior in three ways—leadership, policy and energy. It was also larger than the Pandava army by four akshouhinis.

[100]This is a reference to the conquest by the Pandavas, described in Section 23 (Volume 2). A dvipa is a continent. In the cosmology described in the epics and the Puranas, there are seven dvipas. Jambudvipa is in the centre and Mount Meru is at the centre of Jambudvipa. The other six dvipas are Plakshadvipa, Kushadvipa, Shalmalidvipa, Krounchadvipa, Shakadvipa and Pushkaradvipa. Each dvipa is divided into nine *varsha*s or subcontinents. For example, Bharatavarsha is part of Jambudvipa. While there are some variations in nomenclature across texts, the description given in the text here doesn't fit the standard cosmology.

They are like proud bulls and proud kings of elephants. All of you are like the immortals. All of you are scorchers of enemies and are capable of withstanding enemies. It is my view that even a single one of you would have been enough to bring me happiness, not to speak of when all of you tigers and men and bulls among men are my husbands, like the senses enervating the body.[101] My mother-in-law knows everything and can see everything. Her words cannot be false. She told me, 'O Panchali! O excellent one! Yudhishthira will maintain you in happiness, after he has killed many thousands of kings through his valour.' O lord of men! Now, because of your confusion, I see that you will make this futile. O Indra among kings! If the eldest brother is mad, all the others follow him. Because you are mad, all the Pandavas will become mad. O lord of men! If these brothers of yours were not mad, they should have bound you up with the non-believers and ruled the earth. A person who acts stupidly does not obtain anything that is superior. A person who is on the path towards madness should be treated with incense, collyrium, treatment through the nose,[102] medicines and medical remedies. O supreme among the Bharata lineage! I am the worst of all women in the world. Though I have been oppressed by the enemy, I still wish to remain alive. They[103] have struggled and have obtained this prosperity. But after having obtained the entire earth, you are acting so as to bring a disaster on yourself. O king! The kings Mandhata and Ambarisha were supreme among kings and were honoured by all the kings on earth. Be as radiant as them. In accordance with dharma, rule the goddess earth, with its mountains, forests and islands, and protect the subjects. O king! Do not be distressed in your mind. Perform many sacrifices and offer oblations into the fire. O supreme among kings! Give the brahmanas cities, objects of pleasure and garments."'

[101]To state the obvious, there are five senses.
[102]Inhalation of fumes through the nose.
[103]The other Pandava brothers.

Chapter 1343(15)

Vaishampayana said, 'On hearing Yajnaseni's words, Arjuna again spoke, showing honour to the mighty-armed lord who was his eldest brother. "The rod punishes all subjects. The rod protects them. When everything is asleep, the rod is awake. The learned say that the rod is dharma. O lord of men! The rod protects both dharma and artha. The rod protects kama. Is it said that the rod protects the three objectives.[104] Grain is protected through the rod. Wealth is protected through the rod. You know this and you should accept it. Consider the natural way of the world. Some evil ones do not perform wicked deeds because of their fear for the king's rod, others because of their fear for Yama's rod and others because of their fear of the life hereafter. There are other evil ones who do not perform wicked deeds because of their fear for each other. In this world that has come about, everything is based on the rod. It is because of their fear of the rod that some do not eat each other. Had the rod not protected, they would have been submerged in blind darkness. It controls those who are not disciplined. It punishes those who are wicked. It is because it controls and punishes that the learned know of it as *danda*.[105] Words are the danda for brahmanas, arms that for kshatriyas. Donations are said to be the rod for vaishyas. But it is said that there is no rod for shudras.[106] O lord of the earth! To ensure that there was no confusion among mortals, to protect riches and to establish boundaries in this world, danda was thought of. When danda strides around, dark and red-eyed,[107] there is

[104]Dharma, artha and kama.

[105]Danda means both rod and punishment. *Damana* is to control or subdue. There is a common etymology.

[106]Brahmanas are punished by chastising them with words, kshatriyas through use of weapons and vaishyas by forcing them to donate out of their riches. However, shudras possess no wealth that can be taken away and they are naturally expected to serve. Therefore, no punishment can be imposed on them.

[107]The personification of punishment.

exultation and subjects are not confused. The wicked are not to be seen there. Men who are brahmacharis, householders, in the vanaprastha stage and mendicants remain stationed on their paths because of their fear of danda. O king! If one is not frightened, one does not sacrifice. If one is not frightened, one does not donate. A man who is not frightened does not wish to adhere to agreements. Without severing the inner organs, without performing terrible deeds and without killing like a fisherman, one does not obtain great prosperity. Without killing, there is no fame on earth, nor riches or subjects. Indra became the great Indra after slaying Vritra. The gods who have killed are worshipped much more by the worlds. Rudra, Skanda, Shakra, Agni, Varuna and Yama are killers. O descendant of the Bharata lineage! Time is a killer and so are Vayu, Death, Vaishravana,[108] Ravi,[109] the Vasus, the Maruts, the Sadhyas and the Vishvadevas. It is because of their powers that people bow down before them, but never before Brahma, Dhata or Pushan. These[110] are neutral vis-à-vis all beings, self-controlled and prone to peace. But only a few men, who are peaceful in all their deeds, worship them. I do not see anyone alive in this world who does not act violently. Living beings sustain themselves through other living beings, the stronger live off the weaker. O king! The mongoose eats the rat. The cat eats the mongoose. The dog eats the cat. The carnivorous beast eats the dog. A man eats them all. Behold. That is the way of dharma. Everything, mobile and immobile, is food for living beings. Those are the principles laid down by the gods and a learned person is not confused by this. O Indra among kings! You should become the person you were born to be. Those who are stupid[111] control anger and delight and resort to the forest. Without killing, the ascetics cannot sustain their lives. There are many beings in water, in the earth and in fruits. It is not true that they are not killed. What can be more important than sustaining life? There are

[108]Kubera.

[109]Surya.

[110]Brahma, Dhata and Pushan.

[111]Among kshatriyas.

many beings so subtle that their existence can be determined only through inference. Their bodies can be destroyed through a mere blinking of the eyelids. Men leave the village. They give up anger and pride. But in the forest, they are seen to be confused and live the life of householders with families.[112] They till the ground and destroy herbs and trees. They kill birds and animals. Such men perform sacrifices and obtain heaven. O Kounteya! In my mind, there is no doubt that when the rod is properly applied, the endeavours of all beings become successful. If danda did not exist on this earth, all these beings would be destroyed. Like fish on a stake, the strong will cook the weak. Brahma himself spoke these truthful words earlier. 'When applied rightly, danda protects beings. Look at the fire, once it has been pacified and is not frightened. Scared of the danda, it blazes up again.' If danda did not exist in this world, there would be no difference between the virtuous and the wicked. Everything would be blind darkness and it would be impossible to distinguish anything. There are non-believers and criticizers of the Vedas, those who do not observe the boundaries. But stricken by the rod, even they can be made to follow rules. In this world, everyone is ruled by the rod. The pure man is extremely rare. It is because of fear of the rod that people can be made to follow rules. The rod was thought of by the creator, for the sake of protecting dharma and artha, so that the four varnas could be controlled and did not become confused. If they were not scared of danda, birds and carnivorous animals would have eaten up all the animals and men and all the oblations kept for sacrifices. Had the rod not protected, no brahmachari would have studied, no wonderful cow would have yielded milk and no maiden would have married.[113] There would be an end to the universe and all the boundaries would be broken down. Had the rod not

[112]That is, they could have remained as householders, instead of retiring to the forest.

[113]The suggestion is that studies occur because of the fear of punishment, cows suffer the act of milking because of the fear of punishment and maidens suffer the institution of marriage (as opposed to free love) because of the fear of punishment.

protected, beings would not have recognized property. Had the rod not protected, people would not have been scared and would not have performed sacrifices throughout the year, giving away many kinds of donations, in accordance with the proper rites. Had the rod not protected, people would not have followed the dharma and dictates of the stages of life, nor would anyone have obtained learning. Had the rod not protected, camels, bullocks, horses, mules and asses would not have drawn vehicles, even after they had been yoked. Had the rod not protected, servants would not have listened to their instructions, nor would children have abided by what their fathers described as dharma. All beings are established on the basis of fear of the rod. That is what the learned say. Heaven and the world of men are established on the rod. Where the rod that destroys enemies is applied well, crookedness, sin and deceit are not seen there. When the rod is not raised, dogs are seen to lick oblations. If the rod does not protect, the crow steals the sacrificial cake. Be it through dharma, or be it through adharma, the kingdom has now been obtained. Our duty is not to sorrow, but to enjoy it and perform sacrifices. There are fortunate ones who dwell with their beloved wives. They roam around, attired in pure garments, and happily follow dharma. They eat the best of food. There is no doubt that all efforts depend on artha and that itself is based on danda. Behold the glory of danda. Dharma was declared so that the world could be sustained. There is non-violence and there is violence for righteous reasons. Of these, that which leads to dharma is superior.[114] There is nothing that possesses all the qualities, nor is there anything without any qualities. In all acts, something that is good and something that is evil are seen. Animals are castrated. Their horns are broken off. They are afflicted and made to carry many loads. They are tied down and chastised. This is the way the world goes on. It is on a crooked and decayed path. O great king! Therefore, you should observe the dharma that has been followed from ancient times. Perform sacrifices. Donate. Protect the subjects. Follow dharma. O Kounteya! Slay enemies and protect your friends. O

[114]Righteous violence is superior to non-violence for the sake of non-violence.

descendant of the Bharata lineage! You should not sorrow because you have slain the enemy. O descendant of the Bharata lineage! No sin has attached to you because of that. Someone who kills an assassin advancing to kill him does not suffer the sin attached to killing a foetus,[115] because that anger provokes the anger.[116] There is no doubt that the inner souls of all beings are incapable of being killed. If the soul cannot be killed, then how can it be killed by someone else? Just as a man enters a new house, in that way, beings successively enter new bodies. The old bodies are discarded and the new ones are acquired. People who know about the truth say that the face of death is nothing but this."'

Chapter 1344(16)

Vaishampayana said, 'On hearing Arjuna's words, the intolerant and energetic Bhimasena resorted to his patience and spoke to his eldest brother. "O king! You know about dharma. There is nothing on earth that is not known to you. We always wish to learn from your conduct, but are unable to do so. In my mind, I kept saying, 'I will not speak. I will not speak.' O lord of men! However, I am speaking out of great grief. Listen. Because of your confusion, everything is now uncertain. We have become perplexed and weak. This is the king of the world. He is accomplished in all the sacred texts. How can he be overcome by confusion and cheerlessness now, like an inferior man? You know about the coming and going of the world. O lord! There is nothing that has happened, or will happen, that is not known to you. O great king! O lord of men! This being the case, I will advance an argument about you ruling the kingdom. Listen with undivided attention. There are two kinds of diseases, physical and mental. Each one is generated from the other and they are not

[115]This is being used as an extreme case of the sin of killing.

[116]The anger of the assassin provokes the anger in the slayer.

seen to exist independently. There is no doubt that a physical disease causes a mental one. It is also certain that a mental disease results in a physical one. Someone who sorrows over a physical or mental grief that has already occurred imposes a sorrow on a sorrow and doubles it. The three qualities of a body are cold, heat and wind.[117] When there is harmony between these qualities, that is said to be a sign of health. If one predominates over the others, remedies have been prescribed. Cold is checked through heat and heat is checked through cold. There are three qualities in the mind—*sattva*, *rajas* and tamas. Sorrow is checked through joy and joy is checked through sorrow. Some are in a present state of happiness and remember past sorrows. Others are in a present state of sorrow and remember past unhappiness. But you were not sorrowful in the midst of woes, nor joyful in the midst of happiness. Nor should you remember sorrow in the midst of happiness, or happiness in the midst of sorrows. O Kouravya! Destiny is most powerful. O king! Or, perhaps it is your nature that is afflicting you. In her season, Krishna[118] was in a single garment and was brought into the assembly hall, while the sons of Pandu looked on. Having seen it, why don't you remember that? We were exiled from our residence in the city in deerskins and took up abode in the great forest. Should you not remember that? Jatasura afflicted us, there was a battle with Chitrasena and Saindhava afflicted us.[119] How is it that you have forgotten that? Then again, while we lived in concealment, Kichaka kicked the noble lady with his foot.[120] O scorcher of enemies! You fought a battle with Drona and Bhishma. But you now have to fight this terrible battle in your mind. Arrows will serve no purpose here, nor friends or relatives. In this battle that has presented itself, you will have to fight internally. If you are defeated in this battle and give up your life, you will take up another body and have to fight again. O bull among the Bharata

[117]Meaning, phlegm, bile and wind.

[118]Krishnaa, Droupadi.

[119]Incidents respectively described in Sections 34, 35 and 42 (Volume 3).

[120]The noble lady is Droupadi and this is a reference to the incidents of Section 46 (Volume 4).

lineage! Therefore, you should fight this battle now. O great king! If you win in this, you will become successful. Having determined the nature of beings coming and going,[121] make up your mind. Follow the conduct of your father and grandfathers and rule the kingdom, as is appropriate. It is fortunate that the wicked Duryodhana and his followers were killed in the battle. It is fortunate that you have followed the course of Droupadi's hair.[122] Perform a horse sacrifice in the proper way and give away donations. O Partha! We are your servants and so is the valiant Vasudeva."'

Chapter 1345(17)

'Yudhishthira said, "Discontent, confusion, intoxication, passion, agitation, strength, delusion, pride and anxiety—you are overcome by all these sins and desire the kingdom. Do not be addicted. Be free, calm and extremely happy. The king who rules over this entire earth alone possesses only one stomach. Why are you then praising this course?[123] O bull among men! Desire cannot be satisfied in a day or a month. A desire incapable of being satisfied cannot be gratified in a lifespan. When it is fed, a fire blazes and when there is no kindling, it is pacified. Pacify the fire that has arisen in your stomach with a little bit of food. Conquer your stomach. This vanquished earth will then be conquered for the greater good. You have praised human desire, pleasures and prosperity. But those who do not enjoy objects of pleasure and are weak attain the supreme state. The kingdom's acquisition and preservation, and both dharma and adharma, are based on you. Free yourself from that great burden and resort to renunciation. The tiger, for the sake of a single stomach, creates a

[121]Birth and death.

[122]Droupadi had resolved not to braid her hair until the Kouravas had been killed.

[123]Of asking for more.

great carnage. Other slow-moving animals sustain themselves on that.[124] An ascetic withdraws from material objects and resorts to sannyasa. However, a king is never satisfied. Behold the difference in their intelligence. Those who subsist on leaves, *ashmakuttas*,[125] *dantolukhalas*,[126] those who subsist on water and those who subsist on air are capable of conquering hell. Between a king who rules over every part of this entire earth and one who regards stone and gold as equal, the latter is the successful one, not the king. Do not act because of any intentions. Do not cherish hopes. Do not have a sense of ownership. Resort to the state that is without sorrow in this world and without decay in the next. Those who have no desire do not sorrow. Why are you grieving over desire? If you give up all desire, you will also be freed from these futile words.[127] The paths of *pitriyana* and *devayana*[128] are renowned. Those who sacrifice follow pitriyana, those who wish to be freed follow devayana. Through austerities, brahmacharya and studying, those purified ones are radiant after they free themselves from their bodies and go beyond the grasp of death. Worldly desire is a bond. Freed from the bonds of both desire and action, one attains the supreme objective. It is said that there is a chant sung by Janaka.[129] He was beyond opposite sentiments. He was free and could perceive complete liberation. 'Though I possess nothing, my riches are infinite. If Mithila blazes up, nothing that is mine will be burnt.' Just as a person who ascends a palace on a mountain looks down at the people on the world below, the wise person looks down at evil-minded ones who sorrow about what one should not grieve about. The intelligent person who looks

[124]Sustain themselves on the tiger's prey.

[125]Those who survive on grain ground with stones.

[126]Those who survive on grain ground with their teeth. Literally, those who use their teeth as mortars.

[127]The idea that one can be free from desire, amidst wealth and prosperity.

[128]Respectively, the paths followed by the ancestors and by the gods. Pitriyana involves sacrifices and rites. Devayana abandons sacrifices and rites, in favour of inner contemplation.

[129]This Janaka is not to be confused with King Janaka who was the father of Sita. Mithila was the capital of both Janakas.

and sees what should be seen, has sight. The person who knows what is not normally known is said to be intelligent. There are those who have cleansed their souls, are learned and have attained the brahman. A person who understands their words is greatly revered. When one sees all the different beings to be one and realizes that they are the extension of the brahman, one attains that exalted state, not those who are ignorant, of limited intelligence, without understanding and without austerities. Everything is based on understanding."'

Chapter 1346(18)

Vaishampayana said, 'The king became silent. Arjuna was tormented and overcome by sorrow and grief because of the stakes of the king's words. He spoke again. "O descendant of the Bharata lineage! People speak about the ancient account of the history of a conversation between the king of Videha and his wife.[130] The lord of men made up his mind to abandon his kingdom and resort to a life of begging. The queen of the king of Videha was full of sorrow and addressed him. Janaka gave up riches, offspring, friends, the many jewels and the path of fire[131] and became one who shaved off his head. His beloved wife saw him resort to this life of begging, possessing nothing. He only had a fistful of grain. He was indifferent and without selfishness. He was without any fear. In an isolated spot, the angry and spirited wife approached her husband and spoke words that were full of reason. 'Why have you abandoned your kingdom? It was full of riches and grain. You have adopted a life of mendicancy and are wandering around with a fistful of grain in your hand. O king! Your resolution is of one kind, but your acts are of a different kind. O king! You have abandoned this great kingdom and are satisfied with only a little. O king! In

[130]Janaka was the king of Videha, Mithila was Videha's capital.

[131]The path of performing sacrifices to the fire.

this way, you will now be unable to support gods, guests, devarshis and ancestors. Therefore, your efforts are futile. O king! You have been abandoned by all the gods, guests and ancestors and are wandering around as a mendicant, without any action. You earlier supported thousands of aged brahmanas who knew about the three forms of knowledge.[132] You supported the world and now wish to be supported by others. Having abandoned the blazing prosperity, you are glancing around, like a dog. Your mother is without a son now and the daughter of Kosala is without a husband.[133] For the sake of dharma and kama, eighty kshatriya women served you.[134] Those pitiable ones hoped for the fruits of their actions. Having rendered them unsuccessful, what worlds will you go to? O king! Those bodies depended on you and their salvation is in doubt. Since you are the performer of wicked deeds, you have no superior world, in this world or in the next. Having abandoned the one who is your wife under dharma, you wish to live. Why have you abandoned garlands, fragrances, ornaments and many kinds of garments, living like a mendicant, without any action? You were like a pool[135] for all beings. You were their great cleanser. Having been a tall tree, you now serve others. When an elephant dies, many carnivorous beasts feed on it and so do many worms. But what purpose do you serve? How would you feel if someone broke this water pot, stole this *trivishtabdha*[136]and robbed you of your garment? You have abandoned everything and have accepted this fistful of grain. Even if this is equal to all gifts, what will you give me?[137] If this fistful of grain is all your riches, your pledge will be falsified.[138] Who am I to you? Who are you to me? What favours will you show me now? O king! Rule the kingdom and show me

[132]The first three Vedas.

[133]Janaka was married to the princess of Kosala.

[134]Presumably Janaka's other wives.

[135]Drinking hole, alternatively, refuge.

[136]The three staffs tied together, the mark of a mendicant.

[137]How will you support your wife?

[138]The pledge to support the wife.

the favours of a place, bed, vehicle, garments and ornaments. There are those who have no hope of prosperity. They were without riches. They have no friends. They can renounce. But you have friends, servants and other riches. How can you renounce? There are those who receive a lot and there are those who always give. You know the difference between these two. Who is said to be superior? If one donates to a person who is always asking, even if that person is virtuous and without pride, those gifts are like oblations poured into a forest conflagration.[139] O king! A fire is not pacified until it has consumed everything. In that way, a brahmana who always asks is never satisfied. The Vedas and food are the natural sustenance of virtuous ones in this world. If one who is supposed to give does not give, where will those who desire salvation go?[140] In this world, householders result from food and those who beg result from them.[141] Life results from food. One who gives food, gives life. They[142] emerge from the state of being a householder, but have to resort to householders. Those self-controlled ones criticize the base of their powers.[143] A person cannot be said to be one who has renounced only because he is a mendicant, has shaved his head, or begs. Know that an upright person who happily gives up his wealth is one who renounces.[144] He is unattached, even if he roams around, as if attached. He is alone and has shed all bonds. O lord of the earth! He treats friend and foe equally and is truly free. There are those who roam around in search of alms. They have shaved off their heads and wear ochre robes. But they are tied down by many kinds of bonds and are always thinking about unsatisfied desire. They cast aside the three types of learning,[145] their names, their livelihoods and

[139]A forest conflagration is not a sacred fire.

[140]As a king, Janaka is supposed to give for charity.

[141]From the householders.

[142]The mendicants.

[143]Despite depending on householders, mendicants criticize them.

[144]One can renounce while being a householder and donating.

[145]The first three Vedas.

their sons. They accept the trivishtabdha and garments, but do not have understanding. Know that the ochre robe is not without desire for gain. Those with shaved heads wave the banner of dharma, but it is for the purpose of sustenance. That is my view. O great king! Conquer the world by conquering your senses and support those with ochre robes, those clad in skins, those clad in tatters, those who are naked, those who have shaved heads and those who sport matted hair. Who is superior to the one who maintains the sacred fire, performs sacrifices and gives away animals and other donations? From one day to another, incessantly give, as earlier. There is no dharma superior to that.' King Janaka knew the truth and the world sang about him. He was overcome by confusion. But you should not be confused. This is the dharma that is always followed by benevolent men. Without desire and anger, one should resort to the quality of non-violence. We should protect the subjects and base ourselves on donating. By being truthful in speech and honouring the brahmanas, we will obtain the worlds that we desire."'

Chapter 1347(19)

'Yudhishthira said, "O son![146] I know about the sacred texts and about this world and the next. The words of the Vedas ask one to act and also ask one to renounce action. Though the sacred texts give reasons, they cause confusion. I know what has been certainly prescribed, following the rites. You are only skilled in the use of weapons and base yourself on the conduct of heroes. You are incapable of comprehending the true meaning of the sacred texts. Those who are learned can determine the certainty of dharma. Those who know subtleties can appreciate the true purport of the sacred texts. If you had actually seen the nature of dharma, you would not have spoken

[146]The word used is tata.

those words to me. But those words were spoken by you out of fraternal affection towards a brother. O Kounteya! O Arjuna! Your words are full of reason and I am pleased with you. In the three worlds, there is no one who is your equal amongst those who know the dharma of fighting and are accomplished in all those acts. But the words that I am speaking about the subtlety of dharma will be difficult for you to understand. O Dhananjaya! You should not doubt my intelligence. You know about the science of fighting, but you have not served the elders. You do not know about the conclusions of learned ones who have considered these in their entirety. O son![147] Austerities, renunciation and ritual action—those intelligent ones who have determined the way to the supreme objective have said that each of these is superior to the preceding one.[148] O Partha! You are wrong when you think that there is nothing superior to wealth. I will explain to you why it is not the most important. People who follow dharma are seen to follow austerities and practice studying. The rishis who attain eternal worlds observe austerities. There are those who have not grown beards and other wise ones who dwell in the forest. Though they are without riches, because of their studies, they go to the infinite heaven. There are aryas who abandon the darkness that comes from lack of intelligence and disassociate themselves from objects. They follow the northern path[149] and go to the worlds meant for those who renounce. You see that the southern path[150] is radiant. This is the world of those who follow action, but is a cremation ground. The path seen by those who desire salvation cannot be described. That is the reason renunciation is the most important, though it can only be explained with difficulty. Wise

[147]The word used is tata.

[148]Ritual action is superior to renunciation and renunciation is superior to austerities. There is something wrong in the text. Arjuna is the one who has advocated ritual action, while Yudhishthira has advocated austerities. Therefore, the ordering ought to be the other way round.

[149]The path of the gods.

[150]The path of the ancestors. This leads to rebirth.

ones have followed the sacred texts, wishing to determine what is real and what is unreal, what is here and what is there. They have gone through the words of the Vedas and the sacred texts that are the *Aranyaka*s. They have dissected them like the trunk of a plantain tree, but have not been able to see the essence. Some have attentively rejected and have decided that the atman, in this body with the five elements, has the attributes of desire and aversion.[151] It[152] cannot be seen by the eye. It cannot be expressed through words. Being driven by karma, it circulates in beings.[153] After having realized what is most beneficial, withdrawing all thirst from the mind and casting aside all forms of action, one becomes independent and happy. This is the subtle path traversed by virtuous ones. O Arjuna! This being the case, why are you praising wealth, which is harmful? O descendant of the Bharata lineage! In earlier times, there were people who could see and were learned in the sacred texts. They were always devoted to constant action, donations, sacrifice and deeds. They were learned and provided reasons and it was difficult to dissuade them. But there are foolish ones who rigidly adhere to those earlier texts. They say that it does not exist.[154] Those eloquent ones disregard what is immortal. They roam around the entire earth and speak in assemblies. Though they are extremely learned, they talk a lot. If we do not recognize them, who else will? But there are extremely wise and intelligent and virtuous ones, wise in the store of the sacred texts. They have great intelligence and perform great austerities. O Kounteya! They follow dharma and always obtain happiness through renunciation."'

[151]This is a difficult shloka to understand. The body is composed of the five elements, earth, air, water, fire and space. Rejection probably means the rejection of some doctrines.

[152]The atman.

[153]Through the cycle of death and rebirth, and true knowledge frees one from this cycle.

[154]The atman does not exist, or final emancipation does not exist. Therefore, one should devote oneself to action. These shlokas are not very easy to understand and we have taken some liberties.

Chapter 1348(20)

Vaishampayana said, 'When there was a break in the conversation, the immensely ascetic and eloquent Devasthana spoke appropriate words in reply to Yudhishthira. "Phalguna spoke words to the effect that there is nothing superior to wealth. Listen attentively as I explain this to you. O Ajatashatru! You have conquered the entire earth through dharma. O king! Having won it, you should not give it up without reason. There are four steps on the ladder, established on action.[155] O mighty-armed one! O king! You should ascend it by stages. O Partha! Therefore, perform great sacrifices, with many donations. Rishis perform the sacrifice of austerities and others observe the sacrifice of knowledge. O descendant of the Bharata lineage! You must understand that those who are devoted to austerities also base themselves on action. O Indra among kings! We have heard the words of the *vaikhanasa*s.[156] 'One who does not strive for riches is superior to one who does. There are many sins associated with the pursuit of wealth and they only increase. For the sake of riches, people collect objects with a great deal of difficulty. One who thirsts after wealth is stupid and does not understand that a foetus is being killed.'[157] One may give to the undeserving and not give to the deserving. The dharma of distinguishing the undeserving from the deserving is extremely difficult. The creator created riches for sacrifices and man for protecting them[158] and performing sacrifices. Therefore, all riches should be used for performing sacrifices. Kama follows from that.[159] The immensely energetic Indra surpassed

[155]The four ashramas or stages of life.

[156]Hermits or anchorites.

[157]Sacrifices for the sake of wealth are being condemned. Objects are collected for such sacrifices and it is better not to perform such sacrifices. If sacrifices cannot be performed without wealth, it is best to avoid such sacrifices. Such a pursuit of wealth kills one's own self, the foetus probably referring to one's own self in the cycle of rebirth. This is the belief of the vaikhanasas, being contradicted by Devasthana.

[158]The riches.

[159]The desire for the fruits of sacrifices.

all the gods by performing many sacrifices that were full of food. He became the radiant Indra because of that. Therefore, all riches should be used for performing sacrifices. The great-souled Mahadeva offered himself in a sarvamedha sacrifice and became the exalted god of the gods. He surpassed all the beings in the universe with his deeds. He is the radiant Krittivasa and illuminates them.[160] Avikshit's son, King Marutta, was mortal. But because of his sacrifice, he surpassed the king of the gods. All the vessels used were made out of gold and Shri[161] herself came to the sacrifice. You have heard about Harishchandra, Indra among kings. He performed sacrifices, earned merits and overcame his sorrow. Though he was human, he surpassed Shakra[162] with his prosperity. Therefore, everything must be used to perform sacrifices."'

Chapter 1349(21)

'Devasthana said, "In this connection, an ancient history is recounted. This is about what Brihaspati[163] said, when he was asked by Indra. 'Contentment is the best heaven. Contentment is supreme happiness. There is nothing superior to contentment, since a person is well established in that. When one withdraws from desire, just as a tortoise draws in its limbs, then the radiance of the atman clearly manifests the atman itself. When one is not frightened and does not frighten anyone else, then one triumphs over desire and aversion and sees the atman. Whether in deeds, thought or words, when one is not angry towards anyone and does not injure anyone, then one attains the brahman.'[164] O Kounteya!

[160]Krittivasa is Shiva's name and means the one who is attired in skins. The word for deeds is *kirti* and there is a pun that a translation misses.

[161]The goddess Lakshmi.

[162]Indra.

[163]The preceptor of the gods.

[164]Though not clearly stated, this is the end of Brihaspati's quote.

O descendant of the Bharata lineage! In this way, beings look at this and that, and follow this dharma and that. Understand this.[165] Some praise tranquility, others praise exertion. Some recommend one or the other, others praise both. Some praise sacrifice, other people sannyasa. One praises giving, another receiving. Some say that everything must be renounced and one must be seated in silent meditation. Some praise the kingdom and the protection of everyone, through killing, cutting and piercing.[166] Others prefer solitude. Having examined all this, the wise have determined that the virtuous should have the view that dharma lies in not injuring any being and in non-injury, truthfulness in speech, sharing, fortitude, forgiveness, procreation on one's own wife, gentleness, modesty and steadfastness. Svayambhuva Manu[167] said that riches constituted the most important component of dharma. O Kounteya! Therefore, you should make efforts to protect. A kshatriya who is established in a kingdom must be self-controlled and look on pleasant and unpleasant things equally. He must know the truth about what the sacred texts prescribe for kings and he must subsist on the remnants of sacrifices. He must be engaged in chastising the wicked and supporting the virtuous. He must establish the subjects on the path of dharma and must himself follow dharma. Having passed on the riches to his son, he can retire to the forest and sustain himself on forest fare, in accordance with what is prescribed for hermits, being attentive until his time comes.[168] Such a king acts in accordance with the dharma of kings. O king! Therefore, he is successful in this world and the next. It is my view that *nirvana*[169] is extremely difficult to attain. There are many obstacles along the

[165]Follow the right dharma.

[166]Of wicked ones.

[167]Each era *(manvantara)* is presided over by a Manu. After fourteen manvantaras, the cycle of destruction and creation starts again. In the present cycle of fourteen manvantaras, Svayambhuva Manu was the first and we are now in the seventh manvantara, presided over by Vaivasvata Manu.

[168]Until it is time to die.

[169]The final liberation.

path. Therefore, those who follow this dharma, are devoted to truth, generosity and austerities, have the quality of not causing injury, are devoid of desire and anger, are engaged in the task of protecting the subjects, are based on supreme self-control and fight for the sake of cattle and brahmanas, obtain the supreme objective. O scorcher of enemies! The Rudras, the Vasus, the Adityas, the Sadhyas and large numbers of rajarshis adopted this dharma. They were not distracted. Through their meritorious deeds, they obtained heaven."'

Chapter 1350(22)

Vaishampayana said, 'During a break in this conversation, Arjuna again spoke. He spoke these words to the lord who was his eldest brother, whose mind was cheerless. "O one who is knowledgeable about dharma! You have obtained this supreme kingdom through the dharma of kshatriyas. O best among men! Having conquered it, why are you so severely tormented? O great king! It has been said that being slain in a battle is better for kshatriyas than many sacrifices. Remember the dharma of kshatriyas. It has been said that for brahmanas, austerities and renunciation are the best prescribed dharma for the state beyond death. O lord! Being slain in battle is recommended for kshatriyas. It has been said that the dharma of kshatriyas is extremely terrible, since weapons are always involved. O best among the Bharata lineage! At the right time, they should be slain by weapons in a battle. O king! Even when a brahmana bases himself on the dharma of kshatriyas, his life is praised in this world, because kshatriyas are based on brahmanas. O lord of men! Renunciation, begging, austerities and living off others are not recommended for kshatriyas. O bull among the Bharata lineage! You know about all forms of dharma! You know about everything. You are an intelligent and accomplished king. You can distinguish the bad from the good. Abandon this torment and sorrow and armour yourself for action. In particular, the hearts of kshatriyas are as hard as the vajra. Having vanquished the enemy through the dharma of kshatriyas, you have obtained this kingdom, without any thorns. O Indra among men! Conquer your soul now and devote yourself to sacrifices and donations. Indra was the son of a brahmana, but he became a kshatriya through his deeds.[170] He killed his own wicked relatives eight hundred and ten times.[171] O lord of the earth! Those deeds of his should be honoured and praised. It has been said that this was how he became Indra among the gods. O great king! O Indra among men! When your fever eventually goes, perform sacrifices with many donations, just as Indra sacrificed. O bull among the kshatriyas! You should not sorrow at all about what has already happened. Following the dharma of kshatriyas, they have been purified by weapons and have attained the supreme end. O bull among the Bharatas! What has happened was going to occur. It was ordained. O tiger among kings! No one is capable of thwarting destiny."'

Chapter 1351(23)

Vaishampayana said, 'O descendant of the Bharata lineage! Thus addressed by Gudakesha,[172] Kouravya Kounteya did not say anything in reply. Dvaipayana said, "O Yudhishthira! Bibhatsu's[173] words are completely true. It has been said in the sacred texts that supreme dharma is vested in the status of a householder. O one who knows about dharma! In accordance with the sacred texts and following the stipulations, follow your own dharma. It is not

[170]Indra was the son of the sage Kashyapa.

[171]The wicked relatives are the demons, also descended from Kashyapa. Indra is believed to have attacked the demons 810 times.

[172]Arjuna's name.

[173]Bibhatsu is also one of Arjuna's names.

recommended that you should give up the status of a householder and go to the forest. The gods, the ancestors, the rishis and the servants always sustain themselves on the householder. O lord of the earth! Support them. Birds, animals and other beings also owe their sustenance to householders. O lord of the earth! Therefore, garhasthya is the best of the ashramas. Among the four ashramas, it is the most difficult one to follow. O Partha! Those who are weak in their senses find it difficult to follow. Since you are not distracted, follow it. You possess all the knowledge of the Vedas. You have performed great austerities. You should therefore bear the burden of the kingdom of your father and grandfathers. O great king! Austerities, sacrifices, learning, begging, deprivation of the senses, meditation, solitude in conduct, contentment and donations—in a desire to be successful, these should be followed by brahmanas, to the best of their ability. Though it is already known to you, I will now tell you what it is for kshatriyas: sacrifices, learning, exertion, lack of contentment about one's prosperity, wielding the fierce rod of chastisement, protecting subjects, knowledge of the Vedas, performing all the austerities, good conduct, the earning of many material objects and giving them to the deserving. O lord of the earth! These are the duties for kings. We have heard that, when performed well, they bring success in this world and in that world.[174] O Kounteya! Among these, wielding the rod of chastisement is said to be the best. There is always strength in the kshatriya and the rod is based on that strength. O king! These endeavours bring success for kshatriyas. On this, there is a chant sung by Brihaspati. 'Like a snake swallowing up animals in their holes, the earth swallows up peaceful kings and brahmanas who do not leave their homes.' It has been heard that rajarshi Sudyumna wielded the rod and obtained supreme success, like Daksha, the son of Prachetasa."'[175]

[174]The world after death.

[175]Accounts of Daksha's creation are not consistent. In one version, Prachetasa was a son born through Brahma's mental powers and Daksha was the son of Prachetasa.

Chapter 1352(24)

'Yudhishthira asked, "O illustrious one! Through what deeds did Sudyumna, the lord of the earth, obtain supreme success? I wish to hear about that king."

'Vyasa replied, "An ancient history is recounted about this. There were two brothers, Shankha and Likhita, and they were controlled in their vows. They had separate and beautiful abodes on the banks of the Bahuda river and these were always lovely with trees that had flowers and fruit. On one occasion, Likhita went to Shankha's hermitage. At that time, following his own wishes, Shankha had gone out of his hermitage. Likhita arrived at the hermitage of his brother, Shankha. He knocked down some ripe fruit. Having got them, without thinking about it, the brahmana ate them. While he was eating them, Shankha returned to his hermitage. On seeing him eating them, Shankha asked his brother, 'Where did you get the fruit and why are you eating them?' Embracing his elder brother and greeting him, he smiled and said, 'I got them here.' Shankha was overcome by great anger and replied, 'By taking these fruits yourself, you have committed an act of theft. Go to the king and tell him what you have done. Say, "O best of kings! I have taken something that was not given to me. Know me to be a thief. Follow your own dharma. O lord of men! As a thief, quickly punish me."' O mighty-armed one! Having been addressed in these words, Likhita, rigid in his vows, went to King Sudyumna.

'"Sudyumna heard from his guards that Likhita had arrived. With his advisers, the lord of men advanced on foot to greet him. Having approached the one who knew about the brahman, the king asked, 'O illustrious one! Tell me the reason why you have come. It will be done.' Having been thus addressed, the brahmana rishi replied to Sudyumna, 'You have promised that you will do what has to be done. Now listen and act. O bull among men! I ate fruit that my elder had not authorized. O king! I ate those. Therefore, punish me immediately.' Sudyumna replied, 'O bull among brahmanas! If you think that the king has the authority to wield the rod, then he also has the power to pardon. O performer of auspicious deeds! O observer of great vows! You have been pardoned. Tell me what else you desire. I will certainly act in accordance with your words.' The brahmana rishi was delighted with the great-souled king. But he wished for no other boon from the king than the boon of being punished. At this, the great-souled lord of the earth severed Likhita's two hands.

'"Having been punished, he[176] went to his brother, Shankha, and said in great distress, 'I have been punished for my stupid intelligence. O illustrious one! You should now pardon me.' Shankha replied, 'O one who knows about dharma! I am not angry with you. Nor have you caused me any injury. You violated dharma and that is the reason you have been punished. Now quickly go to the Bahuda and according to the rites, offer oblations to the gods, the ancestors and the rishis. Do not set your mind on adharma again.' On hearing Shankha's words, Likhita performed his ablutions in the sacred river and also performed the water-rites. Instantly, his hands reappeared, like two lotuses. Astounded, he went to his brother and showed him his hands. Shankha said, 'Do not doubt that this has happened because of my ascetic powers and because it has been ordained.' Likhita asked, 'O immensely radiant one! Why did you not purify me earlier? O supreme among brahmanas! Afterall, the strength of your austerities is like this.' Shankha responded, 'I had to act in this way because I was not the one who wielded the rod of chastisement. Other than you, the king and all his ancestors have also been purified.' O best among Pandavas! Through his deeds, that king became supreme. He obtained supreme success, like Daksha, the son of Prachetasa. This is the dharma of kshatriyas, the protection of subjects. Anything else is a wrong path. O great king! Do not unnecessarily sorrow in your mind. O supreme among those who know about dharma! Listen to the beneficial words of your brothers. O Indra among kings! The dharma of kshatriyas is the rod, not the shaved head."'

[176]Likhita.

Chapter 1353(25)

Vaishampayana said, 'Maharshi Krishna Dvaipayana again spoke these words, deep in purport, to Ajatashatru Kounteya. "O son![177] O great king! O Yudhishthira! These brothers of yours dwelt in the forest like ascetics. Their desires that they cherished then must be satisfied. O best of the Bharata lineage! Let these maharathas get what they want. O Partha! Rule the earth, like Yayati, the son of Nahusha. You dwelt in the forest like ascetics and were full of sorrow. But that misery is over and these tigers among men must obtain happiness. O descendant of the Bharata lineage! With your brothers, enjoy dharma, artha and kama. O lord of the earth! After having experienced that, do what you wish to do. O descendant of the Bharata lineage! O Kounteya! You must first free yourself of the debts to guests, ancestors and gods. Only then will you go to heaven. O descendant of the Kuru lineage! Perform the sarvamedha and ashvamedha sacrifices. O great king! After that, you will go towards the supreme objective. Engage your brothers in all the sacrifices, with abundant donations. O Pandaveya! After that, you will obtain unsurpassed fame. O tiger among men! O descendant of the Kuru lineage! We know what you will say. But listen to my words about how a king acts, so as not to deviate from dharma. O Yudhishthira! O lord of men! Those who know about dharma have determined that a person who takes away someone else's property should be fined exactly the same amount. A king who follows the sacred texts, resorts to intelligence and, considering the time and the place, punishes bandits in this way, is right. A king who levies a tax of one-sixth, but does not protect the kingdom, obtains one-fourth of the kingdom's sins. Listen to how a king does not deviate from dharma. If he punishes in accordance with the dharma laid down in the sacred texts, if he does not fall prey to desire and anger, if he treats everyone equally, like a father, he has no reason to be scared. O immensely radiant one! When it is the time for undertaking a task, if a king is afflicted by destiny and distracted, not undertaking the task, this is not regarded as a transgression.

[177]The word used is tata.

However, enemies must be punished, either immediately, or after proper reflection. There must be no alliances with the wicked, nor must the kingdom be sold.[178] O Yudhishthira! Brave ones, aryas and those who are learned must be treated well. In particular, those who possess cattle and those who possess riches must be protected. Those who are extremely learned must be employed in all tasks connected with dharma. An accomplished one[179] does not repose his faith on any single individual, no matter how many qualities he possesses. A king who does not protect, is insolent, proud and arrogant, and is also envious, is said to be one who is uncontrolled. When a king is struck by destiny and all the unprotected subjects are robbed by bandits, this is a sin devolving on the king. O Yudhishthira! If a task is performed with good advice, is based on good policy and is undertaken with enterprise, in accordance with the prescribed rites, that is not adharma. When something is undertaken, depending on destiny, it may, or may not, succeed. However, if there is enterprise, no sin touches the king.

'"O tiger among kings! A story is recounted about this. O king! This is an ancient account about rajarshi Hayagriva. He was brave and unblemished in his deeds. O Yudhishthira! Having killed many enemies in a battle, he was himself slain. The brave one was without any aides and was defeated. Having done all that could be done to restrain the enemy and having protected men, he resorted to the best of yoga. Having performed deeds in that excellent battle, he obtained fame. Vajigriva[180] now finds delight in the world of the gods. In the battle, he was mangled by assassins armed with weapons and attacked by bandits. But he was ready to give himself up. The great-souled Ashvagriva was devoted to his duties. He perfected his soul and finds delight in the world of the gods. The bow was his sacrificial stake. The bowstring was the rope. The arrow was

[178]The text uses the word *panya*, which is a commodity that is bought or sold. This might be *punya*, as it is in some non-Critical versions. In that case—the kingdom must be made pure.

[179]That is, an accomplished king.

[180]Hayagriva, Vajigriva and Ashvagriva mean the same thing. *Griva* is neck and *haya*, *vaji* and *ashva* mean horse.

the smaller ladle. The sword was the larger ladle. Blood was the clarified butter. The chariot, which could go anywhere at will, was the sacrificial altar. The battle was the fire. The best of horses were the four officiating priests. Having offered his enemies and himself as oblations into that sacrificial fire, the spirited lion among kings became free from all sins. Like taking a bath at the end of a sacrifice, he offered his life in the battle. Vajigriva finds delight in the world of the gods. Earlier, he protected the kingdom with intelligence and policy. The great-souled one performed sacrifices and then gave himself up. The spirited one pervaded all the worlds with his fame. Vajigriva finds delight in the world of the gods. He obtained divine and human success. He used the rod and protected the earth, resorting to yoga. That is the reason the great-souled king Hayagriva, who followed dharma in his conduct, finds delight in the world of heaven. He was learned. He renounced. He was faithful. He was grateful. Having performed deeds, he gave up the world of men. There are worlds for those who are intelligent, learned and revered. Having given up his body, the king obtained those. He acquired the Vedas well. He studied. The great-souled one protected the kingdom well. He established the four varnas in their own dharma. Vajigriva finds delight in the world of the gods. Having been victorious in battles, having protected the subjects, having drunk soma, having satisfied the best of brahmanas, having sustained the subjects with the use of the rod and having been destroyed in the battle, he delights in the world of the gods. His conduct was praiseworthy. Virtuous and learned men, themselves deserving honour, show him reverence. He conquered heaven and went to the world meant for heroes. The great-souled one, the performer of auspicious deeds, obtained success."'

Chapter 1354(26)

Vaishampayana said, 'On hearing Dvaipayana's words and on seeing that Dhananjaya was angry, Kounteya Yudhishthira took

Vyasa's permission and replied in these words. "Ruling over this kingdom and its many separate objects of desire do not please my mind now. The sorrow is making me tremble. O sage! On hearing the lamentations of the women who have lost their brave husbands and sons, I can find no peace." Having been thus addressed, Vyasa, supreme among those who know about yoga and knew about dharma, accomplished in the Vedas, spoke the following words in reply to the immensely wise Yudhishthira.

'"A man does not obtain anything through deeds or thought, or by giving anything.[181] Everything that a man obtains progressively in the course of time has been ordained by the creator in successive arrangements. If it is not time, man is incapable of obtaining anything in particular, even by studying learned texts. Even a fool is capable of obtaining riches. Time determines the success of acts. When it is a time of adversity, crafts, mantras and herbs yield no fruits. When the right time arrives and it is a time for prosperity, it is these which ensure success. It is because of time that winds blow swiftly. It is because of time that rain is generated in the clouds. It is because of time that waterbodies have lotuses in them. It is because of time that trees flourish in the forest. It is because of time that the night is dark and cool. It is because of time that the disc of the moon becomes full. When it is not time, there are no flowers or fruits in trees. When it is not time, rivers do not flow with force. When it is not time, birds, serpents, small animals, elephants and large predatory beasts on mountains do not become crazy.[182] When it is not time, women do not conceive. When it is not time, winter, summer and the monsoons do not arrive. When it is not time, one does not die, nor is one born. When it is not time, a child does not begin to speak. When it is not time, youth does not arrive. When it is not time, seeds do not sprout. When it is not time, the sun does not appear. When it is not time, it does not set behind Mount Asta. When it is not time, the moon does not wax and wane, nor do the large waves of the ocean ebb and rise.

'"O Yudhishthira! On this, there is an ancient history that is

[181]This is Vyasa speaking.

[182]This is certainly a reference to sexual desire.

recounted. In great grief, King Senajit sang a song.[183] All mortals are touched by this extremely difficult revolution. All men are ripened by time and die. O king! Some men kill others, and in turn, those men are slain by others. O king! This is the understanding of the worlds. But no one is killed and no one kills. Some think there are killers. Others think that there are no killers. The creation and destruction of beings is determined by their nature. When prosperity is destroyed and one's wife, son or father dies, one cries out in grief. One reflects on this sorrow and acts accordingly. O stupid one! Why do you sorrow? Why do you grieve, since you will also be grieved over? Consider the sorrow amidst all the sorrows and the fear amidst all fears. This body is not mine. Nothing in the earth is mine. He who realizes that what is mine also belongs to others is not confounded. There are thousands of reasons for sorrow and hundreds of reasons for joy. From one day to another, the foolish are submerged in this, but not the one who is learned. In the course of time, there are separate reasons for affection and aversion and beings are whirled around in unhappiness and in happiness. There is only unhappiness and no happiness. This is sometimes perceived. However, unhappiness results from desire and happiness results from unhappiness. There is unhappiness at the end of happiness and happiness at the end of unhappiness. One cannot obtain unhappiness all the time. Nor can one obtain happiness all the time. There is unhappiness at the end of happiness. There is happiness at the end of unhappiness. Therefore, anyone who desires eternal happiness should discard these opposite sentiments. When there is sorrow or torment, when one is senseless with grief, one must abandon the root of that grief, like severing a limb of the body. Whether it is happiness or unhappiness, whether it is pleasant or unpleasant, the one who is unvanquished in his heart will regard this as something that was bound to happen. If you do something that is only a little unpleasant towards your wives or your sons, you will know who, whose, why and how.[184] Those who are

[183]The song is being indirectly reported and is therefore not within quotes.

[184]The sense is that these relationships are driven by selfish motives and therefore, not permanent.

the greatest fools in this world and those who have obtained supreme intelligence are the ones who are in the midst of happiness. Suffering is for those who are in the middle. O Yudhishthira! This is what the immensely wise Senajit said. He knew about cause and effect in this world, about dharma and about happiness and unhappiness. He who delights in the sorrow of someone else will never be happy. There is no end to sorrows, since there is a succession of them. Happiness and unhappiness, existence and non-existence, gain and loss and death and life touch everyone on this earth in turn. One with fortitude is not delighted or angry at this. For a king, it is said that fighting and protection are like the consecration at a sacrifice, appropriate use of the rod is yoga, the renunciation of wealth is the dakshina in a sacrifice and complete knowledge is the purification. By governing the kingdom with intelligence and policy, by controlling selfishness in the soul, by performing sacrifices and by roaming through all the worlds as someone immersed in dharma, after casting aside a body, a great-souled one[185] finds delight in the world of the gods. Being victorious in battle, protecting the kingdom, drinking soma, making the subjects prosper, upholding subjects with the rod of chastisement and dying in a battle, he finds delight in the world of the gods. Having studied all the Vedas and the sacred texts, having protected the kingdom well and having established the four varnas in their own dharma, the king purifies his soul and finds delight in the world of the gods. When a king has ascended to heaven, if men, inhabitants of the city and the country and advisers bow down before his conduct, he is the best of kings."'

Chapter 1355(27)

'Yudhishthira said, "Abhimanyu was a child and was killed. So were the sons of Droupadi, Dhrishtadyumna and the two lords of the earth, Virata and Drupada. In the battle, so were

[185]A king.

Vasushena,[186] knowledgeable about dharma, King Dhrishtaketu and other kings who had come from many countries. I am unable to free myself from the sorrow of having caused the slaughter of my relatives. I am tormented. Because of my fierce greed for the kingdom, I have brought about the destruction of my own lineage. I played on Gangeya's[187] lap and rolled around there. Because of my greed for the kingdom, I have brought him down. I saw him whirled around by Partha's[188] arrows, trembling as if he had been struck by thunder, but glancing only towards Shikhandi. The tall grandfather, lion among men, was like an aged lion. When I saw him covered by sharp arrows, my mind was distressed. Because of the arrows, he fell down from his chariot. He sat down, facing the east, whirled around like a mountain. At that time, I was overcome by dejection. With a bow and arrows in his hand, Kouravya fought for many days with Bhargava, in a great battle in Kurukshetra.[189] For the sake of the maidens, in Varanasi, the brave son of the river had single-handedly fought a battle against the assembled kshatriya kings.[190] With the power of his weapons, he had scorched the unassailable king and emperor, Ugrayudha.[191] He has been brought down by me in the battle. He could himself decide on his time of death. Using his arrows, he did not bring down Panchala Shikhandi, but was brought down by Arjuna. O supreme among sages![192] When I saw him lying down on the ground, covered in blood, a terrible fever overcame me. As children, we were protected and reared by him. I was wicked and greedy for the kingdom. I have slain my senior. For the sake of a temporary kingdom, I have foolishly killed him.

[186]Karna.

[187]Bhishma's.

[188]Arjuna's.

[189]This duel between Bhishma (Kouravya) and Parashurama (Bhargava) has been described in Section 60 (Volume 6).

[190]Described in Section 60 (Volume 6). The son of the river is Bhishma and the maidens are Amba, Ambika and Ambalika.

[191]In the text here, Ugrayudha is a proper name. However, there was no warrior by this name. As an adjective, Ugrayudha may mean a warrior who was fierce in the use of weapons. But that adjective could apply to any warrior.

[192]Yudhishthira is addressing Vedavyasa.

'"The great archer, the preceptor, was worshipped by all the kings. I advanced against him in the battle and wickedly lied to him about his son.[193] My limbs burn because the preceptor told me, 'O king! Tell me truthfully whether my son is alive.' Expecting that I would speak the truth, the brahmana asked me. I lied, by hiding the fact that it was an elephant. Because of my extreme avarice for the kingdom, I was evil and caused the death of my preceptor. In the battle, I put a cloak on the truth. I told my preceptor, 'Ashvatthama has been killed,' though it was an elephant that had been brought down. Having perpetrated such a terrible deed, what worlds will I go to now?

'"Karna did not retreat from the battle and I caused him to be killed. He was my fierce elder brother. Who is more evil-acting than me?

'"Abhimanyu was a child. He was like a lion born in the mountains. In my greed, I made him penetrate the formation that was protected by Drona. I have been as guilty as one who kills a foetus. Since then, I have not been able to glance at Bibhatsu or Pundarikaksha Krishna. I feel extremely sorry for Droupadi. Her five sons have been killed. She is oppressed by grief and is like the earth when it has lost five mountains. I have my share in the sins. I am the destroyer of the earth. Seated here, I will dry up my body. Know that I am the slayer of my seniors. I will fast to death here, so that I am not reborn as a destroyer of the lineage.[194] I will not eat or drink anything. O one who is rich in austerities! Right here, I will dry up my beloved breath of life. Go wherever you wish and grant me this permission. I seek everyone's leave, so that I can cast aside this body."'

Vaishampayana said, 'Partha was distracted because of sorrow on account of his relatives. Vyasa, supreme among sages, restrained

[193]Yudhishthira lied to Drona that Ashvatthama had been killed. This has been described in Section 71 (Volume 7).

[194]Yudhishthira wishes to cleanse himself so that he does not carry forward the sin and be born as a destroyer of the lineage in a future birth. An alternative interpretation is also possible. He does not wish to be reborn as an inferior species, which would also imply a destruction of the lineage.

him and said, "O great king! You should not indulge in this excessive sorrow. O lord! I am telling you again that all this was destiny. The union and separation of living beings is certain. They are like bubbles in the water, which are there, and then are not there. Everything ends in destruction. They rise, accumulate and then fall. Union ends in dissolution. Death is the end of life. Laziness brings temporary happiness, but ends in sorrow. Industry may seem to lead to sorrow, but gives rise to happiness. Affluence, prosperity, modesty, fortitude and success are based on industriousness. Well-wishers do not ensure happiness. Ill-wishers do not ensure sorrow. Wisdom does not ensure artha. Nor is happiness ensured by wealth. O Kounteya! You have been created by the creator for tasks. Undertake them. O king! Success results from that. Otherwise, you will not have control over your atman."'

Chapter 1356(28)

Vaishampayana said, 'Vyasa dispelled the grief of the eldest son of Pandu, who was tormented by grief on account of his kin and wished to give up his life.

'Vyasa said, "In this connection, an ancient history is recounted. O tiger among men! O Yudhisthira! This is known as Ashma's song. Listen to it. King Janaka of Videha was overcome by sorrow, misery and doubt and asked a wise brahmana named Ashma.

'"Janaka asked, 'When relatives and riches come and go, how should a man who desires his own welfare behave?'

'"Ashma replied, 'As soon as the atman arises inside a man's body, all unhappiness and happiness are attached to it. Both of these are possible. But whichever of these he serves, overtakes his consciousness, just as the wind drives away clouds. "I have been born in a noble lineage. I am successful. I am not an ordinary man." His consciousness becomes sprinkled with these three kinds of sentiments. He becomes addicted to pleasures and gives up the wealth accumulated by his ancestors. When this is destroyed, he thinks that even stealing the property of others is good. He transgresses codes of honour and seizes what has not been given. Kings counter such greedy ones like animals with arrows. O king! Such men live for twenty years, or thirty years. They never attain one hundred years.[195] They are full of great misery. Using one's intelligence, one must glance here and there, at the conduct of all beings, and determine a medicine for them.[196] All mental sorrow is because of delusion of consciousness or the onset of a catastrophe. There is no third reason. The various kinds of sorrow a man faces is because of the external or the internal.[197] Old age and death are like two wolves that devour all beings, whether they are strong or weak, short or tall. There is no man who can escape from old age and death, even if it is someone who has conquered the earth, up to the frontiers of the ocean. Whether a being is confronted with happiness or unhappiness, all of it must be accepted and cannot be avoided. O lord of men! They must be faced in young age, middle age, or old age and cannot be avoided. But that which is wished for[198] never arrives. There is separation from that which is pleasant and association with that which is unpleasant. Following destiny, there is prosperity, adversity, happiness and unhappiness. The birth of beings, the giving up of their bodies, and gain and loss, have all been ordained. Smell, colour, taste and touch are naturally determined. Like that, happiness and unhappiness have been ordained. Depending on time, all beings observe sitting, lying down, going, getting up, drinking and eating. Physicians fall ill. The strong become extremely weak. They have women, or become eunuchs. Such is the wonderful progress of time. Birth in a noble lineage, valour, recovery from disease, patience, good fortune and pleasure—all of these are the result of destiny. Even if they do not wish to, the poor have many sons. Even if they wish for many and also try, the rich may have none. Disease, fire, water, weapons, hunger,

[195]The normal lifespan expected for a man.

[196]The king must find an antidote for these suffering subjects.

[197]A little bit of liberty has been taken in translating this shloka.

[198]Freedom from old age and death.

predatory beasts, poison, rope and fall from height—these can be the reasons for a being's death. One's departure is determined by destiny and one follows that reason. No one has been seen to cross it. Nor will anyone cross it. O lord of men! It is seen that a prosperous man may die when he is young, and though he is in misery, a poor person may live for one hundred years. A man who has nothing is seen to live for a long time. However, a person who has been born in a noble lineage is destroyed like an insect. O lord of men! In this world, it is often the case that a prosperous person does not have the capacity to eat anything. But a poor person is capable of digesting wood. Driven by destiny, an evil-acting person or one who is not content, convinces his soul that what he is doing is good and thinks, "I am the doer." Women, gambling with the dice, hunting, drinking and acts that are condemned by the wise—many extremely learned ones are seen to be addicted to various such vices. Because of the progress of time, whether they are desired or not desired, many things are seen to touch all beings. However, the cause is not comprehended. Wind, the sky, fire, the moon, the sun, day, night, the stars, the rivers, the mountains—who has created them and who supports them? O bull among men! Cold, heat and rain are brought about by the circling of time and happiness and unhappiness in men is like that. Herbs, learned texts, oblations and meditations cannot save a man who faces death or old age. Just as a log of wood touches another log of wood in the great ocean, beings approach one another, touch and then drift away. Some men are in the company of women, with singing and the playing of musical instruments. Others are without protectors and depend on others for food. Time acts equally towards both. In this cycle of life,[199] beings may have thousands of mothers and fathers and hundreds of sons and wives. But whom do they belong to? Whom do we belong to? No one belongs to a person. Nor does a person ever belong to anyone. Along the path, one meets large numbers of wives, relatives and well-wishers. Where was I? Where am I? Where am I going? Who am I? Why am I here? Who am I grieving for? Thinking in this way, one can pacify one's mind. One revolves in this cycle of

[199]Through the succession of births.

life, and the association with the ones one loves is temporary. The world hereafter has not been seen. Nor can it be seen. Learned ones know about it. One should not doubt the sacred texts, but be full of devotion. One must follow dharma in acts towards the ancestors and the gods. In accordance with the prescribed rites, the learned must perform sacrifices and follow the three goals.[200] This entire universe is submerged in the deep ocean of time. Old age and death are the giant sharks.[201] But there are few who understand this. There are many physicians who have studied ayurveda[202] and nothing else. Even they are seen to be afflicted by disease. They drink bitter and oily potions. However, they cannot cross death, like the giant ocean against the shoreline. There are chemists who are extremely accomplished in chemistry. They are seen to be shattered by old age, like trees shattered by great elephants. There are those who torment themselves through austerities, are engaged in studying, give generously and perform sacrifices. But even they cannot overcome old age and death. Once beings have been born, days, months, years, fortnights and nights cannot be rolled back. Man is powerless and his existence is uncertain. He must tread this extensive and certain path of time, followed by all beings. Irrespective of whether the soul exists independent of life or whether life exists independent of the soul,[203] we meet our wives and other relatives along the path. There never is any permanent association with anyone. There is none with one's own body. How can there be with anyone else? O king! Where is your father now? Where is your grandfather? They can't see you now. Nor can you see them. There is no man who can see heaven or hell. O king! The sacred texts are the eyes of the virtuous. Act accordingly. Act like a brahmachari. Then procreate and perform sacrifices. Without any malice, repay the debt to ancestors, gods and maharshis. He[204]

[200]Dharma, artha and kama.

[201]Alternatively, crocodiles.

[202]The science of health and medicine.

[203]We have translated this as soul. But this doesn't mean the atman. It means the *linga-sharira*, the subtle body made out of subtle elements, as opposed to the gross body.

[204]The king.

must perform sacrifices. He must procreate and generate offspring, after having practised brahmacharya first. He must divide himself into two.[205] He must worship heaven and this world. In this way, his heart will be freed from that which is false. The king who practises dharma and acquires objects in the proper way extends his fame in all the worlds, mobile and immobile, and keeps the wheel turning.'"

'Vyasa said, "The king of Videha understood all these words, which were full of reason. Having heard this, his intelligence became completely refined. He took Ashma's leave and, with his sorrow pacified, went towards his own house. O one without decay! In that way, free yourself from this grief. You are like Shakra. Arise in delight. You have won the earth through the dharma of kshatriyas. O son of Kunti! Enjoy and do not grieve."'

Chapter 1357(29)

Vaishampayana said, 'Kounteya Yudhishthira, Dharma's son, did not say anything. Pandava Gudakesha[206] addressed Hrishikesha. "Dharmaraja, the scorcher of enemies, is tormented by grief on account of his kin. O Madhava! He is immersed in an ocean of sorrow. Comfort him. O Janardana! All of us are now again faced with an uncertainty. O mighty-armed one! You should dispel this grief." Having been thus addressed by the great-souled Vijaya, the lotus-eyed Govinda Achyuta circumambulated the king. Since he was a child, Dharmaraja could never cross Keshava. He loved Govinda more than Arjuna. The mighty-armed one's[207] arms were smeared with sandalwood paste and were like stone pillars. Shouri seized them and delighted him with these words. His[208] face was beautiful and

[205]This is probably a reference to the son being regarded as the father reborn. Alternatively, it can be a division between brahmacharya and garhasthya.

[206]Arjuna.

[207]Yudhishthira's.

[208]Krishna's.

possessed excellent teeth, with lovely eyes. It was like a full-blown lotus when the sun had arisen. "O tiger among men! Do not indulge in this sorrow that dries up the body. Those who have been slain in the field of battle will not come back. They are like objects one sees in a dream. Once one awakes, they disappear. These kshatriyas have died in the great battle between kings. They did not turn their faces away from the battle. These ornaments of the battle were brave and have died. They did not turn their backs. Nor were they slain while running away. All of those brave ones fought and gave up their lives in the great battle. They were purified through weapons and have attained heaven. You should not sorrow about them.

'"An ancient history is recounted about this.[209] Srinjaya was overcome by sorrow on account of his son and Narada spoke to him. 'O Srinjaya! I, you, and all the subjects, have to face happiness and unhappiness. We have to roam around and can't be free from this. What is there to sorrow about? I will tell you about the deeds of supreme and immensely fortunate kings. Listen. O king! Your sorrow will be dispelled. Hear about these immensely fortunate kings who died. Listen, as I tell you about them in detail. On hearing, your sorrow will be dispelled.

'"'O Srinjaya![210] Hear about Marutta, the son of Avikshit. He died. The gods, with Indra and Varuna, with Brihaspati at the forefront, came to the sacrifice where the great-souled king offered everything. He wished to rival Shakra Shatakratu, the king of the gods. Wishing to ensure pleasure to Shakra, the learned Brihaspati refused to be the officiating priest at his[211] sacrifice. However, for the sake of spiting Brihaspati, Samvarta[212] agreed. O supreme among kings! When that virtuous king ruled, the earth yielded grain, even when it had not been ploughed and was radiant with garlands of holy sanctuaries.[213] At the sacrifice of Avikshit's son, the Vishvadevas

[209]This is Krishna speaking to Yudhishthira.

[210]This is Narada speaking now.

[211]Marutta's.

[212]Brihaspati's younger brother.

[213]*Chaitya*s or holy shrines. These were not necessarily temples.

were the courtiers, the Maruts were the attendants and the great-souled Sadhyas were also present. Large numbers of Maruts drank Marutta's soma. The gifts made surpassed those of gods, men and gandharvas.[214] O Srinjaya! He was four times as fortunate as you and more meritorious than your son. When he died, why are you grieving about your son?

'"'O Srinjaya! We have heard about Suhotra, the son of Vitithi. Maghavan[215] showered gold on him for an entire year. Having obtained him as a lord of men, Vasumati's name became appropriate.[216] When he was the lord of the countries, the rivers flowed with gold. When he was honoured by the worlds, Maghavan showered down tortoises, crabs, crocodiles, makaras and dolphins into the rivers. When he saw hundreds and thousands of fish, makaras and tortoises raining down, Vitithi's son was astounded. He collected the gold that was strewn around and, performing a sacrifice in Kurujangala, gave it all away to brahmanas at the sacrifice. O Srinjaya! He was four times as fortunate as you and more meritorious than your son. When he died, why are you grieving about your son, who did not give anything away, nor perform sacrifices? Be pacified and do not grieve.

'"'O Srinjaya! We have heard about Vrihadratha of Anga. He died, after giving away a million white horses. In the sacrifice that he performed, as donations, he gave away a million maidens with golden ornaments. As donations, he also gave away a million bulls with golden harnesses, followed by thousands of cows. When the king of Anga performed his sacrifice on Mount Vishnupada, Indra was intoxicated with soma and the brahmanas with the gifts. The Indra among kings performed hundreds of other sacrifices too. The gifts given surpassed that of gods, men and gandharvas. No other man has been born, or will be born, who has given away as much

[214]The gifts made by Marutta surpassed the collective gifts made by gods, men and gandharvas.

[215]Indra.

[216]Vasumati is the earth's name and means someone (something) that possesses riches. When Suhotra ruled, the earth was prosperous.

of wealth in the seven soma sacrifices.[217] O Srinjaya! He was four times as fortunate as you and more meritorious than your son. When he died, why are you grieving about your son?

'"'O Srinjaya! We have heard about Shibi, the son of Ushinara. Like a skin, he covered the entire earth. The earth resounded with the mighty roar of his chariot. On a single chariot, he brought the entire earth under a single umbrella.[218] At his sacrifice, Shibi, the son of Ushinara, gave away all the cattle, horses and wild animals that he possessed. O descendant of the Bharata lineage![219] Prajapati thought that amongst all the kings, from the past and from the future, there would be no one else who would be able to bear such a burden, other than rajarshi Shibi, the son of Ushinara. He surpassed Indra is his valour. O Srinjaya! He was four times as fortunate as you and more meritorious than your son. When he died, why are you grieving about your son, who did not give anything away, nor perform sacrifices? Be pacified and do not grieve.

'"'O Srinjaya! We have heard about Bharata, the son of Duhshanta and Shakuntala. He died. He was a great archer and possessed abundant riches and energy. Along the banks of the Yamuna, he tied thirty horses for the gods, twenty along the Sarasvati and fourteen along the banks of the Ganga. He performed one thousand horse sacrifices and one hundred royal sacrifices. Duhshanta's immensely energetic son, Bharata, performed these in earlier times. Among all the kings on earth, no one else could replicate Bharata's great deed, just as mortals cannot fly with the use of their arms. He tied down more than one thousand horses at sacrificial altars. Bharata gave away many treasures to Kanva.[220] O Srinjaya! He was four times as fortunate as you and more meritorious than your son. When he died, why are you grieving about your son?

[217]The seven sacrifices at which soma was offered were *agnishtoma, atyagnishtoma, ukthya, shodashi, vajapeya, atiratra* and *aptoryama*.

[218]That is, he conquered the entire earth and became its emperor.

[219]Within Narada's statement, this doesn't belong, since we haven't been told that King Srinjaya belonged to the Bharata lineage.

[220]When Duhshanta had deserted Shakuntala, the sage Kanva had given shelter to Shakuntala and Bharata.

'"'O Srinjaya! We have heard about Rama, Dasharatha's son. He too died. He was always compassionate towards the subjects, as if they were his own sons. In his kingdom, there were no widows, nor those without protectors. When he ruled over the kingdom, he was like a father to everyone. Rain showered down at the right time and the crops were succulent. When Rama ruled over the kingdom, there was always plenty of food. Beings did not drown in the water. Nor did fires burn unnecessarily. When Rama ruled over the kingdom, there was no fear from predatory beasts. When Rama ruled over the kingdom, the subjects lived for thousands of years and had thousands of sons. They were without disease and were successful in all their objectives. The women did not quarrel with each other, not to speak of men. When Rama ruled over the kingdom, the subjects always followed dharma. Without any calamity, the trees always bore flowers and fruit. When Rama ruled over the kingdom, each cow yielded a bucket of milk. The immensely ascetic one roamed around in the forest for fourteen years. He then performed ten horse sacrifices, at which a lot of gifts were given, with no bars on entry. He was dark and handsome, with red eyes. He was like a mad elephant in his valour. Rama ruled over the kingdom for ten thousand years. O Srinjaya! He was four times as fortunate as you and more meritorious than your son. When he died, why are you grieving about your son?

'"'O Srinjaya! We have heard about King Bhagiratha. He died. At his sacrifice, Indra drank soma and became extremely intoxicated. The illustrious chastiser of Paka, supreme among the gods, was invincible in the strength of his arms and defeated many thousands of asuras. In his sacrifice, he[221] gave away a million maidens, with ornaments of gold. Each maiden was on a chariot and each chariot was drawn by four horses. With each chariot, there were one hundred excellent elephants with golden harnesses. A thousand horses followed each elephant from the rear. A thousand cows followed each horse and there were one thousand goats and sheep behind each cow. When he dwelt in the

[221]Bhagiratha.

mountainous regions earlier, Ganga Bhagirathi was seated on his lap and came to be known as Urvashi.[222] Bhagiratha, descended from the Ikshvaku lineage, performed sacrifices at which a lot of donations were given. Ganga, with three flows,[223] agreed to become his daughter. O Srinjaya! He was four times as fortunate as you and more meritorious than your son. When he died, why are you grieving about your son?

'"'O Srinjaya! We have heard of Dilipa, the son of Ilavila. He died. The brahmanas recount his numerous deeds. In a great sacrifice, the lord of the earth willingly gave away the earth, with all its riches, to brahmanas. In each sacrifice that he performed, the officiating priest received one thousand golden elephants as a gift. For his sacrifices, there was a great and radiant sacrificial stake made out of gold. With Shakra as the foremost, the gods performed their tasks and sought refuge with him. The ring on top of the sacrificial stake was also made out of gold and six thousand divine gandharvas danced around it. In their midst, Vishvavasu[224] himself played the seven notes of the veena and every being there thought, "He is playing for me." No other king could replicate King Dilipa in this. Ornamented in gold, intoxicated women lay down on the road.[225] King Dilipa was truthful and fierce in wielding the bow. Any man who saw the great-souled one went to heaven. There were three sounds that never flagged in Dilipa's residence— the chant of studying, the twang of the bowstring and the words, "I give". O Srinjaya! He was four times as fortunate as you and more meritorious than your son. When he died, why are you grieving about your son?

'"'O Srinjaya! We have heard about Mandhata, Yuvanashva's son. He also died. The gods, the Maruts, extracted the foetus from

[222]Urvashi means someone who is seated on the thigh (lap). In an attempt to rescue his ancestors, who had been reduced to ashes by the sage Kapila, Bhagiratha performed austerities in the Himalayas and persuaded Ganga to descend from heaven.

[223]Ganga flows in heaven, the earth and the nether regions.

[224]Chief of the gandharvas.

[225]The kingdom was safe.

his father's flank.[226] The great-souled one developed in Yuvanashva's stomach, having earlier been generated from the water. The handsome king would later conquer the three worlds. On seeing him lying down on his father's lap, with the form of a god, the gods asked each other, "Who will suckle him?" Indra approached and said, "He will be suckled by me." Thus, Shatakratu gave him the name of Mandhata.[227] For the sake of sustaining the great-souled one, a stream of milk issued forth from Indra's hand, into the mouth of Yuvanashva's son. O king! He drunk from Indra's hand and grew and in twelve days, was like one who was twelve years old. In a single day, the entire earth came under the subjugation of that great-souled one. He had dharma in his soul and, in battle, was as brave as Indra. In battle, Mandhata defeated King Angara, Marutta, Asita, Gaya and Brihadratha from Anga. When Yuvanashva's son fought against Angara in the battle, the gods thought that the stretching of his bow was shattering the firmament. From where the sun rises to where it sets, all of that was said to be the field of Mandhata, Yuvanashva's son. He performed one hundred horse sacrifices and one hundred royal sacrifices. The lord of the earth gave brahmanas *rohita* fish made out of gold and each of these was ten yojanas long and one yojana wide.[228] What was left over was shared out among people who were not brahmanas. O Srinjaya! He was four times as fortunate as you and more meritorious than your son. When he died, why are you grieving about your son?

"'O Srinjaya! We have heard about Yayati, the son of Nahusha. He also died. He conquered the entire earth, with its oceans. O king! He travelled through the earth, throwing a *shami* stick[229] and performing a sacred sacrifice wherever the stick landed, thus dotting it with sacrificial altars. He performed one thousand sacrifices and

[226]Yuvanashva had no son and some sages gave him some consecrated clarified water, meant for his wife. Thirsty, Yuvanashva drank this by mistake and conceived.

[227]Etymologically, *mandhata* can be broken up as—he will suck me.

[228]The rohita fish is a kind of carp, *Cyprinus rohita (rohu)*. A yojana is a measure of distance, usually between 8 and 9 miles.

[229]Stick from the wood of a shami tree, a tree similar to the acacia.

one hundred horse sacrifices. He satisfied Indra of the gods with three mountains of gold. In the battle between the gods and the asuras, Yayati, son of Nahusha, slew daityas and danavas and divided up the entire earth. He abandoned his other sons, with Yadu and Druhyu as the foremost, and instated Puru in the kingdom.[230] With his wives, he then left for the forest. O Srinjaya! He was four times as fortunate as you and more meritorious than your son. When he died, why are you grieving about your son?

'"'O Srinjaya! We have heard about Ambarisha, the son of Nabagha. He died. O supreme among kings! The subjects chose him as their sacred protector. He attentively performed sacrifices and gave brahmanas a million kings who had themselves performed sacrifices. No one had ever performed a task like this earlier, nor will anyone do so in future. Thus did Ambarisha, the son of Nabagha, delight them with dakshina. A hundred thousand kings and another ten thousand kings followed him in his horse sacrifices and went along the southern path.[231] O Srinjaya! He was four times as fortunate as you and more meritorious than your son. When he died, why are you grieving about your son?

'"'O Srinjaya! We have heard about Shashabindu, the son of Chitrasena. He died. The great-souled one had one hundred thousand wives. Shashabindu had a million sons who were excellent archers. All of them were clad in golden armour. Each of those princes married one hundred maidens, who followed him. One hundred elephants followed each maiden and one hundred chariots followed each elephant. One hundred horses, born in the country and adorned with golden harnesses, followed each chariot. One hundred cows followed each horse and one hundred sheep and goats followed each cow. O great king! In a great horse sacrifice, Shashabindu instructed that all these riches should be given away to brahmanas. O Srinjaya! He

[230]Yayati had five sons—Yadu, Turvasu, Druhyu, Anu and Puru. Puru was the youngest. When Yayati became old, and was still addicted to worldly pleasures, he asked his sons to temporarily accept his old age and give him their young age. Since all except Puru refused, they were disinherited and Puru succeeded Yayati.

[231]After dying, they went the way of their ancestors.

was four times as fortunate as you and more meritorious than your son. When he died, why are you grieving about your son?

'"'O Srinjaya! We have heard about Gaya, the son of Amurtarayas. He died. For one hundred years, that king subsisted on what was left over from oblations. Agni wished to give him a boon. Gaya said, "O bearer of oblations! Through your favours, grant me the boons that even when I give, my riches are inexhaustible, my faith in dharma grows and my mind delights in the truth." We have heard that he obtained all these wishes from the fire god. Whenever it was the new moon, whenever it was the full moon and at each interval of four months, the immensely energetic one repeatedly performed sacrifices and this continued for one thousand years. For a thousand years, when he awoke in the morning, he gave away a hundred thousand cows and ten thousand horses. The bull among men satisfied the gods with soma, the brahmanas with riches, the ancestors with *svadha*[232]and his wives with sensual pleasures. He covered a part of the earth with gold. This was ten cubits wide and twenty cubits long, and in a great horse sacrifice the king gave this away as dakshina. O king! O bull among men! Gaya, the son of Amurtarayas, gave away as many cows as there are grains of sand in the Ganga. O Srinjaya! He was four times as fortunate as you and more meritorious than your son. When he died, why are you grieving about your son?

'"'O Srinjaya! We have heard about Rantideva, the son of Sankriti. He died. The immensely illustrious one satisfied Shakra properly and obtained a boon from him. "Let us have an abundance of food and guests. Let my faith never diminish and let me never have to ask anything from anyone."[233] The illustrious Rantideva was extremely rigid in his vows and of their own accord, domestic and wild animals presented themselves before the great-souled one, so as to be sacrificed. Because of the discharge from this mass of hides, a great river was created and this great river became famous as Charmanvati.[234] When the king singled out brahmanas and proceeded to give them one golden

[232]Exclamation made when the ancestors are offered oblations.

[233]This is the boon Rantideva asked for.

[234]The Chambal. *Charma* means hide or skin and Charmanvati is something that has hides or skins.

coin each, they protested. So he gave each brahmana one thousand. There were vessels and implements used in the intelligent Rantideva's sacrifices—pots, plates, frying pans, bowls and cups. There was not a single one that was not made out of gold. Whenever someone spent a night in the house of Rantideva, the son of Sankriti, twenty thousand and one hundred cows were sacrificed. But even then, adorned in bejewelled and excellent earrings, the cooks exclaimed, "There is plenty of broth. Take as much as you want. But now, there is no longer as much meat as there used to be earlier."[235] O Srinjaya! He was four times as fortunate as you and more meritorious than your son. When he died, why are you grieving about your son?

'"'O Srinjaya! We have heard about the great-souled Sagara. He died. The tiger among men was descended from the Ikshvaku lineage and was superhuman in his valour. Sixty thousand sons followed him at the rear. They were like a large number of stellar bodies in a sky without clouds and at the end of the rain, surrounding the lord of the stars.[236] In earlier times, the earth bowed down before him and was under a single umbrella.[237] He satisfied the gods with one thousand horse sacrifices. He gave deserving brahmanas palaces that were completely made out of gold, with golden pillars. They were full of beds and women with eyes like lotuses. The brahmanas got whatever they desired, superior and inferior, and on his instructions, divided this up among themselves. Because of his anger, the earth was dug out and came to be marked with the ocean.[238] It is after his name that the ocean came to be known as Saagara. O Srinjaya! He was four times as fortunate as you and more meritorious than your son. When he died, why are you grieving about your son?

'"'O Srinjaya! We have heard about King Prithu, the son of Vena.[239] He died. The maharshis consecrated him in the great

[235]This is a reflection of the number of guests who were entertained.

[236]The moon.

[237]That is, Sagara was a universal emperor.

[238]Searching for the horse used at the horse sacrifice, which was stolen by Indra, Sagara's sons dug up the earth. The ocean is known as *saagara*, named after Sagara.

[239]Vena was a wicked king and the earth suffered. The sages killed Vena and created Prithu from Vena's dead body. The word Prithu is derived from a

forest. He was known as Prithu because he would extend the world. Someone who saves from injuries is said to be a kshatriya.[240] On seeing Prithu, the son of Vena, the subjects said, "We are attached to him." Because of that affection, he came to known as a raja.[241] The earth yielded crops without being ploughed. There was honey in every hole.[242] When Vena's son ruled, all the cows yielded a bucket of milk. All the men were without disease, were successful in all their objectives and were free from fear. As they wished, they dwelt in their fields or their homes. On his instructions, the waters of the ocean were solidified.[243] The rivers did not swell up and obstruct the advance of his standard. In a great horse sacrifice, the king gave brahmanas twenty-one mountains of gold and each of these was three *nala*s high.[244] O Srinjaya! He was four times as fortunate as you and more meritorious than your son. When he died, why are you grieving about your son? O Srinjaya! Why are you reflecting in silence? O king! You have not listened to my words. If you have not listened, my discourse, though spoken well, has been in vain, like medicine to someone who is about to die.'

'"Srinjaya replied, 'O Narada! I have listened to your words. They are wonderful in their purport, like a fragrant garland. Those rajarshis were great-souled and meritorious in their deeds. Their deeds are enough to dispel my grief. O maharshi! Your discourse has not been in vain. O Narada! Your sight alone has been sufficient to drive away my sorrow. O one who speaks about the brahman! I have listened to your words. However, like one drinking amrita, I am not satisfied. O one whose sight never fails! O lord! I am tormented on

root that means extending or spreading. Prithu was so named because he would extend the earth and the earth (*prithivi*) is named after Prithu.

[240]Literally, a kshatriya is someone who saves from injury (*kshata*). Prithu was thus a kshatriya.

[241]Raja means king. Here, *raja* is etymologically being derived from the word *raga* (affection) or the allied raja (affection).

[242]Of a tree.

[243]This might mean that Prithu fixed the boundaries between the ocean and the land.

[244]A nala is a measure of distance, equal to six feet.

account of my son. Through your favours, let the dead one come back to life. Through your favours, let me be united with my son.'

'"Narada replied, 'Your beloved son, Svarnashthivi, was given to you by Parvata[245] and has departed. But I will give your son back to you. Hiranyanabha[246] will live for one thousand years.'"'

Chapter 1358(30)

'Yudhishthira asked, "How did Srinjaya's son become Kanchanashthivi?[247] Why did Parvata give him? How did he die? At that time, men used to live for one thousand years. Why did Srinjaya's son die while he was still a child? Was he Suvarnashthivi only in name? I wish to know the truth about Kanchanashthivi."

'Vasudeva replied, "O lord of men! I will tell you the details about what actually happened. The rishis Narada and Parvata were worshipped by the worlds. They were maternal uncle and nephew.[248] Once they came down from the world of the gods. The lords, the maternal uncle Narada and the nephew Parvata, cheerfully roamed around in the world of men in those ancient times, discarding food in the form of sacrificial oblations and the food of the gods. Though they possessed powers of asceticism, they wandered around on the surface of the earth. They roamed around here and there, eating the food of humans. They were cheerful and had an agreement. 'Whatever resolution either one of us has, good or bad, will be revealed to the other. If either one fails to do this and falsifies the agreement, he will be cursed.' The maharshis, worshipped in the

[245]The sage Parvata.

[246]Another name for Svarnashthivi. We have interpreted Hiranyanabha as a proper noun rather than as an adjective, meaning one with a golden navel.

[247]Both *kanchana* and *svarna* mean gold, so Svarnashthivi is the same as Kanchanashthivi. Both words mean someone with golden excreta. Suvarnashthivi has the same meaning.

[248]Narada was the maternal uncle and Parvata was his sister's son.

worlds, pledged this. They went to King Srinjaya, the son of Shvitya, and said, 'O child! For the sake of your welfare, we will dwell with you for some time. O protector of the earth! Attend to our needs.' The king acted accordingly and honoured them with hospitality. After some time, in great delight, the king told the great-souled ones who had arrived, 'This is my beautiful daughter and I have only one. She will tend to your needs. Her limbs are lovely and she is virtuous in her conduct. This maiden is known as Sukumari and her complexion is like the filament of a lotus.' Thus addressed, they agreed and the king instructed his daughter. 'Tend to these brahmanas as if they are gods, or your father.' The maiden followed dharma and, instructed by her father, agreed. As instructed by the king, she served them well.

'"While she served them in this way, because of her unmatched beauty, there was a swift and violent urge of desire in Narada. That desire increased in the great-souled one's heart, just as the moon slowly waxes during the bright lunar fortnight. Though he knew about dharma, he was greatly ashamed of his desire and did not tell his great-souled nephew, Parvata. Because of his ascetic powers and through signs, Parvata got to know. Enraged, he severely cursed Narada, who was overcome by desire. 'You voluntarily had an agreement with me. Should there be any resolution in our hearts, good or bad, that would be disclosed to the other. You have falsified that. O brahmana! Those were your words and you are bound by them. Earlier, you did not tell me that you had this desire for the maiden Sukumari. Because of that sin, I will curse you. You are knowledgeable about the brahman. You are my senior. You are an ascetic. You are a brahmana. Despite that, you have falsified the agreement you made with me. In great rage, I am cursing you. Listen to my words. There is no doubt that Sukumari will be your wife. O lord! However, from the time you marry, your own form will be distorted. The maiden, and all other men, will see you as an ape.' As soon as Narada got to know the words spoken by Parvata, he became enraged. The maternal uncle cursed the nephew, 'You possess asceticism. You are a brahmachari. You possess truth and self-control. You are always united with dharma. Despite this, you will not dwell in heaven.' Extremely enraged, those two rishis severely cursed each other. They rushed towards each other, like two angry and excellent elephants.

'"The great sage, Parvata, roamed around the entire earth. O descendant of the Bharata lineage! He was honoured because of his energy. Narada, supreme among those who followed dharma, obtained the unblemished Sukumari, Srinjaya's daughter, in accordance with the rites of dharma. Because of the curse, as soon as the mantras connected with receiving her hand were pronounced, the maiden beheld that Narada had assumed the form of an ape. Despite the devarshi having assumed the form of an ape, Sukumari did not disrespect him. She treated him affectionately. She presented herself to her husband and did not go to anyone else, not even in her mind. Faithful to her husband, she did not wish that a god, another sage or a yaksha should be her husband.

'"After some time, the illustrious Parvata was roaming around in the forest and saw Narada there. Greeting Narada, Parvata said, 'O lord! Show me your favours and let me go to heaven.' Narada saw that Parvata was standing miserably before him, hands joined in salutation. But he was even more distressed and said, 'You are the one who cursed me first and said that I would be an ape. When you spoke to me in this way, I later cursed you in revenge, to the effect that henceforth, you would never dwell in heaven. Since you were like my son, you should not have acted in that way.' The sages then withdrew their curses from each other.

'"Sukumari saw Narada in his prosperity, in a form that was like that of a god. Taking him to be someone else's husband, she fled. On seeing that the unblemished one was running away, Parvata spoke to her. 'This is your husband. You should not doubt that. This is the illustrious lord and rishi Narada, with supreme dharma in his soul. There is no doubt that his heart is completely yours.' The great-souled Parvata entreated her in many ways. When she heard that her husband had been tainted because of the curse, she regained her natural state. Parvata went to heaven and Narada went home. The great rishi, Narada, was a witness to all this himself. O supreme among men! Ask him and he will tell you exactly what happened."'

Chapter 1359(31)

Vaishampayana said, 'At this, the king, Pandu's son, addressed Narada. "O illustrious one! I wish to hear how Suvarnashthivi was born." Having been thus addressed by Dharmaraja, the sage Narada told him the exact truth about Suvarnashthivi. "O great king! It was just as Keshava told you. Since you have asked me, I will tell you about the part that remains. I and the great sage Parvata, my sister's son, went to Srinjaya, supreme among victorious ones, wishing to dwell with him. He honoured us with all the indicated rites. With all our wishes well tended to, we lived in his house. After many years had passed, it was time for us to leave. At that time, Parvata spoke these words to me and they were of grave import. 'We have lived in the house of this Indra among men and have been greatly honoured. O brahmana! Now that the time of residing here is over, we should think about what is appropriate.' O king! At this, I spoke to the handsome Parvata. 'O lord! O nephew! In every respect, this is worthy of you. The king should be delighted with boons and let him obtain what he desires. If you so think fit, let him obtain success through our austerities.' At this, Parvata, bull among sages, summoned the handsome Srinjaya and told him what we had decided. 'O king! We are delighted with the great hospitality you have sincerely offered us. O best among men! With our permission, think of a boon that you desire. However, let it not cause injury to the gods or destruction to men. O great king! It is our view that you are worthy of respect and accept this from us.' Srinjaya replied, 'If you are pleased with me, that is sufficient for me. That is a great fruit and it has been my supreme gain.' When the king repeated this again, Parvata said, 'O king! Ask for a desire that has been in your heart for a long time.' Srinjaya answered, 'I desire a brave son, one who is full of valour and is firm in his vows. He should be immensely fortunate and have a long life. He should be like the king of the gods in his resplendence.' Parvata said, 'This desire of yours will come true. However, he will not live for a long time, since there is a desire in your heart that he should surpass the prosperity of the king of the gods. He will be Suvarnashthivi, since his excreta will be golden. He will be like the king of the gods in his radiance. But protect him from the king of the gods."

'"Narada said, 'On hearing the great-souled Parvata's words, Srinjaya said, 'Through your favours, let it not be that way. O sage! Through your powers of austerities, let my son have a long life.' However, because of his partiality for Indra, Parvata said nothing. The king was miserable and I spoke to him again. 'O great king! When it is time to remember me, think of me and I will show myself to you. When your beloved son has come under the subjugation of the king of the dead, I will give him back to you. O lord of the earth! Do not sorrow. I will again give him back to you in that form.'[249] Having addressed the king thus, we departed, as we desired. As he wished, Srinjaya also entered his own palace.

'"After some time had passed, rajarshi Srinjaya had a son born to him. He was immensely valorous and blazed in his energy. As time passed, he grew, like a giant lotus in a pond. He became Kanchanashthivi, and not just in name.[250] O supreme among the Kuru lineage! This extraordinary fact came to be known throughout the world. Indra of the gods got to know this was because of the boon granted by the great-souled ones.[251] The slayer of Bala and Vritra was frightened[252] and, listening to the counsel of Brihaspati, sought a weakness in the child. He instructed his divine weapon vajra, which appeared in a personified form. 'O lord! Become a tiger. Go and slay the prince. O vajra! Parvata gave Srinjaya his son and if he grows up, he may surpass me in valour.' Having been thus addressed by Shakra, the vajra, the vanquisher of enemy cities, was always near the child, looking for a weakness. Having obtained a son who was the equal of the king of the gods in radiance, Srinjaya was delighted. The king, and all the women belonging to his inner quarters, began to reside in the forest. One day, on the banks of the

[249]That is, alive.

[250]That is, his excreta were golden.

[251]Narada and Parvata.

[252]At the prospect that the child might overthrow him.

Bhagirathi, the child was running around near that mountainous stream.[253] His nurse was the only other person with him. Though the child was only five years old, he was like a king of elephants in his valour. The immensely strong one suddenly ran into the tiger. The king's son trembled as he was crushed. He lost his life and fell down on the ground. The nurse screamed. As soon as the prince had been killed, through the maya of the king of the gods, the tiger instantly disappeared.

'"Hearing the screams and weeping of the extremely distressed nurse, the king himself rushed to the spot. He saw the child lying down dead, covered in blood, and was distressed. It was as if the moon had been dislodged. He raised the mangled torso of his son, covered in blood, on his lap and wept in great grief. His mothers[254] also rushed to the spot where King Srinjaya was. Afflicted by grief, they also wept. At that time, with an attentive mind, the king remembered me.[255] Knowing that he had thought of me, I went and showed myself to him. He was stricken with grief. O lord of the earth! Therefore, I made him hear the words that the brave one from the Yadu lineage has told you about.[256] With Vasava's permission, he was revived by me. It was destiny and it could not have been otherwise. After this, the child, the immensely famous Svarnashthivi, arose. The valiant one delighted the hearts of his father and his mother. When his father went to heaven, the lord ruled the kingdom for one thousand and one hundred years. He was terrible in his valour. He performed many great sacrifices at which large quantities of donations were given. The immensely radiant one satisfied the gods and the ancestors. He generated many sons who were the extenders of the lineage. O king! After a long period, he succumbed to the dharma of time.[257] O Indra among kings! Just as Keshava and the immensely ascetic Vyasa have told you, you must stem this sorrow that has been generated in

[253]The Ganga (Bhagirathi) was a mountainous stream there.

[254]The king had more than one wife.

[255]This is Narada speaking.

[256]The stories of the kings, described in Chapter 1356(29).

[257]That is, he died.

you. Bear the burden of the kingdom that belonged to your father and grandfather. Perform great and auspicious sacrifices and obtain the worlds that are desired."'

Chapter 1360(32)

Vaishampayana said, 'King Yudhishthira was still silent and immersed in grief. The ascetic Krishna Dvaipayana, who knew about the true nature of dharma, spoke to him. "O one with eyes like a blue lotus! The dharma of kings is to protect subjects. Dharma is the standard used to measure people. One must always follow dharma. O king! Follow in the footsteps of your father and grandfather. The eternal dharma of brahmanas has been determined in the Vedas. O bull among the Bharata lineage! That has been the eternal measuring rod, and the dharma of kshatriyas is to protect all this and any man who acts against this must be punished with the use of arms, since this is against the path indicated for the worlds.[258] In one's confusion, one should not take the measuring rod to be something that is not the measuring rod. Whether it is a servant, a son or an ascetic—all those who act in a wicked way must be punished, even killed. If a king does not act in this way, he will commit a sin, since one who does not prevent dharma from being destroyed is guilty of slaying dharma. They[259] were the slayers of dharma and you have killed them and their followers. O Pandava! You were stationed in your own dharma. Why are you sorrowing? According to dharma, the king must kill such people, donate and protect the subjects."

'Yudhishthira said, "O one rich in austerities! I do not doubt your words. O one who is supreme among all those who uphold dharma! Dharma is always in front of you. For the sake of the kingdom, I

[258]Kshatriyas must protect everyone in the pursuit of dharma and punish those who are against dharma.

[259]The Kouravas.

have slain many who should not have been killed. O brahmana! Those deeds are burning and tormenting me."

'Vyasa replied, "O descendant of the Bharata lineage! The doer may be the Lord, or it may be man. Or, as the learned texts say, the fruits in this world may be the consequence of past deeds. O king! If man performs good and evil deeds because he has been so appointed by the Lord, then the fruits also accrue to the Lord. If a man uses an axe to cut down a tree in the forest, the cause can never be the axe, nor does sin accrue to it. The implement cannot take over the fruits of that action. There is no sin if a man uses a weapon to inflict punishment. O Kounteya! One cannot reap the fruits of something that has been done by others.[260] Therefore, vest it on the Lord. Or perhaps it is the case that a man is the doer of both good and bad deeds. In that case, there is nothing like the hereafter. In that case, perform a good deed.[261] O king! There is no one who can act against destiny. There is no sin if a man uses a weapon to inflict punishment. O king! If you think that the world is established on past deeds, then there cannot have been an inauspicious deed, nor will there be. In this world, if it is necessary to assign good and bad deeds, then the king's upraised rod of punishment is the determining factor in this world.[262] O descendant of the Bharata lineage! It is my view that in this world, people are whirled around, performing good and bad deeds and reaping the fruits. This is the truth and I am instructing you to perform good deeds because the fruits from deeds are certain. O tiger among kings! Therefore, abandon this fruitless sorrow in your heart. O descendant of the Bharata lineage! Resort to your own dharma, even if that brings censure. O king! This abandoning of your soul is not proper. O Kounteya! There are rites of atonement

[260]The ones who committed the sin warranting punishment.

[261]There is no hereafter and no birth after death. Therefore, one might as well perform the good deed of ruling the kingdom. The three possibilities of deeds being done by the Lord, man or past deeds are being disposed of.

[262]This is a different line of argument. If everything is based on past deeds, there are no good and bad deeds. Hence, if a classification of good and bad deeds is required, the only one who can do that is the king.

that have been laid down.[263] One must perform them while one has this body. Without the body, one will not succeed.[264] O king! Therefore, while you are still alive, perform those rites of atonement. O descendant of the Bharata lineage! If you do not perform rites of atonement, you will be tormented after death."'

Chapter 1361(33)

'Yudhishthira said, "O grandfather! Because of my greed for the kingdom, sons, grandsons, brothers, fathers, fathers-in-law, preceptors, maternal uncles, grandfathers, great-souled kshatriyas, kin, well-wishers, friends, relatives and many kings who had assembled from many countries have been slain. O grandfather! They have been killed by me alone. O one rich in austerities! Those lords of the earth were always established in dharma. They performed good deeds and drank soma. Having caused such people to be killed, what will I obtain? Thinking repeatedly about this, I am incessantly being burnt. Those kings were prosperous and like lions. The earth is without them now. O grandfather! On seeing this terrible slaughter of relatives, the slaying of hundreds of the enemy and other men in crores, I am being tormented. What will be the plight of those beautiful women? They have been deprived of their sons, husbands and brothers. They are wan and distressed and are falling down on the surface of the ground. They are censuring us, the Pandavas and the Vrishnis, as the perpetrators of terrible deeds. On seeing their fathers, brothers, husbands and sons, all those women are ready to give up their beloved lives and go to Yama's eternal abode. O best among brahmanas! They are driven by affection. I have no doubt about this. It is evident that because of the subtlety of dharma, we will become the slayers of women. We committed an eternal sin by killing

[263] *Prayaschitta.*

[264] If there have been evil deeds, it is better to atone for them in this life, instead of carrying forward the fruits to the next life.

our well-wishers. We will be cast into hell, with our heads hanging downwards. O supreme one! We will perform terrible austerities and free ourselves of our bodies. O grandfather! In particular, tell me about the state of life I should resort to now."'

Chapter 1362(34)

Vaishampayana said, 'On hearing Yudhishthira's words, the intelligent and accomplished rishi, Dvaipayana, thought for some time and then spoke to Pandava. "O king! Remember the dharma of kshatriyas and do not sorrow pointlessly. O bull among the kshatriya lineage! While following their own dharma, those kshatriyas were slain. They desired complete prosperity and great fame on earth. They followed the rules of death and, following time, were killed. They were not killed by you, Bhima, Arjuna, or the twins. Following the dharma of time, those living beings gave up their lives. Time has no mother or father, nor is it partial towards anyone. It is a witness to the deeds committed by people. O bull among men! This[265] is an instrument of time. In its form as lord, it uses beings to slay other beings. Know that time is the essence of deeds and is witness to the good and the bad. Time leads to happiness and unhappiness. Time is the one that yields the fruits. O mighty-armed one! Think of the deeds they[266] performed. Those led to their destruction and they have come under the subjugation of time. Know your own self and the rules and vows that you observe, and also that these deeds have been ordained by fate. An implement constructed by an artisan is under the control of the one who handles it. In that way, the universe is driven by deeds that are controlled by time. On seeing that the birth and destruction of men have no evident cause, sorrow and delight are both pointless. O king! However, your heart has been ensnared by

[265]The destruction in the war.

[266]The ones who have been killed.

that which is unreal. Because of that, perform deeds of atonement. O Partha! It has been heard that, in ancient times, the gods and the asuras fought with each other. The asuras were elder brothers and the gods were younger.[267] Because of rivalry over prosperity, they fought a great battle that lasted for thirty-two thousand years. The earth became a large ocean of blood. At that time, the gods killed the daityas and obtained possession of heaven. The brahmanas, knowledgeable about the Vedas, obtained the earth. However, because they were confounded by insolence, they began to help the danavas. O descendant of the Bharata lineage! They were known in the three worlds as shalavrikas.[268] There were eighty-eight thousand of them and they were killed by the gods. Those who destroy dharma, and those who seek the spread of adharma, should be killed, just as the evil-souled daityas were killed by the gods. If by killing a single person the rest of the lineage becomes virtuous and healthy, or if by killing a family the kingdom is saved, then that must be done. O lord of men! Sometimes, dharma has the appearance of adharma. Learned people should know that dharma may assume the form of adharma. O Pandava! Therefore, control yourself. You are learned. O descendant of the Bharata lineage! You have followed a path that has been travelled by the gods. O bull among the Bharata lineage! People like these do not go to hell. O scorcher of enemies! Assure your brothers and well-wishers. A person who begins wicked acts and does not think about it, and, despite continuing to act in this way, does not feel any shame, then it has been said that all the sins accrue to him. There is no atonement for him. Nor are his wicked deeds ever diminished. You have been born in a pure lineage. Your deeds have been caused by someone else's crimes. You performed those tasks unwillingly. Having performed them, you are repenting. As atonement, a great horse sacrifice is indicated. O great king! Perform that and you will be cleansed of your sin. Having defeated his enemies with the help of the Maruts, Maghavan, the chastiser of

[267]The gods and the demons were descended from the sage Kashyapa, but had different mothers.

[268]The brahmanas who helped the demons. Literally, shala means jackal and vrika means wolf.

Paka, performed one hundred sacrifices one by one and came to be known as Shatakratu.[269] He purified himself and won heaven. He obtained worlds that yield happiness. Surrounded by large numbers of the Maruts, Shakra was radiant and illuminated the directions. Shachi's consort is glorified in heaven by the apsaras. The lord of the gods is worshipped by the rishis and the gods. You have conquered this earth through your valour. O unblemished one! The kings have been defeated through your valour. O king! Surrounded by your well-wishers, go to their cities and kingdoms[270] and instate their brothers, sons and grandsons in their respective kingdoms. Assure the children who are still in the wombs. Delight all the citizens and rule the earth. Where there is no male child, instate a maiden. As a class, women are addicted to desire and will laugh away their sorrow. O descendant of the Bharata lineage! In this way, assure all the kingdoms. Perform a horse sacrifice, just as the victorious Indra did in ancient times. O bull among the kshatriyas! You should not sorrow about those great-souled kshatriyas. Their destruction has been brought on by their own deeds and they have been confounded by the power of death. You have practised the dharma of kshatriyas and have obtained a kingdom that is free from taint. O Kounteya! Follow dharma and after death, you will obtain the best."'

Chapter 1363(35)

'Yudhishthira asked, "After what action does a man need to perform rites of atonement? O grandfather! What must be done to free oneself? Tell me that."

'Vyasa replied, "Having not done deeds that must be performed, having done what is forbidden and having acted in a false way, a man must perform rites of atonement. O Kounteya! A brahmachari

[269]Indra's name is Shatakratu, *shata* meaning one hundred and *kratu* meaning sacrifice.

[270]The kingdoms of the kings who have been slain.

who is asleep when the sun rises, one who goes to sleep before the sun sets, one with malformed nails, one with discoloured teeth, one whose younger brother gets married first, one who marries before his elder brother, one who maligns the brahman, one who is guilty of slander, one who is the husband of a *didhishu*, one whose first wife is a didhishu,[271] one who has violated his vow of chastity, one who kills a brahmana, one who teaches the brahman to an undeserving person, one who does not teach the brahman to a deserving person, one who performs a sacrifice for ordinary people, one who sells the king,[272] one who slays a shudra or a woman, one whose ancestors were contemptible, one who slays an animal without a good reason,[273] one who sets fire to a forest, one who subsists through deceit, one who goes against his preceptor, one who abandons the sacred fire, one who sells the brahman[274] and one who violates an agreement—all of these are sinners.[275] O descendant of the Bharata lineage! Listen attentively as I tell you about deeds that must not be done. Abandoning one's own dharma, following the dharma of another, officiating at the sacrifice of someone who is not entitled to sacrifice, eating something that should not be eaten, abandoning those who have sought refuge, not supporting servants, selling liquor,[276] the killing of inferior species,[277] not performing tasks that one is capable of undertaking, not giving the gifts that must be given every day, not giving dakshina to brahmanas and humiliating them—those who know about dharma say that these are deeds that must not be done. A son who quarrels with his father, one who has

[271]The word didhishu has different meanings—a widow who has remarried, a woman who has married twice, or an elder sister who marries before the younger sister.

[272]Probably meaning a traitor.

[273]A good reason being a sacrifice.

[274]That is, one who sells knowledge.

[275]These are sins that require atonement.

[276]The text uses the word *rasa*. This has multiple meanings, such as salt, juice and spices. Other than liquor, it is not obvious why the selling of any of these other items should be regarded as a sin.

[277]Birds and animals, that is, killing them unnecessarily.

intercourse with his preceptor's wife and one who does not procreate according to dharma—these are people who follow adharma. These are deeds that should not be done and men must perform atonement for them. However, even when men perform these deeds, there are some situations when they are not tainted. If a brahmana who knows about the Vedas picks up a weapon and attacks you in a battle, wishing to kill you, then you are allowed to kill him. O Kounteya! On this, there is a mantra in the Vedas. This is dharma, as proved by the Vedas, and I am telling you this. 'If a brahmana has deviated from his conduct and attacks like an assassin, killing him does not amount to the sin of killing a brahmana. This is said to be rage countering rage.' If a person drinks liquor in ignorance, or because he has been instructed that this will save his life,[278] he should thereafter be brought back to dharma through purification. O Kounteya! I have also told you everything about what should be eaten and what should not be eaten. For all this, purification through rites of atonement is prescribed.

'"A man incurs no sin if intercourse with the preceptor's wife is for the sake of the preceptor. Through a disciple, Uddalaka had Shvetaketu as a son.[279] If one steals for the sake of imparting prosperity to one's preceptor, one is not bound down. That happens if one steals a lot because of desire, or if it is for one's own sake. If one takes from those who are not brahmanas, there is no sin and one is not touched by the crime, as long as it is not for one's own self. Lying is allowed provided it is for the sake of saving one's own life or that of someone else, for the sake of one's preceptor, when it is among women and in connection with a marriage. A vow is not broken if semen is released through a wet dream. Offering oblations into a blazing fire are prescribed as atonement. If the elder brother has become an outcast or has renounced the world, there is no sin from marrying before him. When someone else's wife solicits you,

[278]Presumably by a physician.

[279]Shvetaketu was Uddalaka's son and their stories figure in the Upanishads, particularly Chandogya Upanishad. However, this bit about Shvetaketu being born to Uddalaka through a disciple is not mentioned elsewhere.

there is no taint or adharma from indulging her. One should never kill an animal without good reason or cause such an act to be done. Animals deserve kindness and a violation requires due purification. If one gives to an undeserving brahmana in ignorance, there is no sin, nor if one gives to an undeserving person or does not give to a deserving person, provided there is a reason for this. There is no crime in casting off a wife who is of bad conduct.[280] If such a woman is purified, the husband is not to be blamed. There is no crime in selling soma if one knows the truth about it.[281] If an incompetent servant is discarded, there is no crime. There is no crime if a forest is burnt for the sake of cattle.[282] I have told you about deeds that do not lead to sin when they are done. O descendant of the Bharata lineage! I will now tell you in detail about rites of atonement."'

Chapter 1364(36)[283]

'Vyasa said, "O descendant of the Bharata lineage! Through austerities, deeds and donations, a man is purified, as long as he does not commit wicked deeds again. A person who has killed a brahmana can free himself of the crime of killing a brahmana by eating once a day, roaming around for alms, performing all his tasks himself, holding a skull in one hand and a bedpost in the other,[284] following brahmacharya, by always being enterprising, showing no malice, sleeping on the bare ground and disclosing his deed to

[280]Implicitly, a wife who is adulterous.

[281]That is, it should really be used in sacrifices to the gods.

[282]To create pastureland.

[283]This chapter is about atonement and there are several places where the shlokas are cryptic and not clear. Some liberties have therefore been taken with the text and there is some subjectivity.

[284]A skull and khattanga (bedpost) being held as rod or staff are the signs of mendicancy. The broken bed is symbolic of the giving up of the bed and the comforts of a household.

the worlds. He has to do this for a full twelve years. If he lives on a diet of hardship, a man who kills a brahmana can be purified in six years.[285] If he eats from one month to another, he is freed in three years. If he eats only once a month, there is no doubt that he is freed in one year. O king! If one does not eat at all, one is freed very soon. There is no doubt that one is purified through a horse sacrifice. In this way, there are men who have bathed after a horse sacrifice. There are supreme learned texts which say that all their souls have been cleansed. If one is killed in a battle for the sake of a brahmana, one is freed from the sin of killing a brahmana. If the slayer of a brahmana gives one hundred thousand cows to deserving recipients, he is freed from all sin. If one gives away twenty-five thousand milk-yielding brown cows, one is freed from all sin. At the time of death, if one gives one thousand milk-yielding cows with calves to virtuous and poor people, one is freed from sin. O protector of the earth! If one gives away one hundred horses from Kamboja to self-restrained brahmanas, one is freed from sin. O descendant of the Bharata lineage! If someone gives something that another person wishes for and does not brag about his generosity, he is freed from sin.

'"When a brahmana has drunk liquor, if he drinks that liquor when it is as hot as fire, he purifies himself in this world and the next. Or he can fling himself down from Mount Meru, or enter a fire, or embark on the great journey.[286] He will then be freed from all sin. However, a brahmana who has drunk liquor can again be admitted into an assembly of brahmanas, provided he follows the injunctions of Brihaspati laid down in texts concerning brahmanas.

[285]The translation doesn't capture the nature of the hardship (*krichchha*) diet. In this kind of practice, one only eats in the morning for three days, only in the evening for the next three days, nothing that is not obtained through begging in the next three days and fasts for three more days. This cycle of twelve days continues and one is purified in six years. If this cycle is modified by replacing a seven-day span in odd-numbered months and an eight-day span in even-numbered months, one is purified in three years.

[286]The great journey (*mahaprasthana*) is death. The suggestion is of killing oneself.

O king! If a man who has drunk liquor casts off envy and gives away land, without indulging in that act again, he is cleansed and purified.

'"If one has had intercourse with a preceptor's wife, one should lie down on a heated slab of stone. Alternatively, one should cast one's eyes upwards and roam around, holding one's penis in one's hand.

'"By giving up the body, one is freed from all wicked deeds. If women endeavour to be restrained for a year, they are freed from such deeds. If one observes a great vow, gives away everything that he owns, or is slain in a battle for the sake of a preceptor, one is freed from all wicked deeds. If one acts falsely towards a preceptor or opposes him, one is freed from that crime by giving him something agreeable.[287] If one has deviated from a vow of chastity, one should follow the atonement vows prescribed for a killer of a brahmana. Alternatively, one can wear the hide of a donkey for six months. One will then be freed from that crime. A person who has abducted another person's wife or stolen another person's possessions must observe a vow for one year to be freed from that sin. If a person has stolen the property of another, he must use every means possible to return riches that are of an equal measure. He will then be freed from that sin. O descendant of the Bharata lineage! A younger brother who has married before the elder brother, or an elder brother whose younger brother has married before him, are both naturally freed by eating the hardship diet for twelve nights, or at least for ten. But, to save the ancestors, he[288] must get married. The wife[289] is not tainted by this and no blemish attaches to her. Those who know about dharma say that, after giving birth and after a period, women are cleansed and purified through a *chaturmasya* vow. When there is suspicion about a woman's wicked conduct, it is known that there should be no sexual intercourse with her. However, she is purified through her menstrual flow, like a vessel with ashes.

'"The four parts of dharma are decreed for brahmanas. For kings, it has been ordained that dharma will be reduced by one quarter. The

[287]By giving the preceptor an agreeable gift.
[288]The elder brother.
[289]Of the younger brother.

vaishya's will be a quarter less than that and the shudra's a quarter less than that too. In this way, one determines the seriousness or lightness of the crime and the atonement.

'"If a person kills a bird or an animal, or cuts down a large number of trees, that man should only subsist on air for three nights and proclaim his crime. O king! If a person has intercourse with someone he should not have intercourse with, the atonement has been laid down. For six months, he should sleep in wet clothes and lie down on ashes. These are the decrees laid down in the brahmana texts,[290] explaining all the deeds, the forms of atonement and the detailed reasons. If one recites the *savitri* mantra[291] in a secluded place, while eating little, abjuring violence and hate and speaking little, one is freed from all sin. During the day, one must be under the open sky and during the night, one must also sleep there. Thrice during the day and thrice during the night, one must immerse oneself in the water, wearing one's garments. A brahmana who is observing this vow must not speak to women, shudras and those who have become outcasts because of deviation in their conduct. He will then be freed from any sins that he may have committed in ignorance.

'"The witness to a being[292] obtains good and bad fruits after death. Depending on which of the two[293] is more, the doer reaps the consequences. Donations, austerities and deeds lead to auspicious fruits. In that way, they increase and become greater than wicked deeds. If wicked deeds have been performed, that is a reason to perform auspicious ones. By constantly giving away riches, one is freed from sin. The rites of atonement are in proportion to the wicked deed. However, no atonement is recommended for a *mahapataka*.[294]

[290]The brahmana texts associated with the Vedas.

[291]Another name for the *gayatri* mantra.

[292]The atman.

[293]Good and bad deeds.

[294]A great sin is *pataka* or mahapataka, while a minor sin is *upapataka*. While it is agreed that there are five great or major sins, the listing of those sins varies. But something like killing a brahmana or having intercourse with a preceptor's wife would figure in all such lists.

O king! Eating what should not be eaten and speaking what should not be spoken—for these, atonement depends on whether these are done knowingly or unknowingly. Crimes that are knowingly committed are said to be grievous. Those that are unknowingly committed are light and there is atonement for both. The methods and rites described are capable of cleansing the sin. But those recommendations are for the believers and the faithful. Those rites are never seen to be for men who are non-believers, and unfaithful and those who are prone to insolence and wickedness. O supreme among those who uphold dharma! Good conduct is the dharma of the virtuous. O tiger among men! For the sake of happiness after death, they must serve this. O king! Because of the motives behind your earlier crimes, you will be freed. You wished to save by killing them. Alternatively, you were following the duty of kings. However, if you abhor what you did, follow the path of atonement. Like those who are not aryas, you will then not confront destruction because of your deeds."'

Chapter 1365(37)

Vaishampayana said, 'Having been thus addressed by the illustrious one, Dharmaraja Yudhishthira thought for some time. He then asked that store of austerities, "What should be eaten and what should not be eaten? What is said to be a praiseworthy gift? Who is a deserving person and who is an undeserving one? O grandfather! Tell me that."

'Vyasa replied, "In this connection, an ancient history is recounted. This is a conversation that took place between the Siddhas and Prajapati Manu. The Siddhas were engaged in supreme austerities and vows. In ancient times, they approached the brave lord and Prajapati while he was seated, and asked him about dharma. 'What food should be eaten? What gifts should be given? How should we study? What austerities will we observe? What should be done and what should not be done? O Prajapati! Tell us everything about this.' Having been thus addressed, the illustrious Svayambhuva Manu spoke.

"'"'Listen to me as I expound the true nature of dharma, briefly and in detail.[295] The signs of dharma are: not taking what has not been given, donations, studying, austerities, non-violence, truthfulness, lack of anger and forgiveness. However, if practised in the wrong place and at the wrong time, dharma may become adharma. It has been said that in some situations, not giving, lying and violence are dharma. Those who are learned know that there are two aspects to both dharma and adharma. People who are learned know that there can be both action and withdrawal from action. Inaction leads to immortality and the fruits of action are mortality.[296] One knows that evil acts lead to evil and good acts to the good. This determines whether acts are good or bad, whether they lead to heaven, whether they lead to one's union with heaven, whether they lead to life, or whether they lead to death. However, even if one did not think about it before committing the act, there may be good consequences from an evil act. On considering the consequences, they may have led to uplifting life on earth. But if an act is undertaken without thinking about it, atonement is recommended. If acts are undertaken in anger or out of delusion, without considering the consequences or the reasons, if they lead to torment of the body, or cause pleasant and unpleasant sensations in the mind, then they must be pacified through atonement, like using herbs and mantras. One must also entirely ignore dharma that concerns *jati*, [297] *shreni*, [298] *adhivasa* [299] and family. These are not dharma, because there is no real dharma in them. [300] There may be doubts about what constitutes dharma. In such cases, whatever ten people who know about the sacred Vedas,

[295]This is Manu speaking.

[296]Death and rebirth, immortality meaning freedom from this cycle.

[297]Class or ethnic group.

[298]Guild or association.

[299]Settlement.

[300]The focus is thus on individual dharma, as opposed to dharma of groups or collectives.

or three people who read about dharma, describe as acts that should be done, constitute dharma.

'"'Red earth, red ants, the *shleshmataka*[301] and poison must not be consumed by brahmanas. Brahmanas must also not eat fish that are without scales, frogs and four-footed aquatic animals, with the exception of turtles. Vultures, swans, eagles, *chakravakas*,[302] herons, ducks, curlews, diver-birds, vultures,[303] crows, owls, all predatory birds, all quadrupeds with horns and all quadrupeds that have two teeth or four teeth must not be eaten by brahmanas. Nor must they drink the milk of sheep, mares, she-donkeys, she-camels, cows that have just calved, women and deer. Food offered to a dead man, food cooked by a woman who has just given birth within the last ten days and food cooked by someone unknown must not be eaten. Until ten days have passed, the milk of a cow that has just given birth must not be drunk. One must not eat food given by a carpenter, a person who strips off animal skins, a whore, a washerman, a physician and a guard. Nor should one eat food given by a person who has been thrown out of the village assembly, one who earns a living through dancing girls, a man whose younger brother has married before him, a eunuch, a professional bard and a skilled gambler. One must avoid food given to a prisoner, putrid and stale food, that which has been laced with alcohol, that which has been partly eaten by others and leftover food. Cakes stuffed with meat, sugar cane and vegetables, rice cooked with milk and sugar[304] when it has gone bad, coarsely ground meal, grain and food that has been kept for a long time should not be eaten. Rice cooked with milk and sugar, dishes made of sesamum and grain[305] and meat and cakes that have been prepared unnecessarily[306] should not be eaten. They should not be eaten by brahmanas who are in

[301]Fruit like a plum, *Cordia myxa*.

[302]The brahminy duck.

[303]Two different kinds of vultures are mentioned, *bhasa* and *gridhra*.

[304]*Payasa*.

[305]*Krisara*.

[306]Without a sacrifice in mind.

the householder stage. A householder must eat after worshipping the gods, the ancestors, men, sages and other household gods. A brahmana who dwells in his own household is like a mendicant who is wandering around. If he conducts himself in this way, with his beloved wife, he will obtain the benefits of dharma.

'"'One must not donate for the sake of praise. Or give out of fear, or as a mark of favour to the recipient. One who follows dharma does not give to a person who earns a living through singing and dancing, a jester, a person who is intoxicated or mad, a thief, a physician, one who cannot speak, one who has a pale complexion, one who doesn't have a limb, a dwarf, a wicked person, one born in an inferior lineage and one who has not followed the sacraments. Giving to a brahmana who does not know about the Vedas, or does not know about the brahman, is a dead gift. An inappropriate gift and an inappropriate recipient bring bad consequences to both the giver and the recipient. A man who tries to cross the ocean with the support of a branch of a *khadira* tree[307] or a stone sinks. The giver and the recipient sink in that way. When wood is wet, it does not blaze. An inferior recipient, without austerities, studies and character, is like that. Water in a skull and milk in the bladder of a dog become unclean because of the receptacle. To a man without good conduct, learning is like that. One without mantras, one without vows and one without knowledge of the sacred texts, may be without malice and distressed. One may give to him out of compassion. But even out of compassion, one should give to a distressed person who causes injury. There are brahmanas who have deviated from dharma. One should not give to them, thinking that this is dharma, or that their behaviour is good. This is fruitless. The receptacle is tainted and there is no need to reflect on this. A brahmana who has not studied, an elephant made out wood and a deer made out of skin are similar. All three have nothing but their names. A eunuch has no fruit with a woman. A cow has no fruit with another cow. A brahmana without mantras is like that and is like a bird without wings. Giving to him is futile, since he is like a village that has no granary, like a well that

[307]Acacia.

has no water and like oblations made where there is no fire. He destroys offerings and oblations made to the gods and the ancestors. He is like a stupid enemy who robs one of one's riches. He does not deserve to obtain any worlds.'

'"O Yudhishthira![308] This is the exact truth and it has been recounted to you, as it was said. O bull among the Bharata lineage! This is a great and extensive discourse and deserves to be heard."'

Chapter 1366(38)

'Yudhishthira said, "O illustrious one! O great sage! O best among brahmanas! I wish to hear in detail about the dharma of kings and everything about that for the four varnas. What is the policy decreed for a king in times of distress? While resorting to the path of dharma, how can one conquer the earth? This discourse about atonement and about what should be eaten and what should not be eaten has satisfied my curiosity and has engendered great delight in me. Following dharma and ruling the kingdom are always opposed to each other. That is the reason I am confused and am thinking about it all the time."'

Vaishampayana said, 'The immensely energetic Vyasa, supreme among eloquent ones, who knew everything that was ancient, glanced towards Narada and spoke to him.[309] "O Yudhishthira! O mighty-armed one! If you wish to hear everything about dharma, go to Bhishma, the aged grandfather of the Kurus. He will dispel all the doubts that you have about the secrets. He is Bhagirathi's[310] son and knows everything, everything about all forms of dharma. The river which has three flows, the celestial goddess, gave birth

[308]This is Vyasa speaking again.

[309]That is, spoke to Yudhishthira.

[310]Ganga's.

to him. He has seen all the gods, with Shakra at the forefront, in person. O king! The lord has honoured the devarshis, with Brihaspati at the forefront, and having satisfied them, has studied policy.[311] Ushanas,[312] the brahmana who was the preceptor of the gods and the asuras, knew the sacred texts. All those, with their commentaries, were obtained by that supreme one among the Kuru lineage. In addition, the immensely intelligent one received the large corpus of the Vedangas from Bhargava Chyavana and Vasishtha, who was careful in his vows. In ancient times, he studied the truth about transcendental paths from Kumara, the eldest son of the grandfather, who blazed in his energy.[313] He obtained everything about the dharma followed by ascetics from the mouth of Markandeya himself. O bull among the Bharata lineage! He obtained weapons from Rama[314] and Shakra. Though he has been born as a man, the time of his death depends on his own wishes. Though the virtuous one has no offspring, it has been heard that he will obtain the sacred worlds in heaven. The sacred brahmarshis are always his courtiers. There is no knowledge that deserves to be known that is unknown to him. He is learned about dharma and the true subtleties of dharma and artha. He will tell you. Before the one who knows about dharma gives up his life, go to him." The immensely radiant one, Vyasa, far-sighted in his wisdom, spoke these words.

'Kounteya spoke these words to Satyavati's son, supreme among eloquent ones. "I have created a great carnage among kin and it makes the body hair stand up. I have caused injury to everyone and I am the cause behind the destruction of the earth. He fought fairly and I brought him down through deceit. Therefore, what grounds do I have to question him?" Desiring the welfare of the four varnas, the mighty-armed and immensely radiant one, foremost among the

[311]Studied policy under Brihaspati.

[312]Shukracharya, the preceptor of the demons.

[313]The grandfather is Brahma and his eldest son (born through his mental powers) was Sanatkumara. We have translated *adhyatma* as transcendental.

[314]Parashurama.

Yadu lineage,[315] again spoke to the best of kings. "It is not appropriate that you should be tied down so much through grief now. O supreme among kings! Act in accordance with what the illustrious Vyasa has said. O mighty-armed one! These brahmanas and your immensely energetic brothers are waiting before you, like those afflicted by the summer season wait for the rains. O great king! All the kings who remain and the four varnas from your kingdom of Kurujangala have assembled here. O scorcher of enemies! O slayer of enemies! For the sake of bringing pleasure to the great-souled brahmanas, instructed by the infinitely energetic Vyasa, your senior, for the sake of the distressed well-wishers, us and Droupadi, do what brings us pleasure. Do what ensures the welfare of the worlds." Having been thus addressed by Krishna, the king, with eyes like blue lotuses, arose for the sake of the welfare of the immensely ascetic ones in the world. The tiger among men had been requested by Vishtarashrava[316] himself, Dvaipayana, Devasthana[317] and Jishnu. There were many others who had also entreated him. The great-minded Yudhishthira abandoned the distress in his mind and the torment. He was accomplished in learning and knowing what should be learnt. He was learned in his words and a store of learning. The descendant of the Pandu lineage obtained peace in his mind.

'The king was surrounded by them, like the moon by the nakshatras. With Dhritarashtra at the forefront, he proceeded to enter his own city. Having decided this, the one who knew about dharma, Kunti's son Yudhishthira, worshipped the gods and thousands of brahmanas. He ascended a new and sparkling chariot that was covered with blankets and hides. It was yoked to sixteen white bullocks that were marked with auspicious signs. The maharshis praised and honoured him with sacred mantras. It was as if the moon god had ascended his immortal chariot. Kounteya Bhima, terrible in his valour, grasped the reins. Arjuna held aloft

[315]Krishna.

[316]Literally, the one whom the entire world has heard of. That is, Krishna.

[317]A sage.

a radiant and white umbrella. As that white umbrella was held aloft his head, it looked like a white cloud in the sky and was as resplendent as the king of the stars.[318] Madri's brave sons grasped two whisks to fan him with and these were white, like the rays of the moon. Ornamented, the five brothers ascended the chariot. O king! They looked as if the five elements had gathered together. O king! Yuyutsu followed the eldest of the Pandavas at the rear. He was on a white chariot, yoked to extremely swift horses. With Satyaki, Krishna followed the Kurus. He was on a golden and sparkling chariot, to which, Sainya and Sugriva were yoked.[319] O descendant of the Bharata lineage! With Gandhari, Partha's eldest father[320] advanced ahead of Dharmaraja, on a palanquin borne by men. With Vidura at the forefront, all the Kuru women, with Kunti and Krishna Droupadi advanced on various vehicles, superior and inferior. There were many chariots, ornamented elephants, foot soldiers and those on horses who followed them at the rear. As the king advanced towards the city of Nagasahvya,[321] he was praised with sweet chants by bards, minstrels and raconteurs. The advance of that mighty-armed one was unmatched on earth. There were delighted and healthy people, who created a tumult of rejoicing. As Partha advanced, the men, the residents of the city, decorated the city and the royal road appropriately. There were white garlands, flags and banners. The royal road was made fragrant with incense. The king's palace was full of fragrant powders, scents, many flowers, *priyangu* creepers and garlands. New and firm pots filled with water were placed at the gates of the city. Here and there, there were beautiful maidens and goats. In this way, with his well-wishers, the descendant of the Pandu lineage entered the city through the decorated gate. He was praised through auspicious words.'

[318]The moon.

[319]The names of Krishna's horses.

[320]Dhritarashtra.

[321]Hastinapura.

Chapter 1367(39)

Vaishampayana said, 'When the Parthas entered, the people, the residents of the city, wished to see them and assembled in many thousands. The royal road and the squares were decorated and beautiful. O king! It was like the giant ocean swelling when the moon rises. The large houses along the royal road were bejewelled. O descendant of the Bharata lineage! Full of women, they seemed to tremble at the weight. Because they were bashful, they softly praised Yudhishthira, Bhimasena, Arjuna and the two Pandavas who were Madri's sons. "O Panchali! You are blessed and fortunate, since you serve those best among men, like Goutami tending to the maharshis.[322] O beautiful one! You have followed your vows and your deeds have not been fruitless." O great king! At that time, the women praised Krishna[323] thus. O descendant of the Bharata lineage! Because of the delighted sounds of these words of praise, the city resounded. Having been thus addressed, Yudhishthira passed through the royal road and arrived at the ornamented and radiant royal palace. All the ordinary people, the residents of the city and of the countryside, came there from different sides and spoke words that were pleasant to the ear. "O Indra among kings! O destroyer of enemies! It is through good fortune that you have defeated the enemy. It is through good fortune that you have regained the kingdom, through dharma and strength. O great king! May you rule over the kingdom for one hundred autumns. O king! Protect the subjects through dharma, as Indra does over the thirty gods." At the gates of the royal residence, he was worshipped in this auspicious way. In every direction, he received benedictions from the affectionate brahmanas. The king entered the palace, which was like the residence of the king of the gods. Hearing those victorious sounds, he descended from his chariot.

[322]Goutami means Ahalya, the sage Goutama's wife. There was a drought and there was no food. Because of a boon, Ahalya had plenty of food and tended to the suffering maharshis.

[323]Krishnaa, Droupadi.

'Entering inside, he approached the prosperous gods[324] and worshipped all of them with jewels and fragrant garlands. The prosperous and immensely illustrious one again emerged. He saw the handsome brahmanas who presented themselves. He was surrounded by those brahmanas, who wished to pronounce benedictions over him. He was as resplendent as the sparkling moon, surrounded by a large number of stars. In the prescribed fashion, Kounteya honoured the brahmanas. O Indra among kings! With the preceptor Dhoumya[325] and his eldest father[326] at the forefront, he cheerfully worshipped them with sweets, jewels, large quantities of gold, cattle, garments and many other objects that they desired. O descendant of the Bharata lineage! Auspicious sounds arose and reached up to the sky. These auspicious sounds were pleasant to hear and generated delight among the well-wishers. O king! The brahmanas were learned in the Vedas and their chants resounded like the noise made by swans. It was as if Bharati could be heard there, with meanings, lines and syllables.[327] There was the roar of drums and the beautiful sound of conch shells. O king! Those sounds were heard and proclaimed the news of victory.

'When the brahmanas there became quiet again, the rakshasa Charvaka, disguising himself as a brahmana, spoke to the king.[328] He was a friend of Duryodhana's and was in the form of a mendicant. He was a *samkhya*.[329] He had a tuft of hair on his head.

[324]Clearly referring to some kind of temple inside the palace.

[325]The family priest of the Pandavas.

[326]Dhritarashtra.

[327]The use of the word Bharati causes a problem of interpretation. In a straightforward way, Bharati is nothing but speech personified, especially Sanskrit speech. Meaning is artha, a line or quarter of a shloka is *pada* and syllable is an akshara. But does Bharati mean a reference to the goddess Sarasvati, especially since swans have been mentioned? This is possible, but not necessarily true.

[328]There was a passing reference to Charvaka in Section 77 (Volume 7). There was a famous Charvaka, the founder of a materialist and atheist school of philosophy. This is not the famous Charvaka. The word *charvaka* means someone who is beautiful in speech.

[329]A specific type of mendicant, not to be confused with the samkhya school of philosophy.

He held triple staff in his hand.[330] He was proud and without any fear. He was surrounded by all those brahmanas, who wished to pronounce their benedictions. O Indra among kings! There were thousands of others who had immersed themselves in austerities and rituals. Without taking their permission, the evil and wicked one censured the great-souled Pandavas and spoke to the king. "All these brahmanas have asked me to speak on their behalf. O wicked king! Shame on you. You have slain your kin. O Kounteya! Having caused the destruction of kin, what will you gain from the kingdom? Having slain your elders, it is better to be dead than to be alive." On hearing the terrible words of the rakshasa, the brahmanas were distressed. Afflicted by those words, they roared. O lord of the earth! Together with King Yudhishthira, all the brahmanas were ashamed and greatly anxious and then fell silent. Yudhishthira replied, "I am bowing down before you. Show me your favours. You should not reprimand me. I have just recovered from a catastrophe." O king! O lord of the earth! All the brahmanas shouted, "O king! These are not our words. May you be prosperous." Those brahmanas were learned in the Vedas and had cleansed themselves through austerities. Through the sight of their wisdom, they recognized him.[331] The brahmanas said, "This is Duryodhana's friend and a rakshasa named Charvaka. In the form of a mendicant, he is trying to ensure his welfare.[332] O one with dharma in your soul! We have not spoken in that way. Do not have any fear on that account. Let good fortune wait on you and your brothers." Senseless with anger, all the brahmanas shouted.[333] They were pure and by censuring the wicked rakshasa, killed him. He was burnt and brought down by the energy of the ones who knew about the brahman. It was like the shoots of a tree charred by the great Indra's vajra. Having been honoured, the

[330]A rod with three staffs tied together is the mark of a mendicant.

[331]They saw through Charvaka's disguise.

[332]Though Duryodhana is dead, trying to ensure Duryodhana's welfare by maligning Yudhishthira.

[333]The word used in the text is *humkara*. This means to utter the sound *hum*.

brahmanas congratulated the king and departed. With his well-wishers, the Pandava king was delighted.

'Vasudeva said, "O father![334] In this world, brahmanas have always been revered by me. They are like gods roaming around on earth. They have poison in their speech, but are also easy to please. O father! In ancient times, in krita yuga, there was a rakshasa named Charvaka. O mighty-armed one! For many years, he tormented himself through austerities in Badari.[335] O descendant of the Bharata lineage! Brahma repeatedly offered him boons and he opted for the boon that he should have nothing to fear from all beings. The lord of the universe granted him the supreme boon of fearlessness from all beings, as long as he did not disrespect brahmanas. Having obtained the boon, the rakshasa, immensely strong, terrible in his deeds and infinitely valorous, began to oppress the gods. The gods united and told Brahma, 'His strength is unnatural. Ensure the rakshasa's death.' O descendant of the Bharata lineage! He told the gods, 'I have already thought of a means, so that he confronts his death soon. O king![336] He will be a friend to a king named Duryodhana. Because he will be bound down by affection towards him,[337] he will insult brahmanas. The brahmanas will be incensed at the injury he causes brahmanas. Through the strength of their speech, they will destroy the wicked one and he will perish.' The rakshasa has been killed by the curse of brahmanas and is lying down. O best among kings! O bull among the Bharata lineage! Do not sorrow over Charvaka. O king! Know that all of them have been slain because of the dharma of kshatriyas. Those bulls among kshatriyas were brave and great-souled and have gone to heaven. O one without decay! You must now do what is good. You should not show weakness. Kill the enemy. Protect the subjects. Sustain the brahmanas."'

[334]The word used is tata. This means father, but is affectionately used towards anyone who is older or senior. Yudhishthira was older than Krishna.

[335]Badarikashrama.

[336]Since this is within Brahma's quote, it doesn't belong.

[337]Towards Duryodhana.

Chapter 1368(40)

Vaishampayana said, 'The king who was Kunti's son was freed from his fever. Cheerfully, he sat down on a supreme and golden seat, facing the east. Satyaki and Vasudeva, the scorchers of enemies, were seated on a seat facing him and it was strewn with expensive coverings. With the king between them, the great-souled Bhima and Arjuna were seated on soft seats decorated with gems. Pritha, with Nakula and Sahadeva, was seated on a sparkling seat that was made out of ivory and decorated with gold. Sudharma,[338] Vidura, Dhoumya and Kourava Dhritarashtra were seated on separate seats and seemed to blaze. Yuyutsu, Sanjaya and the illustrious Gandhari sat down where King Dhritarashtra was seated.

'Seated there, with dharma in his soul, the king[339] cheerfully touched the white flowers, the *svastika* signs, the unhusked grain, the ground, gold, silver and jewels. With the priest at the forefront,[340] all the ordinary people came to see Dharmaraja. They brought many auspicious objects with them—earth, gold, many kinds of gems and all the other vessels and equipment required for the consecration. There were full pots that were made out of clay, gold, copper and silver. They were filled with water, parched grain, sacrificial grass and milk. There was kindling of shami, *palasha* and *pumnaga*.[341] There was honey and clarified butter. There were ladles made out of *udumbara*[342] and gold-embellished conch shells. With Dasharha's[343] permission, the priest Dhoumya marked out an auspicious altar that sloped towards the north and the east. The great-souled one and Krishna, Drupada's daughter,

[338]The priest of the Kouravas.

[339]Yudhishthira.

[340]There is a minor inconsistency. This priest can only be Dhoumya and he is seated.

[341]Names of trees.

[342]The sacred fig tree.

[343]Krishna's.

were made to sit on a soft *sarvatobhadra*[344] seat with sturdy legs, covered with the skins of tigers. It was as radiant as the fire. The intelligent one[345] poured oblations into the fire. Pronouncing mantras, he sprinkled water on Yudhishthira, Kunti's son, instating him as the lord of the earth. So did rajarshi Dhritarashtra and all the ordinary people. Cymbals, small drums and kettledrums were sounded. Following dharma, Dharmaraja received all this. He then honoured the brahmanas, who pronounced benedictions on him, in the proper way and gave away large quantities of donations and one thousand golden coins. These brahmanas were accomplished in studying the Vedas and of good conduct. They were delighted and wished the king well. Making sounds like those of swans, they praised Yudhishthira. "O Yudhishthira! O mighty-armed one! O Pandava! It is through good fortune that you have been victorious. O immensely radiant one! It is good fortune that you have obtained this through your own dharma and valour. O king! It is through good fortune that the wielder of Gandiva, Pandava Bhimasena, you and the Pandavas who are Madri's sons are well. You have slain the enemy and have escaped from a battle that has been destructive of heroes. O Pandava! Swiftly do the tasks that must be undertaken next." Dharmaraja Yudhishthira was thus honoured by those virtuous ones. O descendant of the Bharata lineage! With his well-wishers, he received that large kingdom.'

Chapter 1369(41)

Vaishampayana said, 'Having heard the words of the subjects, appropriate to the time and the place, King Yudhishthira

[344]Literally, a seat that is fortunate or auspicious in all directions. This can also be interpreted as a seat that is symmetric in all directions, such as circular, or even in the form of a square.

[345]Dhoumya.

replied to them. "The sons of Pandu are fortunate in this world. The assembled bulls among brahmanas have praised their qualities, whether they possess them or not. It is my view that you have certainly shown us a favour. Without any selfishness, you have spoken about the qualities that we possess. However, the great king, Dhritarashtra, is our father and our supreme god. If you wish to ensure what brings me pleasure, ensure his pleasure and remain under his rule. Having caused a great destruction of the kin, I live for him alone. Constantly and attentively, my duty is to serve him. O well-wishers! If you wish to show your favours towards me, then you should behave towards Dhritarashtra as you used to do earlier. He is the lord of the universe and mine too. The entire earth belongs to him and so do all the Pandavas. In your minds, you should always remember these words I have spoken. Taking the permission of the king, go wherever you wish to." The residents of the city and the countryside took their leave of the descendant of the Kuru lineage.[346]

'Kouravya instated Bhimasena as the heir apparent. He cheerfully instructed that the intelligent Vidura should be the adviser for the six kinds of policy.[347] Sanjaya, who possessed many qualities and could think about what had been done and what should be done, was put in charge of finances and wealth. The king instructed Nakula to supervise the size of the army, make sure salaries were being paid and also take care of the workers. Yudhishthira, the great king, instructed that Phalguna should act against the circles of enemies and punish those who were unruly. The scorcher of enemies instructed that Dhoumya, best among priests, should take care of all the rites laid down in the Vedas and duties connected with the brahmanas. O lord of the earth! Sahadeva was instructed

[346]This might mean either Yudhishthira or Dhritarashtra, probably the former.

[347]Usually, but not universally, understood as discipline, duties of government servants, ensuring law and order, the conduct of courtiers, the removal of obstructions and dealing with other kingdoms. Alternatively, peace, war, marching, halting, creating dissension and defence of the kingdom.

to always remain nearby, so as to protect the king. The lord of the earth joyfully appointed each one to a separate task, depending on what was suitable. The destroyer of enemy heroes, always devoted to dharma and with dharma in his soul, told Vidura, Sanjaya and the immensely intelligent Yuyutsu, "Arise! Get up and accomplish every task for the king who is my father.[348] Perform all the appropriate tasks so that everyone is well. Always act for the residents of the city and the countryside. Having taken the king's[349] permission, follow dharma and perform all those tasks."'

Chapter 1370(42)

Vaishampayana said, 'King Yudhishthira, greatly generous, then had the funeral rites separately performed for all the kin who had been slain in the battle.[350] For the funeral rites of his sons, the immensely illustrious King Dhritarashtra gave away all the objects of desire, full of qualities, cattle, riches, many kinds of jewels and other extremely expensive objects. In a similar way, with Droupadi, Yudhishthira donated for Karna, the great-souled Drona, Dhrishtadyumna, Abhimanyu, the rakshasa who was Hidimba's son,[351] Virata and the other well-wishers who had done good deeds for him, Drupada and Droupadi's sons. He instructed that thousands of brahmanas should separately be given grain, garments, gems and cattle. There were other kings who had no relatives and the king instructed that their funeral rites should also be performed. To perform the funeral rites of the well-wishers, Pandava had many halls, reservoirs of water and lakes constructed. He repaid his debts and ensured that the worlds would not censure

[348]Dhritarashtra.

[349]Dhritarashtra's.

[350]These are funeral rites being performed one month after death, they are shraddha ceremonies.

[351]Ghatotkacha.

him. Having done this, the king followed dharma and protected the subjects. He honoured Dhritarashtra, Gandhari, Vidura, all the Kourava advisers and servants, as he used to do earlier. There were some women whose brave husbands and sons had been slain. Compassionately, the Kourava king honoured and protected all of them. The lord, the king, was full of compassion and non-violence and showed his favours to the distressed, the blind and the miserable with houses, garments and food. Having conquered the entire earth and having repaid his debts to his foes, the king was happy and without any rivals. Yudhishthira enjoyed himself.'

Chapter 1371(43)

Vaishampayana said, 'Having obtained the kingdom, the immensely wise Yudhishthira was consecrated. The pure one[352] joined his hands in salutation and spoke to Dasharha Pundarikaksha. "O Krishna! O tiger among the Yadu lineage! It is through your favours, your strength, your intelligence and your valour that this kingdom of my father and grandfather has again been conveyed to me. O Pundarikaksha! O scorcher of enemies! I repeatedly bow down before you. You have been spoken of as the only man. You are the lord of the Satvatas.[353] I bow down before you. The supreme rishis have praised you under many names[354]

[352]Probably suggesting that the period of mourning is over.

[353]Yadavas.

[354]Obviously, such a numbering is not given in the text. We have given it to suggest the idea that it must have been the intention to mention 100 of Krishna's names. In the listing we have given, it falls short at ninety-five. But that's also because it is not always clear what should be included. For example, should lord of the Satvatas also be included in the numbered list? How about Pundarikaksha? The translations of the names have not been given in the obvious instances.

—(1) Vishvakarma;[355] (2) Vishvatma;[356] (3) Vishvasambhava;[357] (4) Vishnu; (5) Jishnu; (6) Hari; (7) Krishna; (8) Vaikuntha; (9) Purushottama; (10) Aditya, since in ancient times, you were in her womb for seven nights;[358] (11) Prishnigarbha, one who is spoken of as having been born in different forms in the three yugas;[359] (12) Shuchishrava;[360] (13) Hrishikesha;[361] (14) Ghritarchi[362] is a name you are addressed by; (15) Trichakshu;[363](16) Shambhu, the single one; (17) Vibhu;[364] (18) Damodara; (19) Varaha;[365] (20) Agni; (21) Brihadbhanu;[366](22) Vrishana;[367] (23) Tarkshyalakshana;[368] (24) Anikasaha;[369] (25) Purusha; (26) Shipivishta;[370] (27) Urukrama;[371] (28) Vachishtha;[372](29) Ugra; (30) Senani; (31) Satya; (32) Vajasanirguha;[373] (33) Achyuta; (34) Yavana-arinam;[374] (35) Samkriti;

[355]Creator of the universe.

[356]Soul of the universe.

[357]The origin of the universe.

[358]This causes problems of interpretation. The Puranas speak of Vishnu having been born in Aditi's womb on seven occasions. However, the text here clearly says nights, not occasions. Vishnu is one of the Adityas and is Aditi's son. As *vamana* (dwarf) incarnation, Vishnu was specifically Aditi's son. In addition, Devaki, Krishna's mother, was an incarnation of Aditi. In all probability, this refers to the seven sons of Devaki, the first six having been killed by Kamsa.

[359]Four of Vishnu's incarnations in satya yuga, three in *treta yuga* and two in *dvapara yuga*.

[360]Someone who is heard of as being pure.

[361]Lord of the senses.

[362]Someone to whom offerings of clarified butter are made.

[363]One with three eyes.

[364]The lord.

[365]Boar, referring to the incarnation.

[366]The large sun.

[367]With the sign of the bull on the banner.

[368]With the mark of Tarkshya (Garuda) on the banner.

[369]One who can withstand armies.

[370]One who is pervaded by rays.

[371]One who has long strides, a reference to the vamana incarnation.

[372]One who resides in speech.

[373]The hidden winner.

[374]The invader of enemies.

(36) Vikriti; (37) Vrisha; (38) Kritavartma;[375] (39) Vrishagarbha; (40) Vrishakapi; (41) Sindhukshidurmi;[376] (42) Trikaku;[377] (43) Tridhama;[378] (44) Trivid-achyuta;[379] (45) Samrat;[380] (46) Virat;[381] (47) Svarat;[382] (48) Surarat;[383] (49) Dharmada; (50) Bhava; (51) Bhu;[384] (52) Abhibhu;[385] (53) Krishna; (54) Krishavartma;[386] (55) Svishta;[387] (56) Kridbhishagavarta;[388] (57) Kapila; (58) Vamana; (59) Yajna; (60) Dhruva; (61) Patanga;[389] (62) Jayatsena;[390] (63) Shikhandi;[391] (64) Nahusha; (65) Babhru;[392] (66) Divaspriktva;[393] (67) Punarvasu;[394] (68) Subabhru;[395] (69) Ruksha;[396] (70) Rukma; (71) Sushena; (72) Dundubhi; (73) Gabhastinemi;[397] (74) Shripadma; (75) Pushkara; (76) Pushpadharana; (77) Ribhu; (78) Vibhu; (79) Sarvasukshma;[398] (80) Savitra; (81) Ambhanidhi;[399] (82)

[375]The one who makes the path.
[376]The waves that rule the ocean.
[377]The one with three humps.
[378]The one with three abodes.
[379]The one who is known to be undecaying in three ways.
[380]Emperor.
[381]Large.
[382]Ruler of one's own self.
[383]Lord of the gods.
[384]The earth.
[385]The supreme lord.
[386]The one with a dark path.
[387]The one who is worshipped well.
[388]The one who heals healers.
[389]The flying one.
[390]The one with victorious armies.
[391]One with a tonsure.
[392]The brown one.
[393]One who touches the sky.
[394]One who brings riches back.
[395]The extremely brown one.
[396]The harsh one.
[397]One whose axle radiates light.
[398]One who is the subtlety in everything.
[399]The store of waters.

Brahma; (83) Pavitra; (84) Dhama;[400] (85) Dhanva;[401] (86) Hiranyagarbha; (87) Svadha; (88) Svaha; (89) Keshava; (90) Yoni;[402] (91) Pralaya;[403] (92) Krishna; (93) Vishvamagra, the foremost creator of everything in the universe; (94) Vishvajoni, who controls everything in the universe; (95) Sharnga-chakra-asi-pani.[404] I bow down before you." Having been thus praised in the midst of the assembly hall by the eldest Pandava, the eloquent Krishna Pundarikaksha, foremost among the Yadavas, spoke words to delight the descendant of the Bharata lineage.'

Chapter 1372(44)

Vaishampayana said, 'The king dismissed all the subjects and instructed them to return to their own homes. King Yudhishthira then spoke to Bhima, terrible in his valour, the intelligent Arjuna and the twins and pacified them. "In the great battle, your bodies have been mangled by the enemy with many kinds of weapons. You are exhausted and extremely tormented by sorrow and intolerance. O best of men! You have suffered hardships in the forest because of me. You have endured that, like inferior men. Now enjoy this victory in happiness, as you wish. After having rested and recovered your sense, meet me again in the morning." Duryodhana's house was as beautiful as a palace. It was strewn with many gems and full of male and female servants. With Dhritarashtra's permission, it had been given to Vrikodara by his brother.[405] The mighty-armed one received it and entered, like Maghavan. Just like Duryodhana's house, Duhshasana's house was also adorned with the garlands of

[400]The refuge.
[401]The bow.
[402]The origin.
[403]Destruction.
[404]The one who holds the *sharnga* bow, chakra and sword in his hand.
[405]Yudhishthira.

many palaces and was decorated with golden gates. It was stocked with male and female servants and had a lot of riches and grain. On the instructions of the king, the mighty-armed Arjuna received this. Durmarshana's supreme abode was even better than Duhshasana's house. It was like Kubera's residence and was decorated with jewels and gold. Nakula had suffered in the great forest and deserved this. O great king! Dharmaraja Yudhishthira happily gave him this. Durmukha's foremost residence was prosperous and decorated with gold. It had many beds and was full of women who had eyes that were like the petals of lotuses. Sahadeva always did what brought him pleasure and he[406] gave it to him. Having obtained it, he[407] delighted himself, like the lord of riches[408] on Kailasa. Yuyutsu, Vidura, the immensely radiant Sanjaya, Sudharma and Dhoumya[409] went to their own houses. With Satyaki, Shouri,[410] tiger among men, went to Arjuna's residence and entered it, like a tiger entering a cave in the mountains. Those places were stocked with food and drink. They spent the night happily there. Having cheerfully awoken in the morning, they presented themselves before King Yudhishthira.'

Chapter 1373(45)

Janamejaya asked, 'O brahmana! After having obtained the kingdom, what did the immensely energetic Dharmaraja Yudhishthira do next? You should tell me that. O rishi! What did the illustrious Hrishikesha, the supreme preceptor of the three worlds, do? You should tell me that in detail.'

[406] Yudhishthira.
[407] Sahadeva.
[408] Kubera.
[409] There was no reason for Dhoumya to have had a house in Hastinapura.
[410] Krishna.

Vaishampayana replied, 'O Indra among kings! Listen. O unblemished one! I will recount that in detail, about what the Pandavas did, with Vasudeva at the forefront. Having obtained the kingdom, the immensely energetic Dharmaraja Yudhishthira instructed the four varnas to be engaged in their own dharma. He announced that one thousand great-souled snataka[411] brahmanas would be given one thousand golden coins each. He arranged sustenance for the servants and the guests who sought refuge and gratified their desires, even the distressed ones who were prone to debating.[412] He gave tens of thousands of cows to the priest, Dhoumya, and also riches, gold, silver and many kinds of garments. O great king! He behaved towards Kripa as one would towards a preceptor. With dharma in his soul, he was careful in his vows and honoured Vidura. The supreme among generous ones gave food, drink, many kinds of garments, beds and seats and satisfied all those who resorted to him. O supreme among kings! Having obtained peace, the immensely illustrious king honoured Yuyutsu, Dhritarashtra's son. King Yudhishthira offered the kingdom to Dhritarashtra, Gandhari and Vidura and informed them that the kingdom was safe. O Janamejaya! He satisfied everyone in the city in this way.

'With hands joined in salutation, he then went to the great-souled Vasudeva. He saw Krishna seated on an expensive couch, decorated with jewels and gold. He looked like a blue rain cloud atop Mount Meru. Decorated with divine ornaments, his form blazed. He was attired in yellow silk garments and was like a jewel set in golden jewellery. The *koustubha* jewel was on his chest, radiant amidst other gems. He looked like Mount Udaya,[413] with the sun blazing its crown. There was no one like him in the three worlds. He approached the great-souled Vishnu, an idol in human form.

[411]A snataka is one who has completed the brahmacharya stage of studying and is about to enter the householder stage.

[412]Those who used *tarka* (logic) and debated. Clearly, this means heterodox schools that questioned the basis of traditional dharma.

[413]Mountain from which the sun rises.

Smiling first, he addressed him in gentle words. "O supreme among intelligent ones! Have you spent the night in comfort? O Achyuta! I hope all your senses are at ease. O supreme among intelligent ones! We sought refuge with you and the goddess of your intelligence. That is how we obtained our kingdom back and the earth is under our subjugation. O illustrious one! Through your valour, you covered the three worlds in three steps[414] and you have shown us your favours. Hence, we obtained victory and the best of fame. Nor have we deviated from dharma." Dharmaraja Yudhishthira spoke to him in this way. However, the illustrious one was meditating. He remained silent and did not say anything in reply.'

Chapter 1374(46)

'Yudhishthira said, "O infinitely valorous one! It is wonderful that you should be meditating thus. O refuge of the worlds! I hope the three worlds will be safe. O Purushottama! You have resorted to the fourth stage of meditation.[415] O god! You have withdrawn and my mind is surprised. You have stilled the five winds that perform action in the body.[416] You have established all the senses in your mind. You have restrained your senses and your mind in your intelligence.[417] O god! All those groups have been immersed in your soul.[418] Your body hair is still and so are your intelligence and your mind. O Madhava! You don't seem to be here and are like a pillar, a wall or a rock. O Achyuta! You are as still as the blazing flame

[414]A reference to Vishnu's vamana (dwarf) incarnation.

[415]There are three normal states—being awake, sleeping (with dreams) and deep sleep (without dreams and without distractions). There is a fourth stage beyond this, known as *turiya*. This transcends consciousness and one experiences union with the brahman.

[416]This is a reference to the five winds (*vayu*) of *pranayama*—*udana*, *prana*, *samana*, *apana* and *vyana*.

[417]We have used intelligence for *buddhi*.

[418]The atman, the text using the word *kshetrajna*.

of a lamp where there is no wind. O illustrious one! O god! Firm in your resolution, you are as immobile as that. O god! If I deserve to hear it and if it is not a secret, show me your favours and dispel my doubts. You are the creator and the transformer.[419] You are the one who decays and you are the own who does not decay. You are without a beginning and without an end. O Purushottoma! You are the one who is here now. I am bowing down my head before you. With devotion, I am seeking refuge with you. O supreme among upholders of dharma! Tell me the truth about this meditation."'

Vaishampayana said, 'The illustrious one, Vasava's younger brother, then brought his mind, his intelligence and his senses to their usual state. Smiling first, he said, "Bhishma is lying down on a bed of arrows, like a fire that has been pacified. The tiger among men was thinking of me and my mind was concentrated on him. The sound of his bowstring against his palm was like thunder with lightning. Even the king of the gods could not tolerate that. My mind had gone out to him. In earlier times, when he swiftly attacked the assembled circle of kings and abducted the three maidens,[420] my mind had gone out to him. When he fought for twenty-three nights with Bhargava Rama[421] without being overpowered, my mind had gone out to him. In the proper way, Ganga had carried the king in her womb. O father![422] He was Vasishtha's student. O king! My mind had gone out to him. The extremely energetic and intelligent one wielded divine weapons and knew the four Vedas and the Vedangas. My mind had gone out to him. O Pandava! He was the beloved disciple of Rama,[423] Jamadagni's son. He was the store of all kinds of knowledge. My mind had gone out to him. He united his senses, controlled his mind and his intelligence and sought refuge with me. My mind had gone out to him. O bull among men! He knew the past, the present and the future and upheld the best forms of dharma. My mind had gone out to him. O Partha! When that tiger

[419]In the sense of destroyer.

[420]Amba, Ambika and Ambalika. Described in Section 60 (Volume 5).

[421]Parashurama.

[422]The word used is tata.

[423]Parashurama.

among men has ascended to heaven because of his own deeds, the earth will be like a night when there is no moon. O Yudhishthira! Gangeya Bhishma is terrible in his valour. Go to him and carefully ask him about what is in your mind. O lord of the earth! Ask him about the four Vedas, the four rites of sacrifice,[424] the four stages of life and the dharma of the four varnas. Bhishma, has borne the great burden of the Kouravas, and with him, all that knowledge is about to set. That is the reason I am asking you to approach him." When he heard Vasudeva's excellent words, which were full of purport, the one who knew about dharma[425] addressed Janardana in a voice that was choking with tears. "O Madhava! O one who shows honours! There is not the slightest bit of doubt in my mind about the truth of what you have said about Bhishma's powers. I have heard the great-souled brahmanas talk about the immensely fortunate and great-souled Bhishma's powers. O destroyer of enemies! You are the lord of the worlds and there cannot be any doubt about what you have said. O Madhava! If your mind is so inclined towards showing me your favours, then, with you at the forefront, let us go and see Bhishma. When the illustrious sun god has turned around,[426] he will leave for those worlds. O mighty-armed one! Therefore, Kourava should also see you. You are the origin of the gods. You are the one who is destroyed and you are also the one who is not destroyed. You are the storehouse of the brahman. Therfore, seeing you is a true gain." On hearing Dharmaraja's words, Madhusudana instructed Satyaki, who was next to him, that his chariot should be yoked.

'Satyaki departed from Krishna's presence and went and told Daruka that Krishna's chariot should be yoked. The different parts of that supreme chariot were decorated with gold. Its parts were adorned with sapphires and crystals. The wheels were encrusted with gold. It was swift and possessed the complexion of the sun's rays. It was decorated with many kinds of gems and jewels. It blazed like the rising sun. The wonderful standard had Tarkshya[427] atop it.

[424]One associated with each of the Vedas.
[425]Yudhishthira.
[426]Towards *uttarayana*.
[427]Garuda.

It was as swift as thought and its different parts were embellished with gold. Sugriva, Sainya and the best of horses were yoked to it. On hearing Satyaki's instructions, Daruka quickly yoked it properly. O lion among kings! Hands joined in salutation, he then went and informed that it had been readied.'

Chapter 1375(47)

Janamejaya asked, 'The grandfather of the Bharatas was lying down on a bed of arrows. How did he give up his body? What kind of yoga did he resort to?'

Vaishampayana replied, 'O king! O tiger of the Kuru lineage! Purify yourself and listen attentively to how the great-souled Bhishma gave up his body. Pierced by hundreds of arrows, Bhishma was stretched out, like the sun with its rays. As soon as the sun turned towards uttarayana, he controlled himself and immersed himself in his atman. In his supreme prosperity, he was surrounded by the best of brahmanas—Vyasa, known for his learning in the Vedas, Narada, the rishi of the gods, Devasthana, Vatsya, Ashmaka and Sumantu. These, and large numbers of other immensely fortunate and great-souled sages surrounded him. With faith and self-control, they surrounded him, like the moon by the planets. Bhishma was a tiger among men, in his deeds, thoughts and words.

'Lying down on that bed of arrows, he joined his hands in salutation and worshipped Krishna. In a loud voice, he praised Madhusudana, the lord of yoga, Padmanabha,[428] Vishnu, Jishnu, the lord of the universe. He joined his hands in salutation and purified himself. Bhishma was supreme among eloquent ones and had great dharma in his soul. He praised the lord Vasudeva. "O Krishna! I wish to worship you. O Purushottama! May you be pleased with my words, which will be both brief and extensive. You are pure. You

[428]The one with a lotus in his navel.

are the essence of purity. You are the swan.[429] You are supreme. You are the supreme creator. You are in all atmans and you are the lord of beings. You enter and are established in all beings in the universe. You are the qualities in beings. You are the lord of qualities, like a string which holds gems together. Your limbs constitute the universe. You perform deeds in the universe. Everything in the universe is strung together in you, like a garland strung together by a firm thread. You are Hari. You are the one with one thousand heads. You are the one with one thousand feet and one thousand eyes. You are known as the god Narayana. You are the refuge of the universe. You are finer than the finest. You are larger than the largest. You are heavier than the heaviest. You are better than the best. In the *vaka*s, the *anuvaka*s, the *nishad*s and the Upanishads, you are the one who is praised as the performer of truthful deeds.[430] You are truth. You are in the truth of the samas. There are four parts to your atman.[431] You are in all understanding and you are the lord of the Satvatas. Your supreme and secret names are worshipped by the celestial gods. You are the god who was born to the goddess Devaki and Vasudeva, for the sake of protecting brahmanas on earth and they were like two sticks rubbed together to kindle a blazing fire. When one cleanses oneself, controls and withdraws from all desire, desiring the infinite, one sees the unblemished atman of Govinda in one's own atman. In the Puranas, you have been spoken of as Purusha. At the beginning of a yuga, you are Brahma. When the time for destruction has arrived, you are known by the name of Samkarshana. I am worshipping the one who should be worshipped. Your deeds surpass those of Vayu and Agni. You surpass the sun and the fire in your energy. Your

[429]The swan (*hamsa)* is superior to all beings in flight and is often used as a description of the supreme being.

[430]The vakas are mantras. The anuvakas are chapters of the Vedas. The nishads are musical renderings of the mantras.

[431]This can be interpreted in different ways. Each being has the four components of *jivatman*, *paramatman*, mind and consciousness. In the world, the manifestations of the supreme being are worshipped as Vasudeva, Samkarshana, Pradyumna and Aniruddha. The four names of the supreme being are Vishnu, Hari, Nara and Narayana.

atman is beyond the reach of intelligence and the senses. I am seeking refuge with that Prajapati. You are the creator of the universe. You are the lord of everything in the universe. That is how the universe speaks of you. You are the supervisor. You are without decay. You are the supreme state. Your complexion is like that of gold. Though you are one, for the sake of destroying the daityas, Aditi bore twelve different parts in her womb.[432] I am bowing down to the one whose atman is the sun. I bow down before the one whose atman is the moon. He is the king of the brahmanas and gratifies the gods in shuklapaksha and the ancestors in krishnapaksha.[433] You are the blazing and resplendent being who is beyond the great darkness. Knowing you, one goes beyond death. I am bowing down to the one who is everything that there is to be known. In the great ukthas,[434] the large number of brahmanas chants of you as the great one and as the fire in the great sacrifice. You are the soul of the Vedas and I bow down before you. Your abode is in the Rig, Yajur and Sama hymns. You are the five kinds of oblations.[435] You are the seven strands.[436] You are the soul of a sacrifice and I bow down before you. You are the bird named Yajur. The metres are your limbs and the three forms of chanting[437] constitute your head. The *brihat* and *rathamtara*[438] are the eyes. You are the hymns and I bow down before you. When the creators performed a sacrifice with one thousand flows,[439] you were the rishi who appeared. You are the bird with a golden complexion. Your atman is the swan and I bow down before you. I bow down to the one whose atman is speech. He is said to be the eternal akshara.[440]

[432]The twelve Adityas or gods.

[433]In the form of soma offerings.

[434]Verses that are recited.

[435]Clarified butter, milk, grain, cakes and soma (or water).

[436]The seven main Vedic metres.

[437]Rig, Yajur and Sama.

[438]Forms of sama hymns.

[439]Of soma.

[440]Akshara has several meanings. It is the syllable *om*, representative of the brahman, and means something that is immutable. It also means word, speech, syllable or letter of the alphabet.

The words[441] are his limbs. The joints are *sandhi*.[442] The vowels and the consonants are the manifestations. For the sake of the virtuous, you build a bridge from the false to the truth. Your limbs are the use of dharma and artha. I bow down to the one who is the truth. There are those who follow different dharmas. They desire fruits through the pursuit of these different kinds of dharma. They worship you through these different kinds of dharma. I bow down to the one who has dharma in his soul. The maharshis think of you as the unmanifest within the manifest. You are the kshetrajna in the *kshetra*.[443] I bow down to the one who has his atman in the kshetra. I bow down to the one who is the atman of samkhya, who is spoken of in samkhya as the seventeenth and who, firm with the atman in the self, is surrounded by the sixteen qualities.[444] Without sleep, controlling the breath, established in the self and restraining the senses, those who are engaged in yoga see a light. You are the atman of that and I bow down before you. Without any fear of rebirth, peaceful sannyasis obtain the supreme you, beyond the good and the bad. You are the atman of salvation and I bow down before you. At the end of one thousand yugas, you are the blazing flames of fire and devour all beings. You are the atman of the terrible and I bow down before you. Having consumed all beings and having rendered the entire universe into a single ocean, you sleep alone, like a child. You are the atman of maya and I bow down before you. You are the thousand-headed being and your atman is infinite. I bow down before the one who is the atman of this yoga of sleep, in each of the four oceans in turn.[445] You are the lotus in the navel of the one who has not been

[441]Padas, alternatively, lines.

[442]Rules of grammar for combining words.

[443]Literally, kshetrajna means the one who knows the kshetra, kshetra meaning field. Kshetra is usually interpreted as the body and more rarely, as intelligence. Kshetrajna is thus the knower of the field, that is, the atman.

[444]This is a reference to the samkhya school of philosophy. The sixteen qualities are the five organs of sense, the five organs of action, the mind and the five elements.

[445]The four is probably a reference to the four forms of Hari, Krishna, Vishnu and Narayana.

born. The entire universe is established in you. You are Pushkara and Pushkaraksha. I bow down before the one who is the atman of the lotus. The clouds are your hair. The rivers flow through all the joints of your body. The four oceans are in your stomach. I bow down before the one who is the atman of water. You flow through the yugas in the form of days, seasons, *ayanas*[446] and years. You are the cause of creation and destruction. I bow down before the one who is the atman of time. The brahmanas are your mouth, the kshatriyas are your arms, the vaishyas are your thighs and stomach and the shudras find refuge in your feet. I bow down before the one who is the atman of the varnas. The fire is your face. The firmament is the crown of your head. The sky is your navel and the earth constitutes your feet. Your eyes are the sun. The directions are your ears. I bow down before the one whose atman is in the worlds. You are present in objects in the form of *vaisheshika* qualities.[447] You are spoken of as the protector of objects. I bow down before the one whose atman is in all protection. You are the one who sustains beings through food, drink and riches and extends their juice and breaths of life. I bow down before the one whose atman is in the breath of life. You are beyond time. You are beyond sacrifices. You are beyond notions of truth and falsehood. You have no beginning. You are the origin of the universe. I bow down before the one whose atman is in the universe. He is the one who confounds beings through the bonds of affection and hatred. This is for the sake of preserving creation. I bow down before the one whose atman is in confusion. Knowledge about the atman is knowledge one can obtain while still remaining established in the five.[448] Those who obtain that knowledge go to him. I bow down before the one whose atman is in knowledge. His body cannot be measured. His infinite eyes see everything. He is infinite and cannot be measured. I bow down before the one whose atman is in thought. He is matted and always carries a staff. His

[446]Period of six months.

[447]Vaisheshika means specific or distinctive. But this is also a reference to the vaisheshika school of philosophy.

[448]The five senses or the five elements.

body has an elongated stomach. The water pot is his quiver.[449] I bow down before the one whose atman is in Brahma. He wields a trident and is the lord of the gods. He is great-souled and three-eyed. His body is smeared in ashes and his linga is turned up.[450] I bow down before the one whose atman is in Rudra. He is the embodiment of the five elements. He is the creator and destroyer of all beings. He is without anger, without malice and without confusion. I bow down before the one whose atman is in peace. Everything is in him. He is in everything. He is everything. Everything comes from him. He is always made up of everything. I bow down before the one whose atman is in everything. I bow down before the one whose deeds are the universe. You are the soul of the universe. The universe originates in you. Etablished beyond the five,[451] you are the fulfilment of all beings. In the three worlds, I bow down before you. I bow down before you in everything that is beyond those three. I bow down before you in all the directions. You are the refuge of everything. I bow down before the illustrious Vishnu, the origin of the worlds. O Hrishikesha! You are the unvanquished creator and destroyer. I see your divine form in the three paths.[452] I can see the truth about your eternal form. The heaven is pervaded with your head and the goddess earth with your feet. You are the eternal being whose valour is in the three worlds. Your complexion is like the *atasi* flower.[453] You are Achyuta in your yellow garments. Those who bow down before Govinda have no fear. Just as truth is full of Vishnu, oblations are full of Vishnu. Since everything is full of Vishnu, the wicked deeds that I have done will be destroyed. Faithfully, I am seeking refuge with you. I wish to attain the best objective. O Pundarikaksha! O supreme among gods! You will think of what is best. You are the source of learning and austerities. You are Vishnu, who has no origin. I have worshipped the god with my words. May Janardana be pleased

[449]This is a description of Brahma.

[450]This is a description of Shiva.

[451]The five elements.

[452]Heaven, the earth and the nether regions.

[453]A blue flower, *Linum usitatissimum*.

with me." With devotion in his mind, Bhishma spoke these words. Having said this, he bowed down before Krishna.

'Through his powers of yoga, Madhava got to know about Bhishma's devotion and went there.[454] Hari gave him divine knowledge and sight about the three kinds of time.[455] When the immensely wise Bhishma's words ended, those who were knowledgeable about the brahman applauded him loudly, their voices choking with tears. The foremost among brahmanas praised Keshava Purushottama. Then, in gentle words, all of them again praised Bhishma. On discerning Bhishma's yoga of devotion, Purushottma was joyful. He suddenly arose and ascended his vehicle. Keshava and Satyaki advanced on a single chariot. The great-souled Yudhishthira and Dhananjaya were on another one. Bhima and the two twins were on a single chariot. Kripa, Yuyutsu and the suta Sanjaya went on another chariot. Those bulls among men went on chariots that were like cities. These made the earth tremble with the roar of their axles. As he[456] advanced along the road, the best of men was extremely joyful on hearing the words of praise spoken by the brahmanas. There were other men who bowed down before him, hands joined in salutation. The slayer of Keshi[457] was delighted and greeted them.'

Chapter 1376(48)

Vaishampayana said, 'Hrishikesha, King Yudhishthira, Kripa and the others and the four Pandavas rode on chariots that were like cities, adorned with standards and flags. On horses

[454]Krishna had not been there physically and Bhishma had prayed to him in his mind. Before Krishna went there physically, the knowledge was also delivered mentally.

[455]The past, the present and the future.

[456]Krishna.

[457]Krishna killed a demon named Keshi.

that were swift, they quickly went to Kurukshetra. They got down in Kurukshetra, full of hair, marrow and bones. That was where the great-souled kshatriyas had given up their bodies. The bodies and bones of elephants and horses were piled up in heaps, like mountains. The heads and skulls of men were strewn around like conch shells. Thousands of funeral pyres had been lit, with armour and weapons piled on. It looked like a drinking ground that had been used by Death and had just been abandoned. Large numbers of demons wandered around and large numbers of rakshasas frequented it. The maharathas quickly went and saw Kurukshetra.

'While they were going there, the mighty-armed one, the delight of all the Yadavas, spoke to Yudhishthira about the valour of Jamadagni's son. "O Partha! There, in the distance, you can see the five lakes created by Rama.[458] Earlier, he used the blood of kshatriyas to offer oblations to his ancestors. On twenty-one occasions, the lord emptied the earth of kshatriyas. It is only now that Rama has refrained from that task." Yudhishthira replied, "You have told me that Rama emptied the world of kshatriyas twenty-one times. I have a great doubt about this. O bull among the Yadu lineage! O infinitely valorous one! If the seed of the kshatriyas was burnt, how were the kshatriyas generated again? O bull among the Yadu lineage! How were the kshatriyas exterminated by the illustrious and great-souled Rama? How did they prosper again? O supreme among eloquent ones! In the Mahabharata war, crores of kshatriyas have been slain. The earth is strewn with kshatriyas. O Varshneya! O one with Tarkshya[459] on your standard! Sever my doubt. O Vasava's younger brother! O Krishna! Our supreme knowledge comes from you." As they proceeded, the lord who was Gada's elder brother [460] told the infinitely energetic Yudhishthira the complete truth about that account and about how the earth again became full of kshatriyas.'

[458]Parashurama.

[459]Garuda.

[460]Gada was Krishna's younger brother.

Chapter 1377(49)

'Vasudeva said, "O Kounteya! Listen to what I heard when the maharshis were talking about Rama's birth and the reasons behind why Jamadagni's son killed crores of kshatriyas. Those who were born in royal lineages in Bharata[461] were again slain. Jahnu's son was Ajahnu and his son was Ballava. King Kushika, knowledgeable about dharma, was his son. He was an equal of the one with the thousand eyes[462] on earth and performed fierce austerities. He wished to obtain a son who would not be defeated and would be the lord of the three worlds. O descendant of the Bharata lineage! On seeing him engaged in those terrible austerities, the thousand-eyed Purandara knew that he was capable of giving birth to a son who would be his[463] equal. O king! Therefore, having gone there, the chastiser of Paka, the lord of all mobile and immobile objects, himself became Kushika's son, by the name of Gadhi. O king! O lord! His daughter was the maiden named Satyavati. The lord Gadhi gave her to Richika, the son of a wise sage.[464] O Kounteya! O descendant of the Kuru lineage! Bhargava[465] was pleased at this. For the sake of a son for himself and for Gadhi, he cooked some *charu*.[466] Bhargava Richika summoned his wife and said, 'This charu is for you and that one is for your mother. She will give birth to a blazing bull among the kshatriyas. He will be invincible before all the kshatriyas on this earth. He will destroy the bulls among the kshatriyas. O fortunate one! Your son will be steadfast and full of austerities. He will be peaceful in his soul. This charu will make him foremost among the brahmanas.' Having spoken these words to his wife, the intelligent

[461]Bharatavarsha.

[462]Indra.

[463]Indra's.

[464]The text uses the word *kavi,* which means wise, and refers to Richika as the son of Kavi. There was a sage named Kavi. However, Richika was the son of Ourva. Therefore, kavi is being used as an adjective and not as a proper noun.

[465]This means Richika. The entire lineage was descended from the sage Bhrigu.

[466]Mixture of milk and rice used as a sacrificial offering.

Richika, the descendant of the Bhrigu lineage, went away to the forest to engage in austerities.

'"At that time, King Gadhi had decided to visit the tirthas. With his wife, he arrived in Richika's hermitage. O king! Satyavati picked up the two charus and cheerfully gave them to her mother, forgetting in her haste, her husband's words. O Kounteya! The mother gave her own charu to her daughter and ignorantly, consumed her[467] charu herself. The destroyer of kshatriyas was conceived in Satyavati's womb. His form blazed and he was terrible to look at. While he was engaged in the yoga of meditation, Richika saw this. O tiger among kings! He told his beautiful wife, 'O fortunate one! The charu has been exchanged and your mother has deceived you.[468] You will give birth to an extremely powerful son who will be the performer of cruel deeds. Your brother will be born as a store of austerities, immersed in the brahman. Through my austerities, I have given him the universal brahman.' Having been thus addressed by her husband, the immensely fortunate Satyavati trembled. She lowered her head at his feet and said, 'O illustrious one! O great sage! You should not speak such words to me now. "You will have a son who will be the worst among brahmanas."' Richika replied, 'O fortunate one! This is not what I had envisaged for you. You will have a son who is terrible in his deeds. The charu and your mother are the reason for that.' Satyavati said, 'O sage! If you wish, you can create the worlds. But what about me? O supreme among those who meditate! I desire a son who is peaceful and upright.' Richika replied, 'O fortunate one! I have never wilfully uttered a falsehood. Why will I do it after igniting a fire and pronouncing mantras for the charu?' Satyavati said, 'O supreme among those who meditate! Let our grandson be like that. But let our son be like you. I desire a son who is peaceful and upright.' Richika replied, 'O one with a beautiful complexion! I see no difference between a son and a grandson. O fortunate one! It will be according to your words.' Satyavati gave birth to Bhargava Jamadagni. He was peaceful and engaged in austerities. He was

[467]Satyavati's.

[468]This suggests that Satyavati's mother had done this consciously.

peaceful in his soul. Gadhi, the descendant of Kushika, obtained Vishvamitra as a heir. He was united with the universal brahman and was a brahmarshi.

'"Jamadagni, Richika's son, had the extremely terrible Rama as a son. He was foremost among those who knew all forms of learning. He was accomplished in dhanurveda. He was the slayer of kshatriyas and like a blazing fire. At that time, Kritavirya had a powerful son. He was an energetic kshatriya in the Haihaya lineage and his name was Arjuna. He scorched the entire earth with its seven continents[469] and cities, using the strength of his own arms and weapons, but also using supreme dharma. O Kouravya! Chitrabhanu[470] was thirsty and approached him for alms. The powerful and thousand-armed one[471] gave Agni the alms. Chitrabhanu blazed from the valiant one's arrows and burnt down villages, fortifications, hamlets and cities. Because of the powers of that Indra among men, Kartavirya, the one with the great heat burnt down mountains and forests. Aided by the wind and with Haihaya, Chitrabhanu consumed and emptied the hermitage of Varuna's son.[472] O unblemished one! O great king! When his hermitage was burnt down, Apava[473] angrily cursed Kartavirya Arjuna. 'Because of your delusion, you did not spare my forest. O Arjuna! Therefore, in a battle, Rama will burn down and sever your arms.' O great king! After this, the powerful Arjuna always turned to peace. O descendant of the Bharata lineage! He became the generous granter of refuge to brahmanas and brave ones. His extremely powerful sons caused him to be slain through the curse. Those powerful ones were always cruel and became the cause. O bull among the Bharata lineage! In their intolerance, they seized Jamadagni's calf, though the intelligent Haihaya Kartavirya did

[469]*Dvipas*.

[470]Literally, the one with the wonderful and shining light. A name for the fire god, Agni.

[471]Kartavirya Arjuna possessed one thousand hands.

[472]This means the sage Vasishtha, who is sometimes described as the son of Mitra and Varuna.

[473]Vasishtha.

not know about this. O Indra among kings! At this, the lord[474] used his manliness to sever Arjuna's arms and brought the weeping calf back to Jamadagni's hermitage, back from where it was wandering around in the inner quarters.[475] Arjuna's sons lost their minds because of this. Foolishly, they went to the great-souled Jamadagni's hermitage. O lord of men! With broad-headed arrows, sharp at the tip, they severed and brought down his head from his body. This happened when the great-souled Rama had gone out in search of kindling and kusha grass. Rama was overcome with great rage and anger at his father's death. He grasped his weapons and pledged to empty the earth of kshatriyas. The tiger among the Bhrigu lineage used his valour to quickly kill all the sons and grandsons of the valiant Kartavirya. Overcome by great anger, he killed thousands of Haihayas. O king! Bhargava covered the earth with the mud of blood. Thus, the extremely energetic one emptied the earth of kshatriyas. Having done this, he was overcome by great compassion and retired to the forest.

'"Thousands of years passed. The lord was naturally angry and confronted a fierce agitation. O great king! Paravasu was a great ascetic and was the son of Raibhya and the grandson of Vishvamitra. He angrily addressed him[476] in an assembly of men. 'O Rama! When Yayati fell down,[477] virtuous ones assembled at a sacrifice. There were Pratardana and others. Were they not kshatriyas? O Rama! Your pledge has been false. Why do you boast in the assemblies of men? Because of your fear of these brave kshatriyas, you have sought refuge in the mountains.'[478] On hearing Paravasu's words, Bhargava again picked up his weapons and, overcome by rage, again covered the earth with hundreds of kshatriyas. O king! However, there were hundreds of kshatriyas who remained alive. Those immensely valorous ones prospered and became lords of the earth.

[474]Parashurama.

[475]The calf was in the inner quarters of Kartavirya Arjuna's palace.

[476]Parashurama.

[477]Yayati fell down from heaven. This has been described in Section 54 (Volume 4). The point is that some kshatriyas were still alive.

[478]Parashurama resided in Mount Mahendra.

O lord of men! He quickly slew them again, including the children and those who were in the wombs. The earth was again covered. As soon as babies were born from wombs, he killed them again. However, some kshatriya women managed to protect their sons. On twenty-one occasions, the lord emptied the earth of kshatriyas. In a horse sacrifice, he then gave it[479] to Kashyapa as *dakshina*. O king! Wishing to save the remaining kshatriyas, Kashyapa held the sacrificial ladle[480] in his hand and spoke these beneficial words. 'O great sage! Go to the shores of the southern ocean. O Rama! You should not dwell within my dominion.' Because of its fright of Jamadagni's son, the ocean created the country known as Shurparaka, on the other side of the earth. O great king! Kashyapa received the earth. Having made arrangements for the brahmanas to dwell there, he entered the great forest.

'"O bull among the Bharata lineage! The shudras and the vaishyas acted as they wished. They descended on the wives of the foremost among the brahmanas. When there is no king in the world of the living, the strong oppress the weak. There are no restraints and no one is the lord of his own possessions. At that time, the earth entered *rasatala*.[481] At that time, she was not protected in the proper way by kshatriyas, who should be protecting in accordance with dharma. O king! As the earth was submerging, Kashyapa held her on his thigh. That is the reason the earth is known as Urvi.[482] The goddess earth sought Kashyapa's favours and asked that she should be protected by kshatriyas who possessed strength in their arms. 'O brahmana! I have protected some virtuous men who are bulls among kshatriyas. O sage! They have been born in the lineage of the Haihayas. Let them protect me. There is a lord who is a descendant of the Pourava lineage. He is Viduratha's son. O brahmana! The bears have reared

[479]The earth.

[480]Kashyapa was the officiating priest at the sacrifice.

[481]Rasatala is a general term for the nether regions. More specifically, there are seven worlds in the nether regions. Their names vary from one list to another. But rasatala happens to be one of the seven.

[482]*Uru* and *urvi* both mean thigh. Urvi also means the wide one and is one of the earth's names.

him on Mount Riksha.[483] There is another one who is the son of Sudasa. Because of compassion, Parashara's infinitely energetic son has protected him and has performed sacrifices for him. Like a shudra, he performs all the tasks for that rishi and is known by the name of Sarvakarma.[484] Let that king protect me. Shibi's immensely energetic son is known by the name of Gopati. The cows have protected him in the forest.[485] O sage! Let him protect me. Pratardana's son is the immensely illustrious Vatsa. The calves have reared him in a pen.[486] Let that king protect me. There is Dadhivahana's grandson, the son of Diviratha. He is Anga and he was protected on the banks of the Ganga by Goutama. The mighty-armed Brihadratha is foremost on the earth because of his prosperity. The immensely fortunate one was protected on Gridhrakuta by *golangulas*.[487] There are three kshatriyas in the lineage of Marutta. They have been protected by the ocean and are like the Maruts in their valour. Here and there, these sons of kshatriyas have been heard of. Protected by them, I will no longer move. For my sake, Rama, unblemished in his deeds, killed their fathers and their grandfathers in a battle. There is no doubt that it is my duty to honour them.[488] I do not desire to be protected by someone who always lacks valour.' Kashyapa brought together the ones whom the earth had indicated. He consecrated those valorous kshatriyas as the lords of the earth. The present lineages are based on their sons and grandsons. O Pandava! This is the ancient account that you have asked me about."'

Vaishampayana said, 'The foremost among the Yadu lineage spoke thus to Yudhishthira, supreme among those who uphold dharma. He then swiftly departed on his chariot, like the illustrious sun god penetrating the three worlds with its rays.'[489]

[483] *Riksha* also means a bear.

[484] Sarvakarma means someone who performs all the tasks.

[485] Gopati means lord of the cows.

[486] *Vatsa* means calf.

[487] Gridhrakuta is a peak and golangulas are cow-tailed monkeys.

[488] By performing their funeral rites.

[489] All of them were travelling, to see Bhishma.

Chapter 1378(50)

Vaishampayana said, 'Having heard of Rama's deeds, King Yudhishthira was filled with great wonder and replied to Janardana. "O Varshneya! The great-souled Rama is like Shakra. Through his valour and anger, he emptied the earth of kshatriyas. The extenders of the kshatriya lineage were frightened because of Rama and were protected by cattle, the oceans, golangulas, bears and apes. O Achyuta! It is amazing. Men on earth are fortunate that such an act of dharma was performed by the brahmana." O son![490] That is the way Achyuta and Yudhishthira proceeded together. They went to the spot where the lord Gangeya was lying down on a bed of arrows. They saw Bhishma lying down on that bed of arrows. He was like the evening sun or the fire, surrounded by a net of his own rays. That spot, on the banks of the river Oghavati, was extremely auspicious. The sages surrounded and honoured him, like the gods around Shatakratu. From a distance, Krishna, the king who was Dharmaraja, the four Pandavas and Sharadvata and the others saw him. They descended from their vehicles and controlled their agitated minds. They concentrated their senses and approached the great sages. Govinda, Satyaki and the Kouravas greeted Vyasa and the other rishis and then presented themselves before Gangeya. Gangeya was rich in austerities. All the Yadus and the Kouravas, bulls among men, asked about his welfare and then sat down around him.

'Gangeya was fading, like a fire that had been pacified. Somewhat distressed in his mind, Keshava told Bhishma, "O king! I hope your knowledge is as clear at it used to be. O supreme among eloquent ones! I hope anxiety has not affected your intelligence. I hope the wounds from these arrows are not causing great pain to your limbs. Mental pain makes the physical one stronger. O lord! Your father Shantanu, devoted to dharma, granted you the boon that you could choose when to die. But that does not reduce the pain. O descendant of the Bharata lineage! The slightest of stakes generates pain in the

[490]The word used is tata.

body, not to speak of this storm of arrows. O descendant of the Bharata lineage! If you so wish, you can instruct the gods on the origins, the prosperity and the destruction of all living beings. O bull among men! You are revered for your age and wisdom. It is as if the past, the present and the future are inscribed on the palm of your hand. O immensely wise one! For beings, you know about the fruits of dharma and the cycle of death and rebirth. You are a store that is full of the brahman. You were established in this prosperous kingdom and your limbs were without disease. You were surrounded by thousands of women. However, we have seen you hold up your seed. O king! With the exception of Shantanu's son, Bhishma, there is no one in the three worlds who is as devoted to the truth, as immensely valorous, as brave and as conscious of dharma. O father![491] You are about to die and we have not heard of anyone else who, lying down on strewn arrows, is so full of natural power. In truth, austerities, generosity, performing of sacrifices, dhanurveda, the Vedas, non-violence, purity, self-control and engagement in the welfare of all beings, we have not heard of any other maharatha like you. There is no doubt that you are capable of vanquishing the gods, the gandharvas, the *suras*,[492] the asuras and the rakshasas on a single chariot. You are the mighty-armed Bhishma, like a Vasava among the Vasus. The brahmanas always refer to you as the ninth, but you are not the ninth in qualities.[493] O supreme among men! I know who you are. Because of your own capacity and great strength, you are renowned among the thirty gods. O Indra among men! Among men, there is no man on earth who is your equal in qualities, none that has been seen or heard of. O king! In all the qualities, you surpass even the gods. Through your austerities, you are capable of creating worlds, with mobile and immobile objects. The eldest

[491]The word used is tata.

[492]The suras are also gods. But the text uses both the words for gods, devas and suras.

[493]There are eight Vasus. Though Bhishma is himself regarded as one of these Vasus born on earth, he is regarded as a ninth Vasu. However, because of his qualities, he is not ninth in merit.

son of Pandu is tormented because of the destruction of his kin. O Bhishma! Dispel his sorrow. O descendant of the Bharata lineage! You know everything about what is said to be the dharma of the four varnas and the four ashramas.[494] O descendant of the Bharata lineage! This is said to be the eternal dharma, spoken about in the four Vedas, followed by the four officiating priests[495] and stated in samkhya yoga.[496] O Gangeya! There is one single dharma followed, and not contravened, by any of the four varnas and that is also known to you.[497] You know all the *itihasa*[498] and the Puranas. All the Dharmashastras[499] are always established in your mind. O bull among men! With the exception of you, there is no one else in this world who can dispel any doubt that may arise about their meanings. O Indra among men! Using your intelligence, dispel the sorrow that has arisen in Pandaveya's mind. You possess many kinds of extensive intelligence and you should assure the people who are confused."'

Chapter 1379(51)

Vaishampayana said, 'Hearing the words of the intelligent Vasudeva, Bhishma joined his hands in salutation and raising his head a bit, spoke the following words. "O illustrious Vishnu! I bow down before you. You are the origin of the worlds. O Hrishikesha! You are the unvanquished creator and destroyer. I bow down before

[494]The four stages of life.

[495]There are four types of officiating priests—*hotar* (one who recites from the Rig Veda), *udgatar* (one who recites from the Sama Veda), *adhvaryu* (one who recites from the Yajur Veda) and brahman (one who recites from the Atharva Veda).

[496]One of the six schools of philosophy (*darshana*) associated with the sage Kapila.

[497]The text does not indicate what that single dharma is.

[498]Itihasa is history and is specifically used for the two epics.

[499]Specific sacred texts, in the *smriti* tradition, about dharma.

the one who is the doer in the universe, who is the soul of the universe and who is the creator of the universe. You are the objective and you are beyond the five elements. I bow down before the three worlds. I bow down before the one who is beyond the three worlds. I bow down before the one who is the lord of yoga. You are the final refuge of everything. O Purushottama! I have sought refuge in your words and am able to see your divine form in the three paths.[500] I can also see your true and eternal form. Your infinite energy bears up the wind along seven paths.[501] Your head extends up to the firmament and your feet are on the goddess earth. The directions are your arms. Your eyes are the sun and Shakra is established in your valour. In our mind's eye, we see your undecaying form. It has the complexion of the atasi flower. It is attired in yellow garments. It is like a cloud tinged with lightning. With a desire to attain the best objective, I have faithfully sought refuge with you. O Pundarikaksha! O supreme among gods! Think of my welfare."

'Vasudeva replied, "O bull among men! O king! Since you have supreme devotion in me, I have shown you my divine form. O Indra among kings! O descendant of the Bharata lineage! I do not show this self to one without devotion, one with false devotion, or one without self-control. You have always been my devotee and you have always been devoted to the truth and have resorted to control, austerities, truth, generosity and attachment to purity. O Bhishma! O king! It is because of your own austerities that you have been able to see me. The worlds from which there is no return[502] are there for you. O foremost among the Kuru lineage! Fifty-six days still remain in your life. O Bhishma! After that, you will cast aside your body and obtain the auspicious fruits of your deeds. These gods, the Vasus, are astride their celestial vehicles and all of them are like blazing fires. Though they are invisible, they are protecting you until it is the northern solstice. O illustrious one! O foremost among men! As soon as the

[500]Heaven, earth and the nether regions.

[501]Vayu (wind) has seven flows—*avaha, pravaha, nivaha, varaha, udhvaha, samvaha* and *parivaha*.

[502]No rebirth.

sun turns in the northward direction with the progress of time, you will go to the worlds obtained by those with knowledge, and from where there is no return. O Bhishma! O brave one! When you go to that world, all the knowledge you possess will be destroyed. That is the reason all of these have assembled before you, for an analysis of dharma. Yudhishthira's knowledge has been affected by sorrow over his kin, though he is firmly based on truth. Tell him about the union of dharma and artha. Speak meaningful words that will dispel his sorrow."'

Chapter 1380(52)

Vaishampayana said, 'On hearing Krishna's words, full of dharma and artha, Bhishma, Shantanu's son, joined his hands in salutation and spoke these words to him. "O lord of the worlds! O mighty-armed one! O Shiva! O Narayana! O Achyuta! Having heard your words, I am flooded with delight. You are the lord of speech. What can I say in your presence? Everything that can be said exists in your words. O god! Whatever has been done in this world, what should be done, and what is being done, all emanate from you. The worlds are pervaded by your intelligence. In the presence of the king of the gods, who can speak about the world of the gods? Before you, only such a person can talk about dharma, kama and artha in the sacred texts. O Madhusudana! My mind is suffering from the wounds of these arrows. My limbs are weak and my intelligence is unclear. I lack the capacity to talk about anything. O Govinda! These arrows are like poison and the fire and are oppressing me. My great strength is leaving. My breath of life is ebbing away. My inner organs are scorched. My consciousness is distracted. The weakness is affecting my words. How can I be interested in speaking? O virtuous one! O descendant of the Dasharha lineage! Show me your favours. O mighty-armed one! Pardon me. O Achyuta! I will not say anything.

In your presence, even Vachaspati[503] would refrain from speaking. I cannot distinguish the directions, nor the sky or the earth. O Madhusudana! It is only because of your valour that I am still here. O lord! You should yourself quickly tell Dharmaraja about what is beneficial. You are the learning that is there in all the sacred texts. You are the eternal doer in the worlds. When you are present in the world, how can someone like me speak? That will be like a disciple before a preceptor."

'Vasudeva replied, "O one who has borne the great burden of the Kouravas! These words are worthy of you. You are immensely valorous and are established in great spirits. You can see the purpose behind everything. O Gangeya! You have spoken to me about the pain from the wounds of these storms of arrows. O Bhishma! O lord! Through my favours, accept a boon from me. O Gangeya! You will not be affected by debility, unconsciousness, fever, pain, hunger and thirst. O unblemished one! All knowledge will manifest itself before you. Your intelligence will be clear and will not be distracted. O Bhishma! There will always be spirit in your mind. You will like the king of the stars,[504] free of the clouds and without dusk and darkness. Whenever you think about dharma and artha, your intelligence will back this up first. O tiger among kings! O infinitely valorous one! By resorting to your divine sight, you will be able to see the four kinds of beings[505] that have been created. O Bhishma! Through the sight of knowledge, you will be able to see the truth about the four kinds of beings, like a fish in clear water."'

Vaishampayana said, 'With Vyasa, all the maharshis worshipped Krishna with hymns and words from the Rig Veda, the Yajur Veda and the Sama Veda. In every direction, a divine shower of flowers rained down from the sky and fell down at the spot where Varshneya, Gangeya and the Pandavas were. Celestial instruments were sounded and large numbers of apsaras arrived there. Nothing unpleasant was seen anywhere there. An auspicious and pleasant wind began to blow

[503]The lord of speech.

[504]The moon.

[505]Those born from wombs, those born from eggs, those born from seeds and those born from sweat (moisture).

and it carried all the fragrant and sacred scents. The directions were calm and the animals and the birds also became calm. In an instant, the illustrious sun god, with the one thousand rays, was seen in the west, like a fire burning the extremity of a forest. All the maharshis arose and honoured Janardana, Bhishma and King Yudhishthira. Keshava bowed before them, and so did the Pandavas, Satyaki, Sanjaya and Kripa Sharadvata. When those who were always devoted to dharma[506]were honoured in the proper way, they said, "We will return tomorrow," and quickly left, as they wished. Keshava and the Pandavas took their leave of Gangeya. They circumambulated him and ascended their sparkling chariots. The poles of those chariots were decorated with gold and ivory. There were crazy tuskers that looked like mountains. There were horses that were as swift as eagles. There were foot soldiers with bows and arrows. Extremely fast, that army advanced in front and to the rear of those chariots. In front and to the rear, it was like the great river Narmada, separated into two by Mount Rikshavat.[507] In the east, the illustrious moon arose, delighting the army. The sun had drunk up the juice from the herbs and it again restored their original qualities. The bulls among the Yadus and the Pandavas entered the city,[508] which was as radiant as a city of the gods. They were exhausted and entered those supreme and appropriate abodes, like the lord of deer[509] returning to a cave.'

Chapter 1381(53)

Vaishampayana said, 'Madhusudana entered his residence and slept. He awoke when one *yama* was left of the night.[510] Madhava engaged in meditating on all forms of knowledge. After

[506]The sages.

[507]Narmada is believed to originate in Mount Rikshavat, in the Vindhyas.

[508]Hastinapura.

[509]The lion.

[510]A night consists of three yamas. So a yama is four hours.

that, he thought of the eternal brahman. There were those who were learned in the sacred texts and the Puranas, possessing melodious voices. They praised Prajapati Vasudeva, the creator of the universe. They recited, clapped their hands and sang songs. Thousands of conch shells, drums and tambourines were sounded. There were the beautiful sounds of veenas, cymbals and flutes. Like a drawn-out laugh, they were heard to emanate from his residence. Loud and pleasant words, with auspicious sounds, were also heard for King Yudhishthira, mixed with songs and the sound of musical instruments. Dasharha Achyuta arose. He bathed. Joining his hands in salutation, the mighty-armed one lit a fire. Standing before it, he meditated on a secret mantra. There were thousands of brahmanas who were learned about the four Vedas. Madhava promised each of them one thousand cows. Having touched an auspicious object, Krishna then looked at himself in a spotless mirror and told Satyaki, "O descendant of the Shini lineage! Go to the king's residence and ascertain if the immensely energetic Yudhishthira has prepared himself for visiting Bhishma." At Krishna's words, Satyaki quickly went to King Yudhishthira and told him, "O king! The intelligent Vasudeva's supreme chariot is yoked. Janardana is ready to leave for the son of the river. O Dharmaraja! O immensely radiant one! Krishna is waiting for you. You should now do what must immediately be done."

'Yudhishthira said, "O Phalguna! O infinitely radiant one! Let the supreme chariot be yoked. There is no need for the soldiers to go. We will go alone. Let us not afflict Bhishma, supreme among those who uphold dharma. O Dhananjaya! Let the advance guard also refrain. From today, Gangeya will speak about supreme secrets. O Kounteya! I do not desire that ordinary people should assemble there."'

Vaishampayana said, 'Dhananjaya, Kunti's son, paid heed to these words. As instructed, the bull among men had that supreme chariot prepared and informed him. King Yudhishthira, the twins, Bhima and Arjuna went to Krishna's residence, like the five elements assembled together. As the great-souled Pandavas arrived, together with Shini's descendant, the intelligent Krishna went out and ascended his chariot. Astride their chariots, they asked each other whether they had spent the night in happiness. Then the maharathas left on those supreme chariots, with a roar like that of the clouds. Daruka goaded Vasudeva's horses, Meghapushpa, Balaha, Sainya and Sugriva. O king! Goaded by Daruka, Vasudeva's horses tore up the ground with their hooves. Those immensely strong ones departed with great force, seeming to devour the sky. They passed over all of Kurukshetra, the field that was full of dharma. They went to the spot where the lord Bhishma was lying down on his bed of arrows. He was in the midst of brahmarshis, like Brahma amidst a large number of gods. Govinda and Yudhishthira descended from their chariots and so did Bhima, the wielder of Gandiva, the twins and Satyaki. They raised their right hands and honoured the rishis. They then surrounded the king, like the nakshatras around the moon. They approached Gangeya, like Vasava towards Brahma. He was lying down on a bed of arrows, as if the sun had fallen down. On seeing this, the mighty-armed one[511] was struck with fear and timidity.'

Chapter 1382(54)

Janamejaya asked, 'He had dharma in his soul. He was great in spirits and did not waver from the truth. He had conquered his soul. He was immensely fortunate and without decay. Devavrata was lying down on that bed of arrows. Bhishma, Shantanu's son, was lying down on a bed meant for heroes. The Pandavas presented themselves before Gangeya, tiger among men. What conversation took place at that gathering of heroes, after all the soldiers had been killed? O great sage! Tell me that.'

Vaishampayana said, 'Bhishma, who bore the great burden of the Kouravas, was lying down on the bed of arrows. O king! The rishis and siddhas, with Narada at their head, arrived there. There were also the kings who had not been slain, with Yudhishthira at

[511]Yudhishthira.

their head, Dhritarashtra, Krishna, Bhima, Arjuna and the twins. They approached the great-souled grandfather of the Bharatas. They sorrowed over Gangeya, who was like the sun when it has fallen down. Narada, who looked like a god, thought for a short while. Then he spoke to the Pandavas and all the remaining kings. "The time has come for Bhishma to be asked. O descendant of the Bharata lineage![512] Like the sun, Gangeya is about to set. Before he gives up his breath of life, everyone should question him. He knows everything about the diverse kinds of dharma followed by the four varnas. He is aged and has already obtained worlds, for the time when he gives up his body. Quickly ask him about any doubts that you might have." Having been thus addressed by Narada, the kings approached Bhishma. But they were unable to ask him and glanced towards each other.

'Yudhishthira, Pandu's son, then spoke to Hrishikesha. "No one other than Devaki's son is capable of questioning the grandfather. O invincible one! O Madhusudana! You ask first. O son![513] Among all of us, you are the one who knows about the supreme forms of all kinds of dharma." Having been thus addressed by Pandava, the illustrious Keshava approached the unassailable one.[514] Achyuta spoke to him. Vasudeva said, "O supreme among kings! Have you spent the night in happiness? Is your intelligence present and clear? O unblemished one! Is your entire knowledge shining? Is your heart without pain? Is your mind without anxiety?" Bhishma replied, "O Govinda! O unblemished one! Because of your favours, subjugation, confusion, exhaustion, fatigue, languor and agony have just disappeared. O supremely radiant one! Like a fruit in my hand, I can see everything in the past, the present and the future. O Achyuta! Because of the boon you have granted me, I can see everything about the dharma laid down in the Vedas and uttered in Vedanta.[515] The dharma cited for virtuous ones is circling around in my heart. O Janardana! I know the dharma for countries, clans[516]

[512]Narada is primarily speaking to Yudhishthira.

[513]The word used is tata.

[514]Bhishma.

[515]The word Vedanta is usually used for the Upanishads.

[516]Jatis.

and families. The dharma of the four types of ashramas is established in my heart. O Keshava! I understand everything about the dharma of kings. O Janardana! I will state everything that needs to be said. Through your favours, an auspicious intelligence has penetrated my mind. I have been strengthened by meditating on you and seem to be young again. O Janardana! Through your favours, I am able to speak about what is beneficial. Why don't you yourself tell Pandava about what is beneficial? O Madhava! Quickly tell me why you are not doing this."

'Vasudeva replied, "O Kourava! Know me to be the source of fame and everything that is beneficial. All sentiments, good and bad, originate in my soul. Who in the world will wonder if it is said that the moon's rays are cool? In that way, who will wonder that I am full of fame? O immensely radiant one! However, I desire that your fame should be kindled. O Bhishma! That is the reason my greatness has pervaded your intelligence. O protector of the earth! As long as the earth exists, it is certain that your undecaying deeds will circulate throughout the world. O Bhishma! On being asked by Pandava, whatever you say will be established on the surface of the earth, like the declarations of the Vedas. Anyone who himself follows what you have adduced as proof will, after death, reap the fruits of all meritorious deeds. O Bhishma! That is the reason I have granted you divine intelligence. I have granted you a fame that will spread. How can it be extended further? It is certain that as long as a man's fame is spoken of among people on this earth, so long does he possess an undecaying state. O king! The kings who have not been slain are seated around you. O descendant of the Bharata lineage! They wish to ask you about dharma. Tell them. You are aged and senior. You possess learning and good conduct. You are accomplished about the past and future dharma of kings. Since you were born, no one has seen any transgression in you. All the kings know you as someone who is conversant with the dharma of Manu.[517] O king! Address them, like a father to his sons, and tell them about supreme policy. You have always worshipped

[517]The Critical edition says *manudharma*, which brings in Manu. Some non-Critical versions say *sarvadharma*, which means all forms of dharma, without bringing in Manu.

the rishis and the gods. As I see it, you should speak to them without leaving anything out. These virtuous ones have repeatedly asked you and wish to learn about dharma. The wise say that when a learned one is asked about dharma, he must speak. O lord! If one does not answer, one suffers from a sin. Your sons and grandsons have asked you about eternal dharma. They desire learning. O bull among the Bharata lineage! Therefore, you should speak to them."'

Chapter 1383(55)

Vaishampayana said, 'The greatly energetic descendant of the Kourava lineage then spoke these words. "In that case, I will speak about dharma. My speech and my mind are firm because of your favours. O Govinda! You are the eternal soul of all beings. O unblemished one! However, King Yudhishthira must ask me about dharma. In that case, I will be pleased and will speak about dharma. When that rajarshi was born, all the great-souled rishis, with dharma in their souls, were delighted. Therefore, let Pandava ask me. All the Kurus follow dharma and are blazing in their fame. But among them, there is no one who is his equal. Therefore, let Pandava ask me. Fortitude, restraint, brahmacharya, forgiveness, power and energy are always found in him. Therefore, let Pandava ask me. Truthfulness, generosity, austerities, purity, peace, mental vigour and honour—all of these are in him. Therefore, let Pandava ask me. He does not act in accordance with adharma, for the sake of desire, intolerance, fear or prosperity. He has dharma in his soul. Therefore, let Pandava ask me. He welcomes and treats equally relatives, guests, servants and those who seek refuge. Therefore, let Pandava ask me. He is always truthtful. He is always forgiving. He is always learned. He is devoted to guests. He always donates to the righteous. Therefore, let Pandava ask me. He always observes rites and studies. He always follows dharma. He is peaceful and knows the secrets of the sacred texts. Therefore, let Pandava ask me."

'Vasudeva replied, "Yudhishthira has dharma in his soul and is overcome with great shame. Because he is frightened of a curse, he is not approaching you. O lord of the earth! This protector of the worlds has caused carnage of the worlds. Because he is frightened of a curse, he is not approaching you. There were those who should be worshipped. There were those who were devoted. There were preceptors, allies and relatives. They deserved to be honoured. But having slain them with arrows, he is not approaching you."

'Bhishma said, "O Krishna! The dharma of brahmanas is donations, studying and austerities. Like that, the dharma of kshatriyas is to give up the body in battle. Fathers, grandfathers, sons, preceptors, allies and relatives advanced against him on a false cause. He followed dharma and killed them in a battle. O Keshava! There may be wicked seniors who are avaricious and abandon agreements. If a kshatriya kills them in a battle, he is following dharma. If kshatriya relatives challenge one to a battle, one must always fight. Manu has said that fighting is dharma. It leads to heaven and the worlds."'

Vaishampayana said, 'When Bhishma spoke in this way, Dharmaraja Yudhishthira approached humbly and stood in front, so that he could be seen. He grasped Bhishma's feet and honoured him. He[518] inhaled the fragrance of his[519] head and asked him to be seated. Gangeya, bull among all archers, said, "O son![520] Ask me what you wish. O supreme among the Kuru lineage! Do not be scared."'

Chapter 1384(56)

Vaishampayana said, 'Yudhishthira bowed down before Hrishikesha and the grandfather. He took the permission of all the seniors and asked, "Those who are learned about dharma say

[518]Bhishma.

[519]Yudhishthira's.

[520]The word used is tata.

that ruling the kingdom is supreme dharma. O king! I think that it is a great burden. Tell me about this. O grandfather! In particular, tell me about rajadharma.[521] All the beings in the world find a refuge in rajadharma. O Kourava! The three *vargas*[522] are dependent on rajadharma. All the forms of mokshadharma[523] are also clearly based on it. It is like the harness for a horse, or the goad for an elephant. It has been said that the dharma of kings restrains the world in that way. The rajarshis served that dharma earlier. It is becoming confused now, the world will no longer be established and everyone will become anxious. When the sun rises, it dispels the demonic darkness. In that way, rajadharma casts away everything that is inauspicious in this world. O grandfather! O best of the Bharata lineage! O supreme among intelligent ones! Therefore, tell me about the true nature of rajadharma first. O scorcher of enemies! We obtain the truth about all kinds of learning from you. Vasudeva thinks that you are supreme among intelligent ones."

'Bhishma replied, "I bow down before the supreme dharma. I bow down before the supreme Krishna. I honour the brahmanas. I will now speak about eternal dharma. O Yudhishthira! Hear from me a complete account of rajadharma. Listen attentively to everything else that you wish to hear. O best of the Kuru lineage! In the beginning, a king who desires pleasure must worship the gods and the brahmanas in the proper way. O extender of the Kuru lineage! Once one has worshipped the gods and the brahmanas, one is freed of the debts of dharma and is revered by the worlds. O son! O Yudhishthira! You must always strive to uplift yourself. Without the exertion, fortune never makes a king's objectives successful. In general, there are two aspects—destiny and enterprise. But I certainly think it has been said that enterprise is superior to destiny. Even if a task begun does not go well, it is pointless to rue that. O son! If a king is led astray, he must make greater efforts. With the exception of truth, there is nothing that contributes to the success of kings. If a king is devoted

[521]The dharma of kings.

[522]The three objectives, dharma, artha and kama.

[523]Mokshadharma is the dharma that leads to emancipation or liberation.

to the truth, he finds delight here, and in the hereafter. O Indra among kings! Truth is the supreme wealth for rishis too. Like that, nothing inspires as much confidence in kings as adherence to supreme truth. If one possesses qualities and good conduct, is self-controlled and mild, is devoted to dharma and has conquered the senses, if one is extremely handsome and has a broad objective[524]—then one never deviates from prosperity. O descendant of the Kuru lineage! One must resort to uprightness in all tasks. One must reconsider policy and conceal the three.[525] If a king is mild, everyone always disregards him. But if a king is fierce, everyone is troubled. Therefore, act so that you are both. O supreme among generous ones! Brahmanas must never be punished. O descendant of the Bharata lineage! Those who are brahmanas are named as supreme beings in this world. O Indra among kings! The great-souled Manu sung two shlokas about this. O Kouravya! This was about one's own dharma and you should bear this in your heart. 'Fire emerged from water. Kshatriyas emerged from brahmanas. Iron emerged from stone. The energy of each of these is pacified by the source.[526] When iron confronts stone, fire faces water and kshatriyas hate brahmanas, then each of these three is destroyed.' O great king! Knowing this, you must bow down before brahmanas. The best of brahmanas are full of peace and represent the brahman on earth. O tiger among kings! However, you must always use your arms to restrain those who seem to be like that, but actually destroy the edifice of the world.[527] O son! Maharshi Ushanas sang two shlokas in earlier times. O immensely wise one! O king! Listen to them attentively. 'A lord of men, who is following his own dharma, should consider dharma and raise his weapons to even counter someone who knows the Vedas in battle, if that person attacks him. If dharma is being destroyed, the one who protects it is the one who

[524]Without getting bogged down by minute trivia.

[525]These three are left implicit and have to be deduced. One's weaknesses, one's policy and the weaknesses of enemies have to be concealed.

[526]Fire is quenched with water, iron is blunted by stone and kshatriyas are controlled by brahmanas.

[527]Though not directly stated, this seems to mean that the king should restrain imperfect brahmanas.

is following dharma. If one counters anger with anger, the sin of killing a foetus does not result.'[528] O best of men! The brahmanas must be protected in this way. If they commit a crime, they must be exiled to the extremities of the kingdom. O lord of men! But there must be compassion for those who are accused, even those who kill a brahmana, violate the preceptor's bed, or kill a foetus. A brahmana who hates the king must be banished outside the kingdom and it is never recommended that there should be corporal punishment. O supreme among men! You must always be affectionate towards men. For a king, there is no treasure as supreme as the store of men.

'"O great king! There are six kinds of forts that are indicated in the sacred texts.[529] Among all these, it is held that the one protected by men is the most difficult to breach. Therefore, a learned king must act so as to be compassionate towards the four varnas. If a king has dharma in his soul and speaks the truth, he delights the subjects. O supreme among men! However, you should not be indulgent all the time. A mild king follows adharma. He is like a forgiving elephant. In the sacred texts of Brihaspati, a shloka was laid down in earlier times. O great king! It has a bearing on this. I am reciting it. Listen attentively. 'A forgiving king is always subjugated by the inferior, who are like elephant riders who mount the head of an elephant and wound it. Therefore, a king must not be gentle all the time. He must also be harsh. He should be like the sun in the summer, not too cold and not too hot.' O great king! You must always examine friend and foe through direction, examination, inference, analogies and instructions.[530] O one who donates a lot! You must give up all the vices. Even if one indulges in them, one must give up addiction. In the world, people who indulge in vices are always overcome. If a king does not love his subjects, he generates anxiety. The king must always treat them the way a wife treats her embryo. O great king! Listen to the reasons why this is desirable. For the welfare of the embryo, a pregnant woman ceases to follow everything that brings

[528]The killing of a foetus is being equated with the killing of a brahmana.

[529]Those protected by deserts, water, earth, forests, mountains and men.

[530]Of the sacred texts.

pleasure to her mind alone. The king must certainly be like that. O best among the Kuru lineage! He must always follow dharma. For the welfare of the world, he must abandon everything that he likes. O Pandava! However, you must never abandon truth and fortitude. The commands of someone who is patient and firm in meting out punishment are not contravened.

'"O supreme among eloquent ones! You must always avoid cracking jokes with the servants. O tiger among kings! Listen to the reasons why it is wrong to do that. If one involves the servants in pleasure, they disregard the master. They no longer remain in their appointed places and disobey his words. Sent on a task, they think about it and disclose the secret. They ask what they should not ask for. They eat what they should not eat. They become angry and flare up. They lie down on his bed. They resort to deceit, accept bribes and hamper the undertaking of tasks. They indulge in forgeries and cause the prosperity to decay. They dress like the female guards and consort with them. In his[531] presence, they pass wind and spit. O tiger among men! They become shameless and laugh at his words. When the king is cheerful and mild, they mount the king's beloved horse, tusker and chariot. 'O king! It will be difficult for you to do this. You should not have attempted this.' The courtiers, known as well-wishers, speak in this way. They laugh when he is angry. They are not delighted when they are honoured. For various reasons, they always begin to fight with each other. They divulge secrets and cover up their wicked deeds. They treat his commands with mockery and disdain, such as about ornaments, food, bathing and unguents. O tiger among men! They are comfortable with ignoring them, even when they listen to him. O descendant of the Bharata lineage! They censure their own stations and abandon them. They are not satisfied with their salaries and appropriate what belongs to the king. They toy with him as they will, like with a bird tied to a string. They tell people, 'The king is devoted to us.' O Yudhishthira! When the king is mild and cheerful, these and many other sins manifest themselves."'

[531]The master's.

Chapter 1385(57)

'Bhishma said, "O Yudhishthira! The king must always exert himself. Without exertion, a king fades away, like a woman. O lord of the earth! The illustrious Ushanas has a shloka on this. O king! As I recite it, listen attentively to me. 'Like a snake that swallows animals who live in burrows, there are two things that are swallowed up by the earth—a king who does not oppose and a brahmana who does not leave his home.'[532] O tiger among men! Therefore, you must bear this in your heart. You must ally with those one should have alliances with. You must resist those who should be resisted. The kingdom has seven limbs.[533] Anyone who acts against these must be slain, even if he happens to be a preceptor or a friend. O Indra among kings! King Marutta sang an ancient shloka about governing a kingdom, in conformity with Brihaspati's ancient views. 'It is recommended that a preceptor must be abandoned, if he is haughty, cannot distinguish between what should be done and what should not be done, and is inclined to take the wrong path.' To ensure the welfare of the citizens, the intelligent King Sagara, Bahu's son, exiled his eldest son Asamanja.[534] O king! Asamanja had earlier drowned the children of the citizens in the Sarayu. His father censured him and exiled him. The great ascetic Shvetaketu was the beloved son of rishi Uddalaka. But because he falsely made brahmanas follow him, he was abandoned.

'"The eternal duty of kings is ensuring the pleasure of the subjects, protecting the truth and uprightness in conduct. He must not cause harm to the possessions of others. At the right time, he must give what should be given. A king who is brave, truthful in his speech and forgiving, does not deviate from the path to be trodden. His counsels are secret. He conquers anger. He is firm in determining the

[532]Because of excessive attachment for his wife and children.

[533]The king, the army, advisers, allies, the treasury, forts and the geographical expanse of the kingdom.

[534]This story has been recounted in Section 33 (Volume 3). Bahu was also known as Asita.

purport of the sacred texts. He is always devoted to dharma, artha, kama and moksha. The king must always cover weaknesses in the three.[535] There is nothing as important for kings as the control of the wicked. The lords of the earth must protect the dharma of the four varnas. The eternal dharma of kings is to prevent a mixing of dharma.[536] The king must not trust and must not trust too much. Using his own intelligence, he must always examine the good and the bad in the six aspects.[537] A king who can detect weaknesses in the enemy is always praised. So is one who knows the truth of the three objectives[538] and uses the strategy of employing spies. Like Yama and Vaishravana,[539] he must add to the treasury. He should know about the increase and decrease in the status of the ten.[540] He should support those who have no one to support them. However, he must also have an eye towards those who possess support. A king must have an excellent face and must smile before he speaks. He must revere those who are aged and conquer excessive lassitude. He should consider the conduct of the righteous and set his mind on the conduct of the righteous. He must never take away riches from the hands of the righteous. Instead, he must take it away from those who are wicked and give it to those who are righteous. He is himself the one who gives and takes away. Therefore, his soul must be under control and so must those who serve him. He will be pure in his conduct. At the right time, he will give and enjoy. Men who are born in noble lineages, are without disease and are brave and faithful must be employed as advisers. They must be good in conduct. They must not be disrespectful towards relatives[541] and

[535]Probably referring to dharma, artha and kama.

[536]The dharma of the four varnas should not be mixed up.

[537]The six aspects of policy—alliances, war, marching, halting, dividing and fortifying the army and sowing dissension in the enemy.

[538]Dharma, artha and kama.

[539]Kubera.

[540]Advisers, fortified cities, the countryside, the treasury and the army add up to five. There are these five on one's own side and five on the side of the enemy. The king must know about these ten.

[541]The king's relatives.

must not be proud. They must possess learning and be conversant with this world. However, they must also be able to look at the world hereafter. They must be virtuous and devoted to dharma. They must be as immobile as mountains. The king must always reward these aides and they should be his equal in the objects of pleasure that they enjoy. In addition, the king will only possess his umbrella. The king's behaviour towards them, directly and indirectly, will be the same.[542] If he acts in this way, an Indra among kings will never repent. A king who is suspicious of everything, a king who takes everything away and a king who is addicted to wickedness is quickly restrained by his own subjects. However, a lord of the earth who is pure and is engaged in attracting the hearts of the subjects is not devoured by the enemy when he falls. Even when he falls, he rises again. A king who is without anger, not addicted to vices, a king who wields a mild rod of punishment and has conquered his senses, is trusted by beings, as if he was the Himalayas. He is wise. He possesses all the qualities and is engaged in detecting the weaknesses of the enemy. He is extremely handsome. He considers the truth about what is good and bad for the four varnas. He is swift to act. He has conquered his anger. He is high-minded and is extremely easy to please. He is naturally free from disease. He acts and does not boast. He endeavours to complete all the tasks that have been begun.

'"When such a king is seen, that king is supreme among kings. Men in his kingdom roam around fearlessly, like sons in the house of a father. That king is supreme among kings. Citizens who reside in his kingdom know about good policy and bad and do not need to hide their riches. Such a king is supreme among kings. Men who reside in his kingdom are engaged in their own tasks. They do not quarrel and are generous. They are properly protected. They are docile, obedient and humble. They are not inclined to fight. In a kingdom where men find pleasure in donating, he is indeed a king. There is no fraud and deceit. There is no maya. There is no malice. In the kingdom of such a king, there is eternal dharma. He shows proper respect to learning. He is engaged in good policies that bring

[542]He will not differentiate between them and him.

benefits to citizens. He follows the dharma of the righteous and is ready to renounce. He is indeed a king in the kingdom. He uses spies. However, his counsels, what he will do, and what he will not do, is never known to enemies. He is indeed a king in the kingdom. O descendant of the Bharata lineage! There is an ancient shloka that the great-souled Bhargava had sung, which was recited to the king when he was told about Rama's conduct.[543] 'First, get a king.[544] Get a wife after that. After that, obtain riches. If there is no kingdom in this world, how can there be a wife? How can there be riches?' O lion among kings! Therefore, this is the eternal dharma of kings and nothing else. One must clearly protect. The world is sustained on that protection. O Indra among kings! Manu, the son of Prachetasa, recited these two shlokas about rajadharma.[545] Listen attentively to this. 'There are six men who must be avoided, like a broken boat on an ocean—a preceptor who does not speak, an officiating priest who has not studied, a king who does not protect, a wife who does not speak sweetly, a cowherd who wishes to be in a village and a barber who desires to go to the forest.'"'[546]

Chapter 1386(58)

'Bhishma said, "O Yudhishthira! In rajadharma, this is like freshly churned butter. The illustrious Brihaspati praises this and no other dharma. The large-eyed and illustrious Kavya, the great ascetic,[547] the thousand-eyed and great Indra, Manu, the son of

[543]The king in question is Yudhishthira himself, who was told Rama's (i.e., Parashurama's) story (by Krishna) earlier in this section. Bhargava is Parashurama.

[544]That is, choose a kingdom where you wish to live.

[545]Son is to be interpreted as descendant. Prachetasa is Daksha and the Manu in question is Vaivasvata Manu.

[546]The cowherd's tasks are in pastures, not in the village. The barber's tasks are in the village, not in the forest.

[547]Shukracharya, the preceptor of the demons.

Prachetasa, the illustrious Bharadvaja and the sage Gourashira were devoted to Brahma and learned about the brahman. They composed sacred texts about what kings should do. O supreme among those who uphold dharma! They praised the dharma of protection. O one with eyes like blue lotuses tinged with coppery red! O Yudhishthira! Listen to the means of accomplishing this—spies, the act of spying, donations, lack of jealousy, receiving things properly[548] and not receiving improperly, selecting the virtuous,[549] bravery, skill, truth, the welfare of subjects, using fair and foul means to create discord and enmity within the ranks of the enemy, not abandoning righteous people, supporting those born in noble lineages, storing things that should be stored, serving those who are intelligent, finding delight in strength, always glancing towards the welfare of subjects, lack of lethargy in tasks, extending the treasury, protecting the city, distrust, breaking up quarrels between citizens, paying attention to houses that are decayed or falling down, depending on the context, using both kinds of punishment,[550] paying attention to friends, foes and neutrals, weaning away servants who are inclined to move from one's side to that of the enemy, distrust of those on one's own side, assurance towards the enemy, following the policy of dharma, constant readiness for action, not disregarding the enemy and the abandoning of those who are wicked.

'"There are shlokas where Brihaspati has spoken about the rise of kings and the roots of rajadharma. Listen to these. 'Amrita was obtained through enterprise. The asuras were slain through enterprise. It is through enterprise that the great Indra obtained superiority in heaven. It is because of enterprise that a courageous person is superior to one who is eloquent. Those who are clever with words gratify and worship the ones who are courageous in enterprise.[551] Even if he has intelligence, if a king lacks enterprise, he is always oppressed by the enemy, like a snake without any poison.' Even if one is stronger, one

[548]This can be interpreted as fair taxation.

[549]For administrative duties.

[550]Corporal punishment and monetary fines.

[551]This can be interpreted as superiority of kshatriyas over brahmanas.

must not ignore a weaker enemy. A small fire can also burn. A little bit of poison can kill. If an enemy is inside a fortification and only possesses horses, he is capable of afflicting, here and there, a king with a prosperous kingdom. The secret words of a king, the amassing of troops for victory, the deceit in his heart, tasks that are done for specific purposes and the crooked acts that he undertakes—must be sustained by rectitude.[552] Even for the sake of deceiving the people, he must act in accordance with dharma. Sustaining a kingdom is extremely difficult. A person who has not cleansed his soul cannot bear the burden. One has to sustain grievous assaults and the mild cannot tolerate this. A kingdom is like a piece of meat. It must always be supported by rectitude. O Yudhishthira! You must always support it in a mixed way.[553] Even if one confronts a calamity when protecting the subjects, lords of the earth who act in this way accumulate great dharma. I have told you a little bit about rajadharma. O supreme among eloquent ones! Tell me about the doubts that still remain."'

Vaishampayana said, 'At this, the illustrious Vyasa, Devasthana, Ashma, Vasudeva, Kripa, Satyaki and Sanjaya, uttered words of praise. They were delighted and their faces were like blooming flowers. They honoured Bhishma, tiger among men and supreme among those who uphold dharma. With a distressed mind, the supreme among the Kuru lineage[554] gently touched Bhishma's feet, his eyes completely overflowing with tears. He said, "O grandfather! I will ask you about my doubts tomorrow. The sun has drunk the juice of the earth and is setting." Keshava, Kripa, Yudhishthira and the others honoured the brahmanas. Having circumambulated the son of the great river, they happily ascended their chariots. They were good in their vows and bathed in the Dhrishadvati. Having performed ablutions in the water, they observed the auspicious rites. As was appropriate, those scorchers of enemies observed the evening rites. They then entered the city of Gajasahvya.'[555]

[552]The aberrations are justified if there is an overall framework of rectitude.

[553]Part rectitude and part deceit.

[554]Yudhishthira.

[555]Hastinapura.

Chapter 1387(59)

Vaishampayana said, 'At the right time, the Pandavas and the Yadavas arose and performed their morning ablutions. They set out on chariots that looked like cities. They went to Kurukshetra and approached the unblemished Bhishma. They asked if Gangeya, supreme among rathas, had spent the night in happiness. They paid their respects to Vyasa and all the other rishis. Then, in every direction, they seated themselves around Bhishma. The king, the immensely energetic Dharmaraja Yudhishthira, joined his hands in salutation. He paid his respects to Bhishma and asked, "O descendant of the Bharata lineage! The word raja, raja keeps circulating around. O grandfather! What is its origin? Tell me. A man possesses hands, head and neck that are similar to those of others. His understanding, senses and soul are similar. His sense of unhappiness and happiness are similar. His back, arms and stomach are similar. His semen, bones and marrow are similar. His flesh and blood are similar. His inhalation and exhalation are similar. His breath of life and body are similar. His birth and death are similar. All his human qualities are similar. Among all those with bravery and intelligence, why does a single one stand out as superior? The entire earth is full of brave, valiant and noble people. Why does one alone protect it and why do all the people wish to please him? If a single one is pleased, all the people are pleased. When he is troubled, it is certainly the case that everyone is troubled. O bull among the Bharata lineage! I wish to hear the entire truth about this. O supreme among eloquent ones! Tell me the exact truth about this. O lord of the earth! It cannot be a trifling reason that the entire world worships a single person like a god."

'Bhishma replied, "O best among men! Listen attentively to everything, about how, in the beginning, royalty was created in krita yuga. At that time, there was no sovereignty and no king. There was no punishment and no one to chastise. In accordance with dharma, all the subjects protected each other. O descendant of the Bharata lineage! In accordance with dharma, all the men sustained each other. However, they became extremely exhausted and confusion pervaded them. O bull among men! When people were overcome by confusion, this confusion affected their perception and dharma was destroyed. O supreme among the Bharata lineage! All of them were overcome by avarice. The men then hankered after what was not theirs. O lord! Then the vice named desire took over. When they came under the subjugation of desire, passion touched them. O Yudhishthira! O Indra among kings! Because of that passion, they were no longer aware of what should be done and what should not be done, whom one should have intercourse with and whom not with, what should be said and what should not be said, what should be eaten and what should not be eaten, and what was good and what was bad. They accepted what should be discarded. When this world was in disorder, the brahman was destroyed.[556] O king! When the brahman was destroyed, dharma was also destroyed. When the brahman and dharma were destroyed, the gods were frightened. O tiger among men! In their terror, they sought refuge with Brahma. The gods approached the illustrious grandfather of the worlds. They were afflicted by sorrow, grief and fright. All of them joined their hands in salutation and said, 'O illustrious one! The eternal brahman that was present in the world of men has been destroyed. There are sentiments like avarice and confusion there. We are overcome by terror. O original lord! With the brahman having been destroyed, dharma has also been destroyed. O lord of the three worlds! We have become the same as mortals. They poured oblations upwards. We showered downwards on earth.[557] Now that those supreme rites have stopped, we are faced with an uncertainty. O grandfather! Determine what will be beneficial for us. Your power results from our power and that is being destroyed.' Having been thus addressed by all the gods, the illustrious Svayambhu[558] replied, 'O bulls among the gods! I will think about your welfare. Do not be frightened.' Using his

[556]This is interpreted as meaning that the knowledge of the Vedas was destroyed.

[557]The gods showered down rain. Sustained by this, men offered oblations to sustain the gods.

[558]The self-creating one, Brahma's name.

own intelligence, he composed one hundred thousand chapters that described dharma, artha and kama. Svayambhu designated these categories *trivarga*.[559] The fourth one of moksha was a separate objective and a separate category. Within moksha, three categories of sattva, rajas and tamas were spoken of.[560]

'"Preservation, increase and destruction were three categories that were the consequence of chastisement. The self, place, time, means, tasks, aides and causes were said to be the six ingredients of policy.[561] O bull among the Bharata lineage! In this extensive corpus of learning, the three,[562] analysis, livelihood and the policy of punishment are laid down. The means of protecting oneself against aides, protecting oneself against princes, the use of spies and other methods and the use of secret agents are separately indicated.[563] O Pandava! All the techniques of sama, *dana,* danda, *bheda* and the fifth one of *upeksha* are completely laid down.[564] All the secret methods of creating dissension have been described, and also when these secret methods fail. The consequences of success and failure are given. The various kinds of alliances—inferior, middling and superior—based respectively on creating fear, showering honour and offering riches, have been completely described. There is an account of the four kinds of time for departure[565] and a complete description of the three kinds of victory—victory for reasons of dharma, victory for reasons of artha and objectives, and victory that is asura in nature.[566] The three kinds of characteristics associated with the five categories have also

559 The three objectives or categories.

560 Respectively, the qualities of purity, passion and darkness.

561 Place and time are counted as one, so that there are six and not seven.

562 The three Vedas.

563 A king might face treachery from aides and princes.

564 Sama, dana, danda, bheda are the four respective familiar principles of conciliation, gifts (to wean away), punishment and sowing dissension. Upeksha can be translated as both endurance and neglect.

565 Probably very good, good, bad and very bad *muhurtas*.

566 Dharma and artha are not gained from an asura victory.

been described.[567] Direct and indirect kinds of punishment have been recounted. Indirect punishment is of many different kinds. O Pandava! There are eight that are direct—chariots, elephants, horses, foot soldiers, compulsory service, boats, spies and guides for the road[568] as the eighth. O Kouravya! These are the eight direct manifestations of an army. The use and administration of many types of poison and mixtures in mobile and immobile objects has also been described, such as through objects one touches and objects one uses. Enemies, friends and neutral ones have been recounted. There are qualities of roads, qualities of the ground, the technique of protecting, the technique of providing assurance and keeping a lookout for spies. There are different methods for arranging men, elephants, chariots and horses in diverse *vyuha*s and many wonderful techniques of fighting. O bull among the Bharata lineage! There is also information about portents, accidents, fighting well, retreating well and knowledge about making the weapons drink.[569] O Pandava! How is an army freed from a calamity? How is the army's delight increased? What are the times for attacking and destroying? When should one take fright? Techniques of laying trenches and other methods have been described. How does one afflict the kingdom of an enemy through the use of thieves, mountain-dwelling bandits and fierce soldiers? How does one use arsonists, poisoners and spies in disguise? How are foremost members of guilds weaned away?[570] How are the plants uprooted? How are his elephants corrupted? How are his subjects terrified? How are those loyal to him dissuaded? How does one control the roads? The waxing and waning of the

[567]The five categories are the advisers, the countryside, the fortified city, the treasury and the army. These can have three characteristics—superior, middling and inferior.

[568]The text actually suggests that one should take these guides from the country one is at war with.

[569]The word used is *payana,* which means drink. This is not about the blades of weapons being made to drink the enemy's blood. It is about the way those iron blades were crafted, heated and then cooled with water.

[570]Guilds (shrenis) in the enemy's kingdom.

seven parts of the kingdom[571] are described and the extension of the prosperity of the kingdom through the use of emissaries. The development of enemies, neutrals and allies is completely enumerated. How does one grind down and counter stronger enemies? What are the extremely subtle methods used for uprooting thorns? How does one pacify oneself? What are the methods of exercise? How does one use yoga and accumulate objects? Those who are not servants must be sustained and servants must be taken care of. Riches must be given at the right time and one must be free from vices. There are the qualities of a king and the qualities of a commander. There are reasons and tasks and their good and bad aspects. There are signs to discern if someone is wicked and is ensuring livelihoods for those who are dependents. One must be suspicious of everything and avoid being negligent. One must seek to obtain what one does not possess and extend it. In the proper way, this increase must be given away to deserving people. Wealth must be expended for reasons of dharma, artha and kama. The fourth aspect of avoiding vices has also been described there. O foremost among the Kuru lineage! The ten kinds of vices have been described, the most important arising from anger or from desire. O bull among the Bharata lineage! The preceptors say, following Svayambhu, that hunting, gambling with dice, drinking and women are the ones that are born from desire. Harshness in speech, violence, harshness in punishment, inflicting pain on one's own self, suicide and the destruction of one's own riches are mentioned.[572] There is a description of many kinds of machines and their action. How does one counter those of the enemy? How does one shatter his houses? How does one destroy his sanctuaries, trees and boundaries and destroy the tasks he is engaged in? The techniques of spreading out, advancing and stationing have been described. O supreme among warriors! There are the six aspects of cymbals, drums, conch shells, battle drums, the obtaining of supplies and the weak spots of the enemy.

[571]The king, the army, advisers, allies, the treasury, forts and the geographical expanse of the kingdom.

[572]These are the six that arise from anger.

'"What has been obtained[573] must be pacified and the virtuous ones honoured. One must become friendly with these learned ones and learn the methods used to offer oblations in the mornings. What are the auspicious signs followed for the body? What are the food habits and what the rites always followed by believers? One must single-mindedly determine this, using truth and pleasant words. What are the festivals observed by society and what kind of rituals do those residents follow? O tiger among the Bharata lineage! One must always keep an eye on all the rights and livelihoods—direct, as well as indirect. The non-punishment of brahmanas, the use of punishment against the wicked, the protection of the good qualities of followers and relatives, the protection of citizens and the extension of the kingdom has been described. O king! There are thoughts about a circle of twelve kings. Depending on country, race and family, Svayambhu spoke about the seventy-two aspects of dharma.[574] Dharma, artha, kama and moksha were described there. There were many methods to satisfy the desire for riches and the giving away of large quantities of donations. The fundamental tasks and rites and maya and yoga were described. The techniques for poisoning flowing and stagnant waters were described. There were all the methods so that people did not deviate from the noble path. O tiger among kings! All these aspects of policy were laid down in that sacred text.

'"Having composed this auspicious text, the illustrious lord cheerfully addressed all the gods, with Shakra at the forefront. 'This is for the welfare of the worlds and is established in the three objectives.[575]

[573]Newly acquired kingdoms. The succeeding shlokas are difficult to understand. We have interpreted them as learning about these practices in newly acquired kingdoms.

[574]These numbers are about complicated relationships between kings. At the central core is a king, his main ally and the ally's ally. The core king has an adversary, an enemy, a neutral and a king whose kingdom is geographically contiguous to the core king and the enemy, but is not necessarily a neutral. 3 multiplied by 4 gives the number of 12. Each kingdom has six elements—the king, the advisers, the countryside, the fortified city, the treasury and the army. 12 multiplied by 6 gives 72.

[575]Dharma, artha and kama.

This is full of intelligence and is like newly churned butter that has emerged from the Sarasvati.[576] With the use of the rod, this will protect the worlds. It will reward and punish and roam around the world. It will be known as *dandaniti*[577] and the three worlds will follow it. Great-souled ones will place it at the forefront, representing the essence of the six qualities.[578] The greatness of punishment will be evident in all aspects of policy.' O Yudhishthira! Everything has been described here—the extensive corpus of good policy, the learned texts and the Puranas, the origin of the maharshis, the list of tirthas, the list of nakshatras, everything about the four ashramas and the four kinds of oblations,[579] descriptions of the four varnas and the four Vedas, all the descriptions about itihasa, the minor Vedas[580] and good policy, austerities, knowledge, non-violence, the best policy about the true and the false, the serving of seniors, donations, purity, enterprise and compassion towards all beings. All of this has been described here. O Pandava! There is no doubt that everything that exists on earth in the form of speech has been assembled in this sacred text by the grandfather. Everything has been pronounced about dharma, artha, kama and moksha.

'"The illustrious Shankara Shiva Sthanu, the many-formed and large-eyed consort of Uma, received this policy first. The illustrious Shiva knew that the lifespan decreases from one yuga to another.[581] He therefore abridged the text, full of great import, prepared by Brahma. The immensely asectic one then gave this text, known as Vaishalaksha[582] to Indra, who was extremely devoted to Brahma. It had ten thousand chapters. O son![583] The illustrious Indra abridged

[576]As a river, or as the goddess of speech.

[577]The policy of chastisement.

[578]The king, the advisers, the countryside, the fortified city, the treasury and the army.

[579]Associated with the four Vedas.

[580]Probably the Vedangas.

[581]The human span of life decreases progressively from satya yuga to kali yuga. Hence, people wouldn't have the time to read long texts.

[582]Prepared by the one with large eyes, Vishalaksha or Shiva.

[583]The word used is tata.

it to a text with five thousand and this was known as Bahudantaka. The intelligent lord Brihaspati abridged it to three thousand and this is known as Barhaspatya.[584] The immensely wise and great ascetic Kavya,[585] the preceptor of yoga, reduced it to one thousand and recounted it. O Pandava! Thus, knowing that the lifespan of mortals was becoming reduced, at the request of the worlds, the maharshis abridged the text.

'"Once, the gods went to Prajapati Vishnu and said, 'Tell us about one person who deserves to be superior to other mortals.' The illustrious lord, god Narayana, thought about this. Through his mental powers, he created an energetic son named Virajas. O immensely fortunate one! O Pandava! However, Virajas did not wish to rule over earth. His mind was on renunciation. He had a son named Kirtiman, but he too was interested in what was beyond the five.[586] He had a son named Kardama, who tormented himself through great austerities. Kardama Prajapati had a son named Ananga. This virtuous one was accomplished in dandaniti[587] and protected the subjects. Ananga's son, Atibala, obtained knowledge of policy. However, having become the king of the earth, he was overcome by addiction to the senses. O king! Through his mental powers, Mrityu[588] had a daughter named Sunitha. She was famous in the three worlds and gave birth to Vena. But he became a prey to passion and hatred and used adharma against the subjects. The rishis, knowledgeable about the brahman, purified and invoked blades of kusha grass with mantras and killed him with this. The rishis then used mantras to churn his right thigh.[589] At this, a malformed man was created on the ground and he was a dwarf. His eyes were red. His hair was black and he looked like a post that had been burnt. The rishis, knowledgeable about the brahman, asked

[584]Named after Brihaspati.

[585]Shukracharya.

[586]The five elements. He too was interested in renunciation.

[587]The policy of chastisement.

[588]Death.

[589]Because a king was needed.

him to sit down. That is how the cruel Nishadas were created[590] and they dwelt in mountains and forests. Hundreds and thousands of other mlecchas were also created and they made their abode in the Vindhya mountains. The maharshis then churned his right hand. A man was created and his form was like that of Indra himself. He was armoured and his sword was girded. He held a bow and arrows. He was accomplished in the Vedas, the Vedangas and dhanurveda. O supreme among kings! That king possessed the splendour of all of dandaniti. Vainya[591] joined his hands in salutation and spoke to the maharshis. 'An excellent and subtle intelligence that tells me about dharma and artha has arisen in me. What is my task? Tell me the truth about this and instruct me. Tell me about tasks that are full of objectives. Without thinking about it, I will do whatever you ask me to.' The gods and the supreme rishis told him, 'Restrain yourself. Without any doubt, follow dharma. Treat all living beings alike, irrespective of whom you like and whom you don't like. Abandon desire, anger, avarice and price and cast these off far away. Always have your eye on dharma and use your arms to punish all the men in the world who deviate from dharma. In thoughts, deeds and speech, take this pledge. "I will honour and protect the brahman on earth. I will never resort to my own inclinations. Instead, without any doubt, I will follow the policy of dharma and use dandaniti." O scorcher of enemies! Also take a pledge to never punish brahmanas and protect the entire earth against the creation of hybrid varnas.' Vainya replied to the gods, with the rishis at the forefront. 'O bulls among the gods! If the brahmanas and the gods aid me, I will do this.' Those who knew about the brahman agreed with Vainya's words. Shukra, who was a store of the brahman, became his priest. The Valakhilyas became his advisers and the Sarasvatyas followed him. The illustrious maharshi Garga became the reckoner of time.[592]

'"There is a supreme saying among men. 'He is himself the

[590]*Nishida* is an instruction to be seated.

[591]That is, the son of Vena. Also known as Prithu.

[592]Literally, the reckoner of the year, *samvatsara*. The word can also be translated as astrologer.

eighth.'[593] Those who chanted praises were created, bards and minstrels[594] being the foremost. He[595] levelled the earth and made it plain. We have heard that earlier, the earth was uneven. Vishnu, the god Shakra, the other gods, the rishis and Brahma consecrated him to rule over the subjects. O Pandava! The earth herself presented him with jewels. So did the ocean, the lord of the rivers, and the supreme mountains, the Himalayas. O Yudhishthira! Shakra gave him inexhaustible riches. The golden mount, the great Meru, himself gave him gold. The illustrious Naravahana,[596] the lord of yakshas and rakshasas, gave him riches so that he would be capable of following dharma, artha and kama. O Pandava! As soon as Vainya thought of them, horses, chariots, elephants and crores of men manifested themselves. There was no old age, famine, hardship or disease. Because of the protection offered by the king, there was no fear from reptiles and thieves. He milked the earth for the seventeen kinds of grain.[597] Yakshas, rakshasas and serpents, each obtained whatever they wished for. Thus did the great-souled one ensure supreme dharma in the world. He pleased all the subjects and everyone came to call him raja.[598] The word kshatriya is used because he saved the brahmanas from injury.[599] Virtuous ones have said that the earth is famous for being strewn with riches.[600] O king! The eternal Vishnu himself established the rule that no one would ever be able to transgress the king. Through his austerities, the illustrious Vishnu penetrated

[593]Vainya was the eighth because he followed Vishnu, Virajas, Kirtiman, Kardama, Ananga, Atibala and Vena.

[594]Respectively, suta and *magadha*.

[595]Vainya.

[596]Literally, the one whose mount is a man, a name for Kubera.

[597]The word for grain is *shasya* and it is difficult to pin down the number seventeen. Five types are more common—paddy (*dhanya*), beans (*mudga*), sesamum (*tila*), barley (*yava*) and black gram (*masha*).

[598]The word for king is raja. *Ranjita* means pleased or delighted. Since he delighted the subjects, he came to be known as raja, from the root *ranj*. The word for king is actually *rajan* and raja is the nominative, in the singular.

[599]With a play on the words kshata (wound/injury) and save (*trana*).

[600]*Prathita* means extended or famous. The name prithivi for earth is being linked with that word.

the king. O king! That is the reason the world bowed down to and honoured this god among human gods.[601]

'"O lord of men! You must always protect through the use of dandaniti. You must see to it so that it is never afflicted by anyone and use spies for this. The king is equal to everyone else. With the exception that divine qualities exist inside him, there is no reason for everyone in the world to honour him. A golden lotus was generated from Vishnu's forehead. This was the goddess Shri[602] and she became the wife of the intelligent Dharma. O Pandava! Through Shri, Artha was born to Dharma. Therefore, prosperity, dharma and artha are always established in the kingdom. O son![603] When good deeds are exhausted, a person is dislodged from the world of heaven and is born on earth as a king, to follow dandaniti. Such a man on earth is united with the greatness of Vishnu. He is united with intelligence and attains greatness. No one transgresses what has been established by the gods. That is the reason everyone remains under the subjugation of one man. O Indra among kings! Though he is equal to the others in the world, because his good deeds lead to good consequences, everyone follows his words. Whoever glances at his peaceful face comes under his control. He sees someone who is extremely fortunate, prosperous and handsome. O Indra among kings! O lord of the earth! That is the reason the learned pronounce that on earth, gods and human gods are similar. This is the entire account about the greatness of kings. O best among the Bharata lineage! I have said everything. What should we do now?"'

Chapter 1388(60)

Vaishampayana said, 'Yudhishthira again saluted his grandfather, Gangeya. He joined his hands in salutation, composed himself

[601]Kings are like human gods and Vainya was a king among them.
[602]Prosperity personified.
[603]The word used is tata.

and asked, "What is dharma for all the varnas? What is it for each of the varnas separately? What are the views on the four ashramas and for rajadharma? Why does a kingdom prosper? Why does a king prosper? O bull among the Bharata lineage! Why do citizens and servants prosper? What kind of treasury, punishment, forts, aides, advisers, officiating priests, priests[604] and preceptors should a king avoid? When there is a hardship, whom should a king trust? Whom should a king firmly protect himself against? O grandfather! Tell me this."

'Bhishma replied, "I bow down to the great dharma. I bow down to Krishna, the origin. Having bowed down to the brahmanas, I will speak about eternal dharma. There are nine aspects that are applicable to all varnas—lack of anger, truthfulness in speech, sharing properly, forgiveness, procreation on one's wife, purification, non-injury, rectitude and supporting the servants.

'"I will now tell you about the dharma that only applies to brahmanas. O great king! It is said that self-control is the ancient dharma. There are also tasks like studying and teaching that must be completed. All other acts are a consequence of these two acts. If a man is calm and content with wisdom, he should not do anything improper. He should marry, have offspring, practise donations and perform sacrifices. It is said that riches that bring enjoyment must be shared amongst the virtuous. If a brahmana studies, he has accomplished his greatest task. Whether he performs any other task or does not perform any other task, such a brahmana is spoken of as a Maitra.[605]

'"O descendant of the Bharata lineage! I will now tell you about the dharma of kshatriyas. The king must give and not beg. He must perform sacrifices, but not officiate at the sacrifices of others. He should not teach, but can study. He must protect the subjects. He must always show enterprise in killing bandits. He must act valiantly in a

604The officiating priest is for a specific purpose like a sacrifice, while the priest is more like a permanent appointee.

605In general, a *maitra* is a benevolent and affectionate person who is friendly towards all beings. However, more specifically, a maitra is also a brahmana who has attained the highest level of human perfection.

battle. Kings who perform sacrifices, are learned and are victorious in battle conquer supreme worlds. Those who are learned about the ancient accounts do not praise the deeds of a kshatriya who retreats from battle without any wounds on his body. The chief task of a kshatriya has been said to kill. There is no task as important for him as the slaying of bandits. Donations, studying, performing sacrifices, acquisition of goods and their preservation are recommended. However, specifically, a king who desires dharma must fight. The lord of the earth must ensure that all the subjects are established in their own dharma. All their tasks must be properly accomplished, in accordance with dharma. Through protection, the king accomplishes his most important task. Whether he performs other tasks or does not perform other tasks, such a king is spoken of as Aindra.[606]

'"O descendant of the Bharata lineage! I will now tell you about the dharma of vaishyas—donations, studying, the performance of sacrifices, purity and the accumulation of wealth. Like a father, a vaishya must protect all animals. Any other task that he undertakes will be regarded as a wrong task for him. By protecting in this way, he will obtain great happiness. After creating animals, Prajapati gave them to vaishyas. He gave all the subjects to brahmanas and the king. I will tell you about their[607] means of sustenance and livelihood. Out of six cows, he can take the milk from one. Out of a hundred cattle, he can take a cow and a bull. When a cow is dead, he can have one-seventh of the body and horns as his share and one-sixteenth of the hooves.[608] In all the seeds of grain crops, his share is one-seventh.[609] This is his annual maintenance. A vaishya should never have the desire of not tending to animals. If a vaishya is willing, no one else should ever take care of them.

'"O descendant of the Bharata lineage! I will now tell you about the dharma of shudras. Prajapati thought of shudras as a varna

[606]Similar to Indra.

[607]The vaishyas'.

[608]The vaishya thus takes care of animals, but only 'owns' designated shares. When a cow is dead, the shares presumably refer to trade in the dead bodies.

[609]This follows the earlier shloka, so it is not clear whether one means one-seventh or one-sixteenth. It could be either, but one-seventh seems more likely.

marked for servitude. Serving is recommended for the shudra varna. Their great happiness results from serving others. Without any hatred, shudras should serve the other three varnas. A person who has been born as a shudra should never amass anything. If such a wicked person accumulates riches, he will make his superiors subordinate to him. However, with a king's permission, an exception is permitted, or if he[610] wishes to pursue dharma. I will tell you about his means of sustenance and livelihood. It is said that the other varnas must certainly support the shudra. When umbrellas, headdresses, beds, sandals and fans are worn out, they should be given to shudras who are servants. Garments that are torn should not be worn by the three other varnas. Those are meant for shudras and, under dharma, those are their riches. People who are learned in dharma say that when a shudra wishes to serve and comes to any of the other three varnas, work must be found for him. If such a person is weak and aged and doesn't have any offspring, his master must arrange his funeral cake[611] for him. If there is hardship, the shudra must never abandon the master. If the master's possessions are destroyed, he must support the master with anything extra that he has. For a shudra, nothing belongs to him. His riches are his master's. O descendant of the Bharata lineage! The three types of sacrifice[612] have been recommended for the other three varnas. *Svaha* and uttering *nama*s are the mantras recommended for shudras.[613] Using these two, the shudra can himself perform rites and observe *pakayajna*. The dakshina for a pakayajna is said to be a *purnapatra*.[614]

[610]The shudra. That is, the shudra is allowed to accumulate riches under some conditions, such as spending those riches on pursuits of dharma.

[611]*Pinda*.

[612]Connected with the three Vedas.

[613]This and the succeeding shlokas get into complicated questions of interpretation. The simplest interpretation is that shudras were allowed to use the mantras *svaha* and *namaskara*, but not other mantras.

[614]A pakayajna is one where food is cooked and offered to gods, ancestors, guests and birds and beasts. There is the clear suggestion that a shudra would have to perform the sacrifice himself, since no brahmana would be an officiating priest. In that case, where is the question of dakshina? Presumably, dakshina was offered to brahmanas even if they did not officiate. A purnapatra is a full vessel, that is, a vessel full of food.

We have heard of a shudra named Paijavana, who followed the rules laid down by Indra and Agni and gave away one hundred thousand as dakshina.[615]

'"Sacrifices with devotion are recommended for all the varnas. Great devotion is divine and purifies all those who sacrifice. Brahmanas worship the supreme divinity, individually and collectively. They have their own desires, but perform eternal sacrifices.[616] The other three varnas were created from brahmanas. They are like the gods of the gods. What they utter is supreme. Therefore, all the sacrifices performed by the varnas have the same end, even if they result from individual desires. A brahmana who knows Rig, Sama and Yajur must be worshipped like a god. One who does not know Rig, Sama and Yajur is a misfortune for Prajapati. O son! O descendant of the Bharata lineage! Depending on their wishes, all the varnas sacrifice. The gods do not serve the needs of inferior people who are against sacrifices. Therefore, sacrifices with devotion are recommended for all the varnas. The brahmanas always worship their own gods. But they also performed sacrifices for the other varnas. The other three varnas saw that the brahmanas were created for this and this extremely great dharma should be respected by us. Because of this natural dharma, the varnas remain upright. They were created and matured in this way. The Sama was one. The Yajur was one. The Rig was one. But it is certainly seen that the brahmanas are also but one.[617] O Indra among kings! Those who know about the ancient accounts recount a song that was sung about this at a sacrifice, when the Vaikhanasa sages wished to perform a sacrifice. 'When the sun has risen, or just before it has risen, one must be full of devotion and conquer one's senses. One must then follow dharma, light a

[615]One hundred thousand of what is left dangling, probably one hundred thousand purnapatras.

[616]Eternal collective sacrifices, though the desires are individual.

[617]The brahmanas are part of the brahman. However, there seems to be a different suggestion too. The Vedas were originally one, but were divided. In that way, all the varnas originated with brahmanas and were later divided.

fire and pour oblations into it. Devotion is the greatest cause. What was earlier spilt was subsequently not spilt.[618] There are many different kinds of sacrifices and many different kinds of fruits arise from these deeds. A person who knows about all of these is certainly someone whose knowledge is firm. Such a man, who is a brahmana and is full of devotion, can officiate at a sacrifice. It is said that a thief, a wicked person and one who is supremely wicked among the wicked, becomes virtuous if he wishes to perform a sacrifice and performs it. There is no doubt that the rishis praise him as righteous. Certainly, all the varnas must always perform sacrifices. There is nothing in the three worlds that is equal to a sacrifice.'[619] Therefore, it has been said that a man must perform sacrifices without any malice. He must resort to purification and devotion. He must endeavour to the best of his capacity."'

Chapter 1389(61)

'Bhisma said, "O mighty-armed one! O one whose valour is truth! O Yudhishthira! Listen to the four ashramas and the tasks to be performed by the four varnas. It is said that the conduct of brahmanas is vanaprastha, *bhaiksha*,[620] the great ashrama of garhasthya and the fourth ashrama of brahmacharya. A person belonging to the first three varnas[621] will perform the

[618]It is difficult to understand this and refers to the process of offering oblations. What it probably means is that spilt and impure oblations can be rendered pure through mental devotion.

[619]This is probably the place where the Vaikhanasa quote ends.

[620]Earning a living through begging.

[621]The text uses a word that translates as twice-born. This is used for brahmanas, as well as for the first three varnas. The context here suggests the first three varnas.

samskara[622] of getting one's hair matted. He will then perform deeds connected with the sacrificial fire[623] and studying the Vedas. He will then control himself and control his senses. Having performed the tasks required of a householder, he will then leave for vanaprastha, with his wife, or without his wife. He will study the sacred texts known as the Aranyakas and will become learned about dharma. Having already had offspring, he will hold up his seed and advance towards the end where his soul becomes one with the brahman. O king! Sages hold up their seed. A learned brahmana may observe these signs and duties right from the beginning.[624] O lord of the earth! After completing brahmacharya, if a brahmana seeks moksha, his rights to resorting to bhaiksha on this earth are praised. When the sun sets, he will sleep wherever he is. He will have no home and no fire in it. He will subsist on whatever is available. He will be a controlled sage who has conquered his senses. He will be without any desires and will look upon everything as equal. He will be without pleasures and will be indifferent towards everything. Such a brahmana, who has reached a state of tranquility, will advance towards the end where his soul becomes one with the brahman.

'"He will study the Vedas and do everything that he is supposed to do.[625] He will have offspring and enjoy all the objects that bring happiness. He will control himself and observe the dharma of garhasthya, which is perceived to be more difficult than the dharma of ascetics. He will be satisfied with his own wife and approach her when it is her season. However, he will accept the

[622]There are thirteen samskaras or sacraments. The list varies a bit. But one list is *vivaha* (marriage), *garbhalambhana* (conception), *pumshavana* (engendering a male child), *simantonnayana* (parting the hair, performed in the fourth month of pregnancy), *jatakarma* (birth rites), *namakarana* (naming), *chudakarma* (tonsure), *annaprashana* (first solid food), *keshanta* (first shaving of the head), *upanayana* (sacred thread), *vidyarambha* (commencement of studies), *samavartana* (graduation) and *antyeshti* (funeral rites).

[623]The sacrificial fire burns in a household. Since the person is leaving for the forest, this probably means the putting out of the household fire.

[624]Without going through the householder stage.

[625]This is meant for someone who goes through the householder stage.

system of *niyoga*[626] and will not be deceitful or cunning. He will not eat a lot. He will be devoted to the gods and grateful. He will be truthful, gentle, non-violent and forgiving. He will be self-controlled and not be distracted in offering oblations to the gods and the ancestors. He will always give food to the brahmanas. He will not be jealous and will give to everyone, regardless of the marks they bear.[627] The master of the household must always be devoted to performing sacrifices. O son! In this connection, the extremely great maharshis talk about a song that was sung by Narayana. It is full of great purport and full of austerities. I will recount this to you. Listen attentively. 'It is my view that truthfulness, uprightness, the honouring of guests, dharma, artha and sex with one's wife are pleasures to be pursued for happiness, in this world and in the next.' The supreme rishis say that the best ashrama for the virtuous is the maintenance of sons and wives and devotion to the Vedas. If a brahmana is devoted to performing sacrifices and studies properly in the garhasthya stage, he will be completely cleansed of any taint that results from his having been a householder. He will reap pure fruits in heaven. When he casts aside his body, it is said that his desires become endless. They eternally surround him in every direction, with eyes, heads and mouths.[628]

'"O Yudhishthira! One should eat alone.[629] One should meditate alone. One should wander around alone. One should have a single preceptor and serve him, even if he is smeared with mud and dirt. One must always follow the rites of a brahmachari. One must always hold that one's initiation[630] is supreme. One must not question the Vedas and one must always complete one's tasks. One must always serve one's preceptor and bow down before him. One must not

[626]Under the niyoga system, in some situations, a man could have a son through his wife, but through another man.

[627]Irrespective of sect or mode of life.

[628]This is meant for a person who does not control his desires. The desires are seated around him, like servants attending to a master.

[629]This is specifically meant for a brahmachari.

[630]*Diksha*.

withdraw from the six tasks.[631] However, in every way, one must not be addicted to them either. One must not take any task to be an entitlement. One must not serve the enemy. O son! This is described to be the ashrama for brahmacharis."'

Chapter 1390(62)

'Yudhishthira asked, "Tell me about what is auspicious, brings great happiness, is without violence and is revered by the worlds. What can bring dharma and happiness and also lead to happiness for those like me?"

'Bhishma replied, "O lord! Those four ashramas have been laid down for brahmanas. O supreme among the Bharata lineage! The other three varnas also follow them. O king! There are many tasks that have been indicated for kings who wish to attain heaven. But what has been indicated in the sacred texts is not a mere list of examples. It is recommended that all kshatriyas should follow this. A brahmana who follows the conduct of kshatriyas, vaishyas or shudras is regarded as evil in intelligence and censured in this world. He goes to hell in the next world. O Pandava! People give a brahmana who is engaged in wrong tasks names identified with slaves, dogs, wolves and animals. A brahmana who is engaged in the six tasks, follows all the dharmas in the four ashramas, is controlled and has cleansed his soul, is pure and engaged in austerities and is without desire—is spoken of as having obtained the eternal worlds. Whatever tasks a person performs, in whatever form and in whichever place, the qualities that he obtains are exactly proportionate to that. O Indra among kings! You should know that the prosperity associated with studying is reckoned to be greater than that obtained through agriculture, trade and animal husbandry. Destiny is driven by time. Everything is determined by

[631]Studying, teaching, performing sacrifices, officiating at sacrifices, giving gifts and receiving gifts.

the progress of destiny. Under its subjugation, superior, middling and inferior tasks are performed. Some earlier beneficial deeds come to an end.[632] In every direction in the world, it is the brahman who is always engaged in its work."'

Chapter 1391(63)

'Bhisma said, "A brahmana's supreme tasks are to draw the bowstring, the destruction of enemies, agriculture, trade, animal husbandry and tending to others. But he must never do these for reasons of artha.[633] As long as he is in garhasthya, a brahmana must perform the six tasks. When these tasks have been accomplished, a brahmana's residence in the forest is applauded. However, he must avoid serving a king, wealth obtained through agriculture, sustaining himself through trade, deceit, intercourse with unchaste women and usury. O king! A wicked brahmana of evil conduct who deviates from dharma becomes a shudra. Becoming the husband of a shudra woman, being slanderous and treacherous, becoming a dancer and becoming a servant in a village are wicked acts. O king! Whether he meditates and studies the Vedas or not, he is equal to a shudra and a slave and should be seated with them at the time of eating. O king! All of them are equal to shudras and should be avoided in all duties that are for the gods. They are like barbarians who are cruel in their conduct and deserve no honour. By abandoning their own dharma, they cause injury to their own selves. O king! Giving them oblations meant for the gods and the ancestors is tantamount to not giving these at all. O king! Dharma has thus been recommended for brahmanas as well as self-control, purity and truthfulness. O king! In earlier times, Brahma decreed that all the ashramas were recommended for brahmanas. One who

[632]Beneficial deeds in earlier lives, when their fruits are exhausted.

[633]From the point of view of earning a living, these are forbidden occupations for brahmanas, if money is received from these occupations.

is self-controlled, drinks soma, is noble in conduct, is compassionate, tolerates everything, is without desires and upright, and is mild, non-violent and forgiving is a brahmana. One who performs wicked deeds is not that. O king! All those in the world who desire dharma resort to shudras, vaishyas and princes. O son of Pandu! Therefore, Vishnu is not affectionate towards those who do not follow the dharma of their jati and varna. In such a world, there will not be the four varnas among all the people, or talk about the Vedas, or all the different sacrifices, or all the rites amongst people and no one will follow the ashramas.

'"O Pandava! If the three varnas[634] wish to follow the ashramas and act according to what should be done in those ashramas, listen to the dharma that they must follow. O lord of the earth! A shudra must perform acts of servitude, have offspring and follow the instructions of the king. All the ashramas are recommended for him. However, even if he has a little bit of life left or follows *dashadharma*, he must not give up desire.[635] O Indra among kings! For one who follows this kind of dharma, subsistence through begging is not talked about. Nor is it for a vaishya or a prince. A vaishya may have completed all the appointed tasks and may have attained an advanced age. He may have laboured hard. In that case, with the permission of the king, he may pass through the circle of ashramas.[636] O unblemished one! O supreme among eloquent ones! O Pandava! O bull among kshatriyas! There may be a kshatriya who has studied the Vedas, ruled in accordance with the policy for kings, produced offspring and performed similar deeds, drunk soma, protected all the subjects in accordance with dharma, performed royal sacrifices, horse sacrifices

[634]Other than the brahmanas.

[635]This is a difficult shloka to translate, primarily because of dashadharma. This has been interpreted as a shudra being in the tenth (*dasha*) decade of his life. It is much more likely that this refers to the dashadharma or ten principles of Jainism. In any event, the sense seems to be that a shudra should not give up desire and resort to a life of begging.

[636]Under these circumstances, the vaishya may pass beyond the householder stage, abandon desire and live a life of begging.

and other recommended sacrifices, got brahmanas to recite the texts and given them dakshina, obtained victory in battle, whether few or many, and established his son (or someone else from a different lineage who is permitted) in the kingdom, to rule over the subjects, worshipped the ancestors properly in accordance with the sacrifices recommended for ancestors, worshipped the gods with sacrifices and made efforts to honour the rishis with the Vedas. When his death is near, he may wish to enter the next ashrama. O king! Having been passed through the ashramas in due order, he may obtain success. O Indra among kings! Having gone beyond the dharma of a householder, he may become a rajarshi and adopt a life of begging, wandering around as long as he wishes to live. O bull among the Bharata lineage! O tiger among kings! For these three, dwelling in this fourth ashrama is not said to an essential task.[637]

'"Among men, the best dharma to be observed is that followed by kshatriyas. All the dharma and the minor bits of dharma for the other three[638] follow from the dharma of kings. I have heard this in the Vedas. O king! Just as all footprints are lost in that of an elephant, it is said that all the tasks dissolve in this.[639] Listen. All the dharmas can be seen to be based on rajadharma. Men who know about dharma say every other kind of dharma offers little refuge and few fruits. The noble ones say that the dharma of kshatriyas is the great refuge and has many beneficial forms. There is no other. Of all the dharmas, rajadharma is the most important and it protects all the other dharmas. O king! Every kind of renunciation is there in rajadharma and renunciation is said to be ancient and the foremost kind of dharma. If dandaniti is destroyed, the three[640] will be submerged and all the dharmas will be resisted. If kshatriyas abandon the ancient rajadharma, all the dharma of the ashramas will disappear. All kinds of renunciation are seen in rajadharma. All kinds of diksha are said to be in rajadharma. All kinds of yoga are said to

[637]Kshatriyas, vaishyas and shudras need not adopt sannyasa.

[638]Brahmanas, vaishyas and shudras.

[639]The dharma of kings.

[640]The three Vedas.

be in rajadharma. All the worlds are based on rajadharma. Beings are naturally slaughtered. This causes affliction to those who resort to dharma.[641] In that way, if dharma is delinked from rajadharma, one's own dharma will not be followed in any situation."'

Chapter 1392(64)

'Bhishma said, "O Pandava! The dharma of the four ashramas, the dharma of tribes[642] and that of the rulers of the worlds are based on the dharma of kshatriyas. O supreme among the Bharata lineage! All the other dharmas are also in that of kshatriyas. In this world of the living, those who have no desires also base themselves on the dharma of kshatriyas. The eternal sacred texts say that the dharma of those who dwell in the different ashramas have many forms and parts. It is as if there are many gates and it is also not obvious. There are people who profess to speak auspicious words, as if they are certain. However, there are others who do not believe in the certainty of dharma and give instances to the contrary. They say that everything that is for the welfare of the worlds is established in the dharma of kshatriyas. It directly leads to repeated happiness and can be directly experienced by a person. O Yudhishthira! The dharma of brahmanas who have withdrawn from the ashramas,[643] and that of the other three varnas, has been recounted in the ancient and sacred texts. In this world, there is no other good conduct that is equal to rajadharma. O Indra among kings! I told you earlier how, in ancient times, many brave kings went to the immensely energetic Vishnu, the god who is the lord of all beings, the lord Narayana. They wanted to know about dandaniti. Before this, in their own respective ashramas, they had performed tasks and thought these

[641]This is clearly directed against votaries of non-violence and hangs loose.

[642]Jatis.

[643]That is, moved to the sannyasa stage.

to be equal. The kings had followed the words that set out instances as benchmarks and stood around.[644] The gods were the Sadhyas, the Vasus, the Ashvins, the Rudras, the Vishvas,[645] large numbers of Maruts and the Siddhas. They were the first gods, created in ancient times, and they were established in the dharma of kshatriyas. I will now state what determines dharma and artha. In earlier times, the danavas created dishonour and reduced everything to one.[646] O Indra among kings! At that time, there was a valiant king named Mandhata. In ancient times, that lord of the earth performed a sacrifice. He wished to see the god Narayana, without an origin, without a middle and without an end. O tiger among kings! In that sacrifice, King Mandhata placed the two feet of the great-souled Parameshthi[647] Vishnu on his own head. Vishnu adoped the form of Vasava and showed himself and surrounded by kings, he[648] worshipped that lord. O immensely radiant one! A great conversation then took place between that large mass of kings and the great-souled one,[649] about the nature of Vishnu.

'"Indra asked, 'O foremost among those who uphold dharma! Why do you wish to see the one who cannot be measured? Narayana is the ancient and first god. His maya is infinite. His spirit and valour are unlimited. The universe is his form. I am incapable of seeing that god in person. Not even Brahma can. O king! I will grant you whatever other desire exists in your heart. After all, you are a king among mortals. You are based in truth and follow supreme dharma. You have conquered your senses. You are firm in your valour and are engaged in bringing pleasure to the gods. You possess intelligence, devotion and supreme faith. That is the reason I will grant you whatever boon you desire.'

'"Mandhata replied, 'I bow my head down before you. But there is no doubt that I wish to see the illustrious one, the first among the

[644]They wanted Vishnu to determine what kind of dharma was superior and whether rajadharma was superior to the other kinds.

[645]The Vishvadevas.

[646]They mixed everything up and caused confusion.

[647]The supreme lord.

[648]Mandhata.

[649]Vishnu, in the form of Indra.

gods. Desiring dharma, I will give up all objects of pleasure and go to the forest. I will follow that virtuous path, practised by the worlds. The dharma of kshatriyas is extensive. Established in that, I have obtained immeasurable worlds and my own fame. However, there is a dharma that the first among gods is engaged in. That is foremost in the worlds and I do not know how to follow it.'

'"Indra said, 'If you did not possess soldiers, you would have followed supreme adharma. However, if you are not distracted, you will attain the supreme objective. The first god was engaged in the dharma of kshatriyas. It was only later that he resorted to other forms of dharma. The others were created later and have limits. However, the dharma of kshatriyas is special. It is extremely well established and is without limits. All the other dharmas are immersed in this dharma. That is the reason this dharma is said to be the best. In ancient times, Vishnu used the dharma of kshatriyas to crush the enemy[650] and protect all the gods and the infinitely energetic rishis. The illustrious, immeasurable and prosperous one slew those enemies first. Had he not done that, there would have been no brahmanas, no original creator of the worlds,[651] no virtuous dharma and no original dharma. If, in the past, that foremost among gods had not conquered this entire earth, the four varnas and the dharma of the four ashramas would all have ceased to exist, because the brahman would have been destroyed. The hundreds of flows of eternal dharma were seen to be created from the dharma of kshatriyas. The original dharma flows from one yuga to another yuga. However, the dharma of kshatriyas is said to be the foremost in the worlds. Giving up one's one self,[652] compassion towards all beings, knowledge of the worlds, saving, protecting, rescuing the wretched and the distressed—these are to be found in the dharma of kshatriyas, as practised by kings. Those who do not honour, driven by desire and anger, are frightened of the king and do not perform wicked deeds. There are others who are virtuous and follow all forms of dharma. They are righteous in

[650]The demons.

[651]Brahma.

[652]In battle.

conduct and follow virtuous dharma.[653] There is no doubt that as all the beings roam around in this world, the king must follow dharma, observe the signs and protect them like sons. The eternal dharma of kshatriyas is supreme among all forms of dharma and is foremost in the worlds. It is the eternal akshara, it extends up to the akshara.[654] It faces every direction.'"'

Chapter 1393(65)

"'Indra said, 'It is energetic in this way and all the dharmas are secured by it. The dharma of kshatriyas is best among all kinds of dharma. In this world, it must be observed by those like you, who are broad and are like lions. Otherwise, the subjects may be destroyed. The king who is engaged in the yoga of samskara[655] must know that the foremost components of royal dharma are improvement of the earth,[656] not living by alms, protecting the subjects, compassion towards all beings and giving up one's life in battle. The sages say that renunciation is the best and a person who gives up his body is the foremost among all. In rajadharma, everything is always being given up. It is evident how the kings gave it up.[657] It is said that a kshatriya always observes dharma through a lot of learning, serving the seniors, slaying the enemy and brahmacharya.One who desires dharma follows that single ashrama.[658]

[653]Because they are protected by the king.

[654]We have deliberately not translated akshara here. At one level, the word means immutable and imperishable, so that the dharma of kshatriyas is without decay. However, akshara is also a word for the brahman, so that it is possible that the dharma of kshatriyas is being equated with the brahman.

[655]The word samskara has different meanings—refining, polishing, cleansing.

[656]This probably means the act of rendering the ground fit for agriculture.

[657]Gave their lives up in the battle.

[658]Effectively, the householder stage, the sense being that there is no need for renunciation.

In conduct towards ordinary people, he must make endeavours to discard his own likes and dislikes.[659] He must establish and protect the four varnas and engage them in their tasks and rituals. It is said that out of all endeavours and ashramas, the dharma of kshatriyas is the best, because all the dharmas result from it. If all the varnas are not engaged in their own dharmas, one cannot say that dharma is being followed. Men who are cruel and are always engaged in the destruction of their prosperity are said to be like animals.[660] Because the dharma of kshatriyas advances from greed for riches to policy, it is said to be the best of ashramas. The three kinds of learning[661] are said to the objective for brahmanas and this is said to be the ashrama for brahmanas. This is said to be the foremost task for brahmanas. One who acts contrary to this should be killed with a weapon, like a shudra. O king! A brahmana must follow the dharma of the four ashramas and the dharma of the Vedas. Know that there is nothing else for him. If he acts contrary to this, no livelihood has been planned for him. Dharma is evident in one's tasks and without this, he[662] is like a dog. If a brahmana bases himself in perverse deeds, he does not deserve respect. The learned say that someone who is not engaged in his own tasks is not to be trusted. This is the dharma of all the varnas and it is uplifted through the valour in the dharma of kshatriyas. Therefore, rajadharma is the foremost and no other. I think that this dharma of valiant ones is foremost in its enterprise.'

'"Mandhata asked, 'What dharma should be followed by Yavanas, Kiratas, Gandharas, Chinas, Shabaras, Barbaras, Shakas, Tusharas, Kahvas, Pahlavas, Andhras, Madrakas, Odras, Pulindas, Ramathas, Kachas, all the mlecchas, those who are a mix of brahmanas and kshatriyas, vaishyas and men who are shudras, when they reside within the kingdom? How can those like me establish all those who earn a living by being bandits? O illustrious one! I

[659]Be impartial.

[660]This should probably be interpreted as praise of the householder stage.

[661]The three Vedas.

[662]The brahmana.

wish to hear all this. Tell me. O lord of the gods! You are a friend to us kshatriyas.'

'"Indra replied, 'All those who are bandits must serve their mothers and fathers. They must serve their teachers and seniors and all those who live in hermitages. All those who are bandits have a duty to serve the king. Their dharma is said to be the rites of dharma laid down in the Vedas. They must perform sacrifices for the ancestors and, at the right time, must dig wells, create places for drinking water and shelters for sleeping, and donate to brahmanas. Non-violence, truthfulness, lack of anger, living off and protecting what has been inherited, sustaining wives and children, purity and lack of enmity are also recommended. Those who desire prosperity must grant dakshina at all the sacrifices. For all those who are bandits, it is a duty to observe extremely expensive pakayajnas. O unblemished one! These and other techniques were laid down in ancient times. O king! These are the tasks and duties for all the people.'

'"Mandhata said, 'In the world of men, it is seen that bandits exist among all the varnas. Though they disguise themselves, they are present in all the four ashramas.'

'"Indra replied, 'O king! When dandaniti is destroyed and rajadharma is neglected, kingship is demeaned and all the beings are confounded. There will be innumerable mendicants of different types. When this krita yuga is over, alternative kinds of ashramas will be thought of. They will pay no heed to the foremost objective and the ancient dharma. Overcome by desire and anger, they will follow perverse paths. When great-souled ones use dandaniti, wickedness is restrained and the supreme and eternal dharma is established and made to circulate. The king is said to be the supreme preceptor of the world. If a person disrespects him, his donations, oblations and funeral rites never yield any fruits. The eternal king of men originated with the gods. Even the gods exhibit a lot of reverence towards a king who desires dharma. The illustrious Prajapati created everything in the universe. He desired that kshatriyas should follow the dharma of commencement and restraint.[663] I revere and worship the established

[663]Commencement of the virtuous and restraint of the wicked.

kshatriya who remembers that objective and uses his intelligence to encourage dharma.'"

'Bhishma said, "Surrounded by large numbers of the Maruts, the illustrious lord spoke in this way. He then went to his own undecaying and supreme state and residence, that of Vishnu.[664] O unblemished one! In this way, dharma was observed and followed well in ancient times. How can anyone who possesses great learning disrespect kshatriyas? There are those who have engaged and those who have withdrawn.[665] Internally, they face destruction, like those without eyes on a road.[666] In the beginning, a wheel was established and in the beginning, they followed it. O tiger among men! O unblemished one! I have told you about that conduct."'

Chapter 1394(66)

'Yudhishthira said, "I have heard about the four kinds of ashramas followed by men earlier. O grandfather! I am asking you to explain them in detail."

'Bhishma replied, "O Yudhishthira! O mighty-armed one! Everything about dharma, as revered by the virtuous, is known to you, as it is to me. O Yudhishthira! However, you have asked me about differences in practice. O lord of men! O best among those who uphold dharma! Hear about dharma. O Kounteya! O bull among men! All of these are found in those who are of virtuous conduct and engaged in the duties of the four ashramas. O Yudhishthira! If one follows dandaniti without being attached to desire or anger and regards all beings as equal, he is in the ashrama of a mendicant.[667] He knows about acquisition and giving away, about encouraging and restraining and about the appropriate conduct for valiant ones.

[664]One should remember that this was Vishnu, disguised as Indra.

[665]Engaged in action and withdrawn from action.

[666]Because the engagement and withdrawal is not in accordance with dharma.

[667]The reference is to a king, who is then in a state of renunciation.

He is then established in the ashrama of conferring prosperity.[668] O Yudhishthira! When his kin, allies and friends confront a disaster and he rescues and sustains them, he is established in the ashrama of consecration. O Partha! If he performs rites[669] and sacrifices for beings, ancestors and men, then he is established in the broad ashrama of vanaprastha. If a king protects all beings and protects his own kingdom, he is effectively consecrated in many ways and established in the ashrama of vanaprastha. If he always studies the Vedas, is forgiving, worships his teachers and serves his preceptors, then he is established in the ashrama of brahmacharya. O descendant of the Bharata lineage! If he always follows a path that is upright and without deceit and treats all beings in this way, he is established in the ashrama of brahmacharya. O descendant of the Bharata lineage! There are brahmanas who know about the three kinds of learning and are in vanaprastha. If he gives them large quantities of riches, he is established in the ashrama of vanaprastha. O descendant of the Bharata lineage! If he does not cause injury to any being and practises non-violence, he is established in a state that has all the stages. O Kouravya! O Yudhishthira! If he is compassionate towards all, young or old, he is established in a state that has all the stages. O extender of the Kuru lineage! O Kouravya! If he acts and uses his force to save beings and save those who have sought refuge, he resides in the stage of garhasthya. If he protects all beings and mobile and immobile objects and always worships them in accordance with what they deserve, he resides in the stage of garhasthya. O Partha! If he encourages and restrains elder and younger wives, brothers, sons and grandsons, his austerities are like those of garhasthya. O tiger among men! If he protects and worships virtuous ones who look on all subjects as their own selves, he is established in the ashrama of garhasthya. O descendant of the Bharata lineage! O Yudhishthira! When those in different ashramas are welcomed in his house and offered food, he is in the state of garhasthya. A man who is appropriately established in the dharma promulgated

[668]Alternatively, the ashrama of tranquility.

[669]The text uses the word *ahnika*, which means a rite performed twice a day.

by the Creator obtains the supreme fruits of all the ashramas. O Kounteya! O Yudhishthira! It is said that a man whose qualities are never destroyed is the best of men, whatever be the ashrama he is established in. O Yudhishthira! If he acts so as to make everyone dwell and honours according to age and lineage, he is established in all the ashramas. O Kounteya! O tiger among men! A king who protects the dharma of the country and the dharma of families is established in all the ashramas. O tiger among men! At the right time, if he offers riches and gifts to those who should be honoured, he dwells in the ashrama of the virtuous. O Kounteya! Even if he is in the dharma of the tenth decade,[670] if a king glances towards the dharma of all the people, he is said to dwell in an ashrama. When people who are accomplished in dharma and virtuous ones who act in accordance with dharma are protected within the kingdom, the king receives one-fourth.[671] O tiger among men! When kings do not protect those who take delight in dharma and others who follow dharma, they take away their sins.[672] O Yudhishthira! O unblemished one! Those who aid kings in the task of protection also obtain a share in all the dharma obtained by others. O tiger among men! It has been determined that, among all the ashramas, garhasthya is the blazing one. We regard it as the one that purifies. If a man regards all beings as his own self and conquers anger when wielding the rod of chastisement, he obtains happiness after death. This is like a boat that is raised up through dharma and is full of spirit and valour. Its ropes are the bridge of dharma. It is swift, driven by the wind of renunciation, and it will enable you to cross. When the desire in the heart has withdrawn from every object, one is established in the universal essence and attains the brahman. O lord of men! Use yoga to become extremely content. O tiger among men! When you are engaged in protection, you will obtain dharma. There are brahmanas who are engaged in studying the Vedas and the performance of virtuous deeds. O unblemished

[670]That is, even if he is aged.

[671]Of their merits.

[672]The sins devolve on the king.

one! Make efforts to protect them and all the people. O descendant of the Bharata lineage! Dharma is obtained through the ashrama of vanaprastha. However, through protecting, a king can obtain a hundred times the qualities of that dharma. O foremost among Pandavas! The different kinds of dharma have been recounted and you should follow this eternal path, witnessed in earlier times. O Pandava! O tiger among men! If you single-mindedly engage yourself in protecting, you will obtain the dharma of the four ashramas and the four varnas."'

Chapter 1395(67)

'Yudhishthira said, "You have spoken about the four ashramas and also about the four varnas. O grandfather! Tell me about the tasks a kingdom should perform."

'Bhishma replied, "The most important task for a kingdom is the consecration of a king. A kingdom without an Indra is weak and is overwhelmed by bandits. There is no dharma in a kingdom that does not have a king. Everyone devours each other. In every way, shame on a state without a king! The learned texts say that Indra is crowned in the form of a king. Those who desire prosperity should revere the king, like Indra. The Vedas say that one should not dwell in a kingdom without a king. In a kingdom without a king, oblations are not carried by the fire. If a more powerful person desires the kingdom and attacks the kingdom without a king, or if the king has been slain, it is good advice to welcome and honour the invader. There is nothing more evil than to be without a king. If a powerful one is enraged, everything will be destroyed. However, if he looks on everything equally, all will be well. A cow that is difficult to milk confronts hardship repeatedly. However, one that is easy to milk never faces a difficulty. If one bends down, one is not scorched and tormented. A tree that bends down on its own is not afflicted. Because of these analogies, those who are patient bow down before stronger ones. Bowing down before a stronger person is like bowing down before Indra. Those who desire prosperity must always get a king. If there is no king, there is nothing to be gained from possessing riches and nothing to be gained from possessing wives. If there is no king, a wicked person cheerfully steals the property of others. However, when others steal what belongs to him, he wishes for a king. Even the wicked can never obtain peace then. Two steal what belongs to one and many others steal what belongs to two. One who is not a slave is made to become a slave. Women are forcibly abducted. It is because of these reasons that the gods arranged for the protection of subjects. Without a king in this world, no one would wield the rod of chastisement on earth. Like fish on a stake, the stronger would oppress the weaker side. We have heard that subjects without a king have been destroyed in the past. They will devour each other, like fish in the water, preying on weaker ones. We have heard that people got together and arrived at an agreement. 'There are men who are harsh in speech. They wield rods. They abduct the wives of others. They take what belongs to others and act in similar ways. We must discard these.' In particular, they wished to assure all the varnas and treat all of them equally. But having arrived at this agreement, they did not abide by it. Afflicted by misery, all of them assembled and went to the grandfather then. 'O illustrious one! Without a lord, we are being destroyed. Appoint a lord for us. He will be one who will protect us and all of us will honour him.' He appointed Manu, but Manu did not delight them.

'"Manu said, 'I am scared of performing cruel deeds and ruling a kingdom is an exceedingly difficult task. In particular, men are always engaged in false conduct.'"

'Bhishma said, "The subjects replied, 'Do not be frightened. Those deeds will go away.[673] We will give you one-fiftieth of our animals and gold and one-tenth of our grain and thereby increase your treasury. The men who are foremost in wielding weapons and arrows will follow you as their chief, like the gods behind

[673]That is, the bad fruits of any cruel deeds will not vest on the king.

the great Indra. O king! Strength will be engendered in you and you will become unassailable and powerful. You will then happily support all of us, like Kubera did the *nairittas*.[674] The subjects will be protected well by the king and follow their own dharma. One-fourth of that dharma will belong to you. You will easily obtain power through this great dharma. O king! In every way, we promise this to you, like the gods to Shatakratu. Swiftly depart for victory and scorch like the one with the rays.[675] Dispel the pride of our enemies. Dharma always triumphs.' Surrounded by a large army, that greatly energetic one advanced. He was born in an extremely great lineage and seemed to blaze in his energy. On beholding his greatness, like the gods before the great Indra, everyone was filled with fright. They made up their minds to stick to their own dharma. He roamed the earth, like Parjanya showering down rain. He pacified all the wicked ones and employed them in their own tasks. In this way, men on earth who desire prosperity must first arrange for a king. This is for the sake of the welfare of the subjects. They must always bow down before him with devotion, like disciples before a preceptor. In the presence of the king, the subjects must be like the gods before the one with a thousand eyes.[676] When a person is revered by his own people, the enemy also respects him a lot. When a person is disrespected by his own people, the enemy disregards him. When a king is vanquished by the enemy, this brings unhappiness to everyone. That is the reason a king is given umbrellas, conveyances, garments, ornaments, food, drinks, houses, seats, beds and all the required implements. He must protect his own self and become unassailable. He must smile before speaking. When he is addressed by men, he must reply in pleasant tones. He must be grateful and firm in his devotion. He must be prepared to share things. He must conquer his senses. When glanced at, he must be mild, direct and attractive in looking back."'

[674]Nairittas are demons. Kubera is the lord of yakshas and rakshasas.

[675]The sun.

[676]Indra.

Chapter 1396(68)

'Yudhishthira asked, "O bull among the Bharata lineage! Why do the brahmanas speak of the king as a divinity? O grandfather! He is only the lord of men. Tell me that."

'Bhishma replied, "O descendant of the Bharata lineage! In connection with this, an ancient account of what Vasumana asked Brihaspati is spoken of. A supreme among intelligent ones was named Vasumana and he was the king of Kosala. He was accomplished in his wisdom and he questioned maharshi Brihaspati. He knew about the requirements of humility and he observed all the humble modes towards Brihaspati. As is decreed, he kept him on the right and bowed down before him.[677] He was engaged in ensuring the welfare of all beings in the kingdom and asked in the proper way. O lord of the earth! Basing himself on dharma, he wished to know about the welfare of subjects. 'What makes beings prosper and when do they advance towards destruction? O immensely wise one! Whom should they worship, so as to obtain extreme happiness?' Having been asked by the infinitely energetic one, the great king of Kosala, Brihaspati attentively praised the reverence that should be shown to kings.

"'O great king![678] In this world, the king is seen to be the root of all dharma. It is because they are frightened of the king that subjects do not devour each other. The king pacifies this entire agitated and anxious world. Having pacified it through dharma, he rules it. O king! If the sun and the moon did not rise, all the beings would be blind and submerged in darkness and be unable to see each other. Like fish in the absence of water and birds in the absence of perches, they would repeatedly roam around according to their desires and attack each other. They would crush and intolerantly cross each other. There is no doubt that they would soon confront destruction. In that way, without a king, these subjects will be destroyed. They will be blind and submerged in darkness, like animals without a

[677]Vasumana circuambulated Brihaspati in a clockwise direction and then bowed down before him.

[678]This is Brihaspati speaking.

herdsman. If a king does not protect, the strong will abduct the possessions of the weak and kill them when they resist. If a king does not protect, the wicked will violently seize many kinds of vehicles, garments, ornaments and jewels. If a king does not protect in this world, everyone will say, "This is mine," and there will be no property. There will be destruction of the universe. If the king does not protect, wicked ones will oppress and kill their own mothers, fathers, elders, teachers, guests and preceptors. If the king does not protect, many kinds of weapons will descend on those who follow dharma, while those who follow adharma will be accepted. If the king does not protect, those with riches will always be killed, bound and oppressed, and there will be no sense of ownership. If the king does not protect, the sky will be the end.[679] This world will be full of bandits and everyone will descend into a terrible hell. If the king does not protect, seed and grain will not grow. There will be no agriculture and no paths for traders. Dharma and the three types of learning will be submerged. If the king does not protect, there will be no sacrifices and no decreed dakshina. There will be no marriage and no society. If the king does not protect, bulls will not work and there will be no churning of milk in pots. The pens of cattle will be destroyed. If the king does not protect, hearts will be anxious and frightened and the senses will be overcome with lamentations. Everything will be destroyed in an instant. If the king does not protect, one will not be able to stand without fear. There won't be sacrifices throughout the year, with the decreed dakshina being given. If the king does not protect, brahmanas will not engage in asceticism and study the four Vedas. They will not bathe after studying and they will not bathe after austerities. If the king does not protect, all barriers will be demolished and one hand will steal from the other hand. Everyone will run away in fright. If the king does not protect, no one will be touched by dharma. People who are struck will strike back and their own senses will govern them. If the king does not protect, there will be wrong policies and a mixing of varnas. The kingdom

[679]The sense probably is that there will be no worlds in the hereafter for those with good deeds.

will be ravaged by famine. It is because they are protected by the king that men are without fear. They sleep anywhere, as they wish, and leave the doors of their houses open. If men have a king who is devoted to dharma as their protector, no one has to suffer verbal abuse or blows from the hands. If the lord of the earth protects, women, even when unaccompanied by men, can wander fearlessly on the roads, wearing all their ornaments. If the lord of the earth protects, dharma is followed and there is no violence towards each other. Instead, favours are done to each other. When the lord of the earth protects, the three varnas separately perform great sacrifices and attentively study the sacred texts. When the lord of the earth protects, everything is well and the world is productively supported by the three.[680] When the king bears that excellent burden and bears the subjects with a great deal of strength, the world is pleased. In every direction, all the beings always exist because he exists. Had he not existed, they would not have existed. Who will not honour such a person? A king who bears a burden for the happiness of all the people and is engaged in their pleasure and benefit conquers both worlds.[681] If a man harbours evil thoughts towards such a person in his mind, there is no doubt that he will suffer hardships in this life and will be cast into hell after death. No one should disregard a lord of the earth as a mere man. He is a great divinity established in the form of a man. Depending on the occasion, he always adopts five different forms—Agni, Aditya, Mrityu, Vaishravana and Yama.[682] When the king has been deceived through falsehood and burns wicked ones down with his fierce energy, he is then Pavaka.[683] When the lord of the earth uses spies to look at everyone and then travels after providing safety, he is then Bhaskara.[684] When he is angry and destroys hundreds of impure men, with their sons, grandsons and relatives, he is then Antaka.[685] When he strikes all those who follow

[680]Probably the three varnas.
[681]This world and the next.
[682]Mrityu is Death and Vaishravana is Kubera.
[683]That is, Agni.
[684]That is, Aditya, the sun god.
[685]That is, Mrityu or Death.

adharma with the fierce rod of chastisement and shows favours to those who follow dharma, he is Yama. He gives streams of wealth to those who are his benefactors and takes away jewels and many other objects from those who injure him. O king! In this world, when he gives prosperity to some and takes it away from others, the lord of the earth is Vaishravana. Someone who is skilful and is capable of working incessantly, or desires dharma and is not envious of what has been obtained by his lord, should never speak ill of him.[686] One who acts contrary to the king will never obtain happiness, even if it happens to be a son, a brother, a friend, or someone who is like his own self. A fire trailing black smoke, and with the wind as its charioteer, leaves a residue. But when one is seized by a king, there is nothing that is left. One must keep everything protected by him at a long distance, as if it is death. A man must not steal a king's possessions. One will be destroyed if one touches those, like a deer touching a trap. An intelligent person must protect a king's possessions like his own. Those stupid ones who steal the king's possessions descend for a long time into a great, terrible and fathomless hell. He is praised with words like "Raja, Bhoja, Virat, Samrat, Kshatriya, Bhupati and Nripa".[687] Who will not worship such a person? Therefore, an intelligent and accomplished person who is controlled, who has conquered his soul and restrained his senses, who possesses a good memory and wishes to be prosperous, should seek refuge with a lord of the earth. As a minister, the king must honour someone who is grateful, wise, not inferior, firm in his devotion, restrained in his senses, always devoted to dharma and unwavering from his status. Even a forbidden person may be given refuge if he is firm in his devotion, accomplished in wisdom, knowledgeable about dharma, controlled over his senses, brave and superior in his deeds. A king makes a person confident. A king makes a small man great. Where is happiness for someone the king has seized? The king makes someone who approaches him

[686]The king.

[687]All of these are terms for a king and respectively mean delighter of the people, granter of happiness, possessor of prosperity, emperor (supreme one), healer of wounds, lord of the earth and protector of men.

happy. The king becomes great in the hearts of the subjects. He is their objective, their base and their supreme happiness. When men resort to this Indra among men, they conquer this world and the next properly. The lord of men who has ruled the earth with control, truth and affection and, who has worshipped through great sacrifices, obtains great fame and, because of his good deeds, obtains a place in heaven.'

'"The supreme king of Kosala was thus addressed by his preceptor.[688] The brave one made efforts to carefully protect his subjects."'

Chapter 1397(69)

'Yudhishthira asked, "What are the specific duties a king must undertake? How should the countryside be protected? How should he protect against enemies? How should he employ spies? O descendant of the Bharata lineage! How does he obtain the confidence of the varnas, the servants, the wives and the sons?"

'Bhishma replied, "O great king! Listen attentively to the complete account of the conduct of kings—the tasks that a king who is naturally a king must first do. The king must always conquer his soul and then he must conquer his enemies. If a lord of men has not conquered his own soul, how can he defeat the enemy? Victory over one's own self means restraint of the aggregate of the five.[689] Having conquered the senses, a lord of men is then capable of countering the enemy.

'"O descendant of the Kuru lineage! O tiger among men! He must place platoons in forts, boundaries, the groves of cities, all the parks of the towns and the cities, in the midst and in the abode of the king. As spies, he must employ men who have been tested and

[688]This is Bhishma speaking again.

[689]The five senses.

found to be wise, those who can withstand hunger, thirst and heat. They should seem to be dumb, blind and deaf. O great king! Having reflected about it, he must employ spies against all his advisers, the three types of friends,[690] his sons, in cities and in the countryside, and amongst kings who are vassals. The spies should be such that they do not know about each other. O bull among the Bharata lineage! He must know about the spies the enemy has employed in shops, pleasure grounds, assemblies, among beggars, in groves and gardens, amidst assemblies of learned men, brothels, crossroads, assembly halls and dwelling houses. O Pandava! A wise one must counter the spies of the enemy in this way. If one knows everything about the spies, they are as good as destroyed.

'"When the king examines himself and knows himself to be weak, he must seek the counsel of his advisers and have a treaty with the one who is stronger. Even if he knows that he is not weak, an intelligent king swiftly concludes a treaty with the enemy, if he desires to obtain some advantage out of this. A king who protects the kingdom in accordance with dharma appoints those who possess qualities, are great in their enthusiasm, knowledgeable about dharma and virtuous. If an immensely wise king realizes that he is being resisted, he must kill all the people who have injured him in the past and, in every way, counter those who are injurious. A lord of the earth should have nothing to do with someone who can neither help nor hurt him, nor with those who are incapable of saving him from hardships. An intelligent person will march out undetected against someone who has no allies and friends, someone who is preoccupied,[691] someone who is negligent and someone who is weak. A brave one will give the instruction for advancing when the army is strong, nourished and happy. However, before the advance, he must make arrangements for the city. Even if the other one is valiant, a king must never accept subjugation. Even if he is weak in strength and valour, he must try to afflict the enemy. He must oppress the kingdom with weapons, fire and poison and overwhelm it. He must try to cause strife amidst

[690]One's direct allies, allies of allies and enemies of enemies.

[691]Because that other king is busy fighting with someone else.

his[692] advisers and servants. Even if he desires a kingdom, an intelligent person will always seek to avoid war. Brihaspati has said that there are three means of obtaining prosperity—conciliation, gifts and dissension. A learned lord of men will be satisfied with whatever prosperity can be obtained through these.

'"O descendant of the Kuru lineage! For protecting the subjects, an infinitely wise king will take one-sixth of their income as tax. However, even for the sake of protecting the citizens, he must not violently take whatever those in the tenth decade possess, be it a lot or little. There is no doubt that he should look upon the citizens as his sons. In adjudicating disputes, it is his duty not to be partial because of affection. For the task of adjudication, a king must appoint a wise son who can consider all the aspects. A kingdom is always based on proper dispute resolution. The king must appoint his advisers and skilful men who do not cause injury as supervisors over mines, salt, taxes, ferries and elephant corps. A king who always wields the rod of chastisement well will obtain dharma. In the dharma of kings, the rod is always praised. O descendant of the Bharata lineage! The king must always be learned in the Vedas and the Vedangas, wise, a great ascetic and always devoted to donations and the performance of sacrifices. All these qualities must always be collectively established in a king. If a king does not observe the rites, how will he obtain heaven and how will he obtain fame?

'"If a king is oppressed by a stronger king, he must resort to the three kinds of allies and friends[693] and determine what must be done. Those in pens must be set on the roads[694] and villages must be removed. All of them must be made to enter the outskirts of the city. The wealthy and the leaders of the army must repeatedly be assured. The lord of men must himself ensure that the grain is brought in.[695] If it cannot be brought in, it must be completely burnt by fire. The

[692]The enemy's.

[693]Direct allies, allies of allies and enemies of enemies.

[694]Presumably, so that they can go somewhere else.

[695]To guard against a siege and to prevent it from falling into the hands of the enemy.

grain that is still in the fields can be used to wean away the enemy's men, or one's own forces can be used to completely destroy it. The bridges over rivers and the roads must always be demolished. All the stored water must be released. If it cannot be released, it must be poisoned. When such a situation of present and future conflict is at hand, one can ignore policy and decide that it is time to have friendships with anyone who is capable of countering the enemy.[696] The king must cut down the roots of all the small trees that are near forts. However, *chaitya* trees must be spared.[697] The branches of all the old trees must be pruned. However, one must always avoid cutting down the leaves of chaityas. He must erect high walls and casements.[698] The moats must be filled with stakes, crocodiles and fish. There must be doors of straw so that people inside the city can breathe freely. One must act so that these doors are also protected in every way. Machines must be placed atop the heavier gates. He must act so that shataghnis are placed there and are under his control. Timber must be collected and wells must be dug. For the sake of water, wells that have been dug earlier must be purified. Houses thatched with grass must be plastered with mud. Because of the fear of fire, in the month of Chaitra,[699] all straw must be removed from the city. The lord of men must allow food to be cooked only during the night. With the exception of agnihotras, the burning of fires in houses during the day will be avoided. Special care must be taken of fires ignited by artisans and in places where women give birth. It is recommended that fires lit in houses must be covered well. For the sake of the protection of the city, it must be announced that those who light fires during the day will be severely punished. O best of men! Beggars, wagoners, drunkards, lunatics and actors should be driven out. Otherwise, evil may result. The king must act so as to appoint spies from appropriate varnas at crossroads, tirthas, assembly

[696]This is a difficult shloka to translate and some liberties have been taken.

[697]Sacred trees that grow on mounds and are worshipped.

[698]Around the forts.

[699]March–April, the beginnings of the hot season and the last month of the preceding year.

halls and dwelling houses. The lord of men must construct broad royal roads. He must instruct that stores of drinking water and shops are constructed at appropriate places. There must also be stores for riches, stores for weapons and stores for grain everywhere and stables for horses and stables for elephants, with barracks for the soldiers. O Kouravya! O Yudhishthira! There must be moats, highways and narrower roads. No one must be able to detect what is secret. A king who is afflicted by the forces of the enemy must accumulate stores of all kinds of oil, honey, clarified butter and medicines. He must arrange for stores of charcoal, kusha grass, munja grass, red lac, arrows, trees, fodder, kindling and poisoned arrows. The lord of men must arrange for stores of all kinds of weapons—lances, swords, spears and armour. In particular, he must arrange for the collection of all kinds of medicinal herbs, roots and fruits and the four kinds of physicians.[700] Actors, dancers, wrestlers and those skilled in the use of maya should adorn the best of cities and amuse people everywhere. If there is any suspicion attached to servants, ministers, citizens or even kings,[701] he must endeavour to bring them under his control. O Indra among kings! When a task has been accomplished, the doer must be honoured with stores of riches. Honour and various words of appreciation must be appropriate to the person. O descendant of the Kuru lineage! When an enemy has been countered or slain, the king pays off the debts that are indicated for him in the sacred texts.

'"O descendant of the Kuru lineage! Listen to me. The king must protect seven things—his own person, his advisers, his treasury, his army, his allies, his country and his city. The kingdom consists of these seven and they must be protected carefully. O tiger among men! He who knows about the collection of the six, the first three categories and the further three categories, enjoys the earth. O Yudhishthira! Listen to the collection of six that have been mentioned—being seated after concluding a treaty, ensuring a treaty after marching out, being seated after declaring war, seizing[702] after

[700]This is probably a reference to the four kinds of toxins in Ayurveda.
[701]Other kings.
[702]The enemy.

marching out, creating a division in the enemy and seeking asylum with the enemy. Listen attentively to what is said to be the three categories—decay, maintenance of the status quo and increase. The further three categories are the pursuit of dharma, artha and kama at the appropriate time. It is through dharma that a lord of the earth protects the earth for a long period of time. In this connection, Angiras's son[703] himself has sung two shlokas. O son of a Yadavi![704] O fortunate one! You should listen to them. 'Having performed all the tasks well, having protected the earth and having protected the citizens in this way, one enjoys happiness in the hereafter. If all the subjects are unprotected and dharma is disregarded, what will austerities do for a king like that? What will his sacrifices achieve?'"'

Chapter 1398(70)

'Yudhishthira asked, "There is dandaniti and there is the king. O grandfather! Tell me. Are these two equal? And whose success is it going to be?"

'Bhishma replied, "O king! O descendant of the Bharata lineage! Listen to me and I will tell you exactly, with words and reasons, about the great fortune that the success of dandaniti brings. Dandaniti binds down the four varnas to their own dharma. When applied by the lord, it ensures that they do not proceed towards adharma. When the four varnas respect their own dharma and there is no mixing, because of the use of dandaniti, there is peace and the subjects are free from fear. In the proper way, the three varnas will make efforts to perform soma rites. Know that the happiness of gods and men is accumulated from these. You should not entertain any doubt about whether the age results in the king, or the king results in the age. The king causes the age. When the king implements all of dandaniti

[703]Brihaspati was the son of Angiras.

[704]Yudhishthira's mother, Kunti, was born in the Yadava lineage.

properly, the best of ages, known as krita yuga, ensues. When it is krita yuga, dharma prevails. There never is any adharma. None of the varnas finds any delight in adharma. There is no doubt that subjects obtain what they wish and preserve what they have.[705] The rites of the Vedas are performed, without any reduction in qualities. All the seasons bring happiness and are free from disease. Sounds, colours and thoughts please men. There are no diseases then and men with short lifespans are not seen. There are no widows and cruel people are not born. The earth yields crops without being ploughed and the herbs are also like that. There is vigour in barks, leaves, fruits and roots. There is no adharma there. There is only dharma. O Yudhishthira! Know these to be the qualities of krita yuga.

'"When the king abandons one-fourth of dandaniti and follows only three-fourths, treta yuga results. The three-fourths are followed by one-fourth that is inauspicious. The earth yields crops only when ploughed and the herbs are also like that. When the king abandons half of policy and dharma, the age known as dvapara is the result. Half that is inauspicious follows half that is good. The earth yields crops when ploughed, but only a little. When the lord of the earth abandons dandaniti entirely and oppresses his subjects in various ways, then kali enters. Adharma is generally prevalent in kali, but dharma is sometimes seen. The minds of all the varnas turn away from their own dharma. Shudras earn a living through mendicancy and brahmanas through servitude. Yoga and *kshema* are destroyed and there is a mixing of varnas. The rites of the Vedas are without any qualities. All the seasons are devoid of happiness and are full of ill health. Sounds, colour and thoughts of people decay. There are diseases then and one dies before one's span of life is over. There are widows and cruel people are born. It only rains sometimes and crops also grow sometimes. When the lord of the earth no longer wishes to protect the subjects, using dandaniti properly and well, all the juices head towards destruction. The king is the creator of krita yuga, treta and dvapara. The king is the reason behind the fourth yuga too. For creating krita, the king obtains endless heaven. For creating treta, the

[705]Yoga and kshema respectively.

king obtains heaven, but it is not endless. For giving rise to dvapara, the king obtains the portion that is his share. However, for giving rise to kali, the king obtains eternal evil. Such an evil-acting person dwells in hell for an eternal period. Having submerged himself in the sins of his subjects, he reaps the sin of bad deeds.

'"A kshatriya must always know and place dandaniti at the forefront, so that he can obtain what he desires and protect what he possesses. Dandaniti, when administered well, sets boundaries for people and is like a mother or a father, demarcating honour for the welfare of the world. O bull among the Bharata lineage! Know that beings thrive on this. This is supreme dharma and the king must follow dandaniti. O Kouravya! Therefore, protect the subjects in accordance with dharma and policy. Having acted in this way and having protected the subjects, you will conquer the heaven that is extremely difficult to vanquish."'

Chapter 1399(71)

'Yudhishthira asked, "O one who knows about conduct! What kind of conduct must a lord of the earth follow? In this life and in the hereafter, how can he easily obtain objects that give rise to happiness?"

'Bhishma replied, "There are thirty-six qualities, united with another thirty-six qualities. If he possesses qualities and acts according to those qualities, then he will obtain excellence. (1)[706] He must follow dharma without any acerbity. (2) He must shower affection. (3) He must not be a non-believer.[707] (4) He must pursue riches, but without violence. (5) He must pursue kama, but must

[706]There is no numbering in the text. We have used it for ease of understanding. The listing adds up to thirty-seven and not thirty-six. That must be because two of these attributes are being clubbed together, though it is not obvious which.

[707]Nastika.

not be bound down by it. (6) Without any hesitation, he must speak pleasantly. (7) He must be brave, but should not boast about it. (8) He must be generous, but should not give to those who are undeserving. (9) He must be bold, but must not be cruel. (10) He must not have alliances with ignoble people. (11) He must not wage war against his relatives. (12) He must not employ spies who are inappropriate. (13) He must not undertake tasks because he has been forced. (14) Before the wicked, he must not speak about his objectives. (15) He must not speak about his own qualities. (16) He must not take away from those who are virtuous. (17) He must not trust those who are wicked. (18) He must not inflict punishment without examination. (19) He must not disclose his counsel. (20) He must not give to those who are covetous. (21) He must not trust those who have caused injury. (22) He must protect his wife, but without jealousy. (23) The king must be pure, but not compulsively so. (24) He must not be excessively addicted to women. (25) He must not eat sweets that are not healthy. (26) He must humbly honour those who deserve respect. (27) He must be sincere in serving his seniors. (28) Without any pride, he must worship the gods. (29) He must desire prosperity, but not in ways that give rise to censure. (30) He must serve, even if he does not feel affection. (31) He must be accomplished, but must also know the proper time. (32) He must comfort, but not because he wants to use people. (33) He must not show favours and then fling a person away. (34) He must not strike ignorantly. (35) He must slay all the enemies that remain. (36) He must not display sudden anger. (37) He must be mild with those who cause him injury. If you desire welfare, this is the way you should govern the kingdom. The lord of the earth who acts contrary to this confronts supreme hardship. I have stated all the qualities to you. Whoever follows these obtains great fortune in this life and greatness in heaven after death."'

Vaishampayana said, 'Hearing these words of Shantanu's son, King Yudhishthira, surrounded by the foremost among the Pandavas, honoured the grandfather. The intelligent one acted in accordance with what he had been told.'

Chapter 1400(72)

'Yudhishthira asked, "O grandfather! How should the king employ himself in the protection of the subjects so that he does not cause an offence to dharma? Tell me that."

'Bhishma replied, "O son![708] I will tell you briefly about what has been determined to be dharma. If I were to describe dharma in detail, I would never reach the end. There will be qualified brahmanas who are learned, devoted to dharma and immersed in the Vedas and rites. Make them dwell in your house and act as officiating priests. When you get up in the morning, greet your priest by clasping his feet. Make him perform all the rites. When the tasks of dharma have been completed and the auspicious pronouncements have been made, make brahmanas pronounce benedictions for prosperity, success and victory. O descendant of the Bharata lineage! You must possess uprightness, fortitude and intelligence. You must seek to obtain artha, but must give up desire and anger. A foolish king who strives for artha while placing desire and anger at the forefront, obtains neither dharma, nor artha. For matters connected with kama and artha, do not employ those who are avaricious and stupid. In all tasks, those who are intelligent and not greedy should be employed. If a fool is given a position of authority in matters concerning artha, or if an unskilled person is put in charge of a task, or if he is overcome by desire and hatred, he will oppress the subjects with wrong policies.

'"The desire for revenue and riches will come through one-sixth of income collected as taxes, monetary penalties levied on wrongdoers and other levies sanctioned by the sacred texts. The tax imposed on the kingdom must always be in accordance with dharma and in accordance with what has been decreed. The king must be attentive in ensuring unlimited yoga and kshema. If he is like a herdsman and is generous, always attentive towards dharma and without desire and hatred, then men will always be devoted to him and find delight in him. Do not desire to obtain an inflow of riches or gain through

[708]The word used is tata.

adharma. If one deviates from the sacred, one's dharma and artha will both be uncertain. A king who deviates from the sacred texts cannot advance towards accumulation. All that he obtains is destroyed on inappropriate things.[709] If artha alone is the foundation, he harms his own self. In his confusion, he oppresses the subjects by imposing taxes that are not sanctioned by the sacred texts. For the sake of milk, if one slices off the udders of a cow, one does not obtain any milk. In that way, a kingdom oppressed through bad policy does not prosper. A person who is caring towards a milk-yielding cow always obtains milk. In that way, a person who cares for the kingdom enjoys the fruits. O Yudhishthira! If the kingdom is administered and enjoyed while protecting it well, it always leads to an unsurpassed increase in the treasury. When the earth is protected well, it provides grain, gold and offspring to the king, just as a satisfied mother always provides milk to her own and those of others. O king! Be like one who makes garlands. Do not be like one who makes charcoal.[710] If you act in this way and protect, you will be able to enjoy the kingdom for a long time.

'"If the riches are exhausted because of invasion by an enemy, in a desire to collect riches, one can use conciliation and take it from non-brahmanas. O descendant of the Bharata lineage! Even when you confront extreme distress, do not let your mind be disturbed when you see wealthy brahmanas, not to speak of when you are prosperous. You must give them riches, according to your capacity and according to what they deserve. If you comfort them and protect them, you will obtain the heaven that is extremely difficult to get. In this way, protect the subjects according to the conduct of dharma. O descendant of the Kuru lineage! You will then obtain eternal and auspicious fame. O Pandava! Protect the subjects through virtuous conduct. O Yudhisthira! Acting in this way, you will not suffer any anxiety. This is the supreme dharma, the protection of subjects by a king. Protecting subjects in their observance of dharma is the supreme

[709]Even if he obtains artha, he does not obtain dharma.

[710]The maker of charcoal burns trees and plants to make charcoal. The maker of garlands tends to trees and plants.

form of compassion. Those who are learned about dharma think that this is supreme dharma. A king who is engaged in protecting beings performs an act of compassion. If a king fails to protect the subjects from fear for a single day, then it takes one thousand years for him to get out of that sin. If the king performs the auspicious task of following dharma and protecting the subjects for a single day, then he enjoys the fruits in heaven for ten thousand years. There are worlds won through sacrifices, studying and great austerities. By protecting the subjects in accordance with dharma, all those are obtained in an instant. O Kounteya! Endeavour to protect dharma in this way. You will obtain auspicious fruits in this world and have no reason for anxiety. O Pandava! You will obtain great prosperity in the world of heaven. In places where there are no kings, it is impossible to obtain this dharma. Therefore, it is the king, and no one else, who can obtain these great fruits. Use dharma to protect this prosperous kingdom that you have obtained. Satisfy Indra through soma and meet the desires of the ones who are your well-wishers."'

Chapter 1401(73)

'Bhishma said, "O king! It is the king's duty to appoint as a royal priest someone who can protect the virtuous and punish the wicked. On this, the ancient account of the conversation between Aila Pururava and Matarishvana is recounted.[711]

'"Aila asked, 'Where have brahmanas been born from and where have the other three varnas come from? Which of the two is superior? Tell me that.'

'"Vayu replied, 'O supreme among kings! The brahmana was created from Brahma's mouth. It is said that the kshatriya was created from his arms and the vaishya from his thighs. O bull among

[711]Pururava was the son of Ila and was the founder of the lunar dynasty. Matarishvana is Vayu, the wind god.

men! The fourth varna, the shudra, was created later from the feet, for the sake of serving the three varnas. The brahmana was born immediately after the earth was born. For the sake of protecting the store of dharma, he is the lord of all beings. The second varna, the kshatriya, was then made the wielder of the rod for the sake of protecting the earth and protecting beings. The vaishya was created to support the three varnas with wealth and grain and the shudra should serve them. These were Brahma's instructions.'

'"Aila asked, 'O Vayu! According to dharma, tell me whom the earth belongs to. Is it the brahmana, or is it properly the kshatriya, because of his wealth?'

'"Vayu replied, 'Everything that exists in the universe belongs to the brahmana. Those who are learned say that this is because he is the firstborn and because he is accomplished in dharma. The brahmana enjoys only what is his, wears what is his and gives away what is his. The brahmana is the preceptor of all the varnas. He is the eldest and the best. In the absence of the husband, the woman makes his younger brother her husband. In that way, because he is the immediate next, the earth makes the kshatriya her husband.[712] If you desire to obtain a supreme status in heaven and wish to follow the path of dharma, this is the first rule for you, though there is an exception for times of distress. Whoever conquers the earth should offer it to a brahmana who is learned, of good conduct, knowledgeable about dharma, an ascetic, who is satisified with his own dharma and not desirous of the riches of others. Conversant with everything, he will intelligently advise the king about policy. A brahmana born in a noble lineage, accomplished in wisdom, humble in speech and wonderful in his choice of words, will tell the king about the best policy. If a king observes the dharma indicated by the brahmana, listens and is not egoistic and adheres to the dharma and vows of kshatriyas, he will be firm in his wisdom and will be established in fame for a long period. The royal priest has a share in all this dharma. As long as all the subjects seek refuge with the king and follow their own dharma properly, they have nothing to

[712]There is an implied refusal by the brahmana to rule the earth.

fear. When a king protects virtuously, out of all the dharma that is practised within the kingdom, the king enjoys a fourth share of that dharma. Gods, humans, ancestors, gandharvas, serpents and rakshasas survive on what is offered in sacrifices. However, when there is no king, there is nothing. In this way, gods and ancestors survive on what is given to them. And the yoga and kshema of dharma is established in kingship. When it is hot, one seeks happiness in shade, water or breeze. When it is cold, one seeks happiness in fire, the sun or inside a house. The mind is delighted with sound, touch, taste, form and smell. But in all these objects of pleasure, happiness is obtained by a person who is not frightened. One who grants freedom from fear obtains great fruits. In the three worlds, there is no gift that is equal to granting life. The king is Indra. The king is Yama. The king is Dharma. The king has different forms. The king upholds everything.'"'

Chapter 1402(74)

'Bhishma said, "The king must consider both dharma and artha and their differences, which are often unfathomable, and then appoint a priest who is extremely learned in the sacred texts. When the king has a royal priest who has dharma in his soul and is learned in dharma, and the king also possesses similar qualities, everything is well. Those two make subjects, the earlier and the later gods and the ancestors prosper. They should be similarly established in dharma, devoted and extremely austere. They should have fraternal feelings towards each other, revere each other and be similar in temperament. When the brahmana and the kshatriya revere each other, the subjects obtain happiness. When they show each other disrespect, the subjects are destroyed. It is said that the brahmana and the kshatriya are the root of all dharma. On this, an ancient history is recited. O Yudhishthira! Listen to this conversation between Aila and Kashyapa.

'"Aila asked, 'When the brahmana abandons the kshatriya and the kshatriya abandons the brahmana, which among the two should be revered? In such a situation, who should not be revered?'

'"Kashyapa replied, 'In the kingdom of a kshatriya where the brahmana and the kshatriya fight with each other, there is no one to revere and bandits are worshipped. Virtuous ones think that there is no one in control there. Bulls do not thrive, nor do cows. There is no churning in the pots and no sacrifices. When the brahmanas abandon the kshatriyas, the sons do not study the Vedas. The bulls that are born in those houses do not prosper. The subjects do not study, nor do they sacrifice. When the brahmanas abandon the kshatriyas, they[713] degenerate and become like bandits. The two are always connected and support each other. The kshatriya was born from the brahmana's womb. The brahmana was born from the kshatriya's womb. Both of them always depend on each other. Supporting each other, they obtain great prosperity. If that ancient alliance is destroyed, everything becomes confounded. It is like someone who no longer has a boat trying to reach the other shore.Or like a boat tossed around on the giant ocean. The four varnas are then confounded and all the subjects confront a state of destruction. When the tree that represents brahmanas is protected, honey and gold shower down. When it is always unprotected, tears and sin shower down. When a brahmana is not a brahmachari, deviates from studying, but nonetheless seeks protection in Brahma,[714] the gods shower down in strange ways. Terrible misery penetrates there. A person may commit the sin of killing a woman or a brahmana, but is not reprimanded in assembly halls there and is not frightened to approach the king. Then, there is fear for the kshatriya. Extremely wicked persons pile up sin on sin and the god Rudra arises then. The piling up of sin on sin leads to the birth of Rudra. He then kills everyone, the virtuous and the wicked alike.'

'"Aila asked, 'Where does Rudra come from? What is Rudra's form? It is beings who are seen to kill other beings. O Kashyapa! Tell me all this. Where is the god Rudra born from?'

[713]Probably the kshatriyas.

[714]This happens when protection from a kshatriya is absent.

'"Kashyapa replied, 'The soul of Rudra is in the hearts of men. He kills his own body and also the bodies of others. It is said that Rudra is like the stormy wind. His form is like a forest conflagration or the cloud.'

'"Aila said, 'No one can control the wind. Nor do clouds shower down and forest conflagrations are not seen within people.[715] Men are set free and also slain because of desire and hatred.'

'"Kashyapa replied, 'The fire may be lit in one house. But it swiftly burns down an entire village. In that way, the god causes confusion and touches everything, the good and the wicked.'

'"Aila asked, 'If chastisement touches everyone, the good and the wicked, especially because of the sins committed by the wicked, what is the reason to perform good deeds? What is the reason not to perform wicked deeds?'

'"Kashyapa replied, 'Similar chastisement touches those who have not performed wicked deeds, because their sentiments are mixed. They have not abandoned those who perform wicked deeds. Because of mixed sentiments, wet wood is burnt along with the dry. There should never be any mingling with the performers of wicked deeds.'

'"Aila said, 'The earth supports both the virtuous and the wicked. The sun heats both the virtuous and the wicked. The wind blows on both the virtuous and the wicked. The water bears along both the virtuous and the wicked.'

'"Kashyapa replied, 'That is the way of the world. O prince! But it is not like that there.[716] After death, there is a specific difference between those who perform good deeds and those who are wicked. The world of virtuous ones is full of honey and radiant with golden rays into which clarified butter has been poured. It is the navel of immortality. After death, the brahmachari finds delight there. There is no death there. Nor is there old age or unhappiness. The world of the wicked is hell, without any light. There is eternal unhappiness and a lot of sorrow. There, the self sorrows over one's wicked deeds. He descends for many years and cannot find a place to rest. When

[715]Therefore, how can Rudra be inside men?

[716]In the world hereafter.

there is dissension between brahmanas and kshatriyas, the subjects are submerged in intolerable grief. Knowing this, it is the king's duty to make a learned person, one who is not knowledgeable about just one subject, the priest. He is the one who should be consecrated. That is what dharma decrees. According to dharma, the brahmana is said to be the foremost among everyone. Those who are learned about dharma say that brahmanas were created first. Because he is honoured as the first, everything that came later belongs to him. Therefore, the brahmana must be revered and worshipped and he enjoys the best of everything. According to dharma, everything that is best and distinguished must be offered to him. This is a mandatory duty for a king, even if he is powerful. The brahmana makes the kshatriya prosper. The kshatriya makes the brahmana prosper.'"'

Chapter 1403(75)

'Bhishma said, "The yoga and kshema of a kingdom is said to depend on the king. The yoga and kshema of the king depend on the priest. When the invisible fears of the subjects are pacified by the brahmana and the visible ones by the arms of the king, there is indeed happiness in the kingdom. In this connection, an ancient history is recounted. That was a conversation between King Muchukunda and Vaishravana.[717] Having conquered this earth, King Muchukunda wished to test the strength of his own army and attacked the lord of Alaka.[718] King Vaishravana created and released rakshasas on him and that army of nairittas crushed and drove away his forces. When King Muchukunda, the scorcher of enemies, saw that his own soldiers were being slaughtered, he censured his learned priest. Vasishtha, supreme in knowledge about the brahman, performed terrible austerities and drove the rakshasas there away,

[717]Kubera.

[718]The lord of Alaka is Kubera. Kubera's capital is Alaka or Alakapuri.

thereby creating a path. At this, King Vaishravana showed himself before Muchukunda. On the soldiers being slaughtered, he spoke these words. 'Earlier, there were kings who were more powerful than you and they also had priests. However, none of them acted the way you are acting. It is not as if those lords of the earth were limited in strength or in their accomplishment with weapons. They approached and worshipped me, as the lord of happiness and unhappiness. If you possess strength in your arms, you should exhibit it. Why are you depending to such a great degree on the strength of a brahmana?' At this, Muchukunda became angry and replied to the lord of riches. Though he was initially enraged, he reverentially spoke these justified words. 'Svayambhu[719] created the brahmana and the kshatriya from the same womb. Separate powers have been ordained for them and they protect the world. The brahmana is always established in the strength of austerities and mantras. The kshatriya is always established in the strength of weapons and his arms. Together, their task is to protect the subjects. O lord of Alaka! Though you have reprimanded me, this is the way I have acted.' Vaishravana then spoke to the king and his priest. 'Unless it has been ordained, I do not bestow a kingdom on anyone. O king! Know that unless it has been ordained, I do not take it away either. O brave one! I have given you this entire earth. Rule it.' Muchukunda replied, 'O king! I do not wish to enjoy a kingdom that has been given to me by you. I wish to enjoy the prosperity of a kingdom that has been won by my arms and valour.' King Vaishravana was overcome by supreme wonder. On seeing that Muchukunda was established in the dharma of kshatriyas, he honoured this. King Muchukunda followed the dharma and vows of kshatriyas well and ruled over the earth that he had conquered through the valour of his arms. Like that, if a king knows the brahman well and gives precedence to brahmanas, he conquers what has not been conquered earlier and obtains great fame. The brahmana must always have water[720] and the kshatriya

[719]Brahma.

[720]For various religious rituals.

must always have weapons. Everything that is there in the universe is under their control."'

Chapter 1404(76)

'Yudhishthira asked, "To ensure the prosperity of men, what kind of a conduct should a lord of the earth follow? How does he conquer the auspicious worlds? O grandfather! Tell me this."

'Bhishma replied, "O descendant of the Bharata lineage! The king must donate and must perform sacrifices. He must fast, perform austerities and be engaged in protecting the subjects. Following dharma, the king must always protect all the subjects. Without being distracted, he must arise and worship all those who follow dharma. When the king honours dharma, everyone also honours it in every way. When the king acts in this way, the subjects are delighted. He must always hold his rod aloft and must be like death to his enemies. He must slay all the bandits and must not wilfully ignore anyone. O descendant of the Bharata lineage! If a king protects the subjects extremely well, out of whatever dharma is observed by them, one-fourth of that dharma is the king's share. If he protects the subjects in accordance with dharma, the king enjoys one-fourth of their studying, sacrifices, donations and worship. O descendant of the Bharata lineage! If the king does not protect the subjects in any way and if there is something wrong with the kingdom, one-fourth of that sin is enjoyed by the king. It has been said that he gets all of it. Some have determined that he gets half. However, there may be a lord of the earth who is cruel in his deeds and false in his speech. Listen to how that king can be freed from his kingdom and his own treasury. If he cannot restore all of it, he should restore whatever he can, keeping just enough for his own subsistence. All the varnas must protect brahmanas and the property of brahmanas. One who causes injury to brahmanas should not be allowed to remain in the kingdom.

If the property of brahmanas is protected, everything is protected. If their favours are ensured, then the king will have accomplished his objective. Beings depend on Parjanya and birds on a large tree. Like that, men depend on the king for accomplishing all their objectives. If a king has desire in his soul, is always fraudulent in his mind, or is violent and extremely avaricious, he will be incapable of protecting the subjects."

'Yudhishthira said, "I have not sought pleasure in the kingdom. Even for an instant, I have not desired the kingdom. I agreed to the kingdom for the sake of dharma, but there does not seem to be any dharma in it. Since there is no dharma in it, I have had enough of the kingdom. Therefore, for the sake of dharma, I will go to the forest. I will conquer my senses and cast aside my rod. I will worship dharma in the sacred forest and, like a hermit, live on roots and fruits."

'Bhishma replied, "I know your mind and about your qualities of non-violence. However, only through non-violence, you will not be able to accomplish anything great. You are mild, self-controlled, extremely noble and greatly devoted to dharma. However, people do not show you great regard, taking you to be an eunuch, driven by compassion over dharma. Look towards rajadharma, which was appropriate for your father and grandfathers. What you wish to resort to is not the conduct of kings. You have established yourself in non-violence and have thereby created the impotence you should not follow. There are fruits of dharma that can be obtained from protecting the subjects. O son![721] What you wish to follow, through your wisdom and your intelligence, is not the blessing that Pandu and Kunti desired for you. Your father always spoke about valour, strength and spirit for you. Kunti desired greatness, strength and generosity for you. In the worlds of men and gods, ancestors and gods always want offerings of svaha and svadha from their sons.[722] You have been born to practise donations, study, perform sacrifices

[721]The word used is tata.

[722]The exclamation svaha is made when offerings are made to gods. The exclamation svadha is made when offerings are made to ancestors.

and protect the subjects and can either follow dharma or adharma. O Kounteya! Destiny has imposed a burden and a heavier load has been imposed on that. Even if you are fatigued, your fame will not be destroyed. If a person controls himself in every way and bears it without losing his footing, he is without any taint in his deeds, words and success, because of his deeds alone. If someone knows about dharma and stumbles, that is a calamity, regardless of whether he is a householder, a king or a brahmachari. It is better to do a small, generous and virtuous act than to do nothing at all. There is nothing more wicked than not doing. O king! When a person born in a noble lineage knows about dharma and obtains great prosperity, yoga and kshema exist and welfare can be thought of. When a person who knows about dharma obtains a kingdom, he should seize it in every direction—winning over some through donations, others through force, and still others with extremely pleasant words. There are learned ones born in noble lineages, who are afflicted by fear because they may not have a means of sustenance. When they obtain that[723] and are satisfied about their states, what can be a greater dharma than that?"

'Yudhishthira asked, "What is greater than heaven? What is greater happiness than that? What is supreme prosperity? If there is anything that you can think of, tell me about it."

'Bhishma replied, "If complete kshema can be obtained from someone being established,[724] then among all of us, he is the one who has obtained the best of heavens in an instant. I am telling you this truthfully. O supreme among the Kuru lineage! You are the delight of all the Kurus. Be the king. Conquer heaven. Protect the righteous and slay the wicked. O son! Let your well-wishers and the virtuous live and follow you. Be like Parjanya to beings and like a succulent tree to birds. Be dignified, brave, capable of striking, non-violent, victorious over your senses, affectionate and ready to share. Let people live and follow you."'

[723]Because there is a king.

[724]Referring to a king.

Chapter 1405(77)

'Yudhishthira said, "O grandfather! Some brahmanas are engaged in their own tasks, while others are engaged in tasks they should not do. Tell me the difference between them."

'Bhishma replied, "There are those who have the signs of learning. In considering anything, they look to the sacred texts. O king! These brahmanas are celebrated as being equal to the brahman. There are those who are accomplished as officiating priests and preceptors and are engaged in their own tasks. O king! These brahmanas are regarded as the equals of the gods. There are those who are officiating priests, priests, ministers, ambassadors and supervisors of the treasury. O king! These brahmanas are regarded as the equivalent of kshatriyas. There are those who ride horses, ride elephants or chariots, and are also foot soldiers. O king! These brahmanas are regarded as the equivalent of vaishyas. There are also reprehensible ones who are brahmanas only in name. They have abandoned the deeds they should have undertaken by virtue of birth. O king! These brahmanas are said to be the equals of shudras. There are brahmanas who have not studied the sacred texts. Nor have they consecrated the sacred fire. All of these do not follow dharma. The king should make them pay taxes and force them to undertake manual labour. There are those who are employed as ordinary messengers, work as priests in temples, study the nakshatras, work as officiating priests for ordinary people and fifthly, undertake great journeys.[725] These brahmanas are chandalas. If the treasury suffers from a shortage, the lord of the earth should exact taxes from these,[726] with the exception of those who are equals of the brahman and the equals of the gods. The Vedas say that the king is the lord of the riches of those who are not brahmanas and also of brahmanas who perform wrong deeds.

[725]The text uses the word *mahapathika*. Literally, this means someone who undertakes a great journey. But the sense seems to be of a great journey that takes one beyond the seas.

[726]Meaning all brahmanas, with the exception of the categories excluded.

The king must never ignore wrong deeds. If he wishes to follow dharma, he must control and divide them.[727] If a brahmana becomes a thief in a king's kingdom, learned people think that this is the king's crime. O king! If a brahmana who knows the Vedas and is a snataka is forced to become a thief because of lack of means of sustenance, those who are learned about dharma say that it is the king's duty to support him. O scorcher of enemies! If he does not change himself after he has obtained a means of subsistence, then, with his relatives, he should be exiled from the country."'

Chapter 1406(78)

'Yudhishthira asked, "O bull among the Bharata lineage! O grandfather! What kind of a conduct should the king follow, so as to ensure power and prosperity? Tell me this."

'Bhishma replied, "The Vedas say that the king is the lord of the riches of those who are not brahmanas and also of those brahmanas who do the wrong kind of work. The king must never ignore brahmanas who do the wrong kind of work. The virtuous ones say that this was the ancient practice followed by kings. O king! If a brahmana is a thief in the kingdom of a king, that king is regarded as the criminal. Since they hold themselves to be responsible for the deed, all rajarshis have protected brahmanas. In this connection, an ancient history is recounted. The king of Kekaya sung this when he was abducted by a rakshasa. O king! When the king of Kekaya was studying in the forest, rigid in his vows, a terrible rakshasa seized him.

'"The king said, 'There is no thief in my country. Nor is there a wicked person or a drunkard. There is no one who has not consecrated the sacred fire. Why have you then been able to penetrate me? In my dominion, there is no brahmana who is not

[727]The different categories of brahmanas.

learned, without vows. Nor is there one who does not drink soma. Why have you then been able to penetrate me? In my kingdom, there is no one who performs sacrifices without offering dakshina to the officiating priests. There is no one who studies without following the vows. Why have you then been able to penetrate me? They[728] are established in six tasks—studying, teaching, performing sacrifices, officiating at sacrifices, donating and receiving. They are honoured with their proper shares. They are mild and truthful in speech. In my dominion, the brahmanas are engaged in their own tasks. Why have you then been able to penetrate me? They[729] do not beg. They give. They are accomplished in true dharma. They study, but do not teach. They perform sacrifices, but do not work as officiating priests. They protect brahmanas and do not run away from battle. The kshatriyas are engaged in their own tasks. Why have you then been able to penetrate me? They[730] earn a living from agriculture, protecting cattle and trade and do not resort to deception. They are not distracted and perform their tasks. They are good in their vows and truthful in speech. They are ready to share, self-controlled, pure and fraternal in their dealings. My vaishyas are engaged in their own tasks. Why have you then been able to penetrate me? My shudras are engaged in their own tasks. Without any resentment, they serve the three varnas. Why have you then been able to penetrate me? All the women who are in distress, without protectors, weak and afflicted are given their shares. Why have you then been able to penetrate me? I have not destroyed the dharma of specific families or regions. All these have been followed in the proper way. Why have you then been able to penetrate me? In my kingdom, ascetics have been honoured and protected. They have been received well and given their proper share. Why have you then been able to penetrate me? I do not consume anything without sharing. I do not have intercourse with the wives of others. I never sport when I am alone. Why have you then been able to penetrate me? There is no

[728]The brahmanas.
[729]The kshatriyas.
[730]The vaishyas.

brahmachari who is not a beggar. There is no beggar who is not a brahmachari. No oblations are offered without an officiating priest. Why have you then been able to penetrate me? I have not shown disrespect to the aged, the learned and ascetics. When the kingdom sleeps, I am awake. Why have you then been able to penetrate me? My priest is skilled in studying the Vedas. He is an ascetic and knows about all forms of dharma. He is prosperous and is the lord of the entire kingdom. I desire the celestial worlds through donations, truthfulness, protecting the brahmanas and serving the seniors. I should not have any fear from rakshasas. There are no widows in my kingdom, nor those who are brahmanas in name alone. There are no brahmanas who are miserable or thieves. There is no one who has intercourse with someone else's wife. There is no one who is evil in deeds. I should not have any fear from rakshasas. There is no part of my body, not even the space of two fingers, which has not been mangled by weapons, when I have fought for the sake of dharma. Why have you then been able to penetrate me? The people in my kingdom have always sought benedictions for me in the form of cattle, brahmanas and sacrifices. Why have you then been able to penetrate me?'

'"The rakshasa replied, 'Whatever be the circumstance, you always look towards dharma. O Kekaya! Therefore, return to your home in safety. I am leaving. O Kekaya! He who protects cattle and brahmanas and protects his subjects has no reason to fear rakshasas, not to speak of men. Those who have brahmanas at their head, those who are fortified by the strength of the brahman and those who love their guests and wives, are men who have conquered heaven."

'Bhishma said, "You must therefore protect brahmanas. Protected by you, they will protect you. The desire of kings should be that the kingdom should prosper well. Therefore, in particular, brahmanas who perform perverse tasks must be restrained. For the welfare of the subjects, they must be treated separately. The king who acts in this way towards residents of the city and the countryside experiences fortune and obtains the world of Indra."'

Chapter 1407(79)

'Yudhishthira said, "O descendant of the Bharata lineage! It has been said that in times of distress, brahmanas may live by adopting the dharma of kshatriyas. Can they also live by adopting the dharma of vaishyas?"

'Bhishma replied, "When he is incapable of following the dharma of kshatriyas, he can follow the dharma of vaishyas. When the means of subsistence is destroyed because of some hardship, agriculture and tending to cattle is permissible."

'Yudhishthira asked, "O bull among the Bharata lineage! When a brahmana follows the dharma of vaishyas, what commodities can he sell, without being deprived of the world of heaven?"

'Bhishma replied, "Under every circumstance, a brahmana must always avoid liquor, salt, sesamum seeds, animals with manes, bulls, honey, meat and cooked food. O son! If a brahmana sells these, he goes to hell. A goat is Agni. A sheep is Varuna. A horse is Surya. The earth is large.[731] A cow is a soma sacrifice. These must never be sold. The virtuous do not praise the exchange of uncooked food for cooked food. O descendant of the Bharata lineage! However, for the sake of eating, cooked food can be obtained in exchange for uncooked food. 'We will eat this when it has been cooked. Please cook this for us.' If one considers uncooked food with this objective in mind, there is no adharma. On this, there is the ancient conduct of dharma, followed by those who adhered to custom. O Yudhishthira! Listen to this. 'I will give you this. You must give me that in return.' This voluntary agreement is dharma, because there is no force involved. Ancient transactions occurred in this way, accepted by rishis and others. There is no doubt that this is virtuous."

'Yudhishthira said, "O father![732] When all the subjects abandon their own dharma and take up weapons, the strength of the kshatriya

[731]This probably means that land must not be sold.

[732]The word used is tata.

dwindles. How will the king then become the protector and refuge of the worlds? I have a doubt about this. O grandfather! Tell me this in detail."

'Bhishma replied, "As the foremost among the varnas, brahmanas should seek the comfort of their own selves through donations, austerities, performance of sacrifices, lack of injury and self-control. Those among them who possess the strength of the Vedas must arise in every way and increase the king's strength, like the gods do to the great Indra. When the king is weak, it is said that the arms of the brahmanas become his refuge. Therefore, if he knows, he should seek to uplift himself through the strength of brahmanas. When the king is victorious and ensures welfare in the kingdom, all the varnas are immersed in their own dharma and perform their own tasks. O Yudhishthira! However, when bandits are engaged in causing confusion, there is mixing[733] and all the varnas must take up weapons and there is no sin in this."

'Yudhishthira asked, "If all the kshatriyas act injuriously towards the brahmanas, who will then save the brahmanas? What will be the supreme dharma then?"

'Bhishma replied, "In particular, the aged brahmanas must restrain and pacify the kshatriyas through austerities, brahmacharya, weapons, physical strength, deceit and lack of deceit. Brahmanas can do the restraining, because kshatriyas were created from brahmanas. Fire was created from water, kshatriyas from brahmanas and iron from stone. Therefore, the energy of each category is pacified by its own womb. When iron encounters stone, fire comes in contact with water and kshatriyas are injurious towards brahmanas, all three are pacified. O Yudhishthira! Therefore, kshatriyas are pacified by brahmanas, even if they are great and irresistible in energy and strength. When the vigour of brahmanas is mild and the vigour of kshatriyas is extremely weak, all the varnas always act in a wicked way towards the brahmanas. Those who fight then, ready to give up their lives for the sake of protecting brahmanas, are those who have dharma in their souls. All those spirited ones who are

[733]Of the varnas.

enraged and wish to take up weapons for the sake of brahmanas obtain sacred worlds. Those worlds are beyond those meant for the extremely virtuous ones who study, and the ascetics. Those brave ones go to supreme worlds that are beyond those meant for those who fast and destroy their lives in the fire. For learned ones, there is no other dharma than giving up their lives in the cause.[734] One should bow down before those fortunate ones who offer their lives. May we obtain the worlds obtained by those who seek to restrain the enemies of brahmanas. Manu has said that those brave ones conquer heaven and Brahma's world. People are purified when they bathe after a horse sacrifice. That is what happens to the evil and good deeds of those who are killed by weapons in a battle. Because of the time and the place, adharma can become dharma and dharma can become adharma. That is the nature of time and place. Friends can perform cruel deeds and conquer supreme heaven. The virtuous can perform wicked deeds and attain the supreme objective. There are three occasions when the taking up of weapons by a brahmana is not reprehensible—to save himself, to prevent the mixing of the varnas and to restrain the unassailable."

'Yudhishthira asked, "O supreme among kings! When the strength of bandits increases, for the sake of preventing injury, when the varnas are mixed and the varnas are confused, should someone else who is stronger, a brahmana, a vaishya or a shudra, take up the task?[735] Should he protect the subjects against bandits by wielding the rod of dharma? Should he perform that task or is he restrained from doing that? I think that weapons should not be wielded by anyone who is not born a kshatriya."

'Bhishma replied, "If he is a means of crossing over to a shore when none exists, if he is a boat when no boats exist, whether he is a shudra or someone else, he must always be revered. O king! When people are afflicted by bandits, he protects those who have no protectors. Men seek refuge with him and he conveys them to a state of happiness. Therefore, he must be affectionately worshipped, as if he

[734]Of protecting brahmanas.

[735]Because the kshatriyas are weak.

is a relative. O Kouravya! He deserves honour and should be looked upon as a performer of great deeds. What use is a bull that does not bear a load? What use is a cow that does not yield milk? What use is a barren wife? What use is a king who does not protect? What use is an elephant made of wood? What use is a deer made of leather? What use is a cart without a drive and a path? What use is a degraded field? A brahmana who does not study and a king who does not protect are always useless in this way, like a cloud that does not rain. The one who always protects the virtuous and chastises the wicked performs the duties of a king and should always be upheld and instated in this way."'

Chapter 1408(80)

'Yudhishthira asked, "O grandfather! What should be the conduct of those who are officiating priests and how should they endeavour? O Indra among kings! O supreme among eloquent ones! What kind of people should they be?"

'Bhishma replied, "From ancient times, the tasks and conduct of officiating priests have been laid down. They must first be knowledgeable about sacred hymns[736] and the learning of brahmanas. They must always be patient and firm in this one task.[737] They must not be unpleasant in speech. They must be affectionate towards each other.[738] They must be revered and must look on everyone equally. They must possess attributes of non-injury, truthfulness, non-violence, austerities, uprightness, lack of hatred, lack of ego, modesty, forbearance, self-control and tranquility. A person who is modest, truthful, patient, self-controlled, non-injurious towards beings, without desire and harted, possessing the three sparkling

[736]Or metres, *chhanda*.

[737]Of acting as officiating priest.

[738]Other priests.

qualities,[739] non-violent and content with knowledge alone—is said to be worthy of Brahma's seat. O son! These are great officiating priests and all of these must be honoured in the proper way."

'Yudhishthira said, "The words of the Vedas stipulate the giving of dakshina. They say that it must be given. But nothing is said about when that giving is enough. Nor do the sacred texts say enough about riches, for example, what is in accordance with the sacred texts in times of distress.[740] The commands of the sacred texts are terrible, because they do not look towards the capacity of the giver.[741] The ordinances of the Vedas only say that one must faithfully perform sacrifices. However, what will devotion achieve when the sacrifice is performed falsely?"[742]

'Bhishma replied, "One cannot obtain greatness by disrespecting the Vedas, deceit or fraud. You should not think in this way. O son! Dakshina is a part of sacrifice and extend the Vedas. Devoid of dakshina, mantras can never render salvation. However, the capacity to give one full vessel should also be honoured. O son! Therefore, all the three varnas must perform sacrifices in the proper way. The ordinances of the Vedas say that for brahmanas, the king is like soma. One should not try to sell it, since such a means of earning a living is fruitless.[743] If the sacrifice is performed in this way, it will be as if dharma has been sold. The rishis who are learned about dharma have spoken about dharma in this way. The person, the sacrifice and soma must be in accordance with what is proper. A man who has improper conduct is of no use to himself or to others. We have heard it in the sacred texts that the body constitutes the vessels of the sacrifice.

[739]Knowledge of the three Vedas. Alternatively, knowledge of the Vedas, good conduct and lineage.

[740]*Apad dharma* is about dharma in times of distress or hardship. The sacred texts are about standard dharma and have less to say about times of distress.

[741]Who may have limited capacity in times of distress.

[742]This falsehood is in a very specific sense of limited dakshina because of distress. Instead of a cow, food is given. Instead of garments, a piece of barley is given. Instead of gold, a copper coin is given.

[743]For the sake of earning a living, one should not sell soma.

For that reason, conducted properly, only great-souled brahmanas must be engaged. The supreme among the learned texts decrees that austerities are superior to sacrifices. O learned one! Therefore, I will tell you about austerities. Listen to me. Non-violence, truthfulness, lack of injury, self-control and compassion—the learned and the patient know that these are austerities, not the drying up of the body. Not accepting the proof of the Vedas, transgressing the sacred texts and chaos everywhere—these destroy the soul. O Partha! Listen to what has been said about oblations in sacrifices that last for ten days. Consciousness is the ladle. Thoughts are clarified butter. Supreme knowledge is the *pavitra*.[744] All kinds of deceit represent death. All kinds of uprightness represent the objective of the brahman. All this is actually in the realm of the unknown. What purpose will words accomplish?"'

Chapter 1409(81)

'Yudhishthira asked, "O grandfather! For a man who is alone and unaided, even the slightest task is extremely difficult to accomplish, not to speak of running a kingdom. For the sake of prosperity, what should be the conduct of a king's adviser? How should he behave? Whom should the king trust and whom should he not trust?"

'Bhishma replied, "O king! The king has four kinds of friends—those who have the same objective, those who are devoted, those who are natural and those who are artificial.[745] There is a fifth kind of friend, one with dharma in his soul, who serves a single person and not two. He is on the side that has dharma, though he may

[744]Pavitra is two blades of sacred grass, used to sprinkle clarified butter on the fire.

[745]Natural friends are those who are friends by birth, that is, relatives. Artificial friends are those who have been made friends through various means, such as gifts and affection.

also be neutral. Wishing to conquer, a king uses both dharma and adharma. However, to such a person, one should never disclose objectives that would not please him.[746] Out of the four, the two in the middle are the best.[747] The others should always be suspected. However, if a king has to undertake a task himself, all of these should be suspected. It is the king's duty to be never careless in protecting his friends. A king who is careless is overwhelmed by people. A wicked person can become virtuous, a virtuous person can become terrible, an enemy can become a friend and a friend can cause injury. Since a man's mind is uncertain, how can he be trusted? Therefore, the king must ensure that the important tasks are undertaken in his presence. Blind trust can completely destroy dharma and artha. However, not trusting anyone is also worse than death. Trusting amounts to premature death. Trust leads to catastrophe. If one trusts someone, life depends on the person one has trusted. Therefore, the king must trust some people and mistrust others. O son! This is the eternal policy for prosperity. There may be someone who brings riches as soon as one thinks about it. The learned ones say that such a person is an enemy and must always be distrusted. When water flows from one person's field into another person's field, as long as the first one wants the water to flow, he doesn't demolish all the embankments. But when he is worried about too much of water flowing down, he wishes to demolish the embankments. One can discern this through signs and the signs must be used to determine the enemy. When someone is not satisfied with the king's prosperity and is distressed at his decay, it is said that this is the sign of a best friend. If there is someone about whom one can think, 'My destruction is the same as his death,' that person can be trusted, as if he was one's own father. You should try to increase such a person's prosperity in every way and always prevent injury to him, since he is engaged in tasks of dharma. If someone is scared of injury to the king, know that this is a sign that he is the best friend. Those who wish to cause him injury are said to be enemies. There

[746]Instances of adharma should not be revealed to such a person.

[747]Those who are devoted and those who are natural.

may be someone who is always frightened of injury to the king and satisfied with the king's prosperity.[748] A friend who is like this is said to be one's equal. A person who is close to you must be handsome, with a good complexion and good voice. He must be patient and without malice. He must be born in a noble lineage and possess good conduct. Intelligence, a good memory, skill, natural compassion and a capacity to never malign, irrespective of whether one is honoured or dishonoured—these are the attributes of an officiating priest, a preceptor and a friend. Such people must dwell in your house and must be supremely honoured. He can know about secret counsel and also about the objectives of dharma and artha. One can trust such a person, the way one would trust a father. Each task should always be given to one person. Otherwise, there will be dissension. A person for whom duties and fame are the most important, who always sticks to a pledge he has made, who does not hate capable people, who enables others, who does not abandon dharma for the sake of desire, fear, avarice or anger, one who is accomplished and competent in speech—such a person must always be next to you. Brave, noble, learned, powerful, accomplished, born in good lineages, possessing good conduct, patient, without malice—it is your duty to appoint these as advisers and employ them in all the tasks. They must be honoured, given their shares, given good aides and established in their own tasks. Completely immersed in great and important tasks, they ensure great prosperity. They always seek to rival each other and perform these tasks. They consult each other and accomplish the objectives. You must always be frightened of your kin, as if they are death. A kin is like a minor king and can never tolerate the king's prosperity. O mighty-armed one! It is only a kin who is delighted at the destruction of someone who is upright, mild, generous, modest and truthful in speech. However, there is no happiness in not having kin. There is nothing that is worse than that. A man without kin is overwhelmed by the enemy. If a man has

[748]In this sentence, the word 'king' doesn't actually occur in the text and is left implicit. We have introduced it for ease of comprehension and in this particular case, insertion in the text works better than a footnote.

been treated badly by others, kin offer refuge. Kin never tolerate the prospect of kin being maltreated by others. Even if that injury is caused by friends, it is regarded as one to one's own self. There are good qualities in them,[749] but the absence of qualities can also be discerned. He who is not kin, does not do any favours. But he who is not kin, does not use poisoned arrows. In the world of kin, both can be seen—virtuous and wicked. One must always honour them in words and deeds. He must act towards them in a pleasant way and never act in unpleasant ways. He must always act as if he trusts them, even if he actually mistrusts them. It is seen that good and bad qualities are both mixed in them. When a man conducts himself in this way and is not distracted, his enemies are disarmed and become his friends. This is the way he prospers in the circle of kin and relatives. For a very long period of time, he obtains fame and mastery over his friends and enemies."'

Chapter 1410(82)

'Yudhishthira asked, "If the circle of kin and relatives cannot be dealt with in this way, friends may become enemies. What should be one's sentiments then?"

'Bhishma replied, "In this connection, an ancient history is recounted, about the conversation between Vasudeva and Narada, the celestial rishi.

'"Vasudeva said, 'O Narada! A person who is not a well-wisher should not get to know the supremely secret counsel, nor should a well-wisher who is not learned, or a learned person who is not in control of his soul. O Narada! Because you have affectionate feelings towards me, I will tell you something. O one who can go to heaven! Having considered my entire intelligence, I will also ask you something. I do not act so as to become a slave to my kin, by talking to them about their

[749]Meaning, kin.

riches. I enjoy half the objects of pleasure[750] and forgive harsh words spoken to me, which crush my heart, like two kindling sticks rubbed together in a desire for fire. O rishi of the gods! The words that are spoken harshly always torment me. Samkarshana[751] always possesses strength and Gada[752] is again delicate. O Narada! Pradyumna[753] surpasses me in beauty, but I have no aides. O Narada! The others of the Andhaka and Vrishni lineages are extremely fortunate. They are powerful and difficult to assail. They are always full of enterprise. Whether they are on your side, or whether they are not on your side, there is hardship. What can be a greater misery than to have Akrura and Ahuka on the same side?[754] Both of them have always solicited me, but I have not opted for either of them. However, what can be a greater misery than not to have those two on your side? O great sage! I am like the mother of two[755] who are engaged in a gambling match. If I wish for the victory of one, it is like defeat for the other. O Narada! These two always afflict me in this way. You should tell me what is beneficial for my kin and for my own self.'

'"Narada replied, 'O Krishna! Disasters are of two kinds—the external and the internal. O Varshneya! They result from one's own deeds, or those of others. This difficulty is internal and is because of your own deeds. Because of Akrura's power, for the sake of riches, because of desire or because they are frightened by words or deeds, the Bhojas are on his side. You obtained the prosperity for yourself, but gave it away to another.[756] You provided the foundation and

[750]Giving away the remaining half.

[751]Balarama.

[752]Krishna's younger brother.

[753]Krishna's son.

[754]Ahuka was a Yadava king and the father of Ugrasena. Akrura was Ahuka's son-in-law, the point being that Ahuka and Akrura rarely agreed. However, each wanted Krishna to be on his side. The word Ahuka may also refer to Ugrasena himself, that is, the son, not the father.

[755]That is, two brothers.

[756]Kamsa deposed King Ugrasena and became king. Krishna killed Kamsa. However, having killed Kamsa, Krishna did not become the king himself. Instead, he instated Ugrasena and thereby created a problem, by making Ugrasena (Ahuka) powerful.

he[757] is now applauded in words and possesses aides. Like food that has been vomited out, you are incapable of taking it back. O Krishna! You can never take the kingdom back from Babhru[758] and Ugrasena, especially because that will lead to conflict within the clan. That will only be possible after trying hard and performing an extremely difficult task. There will be a great slaughter and perhaps complete destruction. Therefore, use a weapon that is not made of steel, one that is mild, but is capable of piercing hearts. Sharpen that blade and use it to remove their tongues.'

'"Vasudeva asked, 'O sage! How will I know what is the weapon that is not made of steel and is mild? What will I sharpen and use to remove their tongues?'

'"Narada replied, 'Always give as much of food as you are capable of. Be patient, self-controlled and upright. Honour those who must be revered. This is the weapon that is not made of steel. Use words to pacify the hearts, the speech and the minds of the relatives who desire to speak bitter and slighting words. Someone who is not a great man, someone who has not cleansed his soul and someone who is without aides cannot bear a great burden.[759] Raise it aloft on your shoulders. Every one is capable of bearing a great burden on level terrain. Only an excellent bull can bear a load that is extremely heavy over uneven terrain. An aggregation is destroyed if there is conflict within its ranks. O Keshava! You are the foremost of the aggregation. When it has obtained you, act so that the aggregation is not destroyed. Nothing other than prosperity, renunciation and generosity are established in a person who is wise. Ensuring the prosperity of one's own side is fortunate and glorious and ensures a long life. O Krishna! Act so that there is no destruction of your relatives. O lord! Whether it is about the six aspects[760] of policy or marching out on an expedition, you are in control of everything and everything is known to you. O mighty-armed one! The Madhavas, the Kukuras, the Bhojas, the

757 Ahuka.

758 Ugrasena's minister.

759 Of ruling the Yadavas.

760 The king, the advisers, the countryside, the fortified city, the treasury and the army.

Andhakas and the Vrishnis are dependent on you, just as the worlds and the lords of the worlds are. O Madhava! Even the rishis worship your intelligence. You are the preceptor of all beings. You know what has gone and what will come. O foremost among the Yadu lineage! Resorting to you, your relatives enjoy happiness.'"'

Chapter 1411(83)

'Bhishma said, "O descendant of the Bharata lineage! This is the first element of conduct. Listen to the second. The king must always protect the man who extends prosperity. O Yudhishthira! Whether a person is paid or is not paid, if he comes and tells you that the royal treasury is being destroyed and depleted by a minister, you must hear him in secret and protect him from ministers. Ministers tend to kill such informants. All those who destroy the treasury work collectively against the one who protects the treasury and unless protected, he will be destroyed. On this, an ancient history is recounted, about what the sage Kalakavrikshiya told the lord of Kosala. We have heard that the sage Kalakavrikshiya went to Kshemadarshina after he had become the lord of Kosala. Wishing to ascertain what was happening in Kshemadarshina's kingdom, he repeatedly travelled around, with a crow tied in a cage. 'I study the knowledge of crows. Crows tell me what has happened, what will happen, and what is going on right now.' Saying this, with a large number of men, he began to observe the wicked deeds of all those employed by the king, throughout the kingdom. He knew about everything that was going on in the kingdom. He knew everything about the wicked deeds of those employed by the king, here and there. With the crow, the one who was rigid in his vows went to see the king and said, 'I know everything.' He went up to an ornamented adviser of the king of Kosala and, on the basis of what the crow said, told him these words. 'I know what you did on such-and-such an occasion. I know that you stole from the royal treasury. This is what the crow has told me. Swiftly admit or contradict it.' In this way, he spoke to others who had also stolen from the royal treasury. No one heard him speak of anything that was not actually true. O extender of the Kuru lineage! When he was sleeping in the night, all those accused royal employees killed the crow in the night.

'"Next morning, on seeing the crow pierced with an arrow inside the cage, the brahmana went to Kshemadarshina and spoke these words. 'O king! O lord! You are the lord of lives and riches and I seek sanctuary with you. With your permission, I will tell you something that is for the welfare of your city. I have come to you with wholehearted devotion, tormented on account of a friend.[761] Because of the injury caused, I have spoken about your riches being robbed. Like a charioteer with a well-trained horse, I am trying to awake a friend. Because I am intent on ensuring your welfare, I am overcome by great rage. A person who knows and wishes to ensure his own prosperity should always tolerate such advances on the part of a well-wisher.' The king replied to him and said, 'I always desire my own prosperity. Therefore, why will I not forgive what you tell me? O brahmana! If you so wish, tell me what you know. O brahmana! I will act in accordance with the words you tell me.'

'"The sage said, 'I have come to you out of my devotion, to report to you what I know about your policies, your dangers and the threats you are facing from your servants. Learned ones who were preceptors and served kings declared this a long time ago. Only those who have no other means of sustenance should serve the king. Association with kings is like virulent poison. Kings have many friends and also have many enemies. It has been said that those who serve kings face dangers from all of these. O king! Therefore, all the time, they have to be scared of all these. One is incapable of not being single-minded and being distracted when serving a lord of the earth. One who desires prosperity should never be careless. Such carelessness can lead to a king stumbling and if there is such a stumbling, there is no prospect of remaining alive. A learned person must approach the king as if he is a blazing fire. He is the lord of

[761]Referring to the king as a friend.

lives and riches and if he is angry, that lord is like virulent poison. While always making the best of efforts, the man must think, "I am already dead." He must be scared of having said something wrong, having done something wrong, having stood in the wrong way, having sat in the wrong way and having walked in the wrong way. He must watch out for such signs and indications. If the king is pleased, like a god, he can grant every object of desire. However, if he is wrathful, like the fire, he can burn down, from the roots. O king! This is what Maya[762] had said and that is the way it is. I will now repeatedly act so as to extend your prosperity. At times of hardship, an aide like me helps with his intelligence. O king! My crow has been slain, but I am not reprimanding you on account of this. They[763] wish you injury. You should use your intelligence to test for those who wish you well and those who wish you injury. Do not reveal your thoughts. There are those who dwell in your own residence, they do not wish the prosperity of the subjects. It is the likes of those who are hostile towards me. After you have been destroyed, they desire your kingdom. O king! However, they will only succeed if they ally with those who are close to you, not otherwise. O king! Because of fear from them, I will depart and go to a hermitage. O lord! It is they who allied and brought my crow down with an arrow. They sent my crow to Yama's abode as a signal to me. O king! I have seen this through sight gained by a long period of austerities. I used the crow as a hook and crossed this river that is infested with many crocodiles, fish, alligators and a large number of whales.[764] Your kingdom was full of stumps of trees, rocks and thorny scrubs, and infested by tigers, lions and elephants. It was difficult to access and difficult to penetrate, like a cave in the Himalayas. The learned say that a fire should be used to cross a place that is difficult to cross because it is dark, a boat should be used to cross the water. However, the learned also say that there is no means to cross the difficult terrain

[762]The architect of the gods.

[763]The ones who killed the crow.

[764]The text uses the word *timingila*, which is actually an aquatic creature that eats whales.

a king faces. Your kingdom is impenetrable and is enveloped in darkness. Even you are incapable of finding comfort here. How can I? This is not an auspicious place to live in, since the virtuous and the wicked are equal here. There is no doubt that one will be killed here, whether one is good or wicked. One is slain for performing good deeds and one who performs wicked deeds is not slain. One should not remain here for a long time. The learned should depart swiftly. O king! There is a river named Sita, where even boats sink. I think that this trap, which kills everyone, is like that. You are like the fall that confronts those who collect honey, or like a meal laced with poison. Your sentiments are like those of the wicked and you do not follow the conduct of the virtuous. O king! You are like a well that is surrounded by poisonous snakes. You are like a passage to a large river that has sweet water to drink. However, the banks are covered with *kariras*[765] and reeds and it is difficult to reach. O king! You are like that. O king! You are like a swan amidst dogs, vultures and jackals. A creeper attaches itself to a giant tree and, winding around the trunk, increases its abundant growth. It envelopes and surpasses the tree's growth. When there is a terrible conflagration, it burns down both the tree and the creeper. O king! Your advisers fit that image. Cleanse them. O king! You are the one who has nurtured and protected them. Ignoring you, they are seeking to kill someone who loves you. I have dwelt here in fear and have been protected only because they have been careless. It was like living in a house with a snake inside it, or dwelling in a house with a hero's wife.[766] I wished to test the conduct of the king, who was like a fellow resident. Has the king controlled his senses? Has he conquered his inner impulses? Do the subjects love the king and does the king love them? O supreme among kings! Asking these questions, I came to you. O king! I find delight in you, like a hungry person before food. I do not like your ministers. They are like water before someone who is not thirsty. Because I wish to ensure your prosperity, they have

[765] *Capparis aphylla*.
[766] Scared of the brave husband.

found fault with me. There is no doubt that there is no other reason. I do not harbour any enmity towards them. I only wish to point out their faults. However, like a snake that has only wounded its back, one must always be careful about a wicked enemy.'

'"The king replied, 'I will honour you with a lot of expensive objects. I will show you a lot of reverence. O foremost among brahmanas! I will worship you a lot. Reside in my house for a long time. O brahmana! Those who do not like you will no longer reside in my house. But you should tell me about what should be done next. Ensure that the rod is wielded against those who are wicked and the ones who are virtuous are treated well. O illustrious one! Look towards that and guide me about what is beneficial.'

'"The sage said, 'Ignore this sin[767] and weaken them, one by one. Ascertaining their motives, slay one man after another man. When many are guilty of the same crime, they can unite and blunt a thorn. O king! I am telling you this, because of my fear that your secret counsel might be disclosed. We are brahmanas. Our punishments are mild and we are prone to compassion. I desire your welfare, that of your enemies and of my own self. O king! Because I desire your welfare, I am declaring myself to be like your relative. I am the sage Kalakavrikshiya. I am devoted to the truth. Know from the signs that your father revered me as his friend. O king! The kingdom that you obtained from your father confronts a hardship now. At that time, I gave up all objects of desire and tormented myself through austerities. I am telling you this out of affection, so that you do not remain confused any longer. O king! Having obtained the kingdom, depending on your wishes, you can glance both towards its happiness and its misery. O king! How can you be so careless as to have such advisers in the kingdom?'"

'Bhishma said, "At this, great delight was again generated in the royal lineage. The bull among the brahmana lineage was consecrated as the royal priest. The illustrious lord of Kosala brought the earth under a single umbrella.[768] The sage Kalakavrikshiya offered

[767]Of killing the crow.

[768]He became universal emperor, the umbrella being a sign of kingship.

oblations at the best of sacrifices. O descendant of the Bharata lineage! Having heard his beneficial words, the king of Kosala governed the kingdom in accordance with those auspicious words."'

Chapter 1412(84)

'Bhishma said, "There are virtuous ones who are constrained by a sense of shame. They are full of truthfulness and uprightness. They are capable of saying what is proper. Such people should be members of the assembly.[769] O Kounteya! O descendant of the Bharata lineage! For all tasks, choose as aides those who are extremely wealthy, extremely brave, extremely learned brahmanas, those who are extremely satisfied with you and capable of great enterprise. In every difficulty, you should try for people like these. Those who are born in noble lineages and are honoured will never hide their capabilities. Such a person will never abandon you, whether you are happy or troubled, whether you are afflicted or well, and you must sustain such an individual. Your retinue must consist of those born in noble lineages, born within the kingdom, wise, handsome, extremely learned and those who are bold, but are devoted to you. O son! Those born in inferior lineages, avaricious, violent and shameless will serve you as long as their hands are wet.[770] There are those who are loved and share in your prosperity, who are rewarded with superior and inferior objects, those who seek your prosperity and participate in your happiness, those who are learned and whose conduct does not vary, those who are virtuous and follow vows, those who always wish that you are wealthy, are not inferior and speak the truth. Engage them. However, there are ignoble and evil-minded ones who do not know about agreements. Knowing that

[769]*Sabhasada*. This is more than courtier, since there is also a sense of legislative and judicial function.

[770]As long as there are bribes and inducements.

they deviate from pledges, you must be careful about them. When there are many to choose from, one should not choose one, ignoring the many. However, if one is superior to the many, the many can be ignored, depending on one's inclination. These are the signs one sees in the superior person—valour, emphasis on deeds, adherence to agreements, honour shown to capable people, no attempts to rival those who are not rivals, lack of deviation from dharma on account of desire, fear, anger and avarice, lack of arrogance, capability to speak the truth, control over the self and respect for the worthy. Having been examined in every way, such a person should be the adviser in any counsel. He should be born in a noble family, truthful, patient, accomplished, in control over the soul, brave, grateful and upright. O Partha! These are the marks of an excellent person. When these are present, one gets to know such a man. His enemies are disarmed and become his friends. A king who controls his soul, is accomplished in wisdom and desires his own prosperity, should examine the good and bad qualities of his senior ministers and combine men who are wise, born in noble families and born within the country, who are faithful and incapable of being corrupted, and who have been extremely well tested in every possible way. There should be warriors, those who are learned, those whose ancestors have served and others who are not that superior. These men must be adorned with a sense of duty and a desire for prosperity. They must possess morality, natural intelligence, energy, patience, forgiveness, purity, loyalty, firmness and fortitude. After testing their qualities, a king who desires his prosperity must appoint senior advisers who are capable of bearing a heavy load. They must have passed the five tests.[771] He must appoint those who are adequate in speech, brave, skilled in raising resources, born in noble lineages, truthful, knowledgeable about the interpretation of signs and free from cruelty. They must know about the requirements of time and place and seek to ensure the tasks of the master. For the sake of prosperity, these are the kinds of ministers the king must always have.

[771]There were tests of loyalty on grounds of dharma, artha, kama, fear and an overall aggregate one.

'"One who is weak in energy and enterprise will never be decisive. He will certainly generate uncertainty in all tasks. A minister who is not learned, even if he is born in a good family and knows about dharma, artha and kama, is not capable of examining a policy. In that way, one who is not born in a good family, even if he is as learned as one desires, is like a blind man without a leader and is confused in all tasks requiring intelligence. Even if a man is intelligent and knows about the means of implementation, if his resolution wavers, he cannot persevere with the task for a long time. A man who is evil in his intelligence and lacks learning may again simply be engaged in carrying out a task, but is incapable of any special kind of reflection. One should never trust a minister who is not devoted. One should never reveal one's counsel to someone who is not devoted. A fraudulent one will conspire with other ministers and cause hardship to the king, like a fire penetrates a tree through holes created by the battering of the wind. The lord may sometimes be enraged and dislodge someone from his position. He may fling words of anger towards him and later reinstate him. No one except a person who is devoted is capable of tolerating this. Ministers can also be enraged, like lightning mixed with thunder. Wishing for the welfare of the lord, if a person restrains this, considering happiness and unhappiness equally, that is the man who should be sought for the sake of prosperity. If a man is not upright, even if he is devoted, wise and possesses all the superior qualities, he should not learn about the king's plans. When a person allies with enemies and pays no regard to the many citizens, that kind of well-wisher should not learn about the king's plans. If a person is not learned, is impure, stubborn and boastful, serves the enemy and is angry and avaricious, that kind of well-wisher should not learn about the king's plans. If a person is a stranger, even if he is devoted and is as learned as one wants, even if he is honoured and given a share, that person should not learn about the king's plans. If a person has been accused of even a small crime, even if he is honoured well and is appointed again because of his good qualities, that person should not hear about the king's plans.

'"A person who is accomplished in wisdom, intelligent, learned, born within the country, pure and upright in all his deeds, that person deserves to hear the plans. If a person possesses external and internal knowledge[772] and knows his own nature and the souls of others, he is like the king's well-wisher and deserves to hear the plans. If a person is truthful in speech, possesses good conduct, is grave, modest and mild, if he is a father and a grandfather, he deserves to hear the plans. If a person is content, revered, truthful and liberal, if he hates evildoers, if he is brave and understands what needs to be done at different time, he deserves to hear the plans. If a person is capable of looking at all the people equally and can bring them under subjugation through conciliation, then a king who wields the rod should tell him about his plans. A warrior who is learned in policy, whom the citizens and the residents of the countryside trust because he follows dharma, deserves to hear the plans. Therefore, those who possess all the qualities should be honoured well. There should be at least three ministers who know about nature and who aspire for greatness. They should be employed in detecting one's natural weaknesses and that of the enemy. When the foundation is the advice of these ministers, the king and the kingdom prosper. The enemy should not be able to detect one's weaknesses, but one should discern the weaknesses of the enemy. Like a turtle draws in its limbs, one must protect one's own weaknesses. Learned ministers provide policy for the kingdom. The king implements the policy. Other people are like the limbs of that policy. It is said that the essence and root of a kingdom's policy is based on spying.

'"Ministers seek a living on this earth and follow their lord. Having controlled restraints, arrogance, anger, pride and jealousy, the king must always consult ministers who have passed the five kinds of tests. The king must focus his mind and understand the different kinds of advice those three[773] have. After the period of consultation is over, he must tell them his own views and the ultimate decision. If there is a serious matter, he must ask a supreme brahmana who knows about the purport of dharma, artha and kama. He must approach

[772]*Jnana* and *vijnana* respectively, the former learnt from teachers, the latter from one's own self.

[773]The three ministers.

him with devotion and affectionately follow the path indicated by him. Those who know about the process of consultation have always determined and said that this is the process that should be followed in seeking advice. Therfore, counsel should always be implemented in this way and this is capable of ensuring the support of the subjects. There must not be dwarves, hunchbacks, weak people, lame ones, blind people, idiots, women and eunuchs there.[774] No one should move there, in front, at the rear, above, below and diagonally.[775] One should climb up onto a deserted balcony, where the ground can be clearly seen and there is no grass or reeds nearby. Avoiding all the errors associated with speech and gestures, the consultations must be held with the ministers at the right time."'

Chapter 1413(85)

'Bhishma said, 'O Yudhishthira! In this connection an ancient history is recounted, about the conversation between Brihaspati and Shakra.

'"Shakra asked, 'O brahmana! What single step can a man take well, so that he becomes pre-eminent among all beings and obtains great glory?'

'"Brihaspati replied, 'O Shakra! Pleasant speech is the single good step through which a man becomes pre-eminent among all beings and obtains great glory. O Shakra! This is the single step that brings happiness to all beings and by observing this one always becomes the beloved of all beings. If a person never speaks, if he always has a frown on his face and if his speech is not pleasant, he becomes an object of hatred for all beings. A person who glances first, a person who speaks first, a person who smiles before speaking, he is the person whom people favour. Everywhere, even if gifts are given,

[774]At the place where the king holds his consultations.

[775]There should not be distractions from people moving around.

but without pleasant speech, that is like food without seasoning and does not please people. O Shakra! Even if a person does not give anything, but speaks to people in sweet words, he is capable of bringing all the people under his subjugation. Therefore, it is the duty of anyone who wields the rod to be pleasant in speech. That generates results and people do not hate him. Pleasant speech that is soft and sweet and is delivered well is like a good deed and there is nothing that equals it.'"

'Bhishma said, "Having been thus addressed by the priest,[776] Shakra acted entirely in this way. O Kounteya! You should also properly follow this."'

Chapter 1414(86)

'Yudhishthira asked, "O Indra among kings! How does a king succeed in ruling over the subjects, with a specific eye towards dharma, so that he obtains eternal fame?"

'Bhishma replied, "He must be pure in his conduct. He must devote himself to protecting the subjects. He must be cleansed. He will then attain dharma and fame in both the worlds."[777]

'Yudhishthira asked, "What kind of conduct should a king follow and whom should he use? O immensely wise one! I am asking you this and you should tell me. You have earlier spoken about the qualities in a man. But it is my view that all of those cannot be found in a single man."

'Bhishma replied, "O immensely wise one! O intelligent one! It is exactly as you have stated. The man who possesses all these different qualities is extremely rare. But in brief, if one makes the effort, it is not difficult to find good conduct. I will now tell you about appropriate advisers and act according to this. There must be

[776]Brihaspati.
[777]This world and the next.

four brahmanas who are learned in the Vedas and are bold, virtuous and pure. There must be three humble shudras who have been pure in their earlier work.[778] There must be a fifty-year-old suta[779] who is bold and without malice. He will recount the ancient stories and must possess the eight qualities. He must have understanding about the smriti texts and must be humble and impartial. When there is a dispute because of greed for riches, he must be capable of knowing what must be done.[780] When decisions have to be taken about a crime, the king must consult in the midst of those eight[781] ministers and they must be devoid of the seven extremely terrible vices.[782] For the sake of the kingdom, the outcome must be publicized in the kingdom. Through such conduct, one must always look towards the subjects. One must not keep the proceedings a secret, because secrecy runs counter to the task. If the proceeding suffers, that adharma will also afflict you. The kingdom will then be scattered, like birds before a hawk. It will always remain adrift, like a shattered boat on an ocean. When the lord of the earth does not protect his subjects well and uses adharma, fear is generated in his heart and heaven is closed to him. O bull among men! This is also true of a king's adviser or a king's son who follows adharma, because a person who has been appointed to a seat of dharma[783] is the foundation of dharma. When appointed to tasks, if the followers of the king do not act properly, they themselves head downwards first,[784] taking the kings with

[778]The Critical edition excises some shlokas where eighteen kshatriyas and twenty-one vaishyas are also mentioned.

[779]In the sense of bard or raconteur. The eight qualities of the bard are readiness to listen, readiness to learn, ability to receive, ability to retain, ability to reason, ability to be critical, internal knowledge (vijnana) and external knowledge (jnana).

[780]As stated, it is not obvious whether this applies only to the suta, or to all advisers. All advisers seems more likely.

[781]Four brahmanas, three shudras and the suta.

[782]Hunting, gambling with the dice, addiction to women, addiction to liquor, harshness in punishment, harshness in speech and the squandering of riches.

[783]Someone who sits in judgement.

[784]In the next birth.

them. The king must always be the protector of the men who have no protectors. If distressed ones are forcefully oppressed by the powerful, there will be a lot of resentment. When there is a dispute between two parties, it is best to decide on the basis of the strength of witnesses. There must be special scrutiny for those who have no witnesses and are without protectors. The punishment that descends on the wicked must be proportionate to the crime. There must be monetary fines for the wealthy and death and imprisonment for the poor. The king must use decency and blows to control those who are wicked in conduct. The virtuous must be protected through pleasant words and gifts. If a person desires to kill the king, he must be executed through colourful means.[785] This is also recommended for those who make a living out of thievery and those who cause a mingling of the varnas.[786] O lord of the earth! When a lord of the earth applies the rod of punishment well, there is no adharma in this. Instead, this represents eternal dharma. However, if a king uses punishment in an inexperienced way and uses it according to his whims, he does not obtain fame in this world. After death, he goes to hell. He should not impose punishment on another, merely on the basis of hearsay from others. Following the injunctions of the sacred texts, a person should be imprisoned or set free. Even if there is an emergency, the king must never slay a messenger. If he kills a messenger, together with his advisers, he goes to hell. A messenger merely states what he has been asked to. If a king who follows the dharma of kshatriyas kills such a person, this is tantamount to his ancestors being tainted with sin of killing a foetus. It is said that a messenger must possess seven qualities—he must be born in a good family, he must be good in his conduct, he must be eloquent, he must be skilled, he must be pleasant in speech, he must say what he has been asked to and he must have a good memory. The person who protects the gate must have similar qualities and the one who protects his head[787] must also have such qualities. The adviser who is knowledgeable about

[785]The word used is *citravadha* and probably means execution preceded by torture.

[786]Probably meant for those who have intercourse with a person from another varna.

[787]The king's head. This applies to personal bodyguards.

dharma, artha and the sacred texts, who knows about peace and war, who is intelligent, patient, wise and capable of keeping a secret, who is born in a noble family and is truthful and capable—such a person is praised. The commander must also have such qualities. He must know about battle formations, implements of war and warriors and possess valour. He must be capable of tolerating rain, cold, heat and wind and know about the weaknesses of the enemy. He should be able to engineer trust in the enemy, but must never trust anyone. O Indra among kings! It is not recommended that he should even trust his own son. O unblemished one! I have now recounted to you the truth and the purport of the secret texts. I have also told you about the supreme secret—the lords of men should never trust anyone."'

Chapter 1415(87)

'Yudhishthira asked, "What should be the kind of city within which the king should himself dwell? Is it one that already exists, or should he get one constructed? O grandfather! Tell me this."

'Bhishma replied, "O Kounteya! O descendant of the Bharata lineage! The place where he will reside with his sons, brothers and relatives must be properly checked, to ensure that it is protected and there is a means of sustenance. In particular, I will tell you about what must be done about fortifications. Having heard about this, you must make efforts to follow the injunctions. The cities must be constructed with the six kinds of forts in mind, so that there is sufficient prosperity and an abundance of every required object. The six forts are—those in the desert, those on the ground, those in mountains, those with men, those in the water and those in forests.[788] The city must have forts and must be stocked with grain and weapons. There must

[788]This is a reference to the kind of protection a fort will have. For example, one in the water will be protected by natural water or trenches and moats on all sides. Those in the ground will be protected with high walls. Those with men will be protected by warriors and so on.

be firm walls and moats and it must be full of elephants, horses and chariots. There must be learned artisans there and there must be stores of every kind of requirement. It must be populated by excellent and accomplished people who follow dharma. There must be energetic men, elephants and horses and it must be adorned with crossroads and shops. There must be established rules of conduct, so that people are peaceful and without fear. It must be radiant, with the sound of activity.[789] There must be extremely spacious houses. It must be full of brave and wealthy people and must resound with chants of the brahman. There must be congregations and festivals at which the gods are always worshipped. With his faithful advisers and soldiers, the king must himself reside within that city, conducting himself so that his treasury, forces and friends increase. He must restrain all the sins in the city and the countryside. He must make efforts to increase his stores of goods and his stores of weapons. He must increase all the collections of stores, machines, clubs, medicines, firewood, iron, grain chaff,[790] charcoal, timber, horn, bones, bamboo, marrow, oil, fat, honey, medicines, flax, resins from the shala tree, grain, weapons, arrows, leather, sinews, cane, munja grass, *balbaja* grass[791] and bows. The king must always control access to tanks and wells that contain a great deal of excellent water and also to giant trees that are full of juice.[792] He must make efforts to treat preceptors, officiating priests and priests with a great deal of honour. There must be similar treatment for great archers, architects and astrologers. Those who are wise, intelligent, self-controlled, accomplished, brave, extremely learned, born in good lineages and full of enterprise must be appointed for all the tasks. The king must revere those who follow dharma and restrain those who follow adharma. He must make efforts to engage all the varnas in their own tasks. Spies must be engaged within and

[789]Actually, only sound is mentioned. So this could also be the sound of musical instruments.

[790]For use as fuel.

[791]Goosegrass, *Eleusine indica*.

[792]These offer shade.

outside. Having thus got to know, he must employ the people of the city and the countryside in different tasks. In particular, the king must himself attend to spies, the treasury and policy, because everything is established on this. Using spies as his eyes, he must know everything that the people in the city and the countryside wish to do, whether they are neutrals, enemies or friends. He must thus arrange everything, without being careless about anything. He must always honour those who are devoted and punish those who seek to cause injury. He must always perform rites and sacrifices and donate without any hesitation. It is his task to protect the subjects and not undertaking this task is to be censured. He must always think of a means of sustenance and arrange yoga and kshema for those who are miserable, those who have no protectors, those who are aged and those women who are widows. At the right time, the king must honour those who are in hermitages and treat them well with garments, vessels and food. He must always make efforts to stand before an ascetic and tell him about himself, all his tasks and his kingdom. When he sees a person who has given up everything, has been born in a noble lineage and is extremely learned, he must honour him with beds, seats and food. The king can trust him, even in an emergency. Even bandits trust an ascetic. The king will offer his possessions to him and obtain wisdom in return. However, he must not serve them all the time, or honour them excessively.[793] He must seek out one[794] from within his own kingdom, another from the kingdom of the enemy, another who resides in the forests and another who lives in the cities of the vassals. These must be honoured well and a means of sustenance arranged for them, irrespective of whether they reside in the kingdom of the enemy, in the forest, or within one's own dominion. The ascetics are rigid in their vows. And if the king should ever desire to seek refuge with them in a time of hardship, they will offer this refuge. I have now briefly recounted to you the characteristics of the region and the city the king must himself reside in."'

[793]The sense seems to be that if the king is excessive in doing this, enemies may harm these ascetics.

[794]A reference to ascetics the king should befriend.

Chapter 1416(88)

'Yudhishthira asked, "O king! How can a kingdom be protected? How can a kingdom be won over? O bull among the Bharata lineage! I wish to understand this well. Please tell me."

'Bhishma replied, "I will tell you everything about how a kingdom should be protected and about how a kingdom can be won over. Listen with single-minded attention. One must appoint a headman for every village, then one for ten villages, one for twenty, one for one hundred and one for one thousand. The headman protects the village, ascertains any problems the village faces and reports everything about the villagers to the supervisor of ten, who reports to the supervisor of twenty. The supervisor of twenty reports everything about the conduct of the people who live in the countryside to the supervisor of one hundred villages. The village headman will sustain himself on whatever food is produced within the village and this will also be used to sustain the supervisor of ten and twenty. O best of the Bharata lineage! The supervisor of one hundred villages deserves to be honoured well and will be sustained by giving him a large village that is prosperous and well-populated village. O descendant of the Bharata lineage! The king possesses many such. The supervisor of one thousand has the right to choose the best suburb.[795] He is entitled to enjoy the grain and gold that the countryside produces.[796] Whatever needs to be done in a village must be undertaken by the villagers themselves. However, an adviser who knows about dharma must attentively supervise this. In every town, there must be a supervisor who thinks about its welfare from every aspect. He must have the terrible form of a planet located above the nakshatras and himself circulate everywhere. He[797]

[795]The text uses the word *shakhanagara*. This literally translates as a branch town, something that is not quite a town proper.

[796]There is some subjectivity in deciding who is entitled to this grain and the gold. The context suggests that we are talking about the supervisor of one thousand villages and not the king.

[797]This 'he' seems to be the supervisor of the town, rather than the king directly.

must check the sales, purchases, expenses, shops and routes of traders, impose taxes and act so that their yoga and kshema are ensured. He must glance towards the production and expenses of artisans, to ensure that they have a good living and the craft flourishes. The taxes must be commensurate.

'"O Yudhishthira! Earlier, kings levied high taxes and low ones. The lord of the earth must act so that there is no deprivation anywhere. He must glance towards the outcome of a task and then determine taxes. It should never be such that there is no incentive for the work and the outcome.[798] The king must always glance towards this and impose taxes so that both the king and the producer have a share in the outcome of the work. Because of his greed, he should not destroy his own foundation and that of others. The king must be benevolent and restrict his inclination to be avaricious. A king who consumes excessively is known for being hated. If one is hated, how can there be any benefit? One who is loved obtains happiness. An intelligent king will milk the kingdom like a calf that sucks milk. O descendant of the Bharata lineage! If the calf is nurtured, it becomes strong and can sustain hardships. O Yudhishthira! If a calf has drunk too much of milk, it[799] cannot work. A kingdom that has been milked too much is incapable of achieving anything great. A king who tends to the kingdom himself and receives only that which can sustain him obtains great fruits.

'"In this world, kings then accumulate enough for times of hardship. The kingdom becomes the treasury and the treasury becomes his residence.[800] As long as he can, he should show compassion to all those who are close to him and the residents of the city and the countryside who are dependent on him and seek refuge with him. He must first crush the external ones and then enjoy

[798]The sense is that there must be a decent margin of profit, so as to ensure incentives.

[799]This is a straight translation, but the reference seems to be more to the cow than to the calf.

[800]In times of hardship, the subjects willingly part with their resources.

happiness from those who are in between.[801] Thus, people have a share in the happiness and the unhappiness and are not enraged. He must announce the taxes in advance and then repeatedly show himself throughout the kingdom, instilling fear. 'This is the adversity that confronts us. This is the great fear from the circle of enemies. Like a bamboo that has yielded fruit,[802] one cannot contemplate that the danger will disappear. The enemy has arisen and there are many bandits with him. They wish to invade the kingdom and seize me. We are faced with this terrible and fearful danger. I need your riches to save ourselves from this. When the danger is over, I will return all of this to you. However, the enemy will not return anything that it has seized by force. You may have desired this store of riches for the sake of your sons and wives. But they will kill your wives and your own selves. I am delighted at your prosperity, but am appealing to you, like to my own sons. Without afflicting the kingdom, I will show you as much of favour as I can. This is a time of disaster and like good bulls, you must bear the burden. In this time of hardship, you should not act so as to be so enamoured of riches.' A king who knows about the appropriate time should use such sweet, gentle and civil words. He should grasp the reins himself.

'"For those who live on animal husbandry, he must ascertain the size of their pastures, the expenses of their servants, the dangers they face and their yoga and kshema. For those who live on animal husbandry, taxes must be imposed after that. If they are ignored, those who live on animal husbandry will be destroyed and begin to dwell in the forests.[803] Therefore, having thought about this in advance, one must behave mildly towards them. O Partha! After glancing towards their requirements, it is a duty to show conciliation, protection, benevolence, stability, a share in prosperity and good behaviour towards those who live on animal husbandry. There are many fruits

[801]The king must crush those who are external to the kingdom. He can then enjoy prosperity from those who are in between in the sense of belonging to the extremities of the kingdom.

[802]Once there is fruit, the bamboo withers.

[803]They are nomadic and mobile and will therefore leave the kingdom.

that are always yielded by those who live on animal husbandry. They make the kingdom, trade and agriculture prosper. Therefore, one who is perceptive will make efforts to act pleasantly towards those who live on animal husbandry. One should be compassionate and careful and impose taxes that are mild. O son! For those who live on animal husbandry, the generation of wealth is always extremely easy. O Yudhishthira! There is no other wealth that is its equal."'

Chapter 1417(89)

'Yudhishthira asked, "O immensely wise one! O grandfather! If a king is capable and wishes to extend his treasury, how should he behave? Tell me this."

'Bhishma replied, "A king who desires dharma should rule so that he is engaged in the welfare of his subjects and consider the time, the place and the strength. Since he thinks of welfare for them and for his own self, the king should ensure that dharma prevails in the kingdom in every way. He must milk the kingdom like a bee sucks honey and flies away.[804] He must milk the cow bearing the calf in mind, without causing damage to the udders. The lord of men must drink mildly from the kingdom, like a leech. He must treat it the way a tigress carries her cub, not letting it fall, but not biting it. As the kingdom prospers, the taxes can progressively become less and less. Or, if he so desires, he can make them increase progressively. The burden on a young bull is gradually increased. The initial efforts are mild and the halter comes later. If the halter is imposed after good treatment, it does not become intractable. If one makes efforts with care, one is then able to enjoy. It is extremely difficult to behave in the same way towards all men. Having comforted the ones who are the foremost, one can then make the inferior one subservient. Dissension must be engineered among those who are likely to support each other. Having

[804]Without destroying the flower and the plant.

comforted them, he can cheerfully make efforts to use them. Taxes must not be imposed on them at the wrong place, or at the wrong time. Having comforted them in advance, these must be at the right time and follow the proper norms. I have told you about legitimate means. I don't wish to talk about techniques of deceit.

'"Drinking houses, prostitutes, pimps, actors, gamblers and others who are like them must all be controlled.[805] They can cause injury to the kingdom. If they are situated within the kingdom, they hamper gentle subjects. Unless there is a disaster, no one should ever beg. Manu had earlier laid down this dictum for all beings. If no one did any work, nothing would be able to survive. There is no doubt that the three worlds would then be destroyed. The lord and king who does not restrain these people[806] reaps one-fourth of their sins. That is what the sacred texts say. He also obtains one-fourth of all dharma they observe. If one frequents these places,[807] one's prosperity is destroyed. A man who is addicted to desire is incapable of giving up undesirable acts. However, if there is a disaster, one can beg from others. Compassionate people who wish to show pity can then follow dharma and give. But in general, there should not be beggars in the kingdom. Nor should there be bandits. They seize what is good and do not think of anyone's prosperity. Those who favour beings and encourage the prosperity of the subjects, those are the ones who should remain in the kingdom, not those who do not think about prosperity. O great king! Those who take excessive riches must be punished. Those who charge usurious rates must be forced to repay, through fines and taxes. Men must be employed, with many workers, to take care of agriculture, animal husbandry, trade and everything else that is like that. If a man who is engaged in agriculture, animal husbandry or trade suffers even the slightest bit of hardship, the king is to blame. The wealthy must always be honoured with vehicles, garments and food and be told, 'Accept

[805]The word used is *niyamya*. This is best interpreted as regulation, not as a ban.

[806]Wicked ones in general, not just beggars.

[807]The drinking houses and brothels.

these honours and also accept me.' O descendant of the Bharata lineage! The wealthy are referred to as a great limb of the kingdom. There is no doubt that those who are wealthy are foremost among all people. The intelligent person[808] must protect the wise, the brave, the rich, the powerful, those who follow dharma, the ascetics and the truthful. O king! Therefore, be pleasant towards everyone. Protect them through truth, rectitude, lack of anger and non-violence. You will then obtain the army, the treasury, the friends and the earth. Truth and uprightness are supreme. O king! You will then obtain friends and a treasury."'

Chapter 1418(90)

'Bhishma said, "In your kingdom, trees that bear edible fruit should not be cut down. The learned ones have said that according to dharma, roots and fruits belong to brahmanas. If something is left over by brahmanas, other people can consume that. Causing injury to a brahmana, no one must ever take anything away. If a brahmana prepares to leave, saying that he is afflicted and cannot find a means of sustenance, the lord of men must think of a means of sustenance for him and his wife. If he does not refrain, he should be addressed in an assembly of brahmanas in these words. 'Which person will now be able to set limits for him?'[809] There is no doubt that he will then desist. O Kounteya! If he does not, he should be told, 'It is your duty to forget what has happened in the past. This is my command.' Though I do not hold that view, there are those who hold that a brahmana should only be entitled to a means of sustenance. If he does not accept the invitation for only a means of sustenance, one should give him other objects of pleasure. In this

[808] An intelligent king.

[809] The king has found a means of sustenance. Even then, there is no limit to the brahmana's greed.

world, agriculture, animal husbandry and trade provide a means of living for people. Above this, the three kinds of learning[810] ensure prosperity. Those who act contrary to these efforts are bandits. Brahma created kshatriyas so that they could be slain. O king! Slay the enemies. Protect the subjects. Perform rites and sacrifices. O descendant of the Kourava lineage! Be brave and fight in battles. A king who protects those who should be protected is supreme among kings. Those who do not protect them, never obtain any success. O Yudhishthira! The king must always know about all the people. It is for this reason that a man uses other men.[811] Protect those inside from those outside and those outside from those inside. Protect those outside from those outside and those inside from those inside.[812] Always protect everyone. The king must always protect himself and protect the earth. Those who are learned say that one's own self is the foundation for everything. 'What is my weakness? Who are my associates?[813] What hardships can bring me down? What are my sins?' He must always think along these lines. He must appoint secret spies to travel throughout the earth. 'Let them find out if my policy is sound and whether my conduct is praised. Do they like me in the countryside and what is my reputation in the kingdom?' Be knowledgeable about dharma, possess fortitude, do not run away in a battle, live for the kingdom, and live for those who follow the king, for all the advisers and all those who are neutral and also those who praise and censure you. O Yudhishthira! Ensure that all action is implemented well. O son! It is not possible that everyone should only be delighted with you. O descendant of the Bharata lineage! Among all the people, there will be friends and enemies, and those who are neutral. There are those who are equal in the strength of arms and also in the qualities that they possess. How is it that some are superior and succeed in ruling other men? They do this because

[810]The three Vedas.

[811]A reference to the king employing men as spies.

[812]The outside and inside can be interpreted in geographical terms. It can also be interpreted in terms of those who are close to the king and those who are not.

[813]Alternatively, what are my addictions?

those who are mobile devour those who are immobile, those with teeth devour those without teeth and angry and poisonous snakes devour other snakes. O Yudhishthira! You must always make efforts to be careful and act like them. If you are careless, they will descend on you like a *bharunda* bird.[814] I hope the merchants in your kingdom are not afflicted by taxes and that those who tirelessly make efforts in desolate regions are able to buy a lot after spending a little. I hope that those who live on agriculture in the kingdom are not going away because they are oppressed. Those who bear burdens for the king also sustain others. What is given in this world sustains gods and the large number of ancestors and also men, serpents, rakshasas, birds and animals. O descendant of the Bharata lineage! This is how the kingdom sustains itself and this is how it should be protected. O Pandava! I will again tell you about what this prosperity is based on."'

Chapter 1419(91)

'Bhishma said, "Utathya, the son of Angiras, was supreme among those who knew about the brahman.[815] He affectionately told Mandhata, the son of Yuvanashva, about the dharma of kshatriyas. O Yudhishthira! I will tell you completely and in entirety about what Utathya, supreme among those who knew about the brahman, instructed.

'"Utathya said, 'The king exists for the sake of dharma, not for the sake of engaging in kama. O Mandhata! Know that the king is the protector of the world. If the king acts in accordance with dharma, he advances towards a state of divinity.[816] If he follows adharma, he goes to hell. Beings are based on dharma. Dharma is based on the

[814]The bharunda bird is a mythical predatory bird with two heads. If the king isn't careful, others will descend on him, like this predatory bird.

[815]Utathya was Brihaspati's elder brother.

[816]He goes to heaven.

king. A king who administers this properly is a king who is the lord of the earth. It is said that a king who has supreme dharma in his soul and is also prosperous, but happens to be wicked, leads to the gods being despised. It is said that there is no dharma then. When those who follow adharma are seen to be successful in their pursuit of artha, all the people think that this is auspicious and begin to follow them. When the wicked are not restrained, dharma is uprooted, great adharma is followed and it is said that there is fear both during the day and the night. The brahmanas do not follow the Vedas and the vows. When the wicked are not restrained, the brahmanas do not perform sacrifices. O great king! When the wicked are not restrained in this world, the minds of all men are confused, like those who are about to be slain. Having looked at both the worlds,[817] the rishis themselves created the king as an extremely great being, so that there should be dharma.[818] One in whom dharma shines is known as a king.[819] If dharma disappears in someone, the gods know that person to be a *vrishala*. O illustrious one! Dharma is a bull and the gods know one who does away with it as vrishala.[820] Therefore, dharma should not be destroyed. When dharma prospers, all the beings always prosper and when it decays, they decay. Therefore, make dharma prosper. There is no doubt that dharma flows from the acquisition and preservation of wealth. O Indra among men! It has been said that one should lay down the boundaries of what should not be done. Svayambhu[821] created dharma for the power of beings. Therefore, to show favours to subjects, propagate dharma. O tiger among kings! That is the reason the sacred texts have said that dharma is the best. The bull among men who rules his subjects virtuously is a king. One should abandon desire and anger and follow dharma. O supreme among

[817]This world and the next.

[818]This is a reference to the sages creating Prithu.

[819]*Virajate* means to shine or appear beautiful and rajan is king.

[820]Vrishala means a contemptible person. *Vrisha* means a bull, as well as moral merit. *Alam* means 'enough'. A person who says enough of dharma, is a vrishala.

[821]Brahma.

the Bharata lineage![822] Dharma is the best task to be followed by a king. The brahmanas are dharma's womb and must always be revered. O Mandhata! Without any resentment, their desires must always be fulfilled. If one does not act so as to satisfy their wishes, the king confronts fear. The friends do not increase and become his enemies. Bali, Virochana's son, exhibited resentment towards brahmanas.[823] Because of this, Shri[824] was enraged with him and no longer dwelt with him, going instead to the chastiser of Paka.[825] O lord! He[826] was tormented when he saw Shri with Purandara, but this was the consequence of his resentment and insolence. O Mandhata! Therefore, know that you should not enrage prosperity. The sacred texts say that adharma leads to the birth of Shri's son named Darpa.[827] O king! It has led to the subjugation of the gods and the asuras many times. O king! Many rajarshis did not understand this either. Having conquered it, one becomes a king. One who is defeated becomes a slave. Do not serve insolence and adharma. O Mandhata! If you wish to be established for a long time, follow this. In particular, do not associate with those who are intoxicated,[828] careless, infantile and mad. Do not indulge in conduct that is harmful. In particular, always take efforts to be careful of advisers who have been punished, women, mountains, uneven terrain, forts, elephants, horses and reptiles. Do not wander around in the night. Abandon excessive pride, insolence and anger. The king should not indulge in

[822]This is an inconsistency, because the words are being spoken to Mandhata, not Yudhishthira. Bharata and the Pandavas are from the lunar dynasty. Mandhata was from the solar dynasty. There was a lesser known Bharata in the solar dynasty, but he came after Mandhata.

[823]Bali was an asura and was Virochana's son. He was deprived of the three worlds by Vishnu in his vamana (dwarf) incarnation. There are no stories to suggest that Bali was wicked or resentful towards brahmanas. Vishnu restored the three worlds to Indra, who had been deprived by Bali.

[824]Lakshmi, the goddess of prosperity.

[825]Indra killed a demon named Paka.

[826]Bali.

[827]Insolence.

[828]Probably in the sense of intoxicated with insolence.

intercourse with unknown women, eunuchs, promiscuous women, the wives of others and girls.[829] If there is a mixing of varnas, wicked rakshasas are born in the family—eunuchs, those without limbs, those with thick tongues and idiots. When the king is careless, these and others are born. Therefore, for the sake of the welfare of the subjects, the king must take special care. When a kshatriya is careless, great sins result. Adharma is followed and this leads to a mixing of the subjects.[830] It is cold during the summer and it is not cold during the winter. There is no rain, or there is too much of rain. The subjects are penetrated by disease. Terrible nakshatras and planets are seen to rise. Many omens are seen, signifying the king's destruction. When the king does not protect his subjects, he is himself not protected. The subjects decay and he is also destroyed. Two seize the possessions of one and many others seize the possessions of two. Virgins are corrupted. These are said to be the sins of the king. Not a single man can say, "This belongs to me." This is what happens when the king is careless and abandons dharma.'"'

Chapter 1420(92)

'"Utathya said, 'When the king follows dharma, Parjanya showers down at the right time. There is prosperity and the subjects rejoice in happiness. He[831] is like a washerman who does not know how to wash dirty clothes, or washes away the dye in the process. It is the same with brahmanas, kshatriyas, vaishyas and shudras who are no longer established in the various tasks of the four varnas. Labour is for shudras, agriculture for vaishyas and dandaniti for kings. Brahmacharya, austerities, mantras and truth are for brahmanas. The kshatriya who knows good conduct and about how to restrain bad conduct is like a father and a lord of

[829]The word used is *kanya*, meaning girl, as well as virgin. Girl seems to fit better.
[830]Mixing of the varnas.
[831]The careless king.

beings. O bull among the Bharata lineage! Krita, treta, dvapara and kali are all dependent on the conduct of kings. It is said that the king makes the yuga. When the king is careless, the four varnas and the four Vedas and ashramas are all confused. The king is the one who makes beings. The king is their destroyer. The one with dharma in his soul is a maker. The one with adharma in his soul is a destroyer. When the king is careless, the king's wives, sons, relatives and well-wishers all sorrow together. O king! When the king follows adharma, all the elephants, horses, cattle, camels, mules and asses suffer. O Mandhata! It is said that the creator created strength for the sake of the weak.[832] The foundation of everything is immensely weak. O king! When the king bases himself on adharma, the beings who depend on the king and others who depend on those beings, all suffer. I think that the glances of one who is weak, that of a sage and that of a virulent snake cannot be tolerated. Therefore, do not oppress the weak. O son![833] Know that the weak should never be thought of as those who should be disregarded. Otherwise, the glances of the weak will burn you down, together with your relatives. If a family is burnt down by the weak, it is burnt down to the roots and nothing grows there. Therefore, do not oppress the weak. Weakness is superior to strength, since greater strength is superior to strength. When the strong is burnt down by the weak, there is nothing left. If a humiliated and struck person cries out for succour and fails to find a man to help him, the consequent punishment slays the king. O son! When you base yourself on strength, do not oppress the weak. Otherwise, the glances of the weak will burn you down, like a fire that consumes its foundation. The tears shed by those who weep because they have been falsely accused slay the sons and animals of those who have made those false accusations. If not on one's own self, it descends on the son. If not on the son, it descends on the son's son or the daughter's son. Like a cow, the fruits of an evil deed are not immediately reaped.[834] When a weak person is slain and cannot

[832]So that the weak could be protected.

[833]The word used is tata.

[834]One has to wait for a cow to have a calf, before it can be milked.

find a protector, the gods have arranged that a great and terrible punishment should descend.[835] Though they should not beg, when the residents of the countryside are forced to beg like brahmanas, that sin of begging slays the king. When the many royal officers employed by the king in the countryside are engaged in wrong deeds, a great sin devolves on the king. When those employed for good policy are overcome by reasons of desire and greed from riches and extract from those who are distressed and pleading, that is a great sin on the part of the king.

""'A large tree sprouts and then grows. It offers refuge to beings. When it is severed or burnt down, those who have sought refuge in it are also rendered homeless.[836] When those in the kingdom practise the foremost kinds of dharma and follow good conduct, the qualities of the king are spoken about. When they practise adharma and are confused about dharma, his good deeds swiftly turn to bad deeds. When the wicked are known to roam around among the virtuous, the king suffers from kali[837] there. O lord of the earth! When the king punishes those who should not be punished, the kingdom does not prosper. When advisers are honoured in accordance with what they deserve and are engaged by the king for policy and war, the kingdom of that king prospers. He enjoys the entire earth for a long period of time. The king who looks towards good deeds and honours them with pleasant words obtains supreme dharma. When the king enjoys his own share and does not disregard others and slays those who are strong and insolent, that king is said to follow dharma. When the king saves everyone in speech, body and deeds and does not pardon his own son, that king is said to follow dharma. When the king protects those who seek refuge, like his own sons, and does not deviate from any agreements, that king is said to follow dharma. When the king performs rites and sacrifices and faithfully gives away dakshina, disregarding his own desire and

[835]Descend on the king.

[836]The king is being compared to the tree and the royal officers to those who have made homes in the tree.

[837]In the sense of strife and discord.

hatred, that king is said to follow dharma. When he wipes away the tears of the distressed, those without protectors and the weak, and generates delight among men, that king is said to follow dharma. When his friends prosper and his enemies are brought down, when he honours the virtuous, that king is said to follow dharma. When he protects the truth and always gives away land, honouring guests and servants, that king is said to follow dharma. When favours and chastisement are both established in him, that king obtains fruits in this world and in the next. O Mandhata! The king is Yama. He is the supreme lord of those who follow dharma. When he restrains himself, he supports life. When he does not restrain himself, he is wicked. When he receives officiating priests, priests and preceptors well, honouring them and not insulting them, that king is said to follow dharma. Yama controls all beings, without differentiating between them. It is the king's task to duly control the subjects in this way. O bull among men! In every way, the king is like the thousand-eyed one.[838] What he sees as dharma is dharma. You must be careful, learned, forgiving, intelligent, patient and wise, always questioning the spirit of people and separating the good from the evil. You must assuage all the people through gifts and pleasant words. You must protect the residents of the city and the countryside as if they are your own sons. O son! A king who is not accomplished is incapable of protecting the subjects. O son! What is known as the kingdom is an extremely great and difficult burden to bear. Wielding the rod, only a wise and brave one is capable of protecting it. One who is a eunuch and devoid of intelligence cannot wield the rod.

"''There must be handsome ones born in noble lineages.[839] They must be accomplished, faithful and extremely learned. You must examine the intelligence of all of these and also that of ascetics who live in hermitages. In this way, you will know the supreme dharma of all beings and your dharma will not be destroyed, in your country, or in the lands of others. Among dharma, artha and kama, dharma is the

[838]Indra.

[839]As ministers and advisers.

best. The one who knows dharma enjoys happiness in this world and in the next. When men are honoured well, they abandon their chief wives. People should be cultivated through gifts and pleasant words. O son! Great purity follows from care and purity. O Mandhata! Always pay attention to these. The king must be careful and look for weaknesses in his own self and that of the enemy. The enemy should not be able to see his weaknesses. But he must strike at the weak spots of the enemy. This was the conduct followed by Vasava, Yama, Varuna and all the rajarshis. Follow that. O great king! Act in accordance with this conduct, followed by the rajarshis. O bull among the Bharata lineage![840] O descendant of the Bharata lineage! Follow this divine path. In this world and the next, the devarshis, ancestors and gandharvas praise the conduct of infinitely energetic kings who act in accordance with dharma.'"

'Bhishma said, "O descendant of the Bharata lineage! Mandhata was thus addressed by Utathya. Without any hesitation, he acted accordingly and obtained the earth for his own. You should also act well, like King Mandhata. Observe dharma, protect the earth and obtain a place in heaven."'

Chapter 1421(93)

'Yudhishthira asked, "How should a king who is devoted to dharma, and who wishes to establish himself in dharma, behave? O best among the Kuru lineage! O grandfather! I am asking you. Please tell me."

'Bhishma replied, "In this connection, an ancient history is recounted. The intelligent Vamadeva saw the exact truth about this and sang it. There was a king named Vasumana from Kosala. He was powerful and pure. He asked the illustrious maharishi Vamadeva. 'O illustrious one! Instruct me with words that are full of dharma and

[840]This is again an inconsistency.

artha, so that I conduct myself in accordance with them, I remain established and do not deviate from my own dharma.' The supreme among those who meditated, the ascetic Vamadeva, replied to him, as he[841] was seated there, golden in complexion, like Yayati, the son of Nahusha. 'Follow dharma alone. There is nothing that is superior to dharma. Basing themselves on dharma, kings conquered the entire earth. The king who thinks that dharma is superior to success in the matter of artha, and who makes his intelligence truthful, is radiant with dharma. If a king looks towards adharma and acts on the basis of force alone, he is swiftly dislodged from both the first and the second.[842] Because his advisers are wicked and evil, he is a slayer of dharma and deserves to be killed by the people, together with his relatives. He will swiftly perish. If he does not seek artha and is addicted to kama, and if he is boastful, even if he obtains the entire earth, he will swiftly perish. However, if a king concentrates on what is beneficial, is devoid of malice, conquers his senses and is intelligent, he flourishes, like an ocean into which rivers flow. For dharma, artha and kama, he must always think that he is not yet full.[843] The progress of the worlds is based on all these. If he listens to this, he will obtain fame, glory, prosperity and subjects. A person who is proud about dharma, who thinks about dharma and artha, who undertakes action only after thinking about artha, is certain to obtain greatness. If the king is not generous, is not extremely affectionate, if he always wields the rod over his subjects and if he is naturally violent, he will swiftly perish. The stupid one does not use his intelligence to see that he has committed a wicked deed. He is covered in ill fame and, after death, attains hell. If he shows honour, is generous, pure and discriminating about good taste, men seek to destroy any hardships that he confronts, as if those are their own. If he does not have a preceptor to tell him about dharma, if he does not ask others, if he only concentrates on happiness and obtaining

[841]Vasumana.

[842]Dharma and artha respectively.

[843]That is, he must want more of these.

riches, his greatness does not last long. If he shows importance to his preceptor in matters connected with dharma, if he himself glances towards the objectives, if he places dharma at the forefront when dealing with people, his greatness lasts for a long time.'"'

Chapter 1422(94)

'"Vamadeva said, 'When someone who is strong imposes adharma on those who are weak, those who earn a living from him[844] also follow that kind of conduct. They follow the king, who implemented the wicked practices. With those insolent men, that kingdom is swiftly destroyed. When men naturally earn a living from such evil conduct, when he[845] faces a difficulty, even his relatives are prepared to tolerate this.[846] When the king is naturally violent, when he acts without any basis, when he does not follow the indications of the sacred texts, he is swiftly destroyed. The kshatriya who does not follow the conduct that has been followed for a long time, meant both for those who win and those who lose, deviates from the dharma of kshatriyas. A king who is successful in his attempt to seize an enemy in battle, and who does not then show respect to the enemy, deviates from the dharma of kshatriyas. The king must be gracious. If he can, he must show compassion at a time of distress. He will then be loved by the people and not be dislodged from his prosperity. If someone has done an injury, he should repay with something that is more pleasant. If he acts in this pleasant way, a person who is not liked will soon be loved. He must avoid false words. He must do what is pleasant, even if he has not been asked. For the sake of desire, anger or hatred, he should not abandon dharma. He should not avoid answering questions, nor should he be careless in speaking

[844]The king's officers.

[845]The king.

[846]That is, they do nothing to mitigate it.

words. He should not be hasty or malicious. That is how enemies are overcome. He should not be unduly delighted at an act of kindness, nor should he suffer at something disagreeable. Remembering the welfare of subjects, he should not be confused if he encounters a difficulty in the pursuit of artha. The lord of the earth who possesses qualities to always do what is pleasant obtains success in his deeds and prosperity does not desert him. The king must always favour those who have stopped acting against him and are now favourably disposed, as he must those who are devoted. That is the conduct of the virtuous.

"'There are those who are not careless, but attentive. They are wise, extremely devoted and pure. They are capable and faithful. Such people must be employed for important tasks. There are those who may possess good qualities, but do not find delight in the lord of the earth. They are resentful of the master's prosperity. Such people should not be employed for tasks. There are those who are stupid and addicted to their senses. They are greedy, ignoble in their conduct and fraudulent. They have failed the tests and are cruel. They are evil in intelligence and do not possess a great deal of learning. They have squandered away their possessions in drinking, gambling, women and hunting. If the king employs these in great tasks, prosperity does not stay with him. If the king protects himself and protects those whom he is supposed to protect, the subjects prosper and it is certain that he attains greatness. One must use well-wishers who are not recognized to keep an eye on the acts of all the other kings. By this means, the king is not harmed. When one has injured a strong person, one should not be comforted because that person lives a long distance away. Following the conduct of hawks, such people swoop down when one is careless. If one is firm in one's foundation, if one is not evil in one's soul and if one knows about one's strengths, one can attack a weaker person, but not one who is stronger. Having conquered the earth through valour, having protected the subjects through dharma, having been devoted to dharma, a king can be killed in battle. Everything ends in death. There is nothing without disease.

Therefore, the king must be established in dharma and must protect the subjects in accordance with dharma. In the course of time, the earth prospers with five things—arrangements for protection, battle, ruling according to dharma, thinking about counsel and happiness. The king who protects these is supreme among kings. If a king is always engaged in these, he enjoys the earth. No single person is capable of paying attention to all of these together. That is the reason the king must engage these[847] and enjoy the earth for a long period of time. When a person is generous, ready to share, mild, upright and pure, and does not abandon people, people do good things to him. When one knows what is best and acts in accordance with that knowledge, when he gives up his own views, people follow him. When he does not tolerate words about artha and kama because they are contrary, when he is distracted and listens to contrary views only for a limited period of time, when he does not comprehend the intelligence of foremost ones who are in front of him, regardless of whether they have been defeated or not been defeated, he deviates from the dharma of kshatriyas. If he abandons his foremost advisers and makes inferior ones his beloved, he confronts disaster. When he is distressed, he doesn't find succour. When he disrespects relatives with good qualities because of his hatred, when his soul is not firm, when his anger is firm, his prosperity doesn't remain close to him and give him delight. When he acts pleasantly so as to bring those with good qualities under his control, even though they are not close to his heart, his fame is established for a long time. He must not try to accomplish his objectives at the wrong time. The unpleasant must not trouble him. He should not be greatly delighted at something pleasant. He must be engaged in tasks that are healthy. "Which men are devoted to the king? Which seek refuge because of fear? Who among them has the taint of actually being neutral?" Always think of these things. If one is strong, one should never trust those who are weak. If one is careless, they will descend like bharunda birds. If someone is wicked in his soul, he will censure a master who has

[847]The ministers and advisers.

all the qualities and is pleasant in speech. Therefore, one should be scared of such people. Yayati, the son of Nahusha, declared this teaching for kings. "If one is engaged in conquering men, one can slay a supreme enemy."'"'

Chapter 1423(95)

'"Vamadeva said, 'The lord of the earth should prosper through victories without battle. O lord of men! It is said that victory through a war is the worst. If his foundations are not firm, he should not desire to obtain something. If the foundations are weak, a king's pursuit of gains is not recommended. If the countryside is prosperous and wealthy, if the king is loved, if the advisers are satisfied and well nourished, then the king's foundations are firm. When the warriors are well satisfied, content and well entrenched, then the lord of the earth can conquer the earth with the slightest exertion of force. If the residents of the city and the countryside are devoted to him, if they are honoured well, if they possess riches and grain, then the king has a firm foundation. When he thinks that at that time his own power is superior, that is the time when an intelligent one desires the land and the riches of another. When he ignores objects of pleasure, when he is compassionate towards beings, when he protects his kingdom and his own self, he swiftly prospers. When those on his side act well, but he behaves falsely towards them, he then injures his own self, like a forest severed with an axe. If a king is always engaged in killing, there is no end to those who hate him. But if he knows how to control his anger, those who hate him cannot be seen. The knowledgeable person does not engage in tasks that noble people hate. He engages himself in tasks that are beneficial. Then, even if a king indulges in acts of happiness though tasks are incomplete, his own self is not tormented and others do not think ill of him. A lord of the earth who acts in this way towards men conquers both the worlds and is established in victory.'"

'Bhishma said, "Having been addressed in this way by Vamadeva, the king followed everything in his deeds. If you act in this way, there is no doubt that you will conquer both the worlds."'

Chapter 1424(96)

'Yudhishthira asked, "If a kshatriya wishes to defeat another kshatriya in battle, in that victory, how can one follow dharma? I am asking you this. Please tell me."

'Bhishma replied, "When a lord of the earth has arrived in a kingdom, whether he is with aides or without aides, he must say, 'I am your king. I will always protect you. Following dharma, pay me the taxes. Do you accept my power?' If they accept the one who has come, all will be well. There may be virtuous ones who oppose him, though they are not kshatriyas. O lord of men! They are committing a perverse act[848] and must be restrained in every way possible. There may be others who take up weapons because they think that the kshatriyas are incapable.[849] Or they may be extremely proud and think that he[850] is incapable of saving himself."

'Yudhishthira asked, "How should a kshatriya king conduct himself against another kshatriya who advances against him in battle? O grandfather! Tell me this."

'Bhishma replied, "In a battle, one must not fight against a kshatriya who is not armoured and not clad in mail. A single one must speak to another single one, 'Release. I am hurling mine.'[851] If the one who advances is armoured, one must armour oneself. If the one who advances possesses soldiers, one must collect soldiers. If the

[848]Because they are not kshatriyas.
[849]Of protecting them.
[850]The invader.
[851]Referring to weapons.

one who is fighting uses deceit, one must fight back using deceit. If he fights with adharma, one must counter him with adharma. Horses must not be used against chariots. Chariots must advance against chariots. If the adversary is distressed, whether it is to frighten him or for the sake of victory, he must not be struck. There must not be smeared[852] or barbed arrows. These are the weapons of wicked people. One must fight for the sake of victory, not because of anger, or a desire to kill. When two virtuous people are fighting with each other, one of them may face a hardship. One who is wounded or one without offspring must never be struck. His weapons may be shattered. His forces may face a difficulty. His bowstring may have been severed. His mounts may have been slain. A wounded person must be treated in your territory, or he may be sent back to his own home. One who is not wounded must be released. That is the eternal dharma. Svayambhuva Manu said that one must fight in accordance with dharma. Against the virtuous, the virtuous always resort to dharma and this is never destroyed. The kshatriya, who wishes his prosperity and wins through the use of adharma, himself kills his own self. He is wicked and leads an inferior life. It is a duty that the virtuous should defeat the wicked through the use of virtuous means. It is better to use dharma and be killed than to triumph through evil deeds. O king! If one follows adharma, like a cow,[853] the fruits are not immediate. But it follows you and burns down the roots and the branches. If one obtains prosperity through wicked deeds, one becomes addicted to evil. Such a person thinks that there is no dharma and laughs at purity. He is without devotion and advances towards destruction. Though he thinks he is immortal, he is bound by Varuna's noose. Like a large and inflated leather bag, his own deeds make him expand. However, he is then destroyed from the roots, like a tree on the banks of a river. He is shattered, like a clay pot on stone, and there is rejoicing at this. Therefore, a lord of the earth should desire to earn victory through the use of dharma."'

[852]With poison.

[853]The cow has to have a calf before it yields milk.

Chapter 1425(97)

'Bhishma said, "A lord of the earth should not desire to conquer the earth through the use of adharma. Even if a lord of the earth has obtained victory through the use of adharma, who will endorse this? A victory that is full of adharma is not permanent and it does not lead to heaven. O bull among the Bharata lineage! It weakens the king and the earth. There may be an adversary whose armour has been shattered. He speaks and says, 'I am yours.' He joins his hands in supplication. He casts aside his weapons. Such a person should be seized, but not injured. If a person has been conquered through the use of force, a lord of the earth should not fight against him. He should be affectionately made to stay for a year[854] and it will be as if he has been born again. A maiden who has been abducted through the use of valour should not be touched for a year. This is also true of all the riches that have been violently seized. However, the riches should not be sterile. The brahmanas should drink the milk of the cows and everything should be pardoned and restored to what it was.[855] A king must fight with a king. That is what dharma decrees. One who is not a king should never fight against a king. If a brahmana wishes to ensure peace and advances between the two armies that have engaged, one should then refrain from fighting. One should not contravene an eternal agreement that one should not injure a brahmana. If someone who calls himself a kshatriya breaks this agreement, he is not praised. Thereafter, he is not received in assemblies. A lord of the earth who desires victory should not follow a conduct that leads to the destruction of dharma and the violation of an agreement. There is no gain greater than a victory that has been obtained through the use of dharma.

'"When the people have been forced to bow down,[856] they must

[854]In the house of the captor.

[855]This is a difficult shloka to translate. The idea seems to be that property seized from those in the enemy's kingdom must be resorted to the original owners.

[856]The people in the country that has been invaded.

be quickly placated. They must be comforted through gifts of objects of pleasure. This is the supreme policy for the king. If they are forced to bend down and confront oppression in their own country, they will serve the enemies and wait for a calamity to descend.[857] When there is a calamity, they will quickly resort to the enemy. O king! They will be ill-disposed in every way and will desire that the king should face a disaster. One should not abuse the enemy, or struck severely in any way. If struck severely, the man's life may be over.[858] If one possesses only a little, one should be satisfied that a great crime has not been committed. Thus one repeatedly thinks that life alone is left.[859]

'"When the countryside is prosperous and wealthy, when the king is loved, when the servants and advisers are satisfied, the king has a firm foundation. When the officiating priests, priests, preceptors and those with learning are honoured, when those who deserve worship are worshipped, he is said to be a conqueror of the worlds. Having followed this kind of conduct, the supreme among the gods obtained the earth. Following Indra's triumph, other kings desired victory. In ancient times, King Pratardana[860] defeated the king in a battle and conquered the city, leaving the countryside alone. He took away their immortal herbs and grain. However, Divodasa seized the agnihotra sacrifices, the remnants of the fire, the oblations and the vessels and suffered.[861] O descendant of the Bharata lineage! Nabhaga gave away the kingdoms and the kings as dakshina, with the exception of what belonged to learned brahmanas and ascetics. O Yudhishthira! They knew about dharma, but behaved both in superior and inferior ways. I find delight in the ancient accounts of all those kings. The

857On the king.

858This abuse refers to deceit and a fight through unfair means. The injunction against killing thus applies to an unfair fight. Alternatively, it may refer to torturing an enemy who has been captured.

859This is a difficult shloka to translate. It could conceivably apply to the enemy who has been captured.

860The king of Kashi.

861That is, King Pratardana took what should be taken, but King Divodasa took what should not be taken.

lord of the earth who wishes for his own prosperity should seek to obtain victory by acting in accordance with every kind of learning and not use deceit or fraud."'

Chapter 1426(98)

'Yudhishthira said, "O bull among the Bharata lineage! There is no dharma that is more evil than the dharma of kshatriyas. The king mounts a campaign, wages a battle and kills a large number of people. What are the deeds through which a lord of the earth can conquer the worlds? O learned one! O bull among the Bharata lineage! I am asking you. Tell me this."

'Bhishma replied, "By chastising the wicked, by cherishing the virtuous, by performing sacrifices and by giving gifts, kings are purified and cleansed. When kings pursue victory, they cause impediments to people. However, having obtained victory, they make the subjects prosper again. They counter their sins through donations, sacrifices and the strength of austerities. By showing favours to people, they increase their good deeds. One who cuts the crops in a field seems to destroy the dry grass and grain at the same time, but he doesn't actually destroy the grain. In that way, kings release their weapons and seem to slay everyone at the same time. However, they are saved from all sins because they make beings flourish again. He protects the wealth of people and protects them from slaughter and hardship at the hand of bandits. He is the granter of life, riches and happiness and is Virat. The king performs all the sacrifices and gives fearlessness as a dakshina. Having experienced fortune, he attains Indra's world. When he advances to fight for the cause of brahmanas, he offers his own self as the sacrificial post and his sacrifice has an infinite amount of dakshina. He is fearless and scatters the enemy, receiving their arrows. That is the reason the thirty gods do not see anyone superior to him on earth. As long as his limbs continue to be mangled by weapons in battle, he continues to enjoy all the eternal worlds that yield every object of desire. As he moves around,[862] blood flows from his body and that blood cleanses him of all his sins. The pain that he has to bear from those wounds is superior to austerities. This is what is said by those who are learned about dharma. Those who are frightened and display their backs in a battle are the worst of men. They wish to seek refuge with the brave one, like one seeks Parjanya for life. If a brave person comforts them and protects them from fear, people should create his image. However, it doesn't happen like that. If they always honour him, recognizing him for what he has done, that would be proper. But they do not act in accordance with that. People are seen to be the same, but there are great differences between them. When there is a battle, there are those who advance into the tumult of army formations. Brave ones advance against enemy soldiers, but cowards run away, abandoning their companions, and this is not an act that leads to heaven. O son! Do not give birth to those who are like these worst of men, those who abandon their companions in a battle and go to the comfort of their own homes. The gods, with Indra at the forefront, cause discomfort for those who abandon their comrades and wish to save their own lives. They kill them with sticks and stones and burn them up in mats of straw.[863] Kshatriyas who behave in this way are slain like animals. It is adharma for a kshatriya to die when he is lying down on his bed, releasing bile and phlegm and lamenting piteously. Those who are learned about ancient accounts do not praise the deed of a kshatriya who heads towards his destruction without any injuries on his body. O son! A kshatriya's death at home is not praised. It is adharma for those who are haughty to be distressed, like those who are not proud. 'Alas, this is misery! This is unhappiness! This is wicked. This is a sin.' With an emaciated face and with a putrid body, he laments a lot.[864] He envies those who are healthy and desires

[862]In the battle.

[863]The straight translation does not capture the nuance. The word used is *katagni* and is a method of execution used against criminals. Dry grass and straw are tied around the criminal and he is then burnt.

[864]If the kshatriya dies in his bed.

an instant death. Surrounded by his kin, he should create carnage in a battle. He should be severely wounded by sharp weapons. That is the kind of death a kshatriya deserves. A brave one is based on truth and is intolerant. He penetrates the devastation of a battle. When his body is mangled by the enemy, he does not notice it. Having been killed in a battle, he is praised and honoured by the people. He obtains greatness through his own dharma and goes to Shakra's world. Ready to give up their lives, all warriors perform this supreme act of renunciation. A brave one does not show his back and will be with Indra in his world."'

Chapter 1427(99)

'Yudhishthira asked, "O grandfather! There are brave ones who fight and do not retreat. When they die, what worlds do they obtain? Tell me that."

'Bhishma replied, "In this connection, an ancient history is recounted. O Yudhishthira! This was a conversation between Ambarisha and Indra. Ambarisha, the son of Nabhaga, went to heaven, which is extremely difficult to obtain. In the world of the gods, he saw one of his advisers with Shakra. The lord was his own commander, situated on a supreme and divine *vimana* that was full of energy everywhere and was progressively advancing upwards. He saw that his own commander Sudeva, was progressively ascending upwards in great prosperity. Astounded, he asked Vasava, 'In accordance with what is ordained, I have ruled the entire earth, right up to the frontiers of the ocean. Desiring dharma, I have engaged the four varnas in what the sacred texts prescribe. I have observed terrible brahmacharya and served the family of my preceptor. Following dharma, I have studied the Vedas and all the sacred texts meant for kings. I have served food and drink to guests and offered oblations to the ancestors. I have studied under the rishis and have been initiated. I have served the gods through supreme sacrifices.

Following the sacred texts and the recommended principles, I have established myself in the dharma of kshatriyas. O Vasava! I have glanced at armies and have been victorious in battle. O king of the gods! In earlier times, Sudeva used to be my commander. He was a warrior with a calm soul. But how has he surpassed me? He has not performed the best of sacrifices. Nor has he served the brahmanas. He has not satisfied them in accordance with the prescribed rites. O Shakra! How has he surpassed me?'

'"Indra said, 'O son![865] This Sudeva performed the extremely great sacrifice of a battle and so do other men who fight. All armoured warriors who are at the front of an army are consecrated. They thus have the right to observe the sacrifice of a battle. This has been determined.'

'"Ambarisha asked, 'What are the oblations in that sacrifice? What is the clarified butter and what is the dakshina? Who are the officiating priests? O Shatakratu! Tell me this.'

'"Indra said, 'The elephants are the *ritvija*s. The horses are the adhvaryus.[866] The flesh of the enemy constitutes the oblations. The blood is the clarified butter. Jackals, vultures and crows are the *sadasya*s at the sacrifice. They drink the remnants of the clarified butter and eat the remnants of the oblations. Large numbers of spears, javelins, swords, spikes and battleaxes, flaming, extremely sharp and yellow, are the ladles at the sacrifice. There are straight, extremely sharp and yellow arrows, keenly released with force from bows, terrible when they penetrate the bodies of the enemy. These are the larger ladles. There are swords sheathed in scabbards made out of tiger skin. The handles are made out of ivory and, in the battle, they are wielded by arms that are like the trunks of elephants. These are the wooden sticks used to stir. There are

[865]The word used is tata.

[866]There are four types of officiating priests—hotar (one who recites from the Rig Veda), udgatar (one who recites from the Sama Veda), adhvaryu (one who recites from the Yajur Veda) and brahman (one who recites from the Atharva Veda). A ritvija is an officiating priest in general. A sadasya is an assistant priest or a spectator.

blazing, sharp and yellow javelins, spears and battleaxes. They are sharp and made out of steel and the blows from these are the riches. In the battle, blood flows down on the ground. This is the complete oblation. This is a great and prosperous sacrifice and all the desires are satisfied. "Slice. Pierce." These are the sounds that are heard at the vanguard of the army. These are like sama hymns sung by reciters of the sama in Yama's abode. The vanguard of the enemy's forces is said to be the vessel for storing oblations. The large number of armoured elephants and horses are decreed to be the *shyenachit*[867] fire for the sacrifice. Among the thousands who have been slain, the headless torso of a brave one stands up. This is said to be the octagonal khadira[868] post used in the sacrifice. When the elephants are goaded by hooks and shriek, those are the sounds made when *ida* oblations[869] are offered. O lord of the earth! When palms are slapped against palms, this is the sound of vashatkara.[870] In the battle, the sound of the large drum is said to be the three samas chanted by the udgatar. In a battle, if someone is prepared to cast aside his beloved body because a brahmana's possessions are being robbed, his own self is like a sacrificial post and this is a sacrifice with an infinite amount of dakshina. For the sake of his master, if a brave person exhibits valour in the front of the army and does not retreat because of fear, a world like mine is meant for him. There are blue swords that are shaped like the crescent moon. They are wielded by arms that are like clubs. A person who strews the sacrificial altar with these obtains a world that is like mine. If a person is focused on obtaining victory and does not glance to see if he has aides or not, immersing himself in the midst of the army, he obtains a world that is like mine. In the heap of javelins, the drums are like frogs and tortoises.[871] The bones of the brave ones are stones. It is impenetrable because of

[867]When the kindling is piled up in the form of a hawk (*shyena*).

[868]A kind of acacia.

[869]Secondary oblations.

[870]The exclamation vashat when oblations are made.

[871]There is an imagery of a river.

the mire of flesh and blood. The swords and shields are like boats on the river. The hair is the moss and weed. The shattered horses, elephants and chariots are passages. The banners and flags are the reed on the banks.[872] The blood from the slain mounts and armies are the overflowing torrents in the river and it is impossible even for accomplished men to cross. In this inauspicious river, the slain elephants are the giant crocodiles that are borne along to the world of the dead. The swords, cutlasses and flags are like ornaments. The vultures, herons and wild crows are like rafts. It is frequented by those who live on human flesh and it causes terror to cowards. This river is said to be the bath a warrior takes at the end of a great sacrifice. If a person strews the sacrificial altar with the heads of his enemies and heaps of horses and heaps of elephants, his world will be like that of mine. The learned say that if a person regards the vanguard of the enemy's army as his wife's chamber, his own army as the store of oblations, the soldiers to the south as sadasyas, the soldiers to the north as the priest who kindle the fire and the soldiers of the enemy as his wife, he obtains all the worlds. When there are two vyuhas and a space between them, that is always said to be the altar for the sacrifice and the three Vedas are like fires. When a warrior retreats in fear and is slain by the enemy, there is no doubt that he goes to a fathomless hell. If he covers himself with blood from the force of that river, which is full of hair, flesh and bones, he goes to the supreme objective. If someone slays a commander and climbs onto his chariot, he treads with the valour of Vishnu and performs a sacrifice like Brihaspati. He who captures alive a leader[873] or someone who is regarded as his equal, he obtains a world that is like mine. One should never sorrow over a brave one who has been killed in battle. One should not sorrow over a brave one who has been slain, because he obtains greatness in the world of heaven. One should not wish to offer oblations to such a slain one, or bathe, or perform an act of

[872]Of the river.
[873]Of the enemy.

purification.[874] Listen to the worlds obtained by him. If a brave warrior is slain in a battle, thousands of supreme apsaras quickly rush towards him and say, "Be my husband." This sacred austerity is eternal dharma and like the four ashramas for a person who does not run away from the field of battle. One should not kill the aged, children,[875] women, brahmanas, someone with a blade of grass in his mouth[876] and a person who says, "I am yours."[877] I became the lord of the gods after killing in battle Vritra, Bala, Paka, Virochana, with his one hundred kinds of maya, Namuchi, who was difficult to counter, Shambara, who had many different kinds of maya, the daitya Viprachitti, all of Danu's sons[878] and Prahrada.'"

'Bhishma said, "On hearing Shakra's words, Ambarisha accepted them and himself obtained success as a warrior."'

Chapter 1428(100)

'Bhishma said, "In this connection, an ancient history is recounted about when Pratardana[879] and the king of Mithila fought a battle. O Yudhishthira! Listen to this. Janaka of Mithila was invested with the sacred thread of performing a sacrifice through a battle and delighted his warriors. King Janaka of Mithila was great in his soul and knew the truth about everything. He portrayed both heaven and hell before his warriors. 'Behold those radiant worlds, meant for people who are not frightened. They are eternal, full of gandharva maidens, and yield every object of

[874]As part of funeral rites.

[875]There is a typo in the critical edition. It reads *balam*, which makes no sense. It should read *baalam*.

[876]Symbolically, the person pretends to be a cow, as a token of unconditional surrender.

[877]Signifying surrender.

[878]The danavas.

[879]The king of Kashi.

desire. Hell presents itself to those who run away. They immediately descend there and obtain eternal ill fame. Having seen those, having made up your minds to give yourselves up, be victorious. Do not be subjugated in a hell that has no foundation. For brave people, giving themselves up is the foundation for the supreme gate of heaven.' O conqueror of enemy cities! This is what the king told his warriors. They defeated the enemy in the battle and brought delight to that lord of men. Therefore, he[880] must always establish himself in the forefront of the battle. Chariots must be in the middle of the elephants. Horse riders must be to the rear of the chariots. Armoured foot soldiers must be beyond the horse riders. The king who arranges a vyuha in this way is always victorious over the enemy. O Yudhishthira! It has been decreed that it must always be this way. All those who wish to act well and desire to fight well must agitate the army, like makaras in an ocean. They must stand next to each other, delighting those who are distressed. He[881] must protect the land that has been won and not unduly pursue those who have been routed. O king! Those who have given up hope of remaining alive and return to fight again represent a force that is not easy to counter. Therefore, one should not pursue too much. Nor should brave ones wish to strike those who are afraid and are running away. Because they are running away, one should not pursue them. The immobile are devoured by the mobile. Those without teeth are devoured by the ones with teeth. Those without hands are devoured by those with hands. Cowards are devoured by the brave. Though their backs, stomachs, hands and feet are equal, cowards follow the brave. Those who are distressed and scared repeatedly seek refuge with the ones who are brave, joining their hands in supplication. This world hangs from the hands of brave ones, like a young son. That is the reason a brave person deserves respect in every possible situation. There is nothing in the three worlds that is superior to bravery. The brave person protects everything. Everything is established in the brave person."'

[880]The king.

[881]The king.

Chapter 1429(101)

'Yudhishthira asked, "O bull among the Bharata lineage! If one desires victory, how should the soldiers be led, even if one violates dharma a bit? O grandfather! Tell me this."

'Bhishma replied, "Some dharma is based on truth, some more on reason. Some is based on virtuous conduct, some more on implementation.[882] I will tell you about the different techniques of dharma, so that the objectives of obtaining dharma and artha become successful. Bandits, who show no respect, stand in the way of everything. For the sake of countering them, I will tell you what is laid down in the sacred texts. Listen to the different tasks that can be undertaken, so that one is successful in one's objectives. O descendant of the Bharata lineage! You must know about two kinds of wisdom—the straight and the crooked. Knowing about crooked ways, one should not use these, except to counter a danger that has arisen, such as when enemies use dissenstion to strike at a king. Knowing about crooked means, the king can then use these to counter the enemy.

'"Leather from the flanks of elephants, bulls and boa constrictors, stakes, thorns and iron—these are recommended for body armour. Sharp and yellow weapons, red and yellow mail, flags and banners of many dyes and hues, cutlasses, spears, swords, sharp battleaxes and leather for shields—these must be planned for in abundance. The weapons must be ready and the warriors must have practised with them. It is recommended that the soldiers should march in the months of Chaitra and Margashirsha.[883] The crops on the ground ripen then and there is no lack of water. O descendant of the Bharata lineage! At that time, it is neither too cold, nor too hot. Therefore, one should engage then. However, if the enemy is facing a hardship,

[882]This is in the context of a battle and the difference between the four types of dharma is unclear. Conceivably, truth means the dharma of kshatriyas, reason is persuading soldiers to give up their lives, virtuous conduct is encouraging those who are ready to fight and implementation is punishing those who are not ready to fight.

[883]Respectively, April–May or November–December.

for the sake of restraining the enemy, the employment of soldiers is recommended then. An advance along an even road that has water and grass is recommended. Spies who are accomplished in roaming around in the woods must be employed to check these out. Like a herd of deer, the army should not be made to march through newly cleared ways in the forest. Kings who desire victory employ all their soldiers in this way. Camps and fortifications that have plenty of water are recommended. These must be clear and there must be obstacles to an enemy creeping up. A clearing near a forest is thought to be the best in qualities. People who are skilled in warfare think that it possesses many qualities. Foot soldiers who have retreated can regroup, there are hiding places, one can strike at the enemy and there are refuges for times of distress. The army should be like a mountain and fight with the constellation *saptarshi* at the rear.[884] O king! Through this means, one can conquer those who are difficult to defeat. Where there is the wind, where there is the sun, where there is Shukra[885]—victory is there. O Yudhishthira! The wind is superior to the sun, the sun is superior to Shukra, but a conjunction is the best.[886] People who are skilled in warfare praise an even terrain without mud, water and stones for horses. A clear and level terrain without water is recommended for chariots. A terrain with small trees, large bushes and water is recommended for those who fight on elephants. Ground with many fortifications, large trees, clumps of bamboo and cane and hills and woods is recommended for foot soldiers. O descendant of the Bharata lineage! An army with a large number of foot soldiers is solid. When the day is fine, an army with a large number of chariots is praised. During the monsoon, large numbers of foot soldiers and elephants are praised. One must engage after considering all these qualities that have been mentioned and the time and the place. If one employs the soldiers well and advances

[884]The seven rishis, the constellation of Ursa Major. This means that the army will face southwards.

[885]Venus. The sense probably is that these should be to the rear of the army.

[886]The shloka in the text is brief and states that each is superior to the succeeding one. We have expanded it, so that the meaning becomes clear.

after thinking about this, honouring the *tithi* and the nakshatra, one always obtains victory.[887]

'"Those who are asleep, thirsty and exhausted and those who have been routed must not be struck, nor those who are striving for moksha,[888] running away, trembling or drinking and eating. Those who have been severely wounded, those who have been somewhat wounded, those who have been routed, those who are emaciated, those who are completely at ease,[889] those who are engaged in some other task, those who have withdrawn, those who have gone out,[890] those who have withdrawn, though they may have pledged to return, those who are camp followers, those who follow tradition and guard the gates,[891] those who are followers,[892] those who supervise the gatekeepers and those who are shaking must not be struck.

'"The soldiers who cause a breach[893] and those who stem a breach[894] should have the same food and drink as you and it is a duty to pay them double the wages. For these, it is a duty to make the leaders of ten the leaders of one hundred. The brave one who is always attentive should be made the leader of one thousand. Having collected the foremost among them together, one should say, 'Let us take a pledge for the sake of victory in battle. We will not abandon each other. If there is anyone who is frightened, let him retreat right now. Otherwise, after the tumultuous engagement has begun, they will slay and rout us. If one runs away in the battle, one slays one's own self and one's own side. If one runs away, there is destruction of wealth, death, ill fame and a bad reputation. A man who runs away hears harsh and unpleasant words. His lips tremble. His teeth chatter. He throws aside all his weapons. When the lives of

[887]The tithi is the lunar day and the nakshatras must be auspicious.

[888]That is, those who have cast aside their weapons and are meditating and fasting to death on the field of battle, ready to give up their lives.

[889]They are non-combatants.

[890]Gone outside the camp to collect forage or fodder.

[891]They are gatekeepers rather than soldiers.

[892]They are servants rather than soldiers.

[893]In the ranks of the enemy.

[894]In one's own ranks.

his companions are in danger, he abandons them and runs away. His intelligence favours the enemy. Let the enemy face such a state. A person who is reluctant to fight is the worst among men. They can only propagate their own species. But they have nothing in this world, or after death.'[895] The enemy will be delighted in his mind and welcome one who runs away. O son! He will greet him with honour and auspicious sounds, as if he is a victorious well-wisher. O king! When the enemy is delighted at your hardship, I think that this is a more severe sorrow than death. Know that Shri is the foundation for dharma and all happiness. She advances towards the enemies of cowards, but goes to those who are brave. 'We desire heaven and are ready to give up our lives in the battle.[896] Whether we are victorious or whether we are slain, we deserve to obtain the end of virtuous men.' Having taken this oath and ready to give up their lives, the brave ones are not frightened and immerse themselves in the army of the enemy.

'"One should have men armed with swords and shields at the front. The array of carts should be at the rear and the wives should be in the middle. For the sake of countering the enemy, the foot soldiers must be hidden. Those who are at the front must be eager to strike the enemy. Those who are in the front must be reputed, courageous and spirited. They should advance in the front and other people should follow them. One should make efforts to inspire those who are cowards. They should be made to stand close, so that the numbers are seen to be larger. As one desires, a few warriors may be made to fight together, or many may be spread out. When a small number fights with many, the array is called *suchimukha*.[897] When the engagement has started, he[898] should seize the men by the arms and shout, regardless of whether it is true or false, 'The enemy has been routed. The army of our friends has arrived. Strike them without any fear.' Men should create a terrible noise and roar

[895]It is not clear where the pledge ends, but this is as good a place as any.

[896]The pledge begins again.

[897]Literally, the mouth of a needle.

[898]The king or the leader.

and rush after him. They should slap their arms, create a tumult and sound conch shells, *krakachas*[899] and horns. Kettledrums, drums, cymbals and other musical instruments must be sounded and elephants made to trumpet."'

Chapter 1430(102)

'Yudhishthira asked, "O descendant of the Bharata lineage! O king! When men advance into a battle, what should be their conduct? How should they uplift themselves? What should be their form? How should they armour themselves? What should be their weapons?"

'Bhishma replied, "It is recommended that weapons and vehicles should be those they are used to. A man's conduct should be in conformity with practice. Gandharas, Sindhus and Souviras fight with nails and javelins. The Abhiras are extremely strong and their army is skilled in every way. The Ushinaras are spirited and are accomplished in the use of all weapons. Those from the eastern regions are skilled in fighting with elephants and are warriors who fight with deceit. The Yavanas, the Kambojas and those who live around Mathura are accomplished in fighting with bare arms. The southerners use swords and shields. Brave ones who are extremely spirited and extremely strong are born everywhere. I have told you about general indications. Listen to the specifics. Their voices and eyes are like lions and tigers. Their gait is like that of lions and tigers. The eyes of all the brave ones who are strikers are like those of pigeons and sparrows. There are others with voices like deer, glances like leopards and eyes like bulls. Some utter cries that are extremely terrible. When enraged, others have voices like *kinnaris*. With wrathful faces, some thunder like clouds. Some have sounds like young elephants.[900] Some possess

[899]Kind of musical instrument.

[900]Alternatively, young camels.

crooked noses and legs, but they can travel far and strike from a long distance. Some have bodies that are curved like a cat. Some are thin. Others are fair in hair and complexion. These brave ones are restless and difficult to assail. Some have eyes like lizards. Others are mild in nature. Some accomplished men possess the gait and sounds of horses. Some possess robust frames, others are old. Some possess broad chests and symmetrical frames. They are delighted and dance when there is a fight and musical instruments are sounded. Some possess grave eyes. Others have bulging and tawny eyes. They have frowns on their faces. Some have eyes like mongooses. However, all of them are brave ones who are ready to give up their lives. Some have crooked eyes and broad foreheads. Others possess very little flesh. Some have crooked arms and fingers. Some are thin and seem to be made out of veins alone. When the enemy presents itself, they advance with great force. They are difficult to withstand and are like crazy elephants. For some, the tips of the hair seem to blaze in radiance. Others possess stout flanks, jaws and faces. Some have peaked noses, thick necks, fearful forms and thick calves. Others possess excellent necks that can be raised up or lowered, like those of birds. Some possess round heads and faces like snakes. Others have faces like those of cats. When they are wrathful, some make terrible sounds. They roar and rush into battle. They are insolent and terrible and know nothing about dharma. They exhibit how horrible they are. All of them are ready to give up their lives. They dwell in the frontier regions and do not retreat. They place themselves ahead of the soldiers and kill or are killed. They do not follow dharma and have different codes of conduct. They regard virtue as defeat. They act in this wrathful way towards their king too."'

Chapter 1431(103)

'Yudhishthira asked, "O bull among men! What are the acclaimed signs that signify the army's victory? I wish to know about this."

'Bhishma replied, "O bull among men! I will tell you everything about the acclaimed signs that signify the army's victory. Destiny determines this in advance and men are goaded by time. Those who are far-sighted because of their wisdom can see and understand this. Those who are learned about the means of atonement perform meditation and offer oblations. They observe auspicious acts to pacify the ill portents. O descendant of the Bharata lineage! If the warriors and mounts are uplifted in their spirits, it is said that it is certain that the army will obtain victory. Winds blow from the rear and there are rainbows. Clouds shower from the rear and so do the sun's rays. All the jackals, wild crows and vultures become favourably disposed towards it. When they act towards the army in this way, it obtains supreme success. The flames of the fire[901] are clear and the rays rise straight up. There is no smoke and the flames bend towards the south. The oblations emit an auspicious scent. It is said that this is an indication that there will be victory. When conch shells and drums make a loud noise that is deep in tone and those who wish to fight are inspired, it is said that this is an indication that there will be victory. When animals are to the rear or the left of those who are marching or are about to march, that is auspicious. When they are about to kill, if they are to the right, that is said to signify success. However, if they are in front, that is an obstruction. When birds call out in auspicious tones, swans, curlews, woodpeckers and blue jays, the warriors become cheerful and spirited and it is said that this is an indication that there will be victory. When the weapons, shafts, armour and flags are extremely radiant, and so is the sheen and complexion on the faces of the warriors, they become impossible to look at and the army will overcome the enemy. When the warriors are obedient and not insolent, bearing fraternal feelings towards each other, and are always based on purity, it is said that this is an indication that there will be victory. When sounds, touch and the scent that wafts around brings pleasure to the mind and the warriors are full of fortitude, this is the face of victory. For someone who has already

[901]The sacrificial fire.

penetrated, the left side is auspicious. However, for someone who is about to penetrate, it is the right. Things at the rear facilitate success and those in front constrain it.

'"O Yudhishthira! After collecting a large army with the four limbs,[902] you must first try for conciliation. You should endeavour to fight only after that. O descendant of the Bharata lineage! A victory that is obtained through war is to be abhorred. If one thinks about it, victory in a battle depends on the wishes of destiny. Like a great flood of water or a herd of deer that has been terrified, if a large army has been routed, it is extremely difficult to reverse the flight. They begin to flee and even the learned do not know the reason for this.[903] Even if the hearts are firm, a large army is like a mass of *ruru* deer. If they depend on each other, if they are cheerful and ready to give up their lives and if they are extremely firm in their determination, even fifty brave ones can drive away the enemy's army. Or even five, six and seven noble and revered ones, fighting together, and firm in their deterimination, can completely defeat the enemy. You should never advance towards a clash, if it can be prevented. It is said that war should be adopted only after conciliation, dissension and gifts have been tried out. Those who are cowards are scared of soldiers[904] creeping up to attack, looking on it like a bolt of lightning and unsure about where it will descend next. When a body of soldiers gets to know about the intended attack and advances, the bodies of the warriors tremble, and so does the kingdom. O king! The entire kingdom, with its mobile and immobile objects, trembles. Tormented by the heat of the weapons, the marrow in the bodies begins to melt. Therefore, together with severity, conciliation must repeatedly be tried. If the enemy is oppressed too much, it will always attack. One should employ spies to seed internal dissension within the enemy. If the enemy king is superior, a truce is recommended. This is because one will not be able to combine with his foes and act so as to counter

[902]Chariots, cavalry, elephants and infantry.

[903]A reference to the herd mentality.

[904]Enemy soldiers.

him from every side. Forgiveness is the maya of the virtuous. Those who are virtuous are always forgiving. O Partha! Depending on the need, know how to use forgiveness and also when not to forgive. If a king conquers through forgiveness, his fame increases. Even enemies who have committed great crimes begin to trust him. Shambara said, 'Once one has subjugated, one should think about forgiving. However, a piece of wood that has not been completely burnt returns again to its natural state.' But preceptors do not praise this as a virtuous practice. Control must be effortless and without destruction, the way one treats one's own sons. O Yudhishthira! A king who is fierce is hated by the people. However, they also disregard him if he is mild. Therefore, both must be practised. O descendant of the Bharata lineage! Even if one has to strike, one should speak pleasant words before striking. After striking, one should show compassion and sorrow and weep a little. In front of them, one should say, 'I am not pleased that he[905] has been killed. I repeatedly told him that he had not acted in accordance with my words. Alas! I wished that he had remained alive. He did not deserve to be slain in this way. Such excellent men who do not run away from the field of battle are extremely difficult to get. Whoever has killed him in the battle has performed a task that is not agreeable to me.' Having spoken words like this before the ones who survive on the side of the one who has been slain and seizing their hands so as to bring them over to his own side, he must secretly honour the ones who have committed the crime.[906] In this way, in every situation, he must act in accordance with conciliation. An intrepid king who acts in this way knows about dharma and is loved by the people. O descendant of the Bharata lineage! He obtains the trust of all the people. With that trust, as desire presents itself, he will be capable of enjoyment. Therefore, the king must obtain the trust of all people, without resorting to deceit. He who wishes to enjoy the earth should protect it in every way."'

[905]The one who has been killed. The king is speaking to the ones who are around.

[906]The ones on his side who have done the killing.

Chapter 1432(104)

'Yudhishthira asked, "How should a king behave towards an enemy who is mild, one who is fierce and one who has a large army? O grandfather! Tell me that."

'Bhishma replied, "O Yudhishthira! In this connection, an ancient history is recounted about the conversation between Brihaspati and Indra. The lord of the gods joined his hands in salutation and spoke to Brihaspati. Vasava, the destroyer of enemy heroes, approached and asked him, 'O brahmana! How should I be attentive and act towards those who injure me? How can I use techniques to control them, without destroying them? In general, victory is obtained through a clash between armies. But what can I do so that the powerful and blazing Shri does not abandon me?' The radiant one[907] was accomplished about dharma, artha and kama and knew about the precepts of rajadharma. He replied to Purandara, 'When seeking to control those who cause injury, one should not use conflict. That is for those who are intolerant and cannot forgive, it is practised by children. If one desires to kill an enemy, one should not disclose this. Rage, power and intolerance should be controlled and kept within one's own self. Even if there is distrust, one must serve the enemy, as if one trusts him. One must always speak pleasantly. One must never act in an unpleasant way. One should refrain from pointless hostility and abandon any voicing of it. A fowler wanting to catch birds imitates the tones of the birds. A king wishing to subjugate should act in that way. O Purandara! One brings the enemies under one's subjugation and then kills them. O Vasava! Having conquered the enemy, one should never sleep happily. Like a crackling fire, the evil-souled one can arise again. But in general, a clash is not the recommended task for victory. O lord! Having conquered an enemy by winning his trust, one should let him be. However, having consulted with his advisers and great-souled and learned ministers, an enemy

[907] Brihaspati.

may not be defeated in his heart. He may ignore it,[908] or choose to strike back. He may wait for a time to strike, when one is distracted in one's state. He may use trusted men to corrupt the army.[909] He[910] must consider the beginning, the middle and the end and everything that is hidden.[911] Obtaining knowledge and proof, one must corrupt the forces.[912] One should use dissension, blandishments and herbs.[913] However, one should never mix one's clothes with that of the enemy.[914] After having waited for a long time, one can then slay the enemy. One should spend the time in waiting, looking for an opportunity. Large numbers of the enemy should not be immediately killed. If one waits, the victory will be without anxiety. One should not impale a stake that creates a fresh wound. When the right time has come for striking, that is when one should attack again. O Indra of the gods! This is what is indicated for a man who wishes to kill the enemy. However, a man who is waiting for the right time should not let that moment pass. This is the dharma of time. For one who desires this, it is extremely rare for that moment to come back again. Those who are virtuous honour the technique of defeating the enemy's energy. Time always brings success. If something has not been obtained, one should not press. O Purandara! Give up desire, anger and ego. Engage yourself in detecting the weaknesses of those who seek to injure. O supreme among the gods! O Shakra! Mildness, chastisement,[915] laziness and carelessness and different kinds of deceit can destroy the success of those who are not discriminating. These four must be destroyed and deceit countered. Without any hesitation, one will then be able to strike at the enemy. If this is capable of being secretly undertaken with just one person, this is what should be

[908]The defeat.

[909]The victor's army.

[910]This is now a reference to the conquering king.

[911]Such as an incipient rebellion.

[912]Of the enemy.

[913]Probably a reference to poisonous substances.

[914]As a sign of truce, clothing, especially headdresses, was often exchanged.

[915]Excesses of mildness and chastisement.

done. Many advisers can divulge secrets and falsely pass on the responsibility to each other. If it is impossible to do this,[916] one can then have consultations with others. The four limbs should be used against those who are seen and *brahmadanda* against those who are not seen.[917] Dissension should first be used and silence[918] and force thereafter. Depending on the right time, the king must employ these. At a time when the enemy is stronger, one must bow down. However, one must be attentive in seeking for a weakness when he is careless, so that one can kill him. One must bow down, use gifts and speak pleasant words. One must serve the enemy, so that he has no grounds for suspicion. One must carefully avoid all the postures that give rise to suspicion. One should not trust those who have been defeated. Those who have been injured are always awake. O supreme among the gods! O lord of the immortals! There is no task that is as supremely difficult as ensuring prosperity for those who have varied means of subsistence. That is the reason he[919] is spoken of as the generator of different kinds of conduct. One must be engaged in this, restraining both friends and foes. People disrespect one who is mild and hate one who is fierce. Do not be mild. Do not be fierce. Be both mild and fierce. A raging torrent overcomes the riverbank and floods everything with water. If one is careless, the embankments of the kingdom break down in that way. One should not engage against many enemies at the same time. O Purandara! Use sama, dana, bheda and danda. One should use these one at a time. Even if one is skilled, one does not act against all the wicked at the same time. A king who is intelligent knows he is not capable of countering everyone at the same time. When there is a large army of horses, elephants and chariots and

[916]Have consultations with only one person.

[917]Against an enemy who can be seen, the four kinds of forces in the army should be employed. In this context, since the enemy is invisible or far away, brahmadanda can be interpreted as a dependence on destiny. Alternatively, it can be interpreted as resort to rites, sacrifices and mantras.

[918]Silencing the enemy through conciliation.

[919]The king.

there are foot soldiers and many implements of war and that six-fold army[920] is devoted, when one uses one's intelligence to deduce that one is superior in many ways, then, without any hesitation, one can directly strike against bandits. The sacred texts do not recommend conciliation, but punishment.[921] Instead of mildness, one must always advance against the enemy. However, one must avoid the destruction of crops, acts of mixing[922] and excessive destruction of nature. One can use deceit to infuse dissension among people and allow wicked and reprehensible deeds by trusted men, employed against the cities in the kingdom. The lord of the earth will pursue him[923] into the city and conquer all the objects of pleasure inside the city. O destroyer of Bala and Vritra! He must implement the recommended policy for the cities, as is necessary. He will secretly give them[924] riches, while taking away their own possessions. He will cite the sins of those wicked ones and employ them in the cities and the kingdom. There are others who are learned about the texts of love[925] and are adorned with the foresight of knowing the ordinances of the sacred texts. There are extremely skilled ones, accomplished in recounting tales. For bringing down the enemy, these should be considered.'

'"Indra asked, 'O supreme among brahmanas! What are the signs of wicked people? How does one know evil ones? I am asking you. Tell me.'

'"Brihaspati replied, 'He dislikes your good qualities and proclaims your bad qualities behind your back. When others praise you, he is silent and reluctant. Even if there is no obvious reason, one can discern from this silence. Though he seems trustworthy, he bites his lips and shakes his head. He is gracious in public and ungracious in

[920]One has added machines or implements of war to the standard four divisions. The sixth is either the treasury or the supplies.

[921]In a situation where the enemy is weaker.

[922]Mixing poison in waterbodies.

[923]The enemy.

[924]Presumably the conquered leaders.

[925]The text uses the word *ratishastra*, texts of love. This is probably a typo and should be *atishastra*, referring to those who are extremely learned in the sacred texts.

private. When someone is absent, he acts against him. But when that person is present, he says nothing. He eats alone and says, "Today, it is not as it should be."[926] In particular, these signs can be seen in his sitting, sleeping and walking around. If someone sorrows when you are unhappy, that is the sign of a friend. The opposite of this is the sign of an enemy. From anything that is contrary, one can determine the characteristics of an enemy. O lord of the thirty gods! Know from these and the others that I have spoken about, to detect wicked men, since nature is always superior. O supreme among the gods! I have described the knowledge of evil ones. O lord of the immortals! Know the truth of what has been stated in the sacred texts.'"

'Bhishma said, "Hearing the words spoken then by Brihaspati, Purandara, engaged in the destruction of the enemy, acted in accordance with this. At the right time, the slayer of enemies became victorious and brought the enemy under his subjugation."'

Chapter 1433(105)

'Yudhishthira asked, "A king may be devoted to dharma, but may be obstructed by his advisers. If he desires happiness, how should he act when he doesn't possess riches and has been deprived of his treasury and his army?"

'Bhishma replied, "On this, the history of Kshemadarshi is sung. O Yudhishthira! I will tell you this. Listen to it. Kshemadarshi was the son of a king and in ancient times, his strength had decayed. We have heard that he went to the sage Kalakavrikshiya and asked him, 'My prosperity has disappeared and I am immersed in this hardship. I am a man who should have his share of riches and I have tried repeatedly. However, I have been unable to obtain the kingdom. O brahmana! What should I do? O supreme one! There is nothing other than death, theft, seeking refuge or other inferior forms of conduct.

[926]A complaint about the food.

Tell me. You are accomplished in your wisdom. Someone afflicted with disease, mental or otherwise, should seek refuge with someone who is as extremely learned as you are. A man who has broken free and has controlled his desires obtains bliss. He abandons joy and sorrow and obtains wealth that has nothing to do with happiness. I sorrow for those who seek happiness in riches. My large quantity of riches has been destroyed, as if they had appeared in a dream. It is an extremely great and difficult task to abandon riches, even for virtuous ones. We are incapable of giving up what no longer exists.[927] I have been dislodged from my prosperity and have attained this state, where I am miserable and distressed. O brahmana! Instruct me about the other kind of bliss that exists.'

'"Having been addressed by the intelligent prince of Kosala, the immensely radiant sage Kalakavrikshiya replied, 'You already know, because that intelligence has presented itself before you. Act accordingly. Know that everything, I and what is mine, is temporary. Everything that you think of as existing, know that it is non-existent. That is the reason a wise person is not distressed, even when he faces a difficulty and a hardship. Know that whatever had happened and whatever has happened are certainly things that have no existence.[928] Knowing what should be known, you will be able to free yourself from adharma. There was an accumulation of things earlier and there are those that came after that. All of those no longer exist. Knowing this, who will be anxious? Having existed, something no longer exists. Having not existed, something exists. One should not have the capacity to grieve. Why should a man sorrow? O king! Where is your father now? Where is your grandfather now? You cannot see them now, nor can they see you. Beholding your own self to be impermanent, why do you sorrow over them? Use your intelligence to comprehend this. It is certain that you will not exist. O king! I, you, your enemies and your well-wishers will cease to be. Everything will cease to exist. Whether they are twenty years old or whether they are thirty years old, all the men who are here will die

[927]Though the kingdom has gone, Kshemadarshi still hopes to get it back.
[928]In the sense that they are temporary.

before one hundred years have passed. If a man is freed from his great prosperity, if he wishes to ensure his own welfare, he should think that it wasn't his. He should not regard what will come as his either. What has passed should also not be regarded as his. Those who think that destiny is superior are learned and it is said that those are the virtuous ones. It is possible to survive without riches and rule the kingdom. People who are your equal or superior in intelligence and manliness have done that. They have not sorrowed like you. Therefore, you should also not grieve. Why are you not their equal, or superior, in intelligence and manliness?'

'"The prince replied, 'I think that my obtaining the kingdom was also destiny. O brahmana! Everything that was there has been taken away by the greatness of time. O one who is rich in austerities! It has been taken away, as if by a flow of water. I can see the fruits. I must live on whatever I can obtain.'

'"The sage said, 'O one from Kosala! You have arrived at the right conclusion about what will come and what is past. That is the reason you are not sorrowing. Behave in that way about everything. Never desire objectives that cannot be attained, only those that can be attained. Experience what has presented itself and do not sorrow over what has not come. O one from Kosala! You will then find delight in the objectives that have been attained. Now that your sentiments have been cleansed, perhaps you will not grieve over Shri having left. When an evil-minded person confronts misfortune and is deprived of what he possessed earlier, he always censures the creator and is not satisfied with what he now possesses. He thinks that people who are prosperous do not deserve it. That is the reason he is repeatedly immersed in grief. O king! Such a man is proud and is overcome by excessive jealousy. O lord of Kosala! O wise one! In that way, you should not suffer from envy. Though you do not possess prosperity, tolerate that of others. Accomplished people enjoy Lakhsmi, even if she is with someone else. Shri goes to the virtuous and abandons those who hate. Brave men who follow dharma and know about dharma give up Shri and their sons and grandsons. They even give up their own selves. They see that even when they have satisfied their desires, there is a lot that crumbles away. There are others who renounce, thinking that the objectives are extremely difficult to obtain.[929] But though you are wise by nature, you are tormented in your misery. You desire things that should not be desired, noticing that those riches are with others. Use your intelligence to question and abandon the pursuit. Something that is not desirable presents itself in the form of artha. Something that is not artha presents itself in the form of something that is desirable. For some, the destruction of riches is desirable. There are those who look towards prosperity and think that it will bring infinite happiness. There are those who find pleasure in prosperity, disregarding what is superior. In his pursuit of prosperity, all his enterprise is destroyed. O one from Kosala! When something desired has been obtained with a great deal of difficulty and then disappears, the man who was pursuing riches is completely shattered. Men who know about welfare desire dharma alone. They desire happiness beyond death and are indifferent towards what happens in this world. In their greed for wealth, some men are ready to give up their lives. When they are unable to obtain riches, such men think that there is no point in remaining alive. Behold their misery. Behold their stupidity. Because of their confusion, they thirst for riches and live for what is temporary. All these stores are destroyed. Life ends in death. Why should one turn one's mind towards acquiring something that will be separated? O king! Wealth abandons a man, or a man abandons wealth. Knowing that this is certainly inevitable, why should one be anxious over it? The well-wishers and riches of others are also destroyed. O king! Use your intelligence to judge the calamities that you, and other men, face. Restrain, control and focus your senses, mind and words. There are injurious ends, extremely difficult to obtain, that may not be available. These are despicable by nature, or perhaps it is impossible to obtain them. Be content in your wisdom. Be valiant and know. Do not sorrow. Desire a little. Do not be fickle. Be mild, generous and controlled. If you resort to brahmacharya, someone like you will not be confounded. Someone like you should

[929]Some abandon the pursuit of riches to start off with. Others abandon the pursuit after realizing that these are transient.

not resort to the contemptible means of begging for subsistence.[930] That is cruel, wicked and unhappy conduct, meant for cowards. You can subsist on roots and fruits and enjoy yourself in the great forest. Control your soul by being restrained in speech. Show compassion towards all beings. One who finds pleasure in dwelling alone in the forest, is satisfied with a little and enjoys companionship with aged tuskers is like a learned person. The atman will be like a large lake that was once agitated, but is now tranquil. If someone treads this path, I can only see happiness for him. O king! When prosperity is impossible, when one is devoid of advisers, by seeking recourse with destiny, can you think of anything that will be superior?'"'

Chapter 1434(106)

'"The sage said, 'O kshatriya! If instead, you see that there is some manliness left in you, I will tell you about a policy whereby you can get your kingdom back. If you can undertake this, you will perform an everlasting deed. I will tell you everything. Listen to it in detail. If you act in accordance with this, you will obtain great prosperity, the kingdom, control over the kingdom and get the greatness of Shri back again. O king! If this appeals to you, tell me. I will tell you what must be done.'

'"The king replied, 'O illustrious one! O lord! I have sought refuge with you. Tell me about the policy. Now that I have met you, this meeting cannot but be successful.'

'"The sage said, 'Renounce arrogance, pride, anger, joy and fear. Join your hands in salutation, bow down before the enemy and serve him.[931] The lord of Videha is devoted to the truth. Because of your supreme purity, deeds and appeasement, he is certain to grant you a

[930]The text uses the word *kapalin*, which means a mendicant who carries a skull around and begs for a living.

[931]The enemy means King Janaka of Videha.

means of subsistence. You will obtain his favours and become pre-eminent among all the people. You will also obtain aides who are enterprising, without vices and pure. If a person is engaged in his own tasks, restrains his soul and conquers his senses, he uplifts himself and pleases people. He is intelligent and prosperous and will honour you. Having obtained great favours from him, you will become pre-eminent among all people. You will obtain well-wishers and ministers who will give you good advice. Then create internal dissension, like smashing a *bilva* fruit[932] with another bilva fruit. Conclude agreements with his enemies and destroy his forces. Make his mind turn to objects that are not easily attainable—women, garments, beds, seats, vehicles, extremely expensive houses, birds, different kinds of animals, juices, perfumes and fruit. Becoming addicted to these, he will then ruin himself. If you are countered, you should not ignore that. However, if you wish to control the enemy, you should not do anything openly. The wise ones say that one should dwell with one's supreme enemy in his kingdom and by getting him addicted to unusual objects, ensuring the enemy's hardship. One must get him to work on tasks that are great and extremely difficult, such as constructing dams on rivers. Ensure that powerful ones counter him. Let the treasury be frittered away on extremely expensive gardens, beds, seats and other objects of pleasure and happiness. Praise sacrifices and gifts and describe these in the presence of brahmanas, so that they are kind towards you and pursue him like wolves. "There is no doubt that one who is pure in his conduct attains the supreme objective. Such a king obtains the most sacred of spots in heaven."[933] O one from Kosala! When his treasury is destroyed, he will come under the subjugation of the enemy. Whether he is addicted to dharma or adharma,[934] his enemies will take delight in whatever severs the root of his strength and riches. When a man confronts disaster, he blames destiny. When he is swiftly destroyed, there is no

[932]The fruit of the wood-apple tree.

[933]These are examples of the kinds of things that should be said.

[934]The vices are adharma and the sacrifices are dharma, but both deplete the treasury.

doubt that he will think that destiny is supreme. Make him perform the *vishvajita* sacrifice,[935] so that he is deprived of all his possessions. When his objectives are not accomplished and when he is afflicted, he will want to go to an eminent person. Suggest someone from an inferior varna, someone with a shaved head, knowledgeable in the dharma of renunciation. Desiring his own welfare, perhaps he will then resort to renunciation. Employ drugs that are known to have efficacy and are capable of destroying all enemies. Use these vile concoctions to destroy his elephants, horses and men. There are these and many other techniques of deceit that have been determined. O son of a king! If one is not a eunuch, one is capable of using these to conquer.'"'

Chapter 1435(107)

'"The prince said, 'O brahmana! I do not wish to live through fraud and deceit. I do not desire great riches, if they are not obtained through the use of dharma. O illustrious one! I said at the beginning that these should be avoided. I do not want anyone to doubt me and I desire my complete welfare. In this world, I desire to live through a dharma that does not cause injury. I am incapable of doing all this. It is not appropriate for me.'

'"The sage replied, 'O kshatriya! What you have spoken is deserving of you. O one who is wonderful in outlook! You are naturally intelligent. I will endeavour so that both of you attain your objectives. I will bring about an eternal alliance between the two of you. You have been born in a lineage like his. You are non-violent and extremely learned. You are accomplished in ensuring the welfare of a kingdom. Who will not make someone like you an adviser? You have confronted a supreme hardship and have abandoned your kingdom.

[935]A sacrifice that conquers the universe. It is a sacrifice in which one gives away all one's possessions.

O kshatriya! However, you wish to live through non-violent conduct. O son![936] The king of Videha is devoted to the truth and will come to my house. There is no doubt that he will do what I ask him to.'"

'Bhishma said, "The sage summoned the king of Videha and spoke these words to him. 'This one has been born in a lineage of kings and I know what is inside his mind. His soul is as pure as a mirror or the autumn moon. I have tested him in every way and do not see anything crooked in him. You should have an alliance with him. Trust him the way you trust me. O slayer of enemies! Without an adviser, you are incapable of ruling the kingdom. The adviser must be brave and full of intelligence. Both of these[937] cause fear for a king. Look towards the ruling of the kingdom. In this world, a person with dharma in his soul is rare and there is no one like him. This prince is accomplished in his soul. He is established in the path of the virtuous. With dharma at the forefront, you will do well to have him on your side. He will serve you and seize large numbers of the enemy. If he wishes to fight back against you, he will resort to his own dharma of being a kshatriya and try to win back the kingdom of his father and grandfathers in a battle. If you are engaged in your vow of conquest, you will fight back against him. O lord of Videha! However, if you do not fight, he will follow my instructions and remain under your control. Glance towards dharma and cast aside the inappropriate adharma. For the sake of desire or hatred, you should not abandon your own dharma. O son![938] Victory is not permanent. Nor is defeat permanent. One must give food and objects of pleasure to an enemy who has been defeated. Think yourself to be like him, confronting victory and defeat. O son! Those who seek to exterminate all danger end up exterminating their own selves.' He was thus addressed by that bull among brahmanas and replied in the following words, after having honoured and treated him well and taking the permission of the one who deserved worship. 'O immensely wise one! It is exactly as you have said. O immensely learned one! It is

[936]The word used is tata.

[937]Lack of valour and lack of intelligence.

[938]The word used is tata.

exactly as you have said. As you have said, people desire what brings the most benefit. What you have said is the best for both of us. I will follow your words and act exactly in accordance with them. This is supremely beneficial. I do not need to reflect about this.' The king of Videha summoned the one from Kosala and spoke these words to him. 'I have defeated you through the use of dharma, policy and strength. O supreme among kings! However, you have conquered me through your qualities. Though you have been defeated, do not have a low opinion of yourself. I do not disrespect your intelligence. I do not disrespect your manliness. Though you have been defeated, do not think of yourself as having been defeated. O king! Come to my house. You will be honoured and then go to your own house.' Having honoured the brahmana, the two of them trustingly went to the house. The lord of Videha made the lord of Kosala enter his house and honoured him with water for washing the feet, a gift and a mixture of honey.[939] He was honoured back in return and gave him his own daughter, with many kinds of gems. This is the supreme dharma for kings. Both victory and defeat must be endured."'

Chapter 1436(108)

'Yudhishthira said, "O scorcher of enemies! You have described the dharma, the conduct, the subsistence, the means of subsistence and the fruits for brahmanas, kshatriyas, vaishyas and shudras, the conduct of kings, the treasury, the means of making the treasury great, the means of increasing the qualities of the advisers, the prosperity of ordinary people, the six qualities[940] one must think of, the policy concerning the army, the means of knowing the wicked, the characteristics of the virtuous, the signs of those who are equal, inferior and superior, the means to satisfy neutral ones so that

[939]Respectively, *padya, arghya* and *madhuparka*, offered to a guest.
[940]Of the kingdom.

prosperity can be enhanced, the recommended means for sustaining those who have limited resources and about the method indicated in the texts against countries that are weaker. O descendant of the Bharata lineage! You have also described the conduct of someone who desires victory. O supreme among intelligent ones! I now wish to hear about the conduct towards ganas.[941] O descendant of the Bharata lineage! How do ganas prosper? How can they be prevented from breaking up? How do they conquer the enemy and obtain well-wishers? What is the cause of dissension in ganas and how do they confront destruction? It is my view that their sorrow results from the fact that there are many and it is difficult to keep counsel a secret. O scorcher of enemies! I wish to hear everything about this in entirety. O king! Tell me everything about how they can be prevented from breaking up."

'Bhishma replied, "O bull among the Bharata lineage! O lord of men! Greed and intolerance ignite enmity within ganas, families and royal lineages. Avarice begins to consume and intolerance comes after that. These two unite and reinforce each other, until everything is destroyed. They[942] use spies, secret counsel, force, seizure, conciliation, gifts and dissension and other techniques of decay, destruction and fear to weaken each other. Large numbers of ganas that work together are broken apart through gifts. Having been broken, all of them are distressed in their minds and, because of their fear, are quickly subjugated. The ganas are destroyed because of their divisions and, having been shattered, have to bow down before the enemy. Therefore, the ganas must always try to work together. If they are united, their strength and manliness increases and so does their prosperity. When they act together in this way, outsiders seek their friendship. Those who are learned and aged praise a situation where they serve each other. Having not retreated from that object

[941]The word gana has multiple meanings. In this context, it clearly means a small assembly or body. Beyond this, the context makes it difficult to pin it down. It could either mean an aristocracy around the king, or it could mean smaller countries that were like federations, ruled by an aristocracy, without a king.

[942]Different components of the gana.

of unity, they obtain happiness in every way. The best of the ganas follow dharma in conduct, establish themselves in their sacred texts and, following these, become prosperous. They are always engaged in good policy and do not hesitate to punish sons and brothers. The best among ganas prosper because they accept those who are humble. O mighty-armed one! In every way, these ganas are always engaged in ensuring prosperity through spies, secret plans, following ordinances and enhancing the treasury. O king! The ganas are prosperous when they always revere the wise, the brave, those who are great archers and those who base themselves on manliness in all their tasks. When ganas face difficulties and are confused—those who are wealthy, those who are brave, those who are knowledgeable about weapons and those who are accomplished in the sacred texts save them. O supreme among the Bharata lineage! Anger, dissension, fear, punishment, affliction, imprisonment and death immediately lead to ganas becoming subjugated. O king! That is the reason the foremost members of the gana must be given importance. The progress of other people depends mostly on them. O afflicter of enemies! Secret counsels and information about spies must be restricted to the foremost members. O descendant of the Bharata lineage! The entire gana should not get to hear about secret plans. The foremost members of the gana must work together for the welfare of the gana. When members of a gana act separately, have differing views or are divided in some other way, its prosperity suffers and it faces a disaster. When they have broken away from each other and base themselves on individual strengths alone, it is the task of the learned and foremost ones to swiftly restrain them. O king! If there is a conflict within the family and the aged ones in the family ignore this, this ensures that the gotras[943] break away from the gana. One must protect against internal dangers. External dangers are easier to handle. If an internal danger is generated, it severs the roots. If there are sentiments of sudden rage, avarice and natural confusion, and they do not speak to each other, this is a sign of defeat. They[944] are similar in birth. All of them are equally noble

[943]Clans.

[944]The members of the gana.

in lineage. But they are not equal in valour, intelligence, beauty and prosperity. If ganas suffer from the confusion of being disunited, they bow down before the enemy. That is the reason it is said that unity is the great refuge of ganas."'

Chapter 1437(109)

'Yudhishthira asked, "O descendant of the Bharata lineage! Great policy and the path of dharma have many branches. Is it your view that one element of dharma must be pursued the most? In your view, which is the task of dharma that is the most important, so that a man can obtain dharma in this world and after death?"

'Bhishma replied, "It is my view that worship of the mother, the father and the preceptor is the most important. If a man is engaged in this, he obtains great fame and the worlds. O son! O Yudhishthira! If they recognize any task, irrespective of whether it is for dharma or against dharma, it is your duty to honour and implement it. Without their permission, one must not think of something else as dharma. It has been prescribed that their suggestions amount to dharma. They are the three worlds. They are the three ashramas.[945] They are the three Vedas. They are the three fires. The father is said to be the *garhapatya* fire and the mother is the dakshina fire. The preceptor is the *ahavaniya* fire.[946] These three fires are the most important. If you pay attention to these three, you will conquer the three worlds. By always serving the father one can cross this world, by serving the mother, the world beyond this, and by serving the preceptor, Brahma's world. O descendant of the Bharata lineage! O fortunate one! If you conduct yourself well in the three worlds, you will obtain fame and dharma

[945] With the mother, the father and the preceptor, the number is three. It is not evident which of the four ashramas is being excluded, probably sannyasa.

[946] The garhapatya fire is the one that burns in the household, the dakshina fire is the one that burns in the southern direction and the ahavaniya fire is the sacrificial fire into which oblations are poured.

with extremely great fruits. One should not cross their policies. One should not eat before them. One should not censure them. One should always serve them. That is the supreme good deed. O lord of men! Through this, you will earn fame, merits, glory and the worlds. One who honours them is honoured in the three worlds. However, one who dishonours them is dishonoured and all his tasks become fruitless. O scorcher of enemies! A person who always disrespects these three seniors obtains neither this world nor the one hereafter. His fame is not radiant in the world hereafter. After that, nor does he obtain any great benefit. If I give everything away to them, it comes back to me, one hundred times and one thousand times more. O Yudhishthira! Therefore, the three worlds blaze before me. It is said that one good *acharya*[947]is superior to ten learned brahmanas, one *upadhyaya* is superior to ten acharyas and the father is superior to ten upadhyayas. However, a mother is superior to ten fathers and even to the entire earth. In her importance, there is no preceptor who is equal to a mother. However, it is my view that a preceptor is superior to a father and a mother.[948] O descendant of the Bharata lineage! Both the mother and the father unite to give birth, but the father and the mother create the body alone. The birth that is instructed by the acharya is divine. It is without old age and without death. Even if they have caused an injury, the mother and the father must never be killed.[949] If you act in this way, you will not be censured. Nor will they reprimand you. The gods and the rishis know about those who try to follow dharma. One who imparts comprehension, one who speaks about the truth in one's ears and one who grants immortality[950] should be thought of as a father and a mother. Knowing this, one should not act injuriously towards him. When a person has heard about knowledge from a

[947]Preceptor. A preceptor who is an upadhyaya is superior to a preceptor who is an acharya. Etymologically, an acharya teaches only good conduct, while an upadhyaya's teachings are more spiritual.

[948]There is no conflict, because Bhishma is referring to general views, as well as to his own.

[949]This is not a reference to an ordinary individual killing the parents. It is more a reference to the king imposing punishment on the king's parents.

[950]A reference to a preceptor.

preceptor but does not honour him in thought and deeds even when he is present, he must be corrected by other preceptors and those preceptors also deserve to be respected. Therefore, one who desires for the ancient dharma must make efforts to worship and honour all these seniors, giving them their shares. A person who pleases his father also pleases his grandfather. If he is affectionate towards his mother, he reveres the entire earth. If he is affectionate towards his upadhyaya, he worships Brahma. Therefore, if he worships his mother, his father and his preceptor, he pleases the rishis and the gods, together with the ancestors. In one's conduct, one should never disrespect the preceptor, nor the mother and the father, because they are like the preceptor. They should not be censured and they will not reprimand you. The gods, together with the rishis, know that preceptors must be treated well. In thoughts and in deeds, one should not injure the upadhyaya, the father and the mother. A wicked person who does that commits a sin that is worse than killing a foetus. There is no one in the world as wicked as he. We have not heard of any salvation for four—one who harms a friend, one who is an ingrate, one who kills a woman and one who is slanderous. For the acts of men in this world, all this has been created as great instruction. This is most beneficial and there is nothing that is superior to this. Following all kinds of dharma, I have told you this."'

Chapter 1438(110)

'Yudhishthira asked, "O descendant of the Bharata lineage! If a man wishes to base himself on dharma, how should he conduct himself? O learned one! O bull among the Bharata lineage! I wish to know. Tell me. Both truth and falsehood pervade the world. O king! Therefore, if a man is determined to follow dharma, how should he act vis-à-vis these two? What is truth? What is falsehood? What is eternal dharma? When should one speak the truth? When should one utter a lie?"

'Bhishma replied, "Truthful speech is virtuous. There is nothing superior to truth. O descendant of the Bharata lineage! In this world, this is an extremely difficult thing to understand and I will tell you the truth about this. When falsehood is truth and when truth is falsehood, one should not speak the truth and one should utter a lie. A juvenile person is confused about truth that is injurious. One who can discriminate between truth and falsehood knows about dharma. There may be an extremely terrible man who is ignoble and unaccomplished in his wisdom. However, even he can obtain extremely great merits, such as Balaka did when he killed a blind being.[951] What is extraordinary in this? But there can be a person who desires dharma, but acts like one who does not know dharma. On the banks of the Ganga, Koushika perpetrated a great sin. What you have asked me is complicated when it becomes extremely difficult to state what dharma is. It is extremely difficult to enumerate it, even if one resorts to reasoning. The words of dharma were created for the prosperity of beings. It is certain that anything that does not cause injury is dharma. It is said that dharma is anything that holds up.[952] Beings are held up through dharma. It is certain that anything that serves to hold up is dharma. There are some who say that dharma is that which is laid down in the *shruti* texts, but there are other people who do not agree. I cannot find fault with this, since everything is not laid down there. If someone asks, desiring the riches of others, one should not answer.[953] It is certain that not telling them would have been dharma. If one can escape without speaking, one should not speak. However, if not speaking gives rise to suspicion, one must certainly speak. Having thought about it, in that situation, when one consorts with wicked people, uttering a lie is superior to

[951]The Balaka story has been recounted in Section 73 (Volume 7). The hunter Balaka killed a blind beast that was causing injury. The Koushika story has also been recounted in Section 73 (Volume 7). An ascetic named Koushika spoke the truth and caused great harm. There were robbers who pursued some people, desiring their riches, and Koushika told the robbers where those people were hidden.

[952]From the etymological root for holding up, *dhri*.

[953]A reference to the Koushika story.

speaking the truth, even if one has taken an oath. If it is possible, one must never give riches to the likes of those. If riches are given to wicked people, this makes the giver suffer. Even if this involves an injury to one's body, it is better not to give them what they wish. However, there may be witnesses who have to speak to ascertain the nature of the truth. If they do not speak what must be spoken, they are liars.[954] If life is at stake and at the time of a marriage, one should lie. So should one for the sake of preserving riches or for the sake of ensuring dharma for others. However, if he does this out of a desire to share in the dharma of others, he is begging for dharma and is inferior. If someone has promised to pay and later deviates from his duty, he must be compelled by force. If a person deviates from a pledge that has been taken in accordance with dharma, then he establishes himself in adharma. A deceitful person may deviate from his own dharma, but still pretend to live in accordance with it. He is evil and fraudulent in his life and must be restrained in every possible way. All the wicked people in the world are certain to strive for riches. If one tolerates them or if one eats with them, one is wicked in conduct and is certain to fall down. Such a person will be dislodged from gods and men and it will be as if he is dead already. He will be miserable because his riches will be taken away and his remaining alive becomes pointless. One must make efforts to tell him, 'This is the dharma that you should find agreeable.' It is certain that there is no dharma for those who are wicked. If one kills a person who has reached such a state, one does not suffer from any sin. That person has already been slain because of his deeds and is only killing someone who has already been slain. Anyone who concludes an agreement with such a person, whose intelligence has been destroyed and whose life is wicked, behaves like a crow or a vulture.[955] When they are freed from their bodies and rise upwards, they are reborn in those wombs. Whichever is the way in which a man behaves towards one's own self, that is the conduct one should

[954]This shloka breaks the continuity in the argument about not speaking the truth. The argument resumes after this shloka.

[955]Examples of deceit.

show towards him and this is dharma. Deceit should be used against those who are deceitful. Those who are virtuous must be repaid with virtuous conduct."'

Chapter 1439(111)

'Yudhishthira said, "Here and there, beings can be tormented by different kinds of sentiments. How can they tide over difficulties? O grandfather! Tell me that."

'Bhishma replied, "The cited ashramas for brahmanas have already been recounted. If they follow these with controlled souls, they will be able to tide over difficulties. Those who are without deceit, those who meditate, those who remain within the confines of prescribed conduct and those who restrain material desires are able to tide over difficulties. Those who always offer their dwellings to guests, those who are always without malice and those who are always engaged in studying are able to tide over difficulties. Those who follow the conduct of their mother and father, those who know about dharma and those who do not sleep during the day are able to tide over difficulties. Those who have intercourse with their own virtuous wives, at the right season and not outside the season, and those righteous ones who observe agnihotra are able to tide over all difficulties. Kings who give up excessive desire for riches, who are full of the rajas quality and who protect the kingdom are able to tide over all difficulties. Brave ones who give up the fear of death in battles and desire to triumph in accordance with dharma are able to tide over all difficulties. Those who do not commit sins in deeds, thought and speech and impose the rod of chastisement on beings are able to tide over all difficulties. Those who speak the truth, even if life is at stake, and those who set an example to all beings are able to tide over all difficulties. Brahmanas who do not study what should not be studied and are always engaged in asceticism and good austerities are able to tide over all difficulties. Those whose acts do not have fraudulent objectives, those whose words are extremely truthful and those who obtain riches through virtuous means are able to tide over all difficulties. Those who torment themselves through austerities, those who observe brahmacharya in their youth and those who have cleansed through their learning of the Vedas and vows are able to tide over all difficulties. Those who have controlled rajas, those who have controlled tamas and those great-souled ones who are based on truth are able to tide over all difficulties. Those who cause no fear, those who are never frightened and those who look on all people as their own selves are able to tide over all difficulties. Those bulls among men who are not tormented by the prosperity of others and those who refrain from common norms of behaviour are able to tide over all difficulties. Those who worship all the gods, those who listen to all kinds of dharma and those who are faithful and controlled are able to tide over all the difficulties. Those who do not desire respect but respect others instead, and those who pay no attention to any honours they obtain, are able to tide over all difficulties. Desiring offspring, those who perform shraddha ceremonies from one tithi to another and those who are extremely pure in their minds are able to tide over all difficulties. Those who are not enraged, those who pacify the anger of others and those who are not enraged at the servants are able to tide over all difficulties. Those men who have always avoided, since birth, *madhu*, flesh and liquor are able to tide over all difficulties.[956] Those who only eat to remain alive, those who have intercourse only for the sake of having children and those who speak only to state the truth are able to tide over all difficulties. Those who are devoted to Narayana, the lord of all beings, the creator and the destroyer of the universe, are able to tide over all difficulties. His eyes are like red lotuses. He is attired in yellow garments. He is mighty-armed. He is Achyuta. He is your well-wisher, brother, friend and ally.[957]

[956]We have deliberately not translated the word madhu. The text uses a general word for liquor, *madya*, and madhu is mentioned in addition. Madhu could be honey, fermented or otherwise. It could also be a specific kind of liquor, such as *madhvi*.

[957]Krishna was a cousin by birth. He was also linked through matrimonial alliances.

Like a strip of leather, all these worlds are wrapped around his person. He is the lord of riches. His soul cannot be thought of. He is Govinda Purushottama. O bull among men! He is engaged in ensuring Jishnu's[958] welfare. O king! You cannot withstand him. He is Vaikuntha[959] Purushottama. A person who faithfully seeks refuge with Narayana Hari is able to tide over difficulties. There is no need for me to even think about this. A person who reads or hears about this account of tiding over difficulties and a person who has it read out to brahmanas is able to tide over difficulties. O unblemished one! I have instructed you about what must be done, so that a man can tide over difficulties, in this world and in the next."'

Chapter 1440(112)

'Yudhishthira said, "There are those who are not tranquil, but seem tranquil in form. There are those who are tranquil, but have an appearance that is not tranquil. O father! How can we differentiate between such men?"

'Bhishma replied, "On this, an ancient history is recounted about a conversation between a tiger and a jackal. O Yudhishthira! Listen to it. In ancient times, there was a city named Purika. It was prosperous and the king was Pourika. He was cruel and the worst among men, with an inclination to cause injury to others. When his lifespan was over, he obtained an end that is not desired. Because of his wicked earlier deeds, he became a jackal. However, he remembered his earlier life and developed a supreme indifference. He did not eat flesh, even when it had been brought to him by others. He was non-violent towards all beings. He was truthful in speech and firm in his vows. He acted according to his wishes and his food became fruit that had fallen down. The jackal lived in a cremation ground and he liked this.

[958] Arjuna's.

[959] Vaikuntha is Vishnu's name, as well as the name of his abode.

He liked it because he had been born there and no other dwelling place appealed to him. All the others of his species could not tolerate his purity. Though they addressed him respectfully, they tried to make him budge from his intentions. 'You dwell in this terrible grove of our ancestors, yet you desire to be pure. Since you are a flesh-eater, this is a perversity. Be like us. All of us will give you food. This is your food. Therefore, enjoy it and give up this purity.' Having heard their words, he controlled himself. He used gentle and respectful words that were not harsh, but were full of reason, to reply. 'Birth is not important for me. Lineage is created by conduct. I desire for those deeds that will extend my fame. Even though I dwell in a cremation ground, I am seeking to make myself tranquil through meditation. The atman leads to deeds. The ashrama is not an indicator of dharma. While dwelling in a hermitage, one can kill a brahmana. Someone who does not dwell in a hermitage can donate a cow. Is the first not a sin and is the act of donation going to be fruitless? Because of greed, all of you are always engaged in eating. You do not see that you are confused and that you are bound down by these sins. I do not believe in this conduct. This is wicked and reprehensible and takes a person away from the objective. It leads to evil in this world and the next. Therefore, I do not like this conduct.'

'"There was a tiger that was famous for its valour. He formed the view that he[960] was pure and learned. He showed him honour like the ones he himself received and thought that he would appoint him as his own adviser. 'O tranquil one! I know the kind of person you are. Come and spend your life with me. Enjoy the objects of pleasure you desire and do not touch the ones you dislike. We are famous as being fierce. If it is known that you are with us, we will be known as gentle killers and that will be a desirable objective.'

'"He was honoured by the great-souled lord of the deer in these words. Exhibiting a little humility, the jackal replied in these modest words. 'O king of the animals! The words that you have spoken to me are worthy of you. You are searching for advisers who are pure and are accomplished in dharma and artha. O brave one! You are

[960]The jackal.

incapable of ruling this great dominion without an adviser, with a wicked adviser, or with one who seeks to physically injure you. You should get advisers who are devoted to you, those who are not attached to anything else, those who do not shout at each other, those who desire victory, those who are not covetous, those who are beyond deceit, those who are wise, those who are engaged in ensuring welfare and those who are spirited. You should worship these immensely fortunate ones like your preceptors and ancestors. O lord of animals! There is nothing that pleases me more than my present satisfaction. I do not desire happiness, objects of pleasure, prosperity and your refuge. My conduct will not gel with your earlier servants. They will find unhappiness in my conduct and cause dissension between you and me. You are a refuge that is praiseworthy and I respect your radiance. You have cleansed your soul and are extremely fortunate. You are not cruel even towards the wicked. You are far-sighted and great in endeavour. You are broad in your objectives and immensely strong. You are accomplished and all your acts are successful. Your thoughts serve to adorn you. However, someone like me is extremely content and serving another will mean misery. I am inexperienced in serving another and roam around in the woods as I please. For all those who dwell in a refuge with the king, their faults face his rage. A person who lives in the forest is alone. He is without fear and without any ties. If one is summoned by a king, there can be fear in the heart. But for someone who is satisfied in the forest, subsisting on roots and fruit, there is nothing like that. Food and drink are easily procured. On the other side, there is fear. Looking at these, I certainly think that happiness comes from withdrawal. Some servants are punished by kings because of their crimes. But many more virtuous servants are harmed because of false accusations and head towards destruction. Therefore, if the king of the animals thinks that I should perform this task, I wish for an agreement about how I am going to be treated. You must honour what I say and you must listen to my beneficial words. You must remain firmly established in the conduct that you have thought of for me. I will never think of having consultations with any of your other advisers. Those others are politically wise and, wishing to protect themselves, will speak false words about me. I will meet you alone and will privately tell you what is good for you. For any tasks that concern your kin, you will not ask me what is good or bad. Having consulted me, you will not subsequently exhibit any violence towards your advisers. If you are enraged with my kin, you will not bring them down by exercising the rod of punishment.' Thus addressed, the king of animals agreed and honoured him. The jackal became an adviser in the tiger's abode.

'"On seeing that he was so well honoured and engaged in his tasks, the former servants hated him and repeatedly conspired together. They placated the jackal through signs of friendship and made him enter.[961] They were evil in their intelligence and desired to make him a part of the wicked group. They had earlier got used to abducting the property of others. However, now that they were controlled by the jackal, they were incapable of obtaining any of these possessions. They wished to tempt him with accounts of upliftment. They sought to seduce his intelligence with great riches. However, that immensely wise one did not deviate from his patience. Those others decided to bring about his destruction and agreed on a plan. The king of animals desired meat that had been prepared well. They stole it themselves and placed it in his[962] house. He[963] knew everything about who had stolen it, the nature of the plan and the reasons behind it. However, he remained tolerant because of the agreement he had made at the time of agreeing to become an adviser. 'O king! If you desire my friendship, you will not pay heed to a false accusation.' At the time of the meal, the stolen meat could not be seen. The king of animals instructed that the thief should be found. The deceitful ones described this to the king of the animals. 'Your adviser is learned and prides himself on his wisdom. He has stolen the meat.' When he heard about the jackal's fickleness, the tiger was enraged. The intolerant king desired to have him killed. On detecting the opportunity, the former ministers said, 'He is trying to shatter the means of subsistence for all of us. However, these deeds

[961]Enter the group of wicked advisers.
[962]The jackal's.
[963]The jackal.

of his are protected because he has your affection. O lord! But he is not the kind of person that you were told he was. His words suggest that he follows dharma. However, he is naturally cruel. This wicked one wears the deceit of dharma, but is actually false in his conduct. For the sake of furthering his objectives and for the sake of his food, he has deceitfully followed these vows.' On learning that the meat had been stolen and on hearing their words, the tiger instructed that the jackal should be killed.

'"On hearing the tiger's words, the tiger's mother arrived there. She wished to speak some beneficial words and make the king of animals understand. 'O son! You should not accept this. It seems to be full of fraud and deceit. An honest person is being falsely accused by those who are dishonest. Those wicked ones have suffered from the friction caused by his work. Those desiring to cause injury cannot tolerate any beneficial act. They seek to impute taints to a pure person and bring him down. The greedy hate the pure and the weak hate the spirited. Stupid people hate learned ones and poor people hate those who are extremely wealthy. Those who follow adharma hate those who follow dharma and those who are ugly hate those who are handsome. Many learned people are greedy and all of them earn a living through deceit. Wicked ones accuse an innocent person, even if he possesses Brihaspati's intelligence. When the meat was stolen, your house was empty. That virtuous one did not wish to touch it even when it was given to him. Falsehood has the appearance of truth. Truth can seem to be like falsehood. Many kinds of things can be seen, but they need to be examined. The sky seems to be flat. The firefly looks like a spark of fire. But the sky is not flat, nor does the firefly have any fire. Therefore, unless there is a direct witness, everything must be examined. If one does not determine the truth through examination, one is tormented subsequently. O son! This is not a difficult thing to do, for a lord to get someone else killed. In this world, forgiveness is praised and brings prosperity. O son! He was appointed by you and has become famous among the ministers. A capable person is obtained with difficulty and a well-wisher should be supported. If a person is otherwise pure, and is tainted because one accepts the accusations of others, one taints oneself, as well as the minister, and is swiftly destroyed.' At this, a person from the mass of the jackal's enemies presented himself. He had dharma in his soul and told him about the deceit that had been committed.

'"Once his character was known, he[964] was honoured well and freed. The king of animals repeatedly embraced him affectionately. The jackal was exteremely learned about the sacred texts. He was tormented because of the intolerance and, taking the permission of the king of the animals, wished to fast himself to death.[965] However, with tears of affection flowing down from his eyes, the tiger restrained the jackal, who was devoted to dharma. He honoured him and was honoured back in return. The jackal looked at the tiger, who was overcome with affection. In a voice that was choking with tears, he bowed down and spoke these respectful words. 'I was first honoured by you and then later subjected to humiliation. You made an enemy out of me and I should not reside with you any longer. All these only serve to further the cause of the enemy—those who are themselves dissatisfied, those who have been dislodged from their positions, those who have been deprived of their honours, those servants who have themselves brought about their downfall, those who have been brought down by others, those who are weak, those who are greedy, those who are cruel, those who have been flung into prison, those who are proud and have lost their possessions, those who are extremely spirited, but have lost the means, those who are tormented, those who have decayed because of a flood of vices, those who are in hiding and those whose possessions have been seized. You have humiliated me and subsequently wish to instate me. How can you trust me? How can I trust you again? You took me to be capable. You instated me after examining me. You broke the pledge we had made and humiliated me. In the assembly, you spoke about me as a person with virtuous conduct. Had you protected the pledge, you would not have spoken about my bad qualities. Since I have been disrespected, how can you have confidence in me? I will also suffer from anxiety about you and not trust you. You will suspect me. I will be frightened and the enemy will see this as a weakness. Those who

[964]The jackal.

[965]Praya, practised when one has had enough of life and wishes to fast to death.

are not content are very difficult to satisfy. This task will provide a lot of scope for deceit. Those who have come together suffer when they are separated.[966] Those who have come together can also be separated with difficulty. When those who are separated are brought together, there is neither love, nor affection. Sometimes, they are seen to be frightened of each other. While thoughts may focus on the work, gentleness is extremely rare. It is extremely difficult to know about the minds of men, since they are both stable and unstable. Among one hundred, one can find only one who is capable and strong. Suddenly, there is something that makes a man rise to an eminent position. He acts with greatness, intelligence and dexterity, regardless of whether the situation is good or bad.' In this way, the jackal addressed the king with many words that were full of dharma and artha, comforting and delighting him. The intelligent jackal then took his leave of the king of animals. He seated himself in praya, gave up his body and went to heaven."'

Chapter 1441(113)

'Yudhishthira asked, "What must a king do? What acts bring him happiness? O supreme among those who uphold dharma! Tell me everything about this in detail."

'Bhishma replied, "I will certainly tell you this. Listen to what has been determined about tasks. These are the duties of a king and having performed these, he will be happy. However, we have heard an extremely great account about a camel and he should not act in that way. O Yudhishthira! Listen to this. In the age of Prajapati, there was a great camel who could recall his earlier existences. He engaged in great austerities in a forest and was rigid in his vows. At the end of those austerities, the lord was delighted and the grandfather[967] delighted him by graning him a boon.

[966]These shlokas are cryptic and some liberty has been taken.

[967]Brahma.

'"The camel said, 'O illustrious one! Through your favours, let my neck become extremely long. O lord! Let me be able to graze one hundred yojanas in front of me.'"

'Bhishma said, "Having been thus addressed, the great-souled one, the granter of boons, agreed. Having obtained that supreme boon, the camel went to his own forest. Since he had obtained the boon, the evil-minded one became lazy. Confounded by destiny, the evil-souled one no longer wished to go out to graze. There was an occasion when he had stretched out his neck one hundred yojanas to graze, without any exhaustion in his mind. A great storm arrived. The one with the soul of an animal placed his head and neck inside a cave, where they got stuck. Monsoon arrived and a great flood submerged the world. There was a hungry jackal who was shivering from the cold. Afflicted by the water, he and his wife quickly entered the cave. O bull among the Bharata lineage! The flesh-eater was suffering greatly from hunger. On seeing the camel's neck, he began to eat it. The animal[968] realized that he was being eaten. Extremely miserable, he tried to contract himself. The animal flung his neck around, upwards and downwards. However, the jackal and his wife continued to eat him. The jackal killed and ate the camel. When the rains were over, he emerged through the mouth of the cave. Thus, the evil-minded camel was led to his destruction. Behold the great sin that progressively comes about because of laziness. You must abandon such conduct. Resort to yoga and control your senses. Manu has said that the foundation of victory is intelligence. O descendant of the Bharata lineage! Tasks performed with intelligence are the best, those performed with arms are middling and those performed with thighs are the worst, because they are meant to bear loads. O unblemished one! If a person is accomplished and controls his senses, if he listens to secret counsel and if he has excellent aides, then his kingdom lasts. O Yudhishthira! Those who examine the objectives are established in this world. With the help of their aides, they are capable of ruling over the entire earth. Virtuous ones, who know about the ordinances, have spoken about this earlier. You are like the great Indra in your

[968]The camel.

influence. I have also spoken to you about the foresight of the sacred texts. O king! Conduct yourself in accordance with that."'

Chapter 1442(114)

'Yudhishthira asked, "O bull among the Bharata lineage! Having obtained a kingdom, how can a weak king, without any resources, station himself against a stronger one?"

'Bhishma replied, "O descendant of the Bharata lineage! In this connection, an ancient history is recounted about a conversation between the ocean and the rivers. The eternal ocean, the lord of the rivers and the residence of the enemies of the gods,[969] himself had a doubt about this and asked all the rivers. 'I see trees lying down, with their roots and their branches. When you overflow, you bring these down. Though I see others[970] there, I never see any reeds. The reeds that grow along your banks are thin in body and slight of essence. Do you ignore them? Are you incapable? Or have they done you a good turn? I desire to hear all your views on this. When you overflow the banks, why are they not shattered? Why do they not come under your control?' At this, the river Ganga replied in supreme words that were full of meaning. She told the reason to the ocean, the lord of the rivers. 'A tree remains in a single spot. It does not move from that place. Because it foolishly tries to resist us, it is forced to give up that spot. However, when it sees the flood approaching, a reed bends down. The flood passes over it and it remains rooted to its spot. It knows the time and the place and bows down. A tree does not. Because a reed is pliable and does not try to resist, it is not carried away. Herbs, trees and creepers that do not bow down before the force of the wind and the water are overcome.' If a person does not tolerate the powerful onslaught of

[969]The demons reside in the ocean.

[970]Smaller plants.

an enemy who is stronger, he is swiftly destroyed. One who knows the superiority and inferiority in the strength of one's own self and that of the enemy is wise and knows how to conduct himself. He is not overcome. In this way, when a learned one thinks that the enemy is extremely strong, he resorts to the conduct of reeds. That is a sign of wisdom."'

Chapter 1443(115)

'Yudhishthira asked, "O descendant of the Bharata lineage! O scorcher of enemies! How should a learned and mild man behave, when he is abused in an assembly by someone who is stupid, voluble and harsh?"

'Bhishma replied, "O protector of the earth! Listen to what has been sung about this objective. An intelligent person must always tolerate a stupid man with limited intelligence. If he is not angered, he obtains the good deeds of the person who is wrathful.[971] If he is not angered, he passes on his own evil deeds to the intolerant and wrathful one. That other one is afflicted and is quaking like a *tittibha*.[972] He should be ignored. He will be hated by people and will be unsuccessful. A person who is wicked in his deeds will always boast and say, 'In an assembly of people, I have said this about a revered person. He is ashamed and withered. He is standing there, as if he is dead.' A shameless person will thus boast about a task that should not be boasted about. A person who is controlled should ignore such a person, who is worst among men. If someone with limited intelligence says something, it must always be tolerated. Whether that inferior person is praising or censuring, what can he possibly do? He will be as unsuccessful as a foolish crow cawing in the forest. If evil-acting people could achieve something through

[971] The one who is abusing him.
[972] A waterhen.

the use of eloquent words, there would be some purpose in those words. However, those who seek to injure achieve nothing. Those who are engaged in such conduct only establish that they are born from perverse ejaculation.[973] He is like a peacock, exhibiting its genitals while it is dancing. One should never converse with a person who acts in this way. He is impure and finds good conduct difficult. One should not speak to him. A man who speaks of a person's good qualities in his presence and criticizes him behind his back is like a dog in this world and loses all the worlds hereafter. Whatever he gives to one hundred people and whatever oblations he offers are destroyed in an instant, if he criticizes someone behind his back. Therefore, a wise person avoids such an evil-minded one, like a virtuous person avoids the flesh of a dog. When an evil-souled person abuses a good-souled person, he exhibits all his own faults, like a snake extending its hood. If a person is engaged in his own tasks and a second person acts against him in those tasks, that second person's intelligence is like that of an ass that has got submerged in a pile of ashes and dust. You must stay away from men who are like angry wolves, always engaged in abusing people, or those who are like crazy and trumpeting elephants, or those who are like extremely fierce dogs. Such a man treads along the path of the fickle, lacking in control and humility and full of wickedness. Behaving like an enemy, he always wishes to injure you. Shame on such an evil-minded man! If such a person answers you back, do not assume a pained expression. Be at peace. Those who are firm in their intelligence do not approve of the superior consorting with the inferior. If he is enraged, he may slap you with his palm.[974] Or he may fling dust and chaff at you. He may frighten you by baring his teeth. It has been proven that stupid people are violent when they are enraged. Avoid extremely evil-souled and wicked men and tolerate them in assemblies. If a person always reads this illustration, he never suffers from any unpleasantness that is the result of speech."'

[973] A reflection on parentage, bastard. In general, a shameless person.

[974] Literally, the text says five fingers.

Chapter 1444(116)

'Yudhishthira asked, "O grandfather! O immensely wise one! I have a great doubt about policy. You must dispel it. You are one who has advanced our lineage. O father! You have spoken and educated me about evil-souled ones of wicked conduct and the words that they speak. What is beneficial for royal policy? What brings happiness to the family? Now, and in the future, what ensures acquisition and preservation? What is good for the sons and grandsons and what brings prosperity to the kingdom? In terms of food and drink, what is good for the body? Tell me that. When a king is instated in the kingdom and is surrounded by friends, how does he delight the subjects? What happens if he encounters ill-wishers? The forces of love and affection may lead to his being seized by the wicked. Though he should adorn the righteous, he may become subject to his senses. Even if all of his servants have been born in good lineages, they may exhibit bad qualities. The king may not realize the fruits from the appointment of good servants. These are the kinds of doubts I have about the extremely difficult end of rajadharma. You are like Brihaspati in your intelligence and you should instruct me. O tiger among men! You are engaged in the welfare of the lineage. Instruct us. Kshatta[975] is accomplished and wise and instructs us about these things all the time. I will hear beneficial words about the welfare of the family and the welfare of the kingdom. This is like undecaying amrita. Having heard this, I will sleep happily. What kind of servants should one have? What are their attributes and qualities? What are the recommendations about the families of those one entrusts with tasks? Without servants, the king cannot carry out the task of protection alone. O descendant of the Bharata lineage! All those born in good lineages blame the kingdom and one is incapable of ruling the kingdom alone. O father! Without aides, no objectives can be attained. O bull among the Bharata lineage! Having obtained them, one must always protect them."

[975]Vidura.

'Bhishma replied, "If all the servants are learned about jnana and vijnana, if they seek welfare, if they are born in good lineages and if they are gentle, then that kingdom obtains the fruits. If the ministers are born in good lineages, cannot be corrupted and dwell with him, if they are learned about the science of relationships, if they offer advice to the king, if they know about what will happen in the future and can act accordingly, if they are skilled in their knowledge of time and if they do not sorrow over what is already past, then that kingdom obtains the fruits. If the aides are truthful in deeds, looking upon happiness and unhappiness equally and if they are devoted to thinking about prosperity, then that kingdom obtains the fruits. If citizens of the country are never afflicted and never suffer, if they are superior and devote themselves to righteous paths, then that kingdom obtains the fruits. If people in charge of maintaining accounts are always learned and satisfied, if they are engaged in extending the treasury, then that king is a supreme one. If the stores are maintained by learned aides who are engaged in accumulation, if these officers are not avaricious and are protected because of their qualities, if the judicial proceedings in the city give rise to good fruits, if the practices of Shankha and Likhita[976] are observed, then a share in the fruits of dharma is obtained. A king who knows about rajadharma will collect such men and ensure the six aspects of policy. He obtains a share in the fruits of dharma."'

Chapter 1445(117)

'Bhishma said, "In this connection, an ancient history is recounted. Among people, this has always been cited as an instance of good conduct and this illustrates the point. I heard it in the hermitage of Rama, Jamadagni's son, when it was recounted by

[976]The story of these two sages has been recounted earlier.

that supreme among rishis. There was a great forest, inhabited by no other men. There was only a self-controlled rishi who had restrained his senses and subsisted on roots and fruit. He had initiated himself into the task of supreme control. He was tranquil, pure and devoted to great studies. He had cleansed himself through fasting and was always established in the path of the virtuous. The intelligent and righteous one was seated there, looking upon all beings as equal. All the residents of the forest approached him—lions, tigers, *sharabha*s, large and crazy elephants, leopards, rhinos, bears and others that were terrible to behold. All these predatory beasts would ask him about his welfare. They were like the rishi's disciples and did what was agreeable to him. All of them would ask about his welfare and then depart.

'"But there was a village animal that would never leave the great sage and this was a dog. It was faithfully devoted to him and was weak and thin because of the constant fasting. It ate fruits and roots, was calm and acted in virtuous ways. When the rishi was seated, it would be near the great sage's feet. It was severely bound to him by ties of affection and its behaviour was like that of a human. Once, an immensely valorous and carnivorous leopard arrived there. It was cruel, like Death, and the wicked one came there for the sake of the dog. It was thirsty and licked its lips. It lashed its tail around. Since it was hungry, it was in search of some flesh and its mouth gaped. O lord of men! O immensely intelligent one! Listen. On seeing that cruel one advance, to save its life, the dog went to the sage and said, 'O illustrious one! A leopard, the enemy of dogs, wishes to kill me. O great sage! Through your favours, ensure that I face no fear from it.' The sage replied, 'O son! Do not be frightened. You will never face death from a leopard. You will give up your form of a dog and become a leopard.' The dog became a leopard and its complexion became golden. Its limbs were spotted and its teeth were large. It dwelt fearlessly in the forest. However, an extremely terrible tiger arrived there. It was hungry and its mouth gaped open. It desired some blood and approached the leopard, licking the corners of its mouth. On seeing the hungry tiger with a gaping mouth arrive in the forest, the leopard wished to save its life and sought refuge with the rishi. Since they used to live together, the rishi acted affectionately towards it, as he had always done. He changed the leopard into a tiger that was stronger than its enemy. O lord of the earth! On seeing this, the tiger no longer attacked it. Having become a strong tiger that lived on flesh, the dog no longer had any desire to touch and enjoy roots and fruit. A lord of deer always desires residents of the forest. O great king! This tiger also acted in this way. Once, having killed a deer and satisfied itself on this, the tiger was asleep at the foot of a tree. A crazy elephant, which looked like a newly arisen cloud, arrived there. It was huge and its temples were shattered. It was excellent[977] and possessed a broad head. It had superb tusks and was gigantic in form. Its roar was like the rumbling of the thunder. On seeing that mad elephant advance, insolent and crazy, the tiger was terrified of the elephant and sought refuge with the rishi. The supreme among rishis turned the tiger into an elephant. On seeing its form, which was like that of a giant cloud, the other elephant was frightened. It[978] was delighted and roamed around amidst clusters of lotuses and frankincense thickets, adorning its body with pollen from lotuses. The handsome elephant roamed around near the rishi's cottage and time passed. After several nights, a maned lion arrived at that spot and its mane was tawny. The lion was terrible and hailed from mountainous regions, having slain families of elephants. On seeing the lion advance, the elephant was terrified on account of the lion. It was afflicted and, trembling out of fear, sought refuge with the rishi. The sage then turned that king of elephants into a lion and the wild lion ignored the elephant, taking it to belong to the same species. On seeing a more powerful one, the wild lion was terrified and disappeared. The lion dwelt happily in that forest hermitage. However, the other smaller animals that dwelt in the hermitage were terrified to be seen there and were always frightened for their lives. But it so happened with the progress of time that a

[977]This is inaccurate, but there is nothing else one can do. The word used is *padmi* (*padmini* for female elephants). These are elephants with the marks of lotuses on their bodies.

[978]The dog that had become an elephant.

sharabha arrived in the sage's residence, desiring to kill the lion. It was powerful, carnivorous and sought to kill all beings. All beings found it to be fearful. It dwelt in the forest and it possessed eight legs that extended upwards. O scorcher of enemies! The sage turned it[979] into an extremely strong sharabha. The wild sharabha saw the sage's sharabha in front of him and on seeing that it was strong and fierce, quickly fled out of fear.

'"Once the sage had reduced it to the state of a sharabha, the sharabha was full of happiness and always dwelt by the side of the sage. The large numbers of animals in the forest were all terrified of the sharabha. O king! Desiring to save their lives, they fled in all the directions. Always engaged in the killing of animals, the sharabha was extremely satifisied. It was a flesh-eater and no longer desired to be peaceful and subsist on fruits and roots. Desiring blood, the powerful sharabha, born in the womb of a dog, was ungrateful and wished to kill the sage. Through the strength of his austerities and the sight of knowledge, the immensely wise sage divined this and spoke to the dog. 'You became a leopard from a dog and from a leopard you became a tiger. From a tiger you became an elephant with musth and from an elephant you became a lion. From an immensely strong lion you again became a sharabha. Because I was overcome with affection, I had forgotten about your lineage. O wicked one! You desire to act violently towards me, though I have caused you no harm. Therefore, you will go back to your own species. Become a dog.' The stupid one, evil in his soul, became a dog because it hated the sage and people. Because of the rishi's curse, the sharabha again assumed the form of a dog."'

Chapter 1446(118)

'Bhishma said, "Having assumed the nature of a dog, it was overcome by supreme misery. The rishi said 'hum'[980] and

[979]The lion.

[980]Mystical exclamation before a mantra.

expelled the wicked one from the hermitage. In this way, an intelligent king must know about goodness of conduct and purity and about uprightness, nature, spiritedness, lineage, conduct, learning, self-control, compassion, strength, valour, sentiments, tranquility and forgiveness. It is only then that extremely well-trained and skilled servants must be appointed. Without examination, the lord of the earth must not appoint servants. A king who is surrounded by those who have been born in inferior lineages will not obtain happiness. If a person who has naturally been born in a good lineage is reprimanded by the king through no fault of his own, because of the nobility of the lineage, his intelligence will not turn towards wicked deeds. Because of a shortage of virtuous people, if a person born in an inferior lineage is appointed, even if he thereby obtains extremely rare prosperity, once he is censured, he will turn towards enmity. O king! Born in a noble lineage, learned, wise, accomplished in jnana and vijnana, knowledgeable about the purport of all the sacred texts, tolerant, born within the country, grateful, strong, forgiving, self-controlled, with control over the senses, not avaricious, satisfied with one's lot, friendly towards the master and friends, an adviser who knows about the time and the place and is engaged in drawing people to him, one who shows honour, firm in his mind, a constant seeker of welfare, with good conduct in his own areas, knowledgeable about peace and war, knowledgeable about the three objectives,[981] loved by the residents of the city and the countryside, knowledgeable about vyuhas for defence and attack, knowledgeable about how one can cheer the forces, knowledgeable about signs and expressions, skilled about marching and vehicles, learned about the training of elephants, devoid of ego, eloquent, courteous, self-controlled, powerful, reasonable in objectives, upright, one who associates with upright people, well dressed, good-looking, a leader, skilled about policy, possessing the six qualities, flexible, modest, capable, mild in speech, patient, gentle, extremely wealthy, capable of taking measures according to the time and the place—such people should not be ignored and should be made advisers. The kingdom will then extend, like moonlight from the lord of the planets.[982]

[981]Dharma, artha and kama.

[982]The moon.

'"The king must also possess these qualities and must be skilled in the sacred texts. His desire must be supreme dharma and he must be devoted to ruling the subjects. He must be patient, tolerant, pure, swift, exhibiting manliness at the appropriate time, ready to serve, learned, ready to listen, accomplished in reasoning, intelligent, firm in his mind, ready to implement what is fair, self-controlled, always pleasant in speech, forgiving when there is a catastrophe, ceaseless in generosity, ready to act on his own, possessing excellent gates,[983] pleasant to behold, ready to extend a hand to those who are distressed, always engaged in policy indicated by the learned, without ego, without opposite sentiments, without a tendency to act on everything, unwavering in pursuing a task that has been undertaken, a master who is loved by the servants, ready to bring people together, not rigid, always possessing a pleasant demeanour, generous, attentive towards the servants, without anger, extremely broad-minded, ready to use the rod of chastisement, not failing to use the rod of chastisement, a ruler who ensures acts of dharma, one who uses spies as his eyes, attentive towards enemies and always accomplished in dharma and artha. Such a king will possess a hundred qualities and you should be like that. O Indra among men! In sustaining the kingdom, you must search for warriors and excellent men as aides, those who possess all the qualities. The king who desires prosperity should not disrespect them. The warriors must be insolent in battle, grateful and accomplished in the use of weapons. They must know about the sacred texts of dharma and must possess foot soldiers. If they are accomplished in the use of chariots and skilled in the use of arrows and weapons, the king will extend his prosperity and win the earth. The king who is always engaged in attracting people to himself, who is engaged in enterprise and who is firm in friendship is supreme among kings. O descendant of the Bharata lineage! If one can collect one thousand men who are valiant horse riders, one is capable of conquering the entire earth."'

[983]This must be a reference to the organs of sense and action, often referred to as gates.

Chapter 1447(119)

'Bhishma said, "If a king acts so as to engage and employ servants who are unlike the dog, then he obtains the fruits of the kingdom. When the dog transgressed its own state and measure, it was no longer treated well. The dog should have remained in its own place. It transgressed it and became something else. It is a duty for a learned person to appoint servants appropriate to their families and lineages, so that they are engaged in their appropriate tasks. Inappropriate positions are condemned. If servants are engaged in the appropriate tasks, then because of the qualities of those servants, the king obtains fruits. A sharabha should be in a sharabha's place, a lion in a lion's. A tiger should be in a tiger's place, a leopard in a leopard's. As is proper, appoint servants in the appropriate tasks. If one desires the fruits of one's actions, servants should not be appointed in perverse positions. A king who transgresses the norms and appoints servants in perverse positions is foolish and does not delight the subjects. If the king desires his welfare, he should not have stupid, inferior and men born from bad lineages by his side, those who are unable to control their senses. Those who are at the side must be men who are virtuous, accomplished, brave, learned, without malice, without meanness, pure and skilled. Those who are appointed outside[984] by the king must be engaged in the welfare of beings, forgiving, accomplished, naturally pure and satisfied with their own states. A person who is like a lion should always be by the side of a lion. If a person who is not a lion is with a lion, the lion does not obtain any fruits. If a lion is engaged in obtaining the fruits of its deeds, but that lion is surrounded by dogs, because that lion is attended by dogs, it is incapable of enjoying any of the fruits. O Indra among men! In this way, with brave, wise and extremely learned people, who are born in noble lineages, one is capable of conquering the entire earth. O supreme among those who employ

[984]Outside the court.

servants! A lord of the earth must not collect servants who are without learning, without uprightness, without knowledge and without great riches by his side. The king must be attentive towards the servants he has appointed and assure them. These people will then be engaged in the tasks of their master and advance like arrows that have been released. Kings must always endeavour to protect their treasuries. The treasury is the foundation for kings. Ensure the foundation of the treasury. The stores must always be full and stocked with grain. Good people must be employed to take care of them. Have stores of riches and grain. Always engage servants who are skilled in fighting. Skill in the use of horses is also desired. Look towards kin and relatives. Be surrounded by friends and allies. O descendant of the Kourava lineage! Be engaged in tasks that ensure the welfare of the city. I have spoken to you about the desired intelligence and wisdom. O son! The dog is an example before you. What else do you wish to hear?"'

Chapter 1448(120)

'Yudhishthira said, "O descendant of the Bharata lineage! You have said many things about the conduct of kings, about what has been indicated in the past by those who knew about rajadharma. You have recounted in detail the views of those virtuous ones who thought about these earlier. O bull among the Bharata lineage! I am requesting you to again tell me about rajadharma."

'Bhishma replied, "The protection of all beings is the supreme objective for kshatriyas. O lord of the earth! Listen to how this protection can be brought about. A peacock, the devourer of snakes, exhibits colourful plumage. Like that, a king who follows dharma and desires happiness should adopt many kinds of forms—fierceness, deceit, incapability of being controlled, truthfulness and uprightness. He should spiritedly stand amidst all of these. Whatever ensures welfare for a certain objective, that is the colour and form he should adopt. When a king can assume many different forms, even the subtlest of his objectives does not suffer. He must always hide his counsel and be dumb, like a peacock during the autumn. He must speak gently and his body must be smooth and handsome. He should be skilled in the sacred texts. He must make endeavours to guard the gates through which dangers penetrate, like waterfalls, and also be a refuge for brahmanas and virtuous people, when there is a shower of hail and rain.[985] Desiring prosperity, like the crest of a peacock, the king must hold aloft the flag of dharma. He must always wield the rod of chastisement and act attentively, paying attention to the income and expenditure of people, flying from one tree to another.[986] He must fling away insects from the flock with the feet.[987] When his own wings have grown, he should flutter them and cleanse himself. He must identify his enemy's faults and cause agitation to his[988] wings. He must behave the way a peacock acts towards flowers in the forest.[989] He must seek refuge with lofty and prosperous kings who are like mountains, seeking shade and refuge in secret, while one is undetected.[990] Like a peacock submerging itself during the monsoon, undetected and alone in the night, he must go to his wives, following the qualities of the peacock. He must not take off his body armour and must always protect himself. He must not advance into snares and must avoid the nooses. Having destroyed the ground,[991] he must penetrate the dense forest again. Just as the peacock angrily kills the others who are poisonous[992] and does not allow them to reside with him, he[993] must kill the powerful[994] and deceitful ones

[985]There is an implicit image of a peacock passing through waterfalls and avoiding rain and hail.

[986]The implicit image of a peacock again.

[987]The peacock image again.

[988]The enemy's.

[989]The peacock's plumage complements the flowers in the forest. The imagery is a bit stretched, but the king must act in this way.

[990]The image is of a peacock seeking out shade in the mountains.

[991]Like a peacock digging up the ground where there are snares.

[992]The peacock kills poisonous snakes.

[993]The king.

[994]The Critical edition uses the word *baala*, instead of *bala*, and there is a typo.

who seek to injure him. However, unlike the peacock, he must not always be addicted to desire. He must always collect wise people around him, like insects in the deep forest.[995] In this way, like a peacock, the king must protect his own kingdom. If he is skilled, he will adopt a policy that will enhance his own prosperity. He will use his intelligence to control himself and counter the enemy's intelligence. The sacred texts give illustrations to indicate that one's qualities are developed through intelligence. Considering one's own strength, the enemy must be assured through conciliation. The intelligence must be used to reflect, since the intelligence provides counsel to one's own self. One must be calm, devoted to yoga, intelligent and wise, thinking about what must be done and what must not be done. A learned one will keep his counsel hidden and speak only what should be spoken. If he is wise and as intelligent as Brihaspati, he will avoid inferior speech. His nature will be like molten steel, when it has been immersed in water.[996] The lord of the earth will follow the injunctions of the sacred texts to ensure that he himself, and everyone else, is engaged in the appropriate tasks. The inferior, the cruel, the wise, the brave, those who are skilled with money and others who are good with words must all be engaged in their respective tasks. Others who cannot be seen[997] must also be similarly appointed in tasks. They must all be made to follow their appropriate tasks, like notes on the taut strings of a musical instrument. One who acts in an affectionate way towards all beings, without acting against dharma, is as immobile as a mountain and everyone thinks of him as, 'He is my king.' He must look towards dharma and treat everything, pleasant or unpleasant, as equal, like the sun casting its rays and thus dispense judgement. He must appoint those who know about dharma, are middle-aged, without taints, in control of their senses and mild in speech, bearing in mind their lineage, nature and country of origin. They must not be avaricious and must be learned. They

[995]The insects again bring up the imagery of the peacock.

[996]The sense probably is that even if the king is angered, he will quickly cool down.

[997]That is, they are not directly employed in the court.

must be controlled and devoted to dharma. A king who wishes to protect dharma and artha must appoint these for all the tasks. In this way, he acts so as to become the refuge of those who have no refuge. In this way, he is impartially established and having used spies, is content. He must himself consider and act so that his anger and delight are not in vain. If he is firm in his own convictions, his treasury and the earth become full of riches. When the reasons behind his favours and his punishment are transparent, when he is protected and when his kingdom is protected, then that king is a king who knows about dharma. Like the sun rises over cows,[998] he must always look towards the kingdom. He must use his intelligence to know about mobile and immobile objects and will not suffer from any anxiety. The king's accumulation of riches must be appropriate to the time. When he milks the earth every day, he will be like an intelligent person who milks a cow without killing it. A six-legged one[999] gradually collects honey from flowers. In that fashion, the king must collect objects to build up his treasury. Anything that is in excess of the required store should be spent on dharma and kama. A king who knows about dharma must accumulate and also spend. He must never think that any wealth is a trifle. He must never disregard an enemy. He must use his intelligence to know himself and he must not trust those who are limited in intelligence. Perseverance, skill, self-control, great intelligence, patience, valour, knowledge about time and place and attentiveness, whether these are a little or a lot, are the eight kindling logs that lead to an increase in prosperity. When a fire is small but is sprinkled with clarified butter, it becomes larger. A single seed can become many thousand. Even if he hears that his income and expenditure are great, a learned one will not think that anything is too little. Whether the enemy is a child or an adult, or even if he is extremely old, he is capable of slaying a careless man. In the course of time, he can sever the root. Therefore, someone who knows about time is the best among kings. Whether the enemy is weak or strong, if he is driven by malice, he

[998]Protecting the cows.

[999]A bee.

can take away deeds, become an obstruction in the path of dharma and, for a long period of time, take away one's valour. Therefore, a self-controlled person does not ignore the enemy. The enemy must be weakened and one's own stores must be protected. Together with these objectives, dharma, artha and kama exist. An intelligent person does things that are beyond these. Thus, a king resorts to a person who is intelligent. Blazing intelligence destroys the powerful and protected by intelligence, strength increases.[1000] Through intelligence, a prosperous enemy can be made to decline. When one uses one's intelligence and then undertakes a task, this is praised. One who pursues all one's objects of desire is wise. If one possesses only a little bit of enterprise, one is weak in the body. Since he desires prosperity for his own self, he must fill the vessel, even if only a little is available. Therefore, a king who has been seized by the enemy must seek to obtain the foundation of prosperity from everywhere. Even if he has been afflicted for a long period of time, like a momentary flash of lightning, he will obtain honour. Learning, austerities, a great deal of riches—all of these are capable of being obtained with enterprise. The brahman dwells in the bodies of those who are enterprising. Thus, one should know that enterprise is the most important. The intelligent and spirited Shakra, Vishnu and Sarasvati always reside in all beings and, therefore, one must never disregard the body. An avaricious person must be slain with generosity. An avaricious person is always dissatisfied with the prosperity of others. All those who are avaricious may enjoy the qualities of deeds,[1001] but because they abandon dharma and kama, they eventually lose artha too. All those who are avaricious desire the riches, objects of pleasure, sons, wives and prosperity of others. All the sins exist in avaricious people. Therefore, the king must not accept avaricious people.[1002] A person born in an inferior lineage, if he is virtuous and wise, can be used to ascertain the undertakings and all the objectives of those who wish to cause injury. O Pandava! A minister must be known to follow dharma and must be capable of keeping a secret. O king! He must

[1000]One's own strength increases, while that of the enemy declines.

[1001]Good deeds performed in earlier lives. Therefore, they may be prosperous.

[1002]By implication, as advisers or ministers.

be learned, born in a noble lineage and capable of extending the kingdom. O god among men! I have recounted the ordinances of dharma. Use your intelligence to know and follow them. The king who uses his intelligence to follow these is a king who is capable of protecting the earth. Wrong policy that is against the ordinances, or many kinds of deceitful policy, can be seen to produce happiness. But that kind of king has no ultimate end. Nor is there supreme happiness in the kingdom. A king who allies with the virtuous is seen to soon slay enemies who are superior in wealth, intelligence, conduct, honour, endowments of good qualities, evident valour in battle and visible qualities.[1003] One must think of different ways of treading along the path of action and not turn one's mind to obstructions. A man who only looks at the sins[1004] does not obtain prosperity, superiority, great fame and riches. There may be two well-wishers who have been drawn together by bonds of affection, but have later drifted apart. A wise person must know that the two have drifted apart and treat with great gentleness the friend who bears the greater load.[1005] I have recounted rajadharma to you. Using this and your intelligence, protect men. You will obtain auspicious fruits and happiness. Everything in the world is based on the supreme foundation of dharma."'

Chapter 1449(121)

'Yudhishthira said, "O grandfather! You have recounted this eternal rajadharma. This is the lord's[1006] great rod of chastisement and everything is established on this rod of chastisement—in particular, the

1003Since qualities are mentioned twice, the first may be qualities in battle, while the second is qualities in general.

1004In the sense of impediments.

1005This is probably a reference to adjucating a dispute between two people who have formerly been friends. The meaning isn't very clear.

1006The word used is *ishvara* and subsequent sections suggest that Brahma is meant.

gods, the rishis, the great-souled ancestors, the yakshas, the rakshasas, the pishachas and the mortals. In a fierce way, it resides in all the beings in this world. O lord! It pervades everything, is extremely energetic and is the best. You have said that everything that is seen in the worlds—gods, asuras and men, mobile and immobile objects—is touched by the rod of chastisement. O bull among the Bharata lineage! Therefore, I wish to know the entire truth about this. What is this rod? What is the rod like? What is its form? What is its nature? What is its soul like? How was it created? What is its image? How did it become a rod? When does the rod of chastisement, which causes injury to beings, awake? To protect, how does it remain awake, before and after?[1007] How was it known earlier? What are the signs of the rod later? Where is the rod based? What is its trajectory?"

'Bhishma replied, "O Kouravya! Hear about the rod of chastisement and about why it amounts to judgement. In this earth, the rod is the only object through which everything is controlled. O great king! That is the reason judgement is also known by the name of dharma. If it is destroyed, how will beings, who wish to cause injury, be destroyed? That is the reason judgement is known as *vyavahara*.[1008] O king! In ancient times, right at the beginning, this was stated by Manu. 'If the rod is applied well, treating the loved and the disliked equally, then he who protects the subjects in this way is alone like dharma himself.' These words were spoken by Manu in ancient times.

'"But even before that, at the time of creation, there were Brahma's great words, mentioned by Vasishtha. These words were spoken before those other words were uttered, so the learned say that these were the earliest words.[1009] 'In this world, judgement is spoken of as vyavahara. If the rod is applied well, the three objectives[1010] always flow from it.' The supreme rod is divine in form, with trails like fire.

[1007]Before and after an act of chastisement.

[1008]While vyavahara means conduct or behaviour, it also means a lawsuit and judicial procedure.

[1009]Brahma's words were the earliest, because they came before Manu's.

[1010]Dharma, artha and kama.

He is as dark as the petals of a blue lotus. He has four teeth, four arms, eight feet and many eyes. The ears are conical and the hair stands upright. He is matted and possesses two tongues. His eyes are coppery and he is clad in the skin of the king of animals.[1011] The rod always sports this fierce and frightful appearance and is impossible to withstand. The sword, the club, the bow, the spear, the trident, the bludgeon, the arrow, the mallet, the battleaxe, the chakra, the spike, the staff, the cutlass, the javelin and whatever weapons exist in this world—the rod roams around and assumes their forms. The rod roams around, slaying and striking, piercing, severing, smashing, slicing, mangling and uprooting. O Yudhishthira! These names of the rod are recounted—Asi,[1012] Vishasana,[1013] Dharma, Tikshnavartma,[1014] Durasada,[1015] Shrigarbha,[1016] Vijaya,[1017] Shasta,[1018] Vyavahara, Prajagara,[1019] Shastra,[1020] Brahmana, Mantra, Shasta,[1021] Pragyavachana-gata,[1022] Dharmapala,[1023] Akshaya,[1024] Deva,[1025] Satyaga,[1026] Nityaga,[1027] Graha,[1028] Asanga,[1029] Rudratanaya,[1030] Manujyeshtha[1031] and Shivamkara.[1032] The lord is the illustrious

[1011]A lion.

[1012]Sword.

[1013]A sabre or crooked sword.

[1014]Fierce in progress.

[1015]Irresistible.

[1016]The womb of prosperity.

[1017]Victory.

[1018]The ruler.

[1019]The guardian who remains awake.

[1020]Sacred text or command.

[1021]This is repeated.

[1022]The one who returns to the earliest words.

[1023]The protector of dharma.

[1024]The one without decay.

[1025]God, alternatively, the shining one.

[1026]The one who follows truth.

[1027]The one who is always present.

[1028]The one who seizes.

[1029]The one without attachment.

[1030]The son of Rudra.

Vishnu and his sacrifice, the lord Narayana, whose great form is eternal and who is known as the great being. It is said to be Brahma's daughters—Lakshmi, Niti[1033] and Sarasvati. Dandaniti is Jagaddhatri.[1034] O descendant of the Bharata lienage! The rod has many different kinds of forms—good and bad, happy and unhappy, dharma and adharma, strong and weak, good fortune and ill fortune, auspicious and inauspicious, with qualities and without qualities, with desire and without desire, season, month, night, day, moment, without favours and with favours, delight, anger, pacification, self-control, destiny, human endeavour, with salvation and without salvation, with fear and without fear, with violence and without violence, austerities, sacrifices, self-restraint, with poison and without poison, the end, the beginning, the middle, evil sorcery, deceit, intoxication, carelessness, pride, insolence, patience, good policy and bad policy, lack of strength and strength, respect and disrespect, change and status quo, humility, renunciation, the right time and the wrong time. O Kouravya! The rod has many different forms in the world—falsehood, knowing and not knowing, truth, faith and lack of faith, impotence, conduct, gain and loss, victory and defeat, sharpness and mildness, death, getting and not getting, disagreement and agreement, tasks that should be done and tasks that should not be done, strength and weakness, malice and lack of malice, dharma and adharma, shame and lack of shame, success and failure, energy, deeds, learning, strength of speech and intelligence.

'"Had the rod not existed, people would have crushed each other. O Yudhishthira! It is out of fear of the rod that they do not kill each other. O king! It is through the rod that the subjects are constantly protected. Therefore, a king who resorts to the rod obtains prosperity. O lord of men! It swiftly establishes good conduct in the world. Dharma, which is based on the truth, finds

[1031]The eldest Manu.

[1032]The performer of what is auspicious.

[1033]Good policy personified.

[1034]The mother of the universe.

a foundation in brahmanas. Brahmanas are full of dharma and the best among them base themselves on the Vedas. Sacrifices result from the Vedas and sacrifices please the gods. If the gods are pleased, they always give it to Indra.[1035] If Shakra is pleased with the subjects, he gives them food. The lives of all beings always find a basis in food. Thus, subjects obtain a foundation and the rod watches over them. Because of these reasons, the rod manifests itself in kshatriyas. It remains awake and, always and eternally, protects subjects well. It is spoken of in eight names—Ishvara, Purusha, Prana, Sattva,[1036] Vitta,[1037] Prajapati, Bhutatma[1038] and Jiva.[1039] This rod certainly gives him[1040] prosperity. When strength is united with policy, five ingredients result—lineage, strength, wealth, advisers and wisdom. These are said to be the strengths. O Yudhishthira! There is another kind of strength that can be obtained from eight objects—elephants, horses, chariots, infantry, boats, workers, guides and spies. These are said to be the eight kinds of strength. When that eight-limbed army advances, it is united with elephants, elephant riders, horse riders, foot soldiers, ministers, physicians, mendicants, principal investigators, astrologers, readers of omens, treasuries, allies, foodgrains and all kinds of implements. The learned say that it is a body with seven ingredients and eight limbs.[1041] The rod is a limb of the kingdom and the rod provides the power. The lord made efforts so that kshatriyas could bear it. The rod is applied equally to everyone and the rod is the eternal soul. It shows the way towards dharma and there is nothing that kings should revere

[1035]The oblations offered at sacrifices are given to Indra.

[1036]Essence, strength.

[1037]Prosperity, power.

[1038]The soul in all beings.

[1039]Living being.

[1040]The king.

[1041]The kingdom is being compared to the physical body. The seven ingredients are the king, his allies, advisers, the country, the fortified cities, the treasury and the army. To these seven ingredients, the rod of chastisement is being added to account for eight limbs.

more. For the protection of the worlds and to establish people in their own dharma, the creator[1042] engendered this.

'"Judgement comes after this and is seen to be united with it. It is also a characteristic that has been engendered by the creator. Judgement is said to be the soul of the Vedas and obtains its sanction from the Vedas. O tiger among men! While this is the foundation, there is another kind that originates with the ordinances of the sacred texts.[1043] The rod is said to exhibit the characteristics of the lord's[1044] custom. It is known to be based on the customs through which the lord of men exercises the rod. What is seen to be the custom behind the exercise of the rod is said to be the soul of judgement. What is said to be judgement is also the soul of the subject matter of the Vedas. Whatever flows from the soul of the Vedas is said to exhibit the qualities of dharma. When something results from the dharma of customary practice, those with cleansed souls also regard that as dharma. O Yudhishthira! On Brahma's instructions, judgement protects the subjects. It has truth as its soul, it upholds the three worlds and it extends prosperity. Where the rod cannot be seen, eternal judgement doesn't exist either. We have heard that whatever is seen in the judicial process is dharma. Where the Vedas are, dharma exists there. Where dharma exists, the path of virtue is there. Brahma Prajapati was the first. He was the grandfather of all the worlds, with the gods, the asuras and the rakshasas, and with men and the serpents. He is the creator of everything that came into existence. Thus, this judgement flows from the characteristics of custom followed by the lord. That is how we have spoken about this example of the judicial process. If they are not established in their own dharma, the mother, the father, the brother, the wife and the preceptor are not beyond the exercise of the king's rod."'

[1042]Brahma.

[1043]A hierarchy of judgement and judicial process is indicated. The primary one is what is laid down in the Vedas, the secondary flows from other sacred texts and the tertiary is from the exercise of the king's powers.

[1044]The king's.

Chapter 1450(122)

'Bhishma said, "In this connection, an ancient history is recounted. There was a radiant king from Anga and he was famous by the name of Vasuhoma. The king was always engaged in virtuous acts of dharma and great austerities, together with his wife. He went to Munjaprishtha, revered by large numbers of devarshis. The peak of Meru was in the golden mountains of the Himalayas. At Munjavata, Rama had instructed that the matted locks should be seized.[1045] Since then, the rishis, rigid in their vows, have referred to the region as Munjaprishtha and it is frequented by Rudra. He dwelt there, always with much learning and qualities, and was respected by the brahmanas. He became like a devarshi.

'"King Mandhata was an afflicter of enemies and Shakra's esteemed friend. In a cheerful frame of mind, he once arrived there. As Mandhata approached King Vasuhoma, he saw that having performed excellent austerities, the latter stood humbly before him. Vasuhoma gave the king a cow and arghya and asked him if everything was well in his eight-limbed kingdom. Vasuhoma asked the king, who followed the codes of good conduct that had been laid down from ancient times, 'What can I do for you?' O descendant of the Kuru lineage! Mandhata, supreme among kings, was greatly delighted. Having taken a seat, he spoke to the immensely wise Vasuhoma. 'O king! You have studied all of Brihaspati's doctrines. O lord of men! The sacred texts of Ushanas are also known to you. I wish to hear from you about how the rod of chastisement was created. How did it first arise? Why is it said to be supreme? How did the rod come to be firmly established amidst kshatriyas? O immensely wise one! Tell me and I will give you the fees that should be given to a preceptor.'

[1045]The Rama in question is Parashurama. There was another Munjavata near Kurukshetra (mentioned in Section 33, Volume 2), but this Munjavata is being equated with Munjaprishtha. It is not at all clear whose matted locks were being seized, and for what purpose. Munja is a kind of grass and Munjaprishtha means a slope where this grass is found.

'"Vasuhoma replied, 'O king! Listen to how the rod was created for the protection of the world and for maintaining and protecting subjects. It is the eternal essence of dharma. We have heard that the illustrious Brahma, the grandfather of all the worlds, wished to perform a sacrifice and could not find an officiating priest who was his equal. The god then conceived a foetus and carried it within his head for many long years. After it had been borne for a full one thousand years, when he sneezed, the foetus fell out. O scorcher of enemies! Thus the Prajapati named Kshupa was created. O king! That great-souled one became the officiating priest at the sacrifice. O bull among kings! Thus Brahma's sacrifice started. However, because of the cheerful form he had to adopt, the rod disappeared.[1046] When it vanished, the subjects were mixed up. There was no difference between what should be done and what should not be done and between what should be eaten and what should not be eaten. There was no difference between what should be drunk and what should not be drunk. How could there be success? They injured each other. There was no distinction between whom one should go to and whom one should not go to.[1047] One's own property and that of others became the same. They snatched from each other, like dogs after meat. The weak were killed by the strong and no one exhibited any respect. At this, the grandfather worshipped the illustrious and eternal Vishnu, the god who grants boons, and spoke to the great god. "You must certainly show compassion towards these virtuous ones. Arrange it so that there is no mixing up here." At this, the illustrious one meditated for a long time, holding a trident and wearing matted hair. From his own self, that supreme among gods created the rod. And from that was created the policy for observing dharma, the goddess Sarasvati. She was created and is famous in the three worlds as dandaniti. The illustrious one again meditated for a long time, with the trident, supreme among weapons. He made one person a lord over his respective dominion. The god with the

[1046]As a person who was sacrificing, Brahma had to assume a tranquil form, but the rod was fierce.

[1047]A reference to sexual intercourse.

thousand eyes became the lord of the gods. Vaivasvata Yama was made the lord of the ancestors. Kubera became the lord of riches and the rakshasas. Meru became the lord of mountains and the great ocean that of rivers. He decreed that Varuna should be the lord over the divine kingdom of the waters.[1048] Death became the lord of living beings and the fire of energy. The lord announced that Ishana[1049] would be the protector of the Rudras. Vasishtha became the lord of brahmanas, the fire[1050] of the Vasus, the sun of energy,[1051] the moon of nakshatras and Amshuman[1052] of herbs. The supreme lord instructed that Skanda Kumara, the one with twelve arms, would be the king of the spirits.[1053] Time became the one who pacifies, destroys and humbles everything and the lord of the four divisions of death[1054] and happiness and unhappiness. The lord of riches, the king of the yakshas, became the lord of all beings. It has been heard that the one with the trident in his hand[1055] became the lord of all the Rudras. There was that single son named Kshupa, who had been born from Brahma's mental powers. He was given the supreme lordship over all subjects and made the upholder of all kinds of dharma. When the sacrifice started, according to the proper rites, Mahadeva[1056] honoured Vishnu and gave the rod, the protector of dharma, to him. Vishnu gave it to Angiras. Angiras, supreme among sages, gave it to Indra and Marichi. Marichi gave it to Bhrigu. Bhrigu gave that rod, full of dharma, to the rishis. The rishis gave it to the guardians of the worlds and the guardians of the

[1048]The Critical edition probably has a typo here. It says suras, which can only be translated as divine waters. It should probably read asuras, in which case, Varuna would also be lord over the underwater demons.

[1049]Shiva.

[1050]In the form of Jataveda.

[1051]Energy is mentioned twice.

[1052]Amshuman means one with the rays and can refer to either the sun or the moon. Here, it means the moon.

[1053]*Bhutas*.

[1054]Resulting from disease, weapons, one's own acts and Yama.

[1055]Shiva.

[1056]Shiva.

worlds gave it to Kshupa. Ksupa gave it to Manu, the son of the sun god. For the sake of preserving the subtleties of dharma and artha and to protect his own self, Manu, the son of the sun and the god of funeral ceremonies, gave it to his sons. It should be one's duty to apply the rod differentially, according to dharma, and not wilfully, using harsh words of censure, imprisonment, extracting bonds, fines of gold and expulsion. However, physical dismemberment and execution should not be used for trifling reasons, nor should physical punishment, corporal punishment and exile. Right from the beginning, the rod has been awake and has protected subjects. The illustrious Indra remains awake and after him it is Agni, the fire god.[1057] After Agni has remained awake, it is Varuna. After Varuna, it is Prajapati. After Prajapati, Dharma, who humbles souls, remains awake. After Dharma, it is eternal Vyavasaya,[1058] Brahma's son. After Vyavasaya, Tejas[1059] remains awake, for the cause of protection. The medicinal plants and herbs come after Tejas and the mountains after the plants and herbs. After the mountains, the juices and the qualities of the juices remain awake. After that, the goddess Nirriti[1060] remains awake and after Nirriti, it is the stellar bodies. The Vedas are established in the stellar bodies. After that, it is the lord Hayashira.[1061] After him, the undecaying Brahma, the grandfather, remains awake. After the grandfather, the illustrious Mahadeva Shiva remains awake. The Vishvadevas come after Shiva and the rishis after the Vishvadevas. The illustrious Soma[1062] comes after the rishis and the eternal gods after Soma. In this world, the brahmanas remain awake and take it up after the gods. After the brahmanas, kings follow dharma and protect the worlds. After the kshatriyas, it is the eternal mobile and immobile objects. The subjects remain awake in this world and the rod remains awake

[1057]If this remaining awake is interpreted as wielding the rod, this is an alternative line of succession.

[1058]While this word has many meanings, Resolution is best here.

[1059]Energy.

[1060]The goddess of calamity and destruction.

[1061]Literally, with the head of a horse, one of Vishnu's forms.

[1062]The moon god.

among them. The rod is the one who destroys everything and is a lord who is the grandfather's equal. O descendant of the Bharata lineage! At the beginning, in the middle and at the end, time remains awake. Mahadeva Prajapati is the lord of all the worlds. The lord Shiva Sharva is the god of the gods and always remains awake. He is Kapardi, Shankara, Rudra, Bhava, Sthanu and Umapati. Thus, the beginning, the middle and the end of the rod have been recounted. A lord of the earth who knows about dharma must follow the proper conduct and policy.'"

'Bhishma said, "The man who listens to these views of Vasuhoma and having heard, acts properly in accordance with it, is a king who obtains all his desires. O bull among men! You have been told everything about the rod. O descendant of the Bharata lineage! It controls all the people who transgress dharma."'

Chapter 1451(123)

'Yudhishthira said, "I wish to hear what has been determined about dharma, artha and kama. All the advancements in the world are based on these three. What are the foundations of dharma, artha and kama and what is their power? They are sometimes connected with each other and sometimes, they exist separately."

'Bhishma replied, "When people are cheerful in their minds, having determined to pursue their objectives, these three originate in time and are united with each other. The foundation of the body is dharma, and artha is based on dharma. Kama is said to be the fruit of artha. Resolution is the foundation of everything and resolution is based on material objects. All the material objects find success in their being procured. These form the basis for the three objectives.[1063] Withdrawal is said to be moksha. Dharma protects

[1063]The three objectives of dharma, artha and kama are based on the acquisition of material objects.

the body and artha is desired for the sake of dharma. Kama leads to sexual pleasure. But all of these are nothing but dust.[1064] One should pursue whichever of these is nearby and not discard them in one's mind. These begin with dharma and end with kama[1065] and one should renounce them only when one has freed oneself from the tamas quality. A man who is superior in his intelligence can obtain as much of these three objectives in an instant as a person of inferior intelligence can in an entire day. Dharma is stained by jealousy. Artha is stained by secrecy. Kama is stained by excessive addiction. Each quality can be excessively pursued. In this connection, an ancient history is recounted about a conversation between Kamanda and Angarishtha. King Angarishtha greeted the rishi Kamanda when he was seated. Having observed the prescribed norms, Angarishtha asked him, 'A king may be confounded by the force of kama and act sinfully. O rishi! When he repents those, how can the sins be destroyed? In ignorance, one may follow adharma, taking it to be dharma. How can a king restrain that which is practised among men?'

'"Kamanda said, 'A man who disregards dharma and artha and follows kama destroys his own wisdom, because he has abandoned dharma and artha. The confusion that destroys wisdom also destroys dharma and artha. From this is created bad conduct and the trait of not believing.[1066] When the king does not restrain wicked people of bad conduct, people think that this is as if a snake has entered the house.[1067] The subjects do not follow him. Nor do brahmanas and virtuous people. He confronts danger and may even be killed. When one is disrespected, even if one remains alive, the misery is like being dead. Remaining alive with dishonour is pure death. On this, the preceptors have talked about means of destroying sin. He must serve the three forms of knowledge[1068] and treat brahmanas well. He must be

[1064]The text uses the word *rajasvala*, meaning a menstruating woman. That imagery implicitly exists. Beyond that, rajas is dust and there is also the rajas quality of passion.

[1065]An indirect way of referring to dharma, artha and kama.

[1066]The word used for such a person is nastika.

[1067]The king is being compared to a snake.

[1068]The three Vedas.

great-minded and follow dharma. He must marry into a great lineage. He must serve brahmanas who are spiritied and forgiving. Having performed ablutions with water, he must meditate. He must be cheerful and not act in a contrary way. He must seek the companionship of those who follow dharma and avoid association with those who perform wicked deeds. He must placate them[1069] with sweet words and deeds and tell them, "I belong to you." He must recount the good qualities of others. If his conduct is devoid of sin, he will quickly obtain great respect. There is no doubt that he will be able to negate all the wicked deeds that he has committed. What is stated by the seniors is supreme dharma. Act as they say. If you obtain the favours of the seniors, you will obtain the best and supreme objective.'"'

Chapter 1452(124)

'Yudhishthira asked, "O best of men! These people on earth always praise the good conduct that flows from dharma. However, I have a great doubt about this. O supreme among those who uphold dharma! If I am capable of understanding this, I wish to hear everything about this, exactly as it is comprehended. O descendant of the Bharata lineage! How can good conduct be ensured? I wish to hear this. What are its signs? O supreme among eloquent ones! Tell me this."

'Bhishma replied, "O one who grants honours! O great king! In earlier times, Duryodhana was tormented at the sight of your prosperity, when he went to Indraprastha with his brothers. He was laughed at in the assembly hall.[1070] He told Dhritarashtra about this. O descendant of the Bharata lineage! Listen to the account. Having witnessed your supreme prosperity in the assembly hall, Duryodhana seated himself and told his father everything. On hearing Duryodhana's words, Dhritarashtra spoke these words to

[1069]The virtuous people.

[1070] This has been described in Section 27 (Volume 2).

Duryodhana, who was with Karna. 'O son! Why are you tormented? I wish to hear the truth about this. O destroyer of enemy cities! On hearing this, if it is proper, I will instruct you, so that you can also obtain great prosperity, with your servants, your brothers, all your friends and your kin. You cover yourself in excellent garments. You eat food mixed with meat. You are borne on good horses. O son! Why are you grieving?'

'"Duryodhana said, 'In Yudhishthira's abode, ten thousand great-souled snatakas ate from golden vessels. His divine assembly hall is full of celestial flowers and fruit. There are speckled horses of the *tittira* breed. There are many kinds of gems. I saw all that. I saw the dazzling prosperity of the Pandaveyas, my enemies, and it was like that of Indra. O one who grants honours! On seeing this, I am grieving greatly.'

'"Dhritarashtra replied, 'O son! O tiger among men! If you desire prosperity that is like Yudhishthira's, or superior to it, you must follow good conduct. O son! There is no doubt that the three worlds can be conquered through good conduct. For people who possess good conduct, there is nothing that cannot be accomplished. Mandhata obtained the earth in a single night, Janamejaya in three days and Nabhaga in seven nights. All these kings possessed good conduct and self-control. Bought by their good qualities, the earth presented herself of her own accord. On this, an ancient history is recounted. O descendant of the Bharata lineage! In ancient times, Narada spoke about good conduct. Prahrada robbed the great-souled Indra's kingdom. By resorting to good conduct, the daitya subjugated the three worlds. Shakra joined his hands in salutation and presented himself before Brihaspati. He said, "O immensely wise one! I wish to know about what is beneficial." At this, Brihaspati gave him the knowledge that is best and supreme. O extender of the Kuru lineage! The illustrious one spoke about this to Indra of the gods. Brihaspati told him about what was best. However, Indra again asked him about what was superior to that.

'"'Brihaspati said, "O son![1071] There is something that is greater

[1071]The word used is tata.

than this. O fortunate one! O Purandara! Go to the great-souled Bhargava[1072] and he will tell you."'

'"Dhritarashtra said, 'The immensely famous one found out from Bhargava what was best for him. He was delighted at having obtained this knowledge and regained his supreme radiance. Having taken the permission of the great-souled Bhargava, Shatakratu again repeatedly asked Shukra about whether there was anything better. Bhargava, knowledgeable about dharma, told him that the great-souled Prahrada possessed that superior knowledge. Delighted at this, the chastiser of Paka[1073] assumed the form of a brahmana and went to Prahrada. The intelligent one said, "I wish to hear what is best for me." Prahrada told the brahmana, "O bull among brahmanas! I do not have the time. I am engaged in ruling the three worlds and cannot instruct you." The brahmana spoke these words. "When will there be time? When there is a break in your work, I wish to be instructed." At this, King Prahrada, knowledgeable about the brahman, was delighted and agreed. At an auspicious time, he gave him that true knowledge. As is proper, the brahmana observed the supreme conduct towards the preceptor. In every kind of way, he did all that he[1074] desired in his mind. He often asked him, "O scorcher of enemies! How did you obtain all these things? O one who knows about dharma! How did you obtain the kingdom of the three worlds? Tell me the reason." Prahrada replied, "O best among brahmanas! I never show any malice. I never say that I am the king. O son![1075] I control myself and implement what Kavya[1076] says. Anything said by the tranquil ones is always implemented by me. Without any malice, I am devoted to serving at Kavya's feet. I possess dharma in my soul. I have conquered anger. I have controlled myself and have restrained my senses. I have collected the teachings of those who know about the sacred texts, like bees collecting *kshoudra* honey.[1077] I have licked

[1072]Shukracharya, the preceptor of the demons.

[1073]Indra.

[1074]Prahrada.

[1075]The word used is tata.

[1076]Shukracharya.

[1077]A specific kind of honey, that from the *sampangi* plant.

the juices that have oozed out from the tongues of those eloquent ones. I have established myself amidst my species, like the moon amidst nakshatras. What has been stated by Kavya, when it flows from the mouths of brahmanas, is supreme sight and is like amrita on this earth. I have implemented what I have heard." Prahrada told the one who was knowledgeable about the brahman that this was the best. Having been pleased with the servitude, the Indra among daityas spoke these words. "O supreme among brahmanas! I am pleased with your conduct towards your preceptor. O fortunate one! Ask for a boon. There is no doubt that I will give it to you." The brahmana told the Indra among the daityas that he had already obtained one.[1078] Prahrada was delighted at this and asked him to take another boon. The brahmana replied, "O king! If you are pleased with me and wish to ensure my welfare, I wish to have the good conduct that you possess. Let me obtain this boon." Though the Indra among the daityas was pleased at this, he also suffered from great fear. Since this was the boon the brahmana had asked for, he couldn't be one with insignificant energy. Though Prahrada was astounded at this, he agreed to grant what had been asked for.

'"'When the boon had been granted and the brahmana had left, he was miserable. With the boon having been granted and with the brahmana having departed, he began to think a lot. O great king! However, he could not arrive at any conclusion. O son! While he was thinking in this way, an immensely radiant light emerged from his body. This shadow assumed a form made out of energy and left the body. Prahrada asked the immensely gigantic form, "Who are you?" It replied, "I am your good conduct. Since you have abandoned me, I will leave you. O king! I will go to that supreme among brahmanas, the unblemished one who was here as your disciple and was always devoted." O lord! Having said this, it disappeared and penetrated Shakra. After that energy had gone, another image emerged from his body. "Who are you?" he asked. It replied, "O Prahrada! Know me to be dharma. I will go to that supreme among brahmanas. O Indra among daityas! Since good conduct has already gone there, so

[1078]Having been given the knowledge.

will I." O great king! After this, more blazing energy emerged from the great-souled Prahrada's body. "Who are you?" he asked. The immensely radiant one replied, "O Indra of the asuras! I am truth and I will follow dharma." After this being had followed dharma, another being emerged. When this was questioned by the great-souled one, it replied, "O Prahrada! Know me to be behaviour. I will be where truth exists." When it had gone, a giant and white form emerged from his body. Asked, it said, "Know me to be strength. I will be where behaviour exists." O lord of men! Having said this, it went where behaviour had gone. A radiant goddess then emerged from the body. Asked by the Indra among the daityas, she replied, "I am Shri. O brave one! Because of your truth and valour, I dwelt happily with you. But I have been abandoned by you now and will go where strength is." At this, the great-souled Prahrada was terrified. He asked her again, "O one who resides in a lotus! Where are you going? You are a goddess who is always devoted to the truth. You are the supreme goddess of the worlds. Who was that best among brahmanas? I wish to know the truth." Shri replied, "That was Shakra, in the form of a brahmachari. He is the one who has been instructed by you. O lord! He has now robbed you of the prosperity of the three worlds. O one who knows about dharma! You conquered all the worlds through your good conduct. O lord! Knowing this, the great Indra has robbed you of your good conduct. O immensely wise one! Dharma, truth, behaviour, strength and I myself—there is no doubt that all of us find our foundations in good conduct."' O Yudhishthira! Having said this, Shri and all the others departed. Duryodhana again spoke to his father and uttered these words. "O descendant of the Kourava lineage! I wish to know the true nature of good conduct. Tell me the means whereby I can acquire good conduct."

'"Dhritarashtra said, 'The means have earlier been instructed by the great-souled Prahrada. O lord of men! Listen briefly to how good conduct can be obtained. There must be non-violence towards all beings, in deeds, thoughts and words. Compassion and generosity are praised as elements of good conduct. For one's own sake, one must not commit a harsh act that causes injury to another. Nor should one ever do something that one is ashamed of. One should undertake those tasks that warrant praise in assemblies. O supreme among the Kuru lineage! This is said to be the accumulation of good conduct. Even if a king who does not have good conduct possesses Shri, he will not enjoy her for a long time. The roots will fall down. O son! Know this to be the true nature of good conduct. O son! If you desire prosperity that is superior to that of Yudhishthira, this is what you should do.'"

'Bhishma said, "O lord of men! This is what Dhritarashtra told his son. O Kounteya! If you act in this way, you will obtain the fruits."'

Chapter 1453(125)

'Yudhishthira said, "O grandfather! You have said that good conduct is the most important thing for a man. How does hope arise and what is its nature? Tell me this. O grandfather! This great doubt has arisen in me. O destroyer of enemy cities! There is no one other than you who knows the truth and can dispel this. O grandfather! I had a great deal of hope about Suyodhana. O lord! When war was near, I thought that he would act as he had been asked to. A great hope is generated in a man and it becomes everything. When that is destroyed, there is no doubt that he suffers a misery that is like death. The evil-minded and evil-souled son of Dhritarashtra destroyed all my hopes. O Indra among kings! I think that I have been foolish. I think that hope is greater than a mountain with all its trees. O king! Or perhaps it is as immeasurable as the sky. O best among the Kuru lineage! It is extremely difficult to understand it[1079] and it is extremely difficult to obtain. I can see that it is extremely difficult to obtain. Is there anything that is more difficult to obtain than that?"

'Bhishma replied, "O Yudhishthira! In this connection, listen to what happened. This is the history of what transpired between

[1079]Hope.

Sumitra and Rishabha. Among the Haihayas, there was a rajarshi named Sumitra and he went out on a hunt. Having pursued a deer, he pierced it with an arrow with drooping tufts. The deer was infinite in its valour. Despite being struck by the arrow, it continued to flee and the powerful king swiftly dashed after the deer. O Indra among kings! The deer quickly fled through a hollow and in an instant, began to run through flat terrain again. The king was young, enterprising and strong. With arrows, a bow and a sword, he pursued it, like a swan. He plunged through male and female rivers, lakes and woods. Having crossed through places that were difficult to cross, he chased it into a forest. As it desired, the deer sometimes showed itself to the king and sometimes hid itself from the king. It would then speed on, acquiring greater speed. He struck the resident of the forest with many arrows. O Indra among kings! But it seemed to be playing with him and would again approach near. The leader of a herd of deer would then again speed up, resorting to a greater speed. O Indra among kings! It would forge ahead and then again appear nearby. Sumitra, the destroyer of enemies, affixed a foremost and fierce arrow that was capable of penetrating the inner organs and released it from his bow. However, the leader of a herd of deer advanced far ahead, by a distance that was more than one *govyuti*,[1080] beyond the reach of the arrow. It then stood there, seeming to laugh at the king. The blazing arrow fell down on the ground.

'"The deer entered a great forest and the king pursued it there. Having entered the great forest, the king approached a hermitage of ascetics. He was tired and seated himself. The assembled rishis saw him there, with the bow in his hand, exhausted, afflicted and hungry. Following the prescribed rites, they honoured him. The rishis asked that tiger among kings what he wanted. 'O fortunate one! What is the reason behind your coming to this hermitage? O lord of men! Though you are on foot, you have girded your sword and have a bow and arrows. O one who grants honours! We wish to know why you have come here. What lineage have you been born

[1080]Measure of distance, distance from which a cow's bellow can he heard.

in? Tell us what your name is.' O bull among men! O descendant of the Bharata lineage! At this, the king told the brahmanas everything and also about the pursuit. 'I have been born in the lineage of the Haihayas. I am Sumitra, the son of Mitra. I was roaming around, slaying herds of deer with thousands of arrows. I am protected by a large army and the advisers and women are with me. I pierced a deer with my arrow. But though pierced by my arrow, it ran away. While running after it as I desired, I arrived in this forest and near you. My prosperity has been destroyed. My hopes have been destroyed. My enterprise has also been destroyed. O ones who are rich in austerities! Having to abandon the signs of the kingship or giving up the city does not cause me as fierce a misery as the dashing of my hopes. The Himalayas, giant among mountains, the ocean, the great store of water are regarded as vast and so is the space between heaven and earth. O ones who are best in austerities! But I cannot see any boundaries to hope. O ones rich in austerities! Everything is known to you. You know everything. O immensely fortunate ones! I am therefore presenting you with the doubt I have. Which seems to be greater in this world, the hope of a man, or the sky? I wish to hear the truth about this. Which is more difficult to obtain? O ones who are always engaged in austerities! If this is not a secret, tell me, without any delay. O bulls among brahmanas! If you do not regard this to be a secret, I wish to hear. However, if this causes a distraction in your austerities, I will desist. I do not wish my question to lead to a long discussion. These are the reasons I wish to hear the truth about this, in detail. You are always engaged in austerities and are extremely controlled. You should tell me.'"'

Chapter 1454(126)

'Bhishma said, "Then, among those assembled rishis, a brahmana rishi named Rishabha, supreme among rishis, smiled and spoke. 'O tiger among kings! O lord! In earlier times, I visited all the tirthas and arrived at the divine hermitage of Nara and Narayana. There is the *badari*[1081] tree there and the beautiful lake in the sky.[1082] O king! Ashvashira[1083] recites the eternal Vedas there. In those ancient times, I first rendered the recommended offerings to the ancestors and the gods in that lake. I next went to the hermitage. The rishis Nara and Narayana always find delight there. To find an abode, I went a little distance away from the hermitage. There, I saw an extremely emaciated rishi come towards me. He was dressed in rags and hides and he was extremely tall. He was a store of austerities and his name was Tanu. O mighty-armed one! O rajarshi! Many other men have the eight qualities his form possessed.[1084] But I have never seen anyone as lean as him. O Indra among kings! His body was as thin as a little finger. His neck, arms, feet and hair were extraordinary to see. His head was as large as his body and so were his ears and his eyes. O supreme among kings! His speech and movement were feeble. On seeing this extremely emaciated brahmana, I was scared and very distressed. I touched his feet and joining my hands in salutation, stood before him. O bull among men! I told him my name, my gotra and my father's name. Then I slowly sat down on the seat he showed me. O great king! In the midst of those rishis, that supreme upholder of dharma recounted stories that were full of dharma and artha. While he was talking, a king arrived on swift horses, with his army and his women. His eyes were like blue lotuses and he was extremely distressed, thinking about his son, who had got lost in the forest. He was the father of Bhuridyumna[1085] and he was intelligent and immensely illustrious, born in Raghu's lineage. The king said, "I will see my son here. It is here that I will see him." In those ancient times, the king was roaming around, driven thus by hope. However, he also said, "It is also extremely unlikely that

[1081]The jujube tree.

[1082]The celestial Ganga is believed to originate from this lake in the sky.

[1083]With the head of a horse, Vishnu.

[1084]The eight qualities are intelligence, good conduct, self-control, studying, valour, restraint in speech, generosity and gratitude.

[1085]The son's name was Bhuridyumna.

I will ever see the one who is supreme in dharma.[1086] I only have one son and he has perished in the forest. It is extremely unlikely that I will see him, but hopes run high. There is no doubt that I will die and cast aside my body." Hearing these words, the illustrious Tanu, supreme among sages, lowered his head. For some time, he immersed himself in meditation. On seeing him meditating, the king was greatly distressed. Cheerless in his mind, he gently spoke these words. "O brahmana rishi! What is difficult to get and rarer than hope? O illustrious one! If it is not a secret, please tell me this." In the past, because of his misfortune and stupid intelligence, the illustrious maharshi had been insulted.[1087] O king! The brahmana rishi had asked for some riches, a golden pot and some bark for clothing, but his hopes were belied and he was distressed. O supreme among men! Having spoken to the rishi, revered in the worlds, the one with dharma in his soul[1088] worshipped him. But he felt exhausted and sat down. The great rishi offered him arghya, water for washing the feet and showed the king all the due honours, as is recommended for someone dwelling in the forest.

'"'All the sages surrounded that bull among men.[1089] They honoured him and sat down, like the saptarshis around Dhruva.[1090] They asked the unvanquished king about the entire reasons behind his coming to the hermitage. The king said, "I am a king famous in all the directions by the name of Viradyumna. I have come to the forest to look for my son Bhuridyumna, who has got lost. O foremost among brahmanas! O unblemished ones! He is my only son. I have not seen him in the forest and am roaming around here." Having been thus addressed by the king, the sage[1091] remained with his head lowered. He was silent and did not reply to the king. O Indra among kings! In the past, insolent because of his prosperity, the king had

[1086]Referring to the son.

[1087]It will become clear later that Bhuridyumna's father had insulted Tanu.

[1088]Bhuridyumna's father.

[1089]This is Rishabha speaking, not Bhishma. The sages sat down around Tanu.

[1090]Dhruva is the Pole Star and the saptarshis mean the constellation of Ursa Major.

[1091]Tanu.

insulted the brahmana. With his hopes belied, he[1092] had engaged in austerities for a long time. He had resolved, "I will never accept anything from a king, or from any of the other varnas." He had taken this pledge and had abided by it. "Hope agitates men who are foolish. I will fling it away." The king said, "Can hope be made to wear thin? Is there anything else on earth that is more difficult to get? O illustrious one! You have seen the nature of dharma and artha. Please tell me." Remembering everything, the illustrious Tanu, emaciated in his body, reminded the king of the incident and said, "O king! There is nothing that is as emaciated as hope. O king! I have asked many kings and have found that nothing is as difficult to obtain." The king said, "O brahmana! I have understood the purport of your words, about it being emaciated and also not emaciated[1093] and also about the difficulty of obtaining. O brahmana! Your words are the words of the Vedas. O immensely wise one! However, a doubt has arisen in my heart. O supreme one! I am asking you and you should tell me the truth about this. O illustrious one! Tell me, if it is not a secret, is there anyone more emaciated than you? O brahmana! In this world, is there anything that is more difficult to get?"[1094] Krishatanu[1095] replied, "It is rarer to find a petitioner who is satisfied with what he has got.[1096] O son![1097] It is rarer to find a person who does not disrespect a petitioner. There are those who promise to help, but later, do not do so, to the best of their capacities, or do not help those who should be aided. However, even then, the hope that still remains in beings is thinner than I am. There may be a father with a single son who is lost, or absent from home. When one doesn't know what has happened to him, the hope that still remains is thinner than I am. There are aged women who give birth. They, and rich people too, desire sons. O Indra among men! The hope that

[1092]Tanu.

[1093]Hope is strong, but it can be controlled. The objects one hopes for are difficult to get.

[1094]Than the remarkable emaciation of the body.

[1095]*Krisha* means emaciated and the text now refers to Tanu as Krishatanu.

[1096]While not obvious, this may refer to judicial procedures too.

[1097]The word used is tata.

is in them is thinner than I am." O king! Having heard this, the king and his women prostrated themselves and touched the feet of that bull among brahmanas. The king said, "O illustrious one! Through your favours, I desire to meet my son. O brahmana! If you so wish, follow the rites and please grant me this boon." The king, with eyes like blue lotuses, spoke these words. "O brahmana! What you have said is true. There is nothing false in those words." The illustrious Tanu, supreme among the upholders of dharma, laughed. Through his austerities and his learning, he instantly brought the son there. Having brought the son there, he reprimanded the king.[1098] He was supreme among the upholders of dharma and showed himself to be none other than Dharma. He exhibited his own self and it was divine and marvellous to behold. He was devoid of sin and devoid of anger and left for the nearby forest. O king! I saw this and I heard those words. Quickly drive away your hope, which is thinner than what he was.'"

'Bhishma said, "O great king! Thus addressed by the great-souled Rishabha, Sumitra swiftly flung away his hope, which was extremely thin. O Kounteya! You have also heard these words from me. O king! Be as firm as the Himalayas, supreme among mountains. You will see and hear those who are distressed because they pursue objectives. O great king! Listen to me. You should not be tormented."'

Chapter 1455(127)

'Yudhishthira said, "As you have spoken, I have not obtained enough of this amrita. O grandfather! Therefore, speak to me again about dharma."

'Bhishma replied, "On this, an ancient history is recounted about a conversation between Goutama and the great-souled Yama. Goutama's great hermitage was on Mount Pariyatra and Goutama

[1098]Because of what the king had done earlier.

dwelt there for some time. Listen to this. Goutama tormented himself through austerities for sixty thousand years. The cleansed and ascetic sage performed severe austerities. O tiger among men! Yama, the guardian of the world, went to him there. As sage Goutama performed those excellent austerities, he looked at the rishi. Because of his energy, the brahmana rishi realized that Yama had arrived. The one who was rich in austerities joined his hands in salutation and advanced towards him. Dharmaraja[1099] looked towards that bull among men and bowed down before him. Dharma asked him, 'What can I do for you?' Goutama asked, 'How can one free oneself of the debts due to the mother and the father? How can a man quickly obtain the auspicious worlds, which are so difficult to obtain?' Yama replied, 'Austerities, purity, constant devotion to truth and dharma, constant worship of the mother and the father are the tasks one should be attached to. One must perform many horse sacrifices, with dakshina for the officiating priests. A man will then obtain worlds that are extraordinary to behold.'"'

Chapter 1456(128)

'Yudhishthira asked, "O descendant of the Bharata lineage! There may be a king whose friends have abandoned him and who has many enemies. His treasury may have become depleted and his army may have been weakened. What happens to him? His advisers and aides may be wicked. All his secret counsel may have been divulged. His kingdom may gradually be weaned away and he cannot see any course of action. He is weak and may be attacked by a circle of stronger enemies. His kingdom may be in disarray. He may be ignorant about the time and the place. He is unable to use conciliation. And because he is afflicted, he cannot use dissension either. His life may seem to be without purpose. What is a good course of action then?"

[1099]Yama.

'Bhishma replied, "O bull among the Bharata lineage! You have asked me about secret kinds of dharma.[1100] I did not wish to speak about this kind of dharma until I had been asked. O bull among the Bharata lineage! Dharma is more subtle than words and intelligence. If one has served those who have good conduct, and learnt from them, one can perhaps become virtuous. Using one's intelligence to reflect on a task before undertaking it, one may, or may not, become prosperous. In that way, with respect to what you have asked, use your own intelligence to decide what must be done. O descendant of the Bharata lineage! Using the instruments of dharma, there are many ways to advance towards the objective. Listen. If one considers dharma, I do not consider these kinds of action to be dharma.[1101] Prosperous people may bring hardships on themselves and subsequently, it may be held that this was inappropriate.[1102] One can be certain about the outcome of a course of action only after everything has been completed. Whenever a man always looks towards the sacred texts and obtains learning from them, that learning pleases him. If a man is not learned, a course of action may seem wrong. But it seems wrong because of lack of knowledge and that course of action can lead to prosperity. Without any doubt in your mind, listen to the words that I will speak. If the king's treasury is exhausted, his army will decline. The king must try to build the treasury, like a person conserves water in a place where there is no water. This is dharma then, and when it is time, he can show compassion.[1103] These are the instruments of dharma that were followed by people in earlier times. O descendant of the Bharata lineage! There is one kind of dharma for those who are

[1100]Meaning that this should not be talked about in public. Dharma in times of distress figures in the next section.

[1101]The suggestion seems to be that these acts are undertaken in a time of emergency. Therefore, even though they seem to follow dharma, they are not true dharma.

[1102]Because those acts were short-sighted and not in conformity with true dharma.

[1103]In a time of adversity, it is dharma to build the treasury by imposing taxes. When it is a time of prosperity, one can be compassionate and reduce taxes.

capable and another for those in distress. It is said that a treasury ensures dharma and intelligence is superior to dharma.[1104] One who is weak cannot find a means of sustenance by following dharma alone. However, since the acquisition of wealth does not occur in isolation,[1105] it has been heard that, in times of hardship, adharma may acquire the characteristics of dharma. But those who are learned and wise say that adharma results and subsequently,[1106] a kshatriya must act to heal this. Dharma must not be made to decline, but nor should one come under the subjugation of the enemy. Nor, because of the action undertaken, should one allow one's own self to be destroyed. If one is destroyed, one can perform no act of dharma, either for one's own sake, or for the sake of someone else. It is certain that one must use every means possible to preserve oneself. O son! This has been determined by those who are knowledgeable about dharma and skilled about the means of dharma. The sacred texts say that because of the valour in their arms, enterprise is the life of a kshatriya. O descendant of the Bharata lineage! When a kshatriya's means of sustenance have gone, why should he not take from everyone, with the exception of ascetics and brahmanas? It is like a brahmana in hardship officiating at the sacrifice of someone who should not be performing a sacrifice. There is no doubt that in such situations, food that should not be eaten can also be eaten. If someone is distressed, why should gates and paths be barred? If someone is distressed, he can escape through something that is not a door. However, even for a person whose treasury and army have been destroyed and who has been defeated by the entire world, a life of begging is not recommended, nor the livelihood of a vaishya or a shudra. One should first try for one's own dharma, before adopting the livelihood of someone else. At first, one should think of that kind of livelihood to sustain life. However, if there is a disaster, one can then resort to the dharma and livelihood of others. When their means of livelihood have been destroyed, even brahmanas are seen to

[1104]Using intelligence to build up the treasury.

[1105]It can have other adverse affects.

[1106]When the period of hardship is over.

do this. Why should there be any doubt about a kshatriya? This has already been decided. He should take from whoever possesses more and never allow himself to be destroyed. The kshatriya is known to be the slayer and protector of subjects. Therefore, to protect him, it is the duty of the relatives of the kshatriya to appropriate. O king! There is no livelihood that exists without violence. Even a solitary sage, active and roaming in the forest, cannot manage to do that. Nor can one remain alive by following the conduct of Shankha and Likhita. O best among the Kurus! If one desires to protect the subjects, this is especially the case. In times of distress, the king and the kingdom must protect each other. This must always be done and this is eternal dharma. In times of distress, the king protects the kingdom by flooding it with material objects. In a time of distress, the kingdom must also protect the king. When the kingdom suffers from hunger, the king must not hide his treasury, his army, his rod, his friends and anything else that he may have stored. Those who are learned about dharma say that seeds must be saved from one's own food.

'"Shambara, who was great in his knowledge of maya, spoke about this. 'When a kingdom goes into a decline, the life of that king is one of shame. If he knows about the words of Shibi,[1107] why should people be without a means of sustenance?' A king's foundations are his treasury and his army. The treasury is again the foundation of the army. It is the foundation of all dharma and dharma is again the foundation of the subjects. There cannot be a treasury without oppression and without it, how is it possible to have an army? Therefore, one does not deserve to be tainted because of oppression. If a task is undertaken for the sake of a sacrifice, or if rites are followed in the course of a sacrifice, then, because of these reasons, the king does not deserve to be tainted. There are acts pursued for the sake of artha and there are contrary acts pursued for the sake of what is not artha. Those which are for the sake of artha and those which are not for the sake of artha may all seem to have the signs of artha. An intelligent person will use his intelligence to consider all this and then determine the course of action. Some

[1107]Generous king, whose story has been recounted in Section 33 (Volume 3).

objects are of use in a sacrifice, others are of no direct use in the sacrifice and still others may be of use in obtaining the purpose of the sacrifice. But all these are ingredients in conducting the sacrifice. I will tell you about examples, to illuminate the true nature of dharma. A sacrificial post must be severed for the sake of the sacrifice and there are some other trees that stand in the way and obstruct it. It is certain that these must also be cut down. When these fall down, they bring down other trees too. O scorcher of enemies! In that way, there are men who stand in the way of building up a large treasury and without killing them, I see no means of success. Both the worlds can be conquered with riches, this one and the next. What is said about dharma is true—it does not exist where there are no riches. To meet the requirements of sacrifices, every method of obtaining riches must be used. O descendant of the Bharata lineage! The sins from doing the right thing and not doing the right thing are not equal.[1108] O king! O descendant of the Bharata lineage! How can one follow neither of these two? I do not see people who extend their riches in the forest.[1109] A man desires whatever riches he can see in this world and hopes that it might belong to him. O scorcher of enemies! There is no dharma that is equal to the ruling of a kingdom. There is another kind of dharma that is recommended for kings who confront a hardship. Some acquire stores of riches through gifts and deeds, others are ascetics and do this through austerities, and still others choose intelligence and skills. It is said that one without riches is weak and one with riches is strong. One with riches can obtain everything. One with a treasury can overcome everything. The treasury provides dharma and kama, and this world and the next."'

[1108]It is not clear how this is to be interpreted. It probably means that doing the right thing is more important in normal times and not doing the right thing becomes more serious in times of adversity.

[1109]This is an argument against renunciating life.

SECTION EIGHTY-FIVE

Apad Dharma Parva

This parva has 1,560 shlokas and thirty-nine chapters.

Chapter 1457(129): 14 shlokas
Chapter 1458(130): 21 shlokas
Chapter 1459(131): 18 shlokas
Chapter 1460(132): 15 shlokas
Chapter 1461(133): 26 shlokas
Chapter 1462(134): 10 shlokas
Chapter 1463(135): 23 shlokas
Chapter 1464(136): 211 shlokas
Chapter 1465(137): 109 shlokas
Chapter 1466(138): 70 shlokas
Chapter 1467(139): 94 shlokas
Chapter 1468(140): 37 shlokas
Chapter 1469(141): 27 shlokas
Chapter 1470(142): 44 shlokas
Chapter 1471(143): 10 shlokas
Chapter 1472(144): 12 shlokas
Chapter 1473(145): 18 shlokas
Chapter 1474(146): 18 shlokas
Chapter 1475(147): 22 shlokas
Chapter 1476(148): 35 shlokas
Chapter 1477(149): 117 shlokas
Chapter 1478(150): 36 shlokas
Chapter 1479(151): 34 shlokas
Chapter 1480(152): 32 shlokas
Chapter 1481(153): 14 shlokas
Chapter 1482(154): 38 shlokas
Chapter 1483(155): 13 shlokas
Chapter 1484(156): 26 shlokas
Chapter 1485(157): 18 shlokas
Chapter 1486(158): 13 shlokas
Chapter 1487(159): 72 shlokas
Chapter 1488(160): 87 shlokas
Chapter 1489(161): 48 shlokas
Chapter 1490(162): 49 shlokas
Chapter 1491(163): 23 shlokas
Chapter 1492(164): 26 shlokas
Chapter 1493(165): 31 shlokas
Chapter 1494(166): 25 shlokas
Chapter 1495(167): 24 shlokas

Apad *means a misfortune or a calamity. In such situations, the nature of dharma to be followed is different and Bhishma instructs Yudhishthira about this.*

Chapter 1457(129)

'Yudhishthira said, "O descendant of the Bharata lineage! He[1] may be weak. He may be a procrastinator. He may be excessively affectionate towards his relatives. The citizens of the city and the countryside may be disenchanted. He may be without supplies of stores. He may suspect the foremost people.[2] His secret counsel may be divulged. He may be assailed by the enemy. All his advisers may be divided. Despite being weak, he may have to advance against a stronger enemy. When his senses are agitated, tell me what else he can do."

'Bhishma replied, "The external one who seeks to conquer him may be pure and may be accomplished in dharma and artha. He should swiftly conclude an agreement and try to free those parts that have already been conquered. Even if the other person wishes to conquer through adharma, is more powerful and is wicked in his intentions, there should be an attempt to conclude a pact, even if this leads to restrictions on himself.[3] Alternatively, he can abandon the capital and use other means to avoid the calamity. Though that situation[4] continues, as long as he is alive, he can accumulate objects again. There are some calamities that can only be handled by giving up everything. However, no one who knows about artha and dharma should give up the more expensive possession of one's own life.[5] One must protect oneself against being taken captive. How can one find compassion amidst the enemy's riches? If it is possible, one must never give oneself up."

'Yudhishthira said, "Those inside may be enraged and those outside may cause oppression. The treasury may be exhausted. The secret counsel may be divulged. What remains to be done then?"

'Bhishma replied, "One should be swift in concluding a pact,

[1]The king.

[2]His advisers.

[3]These restrictions might amount to giving up some more territory.

[4]Of running away.

[5]This can be interpreted as an injunction against suicide.

or one must be swift in exhibiting one's fierce valour. Or one can swiftly retreat and protect oneself. O lord of the earth! A king can conquer the entire earth with a few soldiers, if they are devoted, nourished and cheerful. If he is slain, he will ascend to heaven. If he is victorious, he will gain the earth. If he gives up his life in the battle, he will obtain Shakra's world. When he has conquered all the people, he must tread gently. If he cannot inspire trust in them through his humility, he should use his shoes.[6] He should retreat only when he wishes to. Should he desire to use conciliation, he should remove all signs from his own self and advance with a friend."'[7]

Chapter 1458(130)

'Yudhishthira said, "The supreme forms of dharma may not be available and people of diverse kinds may transgress it. Every means of sustenance on earth may have been taken over by bandits. O grandfather! When that worst of times arrives, how will a brahmana survive, assuming that out of affection, he does not abandon his sons and grandsons?"

'Bhishma replied, "When such a time arrives, he should survive through the strength of his ability to differentiate.[8] Everything is for the virtuous. There is nothing for the wicked. If someone takes from the wicked and gives it to those who are virtuous, he is knowledgeable about all forms of dharma and ensures a passage for himself. O king! He can seize things that have not been given, thinking, 'These riches are mine and I will give them away,' as long as he does not do this wrathfully and does not cause outrage in the kingdom. If a person uses vijnana to purify his strength,

[6]To run away.

[7]Advance towards the enemy with a friend, removing all signs of royalty.

[8]The word used is vijnana, not jnana. Therefore, it isn't quite straightforward knowledge.

even if he should be censured, he will not be censured, because he is patient and his conduct is based on vijnana. Those whose conduct depends on the exercise of strength find no other means appealing. O Yudhishthira! Their strength is enhanced through the use of energy. Medium people serve the dictates of the ordinary sacred texts, without any discrimination.[9] However, those who are intelligent adopt something that is beyond this. Officiating priests, priests, preceptors and brahmanas must always be treated well and worshipped. Acting contrary to this is a sin.[10] These are the norms of the world and the eternal foresight. This is the standard in which one must be submerged to determine if one is virtuous or wicked. Many who live in villages will angrily say things about each other. A king should not pay attention to these words and act on that basis.[11] Slander must never be spoken, nor heard. The ears must be covered, or one should go somewhere else. The conduct of virtuous people does not encompass slander and calumny. O Yudhishthira! Those who are virtuous only speak about the qualities of righteous people. Two well-trained draught animals, tamed and both capable of bearing an equal load, are good at bearing a burden. The king should be like that. He is the one who really bears the burden, aides come after that. Some think that conduct is the most important indication of dharma. Others do not like this and prefer Shankha and Likhita instead.[12] They do not speak such words out of malice or greed. There are rishis who have held that the perpetrators of wrong deeds must be exiled.[13] However, if someone is like a rishi, there are no norms for this. Perhaps the gods should punish these worst among men, who perpetrate perverse acts. If something is obtained through deceit, dharma suffers. Those who are virtuous must be honoured in every way, because they are the reason for prosperity. This must be accepted in one's heart and it establishes

[9]The sacred texts are meant for normal situations.

[10]The idea is that even in times of adversity, they must not be taxed.

[11]Reward and punishment should not be based on hearsay and slander.

[12]The scrupulous adherence to dharma on the part of Shankha and Likhita, also involving a king punishing a brahmana.

[13]Even if they are brahmanas.

dharma. He who knows about the four qualities that establish dharma is one who truly knows about dharma.[14] Like following a snake, it is extremely difficult to determine the path of dharma. When a deer is pierced, a hunter of deer follows in its footsteps by tracking drops of blood in the grass. That is the way one must follow the path of dharma. O one without decay! O Yudhishthira! You must follow the path of the virtuous with humility. Follow the conduct observed by the rajarshis."'

Chapter 1459(131)

'Bhishma said, "The king must generate his treasury from his own kingdom or the kingdoms of others. O Kounteya! Dharma results from the treasury and establishes the foundation of the kingdom. Therefore, the treasury must be generated and once it has been accumulated, it must be protected. Having protected, he must show compassion. This is the eternal dharma. The treasury cannot be generated through virtue and purity only, or through violence alone. To accumulate a treasury, one must follow a middle path. How can there be a treasury for someone who has no army? How can there be an army for someone who has no treasury? How can there be a kingdom for someone who has no army? How can there be Shri for someone who has no kingdom? For someone of superior conduct, the destruction of Shri is like death. Therefore, the king must increase the treasury, the army and friends. Men disrespect a king whose treasury has been destroyed. They are dissatisfied with little and are not interested in the work.[15] It is because of Shri that a king receives

[14]The four qualities are metaphysics/logic, the Vedas, economic welfare/prosperity and dandaniti. Alternatively, the Vedas, the smriti texts, customary law and what one personally regards to be dharma.

[15]A reference to the rewards a king offers his servants.

the greatest regard. It hides his sins, like garments hide the private parts of women. Men he has earlier injured follow him because of his wealth. They are like dogs,[16] finding delight in an opportunity to kill him. O supreme among the Bharata lineage! How can a king like this be happy?[17] The king must always show enterprise and not be languid. There is manliness in exertion. He must break at the joints, rather than bow down before anyone. He can resort to the forest and roam around with large numbers of bandits. However, he must not roam around with bandits who are against all restraints. O descendant of the Bharata lineage! Among the bandits, one can easily obtain soldiers who are fierce in their deeds. Everyone certainly trembles before a person who does not follow any restraints. Even bandits, who are without compassion, tremble before such a person. He must establish restraints and gladden the minds of people. Even a little bit of restraint is respected by the people. There are some people who have decided that this world and the world hereafter do not exist. One should not trust such a nastika. He is driven by doubt and fear. Bandits regard non-violence the same way as righteous people regard taking from others.[18] However, even among bandits, people find delight in agreements. The slaying of someone who is not a combatant, the ravishing of wives,[19] ingratitude, the seizure of the possessions of brahmanas, the complete destruction of everything and the abduction and confining of women—these are censured even among bandits. O descendant of the Bharata lineage! Since they avoid these, if one has a pact with them, one should not exterminate them completely. That has been determined. Instead of completely exterminating them, they should be brought under one's subjugation. Because one is stronger, one should act violently towards them. O son! Those who

[16]Alternatively, jackals. But dogs is more appropriate. Like vicious dogs, they wish to injure him, but serve him because of his riches.

[17]A king without a large treasury.

[18]Righteous people regard taking from others as adharma and bandits regard non-violence as adharma.

[19]Other people's wives.

exterminate them see their own extermination in every direction. Those who exterminate always have to suffer a fear because of that act of extermination."'[20]

Chapter 1460(132)

'Bhishma said, "On this kind of deed, those who are knowledgeable about ancient accounts recite definitive words. For a kshatriya who knows, dharma and artha are immediately evident and one cannot separate them. But some working of dharma is indirect. 'This is adharma.' 'That is dharma.' Such statements are like the footprints of a wolf.[21] The fruits of dharma and adharma can never be seen. A strong person can use his strength to bring everything under his subjugation and prosper. A strong person obtains Shri, an army and advisers. One without wealth falls and is like a little bit of leftover food. However, even for a strong person, there are many inauspicious things and these ensure that he is not saved from fear. It is only those two[22] true foundations that save him from great fear. I think that strength is superior to dharma. Dharma results from strength. Dharma is established on strength, like mobile objects on the surface of the earth. Just as smoke is controlled by the wind, dharma follows strength. Just as a creeper depends on a tree, dharma provides strength to a weak person. Dharma is under the control of those who are strong, just as happiness is enjoyed by those who possess objects of pleasure. There is nothing that a strong person is not successful at. For the strong, everything is pure.[23] If a wicked person is weak in strength, his stature is reduced. Therefore,

[20]Probably because there will always be some survivors and they will seek vengeance.

[21]They get blurred and a wolf's footprints cannot be distinguished from those of a dog.

[22]Dharma and artha.

[23]Nothing taints them.

everyone is alarmed at him, as if he is a wolf. He is censured and dishonoured and lives a life of unhappiness. A life of humiliation is just like death. When people say that he has been cast aside because of his wicked character, he is severely tormented and is wounded by words that are like stakes. On this, preceptors have spoken about ways of freeing oneself from sins. He must serve the three kinds of learning[24] and tend to brahmanas. He must seek their favours through sweet words and deeds. He must be great-minded and marry into a noble family. He must recount the good qualities of others and say that he will be like them. He must meditate, perform the water-rites, be gentle and not talk a lot. Having performed many extremely difficult deeds, he should penetrate the ranks of brahmana and kshatriyas.[25] Even if many people reprimand him because of this, he should not pay any attention to it. If he does not commit wicked acts, through such conduct he will quickly become greatly respected. He will enjoy happiness and riches and must protect himself through his conduct. He will obtain worship in this world and great fruits in the hereafter."'

Chapter 1461(133)

'Bhishma said, "In this connection, an ancient history is recounted. A bandit who followed restraints was not destroyed after his death. There was a ruler of the nishadas by the name of Kapavya. He was brave, intelligent and a striker. He was learned and was not violent. He protected dharma against any decline and worshipped brahmanas and seniors. His father was a kshatriya and his mother was a nishada. He protected the dharma of kshatriyas. Though he was a bandit, he obtained success. In the morning and in the evening, he would agitate herds of animals in the forest. He

[24]The Vedas.

[25]To serve them.

knew about different kinds of animals and about where they came to drink. He knew about all the different groves and regions and roamed around Mount Pariyatra. He knew about the dharma for all beings. His weapons were firm and he never missed his aim. He could single-handedly defeat hundreds of soldiers. In that great forest, he worshipped his aged and blind parents. He honoured them well and gave them food in the form of honey, meat, roots, fruit and grain that was superior and inferior. He tended to them. He protected the brahmanas who resided in the forest and passed through it. In that great forest, he brought them animals that he had killed. There were some who had doubts about receiving food from a bandit. For these, at the right time, he would leave it outside their houses and leave. There were thousands of dishonourable bandits who were pitiless. They desired to make him their leader.

'"The bandits said, 'You are wise and know about the time and the place. You have good conduct and wield firm weapons. You are respected by all of us. Be our leader and our chief. We will do whatever you ask us to. According to proper policy, protect us, like a mother and a father.' Kapavya replied, 'Do not kill women, those who are frightened, those who are children and those who are ascetics. Do not slay those who are not fighting. Do not forcibly abduct women. Under no circumstances should a spirited warrior slay a woman. Cattle and women should not be harmed and war must not be waged on their account. Grain must not be destroyed and one should not pointlessly create obstructions in ploughing, or in the worship of gods, ancestors and guests. Among all the beings, brahmanas deserve to be freed.[26] One must compensate them, even if one has to give up all of one's property. If they are extremely enraged and chant their mantras, there is no one in the three worlds who will be saved and will not be defeated. A person who speaks ill of brahmanas or wishes for their destruction will be destroyed. This is as certain as the rising of the sun. Dwell here and receive the fruits. Those who do not give according

[26] A brahmana should not be captured.

to their capacity will be attacked by our soldiers. The rod has been intended for the sake of ensuring virtue. It is certain that it is not meant to inflict death. However, it has been said that if a person obstructs virtuous people, it is dharma to kill him. There are some who obtain a living by causing injury to the kingdom. They are compared to worms inside a carcass. However, even if someone is a bandit, if he conducts himself in accordance with the sacred texts of dharma, despite being a bandit, he will swiftly obtain success.' All of them honoured Kapavya's instructions. All of them obtained a livelihood and abandoned their wicked ways. Because of his deeds, Kapavya obtained great success. He acted so as to ensure safety for the virtuous and restrained the bandits from wicked deeds. If someone regularly recounts this conduct of Kapavya, he will never be afflicted by any fear from residents of the forest, or from beings. There will never be any fear from mortals or immortals, from the virtuous or the wicked. O king! He will be like a leader in the forest."'

Chapter 1462(134)

'Bhishma said, "Those who are learned about the ancient accounts chant a verse that was sung by Brahma himself. This is a path through which a king can generate his treasury. 'The wealth of those who perform sacrifices, have good conduct and are noble should not be taken, as it belongs to the gods.[27] A kshatriya should take from bandits and from those who do not perform rites.' O descendant of the Bharata lineage! These subjects are for kshatriyas, who must protect them and also receive from them. The wealth belongs to kshatriyas and not to anyone else. The wealth must be used for the sake of the army, or for the purpose of performing sacrifices.

[27]The text does not indicate where the Brahma quote starts, but this seems to be the obvious place.

Herbs that are inedible are severed and used to cook stuff that is edible.[28] People who are learned in the Vedas say that wealth that is not used as offerings for the gods, the ancestors and mortals comes to no useful end. O king! A lord of the earth who follows dharma should take these riches away. O king! When it is like that,[29] it does not please the worlds and is not treasure. It must be taken away from the wicked and given to the virtuous. If someone makes himself into a bridge between the two, I think that person knows dharma. Some people say that here and there, herbs and animals may originate from injurious sources, but can nevertheless be used for sacrifices. Those who do not perform the rites of sacrifices are like flies that bite and like aggressive ants. That is what dharma pronounces. Dust and *ulapa* grass[30] can rise from the ground. Dharma is like that, subtle and subtler."'

Chapter 1463(135)

'Bhishma said, "On this, listen to this supreme and foremost account. This is about procrastination in deciding what should be done and what should not be done. In a pond that wasn't very deep, there were three *shakula* fishes who were friends. O Kounteya! Among the many other fishes that were there, these became companions. Out of these three that dwelt in the water, one knew when the right time had come, the second one was far-sighted and the third was a procrastinator. On one occasion, fishermen assembled around the pond. Using various outlets, they started to drain out the water to lower spots. On discerning that

[28]The inedible herbs are used as fuel. The inedible herbs are being compared to bandits and those who do not observe rites. Wealth is taken from them and used for sacrifices and the treasury, the edible imagery.

[29]In the hands of bandits and those who do not observe rites.

[30]A kind of soft grass.

the water level was declining, the far-sighted fish told his two friends that a danger had arrived. 'There is a disaster for all of us who dwell in the water. Let us quickly go somewhere else, before the path is destroyed. Those who follow good policy counter a danger before it has arrived. There is no doubt about this. We should decide to quickly go.' The procrastinator replied, 'What you have said is true. But it is my certain view that there is no need for us to hurry.' The one with the right understanding spoke to the far-sighted one, 'When it is the right time, I will not avoid doing anything that needs to be done.' Having been thus addressed, the far-sighted and immensely intelligent one emerged through the single stream that still remained and went into a deeper body of water. When they saw that the water had been drained out from the pond, the fishermen, who earned a living off fish, used different methods to catch the fish. They fluttered around in the pond, which was without any water. Together with the others, the fish that was a procrastinator was captured. When he saw that the fish were being strung together on a rope, the one with the right understanding penetrated into the midst of the ones that had already been strung and seized the rope in its mouth, as if it had already been captured. They[31] thought that all the fish had been captured. They took the fish to a clean bit of water to clean them. The one with the right understanding let go of the rope and swiftly escaped. The procrastinator, evil-souled and inferior in intelligence and consciousness was stupid. It died because it was insensible.

'"In that way, if someone is confused in intelligence and does not realize when the right time has come, he is swiftly destroyed, like the procrastinating fish. If a man thinks himself to be accomplished and does not do at the beginning what is beneficial, he faces a danger, like the fish with the right understanding. If a man acts so as to pacify a danger that has not yet come, he attains the best objective, like the far-sighted fish. The earth is said to be the place. *Kala, kashtha, muhurta, dina, nadya, kshana, lava, paksha, masa, ritu*s that are

[31]The fishermen.

equal, *vatsara*[32]—despite these, time cannot be seen. To obtain success, it is true that there must be good policy too.[33] This is what the rishis have taught in the sacred texts of dharma and artha and the sacred texts of moksha. They also determine the rules for the practice of kama among men. One must examine these properly before embarking on action. If one also considers the time and the place, one obtains the fruits from them."'

Chapter 1464(136)

'Yudhishthira said, "O bull among the Bharata lineage! You have talked about the best kind of intelligence, understanding what has happened and what will happen, and about the destruction that procrastination brings. O supreme among the Bharata lineage! I wish to hear about supreme intelligence for a king, who is confounded because he is surrounded by enemies. You are accomplished in dharma and artha. You are wise. You are skilled in all the sacred texts. O best among the Kuru lineage! I am asking you this. You should explain it to me. What should a king who is encompassed by many enemies do? In accordance with the rules, I wish to hear everything about this. When a king confronts a disaster in the midst of an enemy, there will be many who will range against one and seek to injure him, because of what they have suffered earlier. There will be immensely strong ones acting against him and he will be alone, without allies. How will he be able to take a stand? O bull among the Bharata lineage! How will he know the difference between a friend and an enemy? How will he act against those who are neither friend and an enemy? How will he act against those who are neither friend, nor foe? How will he use his wisdom to discern signs that an

[32]Kala is a small unit of time (roughly one minute), thirty kashthas make 1 kala, one muhurta is forty-eight minutes, dina is a day, nadya means night, kshana is another word for muhurta, lava is two kashthas, paksha is fortnight, masa is month, ritu is season and vatsara is year.

[33]In addition to time and place.

enemy has become a friend? How will such a man act and how will he obtain happiness? Who should he fight with? With whom should he try for a pact? What should be the conduct of a weak person who is in the midst of the enemy? O scorcher of enemies! This is supreme among all the tasks that must be undertaken. Rare is the person who can speak about such things, with the exception of Shantanu's son, Bhishma, who has conquered his senses and does not waver from the truth. A listener is also extremely difficult to get. O mighty-armed one! Therefore, you should tell me everything about all this."

'Bhishma replied, "O Yudhishthira! This question is worthy of someone who possesses your qualities. O son! O descendant of the Bharata lineage! Listen completely to the secrets about a time of adversity. By employing the capabilities of different people in different tasks, an enemy can become a friend and a friend may find himself to be censured. There is always a change in objectives. One must know about the time and the place, determine what should be done and what should not be done, and then decide whom to trust and whom to fight. A wise person always seeks to have peace with those who wish him well. O descendant of the Bharata lineage! But, for the sake of protecting one's life, there can be an alliance with the enemy. A man who is always against alliances is not learned. O descendant of the Bharata lineage! He does not obtain the objectives, or the fruits. If a person uses his reasoning to look towards the objectives and has an alliance with an enemy or counters a friend, he obtains extremely great fruits. On this, an ancient history is recounted, about a conversation between a cat and a rat in a banyan tree.

'"In a great forest, there was an extremely large banyan tree. It was covered with nets of creepers and was frequented by large numbers of diverse birds. Its trunks were like clouds and it offered cool and pleasant shade. Many predatory animals lived there, with enmity towards each other. There was a hole with one hundred mouths at the root of the tree and an immensely wise rat named Palita lived there. Earlier, a cat named Lomasha had happily dwelt in the branches, destroying the lives of the birds. Every day, when the sun had gone down, a *chandala* arrived there, having turned his mind towards enmity. He would spread out nets made of sinews there. Having done this, he would return cheerfully to his home and sleep, waiting for night to be over and for it to be morning. Every night, a large number of animals were always killed there. On one occasion, the cat was careless and got trapped there. At that time, the immensely wise Palita got to know that the enemy, who was always trying to kill it, had got trapped. It wandered around, without any fear at all. As it roamed around in that forest, assured in its roaming, it looked for some food and saw the meat.[34] It climbed up there and began to devour the meat. It laughed mentally, as it stood above the enemy who had got trapped. While it was engaged with the meat, it happened to look up and saw that another enemy had arrived, terrible in appearance. It used to lie down in a giant hole and was like Sharaprasuna.[35] This was an agile mongoose named Harika and its eyes were coppery red. Having smelt the rat, it had swiftly arrived there. It stood on the ground and raised its face upwards, licking its lips at the prospect of a meal. It[36] saw another enemy on a branch, one that lived in a hole in the trunk. This was an owl named Chandraka. Its beak was sharp and it roamed around during the night. It was within the reach of both the mongoose and the owl.

'"In that situation, confronted with that great danger, it began to think. 'Death has presented itself and this is a catastrophe and a great difficulty. There is danger from every side. What should I do to ensure my welfare? I am obstructed in every direction and every direction seems to be the same. Tormented by this fear, I will obtain the ultimate end. There are many difficulties and there is one chance in one hundred of my remaining alive. There is no doubt that disaster confronts me from every direction. If I descend on the ground, the mongoose will violently seize me. If I remain here, the owl will get me, or the cat, after it has severed the noose. However, a person who is wise should not be confused. As long as I breathe, I must try to remain alive. Those who are intelligent and wise and are accomplished in the sacred texts of good policy, are not scared when

[34]The meat left by the chandala as bait.

[35]Someone born in reeds, Kartikeya.

[36]The rat.

they face a danger or a great destruction of prosperity. At the moment, I do not see any means of attaining the objective other than the cat. That animal confronts a disaster and I can do him great service. How else can I remain alive now? There are three enemies who are after me. Therefore, I must resort to my enemy, the cat. I will use the knowledge of kshatriyas[37] and try to ensure its welfare. I have already made up my mind about how I am going to deceive these enemies. The worst of my enemies now faces this worst of hardships. If it is possible, perhaps this fool can be made to understand where his best interests lie. Given this difficulty, perhaps it may be made to have an alliance with me. If one is beset by enemies and if one wishes to save one's life in the midst of a hardship, the preceptors have said that one must have an alliance with a stronger person. A learned enemy is superior to a stupid friend. The prospect of my remaining alive is based on my enemy, the cat. Let me explain to it the means whereby it can save itself. Perhaps this enemy of mine is intelligent.' The rat knew about the time for fighting and the time for an alliance. It knew about artha and objectives.

'"It spoke these conciliatory words to the cat. 'O cat! Are you still alive? I am speaking these fraternal words to you. I wish that you should remain alive. That is best for both of us. O amiable one! You will remain alive, as you used to do earlier. I will save you and even give up my life for your sake. A way to save ourselves completely has presented itself before me. Through that, I am capable of saving you and also ensuring the best for me. Use your intelligence to reflect about the means I will suggest. This is good for you, good for me, and best for both of us. The mongoose and the owl are wicked in their intelligence. O cat! As long as they do not attack me, I am fine. But the shrieking one[38] and the owl with the darting eyes are both glancing towards me. As I am clinging to the branch of this tree, I am becoming extremely anxious. If one treads seven steps together, virtuous people become friends. You are learned. We have lived together. I will act so that you have no fear from death. O cat!

[37]Probably meaning force.

[38]The mongoose.

Without me, you are incapable of severing this noose. If you do not injure me, I will sever this noose. You live at the top of the tree and I dwell at the root. Both of us have lived in this tree for a long time. All this is known to you. Someone who does not trust anyone and someone who trusts a person who should not be trusted—the learned say that these two are always anxious in their minds and should not be praised. Let the friendship between us increase and let this be an agreement between two virtuous ones. The learned do not praise something that is done after the time for it is over. Know that this is full of purpose and reason and this is the right time for it. I desire that you should remain alive. You desire that I should remain alive. If someone wishes to cross a deep and great river with a piece of wood, the wood takes him across, and he takes the wood across too. If we act together in this way, our safety will be certain. I will save you and you will save me.' Palita spoke these words, which were full of purpose and beneficial for both of them. Having said this, it was impatient because time was being lost and looked on, hoping that the reasoning would be accepted. Having heard these excellent words, the cat, the learned enemy, replied in words that were full of reasoning and purpose and deserved to be accepted. It was intelligent and could speak well. Looking towards its own situation, it honoured the rat back in conciliatory words and applauded its speech. Its teeth and claws were sharp and its eyes were like lapis lazuli. Lomasha, the cat, gently looked towards the rat and said, 'O amiable one! O fortunate one! I am delighted that you desire I should remain alive. If you know what is desirable, do it without any reflection. I am gravely afflicted, but you are in a situation that is direr still. Since both of us face difficulties, let us have an alliance. There is no need to think. The time has come. Let us act so that we can ensure our success. If you free me from this difficulty, I will not forget what you have done. I have cast aside my pride and have become devoted to you. I am like a disciple and will work for your welfare. I will follow your instructions. I have sought refuge with you.' When the cat said this and offered to be controlled, Palita again spoke some words that were beneficial and provided arguments and counter-arguments about policy. 'The generous words that you have spoken are not unusual for someone in your situation. You know my ways. Listen to my words, which are for your benefit. The mongoose is giving me great fear and I will crouch under your body. Save me and do not kill me. I am capable of saving you. Also save me from the owl. That inferior one is also seeking to get at me. O friend! I will sever your noose. I am swearing this truthfully.' As Palita came close, Lomasha heard these words, which were full of reason and purpose, and glancing towards it, cheerfully welcomed it with honour.

'"Having thus honoured Palita, the cat, tied to it by a bond of friendship, thought about it patiently. Happily and quickly, it said, 'O fortunate one! Come swiftly. You are a friend whom I love like my own life. O wise one! Through your favours, I will quickly get my life back. I will do whatever I can for you. Make it known to me. I will do whatever you order me to. O friend! We must have an alliance. Once I have been freed from this danger, with my large number of friends and relatives, I will do all the deeds that are for your benefit and bring you pleasure. O amiable one! Once I have been freed from this hardship, I will become yours. I will do whatever brings you pleasure. I am capable of paying you back.' Having persuaded the cat that this was in its own interests, the rat was reassured that the objective could indeed be achieved and entered. Having been reassured by the intelligent cat, the rat fearlessly crouched under the cat's chest, as if it was in the lap of a father or a mother. The rat was curled up under the cat's body. On seeing this, the mongoose and the owl lost all hope and returned to their homes. Palita, knowledgeable about time and place, was curled up there.

'"O king! Waiting for the right time, it slowly began to gnaw through the noose. Afflicted because it was tied up in those bonds, the cat glanced towards the rat. It asked it to sever the noose faster and faster. Palita was severing the noose slowly. The cat continued to urge the rat on. 'O amiable one! Why are you not doing it faster? Do you not wish to accomplish the objective? O destroyer of enemies! Sever the noose before the *shvapacha*[39] arrives here.' Having been thus urged to speed up, the intelligent Palita, accomplished in wisdom,

[39]One who is an outcaste. Literally, one who eats dogs, or eats with dogs.

spoke these beneficial words to the cat which was under its control. 'O amiable one! Be quiet. There is no need to speed up for you, or to be frightened. We know about time and one should not laugh at time. If a task is started, or completed, at the wrong time, it does not accomplish the objective. If a task is started at the right time, it accomplishes great objectives. If you are freed at the wrong time, you will become a great danger to me. O friend! Therefore, we must wait for the right time. Why do you wish to rush? When I see the chandala coming, with a weapon in his hand, I will sever the noose then, since both of us will suffer from fear. At that time, you will be freed and will climb up the tree. There will be nothing except a desire to save your life then. O Lomasha! When you are trying to save yourself and are frightened and terrified, climbing up to your branch, I will enter my hole.' Desiring its own welfare, the rat spoke these words to the cat. However, Lomasha was immensely eloquent and knew about the use of words. It desired its own life. Having itself acted swiftly and well, it spoke these words to the rat, which was not hurrying up. 'This is not the way virtuous and affectionate people accomplish the tasks of their friends. When you faced a hardship, you were quickly freed by me. In that way, you should also swiftly do the task that ensures my welfare. O immensely wise one! Make efforts so that both of us are safe. Is it the case that you are remembering my earlier period of enmity towards you? Behold. That has indeed been a wicked act on my part. It is evident that it has led to a reduction in my lifespan. Earlier, in my ignorance, I may have acted in unpleasant ways towards you. You should not harbour that in your mind. I seek your forgiveness. Show me your favours.' The rat was wise and was honoured because it was knowledgeable about the sacred texts. It spoke these excellent words to the cat. 'O cat! I have heard the words that you have spoken to protect your own interests. You should also know about the preservation of my interests. If there is a friendship that results from fear, or if there is a friendship that is full of fear, then one must make great efforts to preserve it. It is like placing one's hand near a snake's mouth. If a person has an agreement with a stronger person and does not protect himself, he will find it causes him injury, like eating something that is unwholesome. There is no one who is truly an enemy. There is no one who is truly a well-wisher. Interests are bound to interests, like an elephant to a wild elephant.[40] When a task has been completed, no one looks to see who did it. That is the reason all tasks should be left with a little bit still undone. At that time,[41] your task will be determined by fear. You will be focused on running away and won't be able to seize me. Most of the strands have been severed. There is only one that is still left. O Lomasha! Restrain yourself. I will swiftly sever this.' They conversed in this way, both overcome by fear.

'"When the night was over, Lomasha was overcome by terror. It became morning and the chandala named Parigha could be seen, with a weapon in his hand. He was malformed and dark brown. His hips were broad. His head was shaven. He was rough and was surrounded by a circle of dogs. His ears were pointed and his mouth was large. He was aged and terrible in appearance. On seeing him, who looked like one of Yama's messengers, the cat was terrified out of its wits. Frightened, it addressed Palita. 'What will you do now?' On seeing that terrible person, the mongoose and the owl were instantly scared and were filled with hopelessness. The two intelligent and strong ones had contracted an agreement and because of that good policy, could no longer be struck with force.[42] They saw that the cat and the rat had concluded an agreement for the sake of accomplishing their objectives. Therefore, the owl and the mongoose swiftly returned to their own homes. The rat severed the cat's strand. As soon as it had been freed, the cat rushed up the tree. Not only was its terrible enemy freed, Palita was also freed from its fear and entered its hole. Lomasha went up the tree. The chandala looked in every direction and gathered up his snare. O bull among the Bharata lineage! His hopes having been destroyed, in a short instant, the chandala left the spot and returned to his own home.

'"Lomasha was freed from the fear and obtained life, something

[40]Tame elephants are used to trap wild elephants.

[41]When the hunter arrives.

[42]This refers to the agreement between the rat and the cat. There is an inconsistency, because the mongoose and the owl had already left and had gone home.

that is very difficult to obtain. From the top of the tree, it spoke to Palita, in the hole. 'Without having had a conversation with me, you suddenly ran away. I am grateful because you did something good for me. I hope you do not suspect me. You inspired trust in me and you gave me my life. When it is time to enjoy yourself with a friend, why are you avoiding me? If an evil-minded person has an agreement with a friend and does not follow it up later, then, when he faces difficulties, he will not find a friend. O friend! You made me a friend because of my capacity. Having made me a friend, you should now enjoy that friendship. All my friends and all my relatives will show you honour, like a disciple towards a beloved preceptor. I will also worship you, with my large number of friends and relatives. Why will a grateful person not honour someone who has given him life? You are the lord of my body and my home. All the riches that I possess are at your command. O wise one! Be my adviser. Instruct me, like a father. I swear on my life that you need have no fear of me. We may possess strength, but you are like Ushanas[43] himself in your intelligence. If your counsel is united with that strength, victory will be assured.'

'"Having been addressed in these conciliatory words by the cat, the rat, who knew about supreme objectives, wished to ensure its own welfare and spoke these gentle words. 'O Lomasha! I have heard everything that you have said. Now listen to the way I see it. Friends must be examined. Enemies must also be examined. In this world, this is seen in extremely subtle ways and is revered as wisdom. There are well-wishers in the form of enemies. There are enemies in the form of friends. Those who have been won through conciliation do not comprehend this, because they are subservient to affection and greed. No one is born as an enemy. No one is born as a friend. Because of their different capacities, they become friends and enemies. If it is seen that there is a selfish objective of someone being alive because another person is alive, then that other person is a friend, but only as long as there is no other catastrophe. There is no friendship that is permanent. There is no enmity that is permanent. Friendship and

[43]Shukracharya.

enmity result from a specific objective. In the course of time, a friend may become an enemy. An enemy may also become a friend. Self-interest is the most important. If a person does not know about the objective and trusts friends and never trusts enemies, his life becomes unstable. If a person does not know about the objective and turns his mind towards good conduct, regardless of whether it is a friend or an enemy, his intelligence is unstable. One should not trust someone who should not be trusted. One should not even trust someone who should be trusted. The dangers that arise from trust sever the roots. Relationships like father, mother, son, maternal uncle, nephew, matrimonial allies, relatives—all these are based on a purpose. A mother and a father abandon a beloved son who has fallen.[44] People protect their own selves. Behold the essence of selfishness. I think that you are deceitful in your wisdom. Immediately after being freed, you seek to ensure the happiness and safety of someone you should hunt. You descended from the banyan tree to this spot. Earlier, because of your fickleness, you did not realize that there was a snare here. Someone who is fickle cannot do something for his own self, forget others. There is no doubt that a fickle person destroys all tasks. You have spoken pleasant words and have said that I am loved by you. All of that is false. Listen in detail to the reasons. One becomes a beloved because of some reason. Enmity is also because of a reason. In this world of the living, everything is for a purpose. There is no one who is always loved by another. Friendship between two brothers born from the same womb, the affection of a husband and wife towards each other—I know of no affection in this world that is without a reason. If a brother or a wife is enraged, after the immediate reason is over, they naturally become affectionate again.[45] However, other people do not turn affectionate in this way. Some become beloved because of gifts. Others become beloved because of words, and still others because of mantras and offerings. People are loved to accomplish some task. Affection results from a reason. When the reason is absent, it is no longer there. When the reason

[44]Fallen in the sense of having done something reprehensible.

[45]Because of the natural bond of affection.

ceases to exist, the affection also withdraws itself. What reason can I think of, so that I might be your beloved? We should know that there is no connection beyond my being your food. Time changes the reason and self-interest is followed. I am wise. I know about self-interest and accept that people follow it. You should not speak such words to someone who is learned and knows about self-interest. This is the wrong time. There is no longer a catastrophe. You must therefore have reasons of self-interest. I am driven by self-interest and know that war and peace are both fickle. From one moment to another, they change their forms, like clouds. You were my enemy. Later, you became my friend. You have again become my enemy. Behold the fickleness of objective. As long as there was a reason, there was friendship. The reason has now gone and we have gone back to earlier times. With the progress of time, the reason has also gone. You are my ultimate enemy and circumstances made you my friend. With that task having been accomplished, we have returned to our natural enmity. I know the truth about what the sacred texts have laid down. How can I then enter the snare that you have set for me? I have been freed through your valour and you have been freed through my valour. We have favoured each other through our conducts and there is no further association between us. O amiable one! You have accomplished your objective. My purpose has also been met. You have no other purpose with me, other than eating me. I am the food and you are the feeder. I am weak and you are strong. When we are unequal in strength, there can be no alliance between us. I honour your wisdom. Immediately after being freed, you wish to assure me of happiness and safety and wish to hunt and devour me. You were caught because you were in search of food. Having been freed, you have ventured out for food. I know about the sacred texts. You are seeking an alliance with me because you certainly wish to eat me. I know that you are hungry and that it is the time for you to eat. You are seeking an alliance with me, because you wish to hunt and eat me. O friend! You have sons and wives and are looking towards me. You say that you wish to act so as to serve me. But I don't find that appealing. If your beloved wife and sons see me with you, will they be cheerful at this affection? Will they not eat me up? I will not associate with you. The reason for our association is over. If you remember the good deed I did for you, think of what will be auspicious for me now. Will a wise person venture out of his territory when a natural enemy is afflicted and hungry and is hunting for food? May you be safe. I will go far away from you. O Lomasha! Retreat. I will not associate with you. Proximity with someone who is powerful is never praised. O wise one! I must always be terrified of stronger ones, even if they are peaceful. If there is anything else that I can do for you, tell me what I should do for you. I will give everything that you desire, but I will never give up my own self. To protect one's own self, offspring, a kingdom, jewels and prosperity can be given up. For the sake of protecting one's own self, everything should be given up. We have heard that it has been seen that prosperity, wealth and gems, even if they are presently with enemies, return if one acts so as to remain alive. It is said that riches and jewels can be given up, but not one's own self. The self must always be protected, even at the cost of wives and riches. If men act so as to protect the foundations of their lives, having examined the reasons properly, they do not confront any catastrophes that result from their own sins. If the weak know the stronger enemy well and have made up their minds to protect themselves, they cannot be dislodged from that resolution.' Thus did Palita speak these words of censure.

'"The cat was ashamed and spoke these words to the rat. 'I honour your wisdom and the fact that you are devoted to my welfare. You have spoken words that are full of reason, though my views have been different. O virtuous one! But you should not take me to be other than what I am. You have truly granted me my life and my affection results from that. I know about dharma. I know about the qualities. In particular, I am grateful. I am affectionate towards my friends, especially those who are like you. O virtuous one! Given these reasons, you should not avoid me. If you avoid me, I, and all my relatives, will give up our lives. I am spirited and the wise have said that words of censure are enough to instruct people like me. You know about the nature of dharma. You should not suspect that I might be the cause of your death.' Having been thus praised by the cat, the rat thought and spoke these grave and purposeful words to the cat. 'You are virtuous and I have heard the words of reason you have spoken to me. Though I am pleased, I do not trust you. By praising me, or by offering me riches, you won't be able to get me to associate with you. O friend! The wise do not subjugate themselves to the enemy. On this, there was a verse sung by Ushanas. Listen to it. "If one has had an agreement with a more powerful enemy to achieve a common end, one must act in a controlled way. Once the task has been accomplished, one should not trust. In every situation, one must protect one's own life. All one's possessions and offspring exist only as long as one is alive. In brief, the supreme view of all the texts about policy is that one should not trust. Therefore, if one desires the welfare of one's own self, one must completely distrust men.[46] Those who are weak, but do not trust, are not killed by their enemies. But if they trust, even the relatively strong are quickly slain by the weak." O cat! Thus, I must always protect my own self from someone like you. You must also protect yourself from the chandala, whose anger has been generated.' As it was speaking in this way, terror arose in the cat and it swiftly entered its hole. Palita knew about the true purport of the sacred texts and was full of intelligence and capacity. It was wise. Having said all this, it went to another hole. Palita was wise and intelligent, though weak. Because of this, though alone, it was able to overcome many other immensely strong enemies. A learned person must have an alliance with a capable enemy, just as the rat and the cat resorted to each other and escaped.

'"I have instructed you about the path to be followed in the dharma of kshatriyas. O lord of the earth! I have recounted it in detail. Listen to it briefly again. Those two were firm in their enmity towards each other, but acted with supreme affection. They then turned their minds towards subjugating each other. However, by resorting to the strength of its intelligence, the wiser one subjugated the other one. But if care is not exercised, a wiser person can be subjugated, even by someone who is not learned. A person who is scared must act as if he is not scared. Even if he does not trust, he

[46]That is, other men, not in the sense of rats or cats versus men.

must act as if he trusts. One must be careful and not be fickle. If one is fickle, one is destroyed. There is a time for allying with enemies. There is a time for fighting with friends. O Yudhishthira! Those who know about the truth have said that one must always act in this way. O great king! Having thought about this, having understood the purport of the sacred texts and having engaged oneself with care, one must act fearfully, before the cause for fright presents itself. One must determine one's action as if one is frightened and decide on counters. Intelligence results from fear, provided that one engages oneself with care. O king! There is no fear for a person who is frightened of fear that hasn't materialized. However, a great fear is generated for a person who is not frightened, but is careless. One must never offer the counsel, 'Do not be scared.' That leads to ignorance. If one knows, one can go to those who know about a means to get out of the hardship. A person who is scared must therefore act as if he is not scared. Even if he does not trust, he must act as if he trusts. Having comprehended the gravity of the task, he must not indulge in any falsehood. O Yudhishthira! In this way, I have recounted the history to you. O son! Having heard in the midst of these well-wishers, act accordingly. Use your intelligence to first know the difference between an enemy and a friend, the time for war and peace and means of escaping from a difficulty. For a common objective, one must have an alliance with a stronger enemy. One must associate and act in accordance with the agreement. However, having accomplished the objective, one must not trust. O Yudhishthira! This policy is not against the three objectives.[47] Having been instructed and heard, delight the subjects again. O Pandava! Along your path, advance with the brahmanas. O descendant of the Bharata lineage! Brahmanas bring the greatest benefit, in this world and in heaven. O lord! They know about dharma and are always grateful. O lord of men! They are auspicious in their deeds and if revered first, ensure victory. O king! The kingdom is the supreme goal. After that, as is proper, in due course, you will obtain fame, deeds and offspring in the lineage. O descendant of the Bharata lineage! If a king knows

[47]Dharma, artha and kama.

about these excellent words about war and peace, full of specific intelligence, he should always looks towards them and practise them, when that king is encircled by enemies."'

Chapter 1465(137)

'Yudhishthira said, "O mighty-armed one! You have counselled to the effect that the enemy must never be trusted. But if he trusts nobody, how will the king conduct himself? O king! If he trusts, there is a great danger to the king. O king! But if he does not trust, how will a king triumph over his enemies? I have a doubt about this. O grandfather! Dispel this confusion in my mind, which has arisen after you have told me the account about distrust."

'Bhishma replied, "O Kounteya! O king! Listen to the account of the conversation that took place in Brahmadatta's abode between Brahmadatta and Pujani. In the inner quarters of Brahmadatta's palace in Kampilya, a bird named Pujani dwelt for a long time. Like the *jivajivaka* bird, she knew about the cries of all beings.[48] She knew everything. Even though she had been born in an inferior species, she knew about all forms of dharma. There, she gave birth to an immensely radiant son. At the same time, through the queen, the king had a son. Every day, she[49] would go to the shores of the ocean and bring back two fruits to nourish her son and the prince. She would give one fruit to her son and the other to the prince. The fruits tasted like amrita and increased strength and energy. Having eaten the fruit, the prince grew very fast. Once, he got away from the hands of the nurse and began to play with the bird. O Indra among kings! Having taken the bird,[50] which had been born at the same time, to a deserted place, he killed it and returned to his nurse's

[48]The jivajivaka bird is a pheasant. Pujani could probably mimic the cries of all beings.

[49]Pujani.

[50]The baby bird.

arms. After having returned from collecting fruit, the bird saw her dead son lying down on the ground, killed by the child. She was distressed on seeing her slain son and her face became full of tears. Pujani was tormented by grief and spoke these words. 'There is no affection or friendship in association with kshatriyas. They serve you for a purpose. Having accomplished the objective, they abandon you. Kshatriyas should never be trusted. They injure everyone. Having caused the injury, they always seek to pointlessly placate. I will now act in the same way and exact vengeance. He is ungrateful. He is violent. He has destroyed my trust. He has committed a triple sin by killing someone who was born and reared with him, someone who ate with him and someone who sought refuge with him.' Having said this, she used her talons to tear out the eyes of the king's son. Once she had torn these out, Pujani was comforted and again spoke these words. 'If a sin is perpetrated voluntarily, it immediately devolves on the doer. However, if a deed is done in reaction to another deed, it doesn't destroy good or bad merit. Even if such a wicked deed is perpetrated, it doesn't descend on the doer. Instead, it descends on the sons, the sons' sons and the daughters' sons.'

'"Brahmadatta said, 'We committed an injury against you and you have taken a counteraction. Both of us are now equal. O Pujani! Stay with me and do not go.'

'"Pujani replied, 'When one has injured someone else, the learned do not praise remaining there. It is better to withdraw from there. O king! Even if there are words of conciliation, one cannot trust someone with whom there has been an act of enmity. A foolish person will soon comprehend that enmity is never pacified. Once there is enmity towards each other, sons and grandsons are dragged into it. Once the sons and grandsons are destroyed, it carries over to the world after death. Under every circumstance, distrust of those towards whom there is enmity brings happiness. One must never act so as to trust such a person. Otherwise, trust itself will be destroyed. One should not trust someone who should not be trusted. One should not even trust someone who should be trusted. If you so desire, you can make others trust you. But you must not trust others. The mother and the father are the best among relatives.

The wife is wear and tear[51] and the son is nothing but a seed. The brother is an enemy and the friend possesses a moist hand.[52] One's atman alone knows happiness and unhappiness. If there has been enmity towards each other, an alliance is not possible. The purpose behind my staying here has been transgressed. If a person who was earlier terrified by strength has committed an injury, and is now worshipped with riches and honour, he will always be distrustful. A spirited person who was earlier respected and is now dishonoured should no longer dwell in a place where he was first respected and subsequently dishonoured. For a long time, I dwelt in your abode without suffering any injury. But an enmity has arisen now. May you be happy. I will go elsewhere.'

'"Brahmadatta said, 'If one acts as a reaction to an act that has been committed, that is not reckoned as a crime. You have freed yourself of a debt. O Pujani! Stay with me and do not go.'

'"Pujani replied, 'An alliance can never again be forged between someone who has been injured and someone who has caused the injury. The hearts of the one who has been injured and the one who has done the injury know this.'

'"Brahmadatta said, 'There can again be friendship between someone who has been injured and someone who has caused the injury. It has been seen that the enmity has been pacified and there has been no further wicked act.'

'"Pujani replied, 'Enmity can never be overcome. One must not be assured because there has been conciliation. It is childish to believe in trust. Therefore, it is better that I should not be seen. There are those who cannot quickly be seized through extremely sharp weapons, but are captured through conciliation, like elephants with other elephants.'

'"Brahmadatta said, 'Dwelling together leads to affection, even towards someone who may cause one's death. They trust each other, like the shvapacha and the dog. Even among those who have been

[51]The text uses the word *jara*, meaning old age, as well as wear and tear. In this context, wear and tear fits better.

[52]The friend has to be bribed.

enemies, dwelling together leads to gentleness. Like water on the leaf of a lotus, that enmity does not linger.'

'"Pujani replied, 'The learned ones know that enmity arises from five causes—resulting from women, resulting from dwelling places, resulting from words, resulting from rivalries and resulting from injuries. In particular, the kshatriya must kill a person who causes any of these. Considering the place, the strength and other such things, he does this covertly or overtly. Therefore, one must never trust someone against whom an injury has been committed, even if he used to be a well-wisher. The enmity will remain concealed, like fire hidden inside wood. O king! Like Ourva's fire in the ocean,[53] the fire of an enmity is never pacified, be it through riches, punishment, conciliation or teaching. O king! Once the fire of enmity has been ignited and there has been an act of injury, it is not pacified without burning down one of the two parties. If a person has earlier committed an injurious act, even if he is worshipped with riches and honour, he will not find peace or trust. His act gives force to his fear. I have never committed an injurious act towards you, nor you towards me. The trust was earlier unblemished. I no longer have that trust.'

'"Brahmadatta said, 'Every act is done by time and so are all the different kinds of action. Since everything is undertaken by time, who has injured whom? Birth and death occur in the same way. All deeds are undertaken by time and the one who is alive is only an instrument. Some are killed at the same time, others one after another. Time consumes beings, like a fire that has received kindling. O beautiful one! In what we do towards each other, I, nor you, are the principal agents. Time always determines the happiness and unhappiness of living beings. Following time, dwell here with affection. You will not be injured. O Pujani! I have forgiven what you have done. Pardon me.'

'"Pujani replied, 'If time is the principal agent, then there would never have been any enmity. When a relative has been killed, why do other relatives seek vengeance? In earlier times, why did the gods

[53]This story has been recounted in Section 11 (Volume 1). The sage Ourva belonged to the Bhargava lineage and the fire of his rage was cast into the ocean.

and the asuras strike each other? If time determines happiness and unhappiness, existence and non-existence, then, when someone is ill, why do physicians use medicines? If time does the healing, what is the need for medication? If one is senseless with great sorrow, why does one lament? If time is the principal agent, why does dharma accrue to a doer? Your son slew my son and was injured by me. O lord of the earth! After that, I deserve to be captured by you. Because of sorrow over my son, I committed a sin towards your son. Listen to the truth from me. I deserve to be struck by you. Men seek out birds to kill or to sport. There is no third association, other than killing and capture. Because of fear of being slain or being captured, there are those who try to escape. Those who are learned about dharma say that there is unhappiness in death and calamity. Everyone loves his life. Everyone loves his sons. Everyone wishes to avoid misery and calamity. Everyone desires happiness. O Brahmadatta! Old age is misery. The destruction of riches is misery. Misery is dwelling with someone who is injurious. Misery is separation from something one wants. There is misery in enmity and captivity, or in violence and acts caused by women. People are always whirled around between unhappiness and happiness. Some foolish people say that there is no misery in another person's sorrow. But there will be such speculation only among gentlemen who have experienced no grief. How can someone who has sorrowed and has been afflicted with grief speak in this way? A person who knows about the essence of all misery knows that one's own self is no different from another person. O king! O scorcher of enemies! What I have done towards you and what you have done towards me are incapable of being expiated over one hundred years. Because of what we have done towards each other, there cannot be an alliance. Whenever you repeatedly remember your son, there will be a new enmity. Having performed an injurious act, if someone wishes to act affectionately, there can be no alliance with him. It is like an earthen pot that has been shattered. Those who know the purport of the sacred texts have determined that distrust leads to the rise of happiness. In earlier times, Ushanas chanted two verses to Prahrada. "He who trusts the words, true or false, of an enemy, is slain, like those who believe in honey are snared by dry grass.[54] The enmity in a family is not pacified for ten yugas. Even if one man remains in the family, this is spoken about." Kings may hide their enmity and resort to conciliation. But later, they crush the enemy, like a full pot against a rock.[55] O king! One must never trust a person against whom one has committed an evil act. Having injured the other person, one only reaps misery from the trust.'

'"Brahmadatta said, 'Without trusting others, one can never accomplish the objectives. If one is always terrified, it is like being dead.'

'"Pujani replied, 'When there are wounds in the feet, one can only creep along on those feet. Even if those feet are guarded well, one cannot run on them, even for a brief moment. If a person has sore eyes and looks at the wind, it is certain that his eyes will be wounded even more by the wind. If, because of confusion, a person has resorted to a bad path and does not know his own strength, his life will come to an end. If a man ploughs the field without knowing about the rain, his endeavour will be inferior and no crops will be reaped. If a person always eats food that is beneficial, regardless of whether it is bitter, astringent, tasty or devoid of taste, he will be like one who is immortal. If a man does not know the consequences and ignoring wholesome food greedily eats something else, that is the end of his life. Destiny and human endeavour exist and depend on each other. Deeds are resorted to by the enterprising and destiny by the impotent. One must do deeds that are good for one's own self, regardless of whether they are harsh or mild. He who is not devoted to action will always be devoured by some disaster. Therefore, whenever there is doubt over an act, one must exhibit one's valour. Men must give up everything and perform acts that are good for their own selves. Those who are learned say that knowledge, bravery, skill, strength and patience

[54]There are pits covered with dry grass. In pursuit of honey, people don't notice these and fall into them.

[55]There is an implicit image of the king as the rock, the enemy as the pot and the objects in the pot as the temporary blandishments.

are five natural friends and make things happen in this world. It is said that men can obtain residences, metals,[56] fields, wives and well-wishers everywhere. A wise person is always delighted and is always radiant. He does not frighten anyone. Even when there is an attempt to terrify him, he is not scared. If a person is intelligent, his wealth always increases, bit by bit. He bases himself in self-control and undertakes his tasks through skill. Men of limited intelligence are tied to their houses by bonds of affection. They have bad wives who devour their flesh, like female crabs and young crabs.[57] Other men are deficient in intelligence and think of homes, fields, friends and their own country as belonging to them. But one must flee from a country that is afflicted, or is plagued by disease and famine. One must always go and dwell elsewhere and live there, always respected. Therefore, I will go elsewhere. I do not wish to dwell with you. O king! What has been done by your son cannot be accepted. One must keep a bad wife, a bad son, a bad king, a bad relative and a bad country a great distance away. There is no trust in a bad friend. How can there be pleasure in a bad wife? There can be no growth in a bad kingdom. There can be no livelihood in a bad country. There can be no association with a bad friend, because that friendship will always be fickle. When there is a monetary disaster, a bad relative becomes disrespectful. One who speaks pleasantly is truly a wife. One who provides growth is truly a son. If there is trust, one is truly a friend. If there is a livelihood, that is truly a country. Though the king is fierce in his rule, there is no exercise of force. He[58] cherishes the poor and does not avoid an association with them. The wife, the country, friends, sons, allies and relatives—all these possess qualities, and the king has the eye of dharma. A king who is careful and rules is the foundation of the three objectives.[59] The subjects who do not know about dharma

[56] *Kupya*, that is, metals other than silver and gold.

[57] There is nothing in the text to suggest that these young crabs are offspring. Therefore, this is probably nothing more than some crabs eating smaller crabs.

[58] The king.

[59] Dharma, artha and kama.

are restrained and head towards their destruction. A tax can be imposed and one-sixth can be collected as tax. However, a king who does not protect the subjects well is nothing but a thief. If a king himself grants assurance but does not act according to that norm, he is wicked. He will collect the adharma of all the people and go to hell. If a king grants assurance and acts according to that norm, he is known as one who protects the subjects according to dharma and grants every kind of happiness. Prajapati Manu said that a king possesses seven attributes—father, mother, preceptor, protector, Agni, Vaishravana[60] and Yama. By exhibiting compassion towards the subjects, the king is the father of the kingdom. A man who behaves falsely towards him is reborn as inferior species. By nourishing those who are distressed, he is like a mother. Like Agni, he consumes wicked ones. By controlling, he is like Yama. By releasing objects of desire, he is like Kubera, the one who grants wishes. Like a preceptor, he instructs about dharma. He protects like a protector. When the king delights the residents of the city and the countryside with his qualities, he protects with his attributes and with dharma and is not dislodged from his kingdom. He himself knows about the rites followed in the city and the countryside. That king enjoys happiness, in this world and in the next. If the subjects are always anxious and oppressed by the burden of taxes, or overcome by various calamities, then he[61] will head towards destruction. When his subjects prosper, like large lotuses in a pond, he attains greatness in the worlds and enjoys a share in the fruits of all sacrifices. O king! Strife with a strong person is not praised. If one is seized by a stronger person, how can there be a kingdom? How can there be happiness?'"

'Bhishma said, "The bird spoke these words to King Brahmadatta. With the king's permission, she then headed for her desired direction. This was the conversation between Brahmadatta and Pujani. O best among the Bharata lineage! I have recounted it to you. What else do you wish to hear?"'

[60]Kubera.

[61]The king.

Chapter 1466(138)

'Yudhishthira asked, "O descendant of the Bharata lineage! O grandfather! When the yugas progress and dharma decays, when the world is afflicted by bandits, how should one establish oneself?"

'Bhishma replied, "O descendant of the Bharata lineage! I will tell you about the policy for times of calamity. At such a time, the lord of the earth should conduct himself by abandoning compassion. On this, there is the example of an ancient history. There was a conversation between Bharadvaja and King Shatruntapa. King Shatruntapa was a maharatha from Souvira. He approached Kaninka[62] and asked him about his notion of artha. How can one obtain something that has not been got? Having obtained it, how can it be increased? When it has increased, how can it be protected? When it has been protected, how can it be used? The brahmana had determined the nature of artha.

'"When he was asked about his determination of artha, he spoke these words, full of reason, in reply. 'He[63] must always raise the rod of chastisement. He must always exhibit his manliness. He must not have any weaknesses. He must look towards the weaknesses of others, searching for openings. On seeing that the rod is always raised, people will be extremely frightened. Therefore, all beings must be restrained with the rod. This is praised by learned people who have seen the truth. Out of the four, the rod is said to be the most important.[64] When the foundation has been severed, all those who earn a living from it are also killed. When the root of a tree has been severed, how can the branches remain? A learned person first strikes down the root of the enemy's side. After this, he makes all the aides and the allies[65] follow him. At a time of difficulty, without thinking about it, he must follow good counsel, show great valour,

[62]Kaninka is another name for Bharadvaja.

[63]The king.

[64]Sama (conciliation), dana (gifts), danda (the rod/chastisement) and bheda (dissension) are the four elements of policy.

[65]Of the enemy.

fight well and retreat well. He must be humble only in his words. His heart must be like a razor. He must first speak mildly, abandoning desire and anger. To accomplish an objective, he can have an alliance with a rival, but must not trust him. Having accomplished the objective, a clear-sighted person will quickly withdraw from the alliance. Assuming the guise of a friend, the enemy must be assured through conciliation. But one must always be careful about the enemy, since he is like a snake which has entered the house. If the intelligence of the other person can be overwhelmed, he must be conciliated with what has already happened. If the other person is not wise, he can be conciliated with the future. And a learned person can be conciliated with the present. If he[66] desires prosperity, he must join his hands in supplication, take pledges, resort to conciliation, bow down his head at the time of speaking and even shed tears. As long as the time of calamity continues, the enemy can be borne on the shoulder. But when the right time arrives, he[67] must be smashed, like an earthen pot against a rock. O Indra among kings! It is better to blaze for a short period of time like ebony, than to burn without smoke for a long period of time, like chaff of grain. If one knows about the nature of artha, it is futile to associate with an ungrateful person. Such a person only enjoys the riches and is disrespectful when the task has been accomplished. Therefore, in all tasks, something must be left incomplete.[68] To ensure the best for himself, he must act like a cuckoo, a boar, Mount Meru, an empty house, a predatory beast and an actor.[69] He must always be ready to rise up and go to the house of the enemy. Even if the enemy is not well, he must ask him about his welfare. Those who are lazy, those who are impotent, those who are proud, those who are scared of the

[66]The king.

[67]The enemy.

[68]If everything is completed, an ungrateful person will have nothing to look forward to.

[69]He must be like a cuckoo in sweetness of speech, like a boar in destroying enemies, like Meru in loftiness, like an empty house that offers refuge to everyone, like a predatory beast in causing fear and like an actor in adopting different disguises.

disapprobation of people and those who are perennially waiting, never accomplish their objectives. The enemy must not know about his weaknesses. But he must know about the weaknesses of the enemy. He must protect his own weaknesses, like a turtle hiding its limbs. Like a crane, he must think of accomplishing his objective.[70] Like a lion, he must show his valour. He must be like a wolf in attacking. In running away, he must be like a rabbit. Drinking, gambling with the dice, women, hunting, singing and musical instruments can be indulged in, but any addiction is sinful. The bow can be made to resemble a blade of grass and he can sleep like a deer.[71] He should be blind when it is best to be blind and he can even resort to being deaf. A discerning person resorts to valour when it is the right time and the right place. If valour does not pay heed to time and place, it is unsuccessful. He must think about the right time and the wrong time, about his strengths and his weaknesses. He must engage himself only after he has discerned the relative strengths. Having made an enemy bow down through the use of the rod, if a king does not restrain him, he is clinging to death, like a pregnant she-mule.[72] A tree with many flowers may bear no fruit. A tree with fruit may be difficult to climb. Sometimes, a mango may seem to be unripe, or cannot be shaken down. The hope should be appropriate to the time and one must not engage oneself if there is an obstacle. The obstacle is due to a cause and he must speak about the reasons that are behind those causes. As long as the reason for the fear has not presented itself, he must seem to be frightened and seek to counter it. Once the fear is seen to have presented itself, he must fearlessly strike against it. A man will not see anything fortunate as long as he does not surmount an uncertainty. If he surmounts the uncertainty, if he remains alive, he will see the fortune. He must know about what has not yet come. He must sever the danger that has presented itself. However, having pacified it, he must act so as to control it, in case it does not decay, but grows again. When the time for happiness has

[70]The crane waits patiently.

[71]In a time of distress, these are best interpreted as examples of deceit.

[72]Because of the belief that a she-mule dies when she gives birth.

presented itself, those who are intelligent do not think it is good policy to shun it, in the hope of future happiness. A person may have an alliance with an enemy and sleep, happily and trustfully. He is like a person who sleeps atop a tree and awakens only when he falls down. As long as one is capable, whether the task is mild or terrible, one must uplift oneself and act in accordance with dharma. He must tend to all the rivals of his rivals. He must know his own spies and those engaged by the enemy. Spies must be well-appointed in their tasks, in his country and in that of the enemy. Wicked men and ascetics must be made to enter the enemy's kingdom. They act against dharma, are wicked in their conduct and are like thorns to people.[73] They frequent gardens, pleasure grounds, watering places, dwelling houses for travellers, drinking houses, brothels, places of pilgrimage and assemblies. Knowing that they have come, he must control and pacify them. He must not trust a person who should not be trusted. He must not even trust someone who should be trusted. Danger results from trust. One must not trust without examination. Having generated the enemy's trust through assertions of truth and reason, at the right time, when his[74] position is somewhat unstable, one must strike back. He must suspect even those who should not be suspected. He must always suspect someone who should be suspected. There can be danger from someone who should be suspected and its root must be severed. Having generated the enemy's confidence by not striking him, silence, ochre robes, matted hair and garments of hides, he must then leap on him, like a wolf. For the sake of increasing prosperity, those who created obstructions in the way of wealth must be slain—even if it is a son, a brother, a father, or a well-wisher. If there is an arrogant preceptor who does not know the difference between what should be done and what should not be done, and has thus deviated off the path, the rod must be used to chastise him. He must give his enemy gifts. But then, like a bird with a sharp beak, he must rise against him and destroy all his riches. Without having pierced the inner organs, without having performed terrible deeds

[73]Spies sent by the enemy.
[74]The enemy's.

and without having killed like a fisherman, one does not obtain supreme prosperity. No one is born as an enemy. No one is born as a friend. Depending on capacity and circumstances, one becomes a friend or an enemy. An enemy must not be freed, even if he is lamenting piteously. One should not grieve after having killed someone who has caused an earlier injury. However, he must always act without malice and endeavour to accumulate and show favours. In a desire for prosperity, he must also endeavour to punish. Before striking, he must speak pleasantly. After striking, it should be even more pleasant. If the head has to be struck down, he must weep and sorrow. If he desires prosperity, he must placate the enemy, comfort him, show him honour and patience and give him reasons for hope. One should not create enmity over minor matters. One should not try to cross a river using one's arms. The eating of a cow's horn is a pointless exercise. One's teeth are ground down and no juices are obtained. The three objectives have three evils and three bonds.[75] Knowing the bonds that can tie one down, one must avoid the evils. A debt that is not repaid, a fire that has not gone out and an enemy who is not eliminated, repeatedly keep on growing. Therefore, even a trifle becomes difficult to resist. A debt that keeps on increasing and an enemy who has been defeated can lead to terrible calamity, like a disease that is ignored. One must always be careful and complete the task well. When a thorn is not properly cut out, it can create pain for a long time. The enemy's kingdom must be destroyed by killing the men, devastating the roads and destroying the mines. The king must not be anxious and must be as far-sighted about the future as the vulture, as active as the dog, as valorous as the lion, as sceptical as the crow and have a movement like that of the snake. He must seed dissension among the foremost members of the groups and placate those who love him. He must protect the advisers and ensure that they do not create dissension and opposition. He will be

[75]The three objectives are dharma, artha and kama. The bonds are addiction to the fruits these lead to. The evils probably are—pursuit of dharma leads to neglect of artha, pursuit of artha leads to neglect of dharma and the pursuit of kama leads to the neglect of both dharma and artha.

disrespected if he is mild. He will be hated if he is fierce. He must be fierce at a time when fierceness is required and mild at a time when mildness is required. Mildness can be used to kill those who are mild. Mildness can also be used to kill those who are terrible. There is nothing that cannot be obtained through mildness. Therefore, mildness is superior to fierceness. He must be mild at times and terrible at other times. In this way, his tasks become successful and he becomes superior to the enemy. When a learned man is against him, he must not be reassured simply because that person is a long distance away. An intelligent person has long arms and can be injurious, if he has been harmed. He must not cross when the other shore cannot be reached. He must not take what can be seized back again. If the root cannot be taken out, nothing must be dug up. He must not strike if the head cannot be brought down. I have thus spoken to you about deceitful ways. A man should not act in these ways.[76] However, how does one counter the acts of the enemy? For the sake of your welfare, I have therefore told you about these things.' When he heard these beneficial words spoken by the brahmana, the king of the kingdom of Suvira was content. Without any distress in his mind, he acted in accordance with those words. With his relatives, he enjoyed blazing prosperity."'

Chapter 1467(139)

'Yudhishthira said, "When the supreme forms of dharma decay and are transgressed by all the people, adharma transforms into dharma and dharma goes into adharma. Boundaries are broken down and the determination to follow dharma is agitated. O lord of the earth! The world is oppressed by kings and thieves. All the ashramas are confused and the duties are destroyed. O descendant of the Bharata lineage! Fear is seen from desire, confusion and

[76]In a time of catastrophe, a deviation is permitted.

avarice. O king! Everyone is always distrustful and frightened. They use fraud to kill and deceive each other. The country is ablaze and brahmanas are afflicted. The rains do not shower down. Dissension and strife arise. All the means of sustenance on earth are taken over by bandits. When that terrible time arrives, how does a brahmana survive? O lord of men! Because of extreme compassion, he may be unwilling to give up his sons and grandsons.[77] O grandfather! How will he conduct himself? Tell me that. How will the king conduct himself when the world has been rendered impure? O scorcher of enemies! How can artha and dharma be prevented from decaying?"

'Bhishma replied, "O great king! The king is the foundation for the people to obtain yoga, kshema, good rains and lack of fear from disease and death. O bull among the Bharata lineage! I have no doubt that the king is the foundation of everything in krita, treta, dvapara and kali. When a time that causes confusion among subjects arrives, one must live on the basis of the strength of discernment. On this, an ancient history is recounted. It concerns a conversation between Vishvamitra and a chandala in the hut of the chandala. O king! In ancient times, in the intervening period[78] between treta and dvapara, it was ordained by destiny that there should be a terrible drought for twelve years. At the end of the yuga, subjects became extremely aged. As treta gave away and dvapara took hold, the thousand-eyed one[79] did not rain. Jupiter[80] moved in a retrograde direction. The moon abandoned its characteristics and moved along a southern path. There was no dew at the end of the night. There were no collections of clouds. The flow of water in the rivers became less and in some places, it disappeared. Because of destiny, the natural condition and beauty of lakes, rivers, wells and springs were destroyed. The water in waterbodies dried up and water was no longer distributed.[81] There were no sacrifices and recitations of svadha. All the auspicious sounds of vashatkara also

[77]He may be unwilling to give up his life.

[78]Sandhya, the period between two yugas.

[79]Indra.

[80]The text uses the word Guru.

[81]In places along the roads, where there is free distribution of drinking water.

ceased. Agriculture and animal husbandry were destroyed. Shops and markets disappeared. There were no assemblies of people and all the great festivals vanished. Bones and skeletons were strewn around. The place was frequented by large numbers of demons. Most of the cities were emptied. Villages and habitations were burnt up. Sometimes, this was because of thieves. Sometimes, this was because of weapons. Sometimes, this was because of oppressive kings. They were afraid of each other and the desolate spots were also generally empty. No resolutions were made to the gods. The old and the young were abandoned. Cows, goats and buffaloes fought against each other[82] and perished. Brahmanas were killed. There was an end to protection. The stores of herbs were destroyed. The men and the earth turned almost brown then. O Yudhishthira! At that fearful time, dharma was in decay. All the mortals were hungry and ate each other. The rishis abandoned their rituals. They abandoned the sacrificial fire and the gods. They abandoned their hermitages and ran around, here and there.

'"The illustrious maharshi Vishvamitra was without a house.[83] The intelligent one was afflicted by hunger and wandered around in every direction. On one occasion, in the forest, he came upon the houses of violent shvapachas, who killed animals and ate their flesh. The place was strewn with broken pots and the hides of dogs. There were heaps of shattered bones from boars and asses. There were pots made of skulls. It was strewn with garments of the dead and ornamented with used garlands.[84] The huts were decorated with garlands made from the cast-off skins of snakes. The temples bore flags made out of the feathers of owls. There were iron bells and the place was surrounded by packs of dogs. Afflicted by hunger, the great rishi, Gadhi's son, entered there. He made great efforts to search for some food there. Though he was begging for alms, Koushika could find nothing there.[85]

[82]For food.

[83]The lack of a house need not necessarily mean a sign of deprivation, since hermits often didn't possess a fixed residence.

[84]Implicitly, these garments and garlands have been collected from the dead and from cremation grounds.

[85]Vishvamitra was the son of Gadhi and Gadhi was the son of Kushika. Thus, Vishvamitra is Koushika.

There was no meat, rice, roots or fruit, or anything else. Koushika thought, 'Alas! A great hardship has come upon me.' Because of his weakness, in that hamlet of the chandalas, he fell down on the ground. O supreme among kings! The sage thought, 'Do I have any good merits left? How can I avoid a pointless death?' O king! The sage then saw some dog meat hung out from a rope in the chandala's house, from an animal that had just been killed by a weapon. He thought, 'I must steal this now. Other than this, there is no other means for me to remain alive. In a time of catastrophe, it has been determined that even an especially distinguished person can steal. It has been determined that this must be in succession, from an earlier category to the next. One must first take from someone who is inferior and then from someone who is equal. If these are impossible, one can take from an eminent person, even if he follows dharma. I will therefore take it from those who live on the outside fringes. I do not see any sin in this theft. I will steal the meat.' O descendant of the Bharata lineage! Having used his intelligence to determine this, Vishvamitra, the great sage, began to sleep at the spot where he had fallen down. When he saw that it was night and everyone in the chandala hamlet was asleep, the illustrious one arose and gently entered the hut.

'"The chandala was asleep. His eyes were covered with mucus. His voice was broken and harsh and he was unpleasant to look at. He asked, 'When the hamlet of the chandalas is asleep, who is stirring the rope? I am awake. I am not asleep. I am terrible and I will kill you.' At these sudden and forceful words and anxious at the prospect of his actually doing this, he replied, 'I am Vishvamitra.' The chandala heard these words from the maharshi who had perfected his soul and was terrified. He leapt up from his supine position. Tears flowed from his eyes.

'"He joined his hands in salutation, showed a great deal of honour and told Koushika, 'O, brahmana! What do you wish to do here in the night?' Vishvamitra assured Matanga[86] and replied, 'I am hungry and have almost lost my life. I will steal the dog's haunch.

[86]The chandala's name.

The breath of my life is ebbing away. The hunger is destroying my memory. Though I know my own dharma, I will steal the dog's haunch. Despite begging everywhere, I could find no food until I saw some in your house. Then I turned my mind to sin. I will steal the dog's haunch. A thirsty person will drink dirty water. There is no shame for someone who is looking for food. Hunger destroys dharma. I will steal the dog's haunch. Agni is the priest and the mouth of the gods and the illustrious one's footsteps are clean. Just as the one who devours everything still remains a brahmana, know that so will I, according to dharma.' The chandala said, 'O maharshi! Listen to my words. Having heard me, act accordingly, so that dharma is not made to decay. The learned say that dogs are the worst among animals. The worst part of the body is said to be the thighs and the haunches. O maharshi! You did not act properly when you decided to commit this perverse deed. You should not steal from a chandala, in particular, food that you should not eat. Look towards some other means so that you may be successful in remaining alive. O great sage! Do not destroy your austerities because of this greed for meat. You know that this is a forbidden path. You should not act so as to mix up dharma.[87] O supreme among those who know about dharma! You should not abandon dharma.' O king! O bull among the Bharata lineage! Having been thus addressed, the great sage, Vishvamitra, afflicted by hunger, again replied in these words. 'I have been running around for a very long time, without any food. There is no other means for me to remain alive. If one faces a hardship, one should do whatever is possible to remain alive, and if possible, act in accordance with dharma. Indra's dharma is from kshatriyas and Agni's for brahmanas. The brahmana Agni is my strength and I will eat at the time when I am hungry. One should unhesitatingly act so as to remain alive. It is better to be alive than dead. One can follow dharma only if one remains alive. In my desire to remain alive, I will also eat what should not be eaten. I have used my intelligence to determine this earlier. Grant me permission. I am following

[87]Mix up a brahmana's dharma with a chandala's dharma.

the dharma of remaining alive and will cleanse all the impurities through my knowledge and austerities, like stellar bodies dispelling great darkness.' The shvapacha said, 'If you eat this, I do not think that you will obtain your breath of life, a long lifespan, or the satisfaction of amrita. Beg for something else. Do not set your mind on begging for, and eating, dogs. Dogs should not be eaten by brahmanas.' Vishvamitra replied, 'O shvapacha! At a time of famine, no other meat is easily available, or rice. Nor do I possess riches. I am afflicted by hunger and have lost all hope of even being able to move. I think that dog meat will provide the six different kinds of flavours.'[88] The shvapacha said, 'O brahmana! Brahmanas and kshatriyas should only eat five animals that have five claws.[89] If you accept the proofs of the sacred texts, do not pointlessly have a desire to eat what should not be eaten.' Vishvamitra replied, 'When he was hungry, Agastya ate the asura Vatapi.[90] I am afflicted and agitated by hunger. I will eat the dog's haunch.' The shvapacha said, 'Beg for something else. You should not act like this. You should certainly not act in this way. However, since you so wish, take the dog's haunch.' Vishvamitra replied, 'The virtuous act in accordance with dharma and I will follow their conduct.[91] I think that eating this dog's haunch is better than eating food obtained from sacrifices.' The shvapacha said, 'If someone has followed an unrighteous path, this does not become eternal dharma. You should not vainly engage in wicked conduct on the basis of deceitful and false reasons.' Vishvamitra replied, 'Since I am a rishi, I will not do anything wicked, or anything that should not be done. I think that a dog and a deer are the same. Therefore, I will eat the dog's haunch.' The shvapacha said, 'The rishi's[92] right to eat and the act that he did was for the sake of brahmanas. Dharma is that which is not wicked and it must be protected, by whatever means that are possible.' Vishvamitra replied, 'I am a brahmana and this body

[88]Sweet, salty, sour, bitter, pungent and astringent.

[89]Hedgehog, porcupine, lizard, rabbit and turtle.

[90]This incident has been described in Section 33 (Volume 3).

[91]A reference to Agastya.

[92]A reference to Agastya again.

is my friend. In this world, it is worshipped as the most loved. Since I desire to maintain it, I will take this. I am not frightened of any violence that may result from this.' The shvapacha said, 'Do as you wish. There are men who act so as to give up their lives, instead of eating what should not be eaten. They obtain all their desires. O learned one! Since you are afflicted by hunger, do what appeals to you.' Vishvamitra replied, 'There is an uncertainty about what will happen to me after death. Perhaps all my deeds will be destroyed. If I protect the foundation by eating what should not be eaten, I may still return with a cleansed soul.[93] In my knowledge, I am satisfied that the two[94] are distinct, like the skin and sight, and thinking that they are the same is confusion. I am certain that if I act in this way, I will not become someone like you.'[95] The shvapacha said, 'My view is that this downfall is misery. It is because of this that I am committing the evil act of censuring a virtuous brahmana.' Vishvamitra replied, 'Even when frogs croak, cows drink. You have no right to dharma. Do not praise yourself greatly.' The shvapacha said, 'O brahmana! I entreated you as a well-wisher. I felt compassion for you. Therefore, accept what is best. Because of greed, do not eat the dog.' Vishvamitra replied, 'If you are my well-wisher and desire my happiness, then save me from this distress. I know what dharma is. Give me the dog's haunch.' The shvapacha said, 'I am not interested in giving you this. Nor can I ignore my own food being taken away. O brahmana! Both of us will be stained by sins—I, because I am the giver, and you, because you are receiving it.' Vishvamitra replied, 'After perpetrating this wicked act today, if I am still alive and roam around, I will act so as to greatly cleanse myself. Having purified myself, I will obtain dharma. Of these two,[96] tell me which is better.' The shvapacha said, 'The atman is the witness to everything that is done in this world. You yourself know

[93]This shloka is difficult to translate and some liberties have been taken.

[94]The body and the soul.

[95]In the next life.

[96]Remaining alive or dying.

what is wicked here. I think that anyone who is prepared to eat dog meat will not be ready to abstain from anything.' Vishvamitra replied, 'There is no sin in taking it, or eating it. It is always good policy to allow for exceptions. There has been no violence. No false words have been spoken. This can therefore be eaten and there will be no grave sin.' The shvapacha said, 'If this is the reason behind your eating it, it has no rationale from the Vedas, or from dharma. O Indra among brahmanas! Therefore, as you have said, I do not see any sin attached to food that should not be eaten, or from your eating it.' Vishvamitra replied, 'It is not seen that there is a great sin from eating this. If one drinks liquor, one is bound to fall down—these are only words used in this world. This is also true of many other similar deeds. Such deeds do not bring about the slightest bit of downfall.' The shvapacha said, 'If a person is learned, his good conduct restrains him from going to where he should not, from becoming inferior and from being censured. But because of desire, if he nevertheless goes to such a place, he will have to bear the punishment.' Having told Koushika this, Matanga desisted.

'"Having made up his mind, Vishvamitra took the dog's haunch. In a desire to remain alive, the great sage seized those five limbs.[97] The great sage went to the forest, to gratify his wife with this. At that time, Vasava began to rain down. All the subjects were revived and the herbs were generated. The illustrious Vishvamitra performed austerities and burnt his sins. In the course of time, he obtained great and extraordinary success. If a learned person confronts a calamity and desires to remain alive, as long as he is not miserable in his heart and knows of different means, he must cheerfully use every method to save himself. One must thus always resort to one's intelligence and remain alive. If a man remains alive, he obtains what is sacred and sees fortune. O Kounteya! Therefore, resort to the intelligence used by learned people in determining dharma and adharma. Make efforts and conduct yourself in this world accordingly."'

[97]Probably the two hind legs, the two rear thighs and the hind quarters.

Chapter 1468(140)

'Yudhishthira said, "You have instructed me about a terrible thing that is false and lacks devotion. This is the kind of restraint followed by bandits and I avoid it. I am confused and distressed. My bonds of dharma have become weak. I do not have any initiative in following this. How can I even think about it?"

'Bhishma replied, "In instructing you about dharma, I have not depended on the sacred texts alone. This is wisdom and experience and it is the honey that wise people have collected. A wise king will have many means of prevention, from here and there. Progress on the journey does not take place along a single branch of dharma. O Kouravya! When kings ignite their intelligence to follow dharma, they are always victorious. Therefore, understand my words. Kings who desire victory and regard intelligence as the best, are always triumphant. Here and there, using his intelligence, a king thinks of means that are in conformity with dharma. The dharma for kings was not determined as a dharma that only has a single branch. Why has the dharma for weak ones not been described earlier?[98] If an ignorant person sees a fork in the road, he will be confused. O descendant of the Bharata lineage! You should have already realized that intelligence can also offer a dilemma.[99] The wisdom is by one's side, but it flows everywhere, like a river. One must know that the dharma followed by people can have a course and also the opposite course. Some know this properly. There are others who possess an understanding that is false. Understanding the truth of all this, one acquires knowledge from the virtuous. Those who steal[100] from the sacred texts are against dharma. They understand their purport unevenly and vainly seek to explain them. They desire fame in every way and wish to earn a living off this learning. All of them are the worst among men and are against dharma. They are stupid and their views are not ripe. They do not know the true purport. In every

[98]Weak kings will not be able to follow dharma.

[99]This is probably a reference to the confusion between dharma and adharma.

[100]Selectively.

way, their final objective is never to be accomplished in the sacred texts. They steal from the sacred texts and point to what is wrong in the sacred texts. They do not act well when they proclaim their own knowledge. In an attempt to establish their own learning, they criticize the knowledge of others. They use words as their weapons and words as their knives. Their milking of knowledge is fruitless. O descendant of the Bharata lineage! Know them to be the traders of knowledge, like rakshasas. They laugh at dharma and believe that all of it is deceitful. 'We have not heard of any words of dharma in their words, or any intelligence.' When speaking of Brihaspati's knowledge, Maghavan himself said this.[101] There are no words that are spoken in this world without a reason and some are versed in the sacred texts. But others do not act in accordance with them. There are learned ones who have said that dharma is only what people follow in this world. Even if a person is learned, virtuous and instructed about dharma, he cannot understand it on his own. O descendant of the Bharata lineage! He can be intolerant about the sacred texts, or confused in his learning. Even when wise men speak about the sacred texts collectively, insight may be missing. What is praised is intelligent words that are derived from the sacred texts. Even if an ignorant person speaks words that are full of knowledge and reason, that is thought of as virtuous. In ancient times, to dispel the doubts of daityas, Ushanas said, 'Know that if the sacred texts do not possess meaning, they are abhorrent. Knowledge that cannot be defined is non-existent.'[102] Why do you wish to be satisfied with something that has a severed root? Do not resort to words that are false and injurious. You have been created for fierce deeds, but you are paying no attention to what you should do. O king! Look towards my own limbs, decorated with the effects of good policy.[103] Others escaped and are delighted because of this. Brahma created the goat, the

[101]Maghavan is Indra. This probably means that Indra quoted Brihaspati to this effect.

[102]The text does not clearly indicate where the Shukracharya quote ends.

[103]A reference to Bhishma following his own dharma and fighting. His limbs were pierced by arrows and some adversaries escaped.

horse and the kshatriya for similar reasons.[104] Therefore, some[105] are successful in their journey by glancing towards other beings. The sacred texts say that the sin from killing someone who should not be killed is the same as the sin from not killing someone who should be killed. This is certainly a rule which they[106] shun. If the king does not establish them in their own dharma, the subjects face extreme decay. They roam around and devour each other, like wolves. If there is a kingdom where bandits roam around and steal the possessions of others, like egrets snatching fish from the water, that person is the worst among kshatriyas. Choose noble advisers who possess the learning of the Vedas. O king! Rule the earth. Follow dharma and protect the subjects. If a lord of the earth appoints inferior people to tasks and seizes, without knowing the difference between the two,[107] he is a eunuch among kshatriyas. According to dharma, fierceness is not praised. But nor is lack of fierceness. One should not transgress either. Having been fierce, become mild. The dharma of kshatriyas is difficult to follow and there is plenty of affection in you. But you were created for fierce deeds. Rule the kingdom accordingly. Always chastise the wicked and protect the virtuous. O bull among the Bharata lineage! The intelligent Shakra said that this was what should be done in a time of distress."

'Yudhishthira asked, "Do you think that there is a rule followed by bandits that should never be violated? O best among righteous ones! O grandfather! I am asking you this. Tell me."

'Bhishma replied, "One must always serve learned and aged brahmanas and ascetics and also those who are firm and pure in their learning, character and conduct. This is the supreme objective. The conduct towards brahmanas must always be like that towards the gods. O king! If brahmanas are enraged, they can perform many

[104]So that they could be sacrificed.

[105]Some kshatriyas look towards the welfare of other people.

[106]Probably weak kings, or bandits.

[107]Seizes in the sense of levying disproportionate taxation, and not knowing the difference between proper taxation and improper taxation.

acts. The best fame arises from their affection and their disaffection leads to calamity. When pleased, brahmanas are like amrita. When wrathful, they are like poison."'

Chapter 1469(141)

'Yudhishthira said, "O grandfather! O immensely wise one! O one who is accomplished in all the sacred texts! Tell me about the dharma that should be followed by someone who is protecting a person who has sought refuge."

'Bhishma replied, "O great king! There is great dharma in protecting someone who has sought refuge. O supreme among the Bharata lineage! That you have asked such a question is deserving of you. O king! After they protected those who came and sought refuge, Nriga and the other kings obtained supreme success. O great king! It has been heard that a pigeon honoured its enemy when he sought refuge. As is proper, it honoured him and offered him its own flesh."

'Yudhishthira asked, "In ancient times, how did an enemy come and seek refuge with a pigeon? O descendant of the Bharata lineage! What objective did it attain after offering him its own flesh?"

'Bhishma replied, "O king! Listen to this divine account, which destroys all sins. This was recounted by Bhargava[108] to King Muchukunda. O Partha! O bull among the Bharata lineage! In ancient times, King Muchukunda bowed down and asked Bhargava about this. At this, Bhargava recounted the story to the one who wished to listen. O lord of men! He told him about how the pigeon attained success. This account is certainly full of dharma and of kama and artha too. O king! O mighty-armed one! Listen as I tell you this."

'"There used to be a wicked and terrible hunter of birds. Inferior in conduct, he roamed around the earth. He was regarded as death on earth. His limbs were as dark as a raven. He was harsh and

[108]Parashurama.

full of wickedness. His middle was like barley.[109] His neck was thin. His feet were small. His jaws were large. He did not have any well-wishers. Nor did he have any allies or relatives. Because of his terrible deeds, all of them abandoned him. Grasping a net,[110] he would always kill birds in the forest. O lord of men! He would then sell those birds. This is the way that evil-minded one found a means of survival. Without understanding that this was adharma, he followed this for a very long period of time. For a long period, he pleasured with his wife. He was confounded by destiny and no other means of livelihood appealed to him. On one occasion, he was in the forest. A great storm arose and whirled around and brought down the trees. Clouds gathered in the sky and they were tinged with flashes of lightning. In a short period of time, it was as if the ocean was covered with many boats.[111] Delighted, Shatakratu poured down torrents of rain. In a short while, he flooded the earth with water. Because of that torrential downpour in the world, he[112] was terrified and lost his senses. In that forest, he was afflicted with cold. His mind was greatly anxious. The bird-killer could not see any low ground anywhere.[113] The path in the forest was covered in a flood of water. Birds were killed by the force of the wind and vanished. Deer, lions and boars resorted to bits of land and stayed there. All the residents of the forest were terrified because of the strong wind and the rain. They were oppressed by fear. They were afflicted by hunger. Together, they wandered around in the forest. His[114] body was afflicted by the cold. Instead of stopping, he wandered around and in a thicket in the forest, he saw a tree that was as blue as the clouds. Against the background of stars in the clear sky, it looked like a lotus. Lubdhaka[115] was afflicted by the cold and saw that the

[109]Probably meaning a sack of barley.

[110]Alternatively, a cage or a basket for birds.

[111]A reference to the clouds in the sky.

[112]The fowler.

[113]Which would have drained the water off.

[114]The fowler's.

[115]Lubdhaka means a hunter and also a greedy person. We have interpreted it as a proper name.

sky was clear of clouds. O lord! The evil-souled one looked towards the directions and thought that his home in the village was a long distance away from the spot. He therefore made up his mind to spend the night there. O descendant of the Bharata lineage! Joining his hands in salutation, he spoke these words to the tree. 'I seek refuge from whatever gods reside here.' He spread out some leaves on the ground and laid his head down on a stone. In great misery, the slayer of birds slept there."'

Chapter 1470(142)

'Bhishma said, "O king! With its well-wishers, a bird lived on the branches of that tree. Its plumage was colourful and it had lived on the tree for a long time. Its wife had gone out in the morning to roam around and had not returned.[116] On seeing that it was night, the bird lamented. 'There was a great storm and my beloved has not returned. What can be the reason for her not returning yet? I hope my beloved is safe in the forest. Without her, this home of mine is empty now. Her eyes were tinged with red. Her plumage was colourful. Her voice was sweet. Since my wife is not here, there is no purpose in my remaining alive. Her dharma was in devotion to her husband. She was virtuous. She was more important than my life. That ascetic one was devoted to my welfare when she knew that I was exhausted or hungry. She was devoted to her husband. On earth, a man who has a wife like that is fortunate. It has been read that a wife is a man's supreme protector and that in this world, a man who does not have her as a companion along the journey, is helpless. For someone who has been overwhelmed by disease, for someone who has faced a hardship and for someone who is afflicted, there is no medication that is equal to a wife. There is no relative who is equal to a wife. There is no objective who is equal to a wife.

[116]In the earlier chapter, the Critical edition excises some shlokas, where the she-bird had been caught by the fowler.

In accomplishing dharma in this world, there is no aide who is equal to a wife.' Distressed, the bird lamented in this way there.

'"The wife had been seized by the slayer of birds and heard these words. Since her husband was miserable, she was also distressed by grief and thought, 'Someone whose husband is not satisfied does not deserve to be called a wife. With the fire as a witness,[117] a husband becomes a wife's refuge.' The she-pigeon, captured by Lubdhaka, carefully spoke these words. 'I will tell you what is indeed beneficial for you. Having heard, act accordingly. O beloved one! In particular, one must always provide succour to someone who seeks refuge. This fowler has resorted to your residence and is lying down. He is afflicted by cold. He is afflicted by hunger. It is necessary to honour him. If someone who seeks refuge is allowed to perish, the sin is equal to that from killing a brahmana or a cow, who is the mother of the worlds. Following the dharma of different species, that of pigeons has been ordained for us.[118] A knowledgeable person like you must always practise what is proper. If a householder follows dharma to the best of his capacity, when he dies, we have heard that he obtains the undecaying worlds. O bird! You have obtained offspring. You have sons. Therefore, follow dharma and artha and give up all love for your body. Engage in honouring him, so that his mind is cheered.' The ascetic she-bird was imprisoned inside the cage. Extremely miserable, it glanced towards its husband and spoke these words. When it[119] heard its wife's words, which were full of dharma and reason, its eyes overflowed with tears and it was filled with great joy. It glanced towards the fowler, who earned a living from birds. The bird carefully honoured him, following the ordained rites. It said, 'Welcome. What can I do for you? Since this is like your own house, you should not suffer from any misery. Therefore, tell me quickly what I should do. What do you desire? You have sought refuge with me and I am speaking affectionately towards you. If a guest comes

[117]A reference to the rites of marriage.

[118]Since these are pigeons, they can only offer limited hospitality. Alternatively, this might mean that pigeons are meant to be eaten.

[119]The male pigeon.

and seeks refuge, one must tend to him carefully. This is particularly true of a householder who is engaged in the five sacrifices.[120] If a person who is a householder is confused and does not observe these five sacrifices, then, according to dharma, he possesses neither this world, nor the next. Therefore, without any hesitation, tell me. Speak to me carefully and I will do everything. Do not unnecessarily sorrow in your mind.'

'"Hearing these words, Lubdhaka spoke to the bird. 'The cold is constraining me. You should free me from the cold.' Having been thus addressed, the bird carefully covered the ground with dry leaves. The bird then quickly departed to fetch fire. It went to a place where charcoal was burnt and having obtained some fire, brought it back. It kindled a fire in those dry leaves. Having created a great fire, it told the one who had sought refuge, 'Be assured and without fear. Heat your limbs.' Having been thus addressed, Lubdhaka agreed and warmed his limbs. His life having been restored by the fire, he spoke to the bird. 'The hunger is killing me. I desire that you should give me some food.' On hearing this, the bird spoke these words. 'I do not possess any riches with which I can destroy your hunger. We, residents of the forest, survive on what grows here. Like the sages in a forest, we do not possess any stores.' Having spoken thus, its face turned pale. O best among the Bharata lineage! It began to think about what should be done next and condemned its own mode of existence.[121] Having thought for an instant, the bird regained its senses and spoke to the slayer of birds. 'Wait for a while. I will satisfy you.' Having said this, it kindled a fire with dry leaves. Filled with great delight, the pigeon spoke again. 'From great-souled gods, sages and ancestors, I have earlier heard about the great dharma that comes from honouring guests. Show me your favours.[122] I am telling you this truthfully. My mind has certainly been made up on

[120]Sacrifices to gods, sacrifices to ancestors, sacrifices to guests, sacrifices to dependents and sacrifices to one's own self.

[121]Because guests could not be fed.

[122]A guest offers an opportunity to a householder to follow dharma and thus shows favours.

honouring a guest.' Having taken this pledge, the bird seemed to be smiling. O lord of the earth! It circumambulated the fire three times and entered. When Lubdhaka saw that the bird had entered in the midst of the fire, he began to think in his mind, 'What have I done? Alas. Shame on my reprehensible and violent deeds. There is no doubt that I have committed great and terrible adharma.' In this fashion, Lubdhaka repeatedly lamented in many ways. On seeing that the bird had gone, he condemned his own deeds."'

Chapter 1471(143)

'Bhishma said, "On seeing that the pigeon had descended into the fire, Lubdhaka was overcome with compassion and again spoke these words. 'In my stupidity, I have committed a violent deed like this. As long as I am alive, this sin will always be lodged in my heart.' Condemning himself, he repeatedly kept speaking in this way. 'Shame on my great stupidity and the deceitful conduct I have always engaged in. Having abandoned auspicious deeds, I have sought to capture birds. I have resorted to violence. There is no doubt that, by offering me its own flesh, the great-souled pigeon has instructed me. I will abandon my sons and wife and give up my own beloved life. The pigeon, extremely devoted to dharma, has instructed me about dharma. I will offer up my own body and avoid all objects of pleasure. I will shrivel it up, like a little bit of water during the summer. I will endure the torment of hunger and thirst. I will become lean, as if I am made up of veins. To ensure the worlds hereafter, I will observe many different kinds of fasting. Alas! By giving up its own body, it has shown me how guests must be treated. Therefore, I will follow dharma. Dharma is the supreme objective. O supreme among birds![123] Dharma is seen to be that which has been followed by that foremost practitioner of dharma.' Having spoken this,

[123]This is being addressed to the she-pigeon.

Lubdhaka, the performer of evil deeds, became rigid in his vows and resolved to depart on *mahaprasthana*.[124] He discarded his staff, his pointed stick,[125] his net and his cage. He also freed the imprisoned pigeons[126] and departed."'

Chapter 1472(144)

'Bhishma said, "When the fowler had left, the miserable she-pigeon remembered its husband. It became senseless with grief and wept. It lamented in sorrow. 'O beloved! I cannot remember a single instance of your having acted in an unpleasant way. O bird! Even when a spirited woman possesses many sons, when she becomes a widow and is bereft of her husband, her relatives grieve for her. I have always been loved by you and have been comforted and greatly revered by sweet, pleasant and agreeable words. We have sported in valleys, mountains, rivers and springs. O beloved one! We have pleasured in the delightful tops of trees. I have found delight with you, happily roaming through the sky. O beloved one! I have sported with you. Where has all that gone now? What a father gives is limited. What a mother gives is limited. What a son gives is limited. What a husband gives is unlimited and who will not worship him. There is no protector like a husband. There is no happiness like a husband. Abandoning all riches, husbands are the refuges of women. O lord! Without you, there is no point to remaining alive. Which virtuous woman will be interested in remaining alive, if she is without her husband?' Extremely miserable, it lamented piteously in many ways. Devoted to its husband, it entered the blazing fire. And there it saw its husband, attired in colourful garments, astride a celestial vehicle

[124]Literally, the great journey. A person leaves on mahaprasthana when he departs from home and wanders around, awaiting death.

[125]Used for catching birds.

[126]The plural is used. There were other captured pigeons too.

and honoured by great-souled ones who had performed good deeds. It was adorned in colourful garlands and garments and was decorated with every kind of ornament. It was surrounded by the performers of auspicious deeds, astride hundreds of crores of celestial vehicles. The bird had gone to heaven and was joined by its wife. It was worshipped because of its deeds and found pleasure there with its wife."'

Chapter 1473(145)

'Bhishma said, "O king! The fowler saw them in that celestial vehicle. On seeing the couple, he grieved, thinking about attaining a good end. 'Through what kind of austerities can I attain the supreme goal?' Having thought about this, he decided to set about his journey. Lubdhaka, who earned a living from birds, embarked on mahaprasthana. He gave up all efforts, subsisted on air and gave up all sense of ownership, desiring to attain heaven. He then saw an extremely large lake, adorned with lotus flowers. The lake was full of cool and sparkling water and was frequented by a large number of birds. He was afflicted by thirst and on seeing this, had no doubt that he would be able to satisfy himself. O king! Because of the fasting, Lubdhaka was extremely thin. In the forest frequented by predatory beasts, he cheerfully crept along. Having summoned up great resolution, Lubdhaka entered the forest and was grasped by some thorns. His limbs were mangled by those thorns and he was covered with red blood. He roamed around in that desolate spot, frequented by many kinds of animals. As the large trees in the forest rubbed against each other, a great fire was ignited and fanned by the wind. That forest was full of trees and covered with shrubs and creepers. The fire angrily consumed them, as radiant as the fire at the end of a yuga. It blazed with sparks that were fanned by the wind. It fiercely burnt the forest, which teemed with animals and birds. Lubdhaka was delighted in his mind. Desiring to free himself of his body, he rushed towards the raging fire. Burnt by the fire, Lubdhaka's sins were destroyed. O supreme among the Bharata lineage! He then attained supreme success. Devoid of all anxiety, he saw himself in heaven. Like Indra, he was radiant in the midst of yakshas, gandharvas and siddhas. In this way, because of their auspicious deeds, the male pigeon and the female pigeon which was devoted to its husband indeed went to heaven, accompanied by Lubdhaka. In this way, like the she-pigeon, a woman who is devoted to her husband is quickly established in heaven and becomes radiant there. This is the ancient account of the great-souled Lubdhaka and the pigeon. Because of their auspicious deeds, they attained the objective of those who follow dharma. A person who always hears this, or a person who recounts this, will never confront anything inauspicious, even if he is confused in his mind. O Yudhishthira! O supreme among those who uphold dharma! This great dharma provides salvation to even the perpetrators of wicked deeds, such as those who kill cows. But there is no salvation for someone who allows a person who seeks refuge to perish."'

Chapter 1474(146)

'Yudhishthira asked, "O supreme among the Bharata lineage! If a person commits a sin out of ignorance, how can he be freed from it? Tell me about this."

'Bhishma replied, "In this connection, an ancient history is described. This is what the brahmana Indrota, the son of Shunaka, told Janamejaya. There was an extremely valorous king named Janamejaya, the son of Parikshit.[127] In his ignorance, that lord of the earth committed the sin of killing a brahmana. All the brahmanas

[127]Not to be confused with the more famous Parikshit, Abhimanyu's son, and his son, Janamejaya.

and the priests abandoned him. Tormented day and night, the king went to the forest. Abandoned by his subjects, he acted so that he might obtain great welfare. He was tormented by repentance and performed extreme austerities. I will tell you about that history, about how he accumulated dharma. Janamejaya was tormented because of the sin he had committed and departed. He went to Indrota, the son of Shunaka, who was rigid in his vows. Having approached him, he seized his feet and embraced them. At this, the immensely wise one was alarmed and severely reprimanded him. 'You have committed a great sin, like one who has killed a foetus. Why have you come here? What do you wish to do to me? Under no circumstances, should you touch me. Go. Go from this spot. It is certain that your presence does not give me pleasure. There is a smell of blood in you. You look like a corpse. It is inauspicious for you to be near auspicious things. Though you seem to be alive, you are actually dead. You are dead within and your soul is impure. You are only thinking about wickedness. You are awake, but you are actually asleep. You are roaming around, unhappy.[128] O king! Your being alive is futile. You will live in misery. You have been created for wicked and ignoble deeds. In this world, fathers desire sons who will bring great welfare. They perform austerities, offer sacrifices to the gods, worship the gods and are patient. Behold. Because of your deeds, this lineage of your forefathers has gone to hell. All their hopes have been rendered futile and so has their dependence on you. Those who worship brahmanas enjoy heaven, long lives, fame and happiness. But your constant hatred towards them has rendered this futile. Having been freed from this world, because of your wicked deed, you will fall head downwards for many years, though not for eternity. You will be devoured by vultures and peacocks with iron beaks. Once this has happened, you will return again and advance towards a wicked birth. O king! If you think that this world is nothing, not to speak of the one hereafter, in Yama's eternal abode, Yama's messengers will remind you about this.'"'

[128]There is a typo in the Critical edition. It says happy. Clearly, it should read unhappy.

Chapter 1475(147)

'Bhishma said, "Having been thus addressed, Janamejaya replied to the sage. 'You are censuring someone who deserves to be censured. You are condemning someone who deserves to be condemned. You are shaming someone who deserves to be shamed. Nevertheless, show me your favours. All this has come about because of what I have myself done. I am being burnt, as if I am in the midst of a fire. It is not as if my mind is delighted at being associated with my deeds. I certainly suffer because of my terrible fear of Vaivasvata.[129] Without uprooting that stake, how can I possibly remain alive? O Shounaka![130] Suppress all your anger towards me and instruct me. There used to be a great kitchen for brahmanas[131] and I will accomplish that objective again. There must be a remnant to this lineage. This lineage cannot be destroyed. But if we are cursed by brahmanas, if we do not have access to the sacred texts and if we are not conscious of what has been determined in the Vedas, there will be no remnant left. I am in great despair. I am telling you again about what confronts me. Those who are without dharma and without meditation are repeatedly not acknowledged.[132] In the hereafter, their foundation is like that of the Pulindas and the Shabaras.[133] Those who do not perform sacrifices do not obtain any worlds. O extremely learned one! I am ignorant. Impart wisdom to me, like that to a child, like a father to his son. O brahmana! O Shounaka! Be gratified with me.'

'"Shounaka said, 'There is nothing surprising in a wise person performing many appropriate acts. A learned person is not concerned with what has happened or what will happen.[134] Having obtained

[129]Yama.

[130]Shunaka's son, Indrota.

[131]Before Janamejaya killed the brahmana.

[132]A minor liberty has been taken with the text here. As it stands, a translation is difficult.

[133]As examples of barbarians.

[134]He is concerned with the present.

the favours of wisdom, he does not grieve about what other people sorrow over. As if he is stationed on the top of a mountain, he looks on the entire universe with wisdom. Someone who is fickle, someone who is degraded in his soul and someone who is shamed by all the virtuous people and hides himself, does not see the course of action. Knowing that there is freedom from fear, vigour and greatness in the Vedas and the sacred texts, perform a great rite of pacification. The brahmanas are your refuge. If the brahmanas are no longer enraged with you, this will ensure your welfare in the hereafter. This is on the assumption that you are repenting your wicked deed and are looking towards dharma.'

'"Janamejaya replied, 'I am repenting my wicked deed and I will never follow adharma again. O Shounaka! I am looking for someone who will be affectionate and desire my welfare.'

'"Shounaka said, 'O king! Since you have given up your arrogance and pride, I desire to be affectionate towards you. Remain established in the welfare of all beings and remember dharma. I am not summoning you[135] because of fear, weakness or avarice. The gods and the brahmanas will hear the truthful words I speak to you. I do not desire anything from anyone. I am summoning you to a rite of dharma, even though all the beings are uttering words of shame towards you. They will say that I am ignorant about dharma and people who are not well-wishers will speak in this way. If I hear such words from a well-wisher, I will be extremely anxious. There will be some immensely wise ones who will recognize that this is the right course of action.[136] O son![137] O descendant of the Bharata lineage! Know that I am doing this for the sake of brahmanas. For my sake, act so that they may obtain peace. O lord of men! Pledge that you will not show hatred towards brahmanas.'

'"Janamejaya replied, 'O brahmana! I touch your feet and pledge that I will never again injure brahmanas, in words, thoughts and deeds.'"'

[135]To perform a sacrifice.

[136]The performance of the sacrifice.

[137]The word used is tata.

Chapter 1476(148)

'"Shounaka said, 'Therefore, since your senses have been agitated, I will speak to you about dharma. You are prosperous, immensely strong and content and are looking towards dharma. Having been terrible earlier, you have now become extremely distinguished. O king! Favour all beings through your own conduct. In this world, there is good and bad in everything. You were like that earlier. But you are now looking towards dharma. O Janamejaya! You gave up extremely wonderful food and objects of pleasure and resorted to austerities. These things seem extraordinary to beings. There is nothing extraordinary in a weak person becoming generous, or in a miserable person resorting to the store of austerities. It is said that this conduct is close to their state of being. This wretchedness[138] has not been considered properly. Therefore, one must examine it properly. Only then will one appreciate its qualities. O lord of the earth! Sacrifices, donations, compassion, the Vedas and truth—these are the five things that purify. Extremely severe austerities constitute the sixth. O Janamejaya! This is the supreme form of purification for kings. If you accept this completely, you will obtain supreme dharma. Visiting auspicious spots is said to be the supreme purifier. On this, the song sung by Yayati is recounted. "A mortal can obtain a long life, or even live again, by attentively performing sacrifices alone. Thereafter, having renounced, he should observe austerities." Kurukshetra is said to be an auspicious region and Prithudaka,[139] on the banks of the Sarasvati. If a person bathes or drinks there, he need not be tormented about premature death.[140] You must go to the great lakes, Pushkara, Prabhasa and Manasa, to the north. Having gone to Kaloda,[141] one obtains one's breath

[138]That Janamejaya has voluntarily reduced himself to. He is neither weak, nor miserable (in riches).

[139]Pehowa in Kurukshetra district.

[140]Literally, death the next day.

[141]Also known as Kalodaka, Mundkol lake in Kashmir.

of life again. You should go to the confluence of the Sarasvati and the Drishadvati. You must study and observe good conduct in all these places, touching the waters there. He[142] said that renunciation and sannyasa is sacred and supreme dharma. On this, a song composed by Satyavat is recited. "Be as truthful as a child, without any auspicious or wicked deeds. Then, since there will be no unhappiness for all the beings in this world, how can there be happiness?[143] This is the natural state of all beings. In general, this is characteristic of the lives of those who give up all kinds of association and abandon both good and wicked deeds." I will now tell you about the tasks that are best for a king. Use your strength and generosity to again conquer heaven. A man who possesses strength and energy becomes the lord of dharma. For the sake of the happiness of brahmanas, roam around this earth. Since you disrespected them earlier, placate them now. This is despite being condemned and abandoned by many of them. O learned one! Have knowledge of your own self. Do not be enraged and injure them. Be engaged in your own tasks and work towards supreme welfare. A king can be as cold as ice, or as fiery as the fire. O scorcher of enemies! Others can be like a plough or thunder.[144] Do not think that there will be no remnants,[145] or that treatment is not possible. Thinking that there is nothing left of your existence, do not associate with those who are wicked. If one repents one's wicked deed, one is freed from one-fourth of the sin. If one decides that one will not act in this way again, one is freed from a second one-fourth. If one resolves to follow dharma, one is freed from a third one-fourth. A man who desires prosperity should only think about welfare. Those who smell good fragrances also smell like that. Those who smell foul smells also smell like that. A person who devotes himself to austerities is immediately freed from his sins. A person who has been accused is freed if he worships the

[142]Yayati.

[143]Both unhappiness and happiness are transitory illusions.

[144]A plough uproots enemies, thunder scorches them.

[145]Of the lineage.

fire for a year. A person guilty of feticide is freed if he worships the fire for three years. If a person guilty of killing foetuses, saves as many living beings as would naturally have been killed,[146] he is freed. Manu has said that if one immerses oneself in the water and chants Aghamarshana three times,[147] one obtains the benefits equal to those from the final bath after a horse sacrifice. One is swiftly freed from sins and obtains great reverence. Beings seek his favours, as if they are dumb and mute. O king! Once, all the gods and the asuras assembled and asked Brihaspati, the preceptor of the gods. "O maharshi! You know about the fruits that result from dharma and also about those that lead to hell, the world of the wicked. When a person has performed both of these well, which of these triumphs over the other? O maharshi! Tell us about the fruits of deeds. How does a person with auspicious conduct dispel evil?"

'"'Brihaspati replied, "Having ignorantly performed wicked deeds earlier, if a person deliberately performs auspicious deeds, his auspicious conduct dispels that evil, just as a dirty garment is cleansed with a caustic substance. A man who has committed a wicked deed should not think that he has been destroyed. Without any malice and with devotion, he should desire to ensure welfare, just as a hole in a garment can be covered with a good piece. Even after having performed a wicked deed, a man can obtain welfare, just as the sun arises again and drives away all the darkness. If one acts so as to ensure welfare, all sins can be driven away."'"

'Bhishma said, "Indrota spoke in this way to King Janamejaya. Having said this, following the prescribed rites, Shounaka performed a horse sacrifice. After this, the king's sin was cleansed. He was full of prosperity and his form was like that of a blazing fire. The destroyer of enemies entered his own kingdom, like the full moon rising in the sky."'

[146]The number saved is equal to the number of foetuses killed.

[147]This is a reference to the Aghamarshana *suktam* (after the sage Aghamarshana) from the Rig Veda. This is used for consecration ceremonies, ablutions and at times of bathing.

Chapter 1477(149)

'Bhishma said, "O Partha! Listen to this account of an ancient history. This is an account of an ancient conversation that took place between a vulture and a jackal in Vidisha. There were some people who were miserable. There was a child who had not yet become a youth. He died and he was the only possession the family had. They wept and were distracted by grief. They picked up the dead child and advanced in the direction of the cremation ground. They sat down on the ground there. They passed the child from one lap to another and wept. On hearing the sounds of their weeping, a vulture approached and spoke these words. 'He is just one person in this world. Abandon him and quickly go away. Time has brought thousands of men and thousands of women to this place. Did they not have relatives? Behold. The entire universe is full of joy and misery. In due course, there is union and separation. There are those who pick up the dead and come here and there are those who follow them. However, once their lifespans are over, these people also depart. You have spent sufficient time in this cremation ground, frequented by vultures and jackals. It is full of terrible skeletons and is fearful to all beings. Someone who has followed the dharma of time will never become alive again. Whether it is someone who is loved or whether it is someone who is hated, all beings attain this kind of end. Everyone who is born in the world of mortals will indeed die. This is a path that has been ordained by the Destroyer. How can someone who is dead become alive again? People have finished their tasks[148] and the sun is about to set. Return to your own residences and abandon this affection for the son.' O king! On hearing the words of the vulture, they lamented. Abandoning their son on the ground, the relatives departed. They determined that they should abandon their son. They had no hope of his becoming alive. They arose and took to the road.

'"At this time, a jackal emerged from its hole. Its complexion was like that of a crow or a cloud. As they advanced, it told them, 'It is

[148]For the day. The vulture is lying.

evident that humans have no compassion. O stupid people! The sun is still there. Do not be frightened and show some affection. This moment has many forms and perhaps he may come back to life. You have abandoned all affection for your son and have flung him away on the ground. Without any compassion, how can you forsake your son on the cremation ground and go away? This child was sweet in speech and you have no affection for your son. He spoke to please you and you are about to go away. You do not see the affection animals and birds have towards their sons. This is despite their obtaining no fruits from this nurturing.[149] Quadrupeds, birds and insects are beings that are only driven by affection. They will obtain their places in the world hereafter, like sages who perform sacrifices. They take delight in their sons, though this brings nothing in this world, or in the next. We do not see any qualities these beings obtain from this act of nurturing. Yet, when they do not see their beloved sons, they are full of sorrow. After growing up, the mother and the father are never sustained. Do humans have affection? So how can there be grief? This son was the extender of the lineage. Abandoning him, you are going away. For a long time, release your tears. For a long time, gaze on him affectionately. In particular, it must be extremely difficult to abandon something that one loves. When one faces decay, when one has been accused and when one advances towards a cremation ground, it is relatives who stay with that person, and not others. Everyone loves life. Everyone obtains affection. Behold the kind of affection that can be seen in those from inferior species.[150] This one has large eyes, like the petals of a lotus. How can you abandon him and go away? He has been bathed and decorated with garlands, like one who has just been married.'"

'Bhishma said, "Hearing these piteous laments of the jackal, all those men returned, for the sake of the corpse.

'"The vulture said, 'Alas! O ones limited in intelligence! Shame on you. This jackal is cruel, inferior and limited in spirit. Are these

[149]Unlike humans, birds and animals are not sustained by their offspring in their old age.

[150]Animals and birds.

men returning because of what it has said? Why are you grieving over something that has given up the five elements and is like an empty piece of wood? It is immobile. Why are you not sorrowing over your own selves? Perform terrible austerities and cleanse yourself from sin. Everything can be obtained through austerities. What will lamentations achieve? Know that those with bodies must suffer from ill fortune. Everyone must leave this world, giving rise to endless sorrow. Austerities are the foundation for riches, cattle, gold, gems and jewels. These are obtained through the yoga of austerities. Depending on what they have done,[151] beings obtain happiness and unhappiness. Accepting this unhappiness and happiness, beings are born. The son does not get the father's karma. The father does not get the son's karma. Tied down by their good and wicked deeds, they advance along different paths. Carefully follow dharma and retreat from what is adharma. At the right time, act appropriately towards gods and brahmanas. Give up your sorrow and misery and withdraw from affection towards your son. Whether one has performed auspicious deeds, or whether one has perpetrated extremely terrible ones of adharma, the results will be reaped. What role is there for relatives? When relatives leave their beloved relatives here, they do not linger. With eyes full of tears, they abandon their affection and depart. Whether one is wise or stupid, whether one is rich or poor, whether one is auspicious or inauspicious, everyone comes under the subjugation of time. What will you accomplish through grief? Why are you sorrowing over the dead? Time is the lord of everyone and following dharma, he looks on everyone equally. Everyone faces death—youth, children, the aged and even foetuses. This is the way of the universe.'

'"The jackal said, 'You were extremely sorrowful, overcome by affection on account of your son. Alas! The vulture with limited intelligence has diluted that affection. His words were appropriate, chosen well and respectful. That is the reason you have abandoned your affection, which is so difficult to let go, and are going towards the pond.[152] Alas! Separation from a dead son leaves one empty. One

[151]In earlier lives.

[152]To have a bath of purification before leaving.

laments in severe misery, like a cow without a calf. I now know the sorrow that men face on this earth. On seeing the pity associated with affection, I am also shedding tears. One must always seek to strive, though success is determined by destiny. Destiny and manliness combine with earlier deeds. One must always be hopeful. How can there be happiness from despair? Success is obtained through endeavour. How can you leave in this cruel way? He has resulted from your own flesh. His form has been generated from half of your body.[153] He was the extender of the lineage of your fathers. After abandoning him in the forest, where will you go? Stay here until the sun has set and evening has presented itself. Perhaps you will stay here with your son, or take him away.'[154]

'"The vulture said, 'O men! It is now one thousand years since I have been born. I have never seen a dead woman or man come back to life again. Some who died in the womb are born. Some die the moment they are born. Others died after they have attained youth and exhibit valour.[155] The fortune of quadrupeds and birds is temporary. The lifespan of mobile and immobile objects has been determined earlier. There are those who are separated from their beloved wives and those who sorrow over their sons. Tormented by grief, they always go home. Abandoning thousands who were not liked and hundreds who were loved, relatives are extremely miserable and depart. Abandon the one who is without energy. He is like an empty piece of wood. His life is wandering around in vapour. Therefore, abandon him and go. This affection is futile. This concern for him is futile. He cannot see you with his eyes. He cannot hear you with his ears. Therefore, swiftly abandon him and return to your own homes. I have used the dharma of moksha.[156] Though they seem to be cruel, I have spoken words that are full of reason. As I have said, quickly go away to your own respective homes. You have heard words that are full of the knowledge of

[153]This is specifically addressed to the dead son's father.

[154]Take the son away in case he revives.

[155]In battles.

[156]Ultimate liberation.

wisdom. They will give you intelligence and consciousness, though they are harsh. O men! Return.'

'"The jackal said, 'He has the complexion of gold and he is adorned with ornaments. On hearing the words of the vulture, how can you abandon your son? He has the complexion of gold and is adorned with ornaments. He is the one who will offer funeral cakes to the ancestors. There is nothing that prevents affection, lamentation and weeping. But if you abandon the one who has died, it is certain that you will suffer. It has been heard that Rama, truthful in his valour, killed the shudra Shambuka, resorted to dharma, and brought a brahmana child back to life.[157] In that way, rajarshi Shveta's child met his destiny. But since he[158] always followed dharma, the very next day, he could again bring the dead back to life. In that fashion, while you are lamenting, perhaps a siddha, a sage or a god can perform an act of compassion.'"

'Bhishma said, "Having been thus addressed, afflicted by grief and devoted to their son, they returned. Placing his head on their laps, they wept for a long period of time."

'The vulture said, "He has been bathed with your tears. You have kneaded him with the touch of your hands. However, ordained by Dharmaraja,[159] he has entered a long period of sleep. A person who has engaged in austerities is also not spared by destiny. This is the end of all affection. This is the residence of the dead. Thousands of the young and the aged are always abandoned by their relatives on the ground, after they have spent days and nights in misery. Refrain from grief. There has been enough of this bond. It cannot be believed that he will come back to life again. He will not become alive again because of the words of the jackal. Someone who is dead, and has discarded his body, does not get that body back again. Even if hundreds of jackals give up their bodies, this will not happen. In

[157]This is a story from Uttara Kanda of Valmiki Ramayana. A brahmana's son had died because there was adharma in the kingdom, resulting from a shudra engaging in prohibited practices. Rama killed the shudra.

[158]Shveta.

[159]Yama.

hundreds of years, this child is incapable of becoming alive again. The child can only come back to life if Rudra, Kumara, Brahma or Vishnu grants a boon. However, he will not become alive again because of the shedding of tears, because of any assurances, or because of a long period of lamentation. I, the jackal, you and the relatives are all of us travelling in that direction too, accepting our share of dharma and adharma. A wise person should keep unpleasantness, harshness, hatred towards others, desire for the wives of others, adharma and falsehood a long distance away. He must carefully follow the path of truth, dharma, purity, fairness, great compassion towards beings, lack of deceit and lack of fraudulence. While they are alive, those who do not look towards their mothers, fathers, relatives and well-wishers—suffer destruction of dharma. He cannot see with his two eyes. His limbs will never move. His period of being here has come to an end. What will weeping achieve?'"

'Bhishma said, "Having been thus addressed, they were overcome by grief and abandoned their son on the ground. They were tormented by affection for their son. The relatives left for home.

'"The jackal said, 'The world of mortals is terrible. All living beings are destroyed. We live for a short time and are separated from our beloved kin. There is a lot of pretension, fraud, arguing and unpleasant speech. Considering this, coming back here again will only increase sorrow and misery. Even for an instant, the world of humans does not appeal to me. Alas! Shame on the men who are retreating because of the words of the vulture. You are blazing from sorrow on account of your son. Yet, you behave like those who are ignorant. If you have any affection, how can you discard the affection towards your son and go away? On hearing the words of the vulture, you have made up your minds to do that which is wicked. Unhappiness comes at the end of happiness. Happiness comes at the end of unhappiness. There is happiness and unhappiness in this world and there is nothing that does not come to an end. You have laid this handsome child down on the surface of the ground. He has caused grief to your lineage. O stupid ones! After abandoning your son, where will you go? There is no doubt that I can see him alive in my mind, full of beauty and youth, blazing in his prosperity. His destruction was not deserved. O men! You will obtain happiness again. The fire that is tormenting you because of the sorrow over your son's death will be pacified. Once you have suffered from sorrow, you will be able to ensure your own happiness. How can you ensure that if you abandon him in this foolish way and go away now?'"

'Bhishma said, "They thus faced a conflict over dharma and paid heed to these pleasant, but false, words. The resident of the cremation ground waited for the night and for his food.[160] In their midst, he brought them supreme words that were like amrita. For his own objectives, the jackal made those relatives stay.

'"The vulture said, 'This place is full of the spirits of the dead and is frequented by yakshas and rakshasas. It is a terrible and desolate spot and echoes with the screeches of owls. It is fierce and extremely horrible, with a complexion like that of dark and blue clouds. Abandon the corpse and decide to perform the funeral rites. As long as the sun has not set and as long as the directions are clear, abandon him and decide to perform the funeral rites. Hawks are shrieking in harsh tones. Jackals are screaming in fierce tones. Lions are roaring and the sun is about to set. The blue smoke from funeral pyres is imparting a hue to the trees. Hungry beings are finding delight in this cremation ground. In this extremely terrible spot, all of them are brave and energetic. They are malformed and subsist on flesh. They will attack you. Go far away from this spot in the forest. There is fear here. He is like a piece of wood and must be abandoned. Tolerate the jackal's words. If you deviate from knowledge and listen to the futile and false words of the jackal, all of you will be destroyed.'

'"The jackal said, 'Remain here. As long as the sun is shining, there is nothing to be scared about. Driven by affection for your son, as long as you have hope, remain here. Without any fear, confidently weep over him. Confidently, look at him with affection. As long

[160]The jackal is the resident of the cremation ground. The sense is that the jackal used these false words to persuade them to stay till it was night, hoping to feed on the carcass. Had the people left before it was night, the vulture would have fed on the carcass instead.

as the sun is here, remain here. What is the point to the words of that predator?[161] If you accept the fierce and wild words of the vulture, you will delude your own selves and your son will indeed have no future.'"

'Bhishma said, "The vulture said the sun had set. The jackal said that it had not set. They were both hungry and addressed the relatives of the dead person. O king! Both the vulture and the jackal were accomplished in attaining their own objectives. They were hungry, thirsty and exhausted and spoke, seeking support in the sacred texts. Both the jackal and the bird were knowledgeable and learned. Their words were like amrita. They[162] stood up and left. Then they were overcome by sorrow and misery and wept and remained. They[163] were skilled in attaining their own objective. They were accomplished in speaking respectfully. Both of them spoke about knowledge and learning. The relatives were confused and remained there. At that time, Shankara approached. The wielder of the trident spoke these words to the men. 'I am the one who grants boons.' Having been thus addressed, those miserable ones bowed down and remained standing there. They said, 'All of us have been deprived of our single son. We desire his life. You should grant us life by granting that our son becomes alive.' Having been thus addressed, the illustrious one filled his hand with water and granted the child a lifespan of one hundred years. The illustrious one, the wielder of *pinaka* who was engaged in the welfare of all beings, also granted the jackal and the vulture the boon that they should no longer suffer from hunger. They were full of joy at this great benefit and bowed down to the god. O lord! They were delighted and happy that their objectives had been accomplished and stood there. Through a long period of faith and certain and firm devotion, and through the grace of the god of the gods, fruits are swiftly obtained. Behold the god's decision and the determination of the relatives. The tears of the miserable and weeping ones were wiped away. Behold. Certain in their pursuit

[161]The vulture.
[162]The relatives.
[163]The vulture and the jackal.

and through the favours of Shankara, the miserable ones obtained happiness in a short period of time. At their son coming to life again, they were amazed and delighted. O best among the Bharata lineage! All of this was possible because of Shankara's favours. O king! They heard from Bhava[164] about how sorrow can be countered. Taking their son with them, they were filled with joy and entered their city. This is the intelligence that has been indicated for the four varnas. This is the auspicious history, full of dharma, artha and moksha. If a man hears this, he obtains delight in this world and in the next."'

Chapter 1478(150)

'Bhishma said, "On this, an ancient history is recounted. O best among the Bharata lineage! This is a conversation between a *shalmali* tree[165] and the wind. There was a gigantic tree on the slopes of the Himalayas. It had grown for many years and possessed a trunk, branches and foliage. O mighty-armed one! Crazy elephants, afflicted by heat and oppressed by exhaustion, would rest there. So would other kinds of animals. The tree was dense with foliage and was a *nalva*[166] in circumference. It was covered with fruits and flowers and frequented by parrots and *sharika* birds. This was beautiful and supreme among trees. Merchants in search of riches, ascetics, residents of the forest and travellers along the path would rest under it. O bull among the Bharata lineage! Narada saw the large trunk and the branches that extended in every direction. He approached and said, 'You are beautiful. You are handsome. O shalmali! O best among trees! You always please us. O son![167] Birds, animals and elephants have always cheerfully resided under your delicate shade. Your branches, larger branches and trunk are gigantic. Under no

[164]Shiva.

[165]The silk-cotton tree.

[166]A furlong, 660 feet.

[167]The word used is tata.

circumstance do I see any of these being shattered by the wind. O son! Is the wind your affectionate well-wisher? It is certain that the wind always protects you in this forest. The wind uproots large and small trees from their places. Its force dislodges the peaks of mountains. With its fragrant and sacred scent, the wind even dries up the nether regions and also the lakes, the rivers and the oceans. There is no doubt that the wind protects you as a friend. That is the reason you have these many branches, leaves and flowers. O tree! O son! It is seen to be beautiful that these birds sport and find pleasure in you. Their delicate voices can be separately heard. When it is the time for flowering, one can hear these extremely beautiful sounds. The elephants, the adornments of their herds, also take delight. O shalmali! They are afflicted by the heat and find joy on seeking refuge with you. In that way, other kinds of animals are also radiant near you. Those who are in search of riches seek refuge. O tree! You are as resplendent as Mount Meru. There are brahmanas, successful ascetics, hermits and mendicants. I think that your shelter is like heaven. The wind goes everywhere and is fierce. O shalmali! There is no doubt that it protects you because you are a relative or a friend. O shalmali! When the wind approaches you, perhaps you bow down supremely and say, "I belong to you." That is the reason the wind always protects you. I have not seen a tree or a firm mountain that has not been shattered by the wind. It is my view that there is nothing like this on earth. O shalmali! But then again, for some reason, you and your family are always protected by the wind. That is the reason you stand, free from fear.'

'"The shalmali replied, 'O brahmana! The wind is not my friend, my relative, or my well-wisher. Nor is the wind my supreme lord that it should protect me. O Narada! My energy and strength are more terrible than that of the wind. The wind cannot even attain one-eighteenth of my force of life. When the strong wind arrives and destroys trees, mountains and everything else, I resist it with my force. The wind does the shattering,[168] but has been shattered

[168]The wind is named *prabhanjana*, the one who shatters. This is the word used in the text.

by me many times. O devarshi! That is the reason I am not terrified of even an enraged wind.'

'"Narada said, 'O shalmali! There is no doubt that you look at this in a contrary way. There is nothing anywhere that has a strength that is equal to the wind's strength. Indra, Yama, Vaishravana[169] and Varuna, the lord of the waters, are not the wind's equal, not to speak of a tree. O shalmali! When any living being moves on this earth, everywhere, it is the illustrious wind, the lord, who makes the breath of life move. When it exerts itself properly, it reassures all living beings. When it is not properly exerted, men move in perverse ways. This is the nature of the wind and it is the supreme upholder of all life. You do not worship someone who should be worshipped. What can this be, other than lack of intelligence? You have no substance. You are evil in your intelligence. You only speak a lot. O shalmali! Since you have spoken in this false way, I am enraged with you. My anger has been roused at what you have said. I will myself tell the wind about the many wicked words you have spoken. There are other trees that are stronger still—sandalwood, *spandana*,[170] shala,[171] *sarala*,[172] *devadaru*,[173] cane and reeds. They are cleansed in their souls and do not evil-mindedly speak about the wind in this way. They know their own strengths and that of the wind. That is the reason those supreme trees bow down before the wind. You are deluded and do not know about the wind's infinite strength.'"'

Chapter 1479(151)

'Bhishma said, "O Indra among kings! Having spoken in this way, Narada, knowledgeable about the brahman, went and told the

[169]Kubera.

[170]Kind of tree.

[171]*Vatica robusta*.

[172]Pine.

[173]Cedar or spruce.

wind everything that the shalmali had said. 'There is a shalmali tree and its followers on the slopes of the Himalayas. It has a gigantic trunk and many branches. O wind! It shows you disrespect. It spoke many words of irreverence towards you. O wind! O lord! It is not appropriate that I should repeat those words before you. O wind! I know that you are the supreme upholder of all living beings. You are best and the greatest. In your rage, you are like Vaivasvata.'[174] Having heard these words of Narada, the wind went to the shalmali and angrily spoke these words. 'O shalmali! You have spoken disrespectful words before Narada. I am the wind. I will show you my influence and my own strength. I know who you are. O tree! You are known to me. The lord, the grandfather,[175] ended his act of creation with you. Because he ended with you, he showed you favours. O evil-minded one! O worst among trees! That is what has protected you against my valour. Since you have disrespected me as any other natural force, I will show myself to you, so that you know who I am.' Having been thus addressed, the shalmali tree seemed to smile when it replied. 'O wind! Go to the woods and show your enraged self to your own self. Release your anger towards me. What will you do in your rage? O wind! I would not have been frightened of you, even if you had been the lord of beings.' Having been thus addressed, the wind said that it would exhibit its energy the next day.

'"It was night and the shalmali thought about what should be done. It saw that it was not the equal of the wind. 'I spoke inappropriate words about the wind to Narada. I cannot match the wind in strength. It is stronger than me. Narada was right when he said that the wind is always strong. There is no doubt that I am weaker than other trees. However, I do not think there is any other tree that is my equal in intelligence. By resorting to that intelligence, I can free myself from the fear that comes from the wind. There is no doubt that if the trees in the forest used their intelligence, they would always be able to save themselves from any injury on account of the enraged wind. But they are foolish and do not know the wind.

174Yama.

175Brahma.

Unlike me, they do not know how the angry wind blows.' Having made up its mind, the shalmali began to shake itself. It itself cast off its trunk, branches and smaller branches. It cast off its branches, leaves and flowers. Having done this, the tree waited for morning and for the approach of the wind. The wind blew and angrily brought down large trees. It came to the spot where the shalmali was standing. It was without leaves and the tips of the branches had fallen down. The flowers had fallen down. The wind glanced at it and smiling, cheerfully spoke these words to the shalmali tree, which was without any branches. 'O shalmali! In my anger, I would have done exactly this to you and brought down all your branches. You have done this yourself. You are without flowers and the tips of your branches. Your buds and foliage have been destroyed. Through your own evil intelligence, you have come under the subjugation of my valour.' Addressed in these words by the wind, the shalmali tree was ashamed. It remembered the words that Narada had spoken to it and was tormented.

'"O tiger among kings! In this way, if a weak person engages in hostilities with someone who is stronger, he is foolish and will be tormented like the shalmali tree. Therefore, a weak person should have enmity with someone who is superior in strength. If he engages in such enmity, he will sorrow, like the shalmali tree. Even against those who cause grievous injury, great-souled ones do not display their enmity. O great king! Instead, they exhibit their strength gradually and gently. A man without intelligence should not act in enmity towards someone who lives by his intelligence. An intelligent person's intelligence is like a fire raging through dry grass. O king! Among men, there is nothing that is equal to intelligence. O Indra among kings! One might think that there is nothing that is equal to strength. O Indra among kings! O slayer of enemies! You have thus seen that one must tolerate the foolish, the dumb, the deaf and those who are superior in strength. O immensely radiant one! O king! The eleven and seven akshouhinis[176] were not equal in strength to the great-souled Arjuna. The illustrious Pandava, the son of the

[176]Respectively on the Kourava and Pandava side.

chastiser of Paka, roamed around and slew and shattered them in the battle. O descendant of the Bharata lineage! You have been told about rajadharma and apad dharma in detail. O great king! What shall I tell you about next?"'

Chapter 1480(152)

'Yudhishthira said, "O bull among the Bharata lineage! I wish to hear about the true nature of evil's foundation and about how sin propagates."

'Bhishma replied, "O lord of men! Hear about the foundation of evil. Greed alone is the great grasper. Evil is propagated by greed. It is from this that evil, adharma and supreme misery flow. This is the foundation for misdeeds and makes people commit sin. Anger results from greed. Desire results from greed. Confusion and delusion result from greed and so do pride, arrogance, malice and lack of forgiveness. Modesty is abandoned. Prosperity is destroyed and dharma decays. Anxiety and lack of wisdom—all of these result from greed. There are also lack of fairness, lack of reflection and the performance of perverse deeds. One becomes learned in deceit and is proud of one's beauty and prosperity. One is distrustful of all beings. One is crooked towards all beings. One acts injuriously towards all beings. One behaves inappropriately towards all beings. One steals the property of others. One ravishes other people's wives. There is violence in words and thought. There is violence in criticizing. There is turbulence in one's groin and belly. There is the terrible turbulence that is associated with death. There is the violence of envy. The strong impulse to lie is extremely difficult to give up. It is difficult to withstand the impulse of passions. It is impossible to withstand the impulse to hear bad words and boasting. One is malicious, wicked and perpetrates evil deeds. One is rash in every kind of deed and action. At birth, childhood and youth, a man cannot give up the consequences of the deeds that he has done. Though he decays, these do not decay. O extender of the Kuru lineage! One is incapable of satisfying greed through acquisitions. It is always like an ocean, incapable of being filled by deep-flowing rivers. Greed is not satisfied. Nor is desire satiated. O king! Its true nature is not known by the gods, the gandharvas, the asuras, the great serpents and all the large numbers of other beings. One who conquers greed and delusion conquers his soul. O Kouravya! Insolence, hatred, criticism, maligning and malice—these are found in greedy people who have not perfected their souls. There are those who are extremely learned, the repositories of the extremely great sacred texts. They can sever doubt. But on this, even they can have limited intelligence and are afflicted. They become addicted to hatred and anger and are cast out by those who are good in conduct. Though they are harsh inside, their words may be sweet. They are like pits that have been covered with grass. Though they hold up the flag,[177] they are inferior and against dharma. They steal from the universe. They resort to the strength of arguments and follow many different kinds of paths. But because they base themselves on greed and ignorance, they destroy every kind of path. If evil-souled ones, driven primarily by greed, take over dharma, they deform it. But that practice tends to be established. O Kouravya! Arrogance, anger, pride, laziness, delight, sorrow, extreme vanity—these are seen among the greedy and the ignorant. Know that they have not been instructed. They are always full of greed. Ask those who have been instructed. I will tell you about the ones who are auspicious in their vows. They do not have any fear about their conduct. Nor do they fear the world hereafter. They find no delight in flesh, nor are they addicted to the agreeable and the disagreeable. Good conduct is agreeable to them. Self-control is established in them. They are beyond happiness and unhappiness. They are devoted to the truth and the ultimate. Though they are compassionate, they are neither givers, nor receivers. They are always devoted to the ancestors, the gods and guests. They always exert, in every kind of way. They follow every kind of dharma. O descendant of the Bharata lineage! They are engaged in the welfare of all beings. They are prepared to give up

[177]Of dharma.

everything. Having reached the ultimate shore of dharma, they are incapable of being dislodged and moved from their conduct, which was fashioned by virtuous people in ancient times. They are based on the path of virtue and are not frightened, fickle or fierce. They are beyond desire and anger. They are without a sense of ownership and without a sense of the ego. They are good in their vows and firm in their honour. O Yudhishthira! You should worship them and ask them. They do not seek cattle or fame, only dharma. They do perform the functions of the body, because that is necessary. But they do not know fear, anger, fickleness and sorrow. They do not fly the flag of dharma and there is nothing that is secret among them. They do not suffer from greed and delusion. They are upright and devoted to the truth. O Kounteya! You should find delight in them. Their minds are attentive. They find no delight in acquisitions. Nor do they grieve if there are no acquisitions. They are without sense of ownership and without sense of ego. They are based on the truth and look on everything equally. O son! Gain and lack of gain, happiness and unhappiness, pleasant and unpleasant, death and life—these are the same to them, because they are firm in their valour. They are full of intelligence and base themselves on the truth. They are extremely powerful. Attentively and according to your capacity, you should do what brings them happiness and is agreeable. Words used in conversation may be good or bad. Like that, through the working of destiny, all beings may have qualities."'[178]

Chapter 1481(153)

'Yudhishthira said, "O grandfather! You have said that greed is the foundation of everything that is injurious. O father![179] I wish to hear about the true nature of ignorance."

[178]The suggestion seems to be that the acceptance of Bhishma's instructions depends on destiny.

[179]The word used is tata.

'Bhishma replied, "If a person commits a wicked deed as a result of ignorance, he does not know what is good for him. He hates people who observe good conduct and people talk about him.[180] Because of ignorance, he goes to hell. Because of ignorance, he comes to an evil end. Because of ignorance, he suffers misery and is submerged in disaster."

'Yudhishthira said, "I desire to hear about wickedness—its inclination, status, growth, increase and decrease, the source, its working, progress, periodicity, reasons and causes. O king! I wish to hear exactly and completely, about the consequence of ignorance, since unhappiness in this earth has it as its origin."

'Bhishma replied, "Attachment, hatred, confusion, delight, sorrow, arrogance, desire, anger, pride, procrastination, laziness, wishing, aversion, torment, suffering from the prosperity of others—these wicked acts are indicated as ignorance. You have asked about their working, their increase and other things. O mighty-armed one! O lord of the earth! Therefore, listen to this in detail. O descendant of the Bharata lineage! O king! Know that both ignorance and excessive greed are equal in consequences and equal in wickedness. They are the same. The influence of greed is again increased if ignorance increases. If one is constant, so is the other. If one decays, so does the other. Each one has many courses. The source of greed is the great influence of destiny. Even if one has severed greed in every way, the source that is based on destiny remains. Thus, greed comes from ignorance and ignorance comes from greed. Greed is the source of all sins. Therefore, one should avoid greed. Janaka, Yuvanashva, Vrishadarbhi, Prasenjit and other lords of the earth attained heaven because they destroyed their greed. O foremost among the Kurus! In this world, it is evident that you must cast aside greed from your soul. Having abandoned greed, you will follow the path of happiness in this world and the next."'

[180]In words of condemnation.

Chapter 1482(154)

'Yudhishthira said, "O grandfather! O one with dharma in his soul! In this world, what is said to be the best thing for a brahmana who desires dharma and makes the effort to study? Many things are seen as best in this world. O grandfather! Tell me what you think to be best in this world and the next. O descendant of the Bharata lineage! The path of dharma is great and it has many branches. Which are the elements of dharma that are held to be the best? O king! In truth, dharma is great and has many branches. O father! Tell me carefully about all this and about what is the supreme foundation."

'Bhishma replied, "I will indeed tell you about how you may obtain the ultimate benefit. O wise one! You will drink this, which is like amrita, and be satisfied with the knowledge. Each of the maharshis has depended on his knowledge and has talked about a separate aspect of dharma. Self-control is the ultimate among them. The ancients were certain in their foresight when they said that self-control is the supreme quality. In particular, for a brahmana, self-control is eternal dharma. If one is not self-controlled, the success of deeds is not properly obtained. Self-control and generosity surpass sacrifices and studying. Self-control increases energy and self-control is the supreme purifier. A man who is without sin and possesses energy obtains greatness. We have not heard of any dharma that is equal to self-control in any world. Those who follow complete dharma praise self-control as supreme in this world. O Indra among men! Even in the world hereafter, one obtains supreme happiness. Being united with self-control, one obtains great dharma. A self-controlled person sleeps happily. He wakes in happiness. He moves through the world in happiness and his mind is cheerful. A person who is not self-controlled obtains hardship and decay. Because of his own sins, he creates many calamities. Among the four ashramas, this is said to be the supreme vow. I will tell you about the signs that give rise to self-control. Forgiveness, fortitude, non-violence, impartiality, truthfulness, uprightness, conquest of the senses, skill, mildness, modesty, steadfastness, generosity, lack of anger, satisfaction, pleasantness in speech, lack of an acquisitive tendency and lack of malice—these unite and give rise to self-control. O Kouravya! One must also worship the seniors, show compassion towards all beings, be free of slander and tendency to gossip, not indulge in futile conversation and avoid both praise and censure. A self-controlled man does not indulge in desire, anger, greed, pride, insolence, boasting, confusion, jealousy and disrespect of others. He is not censured and is free of desire. He desires little and is not resentful. Such a man is like the ocean and is never filled.[181] 'I am yours. You are mine. They are mine. I am theirs.' The self-controlled person does not say such things about his former relatives.[182] Whatever be the conduct of people in the village or in the forest, such a person does not speak words of censure or praise. He is friendly and good in conduct. He is supremely devoted to his aides. He is free from many kinds of attachment and obtains great fruits in the world hereafter. He is excellent in conduct. He is good in conduct. He is cheerful in his soul and knows about his soul. He obtains reverence in this world and a good end thereafter. There are auspicious deeds in this world. These are practised by the virtuous. He possesses knowledge about these and does not diminish the dharma of sages. He departs and resorts to the forest. He is united with knowledge and conquers his senses. He roams around, waiting for the time.[183] He is capable of attaining the brahman. He has no fear from beings. Beings have no fear from him. He has no fear on account of being separated from his body. He has exhausted his good deeds and has none to accumulate. He acts equally towards all beings and behaves affectionately towards them. He is like a bird in the sky or like an aquatic creature in the water. There is no doubt that his progress cannot be seen.[184] O king!

[181]It is difficult to understand this. A self-controlled man should presumably always be content. Perhaps it means that a self-controlled man is never content with trifles.

[182]The relatives must be former because the self-controlled person has renounced.

[183]For death to arrive.

[184]In the sense that he doesn't leave a visible trail. He does not accumulate any karma.

He abandons his home and attains moksha. He obtains the worlds of energy for an eternal period of time. He renounces all deeds. He renounces all the recommended austerities. He renounces the different kinds of learning. He renounces everything. He does not return to desire. He is cheerful and pure in his soul. He obtains great reverence in this world and heaven thereafter. This is the place of the grandfather[185] and Brahma's essence arises from there. This is always concealed in secret, but can be obtained through self-control. A person who takes comfort in wisdom and possesses intelligence and who does not indulge in hostility towards any being has no fear of returning again.[186] What fear can he have of the world hereafter? There is one sin associated with self-control and a second one does not exist. Because he is forgiving, people think that he is incapable. O immensely wise one! But there is an extremely good quality associated with this taint. Because forgiveness is great, the patient person easily obtains the worlds. O descendant of the Bharata lineage! A self-controlled person doesn't need the forest. A person without self-control also finds nothing there. Wherever a self-controlled person resides, that is his forest and his hermitage."'

Vaishampayana said, 'Hearing these words of Bhishma, King Yudhishthira was cheerful and extremely satisfied, as if he had savoured amrita. He again asked Bhishma, supreme among the upholders of dharma. O extender of the Kuru lineage![187] He told him everything about austerities.'

Chapter 1483(155)

'Bhishma said, "The wise have said that austerities are the foundation of everything. A stupid person who has not been tormented through austerities does not obtain the fruits of his deeds.

[185]Brahma.

[186]Of being reborn.

[187]Janamejaya.

The lord Prajapati created everything here through austerities. The rishis acquired the Vedas through austerities. The siddhas perform austerities in the due order and subsist on fruits, roots and the wind. Extremely controlled, they can see the three worlds through their austerities. Herbs and other medications and the three types of learning[188] are perfected and made successful through austerities. Austerities are the foundation of all endeavour. Everything that is difficult to obtain, difficult to name, difficult to assail and difficult to withstand—all this can be made possible through austerities. There is nothing that can surpass austerities. A sinful man who drinks liquor, seizes objects of others without permission, kills foetuses and violates the bed of his preceptor—can be freed if he torments himself well through austerities. Austerities have many forms and many gates through which they flow. Among the austerities that involve restraint, abstention from food is the best. O great king! Non-violence, truthfulness in speech, donations, restraint of the senses—abstention from food is superior to these austerities too. There is nothing more difficult than giving and no ashrama that surpasses the mother. There is nothing that is superior to the three kinds of learning. Renunciation is the supreme austerity. In this world, the senses protect riches and grain. But in this protection of dharma, artha and austerities, there is nothing superior to abstention from food. The rishis, the ancestors, the gods, humans, the best of animals and all other beings, mobile and immobile—all of them are devoted to austerities. They become successful through austerities. It is through austerities that the gods attained greatness. They always obtained their desirable shares and fruits through austerities. It has been determined that through austerities, one can even attain divinity."'

Chapter 1484(156)

'Yudhishthira said, "The brahmana rishis, ancestors and gods all praise the dharma of truth. O grandfather! I wish to hear

[188]The three Vedas.

about the truth. Tell me about it. O king! What are the signs of the truth? How can it be obtained? Having obtained truth, what does one become? How is all this spoken of?"

'Bhishma replied, "The mixing of the dharma of the four varnas is not praised. O descendant of the Bharata lineage! Without any distortion, truth exists in all the varnas. For the virtuous, truth is always dharma. Truth is the eternal dharma. It is truth that one should bow down to. Truth is the supreme objective. Truth is dharma, austerities and yoga. Truth is the eternal brahman. Truth is said to be the supreme sacrifice. Everything is established in the truth. In this world, truly and in proper order, I will tell you about the conduct associated with truth. In proper order, I will tell you about the characteristics associated with truth. You should hear about how truth can truly be acquired. O descendant of the Bharata lineage! In all the worlds, there are thirteen kinds of truth. There is no doubt that truth is impartiality and self-control. There is also lack of malice, forgiveness, modesty, patience, lack of envy, renunciation, meditation, wisdom, fortitude, constant adherence and non-violence. O Indra among kings! These are the thirteen forms of the truth. The truth is described as immutable. It never undergoes a transformation. It is not against any kind of dharma and it can be obtained through yoga. There must be impartiality towards the desirable and the undesirable, towards one's own self and towards the enemy. When preference and aversion are destroyed, desire and anger are also destroyed. Self-control means one doesn't desire the possessions of others. There is always patience and gravity. There is fearlessness and the pacification of anger. All of these are obtained through knowledge. The learned say that lack of malice manifests itself in generosity and control in the practice of dharma. Those who always base themselves on the truth do not suffer from malice. The virtuous person forgives everyone—those who should be forgiven and those who should not be forgiven, those who are liked and those who are not liked. The virtuous obtain the truth. They do good in secret ways. The modest person never boasts. The dharma of modesty can always be obtained through restraint in speech. The form of forgiveness that is indulged in for the sake of dharma or artha is said to be endurance. This is for the propagation of the worlds and is obtained through patience. If a person renounces affection, if a person renounces objects and if a person gives up love and hatred, he becomes one who renounces—not otherwise. If a person makes efforts to undertake good deeds, without making it obvious and without any attachment, that is said to be nobility among beings. There is fortitude when one does not perform perverse deeds, whether it is in a situation of happiness or unhappiness. A wise person who desires his own prosperity must always pursue this. One must always have sentiments of being forgiving. One must be devoted to the truth. Devoid of delight, fear and anger, a learned person obtains fortitude. Lack of hatred towards all beings, in deeds, thought and words, kindness and generosity—these are the eternal dharma of the virtuous. These are the thirteen separate characteristics of the truth. O descendant of the Bharata lineage! These forms of truth are worshipped and extended. O descendant of the Bharata lineage! It is impossible to speak about the infinite qualities of the truth. That is the reason truth is praised by the brahmanas, the ancestors and the gods. There is no dharma superior to the truth. There is no sin that is worse than falsehood. Truth is the foundation of dharma. That is the reason truth must not be destroyed. The giving of gifts, sacrifices with dakshina, vows, agnihotra sacrifices, the Vedas and other manifestations of dharma result from the truth. One thousand horse sacrifices and truth were held up on a weighing scale and truth surpassed the one thousand horse sacrifices."'

Chapter 1485(157)

'Yudhishthira said, "O bull among the Bharata lineage! O immensely wise one! Tell me accurately about the origin of anger, desire, sorrow, confusion, scepticism, lassitude, intoxication, avarice, jealousy, contempt, slander, intolerance and pity. Tell me about all these."

'Bhishma replied, "Amongst beings, these thirteen are said to be extremely strong enemies. O great king! In this world, all of them unite and serve a man. They distract a man and distracted, he takes delight. They jump like wolves, when they see other men approach.[189] Misery flows from these. Sin flows from these. O bull among the Bharata lineage! Mortal men must always realize this. O supreme among men! I will indeed tell you about the origin, status and destruction of these. Listen attentively. Anger results from greed and is stimulated by the sins of others. O king! It remains dormant through forgiveness. A prosperous person must refrain from it.[190] Desire flows from resolution and grows when one serves it. When a wise person uses his knowledge to discern its true nature, it can no longer be seen and withers away. Scepticism is against the sacred texts and is seen to originate among those who are limited in intelligence. If one possesses true knowledge, it withdraws. Among beings, sorrow results from affection and separation.[191] If one knows that this is futile, it is immediately destroyed. Lassitude results from the practice of anger and avarice. Indifference and kindness towards all beings makes it withdraw. Dispirited people serve malice and that which is injurious. O son! If virtuous people are served, these are destroyed. There are beings who are proud of their lineage, their knowledge and their prosperity. When they discern the reason behind this pride, it is immediately destroyed. O descendant of the Bharata lineage! Envy flows from desire and rivalry. Among those who are mortals, wisdom destroys these. O king! Slander is generated from spiteful words of misguided people, those who are not on one's side. The act of ignoring pacifies this. There may be a powerful person who causes injury and one may be incapable of countering him. Fierce resentment is generated. But compassion makes it withdraw. It is seen that pity[192] always generates pity. If one knows about being devoted

[189]When other men approach, wolves jump upon a man, tear him to pieces, and run away.

[190]Anger.

[191]Separation from the object of affection.

[192]This pity is being used in a negative sense, pity towards one's own state.

to dharma, that pity is pacified. These are said to be the ways whereby these thirteen can be conquered and pacified. All these thirteen sins were there among the sons of Dhritarashtra. You always conquered them in your soul. That is the reason you triumphed over them."'[193]

Chapter 1486(158)

'Yudhishthira said, "I know what non-violence is. I have always seen it among the virtuous. O descendant of the Bharata lineage! However, I do not comprehend violent men and their deeds. Like men avoid thorns, pits and fire, a man must avoid a man who performs violent deeds. O descendant of the Bharata lineage! A violent person is always the worst, in this world and in the next. O Kouravya! Therefore, tell me what dharma has determined about such a person."

'Bhishma replied, "His intentions may be hidden. But his deeds are known. He slanders others, but is censured. He binds others, but is himself tied down. He boasts about his acts of generosity. But he is unfair, inferior, fraudulent and deceitful. He does not share his pleasures. He is insolent. He and his companions are boastful. Such a man suspects everyone. He is foolish and miserly. He always praises his own group and creates enmity in the ashramas, mixing them up. He always indulges in violence and has no particular good qualities or bad ones. He is extremely boastful and spirited. He is extremely greedy and is the perpetrator of violent deeds. If there is a person of good conduct who is devoted to dharma and possesses the qualities, he regards such a person as wicked. Judging on the basis of his own character, he does not trust anyone. Even if the taints of others are hidden, he divulges them. Even if his faults and conduct are similar, he does not talk about them. He thinks that a person who does him

[193]You conquered the sins. Hence, you triumphed over the sons of Dhritarashtra.

good has been cleverly deceived. Even if he gives away riches at the right time to someone who has helped him, he repents this. While others watch, he eats food, licks and enjoys such good food. If a person eats in this way, the learned know him as violent. If there is a person who first gives food to brahmanas and then eats, together with his well-wishers, such a person obtains the infinite in this world and heaven after death. O foremost among the Bharata lineage! The nature of a violent person has been recounted. A man who desires benefit must always avoid such a person."'

Chapter 1487(159)

'Bhishma said, "He who has accomplished his objective, he who is about to perform a sacrifice, he who knows all the Vedas, he who is discharging obligations to a preceptor, a father, or a wife, he who is pursuing the objective of studying—such a brahmana is virtuous and is begging for the sake of dharma. In accordance with their learning, one must give to them, since they have nothing of their own. O supreme among the Bharata lineage! To the others, only dakshina is to be given. There are others for whom it is recommended that uncooked food must be given, but away from the sacrificial altar. In accordance with what they deserve, the king must give every kind of jewel. Brahmanas at a sacrifice must be given food and dakshina. A person who has enough to sustain his dependents and servants for three years or more deserves to drink soma.[194] A sacrifice may suffer because some single ingredient is missing at the sacrifice. Especially if it is a brahmana's sacrifice, a king who follows dharma may take that ingredient away[195] from the household of a vaishya who has many animals, but does not perform sacrifices or drink soma. For the purpose of the sacrifice, the king may take that object away from

[194]Is wealthy enough to perform a soma sacrifice.

[195]And give it to the brahmana.

his household. In his household, a shudra possesses nothing that he actually owns. Therefore, from a shudra's household, he[196] can take away any object that he desires. If there is someone with one hundred cattle who does not have the sacrificial fire, or if there is someone with one thousand cows who does not perform sacrifices, he can seize from those households too, without thinking about it. O lord! Having explained the reason, the king can always take from those who do not donate. The dharma of a king who acts in this way will not suffer.

'"There may be a person who has not eaten six meals. And there may be another person who does not care for tomorrow and does not perform deeds. For the seventh meal, one should take away from such a person.[197] This can be taken from the place for husking, the field, the store, or from anywhere. However, this must be told to the king, irrespective of whether he asks or does not ask. The king who knows about dharma will not follow dharma and punish him. Brahmanas suffer from hunger because of the folly of kshatriyas. Having ascertained about the conduct of a learned person, he must think of a means of sustenance.[198] He must protect him, the way a father protects a son born from his loins. At the end of every year, he[199] must always perform the sacrifice to the fire.[200] In ancient times, there was no alternative to dharma. What was spoken about in dharma was sufficient. However, because they were scared of death in times of catastrophe, the vishvadevas, the sadhyas, the brahmanas and the maharshis allowed for many kinds of substitution. But an evil-minded person who does not follow the primary course and follows the secondary course instead, does not obtain any fruits in the world hereafter. A man must not tell the king about brahmanas.[201] When

[196]The king.

[197]Though not explicitly stated, the person doing the taking is probably a brahmana. Because of poverty, he has not had six meals. That is, he has starved for three days.

[198]The king must think of a means of sustenance for brahmanas.

[199]The king.

[200]Specifically, the sacrifice known as *vaishvanara*.

[201]Presumably about their transgressions.

he is told, he should know that he has no energy, compared to their learning and excellent energy. Their energy is superior. That is the reason the king can never withstand the energy of those who know about the brahman. As a creator, ruler and ordainer, a brahmana is said to be god. Therefore, nothing harmful should be spoken to them. Nor must dry words be spoken. A kshatriya tides over his difficulties through the valour of his arms. A vaishya and a shudra use riches. A brahmana uses mantras and offerings. Mantras are not for maidens, young women, or stupid people. Stupid people cannot serve at agnihotra sacrifices. Nor can those who have not been cleansed. If such a person offers oblations there, he is flung into hell. Those who know about dharma say that if an officiating priest who ignites the sacrificial fire at a *prajapatya* sacrifice is not given a horse as dakshina, it is as if the sacrificial fire has not been ignited at all. There are others who perform auspicious deeds. They are faithful and have conquered their senses. However, they can never perform sacrifices without offering dakshina at those sacrifices. If dakshina is not offered at a sacrifice, this destroys the offspring, the animals and heaven for the performer and diminishes his senses, fame, deeds and span of life.

'"All these follow the dharma of shudras—those who cohabit with menstruating women, those who are without the sacrificial fire and those whose families lack knowledge of the Vedas. There may be a village with its supply of water coming from a well.[202] A brahmana may be the husband of a shudra woman and dwell there for twelve years. In that case, he has become a shudra through his deeds. A brahmana who is married, but sleeps with a woman who is not an arya and whom he has not married, is not thought of as a brahmana. He must sit on grass and at the rear.[203] O king! Hear my words about how he may be purified. If he performs that sin for a single night, the brahmana assumes a black complexion.[204] He can

[202]There is a negative connotation associated with water from a well.

[203]Forsaking the rights of being a brahmana.

[204]He is like a shudra. Brahmanas are associated with the white colour, kshatriyas with red, vaishyas with yellow and shudras with black.

pacify his own sin by observing the vow of standing during the day and sitting during the night for a period of three years. O king! It is said that five kinds of lies are not sin—words of jest that cause no harm, those spoken to women, those at the time of marriage, those for the sake of one's preceptor and those for the sake of protecting one's own life. One who is faithful can obtain sacred learning even from someone who is inferior. It has been determined that gold can be picked up, even from a filthy place. If a woman is a gem, she may be taken from an inferior lineage. This is like drinking amrita from poison. According to dharma, women, gems and water are not tainted. For the welfare of cattle and brahmanas and to protect himself, when there is a mixing of varnas, a vaishya can take up the bow. The drinking of liquor, the killing of a brahmana and the violation of the preceptor's bed—it is thought that these cannot be atoned for, as long as one bears life. The stealing of gold, the theft of a brahmana's property, living a life of pleasure, the drinking of liquor[205] and sexual intercourse with women one should not have intercourse with are sins. O great king! If one associates with those who have fallen, even if they have been born as brahmanas, one soon becomes like them. If one associates with those who have fallen, acts as an officiating priest for them, teaches them, travels with them, sits with them or eats with them, one also falls within a year. For these and other things, atonement has been determined. By following the rites of atonement, one is freed from the calamity within a period of time, as long as one does not indulge in them again. At the funeral rites of someone who has committed the afore-mentioned three, unlike the funeral rites of those who have not fallen down, one need not bother about whether the funeral oblations are offered sideways.[206] A

[205]Though liquor occurs twice, the words used are different. Here, the word used is madya. In the earlier clause, the word used is sura.

[206]This is a messy shloka and needs explanation. For those who have not fallen down, funeral oblations are offered straight into the fire. If they are offered diagonally or sideways, they may fall down on the ground, outside the fire, and wicked spirits may feed on them. The afore-mentioned three sinners are those who drink liquor, those who kill a brahmana and those who violate a preceptor's bed. For these sinners, it does not matter.

person who follows dharma should abandon advisers and preceptors if they follow adharma. If they do not perform rites of atonement, he must not even speak to them. A person who performs adharma can destroy the sin by following dharma and performing austerities. If one addresses a 'thief', one incurs a sin. However, if one addresses a person who is not a thief as a 'thief', one incurs double that sin.

'"A maiden who allows herself to be spoilt acquires three-fourths of the sin of killing a brahmana. The one who does the spoiling acquires the remainder of the sin. Abusing a brahmana is a sin that removes one's status for one hundred years. Touching[207] is even more serious. For killing him, one dwells in hell for one thousand years. Therefore, one must not abuse him and never kill him. O king! As many particles of dust are needed to soak up a brahmana's wound, for that number of years one is whirled around in hell. If a person kills a foetus, he is purified if he is slain through a weapon in the midst of a battle. Or one must offer oneself as kindling into a blazing fire and thereby purify oneself. If one drinks liquor, one is freed from that sin by drinking hot *varuni* liquor.[208] That act burns him. Once he dies, he is purified after death. A brahmana then obtains the worlds. Indeed, there is no other way that he can obtain them. A person who violates his preceptor's bed is evil in his soul and wicked in his intelligence. He must embrace a blazing *surmi*[209] and death will purify him. Or he may himself sever his penis and testicles and holding them in his hands, walk straight in the south-west direction,[210] until he dies and falls down. If he[211] gives up his life for the sake of a brahmana, he will be purified. Or he may perform a horse sacrifice, a cow sacrifice or an agnishtoma sacrifice well and be purified in this world and in the next. A person who has killed a brahmana can hold a skull in his hand for twelve years. He begs

[207]Physically causing harm to a brahmana.

[208]Varuni is a specific kind of liquor and sura is liquor in general.

[209]A red-hot pillar, in the shape of a female figure, used for executing those guilty of adultery.

[210]The text says *nairriti*. This is the south-west direction, the direction presided over by Nirriti, the evil goddess of chaos.

[211]This goes back to the sinner who is guilty of killing a brahmana.

and lives as a brahmachari hermit, loudly proclaiming his deed. In this way, the slayer of a brahmana retires to the forest and performs austerities. Not knowing whether she is pregnant or not, one may have intercourse with and kill an *atreyi* woman.[212] Killing an atreyi is double the sin of killing a brahmana. A person who drinks liquor must be restrained in his food and observe brahmacharya. He must sleep on the ground for three years and perform an agnishtoma sacrifice. Finally, when he has given away one thousand cows and a bull, he will obtain purification. Someone who has killed a vaishya must live in that way for two years and then give away one hundred cows and a bull. Someone who has killed a shudra must live in that way for one year and then give away ten cows and a bull. If one has killed a dog, a barbarian[213] or a donkey, one must observe the same vow as for a shudra. This is also true of a cat, a blue jay, a frog, a crow, a vulture, or a rat. O king! For killing any other living being, the same dharma as for killing an animal must be observed.

'"In due order, I will now tell you about the other kinds of atonement. If one violates another person's bed or indulges in theft, one must live separately for one year. This is said to be three years for the wife of a brahmana who is learned in the Vedas and two years for someone else's wife.[214] A person who makes the sacred fire impure must follow the vow of a brahmachari and only eat during the fourth quarter of the day. He must stand during the day and remain seated at night. For three days, he must arise and not sip any water. O Kouravya! If someone abandons his father or his mother without a valid reason, he becomes fallen. That is the determination of dharma. It has been determined that only food and garments need to be given to wives who are guilty of adultery, especially those who have been imprisoned. Vows imposed on men who violate other

[212]An atreyi woman is a woman whose period is just over. She is ready to conceive. Killing her is equivalent to killing a foetus.

[213]*Barbara.*

[214]There is a contradiction between the two years and the earlier one year. It is possible that the two years is meant for kshatriyas and the one year is meant for others who are not brahmanas.

men's wives must also be imposed on them. If a woman abandons the bed of someone superior and desires that of someone wicked, the king must feed her to the dogs in a place that is frequented by many people. A wise person[215] binds down such a man on an iron bed that has been heated. Wood must be kindled underneath and the perpetrator of wicked deeds burnt there. O great king! This is also the punishment for women who transgress their husbands. If a wicked person is accused for one year,[216] the sin is doubled. If someone associates with such a person for two, three or four years, he must lead a difficult existence for five years. He must beg and observe the vow of a hermit. A man whose younger brother marries though he is yet unmarried, a man who marries before his elder brother has married, the woman who marries the younger brother and the one who conducts the marriage—under dharma, all of them are said to have fallen. All of them must observe the vow meant for someone who kills a hero.[217] Or they may observe *chandrayana*[218] or some other kind of fasting and thereby cleanse their sin. The younger brother who has married must offer his wife to his elder brother, who has not married, as a daughter-in-law. Having obtained the permission of the elder, he then takes her back again. Following dharma, this is the way she is freed and so are the other two.

'"If one has inhuman intercourse,[219] provided it is not a cow, one is not stained, as long as one has not ejaculated.[220] It is known that man is the lord of animals and their eater. However, one must don a

[215]A wise king.

[216]This probably means that the sinner has not performed a rite of atonement within one year.

[217]Other than in war.

[218]A kind of fasting that follows the progress (*ayana*) of the moon (*chandra*). On the full moon night, one only eats fifteen mouthfuls of food. For the fifteen lunar days following the full moon, this is decreased by one mouthful per day. For the fifteen lunar days following the new moon, this is increased by one mouthful per day.

[219]With an animal.

[220]The word used in the text actually translates as showered.

hide with the hair on the outside. One must take an earthen bowl in one's hand. With this, one must beg at seven houses, recounting one's deed. If he eats what he has thus obtained, he is purified in twelve days. If he performs the vow without displaying the signs,[221] he must observe it for one year. Even for men,[222] this is the supreme form of atonement. For all those who are addicted to giving and receiving, that[223] is recommended. Among non-believers, it is said that giving a cow is like giving up a breath of life. If one has eaten the meat of dogs, boars, men, cocks or donkeys, or has drunk urine or eaten excrement, one must perform the atonement of being cleansed again. If a brahmana who drinks soma inhales the breath of someone who has drunk liquor, he can drink hot water for three days, or drink hot milk for three days. He can also drink hot ghee for three days or only subsist on air for three days. These are the eternal modes of atonement that have been indicated. This is especially true for brahmanas and has originated from those who possess true knowledge."'

Chapter 1488(160)

Vaishampayana said, 'Nakula was accomplished in fighting with the sword. During a break in the conversation, he spoke to the grandfather, who was lying down on a bed of arrows. "O grandfather! It is said that the bow is the best weapon. O one who knows about dharma! But it is my view that a well-fashioned sword is the best. O king! When the bow has been severed and when the horses have been killed in a battle, a person is capable of successfully protecting himself with a sword. A brave person wielding a sword is single-handedly capable of warding off those who wield bows and those who wield clubs and spears. I have a doubt and curiosity about this. O king! What is the best weapon for battles? How did a

[221]Without the hide and without proclaiming the sin.

[222]Unnatural intercourse with men.

[223]The act of donations.

sword arise? Who fashioned it and why? O grandfather![224] Tell me about the first person who instructed about the use of the sword." He heard the words of Madri's intelligent son. He knew about all the techniques. He spoke auspicious words that were subtle, colourful and full of purport. He replied to him in words that had vowels and accents. The great-souled Nakula, Drona's son, was skilled in learning and policy. Bhishma was accomplished in dhanurveda and was knowledgeable about all forms of dharma.

'Lying down on the bed of arrows, he said, "O Madri's son! Concerning what you have asked me, listen to the truth. I look like a mountain with minerals flowing from it[225] and you have stirred me. O son![226] In ancient times, everything was in an ocean of water. There was no sky and the surface of the earth could not be discerned. It was enveloped in darkness. It was enveloped in darkness and it was extremely deep to look at. There was no sound. It was immeasurable. The grandfather[227] was born there. He created wind and fire and the energetic sun. He created the sky above and below it, the earth and the nether regions. He created the sky, with the moon, the stars, the nakshatras and the planets, the year, day and night, the seasons, lava and kshana. The grandfather established his body in the worlds. The illustrious one generated supreme and energetic sons—the rishis Marichi, Atri, Pulastya, Pulaha, Kratu, Vasishtha, Angiras and the lord god Rudra. There was Daksha Prachetasa, who gave birth to sixty daughters. All the brahmarshis accepted them for the sake of offspring. All the beings in the universe resulted from them—the gods, the large numbers of ancestors, the gandharvas, the apsaras, the many kinds of rakshasas, the birds, the animals, the fish, the apes, the giant serpents and many others that had different forms and strengths, travelling in the water or on the land. O son! There were plants, those born from sweat, those born from eggs and those born from wombs. Everything in the universe was born, mobile

[224]The text actually says great-grandfather.
[225]Because of the blood.
[226]The word used is tata.
[227]Brahma.

and immobile. The grandfather of all the worlds created all these categories of beings. He then again united them to the eternal dharma that is laid down in the Vedas. The gods, with their preceptors and their priests, remained within the fold of dharma—the Adityas, the Vasus, the Rudras, the Sadhyas, the Maruts and the Ashvins. So did Bhrigu, Atri, Angiras, the Siddhas, Kashyapa, rich in austerities, Vasishtha, Goutama, Agastya, Narada, Parvata, the Valakhilya rishis, the Prabhasas, the Sikatas, the Ghritachas, the Somavayavyas, the Vaikhanasas, the Marichipas, the Akrishtas, the Hamsas, the rishis who were born from the fire, the Vanaprasthas and the Prishnis. All of them based themselves on Brahma's instructions.

'"However, the lords of the danavas transgressed the grandfather's instructions.[228] They were full of anger and avarice and diminished dharma. Hiranyakashipu, Hiranyaksha, Virochana, Shambara, Viprachitti, Prahrada, Namuchi, Bali—these and many other large numbers of daityas and danavas crossed the boundaries set by dharma and enjoyed themselves, having determined to follow adharma. 'All of us are their equals. We are just like the gods are.' Having reasoned in this way, they challenged the gods and the rishis. O descendant of the Bharata lineage! They showed no favour or compassion to any of the beings. They disregarded the three methods and punished the subjects with danda.[229] Because of their insolence, those supreme among the asuras entered into an agreement with them.[230] At this, the brahmarshis presented themselves before the illustrious Brahma. At that time, he was on the beautiful slopes of the Himalayas, in Padmataraka.[231] It was one hundred yojanas in area and was decorated with jewels and pearls. O son! In that supreme mountain, there were groves with blossoming trees. Brahma, the best of the gods, was there, engaged in the success and welfare of the worlds. At the end of one thousand years, the lord made arrangements for a

[228]This is Bhishma speaking, not Vaishampayana.

[229]Since danda has been mentioned, the three ignored methods must be sama, dana and bheda.

[230]The other subjects.

[231]The name of a peak.

grand sacrifice there, following the rites instructed in the *kalpas*.[232] Rishis who were accomplished in performing sacrifices were there. As required, they were capable of undertaking all the acts. The Maruts covered the place and there were blazing fires. The place was radiant and seemed to be decorated with the golden sacrificial vessels. The circle of the sacrifice was resplendent, because it was surrounded by gods.

'"I have heard that the rishis suffered something terrible there. The sparkling moon arises in the sky and surpasses the stars. Like that, it has been heard that a being broke through the fire and arose there. Its complexion was like that of a blue lotus. It possessed sharp teeth and a lean stomach. It was tall and difficult to behold because of its great energy. When it arose, the earth began to tremble. Large waves and whirlpools agitated the great ocean. Meteors showered down and there were grave portents. Branches fell down from the trees. All the directions were disturbed. Inauspicious winds began to blow. All the beings were continuously frightened and afflicted. On witnessing the tumult and the being that had arisen, the grandfather told the maharshis, the gods and the gandharvas, 'This valiant being is known as a sword and I have thought of it. This is for the protection of the worlds and for slaying those who hate the gods.' The sword then abandoned that form and became sharp-edged. It sparkled and was sharp at the edges. It was as if the Destroyer had arisen. Brahma gave the blazing sword to Shitikantha[233] Rudra, the one with the bull on his banner. This was for the purpose of countering adharma. At this, the illustrious Rudra was worshipped by the large number of brahmarshis. The one who was immeasurable in his soul accepted the sword and assumed another form. He was four-armed. Though he stood on the ground, he touched the firmament with his head. Mahalinga[234] glanced upwards and released flames from his mouth. He assumed many different complexions—blue, pale and red. His

[232]The *kalpasutras*, which are a part of Vedanga and indicate the norms to be followed in rites and rituals.

[233]The one with the blue throat, Shiva's name.

[234]Shiva's name.

garment was made out of black antelope skin and was decorated with stars made out of the best gold. There was a giant eye on his forehead and it was like the sun. He was beautiful with two other sparkling eyes and they were dark brown. The god Mahadeva wielded the trident in his hand and he was the one who plucked out Bhaga's eyes.[235] He grasped the sword, which was like the Destroyer, the sun, or the fire. He grasped a shield that was embossed in three places and it looked like a cloud tinged with lightning. The immensely strong and valorous one roamed around in many different kinds of paths. He waved the sword around in the sky, wishing to bring an end to the danavas.

'"He released a roar and laughed loudly. O descendant of the Bharata lineage! Rudra's fearful form was resplendent then. On seeing Rudra's form, all the danavas, wishing to perform terrible deeds, attacked him. They showered down rocks and blazing torches. There were many other terrible weapons, razor-sharp and tipped with iron. That army of the danavas had never wavered earlier. However, because of the force that was generated from Rudra's sword, it trembled and was confused. With the sword in his hand, he moved around, in even faster and colourful ways. All the asuras thought that the solitary person was actually one thousand. He severed, pierced, struck, sliced, shattered and mangled. Rudra roamed around amidst that mass of daityas, like a fire amidst deadwood. The rakshasas were devastated by the force of the sword and their arms, thighs and breasts were severed. Their heads were completely cut down and the great asuras fell down on the ground. There were other danavas who were shattered and afflicted by Rudra's force. They screamed at each other and fled in different directions. Some entered the ground. Others entered mountains. There were others who rose up into the sky. Still others submerged themselves in the water. A great and extremely terrible encounter took place. The earth was then covered with the mud of blood and looked horrible. O mighty-armed one! It was strewn with the large bodies of danavas, wounded and bloodied. They were like mountains, covered with *kimshuka* trees.

[235]At the time of Daksha's sacrifice.

The earth was covered with blood and looked beautiful then. She was like a dark woman, intoxicated with liquor and attired in a red and wet garment.

'"When he had killed the danavas and established supreme dharma in the universe, Rudra swiftly abandoned his terrible form and took up his auspicious form of Shiva. All the maharshis and all the large numbers of gods worshipped the god of the gods because of the wonderful nature of his victory. The sword, the protector of dharma, was still wet with the blood of danavas. Respectfully, the illustrious Rudra gave it to Vishnu. Vishnu gave it to Marichi and the illustrious Marichi gave it to the maharshis. The rishis gave the sword to Vasava. O son! The great Indra gave it to the guardians of the world and the guardians of the world gave the extremely large sword to Manu, Surya's son.[236] They told the first man, 'You are the lord. This sword has dharma in its womb. Use it to protect the subjects. Those who transgress the boundaries of dharma, because of subtle or gross reasons, must be punished and protected by the rod, not as one wills, but following dharma. Harsh words are also punishment and chastisement can also take the form of fining a large quantity of gold. For trifling reasons, a limb of the body must not be severed. Nor should there be execution. Harsh words of censure are indicated as a form of the sword. The sword has different measures[237] and there are also exceptions to these measures.' Having created his own son, Kshupa, Manu, the lord of subjects, gave him the sword, for the protection of the subjects. On earth, Ikshvaku accepted the sword from Kshupa and Pururava from Ikshvaku.[238] Ayu obtained it from him and Nahusha from him. Yayati got it from Nahusha and Puru obtained it from him. Amurtarayasa got it from him and King Bhumishaya from him. O king! Bharata, the son of Duhshanta, obtained the sword from Bhumishaya and Aidabida, knowledgeable about dharma, obtained

[236]This means Vaivasvata Manu.

[237]Different norms of punishment.

[238]The sword thus passed from the solar to the lunar dynasty. But it came back to the solar dynasty.

it from him. From Aidabida, Dhundhumara, lord of men, obtained it. Kamboja got it from Dhundhumara and Muchukunda from him. Marutta got it from Muchukunda and Raivata from Marutta. Yuvanashva got it from Raivata and Raghu from Yuvanashva. The powerful Harinashva, descended from the lineage of Ikshvaku, got it from him. Shunaka got the sword from Harinashva and Ushinara, with dharma in his soul, from Shunaka. The Bhojas and the Yadavas got it from him. Shibi obtained it from the Yadus and Pratardana from Shibi. Ashtaka got it from Pratardana and Rushadashva from Ashtaka. Bharadvaja got it from Rushadashva, Drona from him, and Kripa from him. You and all your brothers obtained the supreme sword from him.

'"The Krittikas are the nakshatra for the sword.[239] The fire is its god. Rohini is its gotra. Rudra is its supreme preceptor. O Pandaveya! Listen to the eight secret names of the sword. Recounting these, one can always obtain victory in the world—Asi, Vishasana, Khadga, Tikshnavartma, Durasada, Shrigarbha, Vijaya and Dharmapala.[240] O son of Madravati![241] The sword is the foremost among weapons. The ancient tales have certainly stated that it was first wielded by Maheshvara. O destroyer of enemies! Prithu created the first bow and with this, Vena's son[242] protected the world earlier. O son of Madri! You must also follow the standard set by the rishis. The sword must always be worshipped by those who are accomplished in war. This is the first principle and this has been explained to you in great detail. O bull among the Bharata lineage! I have told you about the sword's origin and association. If a person listens to the supreme and complete account about how the sword was fashioned, that man obtains fame in this world and eternity in the world hereafter."'

[239]Pleiades. The sword was thus created when Krittika was in the ascendant.

[240]Respectively, sword, the one that severs, another term for sword, the one that is sharp at the edges, the one that is difficult to assail, the one that has prosperity in its womb, victory and the protector of dharma.

[241]Madri.

[242]Prithu.

Chapter 1489(161)

Vaishampayana said, 'When Bhishma said this and became silent, Yudhishthira left his presence and asked his brothers, with Vidura as the fifth, "The conduct of people is based on dharma, artha[243] and kama. Which of these is the most important? Which is medium and which is the least important? If one wishes to conquer all three categories together, which of these must one control? O wise ones! You should speak truthful words and satisfy me."

'Vidura was foremost among those who knew the truth about the progress of artha. He possessed qualities. Remembering the texts of dharma, he spoke these words. "A great deal of learning, austerities, renunciation, faith, the performance of sacrifices, forgiveness, the purification of sentiments, compassion, truthfulness, restraint and richness of the soul—these must be cultivated and the mind must not waver. These are the foundations of dharma and artha and can be subsumed in the single word of 'welfare'. The rishis crossed over through dharma. The worlds are established in dharma. The gods obtained heaven through dharma. Artha is submerged in dharma. O king! Dharma is the supreme in qualities. Artha is said to be medium. The learned ones say that kama is the worst. Therefore, a person must control his soul and make dharma the most important."

'When he stopped, the attentive Partha, who knew the true words about artha, spoke. "O king! This world is the arena of action and such conduct is praised—agriculture, trade, animal husbandry and many kinds of artisanship. Among all these tasks, there is nothing that transcends the need for artha. The sacred texts have said that without artha, dharma and kama cannot occur. A victorious person obtains artha and can pursue supreme dharma. He is capable of following kama, which is difficult for those with unclean souls to pursue. The sacred texts say that dharma and kama take the form of artha. These two can be attained through the successful acquisition of artha. Those who have been born in

[243]There is a typo and the Critical edition says *ardha*.

superior lineages surround the man who possesses artha, just as the beings always worship Brahma. Those who have matted hair, are clad in deerskin, are controlled and have smeared themselves with mud, those who have conquered their senses, have shaven heads, have no offspring and dwell separately—even they hanker after artha. There are others who are bearded and attired in ochre garments, covering themselves with humility. They are learned and tranquil. They are free and have given up all their possessions. Even among them, some seek heaven and others strive for artha. Some follow the practices of their lineages and are established in their own individual paths. There are believers and non-believers, completely engaged in supreme restraint. Lack of wisdom is submerged in darkness and wisdom provides the radiance.[244] A person who possesses artha can maintain his servants in pleasure and exert the rod against his enemies. O best among intelligent ones! That is the reason my view is accurate. Now listen to the words of these two. Their voices are choking with words."

'Madri's sons, Nakula and Sahadeva, accomplished in dharma and artha, spoke these supreme words next. "Whether one is seated, lying down, roaming around or standing, through the pursuit of superior and inferior means, one must always attempt to firmly pursue the acquisition of artha. This is extremely difficult to obtain and is supremely loved. In this world, once one has obtained this, there is no doubt that one can obtain kama. Artha is united with dharma and dharma is united with artha. This is the way amrita is united with honey. Therefore, our view is the following. There can be no kama without artha. How can there be dharma without artha? Thus, people are scared of those who are outside the pale of dharma and artha. Therefore, even if a person thinks that dharma is the most important, he must control his soul and seek to accomplish artha. If people trust a person, he can accomplish everything. One must first pursue dharma and then artha that is in conformity with dharma. Kama should be pursued later. These are the fruits of the

[244]Only some have truly renounced and have seen the light. Others are still ignorant.

successful pursuit of artha." Having spoken these words, the sons of the two Ashvins ceased.

'Bhimasena then spoke these words. "A person without kama does not desire artha. A person without kama does not desire dharma. A person without kama cannot follow the path of desire. Therefore, kama is the best. It is because they are united with kama that the rishis are controlled in their austerities. They eat leaves, fruits and roots. They subsist on air and are greatly restrained. There are others who are engaged in chanting the Vedas, they are devoted to studying. They perform funeral rites and sacrifices and receive donations. Merchants, farmers, herdsmen, craftsmen and artisans are engaged in the tasks of the gods. But it is kama that drives the action. Driven by kama, men enter the ocean. Kama has many different forms. Everything is driven by kama. There is nothing, there was nothing and there will be nothing that is beyond the simple fact of kama. O great king! This is the essence and dharma and artha are dependent on it. Kama is to dharma and artha what butter is to curds. Oil is better than what is left of oilseeds after the extraction of oil. Ghee is better than what is left of milk after churning. Good fruit is better than wood. Kama is superior to dharma and artha. Just as honey comes from the juice of flowers, like that, happiness comes from kama. O king! Serve kama. Pleasure yourself with women who are attired in extremely beautiful garments and are ornamented, mad with intoxication and pleasant in speech. Kama will come to you swiftly. In this group, this is my view. O Dharma's son! You should not reflect about this for a long time. If virtuous people paid heed to these beneficial words, which are not shallow in import, there would be the greatest kindness. One must serve dharma, artha and kama in equal measure. If a man serves only one of these, he is the worst. A person who is accomplished in two is said to be medium. The superior person is engaged in all three categories. He is wise. His well-wishers smear him with sandalwood paste. He is adorned in colourful garlands and ornaments." Having spoken these words, briefly and in detail, Bhima, the younger brother, stopped.

'For an instant, Dharmaraja thought well about the words that had been spoken to him. Extremely learned and supreme among the upholders of dharma, he smiled and spoke these truthful words. "There is no doubt that all your determinations are based on the sacred texts of dharma and that you are acquainted with the proof. You have carefully spoken these words to me and I have got to know about kama. You have said that it is essential in this world. However, single-mindedly, listen to the sentiments in my words. A man who is engaged in neither good deeds nor evil ones, and not engaged in artha, dharma or kama, is freed from all sins and looks on gold and stones in the same way. He is successful in freeing himself from unhappiness and happiness. Beings are born and they die. They face old age and decay. There have been repeated instructions on moksha and it has been praised. But we do not know this. The illustrious Svayambhu[245] has said that one who is not bound down by affection does not suffer these.[246] The learned ones have said that nirvana[247] is supreme. Therefore, one should not act in accordance with what is pleasant and what is unpleasant. However, a person who follows kama does not attach importance to this. I act wherever I have been appointed. All the beings have been appointed by destiny. Know that destiny is powerful in everything. One cannot attain the objective by performing deeds. Know that whatever is going to happen will happen. Even if a person is devoid of the three modes, he can attain this objective.[248] Thus, this is the secret for the welfare of the worlds." These foremost words were pleasant to the mind and full of reason. They heard them and were delighted. They joined their hands in salutation to the foremost one among the Kuru lineage. Those words were extremely beautiful and adorned with letters, syllables and words. They were pleasant to hear and devoid of thorns. O king! On hearing the words spoken by Partha,[249] those Indras among men applauded those words. The one who had never

[245]Brahma.

[246]Birth, death, old age and decay.

[247]Literally, extinction. Being used synonymously with moksha.

[248]The objective being moksha. The three modes are dharma, artha and kama.

[249]Yudhishthira.

been dispirited[250] again questioned the son of the river[251] about supreme dharma.'

Chapter 1490(162)

'Yudhishthira said, "O grandfather! O immensely wise one! O extender of the deeds of the Kuru lineage! I will ask you a question. You should explain this to me completely. What kind of men are amiable and who are the ones towards whom one can have great affection? Tell me who can be depended upon, in the present and in the future. It is my view that a growing store of wealth, kin and relatives cannot occupy the space that well-wishers do. A well-wisher who listens is extremely difficult to get. A well-wisher who does good is extremely difficult to get. O best among those who uphold dharma! You should explain all this to me."

'Bhishma replied, "O king! O Yudhishthira! I will tell you everything in detail. Listen to me about the true nature of men one should have alliances with, and those with whom one should not. O bull among men! O lord of men! Greedy, cruel, one who has forsaken dharma, deceitful, fraudulent, inferior, one who is wicked in conduct, one who is suspicious of everyone, lazy, one who is a procrastinator, one who is not upright, a sufferer, one who has molested his preceptor's wife, one who abandons you at the time of a calamity, an evil-souled person, one who is without shame, one who sees wickedness everywhere, a non-believer, one who criticizes the Vedas, one who cannot control his senses in this world, one who incessantly follows kama, a liar, one who hates people, one who does not adhere to agreements, a person who slanders, one who does not possess wisdom, one who is envious, a person who has made up his mind about doing evil, one who is evil in behaviour, one who has

250Yudhishthira.

251Bhishma.

not cleansed his soul, a person who is violent, a gambler, one who causes injury to friends, one who always desires the wealth that belongs to others, an evil-minded person who is not satisfied even if someone gives him a lot and to the best of giver's capacity, one who always behaves with friends as if they are enemies, one who is enraged for the wrong reasons, one who suddenly loses interest, one who is wicked and swiftly abandons his well-wishers for a benefit, one who behaves foolishly when a trifling and involuntary injury has been done to him, one whose friendship is for an ulterior motive, one who pretends to be a friend but is actually an enemy, one who is confused and is blind to his own good, one who does not find delight in what is beneficial—such a man must be avoided. If a man drinks liquor, is hateful, cruel, devoid of compassion, harsh, takes delight in the sufferings of others, injures friends, is engaged in the killing of beings, is ungrateful and wicked—you must never have an alliance with him. You should never have an alliance with someone who is looking for your weakness.

'"Now listen to me about the ones you should have an alliance with—one who is noble, eloquent in speech, accomplished in jnana and vijnana, devoted to friends, grateful, knowledgeable about everything, devoid of sorrow, possessing the quality of pleasantness, devoted to the truth, one who has conquered his senses, one who is always devoted to physical exercise, one who comes from a noble lineage and has servants and sons, one who is handsome, possesses the qualities, one who is not greedy, one who has conquered exhaustion, one who is bereft of taints and one who is famous. These are the ones a king should accept. O lord! There are also those who act to the best of their abilities, are virtuous and content, are not angered for the wrong reasons, do not suddenly change their inclinations, are not angered when opposed, are mentally accomplished about artha, are devoted to the tasks of well-wishers even if this causes a suffering to themselves, in the manner of a red garment, find delight in their friends,[252] do not suffer from the vices of greed and delusion

[252]A red woolen garment does not change its colour easily.

and pursue riches and young women, do not show such paths to well-wishers, trust and are devoted to their friends, regard gold and rock to be equal in value, do not have fraudulent tendencies towards their well-wishers, are modest in their conduct, are not interested in acquiring riches and ornaments, collect their followers and are always supremely interested in ensuring the prosperity of their master. These kinds of men are the best and a king must have an alliance with them. That is the means for extending the kingdom, like moonlight emanating from the lord of the planets. You must always have alliances with the best of men—those who are always based on the sacred texts, those who have conquered their anger, those who have power, those who take delight in war, those who are forgiving and those who possess the qualities of good conduct. O unblemished one! O king! Among the wicked men that I have mentioned, the worst are those who are ungrateful and kill their friends. Under all circumstances, it is certain that such a person, evil in conduct, must be cast aside."

'Yudhishthira said, "O king! I wish to hear in detail about the reason for not allying with those who kill their enemies and are ungrateful, as stated by you. Please tell me."

'Bhishma replied, "Indeed, on this, there is an ancient history that occurred. O lord of men! It happened in the northern direction, where the mlecchas dwell. There was a brahmana from the central regions. He was dark in limbs and had abandoned the brahman. He saw a village that was full of people and entered there, desiring to beg for alms. A rich bandit lived there and he knew specifically about all the varnas. He was devoted to brahmanas, devoted to the truth and always engaged in donations. He[253] went to his house and begged for alms. He begged for a place where he could reside and alms that would last him for a year. He gave the brahmana all this and also a garment that seemed to be new.[254] He also gave him a mature woman who had then lost her husband. Having obtained

[253]The brahmana.

[254]It was not torn off from an old piece of cloth.

all this from the bandit, the brahmana was delighted in his mind. O king! In that supreme house, Goutama[255] found pleasure with her. He aided in the household work of the bandit who had helped him. He lived in Shabara's[256] prosperous house throughout the monsoon. Goutama made supreme efforts to learn archery. O king! Like the large number of bandits, in every direction, Goutama could always kill the cranes that came within the range of his arrows. He lost all compassion and became addicted to violence. He was always engaged in slaying beings. Because of his association with them, Goutama became just like the bandits. In this way, he resided happily in that village of the bandits. Many months passed and he slew many birds.

'"On one occasion, another brahmana arrived at that spot. He had matted hair and was dressed in rags and hides. He was extremely pure and devoted to studying. He was humble and controlled in his food. He was devoted to the brahman and accomplished in the Vedas. The brahmachari, who hailed from the same country[257] as his beloved friend, came to that village of the bandits. Since he avoided food cooked by shudras, he looked for the home of a brahmana. In the village, which was inhabited by a large number of bandits, he roamed around in every direction. That supreme among brahmanas then entered Goutama's house. When Goutama returned, they met each other. When he returned, he had a load of cranes in his hand and wielded a bow in his hand. His limbs were covered in blood and he appeared at the door of the house. On seeing this flesh-eater, who had deviated and fallen, he still recognized him as the brahmana and in shame, spoke these words. 'Why are you acting in this stupid way? You were born in the lineage of a brahmana. You were known in the central regions. How have you come to act like a bandit? Remember the first and foremost among the brahmanas, renowned for their knowledge of the Vedas. You were born in that lineage! The way you are now, you are the worst of your lineage. Awake and

[255]The brahmana's name.

[256]Being used as a proper name for the bandit, or indicating that the bandit was a hunter.

[257]As Goutama.

realize your own self of truthfulness, good conduct, learning and self-control. O brahmana! Remember your compassion and give up this attire.' O king! He was thus addressed by his well-wisher, who had his welfare in mind. Having decided, he miserably replied, 'O best among brahmanas! I possess no riches. I am not learned in the Vedas. O supreme among brahmanas! Know that I have come to this state in search of a means of subsistence. O brahmana rishi! On seeing you, I know that I will be successful. We will leave together in the morning. Dwell here during the night.'"'

Chapter 1491(163)

'Bhishma said, "When night was over, that supreme among brahmanas departed. O descendant of the Bharata lineage! Goutama also left and headed in the direction of the ocean. Along the road, he saw some traders advancing towards the ocean. In the company of their caravan, he went towards the ocean. O great king! However, in a mountainous cavern, that caravan was attacked by a crazy elephant and most of them were killed. In some way, the brahmana managed to escape. Not knowing the directions but wishing to save his life, he fled in the northern direction. He lost everything—the caravan, the directions, the riches. He fled alone through the forest, like a *kimpurusha*. He eventually managed to reach a road that led in the direction of the ocean and then reached a beautiful forest that was full of large blossoming trees. There were beautiful and flowering mango trees in every direction. That spot was like Nandana[258] and was inhabited by yakshas and kinnaras. There were groves of shala, *tala*, *dhava*, *ashvattha* and sandalwood trees. The best among trees were full of flowers. The beautiful valley in the mountains was extremely fragrant with auspicious scents. Excellent birds warbled and chirped in every direction. There were

[258]Indra's pleasure garden.

the famous bharunda birds,[259] with faces like that of men. In every direction, there were *bhulingas*[260] and other birds that frequented the ocean. Listening to the extremely melodious and pleasant sounds of the birds, the brahmana, Goutama, moved along.

'"He then saw a lovely region that was spread with golden sand. It was wonderful and the region had a complexion like that of heaven. There was a giant and handsome banyan tree and it was rounded. It was adorned with beautiful branches and was like an umbrella. Its root was sprinkled extremely well with water mixed with the best of sandalwood. Covered with divine flowers, it was as handsome as the grandfather's[261] throne. It was supreme and loved by the sages. On seeing it, Goutama was delighted. Surrounded by flowering trees, it looked like the house of a god. He joyfully approached it and seated himself under its branches. O Kouravya! As Goutama was seated there, a pleasant and auspicious breeze began to blow. O king! That sacred breeze touched all the flowers and removed all the exhaustion from Goutama's heart and limbs. The brahmana was touched by the auspicious breeze. He slept happily and the sun set. When the sun set, twilight manifested. The king of cranes was known by the name of Nadijangha. He was supreme among birds and was Brahma's beloved friend. The immensely wise one was descended from Kashyapa. He returned to his abode. Unsurpassed on earth, he was also known by the name of Rajadharma. He was the son of a celestial maiden. He was handsome and learned and was like the lord of the gods in his complexion. He was covered in golden plumage and his ornaments were like the sun. Blazing in prosperity, he was adorned all over his body. He was descended from the gods. On seeing the bird arrive, Goutama was astounded. He was overcome by hunger and thirst and glanced at it, desirous of causing injury.[262]

'"Rajadharma said, 'O brahmana! Welcome. It is through good

[259]The bharunda bird is a mythical predatory bird with two heads.

[260]A bird that lives off carrion. It picks out bits of meat from the mouths of predators.

[261]Brahma's.

[262]He wished to kill the bird for food.

fortune that you have come to my house. The sun has set and twilight has presented itself. You have come to my residence as a beloved and unblemished guest. In accordance with the prescribed rites, you will be worshipped. Leave in the morning.'"'

Chapter 1492(164)

'Bhishma said, "Hearing these sweet words, Goutama was astounded. O king! He was curious and looked at Rajadharma.

'"Rajadharma said, 'I am the son of Kashyapa and Dakshayani is my mother.[263] O bull among brahmanas! You are a guest and possess all the qualities. Welcome.'"

'Bhishma said, "In accordance with the prescribed rites, he gave him all the honours. He fashioned a celestial seat that was covered with shala flowers. That region around the Ganga was traversed by Bhagiratha's chariot and was inhabited by a large number of fishes. Kashyapa[264] properly lit a blazing fire and cooked some extremely large fish, offering them to Goutama, the guest. The brahmana fed on these and was delighted. The great-minded one then fanned him with his wings, so that his exhaustion might become less. When he was seated and rested, he asked him about his gotra. He said, 'I am Goutama, a brahmana.' He did not say anything else. He gave him a celestial bed covered with fragrant leaves and adorned with divine flowers. Goutama happily lay down on it. Once he had lain down on the bed, the eloquent Kashyapa, the king of the cranes, asked him, 'What is the reason behind your coming here?' O descendant of the Bharata lineage! At this, Goutama replied, 'O immensely intelligent one! I am poor. I have come to the ocean with the object of acquiring some riches.' Kashyapa cheerfully replied,

[263]Dakshayani means Daksha's daughter. The sage Kashyapa was married to several of Daksha's daughters and all beings are descended from them.

[264]Descended from Kashyapa.

'O foremost among brahmanas! You should not be anxious. You will be successful. You will return to your home with riches. O lord! It is Brihaspati's view that there are four means of obtaining riches—inheritance, fate, deeds and friends. I have appeared before you as a friend and you are also my well-wisher. I will try on your account, so that you can truly obtain riches.' When it was morning, he asked him[265] whether he was comfortable and said, 'O amiable one! Advance along this path and you will be successful. Once you have travelled three yojanas, there will be a great lord of the rakshasas. He is immensely strong and is known by the name of Virupaksha. He is my friend. O best among brahmanas! Go to him. Because of my telling him, there is no doubt that he will give you as much of riches as you desire.' O king! Having been thus addressed, Goutama was no longer exhausted and departed.

'"O great king! Along the way, as much as he wished, he ate fruit that was like amrita and progressed quickly. There were excellent forests of sandalwood, aloe and cinnamon. He reached a city named Meruvraja, with stone walls. There were ramparts made out of stone and a mechanical gate made out of stone. O king! It was announced to the intelligent Indra among rakshasas that a beloved well-wisher had sent a beloved guest to him. O Yudhishthira! At this, the Indra among rakshasas told his messengers, 'Goutama has arrived at the gates of the city. Quickly go and bring him here.' Men attired in white garments emerged from that supreme city. O great king! The messengers of the lord of the rakshasas went to the city gates and told the brahmana, 'O Goutama! Make haste and come quickly. The king wishes to see you. The brave lord of the rakshasas is Virupaksha and you have heard of him. He wishes to see you swiftly. Therefore, you must make haste.' Because of his amazement, the brahmana's exhaustion vanished and he hurried. Goutama saw the prosperity of the city and marvelled greatly. With the servants, he quickly arrived at the king's residence. At that time, the brahmana wished to see the Indra among the rakshasas."'

[265]Rajadharma asked Goutama.

Chapter 1493(165)

'Bhishma said, "Announced to the king, he entered that supreme house. He was honoured by the Indra among rakshasas and seated himself on an excellent seat. He was asked about his gotra, his code of behaviour, his studies and the nature of his brahmacharya. However, the brahmana told him nothing, other than his gotra. He no longer observed brahmacharya and had stopped studying. The king only got to know about his gotra and asked him where he lived. 'O fortunate one! Where do you dwell? What is the gotra of your brahmana wife? Tell me everything. Do not be frightened. You should happily rest.' Goutama replied, 'I have been born in the central regions. I dwell in Shabara's house. My wife is a shudra who has married again. I am telling you this truthfully.' At this, the king thought, 'How is this possible? What should I do now? How can I obtain merit?' He used his intelligence to think about this. 'This one has been born as a brahmana. He was sent here to me by my great-souled well-wisher, Kashyapa. Since he has always sought refuge with him, I must do what pleases him. He is my brother and relative.[266] He is also a friend who is dear to my heart. This is full moon in the month of Kartika[267] and one thousand excellent brahmanas will eat in my house. He will also eat here and I will give him some of my riches.' One thousand learned and ornamented brahmanas arrived there. They had bathed and prepared themselves. They were attired in long linen garments. O lord of the earth! Those best among brahmanas came to Virupaksha from many directions. He received them as they deserved, following the prescribed rites.

'"On the instructions of the Indra among the rakshasas, blankets were spread out on the ground. O supreme among the Bharata lineage! The servants spread out cushions on these. Seated there, the best among brahmanas were worshipped by the king. O great king! They were as radiant as the lord of the nakshatras.[268] There

[266]The rakshasas are descended from the sage Kashyapa.

[267]October–November.

[268]The moon.

were sparkling, pure and golden vessels, decorated with diamonds. These were filled with excellent rice, flowing with honey and ghee, and offered to the brahmanas. Many brahmanas always received this, in the months of Ashadha and Magha.[269] Honoured well, they always received the excellent food that they desired. But it has been heard that the full moon in Kartika, after autumn is over, was special and brahmanas were given jewels—gold, silver, gems, pearls, extremely expensive diamonds, lapis lazuli, skins of black antelope and skins of ranku deer. O descendant of the Bharata lineage! The immensely illustrious Virupaksha threw away a large pile of jewels as dakshina and told the foremost among the brahmanas, 'Take these jewels, as much as you can, and as much as you wish. O best among brahmanas! Whatever be the vessels you have eaten from, take those too, and go to your own homes.' When addressed by the great-souled Indra among rakshasas in these words, the bulls among brahmanas accepted a sufficient quantity of jewels. All of them were worshipped with those sparkling and extremely expensive jewels. Attired in excellent garments, the brahmanas were delighted. O king! The Indra among rakshasas restrained the rakshasas and again spoke to the brahmanas, who had arrived from many directions. 'O brahmanas! This is one day when you need have no fear from the rakshasas. Amuse yourselves, as you like, and leave quickly.' At this, all the large numbers of brahmanas fled in different directions.

'"Goutama also swiftly grasped a load of gold. O brave one! He bore this with difficulty and approached the banyan tree. He was exhausted and sat down. He was tired and hungry. O king! At that time, Rajadharma, supreme among birds, who was devoted to his friend, arrived and welcomed Goutama. The bird fanned him with his wings and removed his exhaustion. He honoured him and made arrangements for his food. Having eaten and having rested well, Goutama began to think. 'Because of both my greed and my confusion, I have seized this extremely large burden of gold. I have a long distance to travel. There will be no food on the way, whereby I

[269]Respectively, June–July and January–February.

can stay alive. How will I be able to sustain my life?' He thought in this way. He could not see any food that would be available along the route. O tiger among men! The ingrate thought in his mind, 'This lord of the cranes is by my side and he is a heap of flesh. I will kill him and take him with me. I will then swiftly depart.'"'

Chapter 1494(166)

'Bhishma said, "For the sake of protection, the Indra among the birds had kindled a great and blazing fire there and the wind was its charioteer. Having done this, the king of the cranes trustfully went to sleep by the side. Wishing to kill him, the evil-souled ingrate remained awake. With a blazing brand, he killed that trustful one. Having killed him, he was delighted, not seeing the consequences this would lead to. He removed the wings and the feathers and cooked the rest over the fire. Then, taking this and the gold, the brahmana left speedily.

'"After another day passed, Virupaksha told his son, 'O son! Today, I have not seen Rajadharma, supreme among birds. Every evening, he always goes to show his obeisance to Brahma. After this, the bird never goes home without having seen me first. It is now two evenings and two nights since he came to my residence. Therefore, I am disturbed and must find out about my well-wisher. That worst among brahmanas was disunited from studying and the radiance of the brahman wasn't there in him. He has gone there and it is my fear that he might have killed him. I noticed that his conduct was wicked and from signs, could make out that he was evil-minded. He did not perform rites and was terrible in form. He was dark, like the worst among bandits. Goutama has gone there. That is the reason my mind is anxious. O son! Swiftly go to Rajadharma's abode. Immediately find out if the one who is pure in his soul is still alive.' Having been thus addressed, he quickly went to the banyan tree with some rakshasas and saw Rajadharma's skeleton there. Weeping, the intelligent son of the Indra among the rakshasas speedily rushed, to the best of his capacity, to seize Goutama. A short distance away, the rakshasas seized Goutama. They also obtained Rajadharma's body, bereft of the wings, the bones and the feet. Having taken this, the rakshasas hastened to Meruvraja.

'"They showed Rajadharma's body and the ungrateful man, Goutama, wicked in his senses, to the king. The king, with his advisers and priests, lamented on seeing him. Great sounds of lamentation arose in the residence. The city, with the women and the children, were distracted. The king told his son, 'Slay this wretch. As you wish, all of you merrily feast on his flesh. He is wicked in his conduct. He is evil in his deeds. He is dastardly in his soul. His determination is sinful. It is my view that the rakshasas should kill him.' Having been addressed by the Indra among the rakshasas, the rakshasas, terrible in their valour, did not wish to eat him and said, 'He is wicked in his deeds. It is proper that this worst among men should be given to the bandits.' O great king! The travellers of the night addressed the Indra among the rakshasas in this way. Before the lord of the large number of rakshasas, they bowed their heads down on the ground and said, 'You should not give him to us to eat. He is evil.' Having been thus addressed by the travellers of the night, the Indra among rakshasas instructed the rakshasas that he should be given to the bandits. Thus instructed, the servants picked up tridents and clubs in their hands. They chopped the wicked one up into pieces and gave him to the bandits. However, even the bandits did not desire to eat the evil-acting one. O Indra among kings! Predatory creatures did not eat the ingrate either.

'"If someone kills a brahmana, if someone is a drunkard, if someone is a thief, if someone has broken his vows—there are indicated means of atonement. O king! But there is no salvation for someone who is ungrateful. Someone who injures his friends, someone who is violent and someone who is ungrateful is the worst among men. Predatory creatures, worms and other such beings will not devour someone like this."'

Chapter 1495(167)

'Bhishma said, "The rakshasa[270] had a funeral pyre constructed for the king of the cranes. It was decorated with gems, fragrances and garments. O king! The Indra among the rakshasas then followed the prescribed ordinances and performed the funeral rites for the powerful king of the cranes. At that time, the auspicious and illustrious goddess, Dakshayani Surabhi,[271] appeared overhead. O unblemished one! Froth and milk flowed from her mouth and streamed onto Rajadharma's funeral pyre. O unblemished one! The king of the cranes was revived at this. The lord of the cranes arose and approached Virupaksha. At that time, the king of the gods came to Virupaksha's city and told Virupaksha, 'It is good fortune that he has come alive.' Indra told Virupaksha about an ancient curse that had, in earlier times, been imposed by Brahma on Rajadharma. 'O king! When the lord of the cranes did not worship Brahma, the grandfather was enraged and spoke to the Indra among the cranes. "This worst among cranes has foolishly not presented himself before me. Therefore, this evil-souled one will shortly be killed." Because of those words, he was slain by Goutama. Having been sprinkled with amrita, the crane has again been brought back to life.' When this was spoken, Rajadharma bowed down before Purandara and said, 'O Purandara! If your mind is inclined towards showing me favours, let my extremely beloved friend, Goutama, come back to life.' O bull among men! Vasava agreed to these words. He revived Goutama and handed him over to his friend. O king! The lord of the cranes was supremely delighted and embraced his friend, who was still carrying the burden.[272] Then, Rajadharma, the lord of the cranes, took his leave of the evil-acting one and his riches and entered his own residence. The crane went to Brahma's assembly, as he should have. And Brahma honoured the great-souled one as a guest.

[270]Virupaksha.

[271]Accounts of creation vary. In some, Surabhi is one of Daksha's daughters. She was married to Kashyapa and gave birth to cattle. Surabhi is also a celestial cow.

[272]The load of gold.

'"Goutama again reached Shabara's abode. Through the shudra woman, he had many sons who were the perpetrators of wicked deeds. The large number of gods then imposed an extremely severe curse on him. O lord! Over a long period of time, having given birth through his remarried wife,[273] the immensely ungrateful one would go to hell. O descendant of the Bharata lineage! Narada told me all this earlier. O bull among men! I remembered and told you the great account. Everything happened exactly as I have recounted it. How can an ungrateful person obtain fame? What is his status? Where is his happiness? An ingrate is never respected. There is no salvation for an ungrateful person. A man must, especially, never injure his friends. A person who injures his friends obtains a terrible and infinite hell. O unblemished one! One must always have sentiments of gratitude and affection towards friends. Truth comes from friends. Strength comes from friends. The discerning person honours his friends well. The learned avoid a person who is wicked, ungrateful, shameless, injurious towards friends, the worst of his lineage, sinful in his deeds and the worst among men. O best among those who uphold dharma! I have thus spoken to you about the wicked person who was ungrateful and injured his friend. What do you again wish to hear?"'

Vaishampayana said, 'O Janamejaya! On hearing these words spoken by the great-souled Bhishma, Yudhishthira was delighted.'

This concludes Apad Dharma Parva.

[273]Because the wife had been married to someone else earlier.

SECTION EIGHTY-SIX

Moksha Dharma Parva

This parva has 6,935 shlokas and 186 chapters.

Chapter 1496(168): 53 shlokas
Chapter 1497(169): 37 shlokas
Chapter 1498(170): 23 shlokas
Chapter 1499(171): 61 shlokas
Chapter 1500(172): 37 shlokas
Chapter 1501(173): 52 shlokas
Chapter 1502(174): 20 shlokas
Chapter 1503(175): 37 shlokas
Chapter 1504(176): 17 shlokas
Chapter 1505(177): 39 shlokas
Chapter 1506(178): 17 shlokas
Chapter 1507(179): 15 shlokas
Chapter 1508(180): 30 shlokas
Chapter 1509(181): 20 shlokas
Chapter 1510(182): 17 shlokas
Chapter 1511(183): 16 shlokas
Chapter 1512(184): 18 shlokas
Chapter 1513(185): 27 shlokas
Chapter 1514(186): 32 shlokas
Chapter 1515(187): 60 shlokas
Chapter 1516(188): 22 shlokas
Chapter 1517(189): 21 shlokas
Chapter 1518(190): 13 shlokas
Chapter 1519(191): 11 shlokas
Chapter 1520(192): 127 shlokas
Chapter 1521(193): 32 shlokas
Chapter 1522(194): 24 shlokas
Chapter 1523(195): 23 shlokas
Chapter 1524(196): 23 shlokas
Chapter 1525(197): 20 shlokas
Chapter 1526(198): 18 shlokas
Chapter 1527(199): 32 shlokas

Moksha means liberation, as opposed to the pursuit of dharma, artha and kama.

Chapter 1496(168)

'Yudhishthira said, "O grandfather! You have spoken about how one can resort to the sacred rajadharma. O king! You should tell me about the best dharma for those who are in the ashramas."

'Bhishma replied, "There are many doors to dharma and the rites are never unsuccessful. Everywhere, dharma, the path to heaven, truthfulness and the fruits of austerities have been indicated. O supreme among the Bharata lineage! Whatever rules one has thought of, and has determined to observe, is understood to be the only one—there being no other. Whenever one meditates, there is no doubt that detachment is generated and this world becomes like a fabric. O Yudhishthira! When the world is full of deception and many taints, an intelligent man must try to accomplish the objective of moksha for his soul."

'Yudhishthira asked, "O grandfather! When riches are destroyed and a wife, a son or a father dies, how can one use one's intelligence to dispel that sorrow? Tell me that."

'Bhishma replied, "When riches are destroyed and a wife, a son or a father dies, one laments in grief. However, one must act so as to dispel that sorrow through meditation. On this, an ancient history is recounted about the words that were spoken by a brahmana to Senajit, when the king was tormented by grief on account of his son and was distracted with misery. On seeing that his face was sorrowful, the brahmana spoke these words. 'You are as stupid as a millstone. Why are you sorrowing? What are you grieving about? There are those who will sorrow over you and those mourners will also advance to the same end. O king! You, I, and all the others who worship you, all of us will go to the spot where we have come from.' Senajit asked, 'O brahmana! O one who is rich in austerities! What intelligence, austerities, meditation, wisdom and learning can be obtained, so that one does not grieve?'

'"The brahmana replied, 'Behold. All the beings are tied down in misery. For me, my atman is not mine. But the entire earth is mine. What is mine also belongs to others. Because of this intelligence, I am not distressed. Having obtained this intelligence, I am neither delighted, nor distressed. Just as a piece of wood approaches another piece of wood in the great ocean, comes together and drifts apart, that is the way beings meet each other. Sons, grandsons, kin and relatives are like that. One should not be attached to them, since separation from them is certain. He[1] came from what cannot be seen. He has gone to what cannot be seen. He did not know you. You did not know him. Who are you? Who are you sorrowing over? Misery is an affliction created by desire. Happiness results when that affliction of sorrow becomes less. Then again, misery is repeatedly generated by joy. Unhappiness comes after happiness. Happiness comes after unhappiness. Unhappiness is not permanently obtained. Nor is happiness permanently obtained. Friends are truly not the reason for happiness. Enemies are truly not the reason for unhappiness. One cannot obtain riches through wisdom. Nor indeed can riches bring about happiness. One cannot obtain riches through intelligence. Nor is stupidity the reason for penury. It is only a wise person, and no one else, who understands the progress of the world. The intelligent, the stupid, the brave, the coward, the foolish, the wise, the weak, the powerful—all of them enjoy happiness because of destiny. The cow simultaneously belongs to the calf, the cowherd, the master and the thief. But it is certain that the cow actually belongs to the person who drinks her milk.[2] Those who are the most foolish in the world and those who have attained supreme intelligence—only these men can enjoy happiness. People who are in between are miserable. The wise find delight in the two extremes, not in the ones that are in the middle.[3] It is said that happiness is associated with the two extremes

[1]The son.

[2]The others have an illusory sense of owning her. One should not sorrow because of an illusory sense of ownership.

[3]This is a reference to the four states of consciousness—wakefulness (*jagrata*), dreaming (*svapna*), deep sleep (*sushupti*) and pure consciousness (turiya). The wise take delight in wakefulness and pure consciousness, not in dreaming or deep sleep. While the earlier sentence has a reference to the most foolish, it is possible that this is meant to represent the statement of wakefulness, while supreme intelligence is equated with pure consciousness.

and unhappiness with the ones that are intermediate. Those who have obtained happiness through their intelligence and those who are free from opposite sentiments,[4] devoid of jealousy—are never distressed by prosperity or adversity. However, there are also foolish people who have not obtained that intelligence. They have not been able to go beyond excessive delight and extreme misery. There are foolish ones who are bereft of consciousness. They are haughty because of their strength and are given to incessant delight, as if they are like the large numbers of gods in heaven. However, because of their laziness, such happiness terminates in unhappiness. And because of skill, unhappiness can give rise to happiness. Riches and prosperity dwell with those who are accomplished, not with those who are lazy. Whether it is happiness or unhappiness, whether it is unpleasant or pleasant—whatever has been obtained must be enjoyed with an unvanquished heart. From one day to another, there are a thousand reasons for misery and a hundred reasons for joy. Stupid people are submerged in these, but not those who are learned. If a man is intelligent, accomplished in his wisdom, given to servitude[5] and lack of envy, and is self-controlled, having conquered his senses—sorrow cannot touch him. The wise person resorts to this intelligence and guards his consciousness. Sorrow cannot touch a person who knows the origin and the end of everything.[6] The reasons behind sorrow, fright, unhappiness and exertion must be severed from the roots, like casting aside one of the limbs in the body. If objects of desire are cast aside, this fills one with happiness. A man who follows desire is destroyed by that desire. The happiness obtained from the pursuit of desire in this world or the great bliss obtained in heaven is not even one-sixteenth of the happiness obtained from the extinction of desire. The deeds committed in an earlier body, good or bad, and the consequences of those deeds are felt by the wise, the foolish and the brave. In this way, the pleasant and the unpleasant, unhappiness and happiness, incessantly circulate among living beings. Knowing

[4]Like happiness and unhappiness, pleasure and pain.
[5]Of elders, seniors and preceptors.
[6]The brahman.

this and resorting to this intelligence, a person with qualities lives in joy. He disregards all desire and turns his back on all attachment. The wise regard this kind of approach of the heart as equivalent to mental death. A tortoise draws in all its limbs. Like that, such a person contracts desire and with a shining atman, is pleased with his atman. Even if there is the slightest sense of ownership left, that will give rise to repentance and pervade everything. He is not frightened of anything. No one is frightened of him. He has no desire and no hate. He is then immersed in the brahman. He gives up truth and falsehood, sorrow and joy, fear and freedom from fear, pleasant and unpleasant. Having abandoned these, he is tranquil in his soul. That resolute person does not do anything wicked towards any being, in deeds, thoughts and words. He is then immersed in the brahman. He abandons the thirst[7] that is so difficult for the evil-minded to give up, a fear that does not diminish with age and is like a disease that brings an end to life. Having done this, he obtains happiness. O king! On this, a verse sung by Pingala has been heard. This is about how she obtained eternal dharma at a time of hardship. A prostitute named Pingala went to the place meant for the rendezvous, but was rejected by her lover. Despite facing that calamity, by resorting to her intelligence, she found peace.

'"'Pingala said, "I have been crazy for a long time. In my madness, I have dwelt with my beloved. Because my beloved was nearby, I did not pursue the path of virtue earlier. This pillar has nine gates and I will cover it.[8] Even when he[9] approaches, which woman in this world regards him as a beloved? I have been thwarted in my desire. But, in the form of desire, those crafty ones[10] are like hell. They will not deceive me again. I know now and have woken up. Depending on destiny and earlier deeds, failure gives rise to success. I have now

[7]Desire.

[8]The body is the pillar and the nine gates are two eyes, two ears, one mouth, two nostrils, one anus and the genitals. It will be covered with knowledge.

[9]Meaning the brahman. The text does not have a gender. But it is difficult to translate this without using the gender.

[10]Human lovers.

conquered my senses and have obtained the realization that I am without form. I am without any hope and am happy. There is great happiness when there is nothing to hope. Having destroyed hope, Pingala sleeps in happiness."""

'Bhishma said, "The learned brahmana mentioned these and other reasons. King Senajit was comforted and found joy and happiness."'

Chapter 1497(169)

'Yudhishthira said, "This time, which brings about the destruction of all beings, moves on. O grandfather! What is the supreme benefit one should try for? Tell me."

'Bhishma replied, "In this connection, an ancient history is recounted. This is a conversation between a father and a son. O Yudhishthira! Listen to it. O Partha! There was a certain brahmana who was devoted to studying. He had an intelligent son named Medhavin.[11] The son was accomplished in the objective of moksha dharma and was also conversant with the true nature of the world. He spoke to his father, who was engaged in the act of studying. 'O father! Since the lifespan of beings passes so quickly and men are destroyed, what should a wise person do? O father! Tell me about proper yoga and about the progressive way one should follow dharma.'

'"The father replied, 'O son! In brahmacharya, one must study the Vedas. Then, one must desire sons, so that the ancestors can be saved. Next, one must accept the sacrificial fire and perform sacrifices, in accordance with the prescribed rites. Finally, one must enter the forest and strive as a hermit.'

'"The son asked, 'The world is surrounded from all sides and is afflicted. A fall is certain. How can you speak with such patience?'

'"The father replied, 'How is the world afflicted? By what is it surrounded? Why is fall certain? Why are you scaring me?'

[11]The word *medhavin* also means learned or intelligent.

'"The son said, 'The world is afflicted by death. It is surrounded by old age. Day and night, there is downfall. How can you not comprehend this? I know that death does not wait for anyone.[12] How can I wait for it, with my feet tied in that net? As one night follows another night, the lifespan is decreased. Being like a fish in shallow water, how can one then be happy? The learned person knows that every day is fruitless. Before all desires are satisfied, a man encounters death. It is as if a ram is inattentive and is roaming around, feeding on young grass, when a she-wolf grabs him and conveys him to death. Do what is best today, lest you are overtaken by death. Death attracts, even if tasks are left incomplete. Tomorrow's task should be done today, the afternoon's in the forenoon. Death does not wait, to see if a task has been done or is yet undone. Who knows that he will not be approached by death today itself? When one is young, one must accept the pursuit of dharma as the only reason for remaining alive.[13] Observing dharma, one obtains deeds in this world and happiness after death. Overcome by confusion, one strives for the sake of sons and wives. In an attempt to sustain them, one performs desirable and undesirable acts. A man thinks in his mind that sons and animals are important and is devoted to this. While he is thus asleep, death grasps him, like an extremely powerful tiger. He has still not been satisfied by obtaining the objects of desire. Nevertheless, like a tiger grabbing an animal, death takes him away and goes. He is still thinking about the tasks that have been done, those which have been done and those which have partly been done. While he is attached to happiness in this death, he comes under the subjugation of death. This happens even before he has obtained the fruits of the deeds that have been completed. He is attached to the field, the shop and the home and attached to the fruits of deeds, but death takes him and goes away. There is death, old age and disease—and many other reasons for misery. All of them dwell in the body. How can you then remain, as if you are healthy? From the moment a being is born, death and

[12]That is, death touches everyone.

[13]Instead of going through the four ashramas, which is what the father had suggested.

old age pursue him, to bring about his end. Everything, mobile and immobile, is afflicted by these two. The learned texts have said that the pleasure[14] from attachment to dwelling in homes in villages and habitations is just like death. However, this can be contained in the forest. The attachment to villages and habitations binds one down with ropes. The performer of good deeds can sever these. But the performer of evil deeds cannot sever these. A person who does not unnecessarily injure beings through thoughts, words and deeds, is not destroyed by those who seek to take away life and wealth. He is not tied down by his action. When the soldiers of death advance, nothing can withstand them, with the exception of truth and the abandonment of falsehood. There is amrita in truth. Therefore, one must follow the vow of truth and be devoted to the yoga of truth. There is delight, peace and tranquility in truth. It is through truth that one triumphs over death. Both immortality and death exist in the body. Through confusion, one obtains death. Through truth, one obtains immortality. That is the reason I am non-violent and pursuing the truth. I have cast aside desire and anger. I am impartial towards happiness and unhappiness. I am tranquil and look on death, as if I am immortal. I will be a hermit who will be devoted to sacrifices for peace, sacrifices for the brahman, sacrifices through words and sacrifices through deeds, thereby making myself awaken. How can one perform such violent sacrifices that involve the slaughter of animals? How can a wise person acts like a flesh-eater, injure himself internally, and observe the sacrifices of kshatriyas? If a person is single-minded in his words, thoughts, austerities, renunciation and yoga and follows these well, he obtains everything. There is no sight that is equal to knowledge. There is no strength that is equal to knowledge. There is no misery that is like that of attachment. There is no joy that is equal to renunciation. My atman has been generated from the atman.[15] Though I have no offspring, I will base

[14]There is a problem with the text of the Critical edition. It says *devaanam* (belonging to the gods), which makes it impossible to understand it. We have taken it as *devanam* and interpreted it as pleasure.

[15]The first atman is the jivatman and the second atman is the paramatman, the brahman.

myself on the atman.[16] My salvation will come from the atman, not from offspring. There are no riches for a brahmana that are equal to solitude and truth. Basing himself on good conduct, not chastising anyone, resorting to uprightness—he performs the supreme rites. Where are your riches? Where are your relatives? Where are your wives? O brahmana! They will all die. Your atman is hidden inside a cave. Where have your grandfather and your father gone?'"[17]

'Bhishma said, "O king! Hearing the words of the son, the father acted accordingly. You should also conduct yourself in that way, observing the dharma of truth."'

Chapter 1498(170)

'Yudhishthira said, "O grandfather! The rich and the poor observe their own rites. How, and from where, do they face happiness and unhappiness?"

'Bhishma replied, "In this connection, an ancient history is recounted. Shamyaka, who was liberated and had obtained peace, sung a song. In ancient times, a brahmana who had renounced told me this. He was afflicted because of a bad wife, whose conduct was bad. He was also suffering from hunger. 'Since the time he is born on earth, many different kinds of joy and sorrow afflict a man. If he is conveyed along either of these paths,[18] he will not be delighted on obtaining joy, or be anxious on obtaining sorrow. On this earth, you are not following what is best for yourself. Even though you have no desire, you are bearing a heavy burden. If you roam around, thinking all this to be insignificant, you will obtain happiness. A person with nothing sleeps, and awakes, in happiness. Not possessing anything is the medication for happiness in the world. This is healthy and

[16]Meaning, the brahman. He will shun the standard prescription of first having offspring before embarking on vanaprastha and sannyasa.

[17]Reiterating the point that they are mortal.

[18]Conveyed by an external force, destiny.

auspicious. This path is extremely difficult, even for those who have no enemies.[19] But it is easily obtained by those who are virtuous. Glancing at the three worlds, I do not find anyone with possessions who is equal to a virtuous person who is without possessions. I weighed the lack of possessions and a kingdom on a balance and found that the lack of possessions surpassed the kingdom in qualities. Specifically, there is a great difference between the lack of possessions and a kingdom. A prosperous person is always anxious, as if he is in the jaws of death. A fire, the sun, death and bandits have no power over a person who has freed himself from riches and is without hopes. Depending on his wishes, he lies down on the bare ground, using his arms as a pillow. He has obtained tranquility and is praised by the residents of heaven. A wealthy person is afflicted by both anger and avarice and loses his senses. He is wicked, casts sideways glances, has a frown on his face and his mouth is dry. He bites his lower lips with his teeth. He is enraged and terrible in speech. Even if he desires to give the earth away, who will wish to look at him? Dwelling in continuous prosperity confuses a person who is not very discerning. It robs him of his senses, like the wind bearing away autumn clouds. He takes delight in, "I am handsome. I am wealthy. I am noble. I am successful. I am not an ordinary man." His consciousness is sprinkled with these three reasons.[20] Thus sprinkled and attached to objects of pleasure, he is deprived of the riches his ancestors accumulated. When these have decayed, he thinks it is virtuous to appropriate the property of others. He transgresses boundaries and seizes from every direction. The kings then restrain the greedy person, like deer with arrows. These are the many different kinds of sorrows that then touch the man's body. Afflicted by these supreme hardships, he realizes that he needs medication. He abandons the dharma of the world,[21] with everything that is temporary and permanent. Without renunciation, one cannot enjoy supreme happiness. Without renunciation, one can

[19]But have desire.

[20]Probably beauty, wealth and nobility, success not being an independent reason.

[21]The pursuit of desire.

neither sleep, nor be happy in every way.'[22] This is what the brahmana told me in earlier times in Hastinapura, about what had been said by Shamyaka. Therefore, it is my view that renunciation is supreme."'

Chapter 1499(171)

'Yudhishthira said, "If a person undertakes sacrifices and does not possess riches,[23] and the thirst for riches overcomes him, what can he possibly do to obtain happiness?"

'Bhishma replied, "O descendant of the Bharata lineage! A person who looks on everything equally, a person who doesn't make an effort,[24] a person who is truthful in speech, a person who disregards worldly objects, a person who pursues knowledge—such a man is indeed happy. The ancient ones have said that these five are the steps towards tranquility. These are heaven. These are dharma. These are happiness. These are supreme virtue. On this, an ancient history is recounted, about what Manki, who had freed himself from worldly possessions, had sung. O Yudhishthira! Listen to it.

'"Manki was repeatedly frustrated in his pursuit of riches. Finally, with some riches that were left, he bought two bulls and a yoke. Once, he bound them to the yoke and took them out, so as to control them.[25] A camel was lying down in the middle and they suddenly rushed towards it. They approached and fell down on the camel's neck. The enraged camel arose. It ran at great speed, dragging the two bulls with it. Dragged along by the camel, the two bulls were tormented. On seeing that they were about to die, Manki spoke these words. 'If it has not been ordained, even an

[22]It is not clear where the quote from Shamyaka ends. It is possible that the quote ended earlier and the rest of it was spoken by the brahmana.

[23]Required for performing the sacrifices and rites.

[24]For possessions and objects of desire.

[25]That is, to train them in being controlled.

accomplished person is incapable of obtaining wealth, despite his making every effort, faithfully and well. Earlier, I have tried many ways of obtaining riches. But behold the calamity that destiny has inflicted me with. My two bulls have been raised up and are being dragged over uneven terrain. They are being raised up and flung down, as if a crow is tearing at palm fruit or rose apples.[26] My beloved calves are dangling from the camel's neck, like jewels. This is certainly because of destiny and I know that manliness does not exist. Even if there exists something by the name of manliness, if one examines this, one will find that this too is based on destiny. Therefore, someone who wishes to advance towards happiness must be indifferent. A person who shuns all hope of obtaining riches sleeps happily. When Shuka freed himself from everything and went to the great forest from his father's residence, he spoke well.[27] "Between a person who satisfies all his desires and a person who only renounces, the one who renounces is superior to the one who obtains all the objects of desire."[28] There is no end to all desires and one can never attain a state where they are extinguished. As long as he is alive, a foolish person's thirst increases. Refrain from desire. Let tranquility pervade me. Having been deceived by what should not be pursued, it should no longer pervade my body. You desire riches.[29] If I am not going to be destroyed and if you wish to take delight in me, then do not engage me in this futile path of greed. You have repeatedly accumulated riches and they have repeatedly been destroyed. O stupid one! O one who is addicted

[26]This shloka is not very clear and the translation is somewhat contrived. There is a nuance that the translation doesn't also capture. The text uses the word *kakataliya*, which means accident, and there is a story around this. A crow (kaka) sat on a palm-tree and a ripe palm fruit (tala) fell down. The fruit fell down because it was ripe and had nothing to do with the crow. But this accidental or coincidental fall is mistakenly ascribed to the crow sitting on the tree.

[27]The famous Shuka is Vedavyasa's son. The insertion of a quote ascribed to Shuka therefore suggests a later interpolation.

[28]The text does not indicate it clearly. But this seems to be the end of the Shuka quote and it is Manki speaking again.

[29]Manki is addressing himself and his soul.

to riches! When will you free yourself from this desire for wealth? Shame on my folly. This has led me to becoming a puppet in your hands. It is in this way that men who are born become the slaves of others. No person born earlier has ever obtained an end to desire. Nor will any person who is born later. Having abandoned all efforts, I now know and am awake. O desire! It is certain that your heart is as firm as a diamond. That is the reason why, though it is afflicted by one hundred calamities, it does not shatter into one hundred fragments. O desire! I will abandon you and everything that is agreeable to you. Severing what you find to be agreeable, I will obtain happiness. O desire! I know your foundation. You certainly result from resolutions. If I do not have any resolutions, you will not have any foundations. Wealth does not yield happiness on earth. If obtained, it leads to a lot of anxiety. If it is destroyed after having been obtained, that seems like death. Nor does one know whether it can be obtained or not. There is nothing that is a greater misery than its going away after it has been obtained. One is not satisfied when it has been obtained. Instead, one looks for paths to enhance it. Riches are like the tasty waters of the Ganga, since one keeps hankering for more. This is also the reason for my lamentation. I now know and will abandon it. It[30] has sought refuge in the natural elements of my body. As it wishes, let it dwell here, or wherever else it finds happiness.[31] I have no affection for any of you[32] who follow desire and avarice. Therefore, I am abandoning all of you. I will seek refuge with truth alone. My atman will behold all the elements in the body and my mind. I will base myself in yoga, intelligence, learning and spirit and uphold the brahman in my mind. I will happily roam the worlds, without any attachment and without any disease, so that you can no longer try to immerse me in misery again.[33] I have been agitated by you and there is no other path left to me. O desire! Thirst, sorrow and exhaustion have

[30]Desire.

[31]Since Manki has renounced desire, desire can do whatever it wants.

[32]Any other sentiments.

[33]Addressing himself.

always been manifestations of your powers. I think that the sorrow which results from the destruction of riches is the greatest of all miseries. Relatives and friends disrespect the person who has been separated from his wealth. Other than disrespect, in the absence of riches, there are one thousand other taints that are more severe. However, even though riches provide a little bit of happiness, it is mingled with a great deal of unhappiness. In everyone's sight, bandits slay the person who possesses riches. They torment him with many kinds of punishment and always terrify him. After a long period of time, I have realized the stupidity and misery that greed leads to. O desire! You make me follow whatever you get addicted to. You do not know the truth. You are foolish. You are difficult to satisfy. You are never satiated. You are like a fire. You do not consider whether something is easy to obtain, or difficult to obtain. You are as difficult to fill as the nether regions. You wish to fling me into misery. O desire! From today, I am incapable of dwelling with you again. I am free from possessions now. As they will, let the objects be destroyed. I have obtained supreme renunciation now. I no longer think about desire. Because of you, I suffered greatly earlier. I now know myself to be intelligent. Because of the destruction of the riches, I have been deceived. But I can lie down now, without any fever in any of my limbs. O desire! I am casting you away and abandoning all my mental inclinations towards you. O desire! You will not associate with me or find pleasure in me again. I will forgive even those who should not be forgiven. I will not injure, even though I am injured against. I will speak pleasantly to those who hate me and ignore their disagreeable words. I will be satisfied and my senses will be at ease. I will always sustain myself on what has been obtained. You are an enemy of my atman and I will not satisfy your wishes. Know that lack of possessions, lack of desire, satisfaction, tranquility, truth, self-control, forgiveness and compassion towards all beings have now sought refuge with me. Therefore, desire, avarice, thirst and miserliness have been cast away. I have based myself on my spirit. I have abandoned desire, avarice, anger and harshness. I will no longer come under the subjugation of greed and subject myself to misery. Whoever casts aside desire is filled with happiness. Someone who is under the subjugation of desire is always confronted with misery. When a man casts aside the passions that result from desire, he abandons the rajas quality. Sorrow and other hardships always result from desire and anger. I have now immersed myself in the brahman, like entering a cool lake during the summer. I have calmed myself. I have withdrawn myself. I only enjoy happiness. The happiness one obtains in the worlds from the satisfaction of desire and the great happiness one enjoys in heaven are less than one-sixteenth of the happiness one obtains from the extinguishing of thirst. I have slain supreme enemies of the atman, desire being the seventh.[34] I have attained Brahma's indestructible city. I will be happy there, like a king.' Resorting to his own intelligence, Manki became free from all possessions. He abandoned all desire and obtained great bliss with Brahma. Because the bulls had been destroyed, Manki obtained immortality. Having severed the foundation of desire, he obtained great happiness.

'"In this connection, an ancient history is recounted. This is a song sung by Janaka, the king of Videha, who obtained tranquility. 'Though I possess nothing, my wealth is infinite. Even if Mithila[35] is set ablaze, nothing that belongs to me will be consumed.' In this connection, about lack of possessions, there is also what Bodhya, who attained the supreme objective, said. O Yudhishthira! Listen to this. The self-controlled rishi Bodhya was asked by King Nahusha. 'You are without possessions. You have obtained tranquility. You are at peace. You are full of wisdom. O immensely wise one! Instruct me about how one can obtain tranquility. What intelligence should one resort to, so that one can withdraw and roam around in peace?' Bodhya replied, 'I follow the instructions of others, but never instruct anyone. I will tell you about the signs. You can then yourself reflect

[34]Usually, six enemies are mentioned and kama (desire) is one of the six. Since desire has been mentioned as the seventh, the other six are probably the five senses and the mind.

[35]Mithila was the capital of Videha. This King Janaka is different from the King Janaka who was Sita's father.

on those. My six preceptors are Pingala, the osprey, the snake, the bee that is searching in the forest, the one who makes arrows and the maiden.'"'[36]

Chapter 1500(172)

'Yudhishthira said, "O one who knows about conduct! What is the conduct through which one can roam around on earth, free from sorrow? What should a man do in this world, so as to attain the supreme objective?"

'Bhishma replied, "In this connection, an ancient history is recounted. This is a conversation between Prahrada and the sage Ajagara. O king! There was a brahmana who was intelligent and revered by the wise. His consciousness was unblemished. While he was roaming around, he was asked by Prahrada. 'You are at ease, capable, mild, self-controlled, without any desire, free from malice, extremely eloquent, extremely revered in the world and wise. You roam around like a child. There is nothing that you seek to obtain. You do not grieve over anything that has not been obtained. O brahmana! It is as if you are always content. There is nothing that you think about. The beings are distracted, as they are borne along on currents of deeds connected with dharma, kama and artha. But to you, these seem to be illusory. You do not follow dharma or

[36]By excising shlokas, the Critical edition leaves this dangling. Pingala was a prostitute who turned to asceticism after being spurned by her lover. If an osprey desires meat and finds it, other ospreys snatch that piece of meat away. However, there was an osprey that did not desire any meat and was happy. The preceptor is that osprey. A snake is happy and worthy of emulation because it does not try to make a house for itself, but lives in someone else's house instead. The bee searching for honey in the forest does not harm anyone. There is a story about a person who made arrows. He was so busy in his work that he didn't even notice that the king was passing. There is a story about a maiden who roamed alone. Since she did not consort with others, there was no scope of a quarrel.

artha, nor are you engaged in kama. You ignore the objectives of the senses. You roam around free, like a witness. O sage! What is your wisdom? What is your learning? What is your conduct? How did you become like this? O sage! O brahmana! If you think that is beneficial for me, please tell me this immediately.' The intelligent one, who knew about dharma and the conduct of the worlds, was asked in this way.

'"Asked by Prahrada, he gently spoke these words, which were full of import. 'O Prahrada! Behold. The origin, decay, increase and destruction of beings have no evident reason. That is the reason I am not delighted, nor distressed. They are seen to be engaged in their own natural conduct. Everyone is engaged in natural conduct and there is nothing to be tormented about. O Prahrada! Behold. Every kind of union is subject to separation. All stores eventually end in destruction. Hence, my mind has never turned to acquisition. In front of us, every being that possesses qualities comes to an end. If one knows about origin and destruction, what tasks remain to be undertaken? In due course, it is seen that every aquatic creature in this great ocean, be its form gigantic or subtle, confronts destruction. O lord of asuras! I see it as evident that death comes to all beings on earth, and all mobile and immobile objects. O supreme among danavas! When the time comes, all the birds which rise up and roam around in the sky come under the power of death. When the time is right, all the stellar bodies that roam around in the firmament, whether they are small or large, are seen to fall down. Thus, all beings are seen to be attracted by death. Knowing that everything has this general nature, I sleep happily, doing nothing, since there is nothing to be done. If, without trying for it, I obtain a great deal of food, I eat it. There are again many days when I lie down, without having had anything to eat. There are many who give me many different kinds of food, with many different qualities. However, sometimes I get little, with few qualities, or nothing at all. There are times when I eat minute grains, and food from which the oil has been squeezed out. There are also times when I eat the best food, rice mixed with meat. There are times when I sleep on beds and times when I sleep on the bare ground. There are also times when I get a bed inside a palace. I am sometimes attired in rags, hemp, linen and hides. There are also times when I am clad in extremely expensive garments. As I wish, I do not reject objects of pleasure that are in conformity with dharma. but I do not strive for things that are difficult to obtain. I follow the pure vow that is known as *ajagara*.[37] I do not waver from this and have no possessions. This is auspicious and bereft of sorrow. This is infinitely sacred and I have immersed myself in this intelligence of the learned. Foolish ones do not follow it and show it disrespect. I follow the pure vow that is known as ajagara. My mind does not deviate from it. I have not been dislodged from my own dharma. I am restrained in everything and know everything about cause and effect. I am devoid of fear, stupidity, greed and confusion. I follow the pure vow that is known as ajagara. This has no rules about consequences, what should be eaten, what should be enjoyed and what should be drunk. Since everything depends on destiny, nothing is determined in accordance with the time and the place. This contributes to the happiness of my heart and those who are mean do not follow this. I follow the pure vow that is known as ajagara. Because of their thirst, people pursue many kinds of riches. When they don't get them, they grieve. I have used my accomplished intelligence to discern the truth. I follow the pure vow that is known as ajagara. To obtain riches, I have seen distressed people seek refuge with both noble and ignoble men. However, I am relieved of this and have found peace in my soul. I follow the pure vow that is known as ajagara. I know the truth—everything is ordained by destiny. I look on happiness and unhappiness, the acquisition of riches and the loss of riches, love and hatred and death and life equally. I follow the pure vow that is known as ajagara. I have overcome fear, attachment, confusion and insolence. I have fortitude, wisdom, intelligence and tranquility. I am content with enjoying the fruit that presents itself before me.[38] I follow the pure vow that is known as ajagara. I have

[37]Ajagara is the boa constrictor, the python. The belief is that the python does not strive for food, but eats whatever comes to it. If food does not come before a python, it starves.

[38]The image of the python.

no restrictions on where I should sleep and what I should eat. I am naturally united with self-control, restraint, vows, truth and purity. I have transcended the need to store any fruits. I follow the pure vow that is known as ajagara. I have always controlled the thirst in my mind. Based on my atman, I look towards everything with my intelligence. I have transcended the sorrows that come from the pursuit of riches and the lack of riches. I follow the pure vow that is known as ajagara. The heart and the mind strive for the agreeable and the pleasant. But these are difficult to obtain and are transient and I have realized both these aspects. Therefore, I have overcome these. There are learned and intelligent men who have spoken about this in many ways. Those wise ones have sought to establish their own views. They have spoken about this and that and have censured the views of others. But this is beyond debate. I have seen that there are many men who are confused and have been led in separate directions. However, I dwell in the infinite that is beyond all these taints. Having controlled anger and thirst, I roam around among men.' If there is a great-souled man who follows the vow of ajagara in this world, having controlled attachment and having overcome fear, anger, avarice and confusion, he will certainly he happy. He will find delight in this pleasure."'

Chapter 1501(173)

'Yudhishthira asked, "O grandfather! Relatives, deeds, riches and wisdom—which of these actually establishes a man? I am asking you. Tell me."

'Bhishma replied, "Wisdom is the foundation for beings. It is held that wisdom is the greatest of gains. Wisdom is the most beneficial in the world. The virtuous are of the view that wisdom leads to the attainment of heaven. When their riches were destroyed, it is through wisdom that Bali, Prahrada, Namuchi and Manki attained their objectives. What can be greater than that? On this, an ancient history is recounted about a conversation between Indra and Kashyapa. O Yudhishthira! Listen to this.

'"O son! There was a rishi named Kashyapa who was rigid in his vows. There was a prosperous vaishya. Because of his insolence, he brought the ascetic down through his chariot. He fell down and was distressed and was about to give up his life. He angrily said, 'I will die. There is no point to a person without riches remaining alive.' He was seated thus, about to die, and lamented, bereft of his senses. His thoughts were enraged. At that time, Indra appeared before him in the form of a jackal and said, 'All the beings always desire to be born as humans. Among all humans, the status of a brahmana is always praised. O Kashyapa! You are a human and a learned brahmana. This is extremely difficult to obtain. You should not commit this sin.[39] The learned texts have truthfully said that all acquisitions give rise to insolence. You are the form of contentment. But what you are thinking of is full of greed. The virtuous ones who possess hands accomplish their objectives. We desire hands, just as you desire riches. There is no gain that is superior to the obtaining of hands. O brahmana! Without hands, I cannot take out the thorn that is paining my body. For those who possess hands, the gods have given them ten fingers. They can use these to uproot the insects that are biting their limbs. They can act so as to save themselves from the cold, the rains and the heat.[40] They can cheerfully obtain food and enjoy these in beds that are safe from the wind. In this world, they enjoy cattle and employ them to carry burdens. They employ many other means to bring them under their subjugation. Those without hands and those who cannot grind with their tongues[41] do not live for a long time. They have to tolerate many hardships. O sage! It is good fortune that you are not like them. It is good fortune that you are not a jackal, a worm, a rat, a snake, a frog, or some other being born in an inferior species. O Kashyapa! You should be content with this gain. Then again, among all living beings, you are a supreme brahmana. These

[39]Of giving up your life.

[40]By constructing shelters.

[41]Lacking in teeth.

worms are biting me. Look at my state. Because I lack hands, I am incapable of saving myself from them. Despite being unsuccessful in this, I do not wish to give up my life. If I performed this wicked deed, I would descend into an even more inferior species.[42] I am in the state of a jackal and this is about medium among those of wicked species. There are many others who belong to even more wicked species and are greater in evil. Through birth, some are happy and virtuous and others are extremely miserable. However, I do not see anyone who is entirely happy. Having gained prosperity, humans next want a kingdom. Having obtained kingdoms, they wish to become gods. Having become gods, they desire to become Indra. Even if you obtain riches, you will never become a king or a god.[43] Even if you become a god, you will not be satisfied without becoming Indra. You will not be content after obtaining what you desire. The thirst will not be slaked. This is like a fire that is again ignited through the offering of kindling. There is sorrow in you. But there is also delight in you. Since there is both sorrow and joy, why should you grieve? Like birds imprisoned in a cage, restrain the foundations of your senses and confine all your desires and your deeds. If a person does not experience something, there can be no desire on account of that, since it[44] is generated from touch, sight and hearing. You do not remember varuni or the bird known as *latvaka*.[45] There is no food or drink that is superior to these two. O Kashyapa! There are many other distant objects of food and drink. Since you have not experienced these earlier, you do not remember them. Not to eat, not to touch, not to see—I think that this is certainly the supreme rule for a man. There is no doubt that those with hands obtain riches and are powerful. Men use these to reduce other men to a state of servitude. They repeatedly use these to torment, slay, bind

[42]After rebirth.

[43]Since a brahmana cannot become a king and the status of a brahmana is superior to that of a god.

[44]Desire.

[45]The liquor and the flesh of the bird respectively. The brahmana has not tasted these.

and afflict others. They take pleasure in deceit, sport and are happy. Accomplished in their learning, those spirited ones control others through the strength of their arms. They adopt reprehensible and extremely miserable conduct and follow wicked means of subsistence. They become interested in influencing the conduct followed by others. They are bound by their own deeds and this is the working of destiny. Even *pulkasa*s and chandalas do not wish to give up their own lives.[46] Behold the maya and consider others, since you are dissatisfied with your own birth. Look towards the men who have withered arms. There are those who are not healthy. O Kashyapa! Looking towards the others, since you are complete in your limbs, you should think that you have gained. O brahmana! You are well and without fear in this body. You possess all your limbs and are not shamed amongst people. O brahmana rishi! Even if you were to be censured because of a true reason and even if you deviated from dharma, you should not give up your own life. O brahmana! If you listen to my words and act accordingly, you will obtain the best of fruits, as stated in the dharma laid down in the Vedas. Study and, without any distractions, maintain the sacrificial fire. Follow truth, self-control and generosity. Never seek to rival another. Those who study, sacrifice and perform sacrifices for others, how can there be any sorrow in them? They are ornaments among officiating priests. They roam around as they please and obtain great happiness. They are born under auspicious nakshatras, on auspicious lunar days and at extremely energetic muhurtas. But there are also those who are born under extremely inauspicious nakshatras, bad lunar days and extremely weak muhurtas. They descend into the wombs of asuras and their birth deprives them of sacrifices. I used to be learned.[47] I sought reasons and criticized the Vedas. My inclinations were argumentative and I was addicted to pointless debating. I was an exponent of arguments and reasons and spoke about subtle differences. I spoke disparagingly

[46]These terms are often used as synonyms. Pedantically, a chandala is the son of a brahmana mother and a shudra father. A pulkasa (equivalently *pukkasa*) is the son of a nishada father and a shudra mother.

[47]In an earlier life.

about the sacrifices of brahmanas and brahmanas. I was a non-believer and was suspicious of everything. I was foolish and insolent about my learning. O brahmana! Because of that, I have reaped the fruits of being born as a jackal. I have been born as a jackal and after hundreds of days and nights, may again be born as a human. I will then be satisfied and without being distracted, will perform sacrifices and give donations. I will then know what should be known. I will then cast away what should be cast away.' He spoke in this way and the sage Kashyapa arose and said, 'O son! You are accomplished in your intelligence and I marvel at this.' Because of his knowledge, the brahmana was far-sighted. He looked and realized that it was actually Indra of the gods, the god who was Shachi's consort. At this, Kashyapa worshipped the one with the tawny horses.[48] He took his permission and went to his own hermitage."'

Chapter 1502(174)

'Yudhishthira said, "O grandfather! Tell me about donations, sacrifices, tormenting oneself through austerities and the serving of seniors."

'Bhishma replied, "If one's soul turns towards what is not beneficial, if the mind is immersed in sin, then one performs wicked deeds and has to suffer from great hardships. Those perpetrators of wicked deeds are born poor. They starve in the midst of famine. They face difficulties amidst hardships. They are terrified in the midst of fear. They become dead in the midst of death. The performers of auspicious deeds are wealthy. They are festive amidst festivities. They obtain heaven in celestial regions. They obtain bliss in the midst of happiness. They are devoted and self-controlled. Non-believers are bound by their hands and dispatched to desolate spots frequented by predatory beasts and elephants, full of fear from snakes and thieves.

[48]Indra.

What else should one say about them? However, there are those who speak agreeably towards gods and guests. They are affectionate towards virtuous people. The tranquility of their souls takes them along paths that are travelled by those who are correct.[49] Those who do not find reasons in dharma are like shrivelled grain among grains, termites[50] among birds and the worst among men. Ordained destiny follows and swiftly pursues a person, sleeping when he sleeps and accompanying him in everything that he does. It stands when he stands. It walks when he walks. It acts whenever he acts and follows him like a shadow. Whatever acts a man may have done earlier, it has been apportioned that he must enjoy the consequences. Destiny protects the fruits of his own deeds and flings him into these. From every direction, time naturally attracts all beings. At the right time, without being goaded, flowers and fruits blossom on their own. Like that, the consequences of earlier deeds cannot be withdrawn. Repeatedly, destiny determines honour and disrespect, gain and loss, decay and growth, until those have been exhausted. One has oneself determined one's unhappiness. One has oneself determined one's happiness. From the moment one lies down in the womb, one enjoys the outcome of earlier bodies. Whether it is in childhood, youth or old age, whatever auspicious and inauspicious deeds are performed by a person, in exactly that way, he will enjoy this, from one birth to another. A calf seeks out its mother, even in the midst of one thousand cows. In that way, deeds performed earlier follow the doer. A piece of cloth is drenched in water.[51] Like that, subsequent purification through fasting, austerities and repentance can lead to a long period of infinite happiness. One can dwell in a hermitage and perform austerities for a long time. One can wash away sins through dharma and be successful in attaining one's wishes. Like birds in the sky and like fish in the water, the footsteps of a person who is wise in his learning cannot be discerned. There is no need to talk about any

[49]We have translated this as correct. Literally, the text translates as those who are situated on the right (as opposed to the left) side.

[50]Alternatively, white ants or bees.

[51]A dirty piece of cloth is cleaned by washing.

other acts of transgression. One must delicately perform the tasks that will ensure one's own welfare."'

Chapter 1503(175)

'Yudhishthira asked, "From where was this universe created? When there is destruction, where does the world, with all its mobile and immobile objects, go? O grandfather! Tell me this. Who is the one who constructed this world, with its oceans, sky, mountains, clouds, earth, fire and wind? How were the beings created and how were they divided into varnas? What about their purity and impurity? Where did dharma and adharma originate? How do living beings live? Where do they go when they die? Tell me everything about this world and that other world."

'Bhishma replied, "In this connection, an ancient history is recounted, about the great words Bhrigu spoke, when he was asked by Bharadvaja. Bharadvaja saw maharshi Bhrigu seated on the peak of Kailasa, blazing in his energy. He asked, 'Who created this world, with its oceans, sky, mountains, clouds, earth, fire and wind? How were beings created and how were they divided into varnas? What about their purity and impurity? Where did dharma and adharma originate? How do living beings live? Where do they go when they die? You should tell me everything about this world and the world hereafter.' Bharadvaja asked the illustrious maharshi, who was like Brahma himself, about his doubts.

'"He told him everything. 'The maharshis have earlier heard about the famous one named Manasa.[52] He is without beginning and without end. That god cannot be penetrated. He is without old age and without death. He is known as Avyakta.[53] He is eternal. He is

[52]Something connected with the mind or thought. In this context, created from the mind.

[53]The one who is not manifest.

without decay. He is immutable. He is the one who created all the beings that are born and die. He first created a great god named Mahanta.[54] That lord and upholder of all beings created Akasha.[55] Water was created from space. The fire and the wind were created from water. The earth was created from the combination of the fire and the wind. Svayambhu[56] then created a celestial lotus that was full of energy. From that lotus arose Brahma, the store of the essence of the Vedas. He is famous as Ahamkara.[57] All the beings were born from him and he is the creator of all beings. These five elements are the greatly energetic Brahma. The mountains were generated from his bones. The earth is his flesh and fat. The oceans are his blood. The sky is his stomach. The wind is his breath. The fire is his energy. The rivers are his veins. Agni and Soma, the sun and the moon, are known as his eyes. The firmament that is above is his head. His feet are the ground. The directions are his arms. There is no doubt that he is infinite and is impossible to comprehend, even by those who are successful. The illustrious one is known as the infinite Vishnu. He is inside all living beings. However, those whose souls are not cleansed cannot comprehend him. He is the one who created ego. He is the one who thought of all beings. The entire universe was generated from him. He is the one you asked me about.' Bharadvaja asked, 'What are the dimensions of the sky, the directions, the earth and the wind? Tell me the truth about these and resolve my doubts.' Bhrigu replied, 'The sky is infinite and is frequented by siddhas and *charana*s. It is beautiful and has many habitations. It is impossible to decipher its ends. As one ascends, there are regions the moon and the sun cannot see. The stellar bodies[58] are radiant in their own resplendence there, as radiant as the fire. O one who

[54]The great one.

[55]Space.

[56]Meaning Manasa.

[57]*Ahamkara* is usually ego and pride. In this context, a better explanation is that Brahma said, 'Aham'. 'I am he.'

[58]The text uses the word devas. Here, this doesn't mean gods, but means shining or stellar bodies.

is famous for his energy! Where these end, the sky cannot be seen. O one who shows honours! Know that those regions are difficult to reach and infinite. High above and higher still, there are bodies that blaze in their own radiance. Those are the limits of the sky. But they cannot be measured, not even by the gods. The oceans are at the extremities of the earth. It is said that there is darkness where the oceans end. It is said that when darkness ends, there is water. Where water ends, there is fire. There is water at the end of the nether regions.[59] And where this water ends, there is the lord of the serpents. Where this ends, there is the sky again. At the end of this sky, there is water again. In this way, the boundaries of the illustrious one end in water. The fire and the wind are difficult to fathom, even by the gods. The nature of fire, wind, water and the surface of the ground are like that of space. Because one lacks the sight, the differences cannot be understood. The sages read many kinds of sacred texts that have determined the measures of the three worlds and the oceans. But these cannot be seen and one cannot go there. Who can speak about their measure? The siddhas and gods are restricted in where they can go. But even those minor regions seem to be infinite, not to speak of the regions that are actually known as infinite. Its form is like its name, infinite. It is the great-souled Manasa. His divine form sometimes waxes and sometimes wanes. Which other person is capable of knowing him, unless that other person is his equal? The omniscient lord Brahma was created and manifested himself earlier from the lotus. He is the essence of dharma. He is the supreme Prajapati.' Bharadvaja said, 'If he was created from the lotus, the lotus should be regarded as the elder. Why should Brahma be regarded as the first? Remove this doubt of mine.' Bhrigu replied, 'It is the earth that is known as the lotus. Manasa manifested himself in the form of Brahma and needed a seat. Mount Meru extended up to the sky and became the stalk of that lotus. Situated inside it, the lord created the universe and all the worlds.'"'

[59]Strictly speaking, rasatala. There are seven nether regions—*atala*, *vitala*, *sutala*, rasatala, *talatala*, *mahatala* and *patala*.

Chapter 1504(176)

'"Bharadvaja said, 'O supreme among brahmanas! Situated in the midst of Meru, how did the lord Brahma create the different categories of beings? Tell me this.'

'"Bhrigu replied, 'Manasa created many different categories of subjects through the powers of his mind. To protect the subjects, he first created water, since it is the life of all beings and it is through it that all the subjects grow. If it did not exist, everything would be destroyed. Everything is pervaded by it. The earth, the mountains, the clouds and everything else that has form is known to be water. They are its solidified form.'

'"Bharadvaja asked, 'How was water created? What about fire and the wind? How was the earth created? I have great doubts about this.'

'"Bhrigu replied, 'O brahmana! In ancient times, in the period that is known as Brahma's era, the great-souled brahmana rishis assembled and had a doubt about how the worlds were created. They remained silent and immobile, resorting to meditation. Those brahmanas gave up food and subsisted on air for one hundred celestial years. After that, they all heard words that were full of dharma. This celestial and divine voice was heard in the firmament. "Earlier, there was only silent space. It was motionless and immobile. Without the moon, sun and wind, it seemed to be asleep. Then water was created, like darkness emerging from darkness. When that water stirred, the wind was created. An empty vessel without a hole is seen to be silent. But when it has been filled with water, the wind creates a noise inside it. Like that, the infinite space was filled with water. After that, the wind penetrated the water and created a loud noise. Generated from the stirring of the water, the wind whirled around in this way. It reached up into the sky, but was still not pacified. As a result of the friction between the wind and the water, the immensely powerful fire arose, blazing in energy. It rose upwards and removed the darkness that covered the firmament. The wind fanned the fire and brought the sky and the water together. As a result of uniting with the wind, fire became dense. As it descended from the sky, the friction caused its liquid part to solidify and created the earth. The juices, different kinds of fragrances, liquids, beings—the earth is known to be the womb that gave rise to all these things."'"'

Chapter 1505(177)

'"Bharadvaja asked, 'There are five elements[60] that Brahma created first. They pervade this world and are known as the great elements. The immensely intelligent one created thousands of beings. Therefore, why are these five known as the elements?'

'"Bhrigu replied, 'Only those infinite beings that were created with a loud noise are addressed by the appellation "great element". The wind is exertion. The sound is the sky and space. The fire is solidified water. The earth resulted from their friction. The body consists of the five elements. Everything, mobile and immobile, is made out of these five elements and the five senses—hearing, smell, taste, touch and sight, result from them.'[61]

'"Bharadvaja asked, 'If all mobile and immobile objects are constituted from these five elements, why are these five elements not seen in the bodies of immobile objects? Trees do not have any heat. They do not move. Their essence is dense. The five elements are not seen in their bodies. They do not hear. They do not see. They do not know smell and taste. They do not know touch either. How can they be made out of the five elements? They do not have any liquid in them, or fire, or earth, or wind, or space. In any measure of the trees, the elements don't exist.'

[60]Fire, air, earth, water and space (sky), known as *mahabhuta*s, the great elements.

[61]Hearing is equated with space, smell with earth, taste with water, touch with air and sight with fire.

'"Bhrigu replied, 'Though trees are dense, there is no doubt that space exists in them. Manifestations of flowers and fruits are always noticed in them. It is because of the heat in them that leaves, bark, fruits and flowers are seen to decay. They decay and dry and this shows that they possess touch. Crushed by the wind and thunder, fruits and flowers wither away. That sound is received by the ears. Therefore, trees can hear. A creeper winds around a tree and envelopes it from every side. Someone without sight cannot advance along a path. Therefore, trees can see. When trees are healthy, there are flowers and many kinds of auspicious and inauspicious scents and fragrances. Therefore, trees can smell. They drink water with their roots. It is seen that they suffer from disease. Those diseases can also be cured. Therefore, trees possess taste. One can raise water and drink it up through the bent stalk of a lotus. Like that, aided by the wind, trees drink water through their roots. They experience happiness and unhappiness. When severed, they grow again. I see trees as living. They are not without consciousness. The water that has been ingested is digested with the fire and the wind. Depending on the amount of food it has taken, the tree grows and is cool. The five elements exist in the bodies of all mobile objects, though the extent differs from one to the other. It is because of these that the bodies move. The skin, the flesh, the bones, the marrow and veins as the fifth—these things that exist in the body are enumerated as made out of earth. Energy, anger, the eyes, the internal fire and the fire of digestion—these five things in the body are made out of fire. The ears, the nose, the mouth, the heart and the stomach—these five elements in the bodies of living beings are made out of space. Phlegm, bile, sweat, fat and blood —these are the five kinds of water that are always in the bodies of living beings. Prana makes a living being move, vyana provides the impulse to act.[62] Apana advances towards the tongue. Samana resides in the heart. Udana is the state of not breathing and when it penetrates, one can speak. These are

[62]In pranayama, the breath of life is prana and this has five actions—prana (exhalation), apana (downward inhalation), vyana (diffusion through the body), udana (upward inhalation) and samana (digestive breath).

the five kinds of wind that enable bodies to move. The quality of the earth enables smell. Taste is the water in the body. The eyes see because of the fire. One experiences touch because of the wind. Of these, I will recount the qualities of scent in detail. *Ishta*, *anishta*, *madhura*, *katu*, *nirhari*, *samhata*, *snigdha*, *ruksha*, *vishada*—these are the nine types of scent that are known to be extensions of the earth.[63] Sound, touch, sight and taste are said to be the qualities of water. I will tell you about the knowledge of taste. Listen to me attentively. The gods, famous for their souls, have spoken about many kinds of taste. They are sweet, salty, bitter, astringent, sour and pungent. These six kinds of taste are said to be extensions of the water. Sound, touch and form are said to be the three qualities of fire. It is said that the fire sees and makes one see many different kinds of form. Short, tall, thick, quadrangular, triangular, circular, white, black, dark red, blue, yellow, light red—these twelve kinds of form are said to represent the extensive qualities of the fire. Sound and touch are known as the two qualities of the wind. Touch represents the quality of the wind. There are said to be many different kinds of touch—hard, smooth, soft, slippery, mild, terrible, warm, cold, pleasant, disagreeable, delicate and clear. These twelve are said to be the extensive qualities of the wind. It is said that space has only one quality, that of sound. I will now tell you in detail about the many different kinds of sound. Know them to be *shadaja*, *rishabha*, *gandhara*, *madhyama*, *panchama*, *dhaivata* and *nishadaka*.[64] These are said to be the seven types of qualities and signs of space. Though it may exist in drums and other musical instruments, sound is everywhere. It is said that sound is characteristic of space and mingles with the qualities of the air, because it cannot be heard when different kinds of touch are not used. The elements are always mixed with other elements. Water, fire and air are always awake in the bodies of living beings.'"'

[63]With the exception of nirhari, respectively, agreeable, disagreeable, sweet, bitter, composite, gentle, rough and clear. The meaning of nirhari is unclear and probably means a scent that can be smelt from a long distance.

[64]*Sa-re-ga-ma-pa-dha-ni.*

Chapter 1506(178)

'"Bharadvaja asked, 'How do qualities of the earth resort to the body and create fire? How does the wind find a place for itself and flow?'

'"Bhrigu replied, 'O unblemished one! O brahmana! I will recount to you the flow of the air. In the bodies of all living beings, the powerful wind leads to endeavour. There is fire in the head and this protects the body. Prana is the fire in the head and this causes exertion. This is the living being. This is in all living beings. This is the eternal being. This is the mind, intelligence and ego of all living beings. It is also the object of the senses. Everything is sustained in every way by prana. Because of samana at the rear, each of them[65] follows its own course of action. There is a fire at the root of the genital organs and the anus. This is apana. It circulates and bears along urine and excrement. In each of these three,[66] there is a single force that makes all the efforts at action. Learned people refer to it as udana. There is a fire that resides in all the joints of human bodies. This is said to be vyana. The qualities of the fire are circulated by samana. This part of the element circulates in the liquids and the diseases. There is a fire that resides in its own spot between apana and prana. It works with prana and apana and enables the digestion of food. There is a channel that is from the mouth to the anus and ends at the anus. All the other channels in living bodies emerge from this main channel. The different kinds of breaths of life flow and mingle together. The fire that leads to the digestion of food in bodies is *ushma*. Prana bears the force of the fire down to the anus and then sends that fire upwards again. What has been digested resides below the intestine. What has not been digested resides above the navel. All the life in the body is sustained in the midst of the navel. All of them flow out from the heart, diagonally, upwards and downwards. Goaded by prana, these ten[67] convey the juices along the veins. This is

[65]Each of the senses.

[66]Prana, samana and apana.

[67]Probably meaning the five kinds of breaths of life and the five elements.

the path[68] followed by yogis who go towards the supreme objective. They conquer fatigue. They are patient. They drive the atman up to the head. These are the different kinds of prana and apana in the bodies of living beings. That fire always burns inside, just as if it had been placed on a plate.'""

Chapter 1507(179)

'"Bharadvaja said, 'If it is the wind that sustains life, if it is the wind that makes us move, if it makes us breathe and speak, then remaining alive is futile.[69] If heat is the quality of fire and the fire cooks food, if the fire ensures digestion, then remaining alive is futile. When an animal dies, the breath of life is not noticed. The wind departs and the heat is destroyed. If life is equivalent to the wind, if it depended only on the wind, then, it should have been seen to leave into the circle of air and mingle with the wind. If life depended on the wind, then, when it is destroyed, it should have mingled outside, like waters released into the great ocean. If water is flung into a well, or if a lamp is hurled into the fire, then, both of them are instantly destroyed,[70] as soon as they are flung away. How can a living body be constituted out of the five general elements? If one of them does not exist, the aggregate of the other four does not exist either. Water is destroyed if there is no food. The wind is destroyed if breathing is restrained. If one doesn't pass excrement, space doesn't exist. If one doesn't take food, fire is destroyed. Disease, wounds and other hardships make the earth decay. When these five elements are separated,[71] where does life go? What does life know?

[68]The main channel.

[69]Bharadvaja's questions in this chapter are sometimes difficult to translate. But they lead up to the point that life is more than the five elements.

[70]They lose their independent existence.

[71]The text uses the word *panchatva*. This simply means death, that is, when the body is separated into the five elements.

What does it hear? What does it speak? It is said that a cow will save me in the next world.[72] But after having been given away, that animal dies? Whom will that cow save? The receiver of the cow and the giver are both equal; in this world, they both meet with destruction. Where will they meet again? If a person has been eaten up by birds, if he has fallen down from the summit of a mountain, if he has been consumed by the fire, how will he take life again? If the root of a tree has been severed, it does not grow again. Other seeds can sprout. How can someone who is dead revive? In earlier times, only seeds were created and everything circulated from those. Those who die, are destroyed by death. Seeds can only circulate from seeds.'"'

Chapter 1508(180)

'"Bhrigu replied, 'The living being, what has been given and what has been done, are not destroyed. The being goes into another body. It is the body alone that is destroyed. Though the being has resorted to the body, when it is destroyed, the being is not destroyed. It is like the fire not being destroyed when the kindling has been consumed.'

'"Bharadvaja said, 'If it is like the fire and faces no destruction, then it is also the case that when there is no kindling, the fire cannot be seen. When there is no kindling, I know that the fire has been pacified and destroyed. If there is no movement and no existence can be discerned, that is proof enough.'

'"Bhrigu replied, 'When there is no kindling, it is true that the fire can no longer be seen. It goes up into space, because there is no longer any refuge it can adhere to. In that way, after the body has been discarded, the being is located in space. There is no doubt that, like the fire, it cannot be discerned because it is subtle. It is fire that sustains prana and that holds up the living being. The fire holds

[72]The donation of cattle.

up the breath of life and is destroyed when breathing is restrained. Therefore, when the fire in the body is extinguished, the body loses its consciousness. It falls down on the ground and the earth is the destination. This is true of all mobile and immobile objects. The wind goes up into space and the fire follows them. Those three are united and two of them[73] exist on the ground. The wind exists where there is space. The fire exists where there is wind. They are known to have no form. Water and the earth have form.'

'"Bharadvaja said, 'O unblemished one! If fire, wind, earth, space and water exist in all bodies, then what are the signs of a living being? Tell me that. I wish to know about life in the bodies of living beings, since those five come together,[74] one is engaged in the five acts[75] and one is united with the five kinds of discernment.[76] The body is a mixture of flesh and blood, a store of fat, sinews and bones. When that is destroyed, the living being can no longer be discerned. The body of a living being consists of the five elements. When that is not there, who experiences pain and physical and mental sorrow? How can a living being hear, if there are no ears to hear with, or if his mind is elsewhere? O maharshi! Therefore, life is futile. Sight can see everything when the mind is united with the eyes. If the mind is anxious, though the eyes see, they do not really see. Then again, when one is asleep, one does not see, or speak, or hear, or smell. Nor does one experience touch and taste. Who feels joy? Who is angered? Who grieves? Who suffers? Who is the one who desires, meditates, hates and speaks?'

'"Bhrigu replied, 'Just as the five general elements become one in the body, it is like that in the inner atman too. That is the one who knows scent, taste, sound, touch, form and the other qualities. These five come together and become one and are everywhere in the body. The inner atman follows and witnesses these five qualities. It knows unhappiness and happiness. When it is separated from

[73]The water and the earth.

[74]The five elements.

[75]The five organs of action.

[76]The five senses.

the body, it no longer experiences these. When there is no form, no touch and no heat in the fire, the fire in the body is pacified. But though it gives up the body, it is not destroyed. Everything is made out of water. Water manifests itself in bodies. Brahma, the creator of all beings and the worlds, is in the mind and in the atman. Know the atman, which intends the welfare of all the worlds. It is the one which seeks refuge in the body, like a drop of water in a lotus. Always know the kshetrajna,[77] who intends the welfare of all the worlds. Know that tamas, rajas and sattva are the qualities of living beings. Consciousness is said to be the quality of a living being. It[78] strives and makes everything else strive. Those who know about kshetras say that the supreme one has created the seven worlds.[79] When the body is destroyed, the living being is not destroyed. Those who are foolish falsely state that it dies. The living being goes to another body. Death is only the destruction of the body.[80] This is the way it is with all living beings, moving in subtle and unnoticed ways. Using their attentive intelligence, those who know about the subtle truth can see this. Having eaten and having purified his soul, through mediation, every night, before and after sleep, a wise person can see his atman within himself. With a cheerful consciousness, abandoning all auspicious and inauspicious acts, basing oneself on one's joyous atman, one can obtain infinite happiness. Inside the body, there is a fire in the mind and this is known as the living being. Prajapati created this. This is the determination of those who have examined living beings and the atman.'"'

[77]The atman is the kshetrajna, the one who knows the field. The field (kshetra) is the body.

[78]The atman.

[79]The supreme one is the brahman or the paramatman. There are actually fourteen worlds (*lokas*), seven above and seven below. This is a reference to the seven above—*bhurloka, kharloka, svarloka, maharloka, janarloka, taparloka* and *satyaloka (brahmaloka)*.

[80]The text states death in an interesting way, not even using panchatva, but saying *dashardhatva* (half of ten) instead.

Chapter 1509(181)

'"Bhrigu said, 'Brahma Prajapati first created some brahmanas.[81] They were created from his energy and were like the sun and the fire in their resplendence. The lord Brahma then created eternal truth, dharma, austerities, good conduct and purity, so that one could go to heaven. O supreme among brahmanas! Without any sense of ownership, he then created the gods, the danavas, the gandharvas, the daityas, the asuras, the giant serpents, the yakshas, the rakshasas, the serpents, the pishachas, men who were brahmanas, kshatriyas, vaishyas and shudras and masses and masses of other beings. The complexion of brahmanas was white, while that of kshatriyas was red. The complexion of vaishyas was yellow, while that of shudras was black.'[82]

'"Bharadvaja said, 'If the distinction between the four varnas is only on the basis of complexion and that is how the varnas are to be differentiated, then it is evident and can be seen that among the varnas, there has been a mixture of varnas. Desire, anger, fear, avarice, sorrow, anxiety, hunger and exhaustion influence everyone. How can varnas be differentiated on the basis of this? Sweat, urine, excrement, phlegm, bile and blood flow in the bodies of everyone. How can varnas be differentiated on the basis of this? There are an infinite number of mobile objects and so are the categories of the immobile. They have many different complexions. How can one determine their varna?'

'"Bhrigu replied, 'There is no special difference between the varnas. Everything in this universe first consisted of brahmanas. Brahma created all of them earlier and they attained varnas because of their deeds. There were brahmanas who loved desire and objects

[81]These were the original rishis.

[82]It is possible that this is meant to be taken figuratively and not literally. Brahmanas possessed the sattva quality, kshatriyas possessed the rajas quality, vaishyas possessed a combination of sattva and rajas and shudras possessed the tamas quality.

of pleasure. They were fierce and angry and loved courage. They abandoned their own dharma and having turned red in their limbs, became kshatriyas. There were brahmanas who earned a living from animal husbandry and subsisted on agriculture. They did not follow their own dharma, turned yellow and became vaishyas. There were brahmanas who loved violence and falsehood. They were avaricious and turned to all kinds of deeds to earn a living. They were dislodged from purity, turned black and became shudras. In this way, depending on their deeds, brahmanas became other varnas. Dharma, sacrifices and rites are never forbidden to them.[83] In this way, following the instructions of Brahma, all the four varnas were created as brahmanas originally. But in their ignorance, some of them became prone to avarice. Brahmanas who are devoted to sacred texts on dharma and austerities are never destroyed. They always uphold the brahman and observe vows and rituals. There are some who do not know about what Brahma created in ancient times. Among them, there are many kinds of other species—pishachas, rakshasas, ghost and diverse kinds of mlecchas. Their jnana and vijnana has been destroyed. They try to act as they wish. There were subjects who were created as brahmanas and determined to observe their own dharma. Through their own austerities, these rishis then created others. However, their original creation was from that first god and had the eternal Brahma as the foundation. That creation is known as mental and they were devoted to the strands of dharma.'"'[84]

Chapter 1510(182)

'"Bharadvaja asked, 'O supreme among brahmanas! How does one become a brahmana? What about a kshatriya?

[83]All the four varnas have a right to these.

[84]The apparent inconsistency is presumably resolved in the following way. Brahma originally created the first rishis through his mental powers. The others were directly born from them and were indirectly created by Brahma.

O brahmana rishi! O supreme among eloquent ones! Tell me about vaishyas and shudras.'

'"Bhrigu replied, 'A brahmana is said to be someone who has been cleansed and purified by jatakarma and other samskaras,[85] is devoted to studying the Vedas, is engaged in the six tasks,[86] is always devoted to the vows and is devoted to the truth. Truthfulness, donations, self-control, non-violence, lack of injury, forgiveness, withdrawal from improper acts, austerities—where these are seen, that person is said to be a brahmana. A person devoted to the tasks of kshatriyas,[87] devoted to studying the Vedas, one who donates and seizes[88]—such a person is said to be a kshatriya. A person engaged in animal husbandry, agriculture and trade, always immersed in purity and devoted to the study of the Vedas—such a person has the signs of a vaishya. If a person is always addicted to devouring every kind of food, performs all tasks and is impure, if he abandons the conduct prescribed in the Vedas—such a person is said to be a shudra. If the signs are not seen in a shudra, then that shudra is not a shudra. If they are not seen in a brahmana, then that brahmana is not a brahmana. One must use every means to control avarice and anger. Know that these are impure and that the atman must be controlled. For welfare, one must always restrain anger, lack of austerities and jealousy. Knowledge and honour must be protected from disrespect. The atman must not be distracted. A person who undertakes everything without any hope and without any bonds, a person who renounces everything as an oblation, such an intelligent person is known as a true renouncer.

[85]There are thirteen samskaras or sacraments. The list varies a bit. But one list is vivaha (marriage), garbhalambhana (conception), pumshavana (engendering a male child), simantonnayana (parting the hair, performed in the fourth month of pregnancy), jatakarma (birth rites), namakarana (naming), chudakarma (tonsure), annaprashana (first solid food), keshanta (first shaving of the head), upanayana (sacred thread), vidyarambha (commencement of studies), samavartana (graduation) and antyeshti (funeral rites).

[86]Teaching, studying, donating, receiving gifts, performing sacrifices and officiating at the sacrifices of others.

[87]Fighting.

[88]From wrongdoers and for the purpose of donations.

One must be non-violent towards all beings and act as if everyone is a friend. There is no need to disclose it. One should uphold one's atman in secrecy. One must forsake all gifts. An intelligent person must control his senses. One should base oneself of lack of sorrow and freedom from fear, both here and there.[89] The sages are always in control of their souls, self-restrained and always engaged in the observance of austerities. One must conquer desire, which is difficult to vanquish. Even in the midst of attachments, one must cultivate sentiments of not being attached. Everything that can be grasped by the senses has an existence that is manifest. But one must attentively seek to know what is not manifest and grasp the linga.[90] One must grasp prana in the mind and uphold the brahman in prana. If one can free oneself from attachments, there is no need to think of any other kind of attachment. In this way, a brahmana can obtain bliss in the brahman. Constant purity, devotion to good conduct and compassion towards all beings—these are the signs of a brahmana.'"'

Chapter 1511(183)

'"Bhrigu said, 'Brahma is truth. Austerities are truth. Subjects are created through truth. The world is sustained through truth. It is through truth that one goes to heaven. Falsehood is the form of darkness. Darkness takes one downwards. When one is grasped by darkness, one cannot see the light, because one is enveloped in darkness. It is said that heaven is light and hell is darkness. Those who roam around in this universe can obtain both truth and falsehood. In this world, different kinds of conduct can lead to truth and falsehood, dharma and adharma, light and darkness, joy and misery. That which is truth is dharma. What is dharma is

[89]In this world and in the next.

[90]This is a reference to the linga-sharira, the subtle body. When the physical body is destroyed, the linga-sharira remains. When the linga-sharira is destroyed, one merges with the brahman.

light. What is light is joy. That which is false is adharma. What is adharma is darkness. What is darkness is misery. It is said—those who are discerning see that this created world is full of physical and mental misery and that joy also ends in misery. They are not confused. The discerning person seeks to free himself from misery. For living beings, joy is temporary, in this world and in the next.[91] When Rahu devours the moon, the moonlight is no longer radiant. In that way, darkness overcomes beings and the joy of beings is destroyed. It is indeed said that there are two types of joy, physical and mental. In this world and in the next, every kind of conduct is prescribed for the sake of happiness. There is nothing superior to the fruits of the three objectives. These are the specific qualities of dharma, artha and kama. All acts are undertaken with the specific purpose of obtaining happiness.'

'"Bharadvaja said, 'You have said that happiness is the supreme objective behind these three. But I don't accept this. The great rishis do not base themselves on these qualities. Nor do they desire these. It has been heard that the illustrious lord Brahma, the creator of the three worlds, is established as a brahmachari. He does not want the happiness of kama for himself. The illustrious lord, the consort of Uma, overcame kama and pacified Ananga.[92] Therefore, great-souled ones do not want this. This is evidently not a specific quality that the illustrious ones want. O illustrious one! I cannot accept what you have said, that happiness is the supreme objective behind those three. In this world, it is said that there are two kinds of fruits—happiness from good deeds and unhappiness from bad deeds. This is what is commonly said.'

'"Bhrigu said, 'Indeed, darkness results from falsehood. Those who are devoured by darkness follow adharma, not dharma. Those who are enveloped by anger, avarice, confusion and falsehood do not obtain happiness in this world, or in the next. It is said that they suffer from many kinds of disease and hardships. They are oppressed

[91]Happiness in heaven lasts only till one's merits are not exhausted.

[92]Kama is the god of love. Shiva burnt him down to ashes. Since he no longer possessed a body, Kama came to be known as Ananga.

by death, imprisonment and disease. They are tormented by hunger, thirst and other kinds of exhaustion. They suffer from turbulent winds, burning heat, extreme cold and fear and are tormented by many kinds of physical grief. They are also overcome by many kinds of mental grief—the destruction of relatives and wealth and separation from these. There are also old age and death. A person who is not touched by physical and mental grief experiences happiness. None of these blemishes is experienced in heaven. Instead, there are extremely pleasant breezes and extremely fragrant scents in heaven. There is no hunger, thirst or exhaustion. There is no old age and no sin. There is only happiness in heaven. In this world, there are both happiness and unhappiness. It is said that there is only unhappiness in hell. Therefore, that[93] is the supreme objective. The earth is the womb of all beings and women represent the earth. Man is like Prajapati. Know that semen is full of energy. This is the way Brahma created the worlds in ancient times and determined their conduct. Subjects wander around, engaged in their own respective tasks."'

Chapter 1512(184)

'"Bharadvaja asked, 'What are said to be the fruits of donations? What about dharma and conduct? What about austerities, extremely severe austerities, studying and oblations?'

'"Bhrigu replied, 'Sins are pacified through oblations. Studying leads to supreme peace. It is said that one obtains objects of pleasure through donations. Everything is obtained through austerities. It is said that donations are for two purposes, for the sake of the next world and for this one. Out of whatever is given to the virtuous, something accrues in the next world. Whatever one gives to those who are not virtuous leads to objects of pleasure in this world. One obtains fruits in accordance with the donations one has given.'

[93]Happiness.

'"Bharadvaja asked, 'In the conduct of dharma, who should follow what? What are the signs of dharma? How many kinds of dharma are there? You should tell me this.'

'"Bhrigu replied, 'Those who are engaged in following their own dharma are learned. They obtain the fruits of dharma. If one doesn't act in this way, one is deluded.'

'"Bharadvaja said, 'O brahmana rishi! Four kinds of ashramas were ordained in earlier times. You should tell me about the conduct that is prescribed for each of these.'

'"Bhrigu replied, 'In ancient times, the illustrious one[94] laid down four ashramas for the sake of protecting dharma and for the welfare of the worlds. Of these, residing in the household of the preceptor is said to be the first ashrama.[95] He must cleanse himself properly. He must be humble and follow the prescribed rituals. He must be modest in his soul. He must worship the two twilights[96], the sun, the fire and the gods. He must give up excessive sleep and laziness. He must worship the preceptor. He must study the Vedas and listen to them. He must purify his soul. He must perform ablutions thrice.[97] He must follow brahmacharya. He must tend to the fire. He must always serve his preceptor. He must always subsist on begging and single-mindedly give him[98] everything that has been obtained. He must receive all the instructions the preceptor favourably bestows on him.[99] He must attentively meditate on whatever has been obtained through the preceptor's favours. On this, there is a shloka. "A brahmana who obtains the Vedas by serving his preceptor obtains the fruits of heaven and is successful in his desires." Indeed, garhasthya is said to be the second ashrama. I will tell you in detail about all the conduct and signs for this. It is recommended that those who have returned[100]

[94]Brahma.

[95]Brahmacharya.

[96]Morning and evening, sandhya.

[97]Morning, noon and evening.

[98]The preceptor.

[99]The student must not ask the preceptor for instruction, but wait for the instruction.

[100]After studying in the preceptor's household.

follow the ashrama of the householder. With a view to attaining fruits, such a person should marry and observe the conduct of dharma with her. All the three objectives of dharma, artha and kama can be obtained through this mode. One must look towards these and obtain riches through beneficial deeds. The householder should follow garhasthya and obtain riches from the mountains and the oceans. These will be obtained if he studies well and serves the cause of the brahmana rishis. He must offer oblations and practise rituals. Through the favours of the gods, riches will then be obtained. This is said to be the foundation of all the ashramas. There are those who dwell in the residences of their preceptors. There are others who are mendicants. There are also those who have resolved to follow the vows and rituals of dharma. All these enjoy sustenance through shares in alms and sacrifices.[101] Those in vanaprastha must renounce and not store objects. These righteous and virtuous people generally look for medication in being devoted to studying, visiting the tirthas for the purpose of seeing different countries and in roaming around the earth. Without any malice, one must stand up and greet them with pleasant words and gifts, depending on one's capacity. One must give them the best of seats and beds. This must be one's conduct and action. On this, there is a shloka. "If a guest returns from a house with his wishes unsatisfied, he takes away all the good deeds[102] and leaves him with his bad deeds." Therefore, sacrifices must be performed.[103] The gods must be pleased and the ancestors must be satisfied. One must study the Vedas, listen to them and tend to the rishis. For the sake of Prajapati, one must have offspring. On this, there are two shlokas. "One must be affectionate towards all beings, with pleasant words that are agreeable to hear. Censure, the inflicting of hardships and harshness are reprehensible. Disrespect, pride and insolence are condemned. There must be non-violence, truthfulness, lack of anger and austerities, recommended for all the ashramas." A person in the householder stage must always observe the qualities of

[101]Offered by householders.

[102]Of the householder.

[103]This goes back to the duties of the householder.

the three objectives. Wearing garlands, ornaments and garlands, the smearing of the body with unguents, taking pleasure from singing, dancing and musical instruments, pleasant and cheerful objects that bring delight to hearing and sight, the enjoyment of food and drink that is swallowed, licked, drunk and sucked, satisfaction with many kinds of desirable objects and the gratification of sexual desire with one's own wife are allowed. Such a person enjoys happiness and obtains the objective of the virtuous. There may be a householder who follows his own dharma, but observes *unchhavritti*.[104] He gives up all exertion that is for the pursuit of desire and happiness. The attainment of heaven is not at all difficult for him.'"'

Chapter 1513(185)

'"Bhrigu said, 'Those who are in vanaprastha follow the dharma of rishis. They go to sacred tirthas, rivers and streams and deserted and desolate forests frequented by deer, buffaloes, boars, *srimaras*[105] and elephants. They practise austerities. They abandon ordinary garments and objects of food. They are controlled, limited and wonderful in their diet and subsist on wild herbs, roots, fruits and leaves. They sit and lie down on the bare ground, rocks, gravel, pebbles, sand and ashes. They cover their limbs with *kasha*, kusha,[106] hides and bark. They do not cut their hair, beards or nails. They perform their ablutions at the right time. They offer food, oblations and sacrifices at the right time. They do not rest until they have collected the required kusha, flowers and other ingredients required for oblations to the fire. Their skin is cracked everywhere, because of the cold, the heat, the wind and the rain. They observe different kinds of vows and yoga recommended

[104]There are grains left after a crop has been harvested, or after grain has been milled. If one subsists on these leftovers, that is known as unchhavritti.

[105]A variety of young deer.

[106]Both kasha and kusha are kinds of grass.

by dharma. Because of these observances, they are nothing but flesh, blood, skin and bones. They are full of fortitude and spirited in their yoga. They bear their bodies in this way. If a person observes these rituals and conduct, recommended by the brahmana rishis, his sins are burnt, as if by a fire. He conquers worlds that are difficult to win. The conduct of a mendicant[107] is the following. He frees himself from attachment to the fire, riches, wives and family. He casts aside the bond of affection and wanders around. Stone, iron and gold are the same to him. He is not interested in pursuing the three objectives. His intelligence frees him from these attachments. Towards enemies, friends and neutrals, his conduct is the same. In words, deeds and thoughts, he does not injure immobile objects, those born from wombs, those born from eggs, those born from sweat and beings that are in the nature of herbs and plants. He has no abode. He roams around mountains, islands, the roots of trees and temples. He may go to a city or a village for residence. But he will not dwell in a city for more than five nights and in a village for more than one night. For the sake of sustaining life,[108] he will only present himself at the houses of brahmanas who are generous in their deeds. He should not ask for alms that are more than what has been placed in his vessel. He will restrain anger, insolence, delusion, avarice, miserliness, pride, slander, vanity and violence. In this connection, there is a shloka. "If a sage roams around, without causing fear to any being, he never faces fear from any being." He performs the agnihotra sacrifice with his own body. The body is the fire that offers oblations into his mouth. That fire is fed oblations that are obtained through begging. Because of this fire, he transcends the world. As stated, he observes the ashrama of moksha. His resolution and intelligence are properly turned towards purification. He is as tranquil as a blazing body that has no kindling. Such a brahmana obtains Brahma's world.'

'"Bharadvaja said, 'There is a world beyond this world. I have heard about it, but have not seen it. I wish to know about it. You should tell me.'

[107]*Parivrajaka.*

[108]Alms.

'"Bhrigu replied, 'There is a sacred spot towards the north, on the slopes of the Himalayas. It has all the qualities. It is said that this is a supreme world—sacred, tranquil and desirable. The men there have abandoned greed and delusion and do not suffer from any difficulties. They do not perform wicked deeds. They are pure and extremely clean. It is said that this region has such auspicious qualities that it is like heaven. Death comes at the right time and disease does not touch them. Men are devoted to their own wives and do not desire the wives of others. It is amazing that they do not kill each other and do not desire each other's possessions. Since dharma is clearly followed, there is no scope for any doubt. The fruits of all acts are directly obtained there. They possess beds, vehicles, seats, palaces and mansions that have all the objects of desire. Some are adorned in golden ornaments. However, there are also some who only eat enough to remain alive. So as to remain alive, some perform great exertions. In this world, some men are devoted to dharma, while others practise deceit. Some are happy, while others are unhappy. Some are poor, while others are rich. In this world, exertion, fear, delusion and hunger are fierce. There is greed for riches among men and this confuses even those who are learned. There are many kinds of thoughts in this world, about deeds of dharma and adharma. A wise person knows the difference between the two and sin does not touch him. There is fraud, deceit, theft, slander, jealousy, injury towards others, violence, verbal abuse and falsehood. If someone practises these, then his austerities are diminished. However, if a person knows this and acts righteously, his austerities are enhanced. This world is the arena for action. In this world, auspicious and inauspicious deeds can be performed. Good deeds lead to good gains. If one performs inauspicious deeds, the opposite occurs. In ancient times, in this world, Prajapati[109] and the gods, along with masses of rishis, performed sacrifices and austerities, thus attaining Brahma's world. The northern part of the earth is the most sacred and auspicious. People who perform auspicious deeds in this world are born there. There are others who perform wicked deeds and are born as inferior species. There are others who have

[109]Brahma performed austerities in Pushkara, in Rajasthan.

short lifespans and are destroyed on the surface of the earth. They are addicted to devouring each other and are full of avarice and confusion. They circle around here and do not go to the northern direction. If a person serves his preceptor, is controlled and follows brahmacharya, the learned know that he follows the path indicated for all the worlds. I have briefly told you about the dharma that has been ordained by Brahma. A person who knows about dharma and adharma in this world is intelligent.'"

'Bhishma said, "O king! Thus did Bhrigu speak to the powerful Bharadvaja. The one with supreme dharma in his soul[110] was astounded and worshipped Bhrigu back. O king! Thus, everything about the creation of the universe has been recounted to you. O immensely wise one! What do you wish to hear again?"'

Chapter 1514(186)

'Yudhishthira said, "O unblemished one! O one who knows about dharma! It is my view that you know everything. O father! I desire that you should tell me about the recommendations on good conduct."

'Bhishma replied, "Those with bad conduct, bad efforts and bad wisdom, characterized by rashness, are known as the wicked. The virtuous have signs of good conduct. Auspicious men are those who do not pass urine and excrement along royal roads, amidst cattle and in the midst of fields of paddy. After doing this,[111] it is said to be dharma for men to purify oneself by performing ablutions along the banks of a river and offering water to the gods. The sun must always be worshipped. One must not sleep after the sun has arisen. In the morning and the evening, one must perform the sandhya meditation by facing the east and subsequently, the west.[112] After having washed

[110]Bharadvaja.

[111]Relieving oneself.

[112]The east in the morning and the west in the evening.

the five limbs,[113] one must eat silently, facing the east. One must not censure the food one is eating, regardless of whether the food is tasty, or is not tasty. One must wash the hands and then arise. In the night, one must not go to sleep with wet feet. Devarshi Narada has said that these are signs of good conduct. With a desire to purify one's mind and limbs, every day, one must circumambulate a bull, a god, a cow pen, a place where four roads meet and a brahmana who follows dharma. In matters of food, a man who generally does not differentiate between all the guests, attendants, relatives and servants is praised. The gods have ordained that men must eat twice, in the morning and in the evening. In between, it has not been said that one should eat. One should fast instead. At the right time, oblations must be offered. When it is her season, a wise person will go to his wife. He will behave like a brahmachari towards the wives of others. Leftover food from a brahmana is like amrita. It is like milk from a mother's breast. These are truly worshipped by people. The virtuous truly worship them. If a person has abstained from meat,[114] he must refrain from eating meat, even if it has been sanctified by reciting from the Yajur Veda. One must not eat useless flesh.[115] One must also avoid meat from the back. Whether one is in one's own country, or whether one is in some other country, a guest must never be made to fast. Having obtained the desired fruits of action, one must offer them to the seniors. It is a duty to offer one's seat to seniors and respectfully greet them. By worshipping one's seniors, one is united with long life, fame and prosperity. One must not look towards the rising sun. When she is naked, nor should one look towards another man's wife. Sexual intercourse that is in conformity with dharma must be practised, but in secret. The heart is a tirtha among all tirthas. The heart is the purest of the pure. All acts done by a noble person are pure, including the touching of hair. Every time one meets another person, one must ask him questions about his welfare. It has been

[113]The mouth, the two hands and the two feet.

[114]Because of a vow.

[115]Useless flesh is defined as meat that has not been obtained from sacrifices to the gods and the ancestors.

instructed that, in the morning and in the evening, brahmanas must be worshipped. The right hand must be used in an assembly of gods, amidst cows, in performing rites among brahmanas, in studying and in eating. Through this, the stores of a merchant and the crops of an agriculturist increase manifold. Grain, beasts of burden and cattle also multiply. When one has finished eating, one must perform *tarpana* with the hand.[116] One must always say that the payasa and krisara have been cooked well.[117] After shaving, spitting, bathing, eating and recovering from a disease, one must greet everyone with, 'May you have a long life.' While facing the sun, one must not pass urine. One must not look at one's own excrement. One must not sleep with a woman who is a suta. One must also avoid eating with her. One must avoid addressing elders by name or by using '*tvam*'.[118] There is no sin in addressing either juniors or equals in this way. If there is wickedness in the heart, this shows up in deeds. If wicked people conceal their wrong deeds, performed knowingly, from good people, they are nevertheless destroyed. Wicked deeds performed knowingly may be hidden from extremely learned people. Men may not see them. But they are seen by the residents of heaven. A sin committed by a wicked person leads to a further sin. An act of dharma performed by someone who observes dharma follows the doer. A foolish person does not remember the sins that he has committed. However, they circle around the doer. Just as Rahu approaches the moon, those wicked deeds approach that ignorant person. Objects stored with the hope of something are not enjoyed at the right time. The learned do not praise this, because death does not wait for anyone. The learned have said that for all beings, dharma exists in the mind. Therefore, all beings must observe purity in their minds. Dharma must be practised singly. There is no aide in dharma. One

[116]The offering of water to deceased ancestors, with water thrown from the right hand.

[117]Payasa is rice cooked in milk and sugar. Krisara is made out of wheat flour, rice and sesamum. The dessert must be particularly praised.

[118]Tvam is used for juniors and equals. Seniors must be addressed as *bhavan* for males and *bhavati* for females.

should only resort to the ordinances. What will an aide do? Men are born from the gods. The gods have amrita in heaven. If one observes dharma, after death, one enjoys extreme happiness."'

Chapter 1515(187)

'Yudhishthira said, "O grandfather! A man should think about *adhyatma*.[119] Tell me about adhyatma."

'Bhishma replied, "O Partha! You have asked me about adhyatma. O son! It is supremely beneficial and brings happiness and I will tell you about it. Knowing this, men in this world have obtained affection, happiness, immediate fruits and gains and even the welfare of all beings. Earth, air, space, water, and fire as the fifth—these are the great elements and the origins of creation and destruction of all beings. They originate with him[120] and it is to him that these great elements in the beings repeatedly return, like the waves in an ocean. It is like a tortoise extending its limbs and retracting them again. In that way, the creator of beings creates beings and withdraws them again. To create beings, he places the five great elements in all beings, changing the proportions. But the being does not see this. Sound, hearing and the holes[121]—these three originate in space. Skin, touch, exertion and speech—these four have to do with the wind. Form, eye and digestion—these three are said to be of the fire. Taste, liquid secretions and tongue—these three are said to be the qualities of water. Scent, nose and body—these three are the qualities of the earth. There are five great elements and the mind[122] is said to be the sixth. O descendant of the Bharata lineage! The senses and the mind are the source of discernment. Intelligence[123] is said to be the seventh and the

[119]The spiritual, concerning the supreme spirit.

[120]The brahman.

[121]In the body.

[122]*Mana*.

[123]Buddhi.

kshetrajna is the eighth. The eyes and the others are for seeing. But the mind doubts. Exerting intelligence, the kshetrajna is stationed like a witness. Everything that is above the feet, to the rear and to the front, is seen by it. Know that it[124] pervades everything, without there being a gap anywhere. Men must know this and all the senses. Know that the qualities of tamas, rajas and sattva depend on them. A man must use his intelligence to know the coming and going of all beings. If he looks at it in this way, he will obtain tranquility and supreme benefit. The qualities[125] influence intelligence and intelligence influences the senses. The mind is the sixth in all this intelligence. Where will the qualities come from?[126] Everything, mobile and immobile, is pervaded by this. It has been instructed that all destruction and creation results from this. That which sees is the eye. That which hears is said to be the ear. The one which is used to smell is the nose. The tongue tastes. The skin touches and these influence and distort intelligence. If there is a resolution to accomplish something, that is done by the mind. For different objectives, intelligence is established in five separate things. These are said to be the five senses and the invisible entity[127] rests on them. Depending on intelligence, a man can have three kinds of sentiments.[128] Sometimes he is delighted, and sometimes he grieves. Sometimes, there is neither happiness, nor unhappiness. In this way, there are three kinds of sentiments in the minds of men. However, sometimes, one can surpass these three kinds of sentiments, like the ocean, the lord of the rivers, uses its waves to cross the great shoreline. That pure kind of intelligence only exists in the mind.[129] But sometimes, following the rajas quality, it is impelled to act. All the senses then manifest themselves. There is joy in sattva. There is sorrow in rajas. There is confusion in tamas. These are the three. All the sentiments one sees in the world are based on these three. O

[124]The soul.

[125]Sattva, rajas and tamas.

[126]The qualities are confounded by the senses, the intelligence and the mind.

[127]Intelligence.

[128]Sattva, rajas and tamas.

[129]Not influenced by the senses.

descendant of the Bharata lineage! I have thus told you everything about the nature of intelligence. An intelligent person must conquer all the senses. Sattva, rajas and tamas always attach themselves to living beings. O descendant of the Bharata lineage! That is the reason three different kinds of pain, sattva, rajas and tamas, are seen in all living beings. A touch of happiness is the quality of sattva. A touch of sorrow is the quality of rajas. When these are combined with the quality of tamas, confusion is the result. If there is anything joyous in the body or in the mind, that is seen to be the consequence of the sattva quality. Unhappiness is not desired by anyone. This is due to the rajas quality and one should not think about this with fear.[130] There is a state where one is confused and does not know what should be known and what should be done. This is the outcome of tamas. Delight, satisfaction, bliss, happiness, tranquility in thought—when these are seen, that is the quality of sattva. Dissatisfaction, repentance, sorrow, greed, lack of forgiveness—when these signs are seen, those are ascribed to rajas. Insolence, confusion, distraction, excessive sleep, lack of care—when many such traits are evident, that is the quality of tamas.

'"A person may be doubtful about what he has obtained. He will be able to go far, in many different directions. If he is able to control his mind, he will obtain happiness, in this world and in the next. Notice the subtle difference inside between intelligence and the kshetrajna. One of these[131] creates many qualities. The other one[132] creates no qualities at all. It is like a mosquito and a fig being united to each other. They are with each other, but they are also separated from each other. Although they are naturally separate, they are always united. This is like a fish and water being united. The atman possesses no qualities. It only perceives all the qualities. It looks at all the qualities and thinks that it has created them. The senses are inactive and do not know. It[133] uses the seventh, intelligence, to light

[130]Instead, one should try to conquer it.

[131]Intelligence.

[132]The soul.

[133]The atman.

up the paramatman, like a lamp. The kshetrajna sees the qualities that are created by the intelligence. This is certainly the connection between the intelligence and the kshetrajna. There is never any refuge for the intelligence or the kshetrajna. The mind creates intelligence, but never its qualities. When the mind controls the reins[134] well, then the atman becomes visible, like a lamp concealed inside a pot. If a sage discards ordinary acts and always controls his atman, then he may be able to see himself in all beings and attain the supreme objective. A bird roaming in the waters is touched, but is yet not touched. That is the way a person who has obtained wisdom wanders around beings. Using his intelligence, a man must naturally roam around in this way. He should neither grieve, nor be delighted. He should roam around, without any malice. If he is naturally successful in this way, he is always successful in creating the qualities. With that knowledge, he creates the qualities, like a spider creating strands. Some say the qualities[135] are destroyed. Others say that they are destroyed and become invisible. Whether they are manifest, or not manifest, cannot be established on the basis of guesses. Some, basing themselves on their studies, say they remain. Others say that they are destroyed. Considering both views, one must use one's intelligence to decide. One must use one's intelligence to firmly sever these strands in the heart. Having freed oneself, there is no doubt that one will obtain happiness and not sorrow. By bathing in a full river, men cleanse themselves. Know that in this way, filthy people can also purify themselves in knowledge and become extremely learned. A person who is accomplished is not tormented on seeing the further shore of a great river. In that way, a person who knows about adhyatma is only driven by supreme knowledge. A man who has comprehended the ultimate end and origin of all beings looks at it in this way and slowly obtains supreme, using his intelligence. If a person knows about the three objectives, he is freed from what stands before the light. He searches with his mind. He is not interested in anything other than seeing the truth. Because of the different senses, one is

[134]Of the senses.

[135]Of such men. The qualities mean sattva, rajas and tamas.

incapable of seeing the atman. They distract in different directions and are difficult for someone who has not controlled his soul to restrain. A person who knows this is intelligent. What else can be the characteristics of a learned person? Obtaining this knowledge, learned people regard themselves as having become successful. Things which cause great fear to those who are not learned do not cause any fear to those who are learned. There is no other end that is greater than this. But the learned say that the qualities attained are not comparable.[136] If a person acts without attachment, he destroys the effects of his earlier deeds. There is nothing that is disagreeable. If someone tries for the agreeable, his birth on earth will always happen. In this world, people censure those who are afflicted.[137] Behold. They sorrow in many ways. Also, behold. Those who are accomplished do not sorrow. A person who knows about both[138] always accomplishes the objective."'

Chapter 1516(188)

'Bhishma said, "O Partha! I will now tell you about the four kinds of meditation in yoga.[139] The supreme rishis who know this, advance towards eternal success in this world. *Yogi*s engage themselves in this kind of meditation. These are maharshis who are satisfied with their knowledge and have set their minds on emancipation. O Partha! They are freed from the taints of this world and do not return again. The sins associated with their births are destroyed and they become established in their natural states. They are free of opposite sentiments and are always based in their selves. They are always based in freedom. They are without attachments.

[136]Everyone does not progress to the same extent.

[137]By the senses.

[138]Instant moksha and incremental advancements towards moksha.

[139]Dhyana yoga. The number four never becomes clear.

They do not debate. They seek to bring about tranquility in their minds. They are single-mindedly devoted to studying and hold up their atmans. Such a sage is seated like a piece of wood, crushing his senses. He does not hear any sound through his ears. His skin does not know anything through touch. His eyes do not know any form and his tongue does not know any tastes. He smells nothing. Immersed in the yoga of meditation, he experiences nothing. The valiant one does not desire anything that ignites the five categories.[140] The accomplished person withdraws the five categories into his mind. He uses the five senses to control his wavering mind. Since they no longer have a support, they do not wander. The five gates[141] are mobile, but are rendered immobile. Inside, the patient person first controls his mind to the path of meditation. He uses his mind to crush the senses. I have described this path of meditation to you first. Having controlled these first, the sixth one, the mind,[142] is then restrained. It is as fickle as lightning flashing around in the clouds. A drop of water on a leaf is unstable and always moves around. In the process of meditation, the consciousness is first like that. However, after one has meditated for some time, it becomes controlled. However, if the mind again strays into the path of the wind,[143] it becomes like the wind. But a person who knows is not disturbed by this. He strives single-mindedly, without malice. He restrains his consciousness in meditation again, engaged in the yoga of meditation. Engaged in meditation, the sage first accomplishes discrimination, reasoning and judgement.[144] At first, in the process of meditation, the sage first fixes his mind. Disturbed by it, he controls it. A sage must not engage in despair, but must seek to ensure benefit for his atman. Heaps of

[140]The senses.

[141]Of the body.

[142]The five senses having come earlier.

[143]The wind is being used as a metaphor.

[144]The translation doesn't capture the nuance. The terms used in the text are respectively *vichara*, *vitarka* and *viveka*. All three are generally reasoning and judgement. However, in the progression of yoga, these are regarded as higher and higher levels of discernment, vichara being the lowest and viveka being the highest.

dust and ashes from burnt cow dung do not become wet when they are sprinkled with water. Even if they become slightly wet, that dust still seems to be dry. They must be continuously and slowly sprinkled before they become wet. The senses must be slowly controlled, in that way. In this way, the senses are gradually controlled. They are gradually restrained and finally pacified. O descendant of the Bharata lineage! By incessantly pacifying the mind through yoga, one first engages the mind and the five categories in the path of meditation. The happiness obtained through manliness or destiny is nothing compared to what is obtained through the control of the atman. United with such bliss, he remains engaged in the task of meditation. Without any disturbance, the yogi then advances towards emancipation."'

Chapter 1517(189)

'Yudhishthira said, "You have spoken about the four ashramas and about rajadharma. You have separately spoken about many different kinds of history. O immensely intelligent one! I have also heard many true accounts connected with dharma. However, I still have a doubt and you should remove it. O descendant of the Bharata lineage! I wish to hear about the fruits obtained by *japakas*.[145] What fruits are obtained by the japakas who recite in this way? O unblemished one! You should tell me about all the norms that have been laid down for *japa*. What are the different rules and procedures that have been laid down for japakas in sankhya and yoga?[146] What are the ordinances for sacrifices? What is recommended for japa? Tell me all this. It is my view that you know everything."

[145]Japa is the recitation of a mantra in a low tone. A japaka is a person who does this.

[146]Since both sankhya and yoga have multiple meanings, this causes problems of translation and understanding. The following seems to be a reasonable interpretation. In sankhya, the use of no particular mantra is recommended, sankhya being equated with Vedanta. In yoga, there is the recitation of a particular mantra.

'Bhishma replied, "In this connection, an ancient history is recounted, about what transpired in ancient times between Yama, Time and a brahmana. Vedanta has said that renunciation is meditation. The words of the Vedas are about withdrawal, tranquility and resort to the brahman. The paths[147] can be resorted to, or not resorted to. O king! I will tell you about the reasons for resorting to it.[148] It has been said that the mind must be controlled and the senses must be conquered. One must be truthful and tend to the fire. One must immerse oneself in reflection, with meditation, austerities, self-control, forgiveness, lack of jealousy, restraint in food, withdrawal from material objects, frugality in speech and tranquility. This is the way dharma flows. Listen to the mode of abstention now. Those who follow the path of the brahman perform japa and withdraw from rituals. As I have said, all these must be completely renounced. There are three paths one can resort to, external, internal and without any.[149] He must seat himself on kusha grass. He will hold kusha in his hand and tie kusha around his hair. He must surround himself with tattered rags and in its midst, attire himself in kusha. He must bow down before material objects and after that, no longer think of material objects. He must be tranquil in his mind and fix his mind on his mind. With his intelligence, he must meditate on the brahman and engage in japa for his benefit. He must then withdraw from even this and immerse himself in samadhi.[150] Having resorted to meditation, he must use his concentrated powers. Through austerities and self-control, he will purify his atman. He will withdraw from all hatred and desire. He will be without attachment and confusion.

[147]Sankhya and yoga.

[148]This is a reference to resorting to sankhya, without any specific mantra in mind. However, there is an emphasis on rituals. In contrast, in the mode of abstention, there are no rituals, but one meditates on a specific mantra.

[149]These shlokas are not very clear and are also difficult to translate. External probably means external rituals. Internal probably means internal rituals, japa with a specific mantra. However, meditation is also possible without any mantra at all.

[150]The final stage of meditation, where one is completely immersed in the brahman.

He will not sorrow. Nor will he be delighted. He does not think of himself as the doer, nor as the one who enjoys from this action. Nor does he suffer from the action. In yoga, the mind has no sense of ego. Nor does he seek to establish anything. He is not engaged in receiving anything for himself. But he does not ignore this.[151] Nor does he not perform acts. He is engaged in the task of meditation. He is engaged in meditation, having set his mind on meditation. Through the meditation, he obtains samadhi and then gradually gives it up.[152] In that state, he obtains the bliss that is obtained by renouncing everything. He is not interested in this world. He has renounced everything. He gives up his life and merges with the body of the brahman. Or perhaps he does not desire to merge into the body of the brahman then. He follows the path upwards, never to be born again. He resorts to knowledge about the brahman. He is tranquil and without disease. He is immortal and free from all passions. He obtains the purity of his atman."'

Chapter 1518(190)

'Yudhishthira asked, "You have spoken about the supreme ends that japakas obtain. Is this the only end, or is there any other possibility?"

'Bhishma replied, "O king! O lord! Listen attentively to the end attained by japakas. O bull among men! They may also descend into many kinds of hell.[153] If there is a japaka who does not initially follow what has already been stated, or if he cannot complete those rites, he goes to hell. If there is a japaka who shows disrespect, is not satisfied and grieves, there is no doubt that such a person goes to hell. All those who suffer from ego go to hell. A man who insults

[151]Action.

[152]The process of meditation.

[153]In this context, hell is being used in a slightly different sense, as anything that falls short of complete liberation.

others will also go to hell. Those who are confused and perform japa with the objective of obtaining fruits, are also those who desire hell. Those japakas who conduct themselves in the pursuit of riches[154] are also destined for hell and there is no emancipation for them. Those who are confused and perform japa because of attachments descend into a state where they obtain those attachments.[155] If a person is evil-minded and his mind is not stable in wisdom, then his end is also unstable and he goes to hell. There may be a japaka who is foolish and is not accomplished in his wisdom. In his delusion, he goes to hell and having gone there, he has to sorrow. If there is a japaka who performs japa with a firm mind, but fails to complete it, he too goes to hell."

'Yudhishthira asked, "If a japaka has no specific objective and bases himself on the supreme and unmanifest brahman, why does he have to take birth in a body?"

'Bhishma replied, "It is because of the lack of wisdom that one has to go to many different kinds of hell. Japakas are praised. But they have taints in their atmans."'

Chapter 1519(191)

'Yudhishthira asked, "What kind of a hell does a japaka go to? Describe it to me. A great curiosity has arisen in me. You should tell me."

'Bhishma replied, "You have been born from Dharma.[156] You are naturally devoted to dharma. O unblemished one! Listen attentively to these words, which have dharma as their foundation. There are regions for the gods with supreme souls. These regions are of many colours, many forms and many fruits. They are divine and have

[154]These riches can also be interpreted as the special powers obtained through yoga.

[155]That is, they are not freed.

[156]Yudhishthira was born from Dharma.

celestial vehicles and assembly halls that can go anywhere at will. O king! There are many kinds of arenas, with lotuses and sparkling water. The residents of heaven, the four guardians of the world, Shukra, Brihaspati, the Maruts, the Vishvadevas, the Sadhyas, the Ashvins, the Rudras, the Adityas, the Vasus and others are there. O son! But in comparison with the region of the paramatman, these are also hells. This spot has no fear or no objective and is not enveloped in any kind of hardship whatsoever. It is free from both.[157] It is free from the three.[158] It is free from the eight.[159] It is free from the three.[160] It is free of the four characteristics and devoid of the four reasons.[161] It has neither unhappiness nor happiness, nor sorrow or exhaustion. Time is cooked there[162] and time is not the lord there. O king! That region is the lord of time and is also the lord of heaven. The atman alone is obtained there. Having gone there, one does not grieve. This is the supreme region. Hell is not like this. I have accurately detailed all the hells to you. That is the supreme region. Everything else has characteristics of hell."'

Chapter 1520(192)

'Yudhishthira said, "Earlier, you mentioned to me the dispute between Time, Death, Yama and the virtuous brahmana. You should tell me about this."

'Bhishma replied, "In this connection, an ancient history is recounted. This transpired between a brahmana and Ikshvaku, Surya's son. It also involved Time and Death. Listen to the account of

[157]The agreeable and the disagreeable.

[158]Sattva, rajas and tamas.

[159]The five elements, the senses, mind and intelligence.

[160]Distinctions between the knower, the object of knowing and the act of knowing.

[161]Seeing, thinking, hearing, knowing and the reasons behind these.

[162]Time is subservient to the required needs.

the conversation that took place at that spot. There was an immensely illustrious japaka brahmana who was devoted to dharma. He was descended from Kushika and was Pippalada's son. He was immensely wise and knew about the six Angas.[163] He knew about the six Angas and about the one who is not manifest.[164] He was accomplished in the Vedas and dwelt on the slopes of the Himalayas. He performed other austerities for attaining the brahman. He controlled himself and performed japa. He observed such rituals for one thousand years. The goddess manifested herself before him and said, 'I am pleased.'[165] Because he was silent in the midst of his japa, he did not say anything in reply. The goddess was pleased and felt compassion for him. The mother of the Vedas[166] honoured his japa. When the japa was over, he arose and bowed his head down at her feet. Having prostrated himself before the goddess, the one with dharma in his soul spoke the following words. 'O goddess! It is good fortune that you are pleased with me, have appeared before me and have shown yourself to me. If you are pleased with me, may my mind always find delight in japa.'

'"Savitri said, 'O brahmana rishi! What do you desire? What shall I do for you? O supreme among those who perform japa! Tell me. Everything will be as you wish.'"

'Bhishma said, "Having been thus addressed by the goddess, the brahmana who was devoted to dharma replied, 'Let my desire for japa repeatedly increase. O auspicious one! Day and night, let my inclination towards the dharma of samadhi increase.' In a sweet tone, the goddess replied that it would be this way. Wishing to do what would bring him pleasure, the goddess again said, 'You will not go to the hell where other bulls among brahmanas go. You will go to the unblemished region of the brahman, which has not been created by anyone. I will depart now. But what you have wished for will become successful. Single-mindedly, perform japa. Dharma will present himself

[163]The Vedangas.

[164]The brahman.

[165]As will become evident, this goddess is the personification of the gayatri or savitri mantra and his japa was based on reciting this.

[166]The gayatri mantra.

before you. Time, Death and Yama will also present themselves before you. There will be a dispute between them and you on dharma.' Having said this, the illustrious one returned to her own abode. The brahmana continued to perform japa for one hundred celestial years. The intelligent brahmana remained there, completing his rituals. Pleased at this, Dharma presented himself before that brahmana.

'"Dharma said, 'O brahmana! Look at me. I am Dharma. I have come here to see you. Listen to me. You have obtained the fruits that result from japa. You have obtained all the worlds, the divine and the human. You will be successful in passing through all the hells that are inhabited by the gods. O sage! Give up your life and go to the worlds that you desire. If you cast aside your own body, you will obtain those worlds.'

'"The brahmana replied, 'O Dharma! I have obtained all the worlds here. Go to whatever spot brings you pleasure. O lord! Though this body suffers from a lot of joy and misery, I will not give it up.'

'"Dharma said, 'O bull among sages! This body should certainly be cast aside. O brahmana! Go to heaven. O unblemished one! What is it that pleases you?'

'"The brahmana replied, 'O lord! Without this body, I will find no delight in residing in heaven. O Dharma! Go away. Without my body, I am not interested in going to heaven.'

'"Dharma said, 'There has been enough of this body. Make up your mind to give up this body and be happy. Go to the world where there is no rajas. Having gone there, you will not sorrow.'

'"The brahmana replied, 'O immensely fortunate one! I take pleasure in japa and have obtained all the eternal worlds. O lord! I wish to go to heaven in my body, or not at all.'

'"Dharma said, 'O brahmana! Behold. If you do not wish to cast aside your body, Time, Death and Yama will present themselves before you.'"

'Bhishma said, "O lord! There were those three—Vaivasvata,[167] Time and Death. They approached the immensely fortunate

[167]Yama.

brahmana and spoke to him. Yama said, 'I am Yama. You have tormented yourself well with austerities and your conduct is good. I am telling you that you will obtain the best of fruits.' Time said, 'I am Time and I have come before you. Because of your recitations and japa, you have obtained supreme fruits. The time has come for you to ascend to heaven.' Death said, 'O one who knows about dharma! Know me to be death. I have shown my own form to you. O brahmana! I have been urged by Time and have come to take you away.' The brahmana replied, 'Welcome to Surya's son,[168] great-souled Time, Death and Dharma. What can I do for you?' To those who had come, he offered padya and arghya.[169] Extremely delighted, he asked, 'According to my capacity, what can I do for you?' At that time, Ikshvaku was on a visit to the tirthas and arrived at the spot where those lords were assembled together.

'"The rajarshi affectionately honoured all of them. The supreme among kings asked them questions about their welfare. The brahmana offered him a seat and padya and arghya too. Having asked him questions about his welfare, he said, 'O great king! Welcome. Tell me what you desire. According to my capacity, please tell me what I can do for you.' The king replied, 'I am a king. You are a brahmana engaged in the six tasks.[170] I wish to give you some riches. Tell me how much you want.' The brahmana said, 'O king! There are two kinds of brahmanas and dharma is said to be of two kinds. There is attachment and withdrawal. I have accepted the path of withdrawal. O lord of men! Donate gifts to those who are on the path of attachment. I will not accept anything. What can I give you for your welfare instead? O best among kings! Tell me. I will ensure its success through my austerities.' The king replied, 'I am a kshatriya. I do not know the words, "Please give." O best among brahmanas! The only thing we ask for is, "Give us battle."' The brahmana said, 'O king! You are content in your own dharma and in a similar way,

[168]Yama.

[169]Respectively, water for washing the feet and the gift given to a guest.

[170]Studying, teaching, giving gifts, receiving gifts, performing sacrifices and officiating at the sacrifices of others.

so am I with mine. There is no difference between us. Therefore, act as you wish.' The king replied, 'You are the one who first said that you would give according to your capacity. O brahmana! I am asking you. Give me the fruits that you have obtained through japa.' The brahmana said, 'In your words, you boasted that you always asked for battle. Why don't you then ask that I should fight with you?' The king replied, 'It has been said that brahmanas have the power of speech and kshatriyas live through the strength of their arms. O brahmana! That is the reason there has been this fierce duel with words between you and me.' The brahmana said, 'Even now, that is my resolution. According to my capacity, what will I give you? O Indra among kings! I possess wealth. Tell me immediately. What shall I give you?' The king replied, 'You have performed japa for a full hundred years. If you wish to give me something, give me the fruits of that japa.' The brahmana said, 'Take the supreme fruits that I have obtained through japa. Without reflecting, take half of those fruits. Or, take all the fruits of the japa from me. O king! If you so wish, take them entirely.' The king replied, 'O fortunate one! Though I asked for all the fruits of japa, I don't want them. May you be fortunate. I am leaving you. But tell me what those fruits are.' The brahmana said, 'I don't know what fruits have been given to me because of the japa. However, Dharma, Ṭime, Yama and Death are witnesses.'[171] The king replied, 'If you do not even know what the fruits of this dharma are, what will I do with them? O brahmana! Since there are doubts about what they are, I do not desire them.'

'"The brahmana said, 'I will not accept any other words for you. I have already given you my fruits. O rajarshi! Let both your words and mine be true. Earlier, I have never performed japa with any specific objective in mind. O tiger among kings! How will I then know the fruits from japa? You said, "give" and I said "take". Let those words not be falsified. We must be steady and protect the truth. O king! If you do not keep the words that you spoke to me,[172] then, because of the falsehood, a great adharma will

[171]To the fact that there have been some fruits.

[172]Of accepting the fruits.

descend on you. O scorcher of enemies! The words that you have spoken should not be tainted with falsehood. In that way, I am also incapable of falsifying my words. Without any hesitation, I have earlier pledged to give it to you. Therefore, if you wish to adhere to the truth, you should accept it without any reflection. O king! You came here and asked me for the fruits of the japa. Therefore, adhere to the truth and accept what has been given to you. O king! There are no worlds for those who are supremely addicted to falsehood. Their past, or their future, cannot be saved. Sacrifices, studying, donations and rituals are incapable of saving them. O bull among men! In this world and in the next, there is nothing as supreme as the truth. Truth is superior to all the austerities you have performed and all the austerities you will undergo for hundreds and thousands of years. Truth is the single syllable of the brahman. Truth is the single syllable of austerities. Truth is the single syllable of sacrifices. Truth is the single syllable of learning. The Vedas remain awake in truth. The learned texts have said that truth brings the supreme fruits. Truth is dharma and self-control. Everything is established in truth. The Vedas and the Vedangas are truth. The sacrifices and rituals are in truth. Vows and good conduct are truth. Om is truth. The birth of beings is based on truth. Truth is their offspring. The wind blows because of truth. The sun heats because of truth. The fire burns because of truth. Heaven is established in truth. Truth is sacrifices, austerities, the Vedas, hymns, mantras and Sarasvati. We have heard that dharma and truth were weighed on a pair of scales and when they were weighed together, truth was heavier. Where there is dharma, truth is there. Everything is enhanced through truth. O king! Why do you wish to perform an act of falsehood? O king! Fix your sentiments on truth and not futilely on falsehood. Why do you wish to inauspiciously falsify the word "give" that you spoke? O king! I have given you the fruits of my japa. If you refuse to accept them, you will roam around the world, dislodged from your own dharma. Having pledged, if one does not give, and if one does not accept, both are tainted by falsehood. Therefore, you should not act in a false way.'

'"The king said, 'O brahmana! The dharma of kshatriyas is to fight and protect. It is said that kshatriyas are givers. How can I accept from you?'

'"The brahmana replied, 'O king! I did not go to your house and insist. You came here and asked from me. How can you then not accept?'

'"Dharma said, 'Let there be an end to this excessive dispute between you. Know that I am Dharma. Let the brahmana obtain the fruits of giving. Let the king obtain the fruits of adhering to the truth.'

'"Heaven said, 'O Indra among kings! Know that I am Heaven and have myself appeared before you. Let there be an end to this excessive dispute. Both of you are equal in obtaining the fruits.'

'"The king replied, 'I have performed tasks that will ensure heaven for me. O Heaven! Go wherever you want. If the brahmana so desires, I will give him the riches that I have obtained.'

'"The brahmana said, 'In my words, I may have ignorantly stretched out my hand.[173] I now follow the dharma that has the characteristics of not being attached and I am engaged in japa. O king! I have been engaged in withdrawal for a long time. Why do you wish to tempt me? I will perform my own acts. O king! I do not desire your fruits. I am engaged in austerities, studying and good conduct and have accepted the path of withdrawal.'

'"The king replied, 'O brahmana! If you wish to give me the supreme fruits of your japa, then accept some of my fruits and let us divide them. Brahmanas are engaged in accepting. Those born in royal lineages are engaged in giving. O brahmana! If you are learned about dharma, let our fruits be equal. Or if you do not wish to share equally, take all the fruits from me. If you wish to show me your favours, accept what I have earned through dharma.'"

'Bhishma said, "At that time, two malformed men arrived there. They were dressed badly and each of them had his hand on the other one's shoulder. They said, 'You don't owe me anything. It is I who owe you. We are debating in this way and here is a king who is a ruler. I am telling you truthfully. You don't owe me anything. You

[173]For accepting gifts. The text of the Critical edition says, *vakye*, translating as, in words. Non-Critical versions say *balye*, in childhood. Childhood fits better.

are speaking falsely, when you say that you owe me something.' Engaged in this furious debate, they approached the king and said, 'Examine the case, so that neither one of us is censured.' Virupa said, 'O tiger among men! I owe Vikrita the fruits of giving away a cow.[174] O lord of the earth! I wish to return this to him. But Vikrita refuses to accept it.' Vikrita said, 'O lord of men! Virupa does not owe me anything. O lord of men! He is lying to you. This is false.' The king asked, 'O Virupa! Tell me. What do you owe him? It is my view that, having heard, I will do what needs to be done.' Virupa replied, 'O king! Listen attentively to what happened and how I owe a debt to Vikrita. O rajarshi! O bull among men! I will tell you everything. O unblemished one! O rajarshi! For the sake of obtaining riches, in earlier times, he had given away an auspicious cow to a brahmana who was of good conduct and was engaged in austerities and studying. O king! I went to him and asked for the fruits of that act. Pure in his soul, he gave me the fruits of what he had done. Thereafter, after purifying myself, I performed some good deeds. I bought two brown cows[175] with calves and they yielded a lot of milk. O king! O lord! There was a brahmana who was devoted to the conduct of unchhavritti. Faithfully, and following the prescribed rites, I donated these to him. Having received earlier, I now wished to give him twice the fruits.[176] O tiger among men! This being the background, who among us is pure? Who is sinful? O king! We have debated this among us and have come before you. Decide on dharma and adharma and we will accept it with all humility. O lord! If he does not wish to accept the gift that he had bestowed on me earlier, then you must determine the right course for both of us to take.' The king asked, 'Why are you not accepting, when your debt is being repaid now? Grant your permission and receive it quickly.' Vikrita replied, 'He says that he owes me. But what I gave was given away. Therefore, he does not owe me anything. Let him go wherever he

[174]Virupa means deformed. Vikrita also means deformed. Vikrita donated a cow and then donated the fruits of this donation to Virupa.

[175]Kapilas.

[176]Give to Vikrita. Twice, because there are two cows now.

wishes.' The king said, 'He is willing to give, but you do not accept. To me, this does not seem fair. In my view, there is no doubt that you should be punished on this account.' Vikrita replied, 'O rajarshi! I gave him a gift. How can I take it back again? O lord! If it is your view that I am guilty, then please punish me.' Virupa retorted, 'I am willing to give, but you are unwilling to accept. The king is the protector of dharma and must restrain you.' Vikrita replied, 'I myself gave what he asked for. How can I take that back now? I am giving you. Having accepted it, you have my permission to go away.' The brahmana said, 'O king! You have heard what these two have said. Without any reflection, take what I have pledged to give you.' The king replied, 'An extremely grave task confronts us, like a bottomless pit. The japaka is firm in his resolution. How will this end? If I do not accept what has been earned by the brahmana, how will I avoid being tainted with a great sin?' The rajarshi told those two, 'You have accomplished your objectives. Depart now. Rajadharma is vested in me and I must ensure that it is not rendered futile. It has been determined that kings must protect their own dharma. It is extremely unfortunate that the dharma of brahmanas[177] has presented itself before me.' The brahmana said, 'Accept what I owe you. I have heard you ask for it. O king! If you refuse to accept it, it is certain that I will curse you.' The king replied, 'Shame on rajadharma, since it has been determined that I must do this. I must accept what you are giving, so that the two are rendered equal.[178] My hand is stretched out. Earlier, it used to be stretched out only for giving. O brahmana! Give me whatever you owe me.' The brahmana said, 'Whatever qualities I have obtained through the performance of japa and whatever is vested in me, accept all of those.' The king replied, 'O supreme among brahmanas! These drops of water have fallen on my hands. Accept those from me, so that we are equal.' Virupa

[177]That of receiving.

[178]These shlokas are not very clear. On the one hand, there is the dharma of accepting what the brahmana is offering. On the other hand, there is the dharma of kshatriyas not accepting. These two must be balanced and rendered equal.

said, 'Know that we are Desire and Anger and we have goaded you to act in this way. As you have said, the two of you are equal and will be equal in all the worlds. He[179] does not owe me anything. We questioned you for your own sake. Time, Dharma and Death, and the two of us, Desire and Anger, have examined everything about you, in your presence. As you desired, go to the worlds that you have won through your deeds.' I have recounted to you the fruits obtained by japakas and the end, status and worlds conquered by japakas.

'"A person who studies goes to the supreme abode of Brahma, or goes to Agni and enters into Surya. If he is attached, he imbibes that energy. Confounded by attachment, he imbibes those qualities.[180] This is also the case if his body is with Soma, Vayu, the earth or space. If there is attachment, he dwells and acts in accordance with those qualities. However, if he is detached, he is doubtful even if he goes there. He desires for the supreme and eventually penetrates that. He obtains the amrita of all amritas. He is tranquil and it is as if he has no atman. He becomes part of the brahman and is freed from opposite sentiments. He is happy, peaceful and without disease. He obtains the abode of the brahman, from which, there is no return. This is characterized by the single akshara alone. There is no misery. There is no decay. He obtains that region of tranquility. He is devoid of the four characteristics and the six and the sixteen.[181] He passes over Purusha and is immersed in space.[182] However, if he still has attachment in his soul and does not desire all this, he obtains everything that his mind desires. Or he looks upon all the worlds that have earlier been called hells. If he does not desire anything, he is free and finds delight in bliss. O great king! This is the end obtained by japakas. I have told you everything. What else do you wish to hear?"'

[179]Vikrita.

[180]This is not true moksha.

[181]The four characteristics are the four means of obtaining knowledge—the senses, inference, intuition and revelation. The six are hunger, thirst, sorrow, delusion, disease and death. The sixteen are the five organs of sense, the five organs of action, the five kinds of life breath and the mind.

[182]Purusha is probably to be understood as the creator and space (*akasha*) as the brahman.

Chapter 1521(193)

'Yudhishthira asked, "O grandfather! What answer was given then by the brahmana or the king? Tell me this. In accordance with what you have described, what were their ends? What was the conversation between them? What transpired and what did they do there?"

'Bhishma replied, "He[183] accepted the agreement and worshipped Dharma, Yama, Time, Death and Heaven, as they deserved to be honoured. He worshipped all the other bulls among brahmanas who had assembled there. He bowed his head down and honoured all of them. He then spoke to the king in these words. 'O rajarshi! United with the fruits, go to the sacred regions. With your permission, I will devote myself to japa once again. O immensely strong one! O lord of the earth! The goddess[184] granted me a boon earlier—that my devotion to japa would always remain.' The king replied, 'O brahmana! If you are devoted to japa and if your success has been rendered futile, then go with my half and let the fruits of japa remain with you.'[185] The brahmana said, 'In the presence of all these people, you have made great efforts.[186] Therefore, let us be equal and go wherever our ends take us.'

'"Knowing what they had decided, the lord of the thirty gods came there, with all those who had forms of gods, the guardians of the worlds, the Sadhyas, the Vishvadevas, the Maruts, the large stellar bodies, the rivers, the mountains, the oceans, the many tirthas, the austerities, the various rites of the Vedas, the hymns, Sarasvati, Narada, Parvata, Vishvavasu, the Hahas, the Huhus,[187] the

[183]The brahmana.

[184]Savitri.

[185]The brahmana has given away his fruits of japa to the king. The king offers that the brahmana should retain these fruits of his japa and also take half of the king's fruits.

[186]To give me your fruits.

[187]Narada and Parvata are sages. Vishvavasu is a gandharva and the Hahas and the Huhus are gandharvas.

gandharva Chitrasena with a large number of his family members, the serpents, the successful sages, Prajapati, the god of the gods and the unfathomable and thousand-headed Vishnu. Musical instruments like drums and trumpets were sounded in the sky. Celestial flowers were showered down on those great-souled ones. Large numbers of apsaras danced around in every direction.

'"Heaven appeared there in personified form and spoke these words. 'O brahmana! You are immensely fortunate and have become successful. O king! You have also become successful.' O king! Having done what was proper towards each other, those two[188] prepared to withdraw themselves from all material objects. They established prana, apana, udana, samana and vyana in their minds and turned their minds towards prana and apana. They concentrated these at the tips of their noses and below their eyebrows. Using their minds, they gently held them there. They rendered their bodies immobile and were fixed and controlled in their looks. Having seated and controlled themselves in that way, they sent their atmans upwards. A great and blazing mass of energy penetrated the crown of the great-souled brahmana's head and went up to heaven. Great sounds of lamentation arose in all the directions. Worshipped by everyone, that energy entered the brahman. O lord of the earth! The grandfather advanced and welcomed that mass of energy, which was as tall as a man. He again spoke these supreme and sweet words. 'There is no doubt that japakas obtain the same fruits as yogis. The fruits of yoga are directly evident. However, japakas are superior, because I advance to welcome them. Dwell with me.' Having said this, he again imparted consciousness[189] and without any anxiety, the brahmana entered into his[190] mouth. Like that tiger among brahmanas, the king, following the prescribed rites, also entered into the illustrious grandfather.

'"The gods worshipped Svayambhu and spoke these words. 'We have made exertions to come to accomplish the objectives of

[188]The brahmana and the king.

[189]Into the mass of energy.

[190]Brahma's.

the japaka. You have made them[191] equal in honour and equal in obtaining the fruits. We have witnessed the great fruits obtained by yogis and japakas. They can go wherever they wish, passing over all the worlds.' Brahma replied, 'If a person follows the rites and reads the great sacred texts, or the auspicious ones that follow the sacred texts, he also goes to my world.[192] If someone follows yoga in accordance with the prescribed rites, there is no doubt that, after death, he will obtain my worlds. I will now go. To accomplish your objectives, all of you also return to your places.' Having said this, the god disappeared. Having taken his leave earlier, all the gods also returned to their own abodes. O king! All those great-souled ones honoured Dharma and, delighted in their minds, followed him at the rear. These are said to be the fruits and ends obtained by japakas. O great king! This is what I have heard. What else do you wish to hear?"'

Chapter 1522(194)

'Yudhishthira asked, "What are the fruits obtained through the yoga of knowledge, the Vedas and rituals? How can the atman in beings be known? O grandfather! Tell me this."

'Bhishma replied, "In this connection, an ancient history is recounted. This is a conversation between Prajapati Manu and maharshi Brihaspati. Prajapati was supreme on earth and maharshi Brihaspati was foremost amongst the large number of devarshis. In ancient times, the student bowed down before the preceptor[193] and asked him a question. 'What is the cause?[194] Where have mantras and ordinances come from? What are the fruits that brahmanas say are

[191]Japakas and yogis.

[192]The text uses the word smriti. The reference is thus to the original smriti texts and the ones that followed.

[193]Brihaspati was Manu's student.

[194]Behind creation.

attached to knowledge? O illustrious one! Tell me accurately, what are the things that mantras and sounds are not able to reveal? There are those who know about artha, the sacred texts, the subsequent sacred texts[195] and mantras. They perform many supreme sacrifices, at which, they give away cows. What are the great fruits that flow from these? Where are they found? From where have the earth, those on earth, the wind, the sky, aquatic creatures, water, heaven and the residents of heaven originated? O illustrious one! Tell me this ancient account. Men desire and exert for knowledge and their inclination turns towards what they know. But I have no knowledge of that supreme and ancient one.[196] Therefore, how can I avoid being false in my inclinations? I have studied the large material of the Rig Veda, the Sama Veda, the Yajur Veda, prosody, the paths of the nakshatras, *nirukta*,[197] grammar, *samkalpa*[198]and *shiksha*.[199] But I still do not know about the element that is in all nature. You should tell me everything, about the fruits that follow from knowledge and deeds and about how an embodied being gives up a body and again enters another body.'

'"Manu said, 'Anything that is agreeable is said to represent happiness. Similarly, anything disagreeable is said to represent unhappiness. I will obtain happiness from this and not from that—one performs all rites and rituals because of such sentiments. However, those who are engaged in the pursuit of knowledge serve neither happiness, nor unhappiness. Prosody and the yoga of action are because of this desire in the soul. However, if someone is freed from this, he attains the supreme. In the pursuit of happiness, a man engages in many things along the path of action. But he does not go towards the supreme. By freeing oneself from acts, one obtains the supreme. He is without desire and certainly obtains the supreme brahman. Subjects have been created through the mind and through

[195]We have translated *agama* as this, as opposed to *shastra*.

[196]The brahman. This is false because Brihaspati worships something that he does not know.

[197]Etymology in the Vedas.

[198]Concerning rituals.

[199]Concerning accurate pronunciation.

deeds. These are the two virtuous paths, revered by everyone. Acts are seen to have outcomes that are both eternal and temporary. To obtain the eternal, there is no method other than renouncing any desire in the mind. When the night is over and the atman is no longer enveloped in darkness, the eye can lead the atman. Similarly, when a person has the qualities of jnana and vijnana, he can see which inauspicious deeds need to be avoided. When men know, they avoid snakes, the pointed ends of kusha and wells. In their folly, stupid people fall down there. In that way, behold the superior fruits of knowledge. The complete utterance of mantras, sacrifices performed according to the prescribed ordinances, the giving of dakshina, the donation of food and contemplation in the mind—these five are said to be the fruits the atman obtains through action. The Vedas say that deeds have qualities in them.[200] Mantras form the foundations of deeds and mantras also possess these. It is evident that rituals must also have them. Fruits originate in the mind and the embodied being enjoys them. In the world of action, auspicious and sacred sounds, forms, taste, touch and scent can be successfully obtained as fruits. When acts are performed through the body, they are also enjoyed through the body. The body is the frame for happiness. The body is also the frame for unhappiness. However, if any tasks are performed through words, all of them are also enjoyed through words. Whatever acts are performed through the mind, it is the mind alone that enjoys them. Whatever quality and category of action a person desires and acts accordingly, the fruits of his action are also like that. Those qualities become attached and he enjoys the fruits of those auspicious and inauspicious deeds. Like a fish that swims against the tide, one has to confront the deeds one has committed earlier. The embodied being is satisfied because of his good deeds and is not satisfied because of his bad deeds. I will now tell you about the supreme one. Listen to me. He is the one from whom everything in

[200]Sattva, rajas and tamas. Sattva action is driven by a desire for heaven, rajas by a desire for superiority and victory and tamas by a desire to harm others. The intentions are thus important.

the universe has originated. It is through knowing him that one can overcome everything. He cannot be expressed through mantras and words. He is distinct from the many kinds of tastes and scent and sound, touch and form. He is incapable of being understood by the senses. He is the one who is not manifest. He is without complexion. He is the single one. He has created the five kinds of beings.[201] He is not female, male, or neuter. He does not exist. But nor does he not exist. Men who know about the brahman can behold him. Know that he is Akshara, without decay.'"'

Chapter 1523(195)

'"Manu said, 'Wind originated in Akshara. Energy originated in wind. Water originated in energy. The universe originated in water. Everything in the universe originated from the universe. All these bodies eventually enter into the water first.[202] From the water, they then progressively go to energy, wind and space. The enlightened ones who obtain the supreme do not have to return from space. There is no heat, cold, mildness, sharpness, sourness, astringency, sweetness, bitterness, sound, scent or form in that supreme state. One does not feel touch. The tongue does not feel taste. The nose does not feel scent. The ears do not hear sound. In that supreme state, the eyes do not see form. Men who are learned about adhyatma accept that state. The tongue withdraws from taste, the nose from scent, the ears from hearing, the skin from touch and the eyes from the qualities of form. In that supreme state, such a person beholds his own natural state. It has been said that the doer, the act, the facilitators for an act, the inclination, the reasons behind the act and the methods are the soul.[203] But the

[201]Those born from wombs, eggs, sweat, plants and herbs and divinities.

[202]After destruction.

[203]The soul is left implicit in the text. We have added this. Otherwise, the sentence is incomplete.

true doer is the one who pervades everything in the world, just as the mantras have stated. He is the reason behind everything. He is behind the supreme objective. He is the cause. Everything else is an effect. Because of the good and bad deeds performed, a man obtains the good and the bad, sometimes in contradiction to each other. Because of his own deeds, the good and the bad reside in the body, and knowledge is also bound down there.[204] When a lamp is lit, the lamp illuminates everything that is in front. The senses are like lamps on trees. When ignited with knowledge, they illuminate everything. The many advisers of a king cite different reasons, but also come together. Those five in the body[205] are also subservient to supreme knowledge. The flames of the fire, the force of the wind, the rays of the sun and the water in the rivers repeatedly come and go. Like that, embodied beings repeatedly come and go in different bodies. When a person grasps an axe and cuts wood, he sees neither smoke nor fire inside it. Like that, by severing the body, the stomach, the hands and the feet, one cannot see the other one. When wood is rubbed against another piece of wood, one can see both smoke and fire. Like that, a person with excellent intelligence and wisdom, can control his senses to see the supreme in his own natural state. When one is dreaming, one can see one's own body lying down on the ground, as if it is separate from one's own self. Like that, a person with hearing and the others senses, excellent in his mind and in his intelligence, sees himself going from one body into another body. The supreme in the body[206] is not subject to birth, growth, decay and destruction. Unseen, it goes through a process of transition and passes from one body into another body. The eye cannot behold the form of the atman. It cannot be felt by anyone through touch. It does not perform any acts. No one can see it. But it sees them. When a lamp is lit, it assumes a form because of the fire and the heat. That which is inside is also seen to assume form and qualities from the body. Unseen, a man gives up his body and enters another body. He

[204]Because of lack of comprehension, knowledge is bound down.

[205]The senses.

[206]The atman.

casts aside the body formed of the great elements, but still resorts to a form constituted by them. He enters the body of wind, fire, water, space and earth in every way. Depending on their action, hearing and the other senses resort to the five different qualities. The ear is for space, smell is for the earth and sight is for energy and fire. Sweat and taste are said to resort to water. The quality of touch has the property of wind. The objects of the senses, and the five senses themselves, dwell in the five great elements. All of them follow the mind. The mind follows intelligence and the mind follows one's nature. Whatever good and bad deeds may have been performed are received in one's own body. They follow the lead of the mind, just as aquatic creatures follow a favourable current. When a moving object comes into the range of vision, even if it is extremely small, it seems to assume a large form. In the path of intelligence, one can see one's supreme form in one's own form.'"'

Chapter 1524(196)

'"Manu said, 'When the senses are collected together and obtain their qualities, they remember what has been done a long time ago. When the senses are collected together later, through the use of the intelligence, one comprehends one's supreme nature. When all the objects of the senses are simultaneously controlled and, over time, one uses one's strength to prevent them from wandering around, the intelligent person understands himself to be the single supreme embodied being.[207] One passes through the three—rajas, tamas and sattva—and the three qualities and forms of knowledge. In that way, the embodied being penetrates the senses, like wind entering a kindled fire. The eyes cannot see the form of the atman. Touch cannot comprehend it. It is beyond the senses to fathom it. The ears cannot comprehend the soul through hearing.

[207]This is a difficult shloka to translate and we have taken some liberties.

Whichever sense comprehends it is destroyed.[208] Hearing and the other senses cannot fathom the atman on their own. The kshetrajna knows everything, sees everything and witnesses. No man has seen the other side of the Himalayas, or the dark side of the moon. But this doesn't mean that they don't exist. In that way, the atman exists in a subtle way in all beings and is based in knowledge. Something that has not been seen earlier and something that has not been heard of earlier is not necessarily non-existent. Even if one looks, one doesn't always see the universe in the moon. It is like that for those who are not fixed on the final objective. The learned see that form is created and form is also destroyed. Through their intelligence, they can understand the motion of the sun.[209] With the lamp of intelligence, the extremely learned see what is far away. Through their intelligence, they can immediately investigate what should be known. Indeed, nothing can be accomplished without the use of means. Fishermen kill fish by using nets that are made out of strings. Deer are used to capture other deer, birds for other birds and elephants for other elephants. In that way, what needs to be known can be seen through knowledge. As an example, only a snake can see a snake's legs. Through knowledge, inside the body, one can see what is based in the body and deserves to be known. One will not be able to comprehend the senses through the use of the senses. In that way, what is beyond intelligence cannot be understood through the use of supreme intelligence. On the fifteenth day of the dark lunar fortnight, even a subtle form of the moon cannot be seen. That does not mean that it has been destroyed. Know that the embodied being is like that. On the fifteenth day of the dark lunar fortnight, the faint form of the moon is not evident in the sky. In that way, when it is separated from its body, its own body cannot comprehend the soul. Having attained another position, the moon begins to shine again. In that way, having obtained another body, the soul is resplendent again. The birth, growth and decay of the moon can immediately be seen. But the soul is not like that. The birth, growth and decay of

[208]The senses have to be destroyed before the atman can be comprehended.

[209]As opposed to rising and setting.

the body should also be accepted like that. Even in its dark state, the moon possesses a form. One does not see darkness seize the moon and release it. In that way, the release and entering of the soul cannot be seen.[210] Darkness is seen when it approaches the moon and the sun.[211] In that way, the soul can be understood as separate from the body. When the moon and the sun have been freed, Rahu can no longer be seen.[212] In that way, when it has been separated from the body, the soul can no longer be comprehended. Even on the fifteenth day of the dark lunar fortnight, the nakshatras are still united with the moon. In that way, though it has been separated from the body, the fruits of acts performed are still united with it.'"'

Chapter 1525(197)

"'Manu said, 'When the manifest body is asleep, consciousness roams around in his dreams. Like that, consciousness is separated from knowledge and the senses after death. There are both existence and non-existence.[213] When the water is clear, the eyes can see the image in it. In that way, when the senses are clear, knowledge can be used to see what should be known. When the water is agitated, the image cannot be seen. In that way, when the senses are agitated, knowledge cannot be used to see what should be known. Lack of intelligence leads to lack of wisdom. Lack of intelligence taints the mind. When the mind is tainted, the five which are based in the mind[214]

[210]Release from a body and entering another body.

[211]At the time of an eclipse.

[212]An eclipse is believed to be due to Rahu devouring the sun and the moon.

[213]This is a difficult shloka to translate and the interpretation is the following. In dreams, the manifest body is inactive and consciousness is active. After death, consciousness is separated from the senses and from knowledge. Knowledge remains and though the body is no longer existent, knowledge exists in that state of non-existence.

[214]The five senses.

are also tainted. If one is immersed in material objects, one is ignorant and not satisfied. One does not see. Though the atman is pure, not being able to see, it circles around in material objects. Because of the sins, a man's thirst is never satisfied. The thirst is conquered only when one has destroyed the sins. The attachment to material objects has a tendency to perpetuate. The mind hankers for what one should not desire, and the supreme is not obtained. To obtain knowledge, a man must destroy his wicked deeds. When the sight is clear, one sees the atman in one's own self. If the senses are not controlled, one is miserable. When they are restrained, one is happy. Therefore, one must use one's atman to sever that attachment one has for objects of the senses. The mind is above the senses and the intelligence is above that. Knowledge is above intelligence and the supreme[215] is above knowledge. The soul originates in what is not manifest. Knowledge comes from the soul. Intelligence comes from knowledge. The mind comes from intelligence. The virtuous see that the mind is united with hearing and the other senses and sounds and the like. He who casts aside sounds and the like and everything that is manifest is freed from everything that is natural and ordinary. Having been freed, he enjoys immortality. When the sun rises, it creates a circle of rays. When it sets, it withdraws what it had itself created. In that way, the atman enters the body and spreads the rays of the senses, obtaining the qualities of the five senses. But when it sets, it restrains them. A person is repeatedly conveyed along the path of action. Though there is dharma in the soul, he grows old, having obtained the fruits of these deeds. If a person withdraws, material objects also withdraw from him. If a person has beheld the supreme, he abandons objects of desire and desire also leaves him. When the intelligence has rid itself of qualities associated with action and has immersed itself in the mind, there is destruction[216] and one obtains the brahman. This is not something that can be touched, heard, tasted, seen or smelt. This is beyond debate. It is only the spirit that can penetrate that supreme being. Everything created by the mind can be drawn back

[215]The atman.

[216]Of the senses.

into it. The mind can be withdrawn into intelligence. Intelligence can be withdrawn into knowledge. Knowledge can be withdrawn into the supreme. The senses cannot ensure the mind's success. The mind cannot understand intelligence. Intelligence cannot comprehend what is not manifest. The subtle soul can alone see.'"'

Chapter 1526(198)

'"Manu said, 'That which should be known exists in the midst of that knowledge. Know that the mind is only a quality of knowledge. When it is united with the faculties of wisdom, then intelligence is the result. When intelligence is freed from the qualities of action and is immersed in the mind, then wisdom is the result. One is engaged in the yoga of meditation and knows the brahman. If intelligence still possesses those qualities,[217] it circles around because of those qualities and flows down like a stream from the summit of a mountain, heading in different directions. But if one disengages from the qualities and the mind is first immersed in meditation, then one knows the brahman, like gold through a touchstone. The mind pursues the objects of the senses and clouds intelligence. Because it is obsessed with those qualities, it is incapable of seeing what is without qualities. One must close all the doors[218] and base oneself in the mind. Having fixed one's mind, one can then obtain the supreme. When the qualities are extinguished, the great elements are withdrawn. In that way, when the senses are withdrawn, the intelligence circles around in the mind. When intelligence is based in the mind and circles around inside, there are no longer any qualities that the mind is engaged with. When the mind is engaged in the qualities of meditation, it can cast aside its qualities. Devoid of all the qualities, it can know what is without qualities.[219]

[217]Of action.

[218]Of the senses.

[219]The brahman.

There is no vijnana that is capable of proving the existence of what is not manifest. There are no arrangements of words that can express it. How can it be understood through material objects? A person who has cleansed his atman inside can seek to approach the supreme brahman through austerities, inferences and the qualities prescribed in the sacred texts. Freeing oneself from the qualities, one can also follow him in the external path.[220] Because there are no natural attributes, the one who should be known cannot be known through debate. When one withdraws from the qualities, one obtains the brahman, who is devoid of qualities. The intelligence is such that it reaches towards the qualities, like a fire towards kindling. When the five senses are freed from their respective actions, the supreme brahman is also freed and transcends nature. All embodied beings are naturally influenced.[221] When they withdraw, they are freed, and some go to heaven. Man, nature, intelligence, senses in particular, ego and pride are created in beings. Their first creation emanated from that foremost one. The second creation resulted from sexual intercourse and is restrained by rules.[222] Benefit is obtained by observing dharma. The practice of adharma leads to injury. Attachment leads to the normal course.[223] Detachment leads to knowledge.'"'

Chapter 1527(199)

"Manu said, 'When the five attributes and the five[224] are separated from the mind, one can see the brahman, like a gem that is strung on a thread. That thread may be made out of gold, pearls, coral, clay or silver. This is because, as a consequence of

[220]Other than inside one's own self.

[221]Towards performing action.

[222]Such as sexual intercourse between members of the same species.

[223]Of rebirth.

[224]The five senses and their qualities.

its own acts, the atman is attracted and may dwell in cows, humans, elephants, other animals, insects and worms. The body depends on the acts one has performed. In that kind of body, one must enjoy the fruits. Though the earth is sprinkled with the same juices, it follows its nature and yields different kinds of herbs. In that way, intelligence follows the atman and the consequences of earlier deeds. Desire originally comes from knowledge. Resolution first comes from desire. Action flows from resolution. Action is foundation for the fruits. Fruits thus result from action. Knowledge results in action and the atman leads to knowledge. There is knowledge that enables one to know what should be known. This knowledge is virtuous and involves the destruction of ignorance. The destruction of knowledge,[225] fruits, understanding and action leads to divine fruits and knowledge of what should be known. Yogis behold that great and supreme being. Those who are ignorant and only perceive the qualities in themselves do not see it. The form of water is greater than the form of the earth. Energy is greater than water. The wind is greater than energy. Space is greater than the wind. In that way, the supreme is greater than the mind. Intelligence is greater than the mind. It is said that time is greater than intelligence. The illustrious Vishnu, to whom this entire universe belongs, is greater than time. That god has no beginning, no middle and no end. He is without beginning, without middle and without an end. He is without decay. He is beyond all misery, because it is said that misery has an end. He is said to be the supreme Brahma. He is said to be the supreme refuge. Going to him, there are those who are freed from time and material objects and obtain emancipation. Everything is seen to possess qualities. However, the supreme is without qualities. The signs of withdrawal are thought of as eternal dharma. The hymns of the Rig, Yajur and Sama Vedas have a base in the body and flow from the tip of the tongue. But these require effort for success and are also subject to destruction. The brahman cannot be obtained in this way, by relying on things that are dependent on the body. The brahman is without beginning, without middle and without end and cannot be

[225]The inferior kind of knowledge, tantamount to ignorance.

obtained through exertion. The hymns of the Rig, Sama and Yajur Vedas are said to have a beginning. Everything with a beginning has an end. But the brahman is said to be without a beginning. Because there is no beginning and no end, it is infinite and without decay. It is without decay and is without opposite sentiments. It is beyond opposite pairs of sentiments. Mortals do not succeed in seeing or going to the supreme because of their ill fortune, the lack of methods, lack of resolution and because of their deeds. They do not attain the supreme because they are addicted to material objects, because they wish to see something else, or because their minds desire something else. There are other people who see qualities in this world. They desire those qualities and do not desire the supreme, which is without qualities. They are devoted to inferior qualities. How will they know something that has superior qualities? It is beyond qualities and form and one can attain it on the basis of inference. One can know it through the subtleties of the mind and one is incapable of describing it in words. The mind is attracted by the mind. Sight is attracted by sight. It is intelligence that cleans knowledge and knowledge cleans the mind. Through the mind, and by fixing the senses, one obtains the infinite. Accepting intelligence, the mind is enriched. A person may not be interested in the qualities. Like the wind that keeps fire apart from kindling, if he is not driven by greed, he obtains the supreme in this world. When one is disinterested in obtaining all the qualities, the mind always attains what is superior to intelligence. If one is engaged in this mode and disassociates from all the qualities, one merges into the body of the brahman. The atman of a man is not manifest. It becomes manifest through his deeds. While he is destroyed, it becomes unmanifest again. The soul does not act. It is extended by the senses and there is joy and misery. Action is performed. It obtains a body and is united with the senses and finds a refuge in the five elements. However, unless it is goaded by the supreme and undecaying one, it is incapable of performing any action. No man on earth will see its end, but knows that there will be an end. He is agitated and is conveyed to the supreme, like a boat whirled by winds on the ocean. The sun obtains its qualities by spreading its circle of rays. But when it withdraws them, it is without qualities. In that way, in this world, a sage can give up all attachments and enter into the undecaying brahman, devoid of all qualities. It is without beginning. It is the supreme refuge for virtuous people. This is the undecaying Svayambhu. Everything originates in him and everything ends in him. He is eternal and the immortal and undecaying objective. A person who reflects on this obtains tranquility and immortality.'"'

Section 86 will conclude in Volume 9.

The ninth volume will complete Bhishma's teachings in Shanti Parva, that is, it will complete the Moksha Dharma section. Bhishma's teachings continue in Anushasana Parva, specifically, in Dana Dharma. This volume will have roughly half of Dana Dharma Parva.

About the Translator

Bibek Debroy is a member of NITI Aayog, the successor to the Planning Commission. He is an economist who has published popular articles, papers and books on economics. Before NITI Aayog, he has worked in academic institutes, industry chambers and for the government. Bibek Debroy also writes on Indology and Sanskrit. Penguin published his translation of the Bhagavad Gita in 2006 and *Sarama and Her Children: The Dog in Indian Myth* in 2008. The 10-volume unabridged translation of the Mahabharata was sequentially published between 2010 and 2014 and he is now translating the Hari Vamsha, to be published in 2016. Bibek Debroy was awarded the Padma Shri in 2015.